The cloaked assailant looked up, quickly raised his club: a reflex more than a purposeful parry. Hugh's Toledo blade clipped the wooden truncheon at an angle. The wood stripped back and then splintered.

The attacker was thrown back by the blow, alive only because his club had absorbed a cut that would have gone through his collarbone. But, rebounding from his own collision with the house's vinyl siding, the thug turned his momentum into a sideways barrel-roll that brought him back up to his feet in a moment. He sped into the darkness—

And I'm out of time, Hugh thought—and dropped prone just a second before a crossbow bolt sliced through the air where he had been standing. The quarrel impaled the vinyl upon the wood behind it with an almost musical *throoonk*. Hugh did not need to look up to know that this bolt had not been the kind used to stun small game. He jumped to his feet, sprinted along the reverse trajectory indicated by the quivering tail of the quarrel. He found the weapon that had fired it abandoned on the ground twenty yards away, in the lee of the neighboring house's shed. The dark night was quiet all around.

1636

COMMANDER CANTRELL IN THE WEST INDIES

ERIC FLINT
CHARLES E. GANNON

BAEN

1636: COMMANDER CANTRELL IN THE WEST INDIES

Copyright © 2014 by Eric Flint & Charles E. Gannon

A Baen Books Original

Baen Publishing Enterprises
P.O. Box 1403
Riverdale, NY 10471
www.baen.com

ISBN: 978-1-4767-8060-3

Cover art by Tom Kidd
Maps by Gorg Huff

First Baen paperback printing, June 2015

Library of Congress Control Number: 2014009924

Distributed by Simon & Schuster
1230 Avenue of the Americas
New York, NY 10020

Pages by Joy Freeman (www.pagesbyjoy.com)
Printed in the United States of America

With profound gratitude, I dedicate this book to the entirety of the Ring of Fire community, who were enthusiastic in their welcome, and have proven to be a singularly helpful and dedicated group of pros and fans. Their tireless work as researchers, fact-checkers, and proof-readers enriched and improved every page of this manuscript, as well as the other ones I have had the honor of contributing to this series.

—Charles E. Gannon

What he said.

—Eric Flint

Contents

Contents

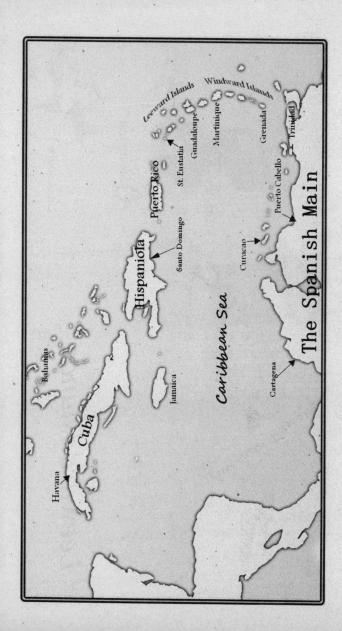

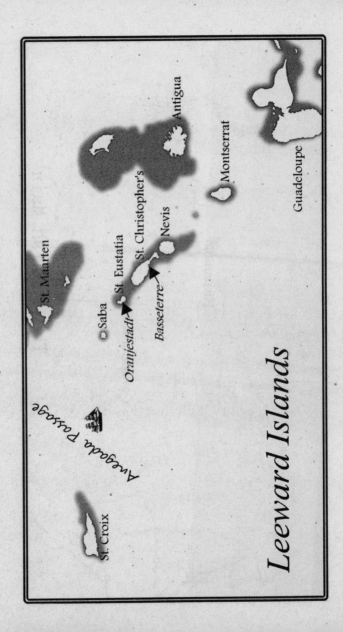

Leeward Islands

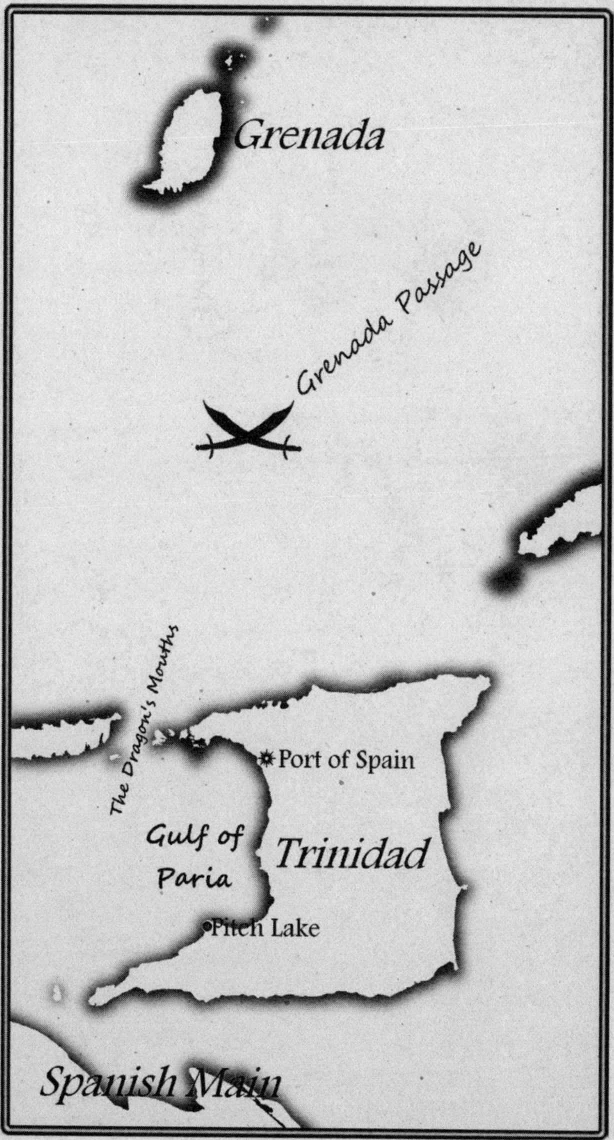
Grenada
Grenada Passage
The Dragon's Mouths
Port of Spain
Gulf of Paria
Trinidad
Pitch Lake
Spanish Main

Part One

April 1635

The heavens themselves, the planets,
and this centre

Chapter 1

Grantville, State of Thuringia-Franconia

Lieutenant Commander Eddie Cantrell looked down at the stump six inches below his left knee as an orderly removed his almost ornate peg leg. Physician Assistant Jessica Porter—formerly Nurse Porter—approached with his new fiberglass prosthetic. The jaundiced-gray color of the object was not appealing. "Wow, that's uglier than I thought it would be," Eddie confessed as the orderly left.

Jessica shrugged. "It may look like hell, but it works like a charm. We've special-cast more than a hundred of these, now." She fitted it tentatively onto the stump, and looked up at Eddie.

He concentrated on how it felt: a little odd—smooth and cool—compared to the wood and leather lashings that had just been removed. He supposed anything else might feel strange now, having spent a year and a half getting used to the cranky, creaky peg leg that had been specially fashioned for him by King Christian IV of Denmark's medical artisans. But now that Eddie paid closer attention to the new sensations

3

of this prosthetic—"Actually, that feels much better. No rubbing."

Jessica snorted in response. "Yeah, it ought to feel better. It's custom-made. That's why we made you stop by when you brought your princess bride with you last fall, to get a wax mold of your—" Jessica missed a beat, floundered. "Of your—your—"

"My stump," Eddie supplied for her. "That's okay; might as well call it what it is." Which, he reflected, Jessica must do dozens of times a week with other amputees. But it was probably different with him. He was a fellow up-timer, a person she had known before the Ring of Fire had whisked their whole town back through time to Germany of 1631. And so, right in the middle of the Thirty Years' War, into which meat-grinder Eddie himself had been thrown.

He looked down at the stump that had gotten caught in those pitiless gears of a new history-in-the-making. "So, that wax mold you took of my stump—?"

Jessica nodded as she secured the new leg. "We filled that mold with a mix of fiberglass and pine resin and presto: your new prosthetic."

Eddie moved the new false limb tentatively. The weight was negligible. "It's hard to believe that's local—uh, down-time—manufacture."

"Every bit of it," nodded Jessica as she stood and stepped back to take a look. "They got the process from us, of course. We made the first few here at the Leahy Medical Center. But after that, there was no stopping all the down-time medical folks, particularly in the new university programs, from dominating the business. Good thing, too: we couldn't have kept up with the demand, here."

"I thought fiberglass would be too hard for the local industries to make."

Jessica shook her head. "That's because you're thinking of the stuff we made speedboats out of, back up-time in the twentieth century. That's ultra-high strength fiberglass. The individual strands were very thin, and very uniform. I doubt any of us will still be alive when that technology makes its debut in this world. But this,"—she tapped the prosthesis; it made a much duller sound than the wood—"this is made of much cruder fibers. Down-timers can make them with a number of different drip-and-spin processes. Then they just pack it into the mold as tight as they can, pour in the pine resin, and, after a little more processing, out comes the prosthesis.

"That's not the end of the process, of course. It needs smoothing and careful finishing where it fits onto the stump. But we didn't stop there," she said, her smile finally returning. "We added something special for you."

"Oh?" Eddie wondered if maybe it had secret compartments. That would be kind of cool.

"Yep. Try stepping on it, then stepping off."

Eddie shrugged: no secret compartments, then. He took hold of his cane, pushed off the examining table, stood tentatively on both legs, then stepped forward with the prosthesis. Well, that felt just fine. And step two—

—almost dropped him to the ground. As his real foot came down and he shifted his primary weight onto it, the heel of the prosthetic seemed to start rising up a little, as if it was eager to take its own next step. It wasn't a particularly strong push, but he hadn't been expecting it, and he flailed for balance.

"Wha—what was that?" he asked, not minding one bit that Jessica had jumped over to steady him.

"That was the spring-loaded heel wedge. Cool, huh? When the sole of the prosthesis is fully compressed, and then you start to shift your weight off it to take the next step, it gives you a little boost. Like your own foot does."

Eddie frowned. "Well, yeah, I guess. But I wasn't ready for it."

Jessica shook her head. "Sorry. Should have thought of that. We don't experience that with the other amputees."

"Why?"

"Well, they're either recent amputees, so they never adjusted to a regular peg leg. Or they come here because someone has told them that up-timers at Leahy Medical Center make the *best* prosthetics, ones with springs in them. So naturally, the first thing we have to do is sit them down and explain every detail, including the phases they're going to go through in getting accustomed to using the new limb. Sorry; I should have observed the same protocol with you, should have warned you."

Eddie grinned and shrugged off her apology, then took a few more steps. Now that he knew to expect that little boost from the prosthetic's heel, it wasn't so bad. In fact, Jessica was right: this was more like real walking, not the flat footed limp-and-waddle he managed with the peg leg and a cane. With this, he could feel the potential for walking like a whole person again, like his old self. He could even imagine how he might be able to work in a little swagger, something to show off to Anne Cathrine . . .

"Eddie, I'm guessing that smug smile means that the prosthetic is a success?"

"Uh, yeah. Thank you, Jessica."

"Not at all. But tell me something, Eddie."

"Sure." He considered sitting, found he was still comfortable standing, something that rarely happened when he had been wearing the peg. "What do you want to know?"

"Well...why did you stay in Denmark once you were no longer being held as Christian IV's own, personal prisoner of war last year? I mean, I know there was the wedding with his daughter, but—"

Eddie nodded. And reflected that in the past, he might have grinned while he explained. But in the past year, life itself had acquired a new gravity that made him less ready to grin and shrug his way through the living or recounting of it. His high school days, not quite four years behind him, now seemed a lifetime away, a collection of memories that rightly belonged to someone else. "Mostly, I stayed up in Denmark because of love, Jessica."

"You mean the princess didn't want to come down here?"

"Oh, no, she was extremely eager to see Grantville." Like pretty much every other down-timer who had the means to do so, the number one locale on Anne Cathrine's list of "places to visit" was the town of miracles that had fallen out of the future into Germany.

"So why not bring the princess back home, Eddie? You get tired of us?"

"Jessica, first of all, Anne Cathrine is not a 'princess.' She's a 'king's daughter.'"

"And the difference is—?"

"The difference is huge. Her mom—her dad's second wife—was nobility, but not high enough for anyone to consider her kids potential inheritors of the throne. It's called a morganatic marriage."

"Thank you, I still read trashy historical romances, so I'm familiar with the term."

"Oh. Sorry. But princess or not, she's one of the brightest apples of her father's eye. He loves all his kids—he's a really good guy, that way—but he's especially fond of Anne Cathrine and her younger sister, Leonora."

"Another blond, buxom beauty, I'm assuming?"

Eddie decided not to point out that Anne Cathrine's hair was decidedly red-blond. "Uh, no, not at all. Leonora is a brunette. And...well, she'll probably be a pretty attractive woman. But she's already sharp as a tack. Not pushy, but has a real sense of her self, of what's right. And doesn't like having her dad determine her future."

One of Jessica's eyebrows elevated slightly. "She sounds like a handful for King Daddy. Good for her. And good for the Princess Anne Cathrine that she chose you."

Eddie shrugged. No reason to add the somewhat embarrassing footnote that Anne Cathrine and he had been surreptitiously "pushed together" by King Daddy, who despite some of his lunatic schemes, understood full well just how advantageous it was to have his daughter married to one of the up-time wizards who had been instrumental in shattering his naval attack on Wismar last year. Happily, Anne Cathrine's heart had already been moving precipitously in Eddie's direction, so King Daddy's stratagems had been, practically speaking, more of an emphatic imprimatur than an imperial order.

Jessica leaned back, arms crossed. "So if she wanted to stay in Grantville for a few weeks or months, instead of three days last fall, why shouldn't you and she have done so?"

"Because of how it would have looked, Jessica. I was the king's hostage after Luebeck, and his convalescent patient." He gestured down toward his leg. "But instead of ending up as a diplomatic football, I became part of the whole war's diplomatic solution."

"How's that?"

"Well, you know the old story: how 'young lovers' from two sides of a conflict become the basis of peace between enemies. Funny how a little intangible 'feel good' stuff like that can go a long way to easing tensions, making things a little smoother at the truce, and then the treaty tables. Which rolled right on into the deals that led to Denmark's entry into a restored Union of Kalmar with Sweden."

"Okay, but all that was finished even before you got married. So why not come back sooner?"

"Well, that whole 'young love' angle could also have lost a lot of its fairy-tale glow unless we got married pretty quickly, since, er ... since—"

"Since there was no way of knowing how long it would be before the young wife might become a young mother. And how it might embarrass King Daddy if there were fewer than eight months between bridal bed and birthing bed."

"Uh ... yeah. Pretty much." Eddie hated that he still—*still*—blushed so easily. "And once I was officially part of the family, I needed to get introduced all around

Denmark. And any noble that did not get to host us for a short stay or a party or some other damned meet-and-greet event was sure to get their nose out of joint. And of course, the order in which we went to all these dinners and dances was how King Christian demonstrated this year's pecking order amongst his aristocracy."

"And he got to show off his own prize-stud, up-timer wizard, bought fair and square at the territorial negotiation table last summer."

"Yup." Although, truth be told, Eddie had found the whole circus of his semi-celebrity more than a bit of an ego-boost. Who would have ever guessed that his marginal nerdiness would one day make him a star? Back up-time, in the twentieth century, his identity as gamer, military-history nut, and educated layman on all the related technologies had made him one of the boys that the hot-looking high school girls had looked straight through—unless they needed help with their homework. But here in the seventeenth century, those same qualities, along with his service and wounding in the recent Baltic War, had made him the veritable crown prince of geek chic.

Of course, the down-timers didn't see the geekiness at all. To them, he was simply a young Renaissance Man, a creature all at once unique, and brave, and furnished with powerful reservoirs of knowledge that were surprisingly deep and unthinkably wide. And Anne Cathrine was his first and most ardently smitten admirer. Which suited him just fine since, reciprocally, he was her biggest fan, as well.

"And so as soon as King Christian was done with you, your prior master, Admiral Simpson, snatched you back to Luebeck?"

"Well, Admiral Simpson never stopped being my C.O., even when I was a prisoner of war. Afterward, too. So when you get right down to it, all the gallivanting I did in Denmark was really an 'extended leave to complete diplomatic initiatives.'" Eddie swayed into motion, put his right hand out, used the cane in his left to steady himself. "Jessica, thanks so much. The prosthesis—the leg—feels so natural. It's going to make a huge difference in my life."

Jessica smiled. "Well, that was the objective. And you've got a lot going on in that life. Seems, in some ways, that the Ring of Fire has been a good change for you." She glanced down; her smile dimmed. "I mean, I'm not saying that it was worth losing a leg over, but—"

"I know what you mean, Jessica. Without the Ring of Fire, I'd probably have been working a nowhere job, trying to figure out a way to pay for college as the weeks and months mounted up, and I had less and less in the bank to show for them. Sure, I'd have both legs—"

"But you wouldn't be so alive, wouldn't have so much to look forward to?"

"Yeah, I think that's it. Up-time, I just might be surviving day after dull day in my parents' basement, but here, I'm living life. For real. And so is she."

Jessica frowned, not understanding. "'She'? Who? The princess?"

Eddie nodded, released Jessica's hand, and started moving—with surprising ease and surety—for the door. "Yup."

Jessica held him with her wondering voice. "How did the Ring of Fire make her—well, more alive?"

Eddie turned. "It didn't *make* her more alive, Jessica. It *kept* her alive. In the old history, Anne Cathrine died on August 20, 1633. But for some reason, when we arrived here in 1631, our actions sent out waves of change that radiated into her life as well. Who knows? Maybe a ship carrying plague didn't make it to Copenhagen, or she missed a dance where she was exposed to typhus, or any one of another million possible rendezvous with death that she was prevented from making. All I know is that she's here now, and very alive. But back up-time, where she was part of what we called 'history,' she was dead ten days after her fifteenth birthday."

Jessica's mouth was slightly open. She seemed to be searching for something to say. And was failing.

Eddie nodded. "Thanks again, Jessica," he said. "Say hello to your folks for me." He swung around the door jamb, tugging the door closed behind him.

Chapter 2

Grantville, State of Thuringia-Franconia

Colonel Hugh Albert O'Donnell, the expatriate Earl of Tyrconnell, slugged back the contents of the small, clear shot glass. The liquid he gulped down burned from the top of his gullet to the bottom of his gut and filled his head with fumes that, he still suspected, might be poisonous. But at least this time he wasn't going to—

The burn flared at the back of his throat and he coughed. And choked and sputtered. He looked up at his hosts—Grantville's two Mike McCarthys, one Senior and one Junior—who looked on sympathetically. The older man also seemed to be suppressing either a grimace or a grin. Hugh put the shot glass aside politely.

"Can't stomach moonshine, eh?" There was a little friendly chiding in Don McCarthy the Elder's tone.

"Alas, and it pains an Irishman to say it, I cannot. It is not as similar to *poteen* as you conjectured. And it has not 'grown on me' as you Americans say—not the least bit, these past six nights. My apologies."

13

"Ah, that's all right," said Mike the Younger, who disappeared into the kitchen and promptly returned with a perfectly cast squat bottle, half-filled with liquid of a very promising amber color. "Want to try some bourbon?"

Hugh struggled to understand. "Is it a drink of that line, of that family?"

"'Of that line—?' Oh, you mean the Bourbons of France? No, no: this is American whiskey—*uisce beatha*—made in some of the Southern States. Interested?"

At the words "whiskey" and its Gaelic root-word, *uisce beatha*, Hugh felt his interest and even his spirits brighten. He sat a little straighter. "I am very interested, Michael."

Smiles and new drinks all around. But the small glasses were poured out very carefully this time, as though the "bourbon" was precious nectar—and then Hugh realized that indeed it must be. The label, the bottle, the screw-on cap: all bore the stamp of machine-manufactured precision. This was a whiskey from almost four hundred years in the future. It would be a long wait indeed before any more was available. Hugh resolved to savor every drop. He raised his glass. "*Slainte.*"

"*Slainte,*" replied Michael McCarthy, Sr. with a quick, wide smile.

Michael the Younger mumbled something that sounded more like "shlondy." He obviously saw the grin that Hugh tried to suppress. "Maybe you can teach me how to say it later?" Mike Jr. wondered sheepishly.

Marveling at the taste of the bourbon, Hugh nodded. "If my payment is more bourbon, you may consider yourself furnished with a permanent tutor in the finer points of Gaelic." Hugh felt his smile slip a little. "Well, as permanent as a tutor may be when he must leave on the morrow."

"Hugh," began Mike Jr., "I'll say it again: Dad and I would be happy—very happy—if you'd reconsider and stay a few more days."

O'Donnell waved his hand. "Forgive me for having struck a melancholy note. Let us not ruin this fine drink with dark thoughts. Besides,"—he hoped his light tone would change the mood—"the name of this whiskey reminds me that I need to practice my French pronunciation. Which, up until now, has usually been employed in the exchange of pleasantries over the tops of contested revetments and abatis."

The answering smiles were polite, not amused. Michael Sr. rolled the small glass of bourbon slowly between his palms. "Why are you brushing up on your French?"

Hugh sighed. "A man must eat, Don McCarthy."

"I'd have thought that would hardly be a worry for you."

Hugh shrugged. "While I was in the employ of the king of Spain, you would have been quite right. But I am no longer the colonel of a regiment, nor a knight-captain of the Order of Alcantara, nor may I even remain a servant of my own godmother, Infanta Isabella of the Lowlands, since she remains a vassal of Philip IV of Spain. I am, as you would say, 'unemployed.'"

Don McCarthy leaned back. "So—France. You are becoming a true soldier-of-fortune now."

"You may say the dirty word: yes, I am now a

'mercenary.' I have little choice. So too for all us Irish 'Wild Geese' in Spanish service. Our employer's 'alliance' with England runs counter to any hope that Philip will make good his promise to liberate Ireland. It is a failure that is anticipated in your own histories—although there, the reasons were somewhat different. Besides, I do not wish to find myself fighting you."

"Fighting *us*? How?"

"How not? Spain's enmity toward your United States of Europe is unlikely to abate soon. So, if I am not willing to become the physical instrument of that hatred, I must take service elsewhere. And that decision reflects not just my loyalty as your friend, but the practicality of a seasoned officer: becoming a military adversary of the USE seems best suited to those who are in an intemperate rush to meet their maker."

Michael Sr. smiled a bit. Michael Jr. frowned a bit. Hugh leaned toward the latter. "What is it, Michael?"

"Nothing. Just thinking, is all."

"Thinking of what?"

Michael Jr. seemed to weigh his words very carefully before he spoke. "Well, Hugh, we might be working for the same boss, soon."

"You, Michael—working for the French? How could that be? Just last year, they attacked the USE."

"Well, yes . . . but that was last year. We have a treaty now."

"Michael, just a few days ago, did your own father not quip that the honor of nations is, in fact, an oxymoron?"

"Dad did, but I'm not counting on French honor." He snorted the last two words. "I'm thinking practically.

My guess is that the French are going to be lying low for a while, at least with regards to the USE. So it should be safe for me to do a short stint of work for the French, just to make some extra money. To handle some extra expenses."

Hugh frowned, perplexed. Then, through the kitchen doorway, he saw Mike Sr.'s German nurse bustling busily at a shelf lined with his many special ointments, potions, and pills.

Michael Sr. spoke up. "Yep, I'm the 'extra expense.'"

"Perhaps I remember incorrectly, but isn't your wife—?"

"A nurse. Yes, but she's needed elsewhere, and there's not a whole lot she can do for me that any reasonably competent person can't."

"And the USE does not provide you with adequate care in exchange for both your wife's service, and your son's?"

"Oh, they provide, but it's pretty costly, taking care of a crusty old coot like me."

Hugh smiled, not really understanding what a "coot" was or how it might acquire a crust, but he got the gist by context.

Michael leaned towards his father, subtly protective. "So I found a way to make a lot of money pretty quickly, I think. But it involves going over the border."

"To France."

"More specifically, to Amiens."

Hugh started. "You mean to work for Turenne?"

Michael nodded, looked away.

Hugh did his best to mask his surprise. "Really? Turenne? And his technical, eh, 'laboratories?'"

Michael nodded again. "I negotiated the leave of

absence a while ago. My bags are pretty much packed. Literally."

"And Stearns, and Gustav, will allow you to provide technical assistance to Turenne?"

Michael shrugged, still looking away. "This down-time version of America is still a free country. We brought that with us and kept it. Mostly. Besides, I'll only be showing the French how to achieve something that I'm sure they've already studied in our books."

Hugh nodded, wondered what this "something" might be, and also if there might be some way for Michael and he to combine their westward journeys. He leaned back, feeling a surge of relief at even this nebulous prospect of having a comrade as he began to seek his fortune in France. It was a relief to think one might not start out on a new career completely alone, almost as comforting as the fire which threw flickering shadows around the walls and even painted a few on the back of the front door.

Six days ago, Hugh had knocked on that front door—unannounced—to begin his second visit to Grantville. This was a considerable departure from the formality of his first visit, made about three months earlier.

That initial visit had been something of a low-level affair of state. Technically still the earl of Tyrconnell (in everyone's opinion but the English), Hugh Albert O'Donnell's name was known to some up-timers not only in reports from this present, but also from the tales of their own past. And it had been that past, and the future that had followed from it, that Hugh had come to explore.

Grantville's official libraries had been helpful in

the matter of general history, but had little mention of Hugh or his illustrious forebears. Rather, it was his first passage through the front door of the McCarthy house that changed his world forever. Although it was Michael Jr. who had invited Hugh to use their home library, it was the father—an elderly ex-miner suffering from black lung—who was the more ardent (or at least outspoken) Fenian, possessing an impressive collection of both historical and contemporary texts on the subject. Like some enfeebled but passionate bard, Michael Sr. could recall twice the number of tales that were in the books, and was singularly well-versed in the lore of Ireland's many troubles—troubles which had continued on, Hugh was devastated to learn, for almost another four centuries.

On the last day of his first visit, Don McCarthy had waggled a gnarled finger at him. "Sir O'Donnell—"

"Don McCarthy, this will not do. I insist that you address me simply as 'Hugh.'"

"Then stop calling me 'Don McCarthy'—'Hugh.'"

Hugh could not stop the smile. "You are the eldest of your family and have the wisdom of many years. I would be a boor not to title you 'Don.'"

"Don" McCarthy made a gruff, guttural sound. He had learned that, although the thirty-year-old earl was always gentle with his hosts, he had a winning way of getting what he wanted. "I have a book," the elder McCarthy grumbled at last.

"You have many."

"Yeah—well, this one talks about you."

"I am mentioned in many of the—"

"No, Hugh. This one has a special chapter about you. About your family, your life—your death."

Hugh felt the hair on the back of his neck rise up straight and stay that way. The old McCarthy patriarch reached up a slender journal. Hugh remembered taking it with the same mix of avidity and dread that he would have felt if given the chance to handle one of the legendary serpents that possessed both the power to kill and confer immortality.

And the chapter, written in 1941 by Brendan Jennings, OFM, had proven to have both such powers. In his first hurried read of *The Career of Hugh, Son of Rory O'Donnell, Earl of Tyrconnell, in the Low Countries*, Hugh discovered that he and the last of his men were to die in 1642, only seven years hence, in the service of Spain, fighting the French at sea off the coast of Barcelona. And thus was sparked his resolve to leave direct Spanish service and encourage his men to consider carefully any offer that might draw them away from their benefactress—and his aunt—Archduchess Isabella of the Spanish Lowlands. It was a decision that might simply lead him to an even earlier death, Hugh reasoned, but that was only one possibility. And so, he hoped that he, and many of his men, had been granted a new lease on life.

But within a few minutes, Hugh discovered the darker curse lurking in the pages of the book. It indicated that his wife had died in 1634. And so she had. Eighteen-year-old Anna Margaritte de Hennin had often visited the court of the infanta Isabella, who had been instrumental in brokering Hugh's marriage to her. What had started as an act of prudent policy had blossomed (as Isabella had wryly predicted) into a passionate romance, but one which had ended in bitter tragedy. Anna Margaritte lost both their first child and her life in the week before Christmas, torrents of post-partum blood pouring out of her as if some demon within could not kill her quickly or thoroughly enough.

Hugh stared at the book. The warning had been here. It had been here since the American town had materialized in the middle of Germany in 1631. It had been here before he had married Anna Margaritte. Before they had spoken of children. The warning of Anna Margaritte's death in childbirth had been here, waiting. And he had not come, had not read it.

And so they had conceived a child in blissful igno-rance and she had died in horrible agony.

Hugh did not remember leaving the McCarthys' house. He remembered putting the book down care-fully, remembered gathering most of his belongings and notes, and the next thing he knew, he was riding west, into the deepening night. His two guards caught up with him, frenzied with worry, three hours later.

After returning to his regiment, Hugh spent days recovering from the shock of what he had read, and then weeks thinking about what course of action he should take, and when.

At last, just before spring, he began writing the most difficult and delicate letter of his long career as a correspondent with kings and cardinals, princes and pontiffs. When he completed the letter in early April, he leaned back and tried to see anew this document that had even plagued his dreams. And so, skipping the long prefatory parade of titles and overblown felicities, he read the beginning of its second paragraph with, he hoped, fresh eyes:

*"So as not to besmirch the names and honor
of my kind patrons—who ensured I kept my
own titles when my sires died—I regretfully
announce my resolve to take leave of their
service, that I may better serve my native
country and kinsmen. This decision in no
way signifies any deficiency or decrease
in the love and esteem in which I hold
my many benefactors. I have naught but
gratitude for their innumerable kindnesses,
and I depart their service heavy with the
sorrow that I shall surely never know the
like of their love again."*

And, given the many contexts (and pretexts) that
had gone into the making of Hugh's current situation, he reflected that his words were true enough
on all counts. The persons who had truly been his
surrogate family—Archduchess Infanta Isabella; Sister
Catherine, prioress of the *Dames Blanches*; Father
Florence Conry of St. Anthony's—had been generous,
compassionate, even loving. And of his more distant
benefactors—the careful Philip, his recidivistic court,
and its hopelessly blinkered courtiers—he could only
say that their "love" had indeed been unique. No group
of "benefactors" had ever stood in such a strange and
often awkward relationship to its dependents as had
the Spanish crown to the relatives of the exiled Irish
earls O'Donnell and O'Neill.

Three days later, Hugh was finally able to bring
himself to fold the letter and press his seal down
deep into the pool of red wax that bled across the
edge of the top sheet.

The following morning he posted the letter to his patrons and lieges, sought permission for a leave of several weeks, received it, dashed off a missive to the McCarthys that might or might not arrive before he did, and set off for his second visit to Grantville, alone.

He had arrived at their fateful yet welcoming front door six days ago. He had ventured back out beyond it a few times, but had spent most of the days—and nights—reading. Reading reading reading. And when he was not reading, he was making notes, comparing accounts, examining how the dominoes of polities and personalities had fallen during what the up-timer histories called the Thirty Years' War. Judging from how current events had already veered dramatically away from those chronicled in the up-timer books, Hugh quickly concluded that although the current wars might or might not last as long as Thirty Years, they would have an even more profound and lasting effect upon the map—and life—of Europe. And, no doubt, the world beyond.

But ever and again, he would find something that reminded him of how his late arrival to Grantville and its histories had allowed him to follow the fateful track of that other future just a few months too long. Too long for his wife, his son, and at least a hundred of his regiment who had been lost fighting for the interests of a Spanish king who, it was now clear, would never fight for their interests.

And on this, the sixth night of his stay, while sitting in the worn living room of Don McCarthy, these specters of regret had been gathering within Hugh once again as Michael McCarthy, Jr., had emerged from the kitchen with the dreaded "white lightning" that the up-timers seemed to consider divine nectar. He had found himself recalling all the faces that had come to swear allegiance under his banners, and which were now buried in the loam of foreign fields.

He broke out of his silent reverie without preamble. "I could no longer command a unit that bore my name like a lure, so as to attract the *cultchies*—the simple country boys—like bees to pollen."

The McCarthys did not comment as the first round of moonshine was poured out, but he felt their eyes.

"It was hard watching them die in foreign service, far from home, dismally used. But I could make myself do it, so long as I was able to believe we were purchasing the good opinion of our Spanish allies, that we were securing their permanent regard for our honor and character, as well as skill on the battlefield. And that, therefore, Philip would finally be moved to act—if only to keep faith with the promises he had made to men of such quality and integrity." He took a look a small sip of the white lightning. "What a fool I was."

Michael Sr. responded in a low, steady voice. "Hugh, you were brought up by good people to be a good man, and true. But nations—even those ruled by kings who claim to prize honor and loyalty—cannot keep faith with those same virtues. It's in the nature of nations to make promises they don't keep. Unfortunately, no man can know beforehand which of the promises made to him will turn out to be the worthless ones."

Hugh heard the attempt to take the onus off him. He shrugged it off. "I was gullible—in this and other matters. I was not merely a child but a simpleton to believe the initial priestly rubbish about Americans as the spawn of Satan himself. If I hadn't put such faith in Philip's court clerics, I might have thought for myself and come here earlier. I might have read my own future—and in it, seen and avoided Anna's death in childbirth."

"You could not have known." Don Michael's tone was soft yet strangely certain.

"I could have. I could have found better care for her."

"She was Flemish aristocracy. She had the finest doctors of Europe."

"The finest doctors of Europe, even of the Lowlands, are not *your* doctors. My reading has not been confined to the future plight of Ireland, Don McCarthy. I have spent many hours in your libraries. I have learned of obstetrical bleeding, of *placenta previa*. And so I learned that what killed my wife was ignorance: my ignorance, our ignorance."

"Son,"—and McCarthy sounded sincere in affixing that label—"son; you couldn't have read that in time to save her."

"With respect, Don McCarthy, you were here almost three years before her *accouchement*. At any time, I could have—"

"No, Hugh. I'm not saying that the books were not here to be read. I mean that you weren't ready to read—and *believe*—them." He looked to his own son, whose often unreadable gray eyes were crinkled in what appeared to be pain.

And suddenly Hugh understood that these strikingly plain-mannered beings had been trying to lead him to the realization that now snapped on in his mind like one of their impossible "light bulbs":

—it was Anna's *death* that had jarred him enough so that, shaken from his old perspectives, he could see the world through the new lenses brought by the up-timers. Before she had died, he would not have traveled to read, nor have believed or trusted the content of, the books in Grantville that might have saved her. But when their unborn child had killed her by tearing out the very root of the umbilicus that had already choked him, Hugh's happy complacency ended. Their two deaths had midwifed the birth of his new consciousness.

The change had not been instantaneous. His former habits of thought had not died suddenly, as if decapitated by the single blow of a headsman's axe. No, it had been like a fall from a great height, starting when the midwives and doctors left him alone with Anna's haggard corpse and the tiny, blue-black body of he who was to have had his father's name, and titles, and boundless love. Sitting there with that tiny form in his hands, Hugh had started falling into a hole at the center of himself: falling falling falling—

And when he finally awakened from that long fall, weeks later, he opened his eyes upon a different world. It was a world that was unguided by Divine Providence, and in which his kinsmen had languished and died hoping hopeless hopes. And then had come the strange letter from Grantville.

It had been a strange letter indeed. It conveyed, first and foremost, condolences—of which there had been many others, most far more grandiloquent in their invocation of tragedy and the mysterious will of God. In contrast, this letter—from an up-timer named Mr. Michael McCarthy, Sr.—while clearly heartfelt, had been singularly straightforward and plainspoken. Yet, it landed like a thunderbolt before Hugh's eyes. In part, this was because he had never thought to receive any such expression of solicitude from an up-timer. But even more arresting was McCarthy's lament that the death of Hugh's wife and heir were also "terrible blows to all O'Donnells—and to the many generations of patriotic Irish who came after you."

This added a strange, almost surreal dimension to his loss. Posterity had, somewhere, already been lastingly impacted by the death of his child and his wife. And the more Hugh reflected on that, the more he felt it grow like a tapeworm in that part of his mind that digested new facts. He and his line were known in the future. And that future could be discovered by going to Grantville.

And so he had. And now he sat in Don Michael McCarthy's living room, sharing this magical bourbon with him and his son. He sighed, sipped again, wondered if life was really any less capricious than the unpredictable dance of flames in this hearth built from eerily identical up-time bricks. He watched the fire send flickering shadow-demons capering along the walls. But less energetically now; it was burning low.

Michael Jr. noticed the fading flames and got up; he gestured for Hugh to remain in his seat. "I'll get another few pieces of wood. Stay put." He looked for his coat. "Damn. That's right; it's in the wash."

Hugh tried to hide his smile. Michael had attempted to ride Hugh's war-trained charger earlier in the day. The high-spirited stallion had been tolerant enough when the up-timer was in the saddle, but was impatient with his awkward attempt at dismounting. One sharp, tight turn had flung coat-wearing Michael down into the mud and manure.

Hugh rose. "Michael, I will—"

"You will not. You're my guest."

Hugh took his distinctively embroidered cape from the knob on the coat-closet door, revealing his scabbarded sword. "Then at least stay warm in this."

Michael seemed ready to decline, then nodded his thanks and took the cape. Hugh sat back down, contemplated the firelight sparkling through the bourbon, wondered what foreign fire he'd be staring into a year from now.

Presuming that he was still alive to do so.

Chapter 3

Grantville, State of Thuringia-Franconia

Eddie emerged onto the rapidly dimming streets of Grantville and pushed up his collar against the faint chill. *You'd think after spending almost a year and a half on the Baltic I'd have a little better resistance to cold, but no.* Having recovered from borderline hypothermia while recuperating from the amputation had left him weakened for quite a long time. In particular, he had been susceptible to chest colds that, up-time, would have been annoyances cleared up by any halfway decent decongestant. Down-time, they were potential death sentences in his then-weakened state. And ever since, cold weather cut through him like a knife.

He strolled west, deciding to take a look at the three trailer homes that had served as his first down-time abode. He smiled to think of the early days when he and Jeff Higgins and Larry Wild and Jimmy Andersen had played D & D there, the game having acquired a strange significance given their displacement in time. It wasn't because of the "historical value" of the game—because there wasn't any; role-playing games were about excitement, not accuracy—but because it was somehow a symbol that not everything had changed with their arrival in war-torn Germany. Not every waking minute was toil for food, scrambling to preserve or rebirth technology, find allies, and repel utterly murderous foes. A quick session of D & D, where imaginary warriors and wizards strove to slay evil trolls and troglodytes, was also a reassurance that life had not boiled down only to a mere continuation of existence. There was still time for fanciful adventures, for larking about a fictional world with his very real friends.

But then Jeff had married a down-time firebrand named Gretchen Richter, and her entire loosely-associated clan had moved in. Overnight, fancy had given way to kid-powered frenzy. And that, too, had been reassuring and endearing in its own way. It was as though the house was constantly alive with rambunctious sounds of hope, thanks to all the healthy, lively children that were forever charging around and through its small rooms and tight hallways. Yes, in all its permutations, Eddie reflected, it had been a good house.

He almost walked past the tripartite structure, so changed was it. Gone were the bright, albeit fading, colors of the siding. The local tenants (who paid a pretty penny for the privilege of living in an up-time domicile) had given it a second layer of wood shingles, dug a number of discreet latrines in the back to relieve the burden on the indoor plumbing, tidied up the yard, and replaced two of the doors (and their frames) with solid local manufactures. They had also erected what looked like a huge, wooden carport over the entire structure, evidently in an attempt to preserve the metal and vinyl conglomeration from the elements. However, it created the impression that this was not so much a home as it was an oversized shrine commemorating trailer parks everywhere.

Through the windows, oil lamps glowed to greet the dusk, and then shadows moved with slow purpose toward the largest of the kitchens. A brief pause and then a sharp white-yellow light seemed to blot out all the other fire-orange glows about the house. Clearly, someone had turned on an electric light. Immediately, silhouettes of all sizes began gathering around it, some bearing what looked like outlines of cooking implements, others arriving with already-open books.

It looked ritualistic, Eddie admitted, but he knew damned well it was not some strange species of cargo-cultism, a trait Larry Wild had often ascribed to the down-time Germans before he was killed off the coast of Luebeck almost two years ago. This was the prudence of practically-minded folk, amplified by the parsimony of war survivors. Germans who had lived through the now-truncated Thirty Years' War were generally not spendthrifts. Every resource they had was kept as long as possible, its life extended by using it only when absolutely necessary. And when that intermittent and gentle use nonetheless wore it out, the object was repurposed—right down to its last component. Objects with limited service lives became especially revered objects: not because of their wondrousness, but because of the mix of singular utility and utter irreplaceability that characterized them. It would be a long time before the up-time boosted labs and workshops of even the best down-timer engineers and inventors were producing freon filled cooling compressors or a wide selection of vaccines or antibiotics.

But the down-timers were also coming up with new compensatory technologies, one of which now intruded upon Eddie's reverie. Just down the street from where he stood staring at the house that had been his first haven in this often frightening new version of the Old World, he heard a distant toot. Like a child's train whistle, but louder. He turned and, already moving far faster than he ever had with his peg leg, Eddie Cantrell hobble-ran in an attempt to catch the new monorail trolley that was approaching the stop on East Main Street, just a block behind him.

The strange vehicle chugged slowly into view: a simple wooden front car that resembled a rough-hewn and vastly shrunken version of a San Francisco cable car. Except there were no cables, and there was only one track, comprised of split logs, their flat-cut centers lying flush upon the ground, their sun-bleached hemicircular trunks facing up. The operator reached down, disengaged the drive-gear, applied brakes. The train slowed and the passengers in the front car swayed, as did the crates and boxes in the high-sided freight car behind it.

Eddie timed his hobble so as to wave his cane and shout when he came down on his good leg. "Hey, wait up!"

If the operator heard him, he gave no sign of it. Instead, he stepped down to help an elderly passenger up into the lead car.

Which, on closer inspection, was a radical departure from any form of up-time rail transportation Eddie had ever seen. In addition to the two, flanged, steel track-wheels—salvaged from small automobiles, and now leather-strapped on their contact surface with the rail—there was, for lack of a better term, a larger wagon wheel attached to the side of the car as an outrigger. It kept the car upright, and ran along the smooth up-time roadbed. The front car's very small steam engine, puffing faintly, was of entirely down-time manufacture. Not terribly efficient, and both heavy and crude, but none of that mattered: it provided reliable power to the up-time car wheels that pulled the car along the wooden track at a comfortable six miles an hour or so.

"Hey!" shouted Eddie again, and this time, missed the timing with his cane. But his new foot's spring-compressed heel popped him into his next step, and what should have been a nasty fall turned into an arm-flailing stumble.

Which apparently attracted the attention of the operator. "I wait!" the man assured him loudly, squinting at Eddie's gait. "We always wait for our soldiers."

Eddie waved his thanks, noted the driver's extremely thick accent. Swabian, from the sound of him, likely rendered homeless by the border wars between the up-timers' first allies—the Swedes of Gustav Adolf—and the upstart dukedom of Bernhard, originally one of the dukes of Saxe-Weimar. As had so many other refugees from all the neighboring provinces of Germany, this driver had probably come to Grantville to find his fortune—and no doubt, from his perspective, had accomplished just that. There was a palpable eagerness as he turned from seating the elderly passenger and came forward to offer a hand to Eddie.

The prompt, energetic gesture radiated that special pride particular to those down-timers who operated the new machines that their own artisans had crafted from up-time ideas and inspirations. It was as though they were simultaneously saying, "See? We are helping build this new world with you!" and "Do not discount us: we are just as smart as you are." In truth, given how little of the up-time science and engineering they understood when Grantville first fell out of the future, and how much of its technology they were now mastering and adapting, it was arguably true that, on the average, the Germans were smarter than the up-timers. Markedly so, in a number of cases.

Eddie smiled his thanks at the driver and accepted the hand up into the passenger car. With only room for twenty, who were currently packed in like sardines, there was no seat left for him. Seeing the unnatural stiffness of Eddie's left leg, one of the comparatively younger men stood quickly, gestured towards his spot on a transverse bench. Eddie smiled, shook his head with a "Thanks, anyhow," and held on to the rail as the car lurched forward to resume its journey with a sigh of steam.

The other passengers were mostly mothers with children, older folks, and two other amputees. One of the passengers seemed to be a workman, hand truck tucked tight between his legs. *Probably delivering the cargo in the back*, Eddie surmised.

They had hardly gone a block when the driver stifled a curse and backed off the steam, letting the little train begin to coast. Seeing Eddie's interest, he pointed forward. "Another train. I must pull off."

Eddie saw the oncoming train, almost a twin to the

one he was on, approaching from about two blocks away. But there was only one rail. "Um . . . how do we—?"

The driver seemed gratified, rather than annoyed, by the question. "See ahead, the curve into the smaller cross-street we approach?"

"Yeah, you mean Rose Street?"

"Yes. We take that curve and wait."

"Like a train being diverted into a siding."

"Yes. But it is only one track, so we slow down to wait in the little street."

And applying the brakes gently, they slid around the relatively tight curve with only a slight bump. But the operator frowned at the brief jolt.

"Problem?" asked Eddie.

"Not with the train; with the track," he answered. "It is wood. It wears out quickly at the joints."

"Then why use wood?"

He smiled. "Because wood is also very cheap. So is the cost of putting new track into place. Much cheaper than iron. Or steel. Maybe you forget that, since there was so much of that metal in the future?"

Eddie smiled back. "Yeah, there was—but no, I didn't forget. I deal with that problem every day."

The driver's slightly graying left eyebrow rose. "Yes, and so?"

"I work with Admiral Simpson. Building the new navy."

"Ah. Of course you would know about iron shortages, then." He paused, looked at Eddie more closely. "So you are . . . are Commander Cantrell, yes? The hero?"

Eddie felt a rapid flush. "I was just—just doing my job."

As the other engine huffed past, the man's eyes

strayed to Eddie's left leg. "I think you did a little more than just your job, maybe." He looked up. "I am honored to have you on my train." His English became slightly more precise. "Where may I take you, Herr Commander Cantrell?" There was also a hint of a straighter spine and the faintest bow. Not enough to imply a new, distant formality, but enough to show acknowledgement and respect.

"Oh, just up the street to—"

"The Government House? We shall be there very soon."

"The Government House?" Eddie echoed. "What's that?"

The man smiled. "It is officially called the 'Administrative Annex'—the old presidential office building. It is where all the decisions were made before the capital was moved to Bamberg. But as you must know, there are still many decisions being made there. And I suspect it will continue to be so."

"But then why relocate the capital to Bamberg?"

The driver smiled sagely. "Oh, Bamberg will certainly be the center of attention, and home to most of the bureaucracy. All the fine lords and burgermeisters will journey there and make speeches and drink too much and diddle the barmaids—if their wives have not made the journey with them."

"And here at the Government House?"

"Here is where the business of putting certain decisions into practice will remain. Certain sensitive decisions. It is interesting to see which offices remain here—renamed, but still here. Offices which must make important decisions very quickly. And how else should it be? Here, all the leaders, all the decisions, are still only a phone call away. But here, also, there are many up-time radios and the people who know best how to use them. Here is running water, and electricity for computers, and heat and light for winter hours that reach far into the night." He shifted a gear, opened the throttle, looked behind, and began to reverse back out onto the main line of the track that ran along East Main. "Bamberg is certainly the capital, the center for important talk. But Grantville, Commander Cantrell, remains the center for important action." And with that, he shifted the train's gear back into its original position, tugged the whistle cord, and, as if to give emphasis to that hoarse toot, opened the throttle to resume their journey to Government House.

Chapter 4

Grantville, State of Thuringia-Franconia

Hugh sighed and sipped his bourbon again. Michael McCarthy, Jr., having shrugged into O'Donnell's heavy, distinctively embroidered cloak, thumped through the front room and out the front door.

Hugh let his head lean back on the sofa and closed his eyes, savoring the smooth aftertaste of the bourbon and letting the faces and voices of the past fade away. In their place, he let the utterly mundane sounds of the guttering fire and Michael Jr.'s progress fill his mind. Over the hissing crack of logs rapidly breaking down into embers, he heard Michael trot down off the porch and around to the garage-become-stable. A moment later, Hugh's charger greeted the up-timer with a congenial nicker.

And then, Hugh heard a fast, sliding patter of stealthy human feet: the almost liquid sound of an assassin closing on his target.

Hugh bounded out of the McCarthys' sagging sofa. He landed next to the coat-closet, hip-pinned his sword's scabbard against that door, and drew the saber in one, clean sweep, still moving as he did. He was already sprinting through the abbreviated foyer when a crossbow quarrel—almost certainly a blunt, from the sound of it—smashed loudly through the garage-side window closest to the front door. Someone had seen him moving, had taken a shot.

But why a blunt quarrel? wondered Hugh. That fleeting puzzlement didn't slow him any more than the front stairs. He leaped down all five, already running as he landed. As he approached the corner of the house, he heard a dull thud, a grunt, and the muffled bump of someone bouncing off the pliable up-timer wall-shingling that they called "vinyl siding."

Hugh went low as he snaked around the side of the house, saw Michael Jr. face down on the ground, a cloaked figure over him, club ready, reaching toward him—

But not trying for a quick kill—a split-second observation which, again, did not delay Hugh. Trusting that the unseen crossbowman had not had time to both reload and aim his weapon, he leaped forward, saber whirring back and then forward with the speed that only a trained wrist can deliver.

The cloaked assailant looked up, quickly raised his club: a reflex more than a purposeful parry. Hugh's Toledo blade clipped the wooden truncheon at an angle. The wood stripped back and then splintered.

Michael's attacker was thrown back by the blow, alive only because his club had absorbed a cut that would have gone through his collar-bone. But, rebounding from his own collision with the house's vinyl siding, the thug turned his momentum into a sideways barrel-roll that brought him back up to his feet in a moment. He sped into the darkness—

And I'm out of time, Hugh thought—and dropped prone just a second before a crossbow bolt sliced through the air where he had been standing. The quarrel impaled the vinyl upon the wood behind it with an almost musical *throoonk.* Hugh did not need to look up to know that this bolt had not been the kind used to stun small game. He jumped to his feet, sprinted along the reverse trajectory indicated by the quivering tail of the quarrel. He found the weapon that had fired it abandoned on the ground twenty yards away, in the lee of the neighboring house's shed. The dark night was quiet all around.

Staying low—as a lifetime of habit and training had taught him—Hugh frog-trotted back to Mike Jr., who was already raising himself up on his elbows. The displaced earl of Tyrconnell put an arm on his friend's not-inconsiderable bicep. "Here. Let me help you, Don Michael."

For a moment, Hugh thought that his middle-aged host was going to refuse. Then he felt the arm sag a bit as Michael grunted his gratitude and allowed Hugh to roll him into a sitting position, back against the house. But he was evidently not too stunned to speak. "So now I'm 'Don Michael,' too? What does that make me—royalty?"

"Aristocracy," Hugh corrected gently, wondering how the up-timers could command such wonderful knowledge of machinery and the physical sciences, and yet make social errors that would mark even a five-year-old down-timer as slow, perhaps simple. "I should have used the title before now."

"Before now, you were using it only on my da. I figured that was because he's almost eighty. So am I really 'aristocracy'—or just another old coot who can't defend himself any longer?"

The answer came from the corner of the house. "Speak for yourself, sonny boy." Michael McCarthy, Sr., was there, on his feet and unaided, but with one hand firmly clutching the corner-board for support. The gnarled fingers of his other hand were wrapped around the grip of a .45 automatic.

Michael Jr. goggled. "Da—you shouldn't be walking on your own. And is that your pop's old service pistol? I didn't know you kept—"

"Plenty you still don't know about me, Junior," interrupted Michael McCarthy, Sr. He tried to suppress a wry grin, almost did, but then his efforts were undermined by a bout of violent, phlegmy coughing.

Hugh was over to the ailing father in a moment. Michael Jr. following only a second behind, remonstrated, "Dad, you shouldn't be up—"

"Someone was shooting at my son and my guest—and damn if he didn't bust a window, too. So yes, you're God-damned right I got up, and brought a little bit of persuasion with me." He shook the .45 for emphasis—just as his wheezing phrases became a spasmodic coughing fit that was painful for Hugh to hear. He'd heard similar sounds often enough. War-time camp conditions in the Lowlands had killed almost as many of his men as blades and bullets. Now, lessons learned from up-timer books had begun to change that. Dramatically. But for a chronic condition such as Michael Sr.'s, there was little to do but delay the inevitable.

As they helped Michael Sr. back around the corner of the house, the door banged open and spat out the old man's German nurse, Lenna. Her fierce glance conclusively damned the two younger men for all the martial (and therefore male) idiocy that plagued the world. She almost shoved them aside in her outraged urgency to help Michael Sr. up the stairs, but at the top, he stopped, turned, snapped the .45's safety into place, and tossed the weapon down to Michael Jr.

Who stared at it, and then him.

"You're going to need it," the old man said, almost apologetically, and then disappeared into the darkness of the unlit doorway.

Michael Jr. stared after him and then back down at the gun.

Hugh put a hand on his shoulder. "Michael, are you hurt?"

Michael waved the concerns away with his free hand. "Nah. Hell, I've caught worse when a wrench slipped off the hood of a car I was working on. But what about you? Are you okay?"

Hugh paused, as he often did when Americans used that strange word, "o-kay." It had too many meanings, and each had its own maddeningly distinct contextual rules. "I was not injured—this time."

"'This time?' What do you mean?"

"I mean that I must assume that there will soon be another attempt on my life."

"Whoa—an attempt on *your* life?" Mike rubbed his head. "If this growing bump and my short-term memory don't lie, it was *me* they were trying to kill."

Hugh smiled, reached up, put a gentle index finger on the cloak Michael was wearing. It was the ornately distinctive one he had borrowed from Hugh just minutes before. "You took a blow that was meant for me, Michael."

He stared for a moment before asserting, "Well, then let's get over to the police station right away and—"

"It is not necessary that we involve your nation's public militia, Michael."

"The hell it isn't, Hugh. Look, you are a foreign dignitary, and someone just tried to assassinate you on our turf. And worse yet, they obviously had you under observation in *my* home."

"Michael, I am no longer a foreign dignitary. I have resigned my rank and titles in Spanish service, and my earldom is attainted. I am, as some of your novels would put it, 'just a regular guy,' now."

"Bullshit. Regular guys don't attract assassins. I'm taking you to the Army—"

"Michael, your kindness is a great honor, but I must refuse. I am not here in any official capacity. I am but a man visiting my friends."

"Then—as your friend—I insist that you come back into the house until we can figure out—" Michael ceased speaking as soon as Hugh began to shake his head.

"Michael, would you have me repay your kindness and friendship by bringing death over your doorstep? These two blackguards showed unexpected—indeed, inexplicable—restraint in their first attempt on my life. They are unlikely to do so next time. So, no, my friend, I will not further endanger you and your good father by accepting the hospitality of your hearth again. I must leave. Now."

Mike stared up at Hugh for three full seconds. Then he looked at the .45 in his own hand and nodded. "Okay. Then I'm coming with you."

Before Hugh could utter a negation through the

surprise and secret gratitude that washed over him, Mike had pounded back up the stairs, across the porch, and through the front door that had changed Hugh's life. And if the fates were as kind as they were strange, perhaps he and the younger McCarthy would not merely share the road to Amiens, but share professional fortunes as well. After all, any business with Turenne would ultimately be concerned with military matters—and Hugh had a long and varied acquaintance with those. Of course, it was too early to broach the topic of any kind of joint enterprise with Michael just yet, but the journey ahead would afford ample opportunities to casually learn more about the American's business in France, and if there was any way a displaced Irish earl might help with it...

Mike wasn't gone long—five minutes at most—before he reemerged, backpack in one hand, his other tucking the .45 under his belt. "I'm just about ready to go."

"But—doesn't your family have only one horse?"

"Yeah, but she's *my* horse. Besides, my stepmother is doing her nursing in another city and Dad ain't riding again any time soon."

"Are you sure this is a good idea?"

"You mean, because you're someone's target?"

"Yes."

"Well, I've been thinking about that. Actually, if I come along, it still might put you in danger. I *could* be the guy those assassins were trying to kill."

"Michael, admittedly you are a most important person. As a senior instructor at the technical college, I'm sure any number of foreign powers have a pointed interest in you. But you *were* wearing my cloak when you were attacked. And if anyone wished to assassinate you, they could have chosen a hundred other moments that would be both less complicated and more subtle. I am forced to conclude that I was the intended target."

"Okay—but then wouldn't there also have been a better time to get *you*?"

"In my case, this timing might actually *help* to explain why they made their attempt here and now."

"How so?"

"If an English agent got hold of my letter of resignation during its progress to Philip, then they will have learned that I no longer enjoy the relative protection of my official positions and my own regiment. They might very well send assassins—or maybe kidnappers— to intercept me before I can secure the protection of a new patron. After all, John O'Neill and I are still declarable as princes of Ireland. As offspring of royal blood, we remain worrisome to the English occupiers."

"Yeah, but England seems to have toned down a little bit on the 'Irish Question' right now."

"Officially, yes. And largely thanks to you Americans. But that might be why these assassins tried to use nonlethal methods, at first. King Charles—or factions in his court—might find it less complicated to simply imprison me in the Tower of London."

Michael nodded. "Okay, so maybe you *are* the bullet-magnet. But there's something else you should know, Hugh."

"Yes?"

"It's also possible there's been some loose talk about the technology that I'm bringing to Turenne."

"Others know about it?"

"A few. One is going to have to come with us."

Hugh did not try to stop his eyebrows from rising.

Mike hurried on. "Yeah, I know: another fellow-traveler is probably not what you were bargaining for. But this guy is part of the package. Turenne is going to need him. At least for the first few months. And if this guy, or any of his friends, talked, and rival powers heard the whispers, then—"

"—then they would want to make sure that Turenne will not enjoy the advantage of this new technology," Hugh finished for him. "So first they would try to take you hostage and secure the advantage for themselves, but failing that, they might resort to a more 'permanent' solution—"

"Right, which would make *me* the bullet magnet. Again."

Hugh smiled. "Evidently, we cannot know with certainty who is endangering whom. So we will share the peril equally. Now, you mentioned that we must pick someone up on the way. Who is this person?"

Mike started walking toward his nag. "He's a toy-maker."

"A toymaker? What kind of toys does he make?"

"Secret toys."

"Truly? Tell me, Michael, what kind of toy would need to be kept a secret?"

"I'll tell you as we ride."

Chapter 5

Grantville, State of Thuringia-Franconia

Ed Piazza, President of the State of Thuringia-Franconia rubbed his eyes. "Are those the latest production reports, Anton?"

Anton Roedel, former clerk for the city council of Rudolstadt and now Executive Secretary to the President, nodded. "Yes, Mr. President. The production numbers from the new coal mines should not be considered a basis for long-term projection, though. Their operating managers indicate that—"

"Yes, Anton," Piazza smiled, "I was listening when you read their letters to us."

Farther down the conference table—a battered brown institutional slab that had started life in the teacher's lounge of Grantville's elementary school—Vince Marcantonio, Piazza's chief of staff, stretched and groaned. "Please tell me that's the last of the reports, Anton."

"Yes sir, I thought it prudent to conclude with—"

There was a knock on the door.

Warner Barnes of the State Department sighed. "Now what?"

Francisco Nasi, Mike Stearns' spymaster, shrugged. "That would be the arrival of 'unofficial' official business."

"Huh?"

Piazza grinned. "C'mon, Warner, you've worked in the State Department long enough to recognize euphemistic 'code' when you hear it."

"Oh no," Barnes sighed, "not covert crap. Not now. That shit takes forever, and I want to get home."

"Before the evening gets cold?"

"Before my *dinner* gets cold and my wife blows her stack. This happens every time you and Francisco come back from Bamberg with a 'special agenda' for us to go through. This time, I don't think I've even seen her in the past seventy-two hours. She's out the door before I'm out of bed. I get back after she stops waiting up. You're a damned home wrecker, Mr. President."

Piazza nodded. "My apologies, but let's not keep our 'unexpected' guest waiting." Raising his voice, he called, "Come in!"

"Watch," growled Secretary of the Interior George Chehab from his sulky slouch at the very end of the table, "I'll bet this becomes the longest, drawn out business of the whole damned evening. Mark my words—"

But then his jaw shut with a snap, followed by a guilty gulp: Eddie Cantrell stuck his head into the room. He looked a little puzzled as he scanned all the faces.

"Uh...hello, Mr. President, gentlemen. I'm sorry if I'm interrupting. I was told you'd be concluded by this ti—"

Piazza smiled and waved him in. "There's always more work to do than there are hours in which to do it, Eddie. No worries."

The recording secretary looked at Eddie, then Piazza, then turned a new page, and started scribbling.

Eddie glanced uncertainly at Anton and back again to Piazza.

Piazza nodded faintly, so faintly that he was pretty sure that the only two people who saw it were Eddie, who was looking straight at him, and Nasi, who saw everything, anyway. "No need to itemize the report from Admiral Simpson, Eddie. Just leave it with us. We'll probably go over it after Mr. Roedel departs."

Anton seemed to start slightly, then resumed his scribbling.

Eddie nodded. "I understand, sir. Perfectly."

And he and Piazza shared a smile, just as they shared a complete understanding of why a review of the report was being deferred. By waiting until Anton was gone, there would be no official record of Admiral Simpson's strident, not to say fulminative, arguments about the materials, money, specialists, priorities, and other assets he wanted—no: needed!—in order to have a snowball's chance in hell of getting a blue water navy ready by the promised date.

"Those folders under your arm," Piazza said, nodding at the leather-bound attachés that passed for "folders" in Early Modern Germany, "I take it they also contain brand new requests from Admiral Simpson?"

Eddie's smile was rueful. "Yes, Mr. President. They most certainly do."

"And what would the esteemed admiral want now?"

"Well, pretty much everything he wrote you about last month. Except lots more of it."

Piazza put out his hand for the folders. Eddie moved to walk them over. Piazza saw the limp, remembered the missing leg, jumped to his feet to get the folders, mentally cursing his forgetfulness and excusing it at the same time. *Damn it! Eddie was just a kid—just a smart, awkward kid—only four years ago, staring at cheerleaders, dealing with acne, and coping with the low ceiling of his possibilities in a small West Virginia mining town. And now he's a handicapped veteran. But I still see that kid, when I look at him.*

And that was when Piazza saw the look on Eddie's face: that "kid" wanted to walk the folders over himself. And the way he held himself as he limped closer—straighter, in a military posture—shamed the image of Eddie Cantrell, Nice Kid, forever out of Piazza's mind. He was sad to see that old image go, but felt an almost tearful pride at the image that had now permanently replaced it: Lieutenant Commander Edward Cantrell, veteran and hero at the tender age of twenty-three.

Piazza extended his hand for the folders that Eddie could now reach out to him and he said, quietly, and as seriously as he had ever said anything in his life, "Thank you for bringing these to us, Commander Cantrell."

"My pleasure, sir."

"—*And my duty,*" Piazza heard as the unspoken subtext behind those words. He nodded. "Before you go, Commander, we have something that you need to take with you."

"A return communiqué, Mr. President?"

Piazza smiled. "No, Commander." He turned. Francisco Nasi held out a large, varnished wood box, with a strangely intense look in his dark eyes, as if he was hoping they would convey something that he could not, or dare not, frame as spoken words.

"Sir?" said Eddie, puzzled, as Piazza turned and proffered the box to him.

"Open it."

Eddie did and seemed to redden for the briefest moment. "Is this—?"

"That's the finished medal, Commander. Allow me."

Piazza took the box back, lifted out the first Navy Cross that the United States of Europe had awarded to a living recipient, and put it around Eddie's neck. Who straightened and saluted.

Piazza straightened, "For your actions in and around Wismar, 1633, as per the citations read at the official ceremony," and saluted back. Then he relaxed a bit. "I know you did this last year in Magdeburg, with all the pomp and circumstance, but since the artisans and politicos were still arguing over the final design of the medal, and hadn't gotten around to—"

"Thank you, sir." Eddie looked Piazza in the eyes and then around the table. "It means more than I can say that you—that all of you—did this." All present had risen and come to attention as the real medal was conferred. Then Eddie frowned and glanced back in the box. "Uh—"

"Yes, Commander?"

"Kind of a big box for a medal, sir. And damned heavy."

Piazza smiled again. "I thought a congratulatory gift was in order. To commemorate the occasion and to help you in your future endeavors."

Eddie lifted out the wooden panel upon which the medal had rested. He stared, and then looked up at Piazza. "How did you know?"

Francisco Nasi may have smiled briefly. "I was sitting

just down the table from you at your state dinner in Magdeburg last year. Perhaps you remember having a friendly dispute with the admiral over preferred side arms?"

Eddie lifted out the gift with almost reverent hands. An almost slender automatic pistol caught the light and sent gleams skittering off a blued hammer. "An HP-35. Manufactured just after the World War II, if I read the markings correctly."

Piazza grinned. "You do. Although you may be the only person in this world who would call it an HP-35. 'Browning Hi-Power' was the preferred term in the States, Commander."

Eddie, completely oblivious to Piazza's correction, turned the weapon over to confirm that no magazine was inserted. "How—where did you find this?"

Piazza looked down, shrugged, and was slightly annoyed when Nasi almost drawled, "Actually, it wasn't hard to find at all. It seems a person we know very well had it in his possession. Had an opinion of the gun similar to your own, Commander, and chose it over many others. Even though it was distinctly nonregulation in your up-time US Army. This person has often claimed that it never failed him, and that he preferred the larger magazine size to the stopping power of the larger . . . er, 'forty-fives'?" Nasi sent a glance at Piazza, checking his terminology.

Eddie followed Nasi's gaze. "You, Mr. President? This is *your* gun?"

"*Was* my gun, Commander. It is yours, now. Use it with pride and honor. As I know you will."

"Sir, I can't take it. I couldn't—"

"Rubbish, Commander. You've already taken it. And

it's the right gift for a young man who has no choice but to go in harm's way with only one leg. By comparison, I am an increasingly paunchy man whose fate is to sit at a big desk although I have two perfectly good legs. Seriously, now, who has more use for that gun? Who needs every bit of advantage they can get?"

Eddie's eyes raised from the weapon and fixed on Piazza's face, assessing. "Mr. President, you're about fifty-five, now, right?"

"Not a day over fifty-four. Don't put me in the grave any earlier than I have to go, Commander!"

"So during your tour in the Army, you were in—?"

"Yes, I was there, Commander. And since the Browning worked in the jungles on one side of this planet, I'm pretty sure it'll work just as well in the jungles on the other side. I hope you don't have to use it at all, of course, but if you do, you may find it's nice to have a thirteen-round magazine when you can't usually see what you're shooting at very well—if at all." He left unspoken the fact that there were plenty of Glocks and M-9s to be had, which boasted even larger magazine sizes. But the Hi-Power was renowned for its reliability and kindness to small-handed or easily unbalanced shooters—as Eddie Cantrell now might be.

Eddie looked down and held the gun firmly with both hands, almost as if it were a holy relic. For a second, Piazza saw the eager, earnest kid again.

Eddie looked up. "I don't know what to say, Mr. President."

Piazza laughed. "I think 'thanks,' will be sufficient. Otherwise, I can tell you're going to get maudlin on me. Well, more maudlin. Now look here, Commander, I do have one bone to pick with you."

"Sir?"

"How dare you come down to Grantville and not bring your bride?"

"Sir, I didn't think that protocol—"

Always Earnest Eddie. "Protocol be damned, Commander, we just wanted to see her again."

"'See her,' sir?"

Really? You still don't get the ribbing? "See her, Commander. Perceive her form. Appreciate her beauty. Feast upon her feminine pulchritude with our own, envious eyes. You get the picture?" And he grinned.

Before Eddie could get the surprised look off his face, George Chehab rasped, "How could you not know what we meant, son? She's a class-A knockout, that Danish Ann Margaret of yours."

"Uh, Mr. Chehab, her name is actually Anne Cathrine."

"Trust me son, she is a young Ann Margret. But more curvaceous."

"Now George," warned Vince Marcantonio, "let's not get too blatant in our admiration of the young lady."

Chehab smiled and shrugged. "Okay, but damn, I confess to disappointment that she didn't come down with you, Commander: severe, genuine, personal disappointment. She's as charming as she is beautiful, and we'd have liked to show her more of Grantville last year."

Eddie nodded. "Yes, sir. A return visit tops our list of things to do. When time permits."

And the room became quiet again, the jocularity chased out by the shadow of things to come. Serious things. Time to get back to and conclude the matters at hand, Piazza admitted. "Well, Commander, we are very glad to have seen you and presented you with your long overdue medal—and gift. I take it you will be returning to your duties immediately?"

"Yes, sir."

"Not even time to sneak a quick visit to Copenhagen?"

Eddie shook his head. "No, sir. Much as I'd like to. What with being a new husband and all."

"Amen to that," breathed Warner Barnes sympathetically, who knew because Piazza had briefed them months ago, that Anne Cathrine was "inexplicably" not with her husband in Luebeck. Of course, there was a simple, if unpleasant explanation for her absence: she had been purposely kept away from Luebeck at the behest of a group of Swedish officers. Anne Cathrine, they correctly asserted, was inquisitive, clever, enthusiastic, and probably could have deduced military secrets from fragments of conversations overheard in Eddie's quarters. Of course, the great majority of the command staff also held that she'd have been even more likely to die rather than give up those secrets. But there had been concerns among some ultranationalist Swedes that a new bride—and a Danish one, at that—should not be in close proximity to secret projects and documents. Nonsense of course, and driven by their distrust of Copenhagen's loyalty to Stockholm in the forcibly reforged Union of Kalmar. But those officers wielded enough political power that some concessions had to be made, and this one was consented to because it imposed politically-inconsequential costs upon only two persons: a love-lorn and sex-starved new husband named Eddie Cantrell and his pining bride.

"That's hard, lonely duty you've pulled up north, Commander," nodded Piazza.

Eddie either misunderstood or was trying to change the topic. "Well, I do like learning how to sail and command a ship, but much of the Baltic is iced over and all of it is cold and stormy as hell in February and March. Every time a training tour is up, I'm grateful to be back in HQ for another few weeks. Suddenly, sorting through an endless stack of papers doesn't seem so bad, when you're doing it in a nice, warm office."

"Well, I'm sure a lot more papers have accumulated in your absence. You certainly have done quite a job of depositing a hefty new pile here with us." Piazza gestured to the leather folios on the table.

Eddie glanced at the "folders" and nodded, taking the president's hand. "It's been a pleasure to see you again, sir."

"And you, Commander. Safe travels. And I almost forgot to ask: how are construction schedules holding up in the shipyards?"

"They're passable, Mr. President," an answer which Eddie punctuated by one moment of extended eye contact, a moment that was, again, probably lost on everyone except Nasi. Sagging a little, Eddie leaned on the table for support. "But everything will come together eventually." And with that, his finger grazed across the exposed corner of the bottom-most folio.

Which was all code for: *construction is on schedule and the new technologies have reached production phase, details of which are in this folder I just touched.* And the delivery of that message, and the coded details scattered as harmless phrases throughout the papers in that folio, were the only reasons that the young commander had actually been sent down to Grantville.

The new prosthetic had been a great cover-story—flawless, actually—but the coded reports on Simpson's classified projects, and his actual completion and readiness dates, could not be entrusted to airwaves or routine couriers. Even secure couriers were problematic because there was always the chance that their role was already known and that they would be waylaid at a most inopportune moment.

No, the best means of sending secret data—for which the codes were the second, not the first line of defense—was to send them in plain sight, so to speak. And that meant using a routine contact, such as Admiral Simpson's staff expert on technology initiatives and fellow up-timer, to convey a single secure communiqué as part of a perfectly plausible trip that had been planned upon months ahead of time. And it meant that there were only three people who had known the identity of the courier in advance: Simpson, Piazza, and the courier himself—Eddie Cantrell.

Who had now reached the door. He turned, saluted, received their returns, and with one boyish smile—like a parting endearment from his rapidly disappearing former self—he was gone.

Anton Roedel finished his scribbling. "Mr. President, shall I read back the—?"

There was a knock at the door. Anton speared it with a glance sharp enough to gut a fish. "Sir, are we expecting another—?"

Nasi interrupted smoothly, with a friendly smile. "That will be all, Mr. Roedel. Please drop off the evening's secure communiqués at the encryption office, will you?"

Roedel's eyes went back to the door briefly. "Yes, but—"

"We need those messages to go out as soon as possible, Mr. Roedel. So please, waste no time delivering them to the encryptionist on duty."

Roedel glanced at Piazza who nodded faintly at the secretary and added a placating smile. "On your way, now, Anton."

Who evidently was still miffed at being sent out when, clearly, there was yet another unexpected visitor waiting beyond the door. Chin slightly higher than usual, Anton Roedel gathered his papers and notes, squared them off, put them carefully in his own leather folio, and exited like a spurned ex-girlfriend.

It was Nasi who, three seconds after the door closed behind Roedel, called out "Come in."

The person who entered through the door Eddie had exited was small, slightly stooped, and dressed indifferently, a hint of seediness in the worn seams of his coat and his britches. He looked around the room's lower periphery, not raising his eyes to meet any of those looking at him. Pressed to categorize him, Piazza would have guessed him to be a vagrant who had somehow, impossibly, strayed off the street, past the guards, and into the highest offices of the State of Thuringia-Franconia.

Nasi nodded at the man, who exited far more swiftly and eagerly than he had entered.

Warner frowned, looked at Nasi and then around the table. "What, no message? Was the guy—lost?"

Nasi shook his head. "No, he was not lost. He was the message."

"What?"

Chehab leaned forward. "The messenger coming through that door could have been one of three persons. Each one meant something different, so their face was their message, you might say."

"And this one means—what?"

Nasi looked at Piazza. "It means that a pair of mechanics who were reported in town four days ago have just now departed."

Warner blinked. "Mechanics?"

Chehab shrugged, looked away. "Fixers. Freelance wiseguys."

Warner blinked harder. "What? You mean hit men, assassins?"

Nasi smoothed the front of his shirt. "Not necessarily."

"And what does *that* mean?"

"It means it depends who hired them and what for." Piazza looked over at Warner with what he hoped was a small, reassuring smile. Warner Barnes was a relatively new and infrequent member of the group and wasn't familiar with how, or what kind of, things were done in this "sleepy subcommittee"—which also functioned, unadvertised, as the State of Thuringia-Franconia's intelligence directorate.

Warner still hadn't read between the lines. "And we just stood by while these two murderers were walking our streets?"

Piazza shrugged. "What would you have had me do? We don't have any outstanding warrants on them."

Nasi added, "They do not even stand accused of any crime."

Warner sputtered. "Then how do we know they're assassins, mechanics, or whatever?"

"Via the good offices of our preeminent international banker, Balthazar Abrabanel. His discreet connections with the Jewish 'gray market' frequently provide him with information about persons like these. They are often called upon to aid in, er, 'collections.'"

Piazza leaned in. "And we have confirming reports of their identities and reputations from the Committees of Correspondence. These two aren't political activists, but are well-known to the, um, action arms of the Committees."

"And Abrabanel and the Committees—they actually hire thugs like these?"

"Not often. And never these two in particular."

"Why not these two?"

Nasi shrugged. "Well, as has already been implied, this pair has a reputation for preferring to resolve matters . . . too kinetically."

Warner goggled. "So they're rougher than the average brute and we let them walk around our town, unwatched? All because some of our shadier contacts know who they are? Listen, Ed—"

Piazza shook his head. "Warner, they're not a concern of ours."

Warner gaped, tried another approach. "Okay, if you say so. But maybe we should put a tail on them while we make a quick inquiry into their whereabouts while they were here, make sure they didn't use their visit to harm any of our—"

Piazza looked at Nasi, who in turn looked at Warner, and interrupted him sharply. "Mr. Barnes. Allow me to be quite clear about this: those two men are gone. And being gone, they are to be left alone. Entirely alone. That is this committee's official policy on the matter. Is that understood?"

Warner blinked in surprise, probably more at the tone than the instructions, Piazza suspected. "Okay, yes, Don Francisco. Although I just wish I understood why—"

Piazza stood, making sure that his chair made a loud scraping noise as he did, which momentarily silenced Barnes. The president rubbed tired eyes and then stared straight at Warner before he could resume his objections. "It's been a long day, everyone. Let's go home."

Part Two

May–June 1635

The ladder to all high design

Chapter 6

Amiens, France

"Lord Turenne, we have finished searching their gear. Nothing suspicious, sir."

Turenne nodded and dismissed his orderly with a wave. He had watched from a narrow casement window when, hours ago, the strange trio had first approached the portcullis of his "testing facility." They had surrendered their arms as though they expected to do no less, submitted to the further indignity of a close personal search, and were then led into the courtyard to await a more thorough check of their rucksacks and gear.

While waiting on that process, Turenne had compared their self-written letters of introduction with the fragmentary dossiers he already possessed on two of the three men. The French intelligence was patchy at best, but confirmed that such persons did exist, that the individuals in the courtyard answered to their general descriptions, and that the positions and abilities they claimed in their letters certainly conformed to those attributed to them by the analysts in Paris. But neither source provided any clue as to why the group's two persons of note might be traveling together or why they desired an audience with Turenne himself. However, they had both been clear and politely specific regarding that latter point: they were not interested in speaking with the senior military authorities in Paris, nor Turenne's chief of staff Robert du Barry. They required an audience with Turenne. Otherwise, they explained—again politely—they would take their leave, and take their proposal elsewhere. Given his busy schedule, Turenne would normally have dictated a brief note, wishing them *bon chance* and pleasant travels to whoever was the next influential person on their list.

But one of the two credentialed strangers was an American technical expert. The other was the storied son of an exiled Irish earl, and had played a pivotal role in repulsing Frederik Hendrik's drive on Bruges just four years ago. If Turenne had ever encountered a more peculiar pair of traveling companions, he could not recall it.

There was the anticipated knock on the door. Turenne elected to stand. "Enter."

Du Barry, along with two guards armed with Cardinal breech-loading carbines, brought the unlikely duo into Turenne's office. Du Barry looked to Turenne, who waved a desultory hand at him. "I am safe here, Robert. You may go."

With a backward bow, du Barry and the two guards departed—and headed to join two other guards secreted in small rooms adjacent to this one, the entrances concealed behind bookcases and mirrors. The code "I am safe here" had sent them to these secret stations to oversee their viscount's protection.

However, as the door closed behind Turenne's security entourage, the land-displaced Irish earl and the time-displaced American looked at the walls, and then exchanged glances. Then they looked at Turenne. And smiled faintly.

So much for preserving the impression of trust and a private meeting. Turenne surprised himself by returning their smiles. "Please understand, gentlemen, in my position, to be contemptuous of possible risk is to be contemptuous of one's own life."

The taller and younger of the two spoke. "We understand completely, Lord de la Tour d'Auverge."

He waved away that title like cobwebs. "My dear Comte, er, *Earl* of Tyrconnell, let us dispense with these titles. They are so cumbersome, particularly mine. I am simply Turenne."

"And by that usage, I am simply O'Donnell."

"And your companion?"

The American stepped forward, hand half-extended, but then he glanced at the room's bookcases and mirrors. *Mon Dieu, is it so obvious?* Turenne came around his desk. As he extended his hand in the American fashion, he imagined a nervous du Barry whelping kittens in his sally port. "I welcome your hand, *Monsieur*—?"

"McCarthy, Michael McCarthy. Junior. A pleasure, Lord Turenne."

Plain manners and plain spoken, but forthright, honest, and unbowed. Turenne had heard this about most of the Americans. To many of his aristocratic peers, it made the up-timers intolerable abominations, like ogres who had learned enough of the ancient virtues of Athens and Pericles to become both supremely ridiculous and dangerous at the same time. But Turenne found the effect refreshing. He could already anticipate how, with a man of this demeanor, one could get to ideas, could get to agreements, and could get down to work, very quickly. And without the interminable folderol of titles, and protocols, and curtsies. "I welcome both of you to my, well, you might call them 'experimental laboratories.'" And with that greeting, Turenne resumed his seat. And waited.

O'Donnell heard the unasked question in the silence. "We apologize for taking the liberty of seeking you at your place of work, and with no proper application for an audience. But our circumstances and the import of our proposal are both such that this direct approach seemed best, if regrettably brusque."

"I see. Which explains much, Lord O'Donnell, since you could certainly have asked one of your correspondents for a thoroughly adequate introduction." *Or could have used them to bypass me altogether,* Turenne observed silently. "Unless I am misinformed, your seal is well-known to the pope and Philip of Spain."

Hugh nodded. "It is."

"Yet here you are, on my doorstep, without any of the letters of introduction which would have assured you of immediate audience, and spared you the distasteful experience of being searched and examined like a common highwayman."

The American answered. "Had Lord O'Donnell secured those letters, he would also have alerted those same persons to our meeting with you."

Turenne nodded and looked at the displaced earl. "Lord O'Donnell, if I am not mistaken, you have been in the court, and then direct service, of Archduchess Infanta Isabella of the Spanish Lowlands, since you were two years of age. Have you now chosen to seek service elsewhere?"

The Irishman's face took on a melancholy expression. "I had little enough 'choice' in the matter, given what the histories of Grantville have shown me."

"I can sympathize, sir. My own career was changed as a result of those documents. Cardinal Richelieu advanced me on the strength of deeds I had not yet performed, and now, never can, for that history has been irreversibly changed. Is it the same with you?"

"According to their books, I am a dead man in seven years."

Turenne felt his stomach contract, suddenly cold. "*Mon Dieu*—Lord O'Donnell, my apologies. I had no idea, or I would not have spoken with such insouciance."

O'Donnell waved aside the apology. "We all have different fates. And that was mine if I remained in Spanish service. And probably the fate of many hundreds of my countrymen, as well. And all for naught."

Turenne had read a précis of the European histories that had arrived with Grantville. "Sir, again you have my sympathies, but I must also be frank. I see no promise that the new history we are now embarked upon will make France any more ardent a supporter of Irish interests. Given the recent combination of our fleet and England's to defeat the Dutch, I must sadly project that there might even be less reason for hope."

"I do not place my hope in France, Lord Turenne. I place it in you."

The surprise of those words left Turenne both baffled and a bit wary. "Me? Why me?"

But it was McCarthy who answered. "Because, Lord Turenne, your nationality isn't what's important in this case. What's important is that you obviously understand, *really* understand, the kind of changes my town has brought to your world."

"Your opinion flatters me, Monsieur McCarthy. But then why is the earl of Tyrconnell not joining his banner to that of your USE, and Grantville in particular? It is the very embodiment of those changes."

"Which is probably why that's not the wisest choice for Lord O'Donnell. His former liege King Philip isn't exactly a fan of ours, and vice versa. Besides there's the matter of his men's Roman Catholicism."

Turenne nodded. Of course. Many of O'Donnell's "Wild Geese" were extremely devout Roman Catholics, and most had been driven from their lands to make room for resettled Protestants. Their religious fervor and grudges would be a poor fit for the USE, which, despite its lopsided polyglot of different faiths, was founded upon the strong military spine and current leadership of the Swedish Lutheran Gustav Adolf. "So then, Mr. McCarthy, I suppose it is *your* presence which is the greater mystery. As I understand it, you still retain your post as a Senior Instructor at Grantville's Technical College. If I also understand correctly, I would be a fool not to detain you on the spot and make your future freedom contingent upon your helping us with any number of mechanical challenges that my researchers currently find insurmountable."

McCarthy smiled. "But you won't do that."

Turenne kept himself from bristling at the American's self-assured tone. "Oh? And why not?"

"Well, first, it's not the kind of man you are."

"Indeed? And just how would you know what kind of man I am?"

"I know about the letter you wrote to Mike Stearns last year, expressing regret that your men killed Quentin Underwood during their raid on the oil field at Wietze."

Turenne suppressed any physical reaction to McCarthy's observation, even as he thought: *Interesting: that epistolary gesture has borne some diplomatic fruit, after all.*

McCarthy continued. "Detaining me would also ruin any hope of accord with Lord O'Donnell, thereby permanently and personally inflaming the Irish regiments in the Low Lands against you and France. But most important, forcing me to work for you wouldn't accomplish anything, since you obviously know that men who work against their will neither give you their best work, nor can they be trusted."

Turenne nodded. "All true. But I find it odd that you do not include your status as an American as a further restraint upon me. After all, keeping you against your will could be inflamed into an international incident."

McCarthy shifted. "If I were here as a representative of the USE, that would be true. But I'm not here in that capacity."

Turenne studied McCarthy carefully. "No?"

"No, Lord Turenne. Right now, I'm a free agent."

"You have renounced your citizenship in the USE?"

"No. But I've never taken a day off from my work at the college. It took me a few months to persuade my bosses, but I arranged to take all those days at once, added to a leave of absence. They didn't like that much, but they don't really have any one else with my skills." He shrugged. "I can do as I please with that time."

"And it pleases you to come here for—a visit?"

If McCarthy found the bathos amusing, he gave no sign of it. "I came here to make money, Lord Turenne."

Who, being unaccustomed to such a frank admission of monetary need, neither expected nor knew how to respond to McCarthy's statement. And it seemed that McCarthy himself had not been entirely comfortable uttering it. Unsure how to navigate this delicate impasse, Turenne leaned back—

—just as O'Donnell leaned forward: "Lord Turenne, Mr. McCarthy is a proud man. His father, Don McCarthy, is severely ill and requires constant and increasing care. More care than Michael can readily afford."

Turenne experienced a moment of utter social disorientation. "But does not the American government—?"

"With your indulgence," interrupted the Irish earl smoothly, "neither the USE nor Grantville itself provide for the private needs of even its most important personages. Within reason, they are expected to see to their own expenses."

Turenne looked at Michael and found two subtly defiant but pride-bruised eyes looking back at him. If this was an act, it was an extraordinarily good one. "I see," said Turenne, who remembered something else connecting pride and the name "McCarthy" in the intelligence he'd read on Grantville. Specifically, the McCarthy family was noted as holding an extensive book collection, and ardent political sympathies, that were both radically pro-Irish. And here sat an uptimer named McCarthy with a displaced Irish earl. The pieces were coming together. "So now I know why you are here. But I still have no idea what it is you wish to propose."

McCarthy's posture did not change, but his eyes

became more expressive, less defensive. "We propose to help you with some of your current 'logistical initiatives,' Lord Turenne."

Turenne was not sure whether he should be amused or aghast at the blithe certainty underlying such an offer. "And just what initiatives are those, Mr. McCarthy?"

"Well, to start with, I think we have a way to help you achieve some of your long-term objectives in the Caribbean."

Turenne frowned. "Mr. McCarthy, I am rather busy, but out of deference to your background, I made time for this meeting However, I hardly think that France needs to consult with you—or, respectfully, the earl of Tyrconnell—on its strategic posture in the Caribbean."

McCarthy shrugged. "I don't propose to advise you on general regional strategy, Lord Turenne. I have a very specific objective in mind."

"Oh? And that would be?"

"Trinidad."

Turenne leaned back a little and narrowed his eyes. With every passing second, the conversation was becoming more interesting and also more dangerous. Michael McCarthy, Jr., and perhaps higher-ranking Americans, had been doing their homework, evidently. And now began the delicate dance—for which Turenne had little taste—of learning how much the Americans knew and conjectured, even as McCarthy might now be trying to determine the same thing about him and France's own speculations. Turenne studied the expressionless up-timer and thought: *he is a mechanic, a man who works with wheels. And he himself may be filled by wheels within wheels. A spy? Perhaps. But perhaps an emissary, as well. And both roles would require extreme discretion at this point.*

"Trinidad," echoed Turenne eventually. "An interesting location to focus upon. Why there?"

"The petroleum deposits at Pitch Lake. They're right on the surface."

"True. But why would I want to travel across the Atlantic for oil?"

"For the same reason you took all the engineering plans from the oilfield at Wietze before you disabled the facility. You wouldn't have been interested in those plans if you didn't realize that France needs its own aircraft, vehicles and other systems dependent upon internal combustion engines. And that, in turn, means France *must* have oil. And getting oil quickly necessitates owning surface deposits that you can access with only minimal improvement to your current drilling capabilities."

Turenne acknowledged the truth of the deductions with a wave of his hand. Denying something so obvious would only make him seem childish. "So, even if we accept your conjecture, I am still no closer to getting oil, even if I am willing to cross the Atlantic. Pitch Lake is held by the Spanish."

"It is on a Spanish island. That's not quite the same thing."

So they also had access to tactical intelligence on Trinidad. That was interesting. "You seem unusually familiar with, and sure about, the disposition of Spanish forces on Trinidad," he said.

McCarthy nodded. "A young American visited the island not too long ago, on board a Dutch ship. They landed near Pitch Lake and there were no Spanish to be seen, just a few of their native allies. So as regards Pitch Lake, either the Spanish don't know what they're sitting on, don't know what to do with it, or don't care about it."

A concise and accurate summary of all the possibilities. But the dance of dueling intelligence portfolios was not yet over. "Even if it is true that the Spanish have no town or garrison at Pitch Lake, it does not follow that the Spanish are inherently uninterested in it. It is a relatively short sail to Cumana and even Puerto Cabello, where they have a considerable depth of power. In order to hold out against a response from those bases, one would need a small flotilla, at least, to hold Pitch Lake."

"That presumes the Spanish are even aware you have taken possession of it." And McCarthy almost smiled.

So here at last was the first hint of something mysterious, unprecedented: a sure sign that the conversation would soon turn toward an unforeseen up-timer capability, upon which this pair was obviously basing their proposal. "And you have a way to ensure that the Spanish would remain unaware if Pitch Lake were to be seized?"

"Not permanently, but long enough that you wouldn't need to commit large forces to landing and initial defense. Sizable forces would only be needed once Pitch Lake was securely invested and held, to further fortify and secure it against Spanish attempts at reconquest."

"You speak of summoning 'sizable forces' as if I was the French military commander of the Caribbean, Mr. McCarthy. I assure you, I have no such authority. Nor does our senior factor on St. Christopher."

"I am aware of that, Lord Turenne. That is why our proposal for seizing Pitch Lake calls for only one ship."

"One ship?"

"Yes, Lord Turenne. A prize hull, currently at moorings in Dunkirk. The *Fleur Sable.*"

Turenne frowned. The *Fleur Sable* was a severely damaged Dutch cromster, recently taken by the "privateers" operating out of Dunkirk. She had earned mention in his intelligence dispatches when two confidential agents in her crew—one English, one French—both attempted to negotiate with the victorious pirates in the name of their respective governments. Heads (theirs) had rolled in the confusion and the ship, a potential item of international embarrassment, remained unsold and unrepaired. As Turenne remembered her, the oversized *Fleur Sable* was square-rigged at both the fore- and mainmasts and lateen-rigged at the mizzenmast, meaning that she was not only capable of making an Atlantic crossing in good shape, but also had reasonable maneuverability in capricious winds.

Turenne looked at his two visitors with newfound regard. They had selected this hull carefully and well. And they obviously knew that, given his contacts and authority in the region, Turenne could acquire a single battered (and therefore under-priced) hull for "experimental purposes" easily enough. But that did not dispose him toward ready agreement. "And how do you expect me to crew this Dutch sieve?"

O'Donnell answered. "Among the ranks of the Dunkirk privateers, there are currently French sailors, and even a few officers, who were unjustly dismissed from Louis XIII's service in disgrace. As I hear it, almost all of them wish to return to his service, and success on a mission such as this might dispose him to hear their appeals with greater favor."

Turenne was careful to make no motion, change not one line in his face. *Merde! The audacity—and elegance—of the plan!* And it just might work, if this odd pair did indeed have some way of seizing Pitch Lake without being intercepted first or detected shortly afterward. "His Majesty might indeed see fit to restore such men to his favor and service, but I am of course powerless to make such a promise."

O'Donnell smiled. "I fully understand, Lord Turenne."

Turenne wondered whether Richelieu would want to send him a medal or send him to the headsman when this operation was finally revealed. But France needed oil, easy oil that could be reached by her neophyte drillers, and Trinidad's accommodating seeps and shallow deposits were a matter of record, well-detailed in the books at Grantville. But there were still problems with the plan. "Of course, you have not yet discussed who will land on Trinidad itself and take control of Pitch Lake."

The big-shouldered Irish earl nodded. "Well, let us begin by acknowledging that this force cannot be made up of French soldiers, lest you officially embroil your sovereign in an attack upon Spain."

"Exactly. So who would serve as the landing party and foot soldiers?"

O'Donnell cleared his throat. "My men. Five dozen, hand-picked."

I should have seen that coming. "And they will serve France because...?"

"Because you will provide sustenance for the rest of my *tercio* while they are on this mission."

"And so let us presume you have reached and invested Pitch Lake with your forces. In whose name do you intend to claim it, for what country? Ireland?"

"A tempting idea, but rather futile, wouldn't you agree? No, I will take it as a private possession, for sale to the highest—or preferred—bidder. So you see, my part of this operation is to be a purely corporate venture."

Turenne's head was dizzy with the possibilities and pitfalls. Corporations seizing national holdings? Was the word "corporation" just a legitimizing euphemism for "free company?" Would private ownership by dint of military conquest be recognized by any other sovereign state? On the other hand, what would national recognition matter if the "corporate" forces held it firmly? And the Dutch East India company had already made several forceful rebuttals to the common monarchical contention that all the lands of the Earth rightly belonged to sovereigns, who then bestowed their use upon a descending pyramid of vassals.

However, despite the foreseeable legal wrangling, Turenne saw one other certainty clearly enough: by proposing that he take Pitch Lake as a private entity, O'Donnell was allowing France to remain blameless of overt conquest. Of course, once O'Donnell's seizure of Pitch Lake was *fait accompli*, it was almost certain that Richelieu would move quickly to purchase the site. And then France would have its oil, and Turenne would be able to fuel the machines needed for the nation's defense. But still, the most nagging problem of all was that—"Logic and precedent dictates that the operation cannot be carried out by one ship. Unless, as you claim, your single ship can arrive at Pitch Lake completely unseen and land its small force intact, having suffered no losses in chance encounters. And so I must ask: can you do this?" He looked at McCarthy, certain from O'Donnell's expression that the answer did not lie with the Irish earl. "Can your American technology turn a small ship invisible?"

"No, but if you can see far enough ahead, you can detect and dodge opposing ships. Before they detect you."

"And do you have some means of seeing farther ahead than the lookout in a crow's nest?"

"I don't," said McCarthy. "But a friend of mine does."

"Oh? What friend? The German fellow you came with, the one downstairs?"

"Yes, sir."

"And what does he do? Build very tall masts?"

"No, sir. He builds hot air balloons."

Turenne, despite his well-practiced self-control, couldn't keep himself from snapping forward in his chair. "He builds *what*?"

"Hot air balloons, Lord Turenne. Right now, Siegfried's got a model that carries about twelve pounds aloft." McCarthy shrugged. "I think with a little guidance, some material support, and access to the inventories of your silk merchants—"

Turenne was on his feet, calling to the door and then the walls. "Orderlies. Please bring in the other visitor." After nodding briefly at O'Donnell, he turned back to the up-timer. "Mr. McCarthy, did you have plans for this evening?"

"Well, yes. I—"

"Your plans have just changed." Turenne finally smiled at the American. "And if all your hypotheses are correct, you will need to clear your itinerary for the next six months."

Chapter 7

Off Luebeck, Baltic Sea

Eddie watched the slide and tilt of the inclinometer diminish, peripherally saw that his ship's hull was nearing the center of a long, smooth trough between the modest Baltic swells, and shouted, "Fire!"

The second gunner pulled the lanyard; the percussion lock atop the breech of the eight-inch naval rifle snapped down.

Flame jumped out of the weapon's muzzle. The blast shook the deck, rattled all the ship's fixtures, and buffeted Eddie's clothes and those of the gun crew as if, for a moment, they had been standing sideways to a hurricane. The gun leaped backward in its carriage, slamming furiously against its hydraulic recoil compensators as smoke gushed out of it in a long, lateral plume.

A moment later, water geysered up approximately half a mile off the starboard beam.

Beside Eddie, Admiral Simpson adjusted his binoculars slightly. "Thirty yards long of the target, Commander Cantrell, but you were dead-on the line. Your azimuth needs no adjustment."

"I just wish I could adjust the waves," Eddie muttered.

Simpson's wooden features seemed ready to warp. Eddie knew to read that as a small, but well-suppressed smile. "Sounds like a request for the twentieth-century luxury of electric ignition systems, slaved to adequate inclinometers."

Eddie tapped the deck fitfully with his false foot. "I guess so, sir." Chagrined that he hadn't hit the target once in ten attempts, he was reluctant to stop this part of the gun's first sea trial, but the protocols were set. "Swap out the ignition system," he ordered the gun crew.

Simpson raised an eyebrow. "You look annoyed, Commander." His tone turned ironic. "Well, don't fret over getting a proper inclinometer. I'm sure the arbiters of our destiny, the Department of Economic Resources back in Grantville, will put it on the top of their 'to fund' list when they get these test results. Even though they ignored my seven-page brief which predicted this outcome."

Eddie was glad that Simpson hadn't phrased his facetious assessment of the navy's budgetary overseers as a request for his subordinate's opinion of them. Because, truth be told, Eddie could see both sides of the funding argument. Grantville's resources were pinched more tightly than ever. Despite being part of the populous and productive State of Thuringia-Franconia, the town-become-a-city had less, rather than more, wiggle room when it came to supporting cutting-edge technologies.

It hadn't started out that way, of course. When Grantville had materialized, no one understood what it represented in terms of knowledge and advanced materials. Hell, there had been a lot of people who simply refused to believe in its existence. But then, with its decisive intervention in the Thirty Years' War in support of Gustav's Swedes, Grantville became an object of intense scrutiny. And as it integrated into the economic and fiscal life of the United States of Europe that it had largely midwifed into existence, and the broader domain of world events, its singular features came under singular pressure. Every monarch, great and small, wanted devices from the future, yes, but that wasn't the greatest drain. It was all the extraordinary down-time innovators who realized the potentials of steel, of rubber, of electric motors, of plastic, and then designed genius-level devices or processes based on them. All they needed was just a modest amount of x, y, and/or z, and they could usher in a bold new era of—well, whatever bold new era their invention was sure to usher in.

The crowning irony of it was that, after you filtered out the crackpots (which was usually not very difficult; they tended to be self-eliminating), the great majority of these extraordinary innovations would probably have done exactly what their inventors claimed: they would have revolutionized some aspect of life as it was in the 1630s.

But there were thousands of such innovators, and only one Grantville. Only one source for all that up-time-quality steel, and rubber, and plastic, and everything else that was both handmaiden and midwife to these new inventions. And while Mike Stearns had led Grantville in the direction of sharing out its unique wealth rather than hoarding it, there were practical limits as to how far that could go. By now, the daily influx of inventors, treasure seekers, and curio hunters into the precincts of Grantville had emerged as both a singular fiscal opportunity (inns, hotels, eateries, short-term rental properties had sprung up like weeds) and a singular civic headache (congested streets, overburdened utilities, inflation, and a far more complicated and multi-lingual law enforcement environment). And straddling it all was the State of Thuringia-Franconia's beleaguered Department of Economic Resources, which had to set policy on how the town's unique resources should be meted out.

John Simpson understood their job, may have even had a species of theoretical sympathy for it, but he was a man who had been given an official mandate that had also become his personal mission: to build a navy which, with its small number of hulls, could defeat any conventional force in the world. And the primary factor in achieving that extraordinary potency was up-time technology, either in terms of design, or in terms of actual up-time machinery. Unfortunately, it was that latter desideratum over which the admiral and the Department of Economic Resources, or DER, eternally wrestled, since there could be no increase in the amount of advanced technological systems. Grantville was almost four hundred years away from the riches of the American military-industrial complex, or even Walmart. There were never going to be any more motors, tires, televisions, or computers than there were right now. Not for a century or two, at the very least. And almost everything that Admiral Simpson wanted for his Navy, a hundred other people wanted for some other project.

The electronic inclinometer and fire-control system was, Eddie had to admit, one of those resource wrestling matches about which he felt the most profound ambivalence. On the one hand, that system was not technically *essential* to the operation of the new ship's guns. And there was no accomplishing it "on the cheap." Down-time materials and technology were simply not up to the task of fabricating one that was sufficiently sensitive and reliable.

But if he had had a system that could measure the attitudinal effects of wave action on his hull, and then send an electric pulse to fire the gun the moment that the ship was level, he would have been able to hit today's target—a forty-foot by twenty-foot wood framework mounted on a barge—on the fourth, or maybe even the third, try. Instead, after the first three shots—which had been required to make the gun's basic azimuth and elevation adjustments—he still kept missing the target by thirty or forty yards. But not because his targeting was off, or his crew was sloppy, or the ammunition was of irregular quality. No, it was because of these comparatively tiny three- and four-foot swells.

The roll in the deck beneath his feet was almost imperceptible. From moment to moment it rarely varied by more than one degree. But since that motion was not predictable, and since a fraction of a degree was all it took for him to drop a round short or long, it represented an irrefragable limit upon his accuracy. It was a random variable over which he had almost no control.

What little control he did have was through the combined sensory apparatuses of a down-time inclinometer and his own eyes. But the inclinometer, although the best that could be fashioned by exacting down-time experts, was simply a very well-built three-axis carpenter's level: it was not sensitive or responsive enough. And of course, the human eye was an invariably unreliable instrument—although when combined with trained human judgment, it could furnish by prediction much of what the inclinometer could not provide quickly enough.

That precision provided by electronic firing controls was simply not important to naval weapons and tactics of this era. The contemporary down-time guns were fairly primitive smoothbore cannons that evinced all the individual idiosyncrasies of their unique, by-hand production. And so, lacking the range and uniform performance of up-time weapons, it was inevitable that they were most effective when fired at very close ranges, and in volleys. That way, some balls were sure to hit.

Obviously, such weapons would have derived much less benefit from an inclinometer-controlled firing system. As Eddie had explained to Anne Cathrine, putting an up-time inclinometer on a down-time cannon was a lot like putting four-wheel disc brakes and airbags on an ox-cart. She had simply stared at that reference, so he had tried another one: it was like putting lip-paint on a pig. She got that right away.

But with the new eight-inch, breech loading, wire-wrapped naval rifles that Admiral Simpson had designed for these steamships, the want for truly accurate and speedy inclinometers was making itself felt. Profoundly. The extraordinary range and accuracy of these weapons made them, ironically, far more vulnerable to the inherent instability of a sea-going ship. This had not been so important a consideration during the Baltic War, where engagement ranges had been short, the waters relatively calm, and the hulls had been comparatively bargelike and stable. But now, highly responsive fire control was a paramount concern. The hulls that were the prototypes for Simpson's blue water navy—a large one similar to a bulked-up version of the Civil War era USS *Hartford*; the other, a slightly shrunken equivalent of the USS *Kearsarge*—were ocean-going, and if they stood high, rolling seas well, it was in part because the shape of their hulls helped them stay afloat by moving as the water did. Ironically, they were far less stable firing platforms, but fitted with guns that required, and would richly reward, superior stability. Or fire control correction.

Simpson had won the fight to get the guns he needed, and their recoil carriages, but not the electronic inclinometer and fire-control system. Eddie could see the value in both sides of that latter argument, which had essentially boiled down to, "there are finite resources and the navy can't have first pick of all of them," versus, "why go to the expense of creating the most powerful and lethal guns ever seen on the planet only to give them the same sights you would find on a zip gun?"

As time had worn on, Eddie's sympathies had moved increasingly toward Simpson's own—probably, he conceded, because he would soon have to ship out in one of these new hulls and wanted to be able to reliably smack the bad guys at distances of half a mile. By way of comparison, the down-time cannons were notoriously ineffective beyond one or two hundred yards, and were laughable at four hundred. And so if that made engagements with such ships a very one-sided proposition—well, Eddie had learned personally that in war, mercilessly exploiting an advantage wasn't "unsporting." It was sound tactics. Indeed, anything else was the sheerest insanity.

"Commander Cantrell?"

Eddie swam up out of his thoughts, saw blue waves and then Simpson's blue eyes. "Uh . . . Yes, sir?"

"The gun crew has swapped in the new ignition system. You may commence firing at your leisure." Simpson put the binoculars back up to his eyes.

Eddie stared unhappily at the fast-fuse that was now inserted into the aperture that had, minutes ago, been fitted with a percussion cap nipple. The hammer for that system was now secured in a cleared position.

The gun chief, a Swede, saluted. "Ready to begin firing, Commander."

Eddie sighed. "Reacquire the target, Chief."

"Aye, sir." He stared through his glass, then nodded. "Reacquired, sir. Range and bearing unchanged."

"Very well," answered Eddie, "stand by for the order to fire." Eddie felt for the wind, watched the pattern of the swells, looked for another long, flat trough between them—and saw one. He glanced at the inclinometer. The yaw and pitch were too small to register and the roll was subsiding, the bead floating gradually toward the balance point. Eddie saw it move into the middle band, approach dead center—

"Fire!"

The second gunner touched the glowing match at the end of the handlelike linstock to the fuse. It flashed down in a lazy eyeblink: quick, but far slower than the near-instant response of the percussion-cap ignition system. The gun discharged, sending out its sharp blast of sound and air pressure.

But that lazy eye blink had been a sliver of a second too long. The ship had rolled a fraction past the perfect level point of the inclinometer. Water jetted up almost one hundred yards beyond the target, and very slightly to the left.

"And that shot," observed Simpson, "had the advantage of being fired at an already ranged and acquired target."

"I may have timed the swell incorrectly, Admiral."

"Nonsense. Your timing was as good, or better, than during the trials with the percussion lock. You know the reason for the greater inaccuracy as well as I do, Commander."

Eddie nodded. "The fuse delay. There's just no way to compensate for that extra interval."

"Precisely. The comparative difference in the burn-time of powder fuses reduces the accuracy of the weapon so greatly that it's barely worth the cost of building it. Percussion caps not only ignite much faster, but with far greater uniformity. But let's not leave any room for argument. Since the bean counters in Grant-ville want concrete justification to release funding for a uniform provision of the percussion system, we shall give it to them." He watched the second loader turn the breech handle and pull sharply; the half-threaded breech block swung open and fumes rolled out, along with a powerful sulfur smell. "Give every shot your best estimate, Commander. I don't want any more trouble with the DER than is absolutely necessary."

Eddie squinted, stuck a finger at the horizon two

points off the port bow. "Looks like we may have some other trouble before that, Admiral."

Simpson frowned, looked, spied the almost invisible gray-sailed skiff that Eddie had just noticed, bobbing five miles to the southeast. Grumbling, the admiral jammed the binoculars back over his eyes, then was silent. Eddie saw his jaw work and a moment later, Simpson uttered a profanity which was, for him, so rare as to be shocking.

"What is it, sir? Pirates?"

"Worse, Commander," Simpson muttered through clenched teeth. "Unless I am much mistaken, that is the press."

Chapter 8

Luebeck, United States of Europe

At a nod from Simpson, the two Marine guards stood at ease, but remained flanking the man who had hired the skiff. The fellow did not look particularly anxious. Then again, he did not appear particularly comfortable, either.

Simpson took his seat; he glanced at the chair beside him, which Eddie quickly occupied, grateful to be off his one real leg.

Simpson scanned the few scant reports he had on the man and his activities. Scanned them long enough to have read them five times over, Eddie realized.

The man from the skiff cleared his throat. "Admiral, I wonder if I might—"

"Herr Kirstenfels—if that is your real name—I have not finished studying the information we have on you and your actions today. I will speak with you when I have concluded."

"But Admiral, I only—"

It was quite clear what he wanted: a chair. But Simpson, who had kept this slightly pudgy man from sitting since he was taken into custody, simply waved him to silence.

Herr Kirstenfels shifted his feet but did not resume his request.

After another minute, Simpson put down the papers and folded his hands on the desk in front of him. "Herr Kirstenfels, I presume you are aware that you not only put your own life at risk, but also the owner of the skiff?"

"Yes, Herr Admiral, I know this now. May I please have a seat?"

Simpson frowned. "Herr Kirstenfels, you are hardly in a position to request anything, but I will allow you to be seated." The admiral pointed out a chair to one of the Marine guards, who promptly fetched it and put it behind the detainee. Who sat on it and winced: it was as small, hard, and ugly a chair as humans could craft. Which, as Eddie knew from prior witness, Simpson kept on hand for exactly this purpose. "Now, I wonder if you know how much trouble you are in."

"Perhaps I do not."

Eddie suppressed a frown. Kirstenfels' admission sounded humble enough, but it also sounded faintly coy. Not what one would associate with an appropriately cowed, even intimidated, civilian. The undertone in his voice did not suggest fear, but watchful maneuvering. *Hmmm...did we catch this guy, or did he want to get caught?*

What Simpson had heard, if anything, was not suggested in his response. "I shall provide a brief outline of the situation in which you find yourself, Herr Kirstenfels. You entered a test range during official operations. You did so with the admitted intent to

observe our weapons trials. Since we did not announce
the trials publicly, I must conclude that you bribed or
extorted that information out of a representative of the
USE's armed forces or government. And that alone
constitutes grounds for a full investigation by my staff."

If Simpson had meant to frighten Kirstenfels, it
apparently had not worked. The smallish man merely
nodded, listening carefully to each of the specifications
read against him. When the admiral had concluded,
he reflected momentarily, and then asked, "But have
I broken any laws?"

Simpson's color changed slightly. "That remains to
be seen."

"Pardon me, Herr Admiral, I should have been
more precise. Were any of the actions you cited just
now legal violations?"

"Your presence on the test range certainly was. Your
possession of information regarding the trials may be."

"Well, Admiral Simpson, as to the latter, I did not
suborn or solicit information illegally."

Eddie noticed, and so did Simpson, judging from
the slight stiffening of his neck, the carefully official
language.

Kirstenfels expanded upon his claim. "I simply
overheard the conversation between some of the land-
based test crew talking about the gun with the sailors
who were preparing to go out with it on today's trial."

—*A convenient and utterly incontestable alibi,*
Eddie conceded silently.

"And as far as being on the range during the test
is concerned, I do not know how that could be illegal, Admiral."

"What do you mean?"

"I mean, if the trial was supposed to be a secret, how could anyone know it was illegal? Since your men were speaking about the weapon tests in a public place, I rather assumed it was not secret. And I never did hear anything about that stretch of the Baltic being off-limits to the public."

"That is because 'the public' does not often venture into those particular waters, and because we had distributed navigational restrictions to all the ship operators and owners currently in port."

"Ah. But that is still not a declaration of illegality, Herr Admiral. Rather, it is an official attempt to make the area temporarily unreachable to the public. Those are two very different things. Wouldn't you agree?"

John Simpson was motionless, but Eddie could read that as one of the clear signs of growing fury. Simpson had a particular sore spot when it came to the press. In his view of up-time events, they had been uncharitable to his country and his comrades in the way they depicted the Vietnam War, in which he had lost his own foot. The press had once again been opportunistic and accusatory when he was a captain of industry afterwards. And Eddie could see that Simpson would soon leave a crater where this hapless reporter was now sitting, if he gave voice to even a small measure of his rage. Which was not in the interests of the Navy—

But Simpson surprised Eddie by exhaling at a slow, controlled rate and then smiling, albeit without the faintest hint of genuine amity. "Well, Mr. Kirstenfels, it seems you wanted to get access to me for an exclusive interview. And now you have it, don't you?"

Kirstenfels stammered for a moment, obviously

surprised at being sniffed out so quickly. "Er ... well, yes, I suppose that may have been part of my—"

"Come now, Mr. Kirstenfels, what else would be sufficient motivation to sail near a live-fire range? Certainly nothing having to do with our guns."

"Well, in point of fact, your guns are a matter of keen interest to me."

"So it seems. I have reports that, during the land-based proving trials, some of our perimeter guards escorted you back beyond the no-trespassing line." Simpson's restored smile was anything but genial. "You are an artillery enthusiast, perhaps?"

But Kirstenfels, despite his unprepossessing appearance, turned out to have more than his share of sand. "Perhaps, but not in the way you mean, Admiral Simpson."

"Then why don't you explicate?"

"Thank you, Herr Admiral, I will."

And Eddie could tell from Simpson's suddenly rigid jaw, that he had just given the reporter what he wanted: not merely an opening, but an invitation.

The reporter had produced a pad and one of the new, if crude, pencils that were starting to show up in a variety of forms. "You see, Admiral Simpson, I have been duly impressed by the tremendous range and accuracy of your new guns."

"They are not really new," Simpson corrected.

Kirstenfels nodded. "No, of course not. They are modeled on the ten-inch naval rifles you used in the Baltic War, except these are breechloaders rather than muzzle-loaders. But I was surprised to see the mounts for them being readied on the frigate-style ships you are building at your secure facility in Luebeck."

"Oh, and why is that?"

"Well, for the very reason you demonstrated on the water earlier today. Guns such as those require a very stable ship in order to be accurate. The monitors you first put them on have exactly that kind of stability in the mostly calm waters where you employed them, but not the sea-going frigate-style hulls you are currently fitting with steam engines."

Well, Eddie reflected, the steam-engine "secret" was going to come out at last. Which was just as well: it had always been pretty laughable as a "classified" project. After all, it was simply a logical progression to move from steam-powered monitors to steam-powered blue-water ships. In fact, all their projections had presumed that some external observers would have surmised, and then confirmed, that development long ago. Eddie and Simpson privately conceded that Richelieu had probably received definitive intelligence reports on that aspect of the ships' construction no later than March.

But "investigative reporting" was a new phenomenon, and frequently, even the best down-time newspapermen missed telltale clues of what might be transpiring simply because they did not have nuanced enough knowledge of up-time technology to understand how small details were often indicative of whole stories. It was the old problem of the expert tracker who is tasked to find an animal he has never seen or heard of.

But in this case, Kirstenfels was a reporter who obviously understood the greater significance of the (literally) "smoking gun" he was investigating. "My reading in Grantville last month suggests that those long guns would be almost useless while riding up and down the swells of the Atlantic. But there are other bodies of water—strategically significant bodies of water—for which they might be far more suited."

Eddie saw no hint of reaction in Simpson's perfect poker face, but reasoned that his CO's observations must be similar to his own. Kirstenfels evidently knew a lot about his topic, but probably did not understand the ignition variable: that with calmer seas and a percussion cap instead of a fuse, the rifles would be fairly accurate out to their medium ranges. But he certainly did understand the broader strategic implications of putting guns like those on ships that could travel on the ocean. Even if these ships were not being built for high seas battles, they might be intended to sail and steam into engagements on calmer, bounded bodies of water.

"I am speaking, of course, of their potential usefulness in the Mediterranean," finished Kirstenfels.

Which was both a correct and an incorrect guess, Eddie allowed. Eventually, that was where the new class of ships would probably be needed and hopefully, be decisive. But before then—

Simpson raised an eyebrow. "Mr. Kirstenfels, that is, to put it lightly, a most improbable surmise. What could possibly possess the USE to become embroiled in a Mediterranean conflict?"

Kirstenfels actually hazarded a small smile. "I could think of several possibilities. Ottoman expansion. Any serious threat to Venice, where the USE—and Grantville in particular—is heavily invested. An increase in the Spanish adventurism on or near the Italian peninsula, possibly including an attempt to eliminate Savoy's small but troublesome fleet."

He settled back in the chair that had been built—unsuccessfully, evidently—to prevent such relaxed postures. "However, the specific nature of the conflict is hardly the key datum in my surmise, Herr Admiral. I have been studying the ships you are building. They are high weather designs. That is more than you need if you were just going to punt around the Baltic."

Simpson's chin came out defensively. "Perhaps you've overlooked how rough the weather gets up here. In all seasons."

Kirstenfels nodded politely, but didn't look away. "Yes, but by that reasoning, then your choice of smaller craft becomes even more puzzling. The smaller hulls you've been procuring for portage on the larger ones are invariably very shallow-draft. They are lateen or yawl-rigged, have low bows, are narrow in the waist. Not for the Baltic." Kirstenfels glanced out the lead-mullioned windows at the choppy gray swells beyond the bay. "Five months out of the year, these waters would swamp such boats on a regular basis. They are, however, perfectly suited for the Mediterranean: river and inlet scouting, touching on shallow coastlines, and regular ship-to-ship and ship-to-shore exchanges."

A slow, ironic smile had been growing on Simpson's face as the reporter laid out his case. Kirstenfels' answering frown deepened as the admiral's grin widened. "This amuses you, Admiral?"

Simpson seemed to stifle a chuckle. "Oh, no, no. Please continue. I like stories. Particularly fanciful ones."

For a moment, Eddie glimpsed Kirstenfels without his mask of bourgeois suavity and well-groomed calmness. Intent and beady eyes stared and calculated, unaware that he had just been taken in by his own gambit, that the ships' ultimate goal was the Mediterranean—just not yet. But all hungry newsman Kirstenfels knew was that his finger had slipped off whatever sensitive spot had first irked Simpson, that the story which he had been building was about to slip away from him. He was annoyed, anxious, resentful at the easy unvoiced mockery with which his hard-gained evidence was being dismissed, and his conjectures along with them.

Kirstenfels' eyes lost that brief feral glaze. He tried a new tack. "Well, since you enjoy fanciful tales, let's try this one. That the fleet you're building is not bound for the Mediterranean at all, but for waters with somewhat similar characteristics and sailing requirements. Specifically, the Caribbean."

Simpson seemed to allow himself to smile. "Ah, now there's a new one. Tell me more."

Kirstenfels didn't get rattled this time. "I'd be happy to, Herr Admiral. Beyond the indisputable fact that the flotilla you are currently building would be supremely well-suited for operations in those waters, some of you Americans are likely to be relatively familiar with those waters. And you have a special interest in projecting your power into the New World, since the Caribbean has something the Mediterranean doesn't."

"Oh? Like what?" Simpson seemed to be trying to hide a smile once again.

"Like Trinidad. Like Pitch Lake. Like easily reached oil."

Simpson allowed the smile to resurface but it was faintly brittle, and Eddie knew what that meant: *that surprised him. And now Kirstenfels has hit the nail right on its head. If I don't do something, he's*

going to see and figure out the meaning of the look
on Simpson's face and then the cat will truly be out
of the bag—

Eddie grinned, covered his mouth hastily.

Kirstenfels looked over at him sharply. "I have said
something amusing, Commander?"

Eddie put on a straight face, shook his head ear-
nestly. "No, Mr. Kirstenfels. I'm just, well, surprised
that you figured out our secret."

"Your secret?"

"Yes, sir. About taking the flotilla to the Caribbean.
It's no good for us to deny it any longer, now that
you've put all the facts together."

Kirstenfels' frown returned. And Eddie could see
the wheels of presupposition turning behind his gray,
uncharitable eyes: *I know they will not tell me the
truth, so my guess about the Caribbean must be
incorrect. But they want me to believe it in order
to throw me off the real scent. Of course, I should
check to see if this, too, is just a ruse—*

Kirstenfels looked at Simpson whose face was once
again wooden. "So, Admiral, since we are free to talk
about the Caribbean, then—"

With a sharp look at Eddie, he cut off the reporter,
"I cannot comment on any operations we might, or
might not, have planned for the Caribbean." The faintest hint of the histrionic had crept into his voice, at
which Eddie nearly smiled: *very well played, Admiral.*

And Kirstenfels had obviously taken the bait. The
instant he heard that slightly theatrical tone in Simpson's
prohibition on further conversation about the Caribbean,
a tiny smile crinkled his lips. Eddie could almost see
the thought bubble over the newsman's head: *So, the*

admiral play-acts at upset and worry. The two of them hope to mislead me into thinking my guess about the Caribbean was accurate. All in order to divert me from my first, best hypothesis: that they really are preparing for action in the Mediterranean. A smug expression flitted across Kirstenfels' features and was gone all in the same instant, but Eddie knew the look of vindication and triumphant certainty when he saw it.

Simpson had folded his arms. "Is there anything else, Mr. Kirstenfels?"

The newsman rose, cap in his hands. "No, thank you, Admiral Simpson. Am I free to go?"

Simpson looked as though he had swallowed a gill of spoiled vinegar. "Unfortunately, you are, Mr. Kirstenfels. But any subsequent incidents will have consequences. You have been directly and personally warned not to pursue any further investigation into the ships we are building here or their potential uses. If you disregard that warning, I will hand you over to a judge to determine just how profound your disloyalty is in the eyes of the government of the USE. The Marines will see you out."

"And I presume I am not allowed to ask any questions of your men that might be construed to be an inquiry into their ultimate destination in the Mediterranean?"

"Or the Caribbean," Simpson added peevishly. If Eddie hadn't known better, he would have truly believed that the admiral was now irritated at having to play-act at such lame and obvious conceits as prohibiting Caribbean inquiries.

"Or the Caribbean," Kirstenfels agreed, almost facetiously from the doorway. "Good day, gentlemen."

Simpson stared at the door for five silent seconds before turning toward Eddie and matching his smile. "Thanks for the quick thinking, Commander. He had me on the ropes for that first second, when he hit on the Caribbean."

"My pleasure, Admiral. You're quite the poker player. Masterful last bluff, by the way."

The older man's smile became slightly predatory. "Do *you* play poker, Commander?"

"Not with you, sir."

"Ah. Well, in this case, that caution might indeed be more helpful than a gamesman's daring. At any rate, I'm sure we'll be hearing about our Mediterranean flotilla any day now."

"Yes, but Kirstenfels' report will be so premature that it will actually be meaningless."

"'Premature,' Commander?"

"Yes, sir. As you pointed out honestly enough, we have no reason to go down there. But you left out an important qualifying word: '*Yet*.'"

Simpson's rare light-hearted mood extinguished as sharply as a candle in a cold breeze. "Situations can change very dramatically and very quickly, Commander. We could find ourselves wishing for a Mediterranean fleet much sooner than our own timelines of 'international eventualities' suggest. But enough: we've lost a lot of time misdirecting that ambulance chaser. What's the latest status update on the New World mission, Commander?"

Chapter 9

*Convent of the Dames Blanches,
Louvain, The Low Countries*

"Your Highne—I mean, Sister Isabella?"

The urgency in the novitiate's tone caused the infanta Isabella to start—that, and a brief pulse of religious guilt. Once again, Isabella's thoughts had drifted away from her devotions and novenas and veered into memories of her long-dead husband Albert and poignant fantasies of a family that might have been. "What is it, my child?"

"There is a . . . a penitent here to see you."

"A penitent?" Isabella sat a bit straighter. Sister Marie was neither a very mature nor a very wise novitiate, but she certainly knew that only priests could hear confessions and that they generally did not situate themselves at convents to do so. So this "penitent" was clearly someone traveling incognito, a subtlety which had obviously eluded, and therefore baffled, the country-bred novitiate.

Isabella smoothed her habit, touched her neck as if to assure herself that it was still there, and nodded. "Show the 'penitent' in."

If the young nun was surprised that the sister who was also the archduchess of the Spanish Lowlands was willing to receive a "penitent" in the unusually well-furnished room that had been set aside for her biweekly retreats, she gave no sign of it.

But when Sister Marie returned, she was decidedly flustered.

"Sister Isabella...this penitent...I am not sure. That is, I think...I fear I have—"

"Yes, he is a man. Do not be alarmed, child. None of the men I know bite. At least, they don't bite nuns. Usually."

Sister Marie first flushed very red, then blanched very white. She made a sound not unlike a whimpering squeak, then nodded herself out and the visitor in.

Isabella smiled as she turned. So which one of her many renegade charges had been resourceful enough to find her here—?

She stopped: a large figure draped in a cloak of gray worsted had already entered and sealed the room. The cloak was ragged at the edges, loosely cowled over the wearer's face. Whatever else Isabella had expected, this rough apparel and stealthy approach was not merely discomfiting but downright—

Then the hood went back and she breathed out through tears that, at her age, came too readily and too quickly for her to stop. "Hugh." And suddenly, in place of what the wool had revealed—a square chin, strong straight nose, and dark auburn hair—she saw:

—the cherubic face of her newest page, sparkling blue eyes taking in the wonders of her formal, or "high," court for the first time. Sunbeams from the towering windows marked his approach with a path of luminous shafts, which, as he walked through each one, glanced back off his reddish-brown hair as flashes of harvest gold. When summoned, his final approach to the throne was composed, yet there was mischief hiding behind the tutored solemnity of his gaze.

Isabella had affected a scowling gravity with some difficulty. "Are you sure you are prepared to be a page in this court, young Conde O'Donnell?"

"Your Grace, I'm sure I'm not!" His voice was high, but strong for his age. "But I will grow into this honor, just as I grow into the clothes you and the good archduke always send me." And then Albert had laughed, and so had she, and the little boy smiled, showing a wonderful row of—

His white teeth were still as bright now as then, she realized as she reached out and put two, veined, wrinkled hands on either side of Hugh's face. "My dear boy. You have returned."

"Dearest Godmother, I have."

And the pause told her, in the language of people who have long known each others' hearts, that he had not just returned from Grantville, but from the long, dark travail that had started when he had turned away from his young wife's winter grave almost five months ago. There was light in those dark blue eyes once again.

"Tell me of your trip to Grantville."

He did. She listened, nodded several times. "And so you have decided to leave Spanish service."

He blinked. "You have your copy of the letter? Already?"

"Of course. And you most certainly make an eloquent appeal for the home rule of the Netherlands, and link it to your own cause most cleverly."

"So you think well of this?"

"Of the letter? The writing is like music, the idea eminently sound, and sure to save thousands of lives. And, of course, Philip will not countenance it."

"Perhaps not. But I must try. Even though Olivares is obstinate about retaking the United Provinces."

"So now you have ears at Philip's court, too?"

"No, but I see what's happening to his treasury. Yet he remains dedicated to spending countless *reales* to retain lands that have already been, *de facto*, lost to the crown. Once Fernando declared himself 'King in the Low Countries,' no other political outcome was possible. But Olivares has no prudence in the matter of the Lowlands. He spends money like a drunken profligate to prop up the economy while slashing even basic provisioning for its *tercios*. His fine faculties no longer determine how he reacts to events here. He is driven by pride and obstinacy."

She smiled. "I will make a prince of you yet, my dear Earl of Tyrconnell. You have a head for this game."

"That is because I have a peerless tutoress. Whose many wiles still surprise me: how did you get hold of my letter weeks before my man was to deliver it?"

"Dear boy, do you not think that I know what confidential agents you employ, and that I keep them better paid than you can afford?"

She saw surprise in his eyes and remembered how the first sight of them had been a salve to her wounded soul. He had arrived in her privy court as a stumbling toddler, shortly after she had lost her third—and last—child in infancy. In those days, she thought her attention to little Hugh's education and fortunes was merely a clever self-distraction from her own sorrows. But now, being surprised by him like this, and finding her heart leaping up with a simple joy, she realized, perhaps for the first time, that he had been a surrogate for her losses, her childlessness. And he—fatherless a year after he arrived, and his mother a shadow figure trapped in the English court—had been, for all intents and purposes, an orphan, as beautiful and bright a child as might have stepped out of Eden. But there had been ambitious serpents all around, serpents sly and protected by titles, so she had often been compelled to protect him by employing methods as subtle and devious as theirs.

And she would still need to protect him now. "I must say that the timing of your decision to leave Philip's employ is . . . dismaying, my dear."

"Not as dismaying as finding that my godmother's intelligence network includes my own servitors."

"Hush, Hugh. How else could I know if one of them had finally been suborned by enough English pounds to betray you? But this time, it simply alerted me to your impending departure."

Hugh's eyes dropped. "What I found in Grantville left me no choice *but* to depart. Even if I was willing to go on to the fate those histories foretold, I cannot also lead my countrymen into pointless deaths. But I know well enough that Philip will not deem those sufficient grounds for my resignations, not even if he were to suddenly give full credence to the revelations of Grantville. All that he will see is that I have become a base ingrate."

Isabella smiled. "Perhaps. But here is what *I* see." She laid one hand back on his cheek, hating the palsied quiver in it that she could not still. "I see a man who blamed himself, and maybe the Spanish clergy's initial nonsense about the 'satanic' Americans, for his wife's death. And I see a nobleman who had to discover and act upon what the future held in store for his land and his people. And so you went to Grantville. And you have acted as you must. Now, tell me: having visited twice, what did you think of the Americans?"

"They are . . . very different from us." Hugh looked up. "But I had suspected that, particularly after they sent me both condolences for Anna and an invitation to visit them all in one letter."

"Yes, their manners are often—curious. Sometimes even crude. But on the other hand, so many of our courtesies have lost the gracious intentions that engendered them. The American manners are—well, they may be simple, but they are not empty. But enough of this. If you come to me disguised in this rude garb, I presume we cannot have much time, so—to business."

"Yes, Godmother. In part, I had come to tell you to expect the copy of my letter to Philip within the week. Which you have had for over a month, I gather. But I also came to tell you something else."

"Yes?" Such hesitancy was most unlike Hugh, and she felt her fingers become active and tense.

"My men will not all stay in your employ."

She closed her eyes, made sure her voice remained neutral. It would not do to impart the faintest hint to Hugh that she knew more about his most recent activities and the condition of his *tercio* than he did. "I presumed some of your men might wish to leave, since Philip has not sent sufficient pay in many months. A reasonable number are free to go at once. I will see to their release from service. But I cannot afford to have an entire *tercio* disband overnight. It will take some months to achieve a full release. And we will have to weather a torrent of displeasure from Madrid."

"And my many thanks for bearing the brunt of Philip's imperial temper, but that is still not what I came to tell you."

Isabella became nervous again. Her intelligence on Hugh's movements and meetings was uncommonly good and multisourced. But surprises were still possible, and at this point, the smallest surprise could derail the delicate plans she had set in motion.

"Godmother, it may yet transpire that Philip will think worse of me than merely being an ingrate. Though Spain may have made some temporary alliances of convenience, her interests are still ranged against almost every other nation of Europe. And so, if my employ is not with Philip, I might find myself confronting his banners, rather than beneath them."

Despite anticipating this, Isabella still felt a stab at her heart, wondered if it was emotion or the frailty of age. "Dear boy, this is dire news."

"How can it be otherwise, dearest Godmother? But before I depart to—to distant places, I want you to *know* this:"—and he stopped and reached out a hand to touch her cheek, down which tears promptly sped in response—"I will never suffer my sword, or those of my men, to be lifted against yours."

"I remain a vassal of Philip, so how can you make such a promise?"

Hugh looked at her steadily. "I make my oath and I pledge my life upon it." And then he studied her more closely, a hint of a smile at the corner of his mouth. "But I foresee that my promise may not be so difficult an oath to keep as you suggest. I see other changes afoot, Godmother. Don Fernando proclaims himself the king in the Low Countries, but not the king *of* the Netherlands? What careful distinctions. They almost seem like mincing steps and mincing words, if I didn't know him—and you—better."

As his smile widened knowingly, she felt another stab of panic: *does he suspect our plans? He must not! Not yet, anyway—for his own sake.* And his next words did indeed quicken her fear that Hugh might have stumbled upon the subtle machinations she had activated for his eventual benefit and of which he had to remain unaware, for now.

"And Fernando's careful steps towards greater autonomy also lead me to wonder: which Americans have had your ear in the privy chambers? And how has Philip reacted to your receiving their counsel, and to Fernando's unusual declaration? No, do not tell me. If I do not know Philip's will on this matter, or your plans—and you do not know mine—then Philip can never accuse you of being a traitor to his throne, no matter what might occur."

Isabella managed not to release her breath in one, great sigh of relief. No, he had no specific information. He discerned the looming crisis—the inevitable conflicts with Madrid—but nothing more specific. Thankfully, he had not learned of their plans or his envisioned role in them.

Hugh was now completing and expanding the oath with which he had begun. "So finally, know this too, Godmother. Once I have returned from my travels, if you call for my sword, it is yours. And, if Don Fernando finds himself estranged from his brother's good opinion, and still in your favor, he may call for my sword as well."

Until that moment, Isabella had always cherished a view of Hugh as the wonderful, smiling boy that had made her childless life a little more bearable. Now, he was suddenly, and completely, and only, a man and a captain, and, possibly, an important ally in the turbulent times to come. The ache of her personal desolation vied with the almost parental pride she felt for the boy who had become this man. The contending emotions washed through her in a chaotic rush and came out as another quick flurry of tears. Through which she murmured, "*Via con Dios*, dear Hugh. Wherever you may go."

He smiled, took his hand from her cheek, and put his lips to her forehead, where he placed a long and tender kiss. She sighed and closed her eyes.

When she opened them, he was gone.

Amiens, France

As du Barry entered, Turenne looked up. "What news?"

"We have word concerning the earl of Tyrconnell's clandestine northward journey, sir. He slipped over the border into the Lowlands without incident four nights ago. Soon after, he apparently began the process of bringing the first group of troops down to us, the ones that will go with him to Trinidad."

"Excellent. And how do you know this?"

"Reports from our watchers near his *tercio*'s bivouac report a smallish contingent making ready for travel. Several hundred more seem to be making more gradual preparations for departure."

"I see. Did Lord O'Donnell ask for their release from service at court in Brussels?"

"No, sir."

"Then how did he manage it?"

Du Barry reddened. "I regret to say we do not know, Lord Turenne. Once he crossed the border, our agents were not able to keep track of him. He is far more versed in the subtleties of those lands and those roads. For a while, we even feared him dead."

Turenne started. "What? Why?"

"The very last reports inexplicably placed him in Colonel Preston's camp just outside of Brussels during a surprise attack upon a council of the other captains of the Wild Geese *tercios*. Our observer necessarily had to hang well back, so as not to be picked up in the sweeps afterward. By the time he returned, he could find no trace of O'Donnell, nor pick up his trail."

Turenne thought. "Is there any chance the earl himself staged that attack? As a decoy to distract our observers, and to escape in the confusion of its aftermath?"

Du Barry shrugged. "Not unless Lord O'Donnell was also willing to sacrifice a number of his own men to achieve those ends, sir. And his reputation runs quite to the contrary of such a ruthless scheme. His concern for his men is legendary, and a matter of record. The only friction he ever had with his god-mother the archduchess, other than some puppyish clamorings to be sent to war too early in his youth, were his complaints over the recent welfare of, and payrolls for, the common soldiers of his *tercio*."

"Complaints for which he had good grounds, as I hear it."

"Indeed so, Lord Turenne. Although his godmother herself has had no hand in causing the *tercios*' pay to be in arrears. That is determined by the court at Madrid." Du Barry shifted slightly "While on the subject of the earl of Tyrconnell's Wild Geese, sir: is it your intent to really allow hundreds of them to cross over the border into France in one group? I suspect there might be some, er, pointed inquiries, if you were to add so many mercenaries to your payroll, and all at once."

Turenne stared at his chief councilor and expediter. "What are you driving at, du Barry?"

"Sir, with the recent increased tensions at court between Cardinal Richelieu's faction, and that of Monsieur Gaston, a sudden hiring of hundreds, and eventually perhaps thousands, of new foreign mercenaries could appear to be motivated by domestic rather than foreign worries."

"Ah," sighed Turenne with a nod. "True enough, du Barry. And if it reassures you, I do not intend to allow the earl of Tyrconnell's larger force to cross into France until we have full satisfaction in the matter of the tasks which lie before him in the Caribbean. However, in the meantime, we will provide for them as promised by sending the necessary livres over the border to the sutlers for their camps. We cannot hire them outright as long as they remain in service to Fernando and, I presume, Philip. So any money sent to them directly would be rightly construed as a sign that we had engaged their services while their oaths were still with their original employers. They, and we, would be rightly accused of base treachery.

"But mere provisioning cannot be so construed, for they are simply the designated beneficiaries of largesse which their countryman Tyrconnell has purchased for them. And so, even before they come to our colors, we will have bought their loyalty with 'gifts' of food for their hungry families. And by letting them clamor ever louder for permission to march south, we acquire something that I suspect Lord O'Donnell has not foreseen."

"And what is that, sir?"

"Leverage over the earl himself."

Du Barry frowned. "Now it is I who do not understand what you are driving at, Lord Turenne."

Turenne smiled. "Let us presume that the Wild Geese in Brussels' employ are becoming ever-more desirous of being allowed into France. Now let us also presume that the earl of Tyrconnell succeeds in his bid to wrest Trinidad from the Spanish. We may still need leverage over him in order to ensure that we remain the recipients of what he has seized.

"I hope, and believe, that Richelieu's factors in the New World will offer the earl a fair price, and promptly. The ship dispatched by the *Compagnie des Îles de l'Amérique* to discreetly observe O'Donnell's progress carries not only the cardinal's personal agent, but also a great deal of silver.

"But if the negotiation with O'Donnell does not come off as planned—well, we must retain an incentive to compel him to turn the oil over to us. And if we still have the power to deny his increasingly desperate men entry to France at that time, he will have an additional incentive to look with particular favor on any terms our representatives offer him."

Du Barry nodded, then asked in a careful voice, "Would he not have an even greater incentive to comply if we already had his men in our camps, unarmed and vulnerable to our . . . displeasure?"

Turenne frowned. "I will go only so far, du Barry. Leverage should not become synonymous with extortion, or kidnapping. I refuse to offer physical shelter to men that I actually intend to use as hostages. Let others play at such games: I shall not. I will keep my honor, my good name, and my soul, thank you. Besides, our agents in Brussels report that whispers about the Wild Geese's possible departure en masse have fueled official concerns regarding their loyalty. Those concerns may be manifesting as even further constraints upon their provisioning. Furthermore, the commanders of the Spanish *tercios* are finding their Irish comrades increasingly worrisome and are pleading with Philip to remove them entirely."

Turenne stood and poured a glass of wine as he outlined the logical endgame of the evolving political situation in the Spanish Lowlands. "Consequently, as the poverty of the Wild Geese increases, so will their desperation. Given another half year, they will all be clamoring to come to Amiens, where we shall be happy to accept them at rates favorable to us. And the earl of Tyrconnell, being a true, albeit young, father to his men, will not deny them that livelihood."

Du Barry edged closer. Turenne took the hint and poured out a second glass with an apologetic smile. "Do not worry, du Barry. Matters are in hand."

Du Barry took the glass; he raised it slightly in Turenne's direction. "I toast the assured success of your plans, my lord, for they are so well-crafted as to need no invocation of luck."

Turenne halted his glass's progress to his lips. "Plans always need invocations of luck, du Barry. For we can only be sure of one thing in this world: that we may be sure of nothing in this world. A thousand foreseeable or unforeseeable things could go wrong. But this much we know, for we have seen it with our own eyes: France has a workable observation balloon, now. But the rest, this quest for New World oil?" Now Turenne sipped. "I avoid overconfidence at all times, my dear du Barry, for I am not one to snub fate. Lest it should decide to snub me in return."

Chapter 10

Thuringia, United States of Europe

Major Larry Quinn of the State of Thuringia-Franconia's National Guard led the way down the last switchback of the game trail, which spilled out into a grassy sward. That bright green carpet of spring growth sloped gently down to where the river wound its way between the ridge they had been on and the rocky outcropping that formed the opposite bank.

Quinn looked behind, as the other two people in the group were navigating the declination. One, a young man, did so easily. The other, a middle-aged woman, was proceeding more cautiously.

Larry smiled. Ms. Aossey had never been particularly fleet of foot, even when she had been his home room and science teacher in eighth grade. And she was more careful now. Which, Larry conceded, only made good sense: a broken leg in the seventeenth century was nothing to take lightly, not even with Grantville's medical services available.

The young man with Ms. Aossey looked back to check her progress, putting out a helping hand. She accepted it with a brief, sunny smile. He returned a smaller one, complete with a nod that threatened to become a bow.

Larry's own smile was inward only. The understated politesse he had just witnessed was typical of twenty-year-old Karl Willibald Klemm. Larry had spotted the telltale signs of intentionally suppressed "good breeding" the moment the young fellow arrived in his office, having been referred there by Colonel Donovan of the Hibernian Mercenary Battalion.

Although admitting that he was originally from Ingolstadt, Klemm had not divulged the other details of his background so willingly. And Larry understood why as soon as the young Bavarian's story started leaking out. At fourteen years of age, Klemm had been recruited to play for the opposing—and losing—team in the Thirty Years' War. As a Catholic, Klemm explained that he'd been impressed into Tilly's forces in 1632, but not as a mercenary. He had been made a staff adjutant for a recently-promoted general of artillery. That general had not survived the battle against Gustav Adolf at Breitenfeld. At which point Klemm decided that his next destination would be any place that was as far away from the war as he could get to on foot.

Larry Quinn had been unable to repress a smile at the young man's careful retelling of the events surrounding his induction. Young Klemm had been "impressed" by Tilly's own sergeants at the age of fourteen, and then just happened to be assigned to a general of the artillery. Larry had wryly observed that this was not typical of the largely random acts of impressment whereby youths had been made to serve under the colors of both sides, usually as unglorified cannon-fodder.

Klemm had the admirable habit of staring his questioner straight in the eye when addressing a ticklish topic. No, Klemm admitted, he had not been randomly recruited. He had been plucked out of school by members of Tilly's own general staff.

And at what school had that occurred?

Again, Klemm had not batted an eye, but his jaw line became more pronounced when he revealed that he had been in classes at the University of Ingolstadt.

The rest of Larry's questions met with similarly direct, if terse answers. Yes, Klemm had been in his second year of studies at the tender age of fourteen. Yes, he had been in mathematics, but also the sciences and humanities. Yes, he supposed the work did come easily to him, since he was usually done before the most advanced students in each of his classes. Except in the humanities. But he somberly observed that this "failing" was because he often lacked the adult sensibilities to adequately unpack the layered meanings in most art. He had still been "just a boy" at school. Then, he had gone to war.

Tilly's "recruiters" had apparently been well-briefed by young Karl Klemm's predominantly Jesuit tutors. The youth not only had an extraordinarily sharp and flexible mind, but possessed what later researchers would call an "eidetic" memory. Larry doubted the existence of such savantlike powers, but was suitably impressed when Klemm scanned a paragraph, then a list of numbers, then a set of completely disparate facts, and was able to recall them perfectly afterwards.

Given the data-intensive nature of the artillery branch, it had been perhaps inevitable that Klemm had been assigned there. It had been the intent of his recruiters for him to function as a human calculator during sieges and other extended shelling scenarios. There, the ruthless laws of physics dictated results more profoundly than upon the fluid battlefields where human unpredictability, and even caprice, played a greater role in determining outcomes.

But that rear-echelon role hadn't kept Karl Klemm from seeing the full scope of horrors on display in the Thirty Years' War. Nor had it insulated him from the vicious attitudes of an increasing number of the Catholic troops. Not only were Tilly's men weary with war, they had been forced to forage from (then pillage, and ultimately sack) towns, both enemy and allied, for supplies. Predictably, with its ranks swollen by amoral and brutish mercenaries whom Klemm could hardly distinguish from highwaymen, the rank-and-file of Tilly's army was not receptive to a clever young fellow who was clearly the darling of the army's highest, aristocratic officers. The resentment and hate that the soldiers could not express toward those officers themselves was redirected toward this younger, more vulnerable object of their approbation. And so young Karl Klemm had learned to keep his head down and his gifts hidden.

He had approached the Hibernian Mercenary Battalion without referring to his background with the enemy's army or his unusual skills. Rather, he had heard they were looking for persons who might be handy at refurbishing broken up-time firearms. He had applied to become a mere technician. But one of the battalion's two proprietors, Liam Donovan, had the shrewd eye of a professional recruiter and saw much more than that in young Klemm. And so had sent him on to Larry's office.

That had been when Karl was thin, jobless, and shivering in a coat much too old to ward off the frigid fangs of the middle weeks of February. Now, three months later, in a riverside meadow, releasing Lolly Aossey's hand as if handing off a partner in a gavotte, he seemed a different person.

"Karl," Larry called.

"Yes, Major Quinn?"

"Has Ms. Aossey finished boring you today?"

Lolly rounded on Quinn, who was smiling mischief at her. "So I was a boring teacher, Larry?"

"Not usually, Miz Aossey, but let's face it: a fifty-minute lesson on earth science is now a reasonable replacement for the sleeping aids we left back up-time."

"Hmpf. Do you agree with Major Quinn, Karl?"

Klemm knelt to study the soil. "I cannot speak for anyone else, but I find geology rather fascinating."

That's Karl, ever the diplomat. Larry looked back at Lolly. "So why did you want to come down here from the hills?"

Lolly walked over to where Karl was strolling, now running his hands along the sheer skirts of the ridge as he studied the strata of its rocky ribs. "So that Karl could look at what surveyors and drillers would designate extremely soft 'unconsolidated formations.'"

"And what are those?"

Lolly turned to look at Klemm with one slightly raised eyebrow. Karl, seeing that as his cue, supplied the answer promptly. "An unconsolidated rock formation takes the form of loose particles, such as sand or clay."

"You mean, it's not really rock."

"No, Larry," scolded Lolly. "That's not what it means at all. Sand, for instance, starts out as solid rock."

"Like gravel."

Ms. Aossey nodded. "Exactly."

"So how is coming here better than going to a sand pit?"

"Because, Larry, a sand pit such as you mean is not a natural occurrence. And that's what Karl needs to see, to experience: the formations that arise naturally around such earths, and vice versa."

Karl brushed off his hands, put them on his narrow hips, looked at the rock thoughtfully, then at the ground. "And unless I am much mistaken, Ms. Aossey wishes me to become especially familiar with the compositions particular to alluvial or coastal deposits. The other two times we have gone on a field survey, we visited similar environments."

Lolly stared at Klemm. She said, "Very good, Karl," and clearly meant it, but there was also a surprised, even worried tone in her voice.

Quinn kept himself from smiling. The problem with training clever people for even highly compartmentalized confidential missions was that their quick wits could often defeat the information firewalls erected by the planners. From a few key pieces, they could begin to discern the shape, or at least the key objectives, of the operation.

Karl Klemm demonstrated that propensity in his next leading comment. "In fact, I find it puzzling that we are spending so much time in areas with these formations."

Lolly, who was inspecting some small outcroppings of marl that disturbed the smooth expanse beneath their feet, distractedly asked, "Why, Karl? They are good challenges for you: not always the easiest areas to read, geologically. They can be quite tricky unless you know what to look for."

"So you have taught me. And very well, Ms. Aossey. But that still begs the question of why we are studying them at all."

Lolly stopped, a bit perplexed. Quinn now had to hide a small smile. He was no geologist, but he had learned to read people pretty well, and he could see where Karl Klemm was headed. Lolly didn't, apparently. "We study them because they are some of the formations you might encounter when you travel with Major Quinn to the New World."

"Yes, I might. But it seems odd to focus so heavily on these formations, since I will not be expected to survey them closely, let alone exclusively." Karl poked at an upthrust tooth of marlstone. "Or will I?"

Lolly shot a surprised and alarmed glance at Quinn, a glance which said: *Oh. My. God. Could he have guessed where* exactly *you're taking him? And why? And if that cat is out of the bag, does he have to be sequestered until you leave?*

Quinn simply shrugged.

Lolly Aossey crossed her arms tightly. "Well, Karl, you never know where people might want to dig. Or for what."

"That is true, although one immediately thinks of the New World's coastal oil deposits. However, it does not stand to reason that the USE would be interested in those, or any, oil deposits known to reside in unconsolidated rock formations."

"And why is that?"

"Because we cannot tap such deposits, not with our current drilling technology. A cable rig will not work. The constant pounding collapses the walls of the hole. To drill in soils such as these, which in the New World predominate around the Gulf coast oil deposits, you would need a rotary drill. A technology which we do not yet possess." He looked up from the marlstone. "I am correct in my conclusions, yes?" He did not blink.

Quinn watched and heard Lolly swallow. Looking like an adolescent who'd been caught telling a lie to her parents, she spread her hands in gesture that marked her next utterance as both an explanation and appeal. "Well, Karl, now about that rotary drill—"

Chapter 11

Undisclosed location near Wietze, USE

Ann Koudsi finished her morning cup of broth—it had been unseasonably chilly overnight—and nosed back into her books and progress charts again. As the second in charge of the rotary drill test rig, and ultimately, the superintendent who would be responsible for the new machine and its crew in the field, it was her job to be The Final Authority on all things pertaining to its operation. That, in turn, meant minor or full mastery of a wide range of topics, including practical geology, mechanical engineering, the physics of pressurized fluids and gases, and even organizational management. To name but a few.

So it was not merely frustrating but alarming and infuriating when, once again, concentration on the words, and charts, and formulae did not come easily. Indeed, she discovered that she had been reading the same line about assessing imminent well-head failures because, instead of seeing it, she was seeing something else in her mind's eye:

Ulrich Rohrbach, down-time crew chief for the rig.

Which was not just foolishness, but utter, stupid, and dangerous foolishness. As she had kept telling herself over the last nine months. It was foolishness to allow him to court her at all. Foolish that they had started taking all their meals together. Foolish that they had spent Christmas visiting what was left of his war-torn family: a widowed sister and her two perilously adorable kids. More foolish still when they had started holding hands just before Valentine's Day, a mostly up-time tradition which he had somehow learned of (Ann secretly suspected their mutual boss, Dave Willcocks, of playing matchmaker). And most foolish of all had been their first kiss as they were laughing beneath the Maypole just weeks ago.

And there were so many reasons *why* it was all extraordinarily foolish. First, Ulrich was a down-timer, albeit a perfect gentleman and more patient than any up-time American would have been in regard to the glacial progress of their relationship. It was foolish because Ulrich barely had a fourth grade education, although, truth be told, his reading had become much faster and broader in the past half year and revealed that his mind was not slow, merely starved. And it was foolish because he just didn't look the way she had imagined the man of her dreams would look: he was not tall, dark, or particularly handsome. But on the other hand, he had kind eyes, thick sandy hair, dimples, a wonderful bass laugh, and a surprisingly muscular build, which, compacted into his sturdy 5'8" frame, would have put any number of up-time body-builders to shame.

And what had been especially foolish about their first kiss was her own response: not merely eager, but starved. She had absolutely embarrassed herself. And why? Because, as she learned when she started flipping backward through the months on her mental calendar, it had been at least—well, it had been a long, long, *long* time since she had had sex.

So all right, maybe her physical reaction—her *over*reaction, she firmly reminded herself—to the kiss had been understandable. But Ulrich wasn't likely to understand it. Or, more problematically, he was all too likely to understand it the wrong way: that her sudden avid response had been to *him*, personally, rather than to his, er, generic maleness. And so how would she explain that to him so that he wouldn't get more attached or more hopeful?

Are you sure that's really what you want to do? said a voice at the back of her mind, the one that had been growing steadily louder and more ironic for the past three weeks.

Her response was indignant and maybe a little bit terrified. Of course she wanted to let Ulrich know that she wasn't interested in him, *per se.* She had work, *important* work, to do. And after all, where could a relationship with him wind up?

Well, let's see, said the voice, *it could start in bed, then move to a house, which would quickly acquire some small, additional inhabitants—*

Ann Koudsi stood up quickly, her stomach suddenly very compact and hard. She did not want to get married to a down-timer. No matter how nice, or how good-natured, or how gentlemanly—or how damnedly sexy—he was. It wouldn't end well.

Right, agreed the grinning voice, *because it wouldn't end at all. Just like it hasn't ended for the hundreds of other up-time-down-time marriages that have occurred over the past few years.*

She paced to the bookshelf to get a book she didn't need, opened it, furiously thumbing through the index for she had no idea what.

Unless, said the voice, *what it's really about is home.*

Ann stopped thumbing the pages, forgot she was holding the book.

Yes, that's it, isn't it? If you marry a down-timer, it's the final act of acceptance that you're here in the past for good. That so much of your family, so many of your friends and almost everything else you ever knew and loved, is gone like that awful song said: dust in the wind. You won't embrace anyone in this world because you won't let go of the people in the other world.

Ann discovered she had clutched the book close to her chest, could feel her heart beating with a crisp, painful precision.

But here's the problem, girl: you can't hold on to what isn't there, what no longer exists. And if you wait too long, if you push Ulrich away too hard, you just might lose the best thing—the best man—you've ever laid eyes on in this world or the—

A distinctive metallic cough broke the stillness of the remote, steep-sided glen in which they had set up their test rig. Ann looked up, disoriented and startled. That was the drilling rig's engine, starting to run at full speed. But today's test run had been cancelled—

Then she detected an almost subaudible hum: the rig's turntable was spinning at operating RPMs.

Ann dropped the book and was out the door, sprinting for the drill site, which was located in a dead-end defile a quarter mile away. There was no fire-bell or even dinner-gong to ring to get them to stop, because other than the three cabins for the workers and the one for the senior site engineer—her—there was no one else nearby. And nothing with which to make alarm-level noise. "No reason to attract undue attention," Professor Doctor Wecke of the Mines and Drilling Program of the University of Helmstedt had explained coyly to her when she had accepted the position. She had wondered at the isolation of the site and then wondered if Wecke's caution about gongs and the like wasn't a bit ridiculous. Why worry about noisemaking bells when you spent most of the day running a loud, crude, experimental rotary drilling rig?

As she ran, Ann saw the expected plume of steam from the rig's engine obscuring the black cloud of its wood-fired boiler, and glimpsed a small figure well ahead of her, also running toward the drill site. That figure was moving very quickly and angling in from the main access road that led off to the rig's supply and service sheds. Then she saw its gray-dyed down-time coveralls. Distinct from the typical brown ones of the rank and file workers, that could only be Ulrich. He must have heard the engine start, too. Had probably been in the materials depot, checking the quality of the new casing before it went in the hole to shore up the soft, unconsolidated walls that would be left behind by the next day's digging.

The next *day's digging:* that deferral to tomorrow had not been merely advisable, but essential. Today's run *had* to be called off because too many of the main crew, the veterans, were down with the flu. It was one of those brief but vicious late spring bugs that spreads like wildfire, burns through a body by setting both brow and guts on fire (albeit in different ways), and then burns out just as quickly. Even old tough-as-leather Dave Willcocks, head of the rotary drill development team and liaison to the academics and financiers back at the University of Helmstedt, had fallen victim to the virus. Which was a source of some extra concern at the site and beyond: this was the first sign that Willcocks was anything other than indestructible, and at seventy years of age, there was no knowing if this was just an aberration in his otherwise unexceptioned robust health, or the first sign of impending decline. Ann had seen, all too often and too arrestingly, that people aged more quickly in the seventeenth century, and the transition from good health to decrepitude could, on occasion, be startlingly swift.

Ulrich had reached the rig, seemed to dart around looking for something. Or someone, Ann corrected. He was clearly trying to find who was in charge, who had overridden today's suspension of operations.

From far behind her private cabin, Ann heard another engine kick into life with a roar. That was an up-time sound, the engine on Dave Willcock's pick-up truck. Good, so that meant he was on his way. Ann didn't like that he was up and about, but right now, her strongest sensation was relief. No one back-talked Willcocks. His word was law on site, and that was what was needed to shut down the rig without a moment's delay. Without Dave or Ulrich or her there to oversee the commencement of operations, there was no telling what errors might be made.

Ulrich had reached the platform upon which the

derrick was built. Now only a hundred yards off—
but with a wind-stitch suddenly clutching at her left
side—Ann could see him engaged in a shouting match
with someone up there. Someone very tall and very
lean and very blond, almost white blond—

Oh shit, Ann thought, *he's arguing with Otto Bauernfeld.* Bauernfeld was the senior overseer for Gerhard
Graves, who was the nosiest and most intrusive of all
the investors. Imperious and contemptuous both, the
Graves family had tried double-crossing David Willcocks and his associates when they undertook their
first joint drilling project, a simple cable rig. So this
time, Willcocks, his team, and now the university, had
unanimously wanted to reject Graves' money—but they
simply couldn't afford to. The project would not have
been possible without Gerhard Graves carrying twenty
percent of the upfront costs. And Otto Bauernfeld,
as Graves' visiting factotum, had adopted an attitude
to match his master's: presumptuous, dictatorial, and
arrogantly dismissive of the rank-and-file workers.
"Shit," Ann repeated. Aloud, this time.

She sprinted the last thirty yards to the gravel-
ringed drill site, earning stares as she went. Pebbles
churned underfoot, slowing her down, but she was
able to catch the shouted exchange between Ulrich
and Otto Bauernfeld as she traversed the last few
yards of loose stone.

"You must shut the rig down, Herr Bauernfeld.
Mr. Willcocks has ordered us not to drill today, not
even to—"

Bauernfeld looked far down his very long nose at
the medium-sized but very powerful Ulrich. "Who are
you, and why should I care?"

"I am Ulrich Rohrbach, the site foreman and design consultant. I must ask you to—"

"I do not take orders from you, workman. Now, do not obstruct me any further."

"Herr Bauernfeld, I must insist: on whose authority do you ignore and violate Project Director David Willcocks' strict prohibition against drilling today?"

"I ignore it based on the only authority that truly matters on this site: that stemming from my patron's heavy investment in this project. Which you should understand. I am here for one day—one day, and no more—and must see the progress you have made in developing this drill. My superior expects an impartial report, and he shall have it."

"Herr Bauernfeld, with a little warning, I could have—"

"You are a worker. And an employee of Herr Willcocks. Who will be pleased to tell me whatever he thinks will please my employer. But Herr Graves wants the truth and I know how to get it for him." Bauernfeld stuck this thumbs into his belt and leaned back, quite pleased with himself. "It was simply a matter of getting the crew to run the drill without your interference. Which they did readily enough, when I told them who my superior was, and the personal consequences they would face if they displeased him. So, now I shall see the operation as it truly is, and with my own eyes."

"You are not seeing the operation," Ann panted.

Bauernfeld halted as she gasped for breath, and then doubled over to ease the cramp in her gut. Still looking up, she could see the uncertainty in his eyes, the waver in his demeanor as he tried to decide where she fit into his complex constellation of class and professional relationships. A woman of no particular birth, but an up-timer: a person who actually worked alongside laborers, but also a person of considerable achievement and education. There were no ready social equations that defined her place in his social scheme of things.

But then his eyes strayed to her clothes: grimy, practical coveralls, gray like Ulrich's. Something like a satisfied smile settled about Bauernfeld's eyes. "Frau Koudsi, the rig's motors are running and the drill-string has been lowered. And now—see? It is turning: the drilling has begun. So I am most certainly seeing the operations of your drill."

"Proper operations involve more than turning on the machines." Ulrich's voice was so guttural that he sounded more animal than human.

Bauernfeld speared him with eyes that suggested he would have preferred to respond with the back of his hand instead of his tongue. "Your workers know the steps well enough, I perceive."

"You perceive wrong, then, you ass." Ann felt herself rising on her toes to make her rebuttal emphatic. "These aren't our first crew. Almost all of them are second crew. Replacements who usually carry gear, clean the facility. They're like apprentices at this stage."

Bauernfeld became a bit pale. "And the—the journeymen, or 'first crew,' as you say?"

Ulrich waved an arm angrily back at the workers' sheds. "Back there. In bed. Sick with the same flu that has Herr Willcocks in bed, and why we shut down operations today."

Bauernfeld was now truly pale. "But... all seems to be in order. These men know their tasks."

"Do they?" shrieked Ann over the motor and the drill, wondering how long they had to convince Bauernfeld to tell the class-cowed workers shut the rig down—or how long it would take for Dave Willcocks to drive down here, if he wouldn't listen to reason. "Did you flush the mud hose? Did you check its flexibility? Did you check where it connects to the kelly for signs of wear or fraying? Did you turn the drill in the hole long enough to warm the mud already there *before* putting weight on the bit? And did you warm the new mud in the tanks before pumping it in?"

Bauernfeld scowled at the last. "And how could the temperature of mud possibly matter?"

Ann pointed behind her at the mud-tank. "*That* mud is being pumped down in that hole, Herr Bauernfeld. At extremely high pressure. Among other things, it scoops up the shavings—the debris made by the drilling—and dumps it there, in the shaker tray, where the debris is removed and the mud is returned to the system."

With uncertain eyes, Bauernfeld followed the progress of her pointing: from mud pit, to mud tube, to where it connected to the swivel atop the drill string, to where the return tube dumped the fouled mud into the shaker tray. "And to do this," he said slowly, "the mud must be warm?"

Ulrich leaned in, face red, voice loud with both urgency and anger. "No, but it cannot be *cold*."

"But why?"

Ann rolled her eyes. *Can Bauernfeld really be so stupid? Well, he might be.* "Look, you sit down to breakfast and get thin, hot porridge. How easy can you pour it into your bowl?"

Bauernfeld shrugged. "Easily enough."

"Right. Now let it get cold. Try pouring it."

Bauernfeld's eyebrows lowered, but then rose quickly. "It is thicker. It will be harder to—"

"Exactly, and that's why the mud can't be too cold. But last night we had a hard frost, and the men running the drill haven't dealt with this. They don't know how the resistance builds, particularly with the shavings collecting because the thicker mud can't clear them quickly enough. They have no idea what that could do to—"

Ann heard a faint groan in the mud-carrying standpipe where it ascended the nearest leg of the derrick. "Uh oh," she breathed and looked up at the swivel.

Ulrich was already staring at it but with a surprised expression. "Looks like the swivel coupling is holding," he breathed. Carefully.

Ann nodded, was aware of Bauernfeld's confused gape. He followed their eyes, but did not know what to look at. Which in this case was the swivel atop the spinning drill string. That had been the most problematic piece of machinery to make reliable and robust. Not the swivel itself—that was a fairly straightforward fabrication job—but where the flexible mud hose connected to it.

While the hose did not fully "spin" with the swivel, there was a lot of random and varying motion imparted to it as the drill string sped up, slowed down, encountered resistance, spun free. In short, the linkage between hose and swivel had to be both strong and flexible.

And that was a difficult requirement for seventeenth-century materials. There was no rubber available, yet.

That would involve tapping New World trees en masse or growing them elsewhere. And synthetics were a pipe dream, an up-time reality that was now a distant fantasy. So they made do with leather. Layered with canvas. Stitched carefully. Reinforced by brass rivets and clamps, where feasible. And at the connecting collar, where the changes in pressure and torque were most intense, precious (which was to say "retooled up-time") steel rings added extra reinforcement.

And so far, despite the rapid spin-up and overly thick mud, the epicenter of their engineering headaches and operational worries was holding up. Ann felt a smile try to rise to her lips. *Heh, progress at last—*

But that impulse did not last longer than the eye-blink which refocused her on the very real dangers of continuing operations. So the mud hose's linkage to the swivel was good: so what? The mud was too cold, meaning there were about a dozen other failure points that could be potentially—

The groan in the standpipe returned as a loud surging wail and the whole tube began shuddering, the oscillations racing up its gantry-ascending length.

Ann turned to the engine operator, prepared to talk him through the spin-down instructions—

But Bauernfeld had gone completely pale, discerning in the combination of her desperate motions and the quaking of the standpipe, that he was standing right next to an impending disaster. "Shut it off!" he screamed at the engine operator, "Turn the engine off! Stop the drill string!"

"NO!" Ann and Ulrich howled together. But it was too late.

The disaster was already unleashing itself when

Bauernfeld shouted his crude, and therefore counterproductive, orders. The standpipe, shaking mightily, now put pressure on a connection which had never been a major point of design concern: that point where it joined to the mud-hose, which hung free between the gantry leg and the swivel atop the drill string. However, since that hose was more rigidly affixed to its point of connection with the standpipe, the excessive pressure in the system now made it shudder violently. At the very fringe of where it met the pipe's connecting collar, a brass rivet popped, a seam opened—

"Run!" Ann shouted. "Clear the rig!" And then she felt a blow on her back. The air was driven out of her, and she was flying—but being carried, too. The momentary disorientation became realization: Ulrich had tackled her off the platform. And a powerful emotion rose up to meet that realization. *I love him. I do! I know that now. But this is going to hurt. And we could still die. Very easily.* And yet, her eyes never left the rig.

With a screaming pop of suddenly released pressure, the mud hose stripped itself off the top of the standpipe, flinging the attachment collar high into the air. Freed, the hose's sudden wild writhings resembled the overdose-death throes of a mud-vomiting anaconda. One worker, among the youngest, staring openmouthed at the sudden spectacle before him, did not move in time. The hose spasmed through a vicious twist and cut him open from chest to navel, viscera flying in all directions. Almost bisected, he was dead before he hit the ground.

The wild whipping and slashing caught two more persons. Bauernfeld himself managed to dodge the hose, but his left hip and groin were caught in the spray pattern of the mud. Although quickly losing pressure, that viscous jet was still spewing with a force well above one hundred PSI. Bauernfeld went down with a warbling shriek of pain and surprise, white bone showing through a wash of blood and shattered intestines—less than two seconds after he had shouted his final orders.

Those orders now went into full, monstrous effect. The partially trained rig operator not only cut the engine, but, hearing Bauernfeld's "stop" order, had thrown the long lever that engaged a large, counter-weighted arresting gear.

The effect on the drill-string was dramatic. With many tons of pipe already spinning in the three hundred foot hole, there was simply no way to, as Ann's mother used to say, "stand on the brakes." Instead, the arrestor groaned, its cable snapped, and the counterweights were launched sideways, one smashing down a nearby utility shed, the other tracing a ballistic arc into the side of the ravine.

But, even though it was brief, that sudden, strong resistance at the head of the drill pipe forced a rapid drop in rotational speed of its uppermost lengths. However, the much weightier part of the entire drill string assembly was still turning in the hole, its massive inertia being what had quickly shattered the braking mechanism, which had only been designed to gradually slow, not immediately stop, the string.

Now, the differences in inertia and resistance at the two ends of the drill string simply tore it apart. The threaded ends which joined the top pipe in the hole with length that was still free-spinning above it

screeched and gave way in a shower of sparks. The
lower length of pipe, grinding shrilly against the sides
of the borehole, slowed quickly, but its single sweep
smashed everything in its path. The upper length, no
longer anchored on the bottom, swung wide and fast,
ripping free of the kelly and swivel. It spun away like
a side-slung baton, clipping the northernmost leg of
the derrick, and swatting three workers aside like so
many inconsequential—and now quite shattered—flies.
The combined kelly-and-swivel assembly swung around
like a misshapen bolo, cracked through two gantry
struts and spent the rest of its energy by slamming
full on into yet another of the derrick's legs.

Showered by the mud spewing up from the shattered standpipe, Ann swung to her feet, blinking—
when Ulrich retightened his arm around her waist
and started running away—

—Away from the groaning, tilting, unraveling derrick that pushed slowly down through the curtain of
mud as it toppled toward them.

Ann got her own feet under her somehow and, with
Ulrich now pulling her by the hand, they sprinted
away. This time, Ann did not look back.

She heard the smash, felt the ground shiver a
moment before the slight concussive wave of the impact
buffeted her back. Splinters, whining like darts, bit
into her right thigh and buttock. She only ran harder.

Which was just as well. More debris, ejected upward,
came down in a lethal torrent where she had been
running just two seconds before.

A pulley, rolling on its edge, wheeled past her
briskly, lagged when it reached the gravel perimeter
of the site, wobbled lazily and fell over. As if that

was a signal to Ann and Ulrich that the danger was indeed past, they turned, still holding hands.

The rig was gone. Except for four feet of the drill pipe that had sheared off while partially in the bore hole and two feet of savaged standpipe that had not gone over with the derrick, nothing was left standing upright on the platform. The steam engine had been ruined by debris, its boiler knocked over and the firebox already flaring dangerously. Mud oozed outward and downward in all directions. Smoke—black, brown, and gray—fanned upward into the sky. The workers who had cleared the rig in time were already being joined by members of the sickly "first crew," who, wan and haggard, spread out through the wreckage with them, searching for survivors.

Behind them, brakes screeched, gravel spattered, and a car door opened. A moment later, Dave Willcocks, looking haggard and pale, was standing alongside them, staring at the ruin that had been their grand experiment. "Jesus Christ," he swore. But he didn't stare at the wreckage for more than a few seconds before heading toward the disaster to assist in the rescue work, just a few steps behind Ann and Ulrich.

The time that followed was without a doubt the most gruesome experience in Ann's life. The scale of the blunt force trauma inflicted on fragile human bodies by the disintegrating oil rig was genuinely incredible. It was as if the gods of the earth, awakened and risen in fury, had just torn people apart.

She couldn't even find any flicker of vengeful satisfaction in Bauernfeld's fate, although he'd been directly responsible for the disaster. The wound that had killed him was . . . horrible, a perfect illustration of the old saw *I wouldn't wish that on my worst enemy.*

Eventually—thankfully—the immediate rescue work was over. Those who'd survived had been stabilized and had been taken away to receive real medical care. Repairing the property damage would take a lot longer, but there was no immediate urgency involved. So, tired and blood-spackled themselves, Ann and Ulrich and Dave Willcocks came back together to discuss the situation.

"I heard about Bauernfeld coming here," said Willcocks. "Got the message from your runner, Ulrich, the same moment I heard the rig start. His doing, I take it?"

Ann looked out of the corner of her eye. Ulrich frowned at David Willcocks' question, looked away, clearly trying to fabricate a face-saving story for a man who was now dead. An incompetent, arrogant man whom Ulrich would probably now risk his own good reputation to protect.

Ann turned and looked Willcocks in the eye. "Yes, this was Bauernfeld's doing. All so he could make a report to Gerhard Graves without any input or 'interference' from us." She turned her eyes back to the smoking ruins. "I'd say his methods were ill-considered."

Another car door opened and closed behind them. Footsteps rasped on the gravel, and then Dennis Grady, head of contractors for the State of Thuringia-Franconia's Department of Economic Resources, their project's other fiscal godfather, came to stand beside Ulrich.

Ann started. "Mr. Grady, what are you doing up here?"

He looked away from the devastation with a baleful expression. "Why, to check on your progress."

Ann—broken-hearted but also quite suddenly aware that not only was she in love with Ulrich, but had been for almost three months now—felt conflicting emotions of joy and loss roil and bash into each other. They came out of her as a burst of laughter. "Our progress! Wow, did you pick the wrong day for a visit, or what?"

Grady shrugged. "Machines can be rebuilt, if they're worth rebuilding."

Grady's serious, level tone was like a bucket of cold water in Ann's face. *So this isn't the end of all our work, maybe?* "And what determines if they're worth rebuilding?"

"Well, how was the rig doing before this happened?"

"That is the irony of this disaster, Herr Grady," Ulrich sighed. "Tomorrow, we were scheduled to get to four hundred feet. And the equipment had been working quite well. We had to be careful not to push the system too much. The mud flow cannot keep up with our top operating speeds."

"Why?"

Ann thought Dave Willcocks might explain, but instead he nodded at her to continue, smiling like a proud uncle. She shrugged, answered, "The rate that we get fresh mud in the hole determines how much we can cool the system. It bathes the hot drill bit, removes extra friction by carrying away the cuttings. But the mud hose is the bottleneck. We can't push the pressure in the hose over two hundred fifty psi without risking a rupture. That reduces how much we can cool the system, and how fast we can clear cuttings out of the hole. And that determines our upper operating limit."

"But if you stay beneath that limit—?"

"We were making good progress, and this design was holding up pretty well."

"We still have challenges," Willcocks put in. "We've got to have better threading between the separate sections of drill pipe. And I'm not sure that we've got enough horsepower from the current steam engine to really do the job when we get under six hundred feet."

"But in principle, this design is functional?"

"Functional, yes. Ready to drill, no."

Grady shook his head. "But I didn't ask you about readiness."

David frowned. "Two months ago you did."

Grady shrugged. "That was two months ago. Things change."

"Like what?"

"Like never you mind. Look, it was always a long-shot that you'd have a rotary drill ready for the New World survey expedition, anyhow. And as things are developing, we won't need it until next year, probably. By which time, I expect it will be ready." Grady glanced at the smoldering ruin, through which rescuers were picking their careful ways. "Well, *this* one won't be ready, but you get what I mean."

Ann almost smiled, but it felt wrong, somehow. "Thanks, Dennis. I wish I could be happier. But we've lost so much: so many people, so much hard work, and a chance to set foot in North America again."

"Oh, now hold on," said Grady. "Just because you won't have a rotary drill, doesn't mean you're not still going along for the ride to the New World. We need your scientific and technical skills on site, and there *are* drills besides your rotary wonder, you know."

Ann shrugged. "I ought to know. We were working cable rigs at Wietze for the better part of two years."

"And you'll be working them again, half a world away."

Ulrich looked flustered, possibly heart-broken. "So then, if Ms. Koudsi is—is gone, who shall resume building the rotary drill?"

David kicked at the gravel. "I guess that would be me and the technical assistants that have been helping you out here. And I could bring up Glen Sterling from Grantville. And actually, we did learn something important about the drill design today: that the weak point is no longer at the juncture of the swivel and the mud hose, but at the juncture of the mud-hose and the standpipe."

"So how much time do I have to help David with the improved model before I leave?" Ann asked Dennis, while looking at Ulrich.

"None, I'm afraid," answered Grady. "We've got to get you up north for special training and equipment familiarization. Besides, there's not going to be much breakthrough engineering going on for a few months. I figure it will take that long just to get all the drill pipe and casing out of the ground." He looked at David for confirmation.

Willcocks nodded. "Gonna be a bitch of a job. But it will be our golden opportunity to own the next rig outright, without worrying about financiers."

Grady frowned. "Oh? How's that?"

"Herr Graves' representative caused this failure. Every surviving witness will testify to that. And from what Herr Bauernfeld told me on the way down here, he had papers in his bags indicating that he has a 'clear mandate from his employer' to ensure that he saw the rig in operation without me or any of my supervisors around to meddle with it. I told him that wasn't permissible. Sent a letter to his boss on the topic, too.

"But he disregarded multiple direct orders from the lawful site operators and majority owners, and went ahead with his 'private test.' So he and his employer are directly culpable for all this—the loss of life, the loss of the rig, and the expense of recovering all that pipe and casing, since it's too rare and costly to leave sitting in the ground." David's grin was one of savage revenge, not mirth. "It's going to cost that bastard Graves his stake in this whole operation to be able to walk away from this disaster without getting roasted alive by the courts."

Grady nodded. "Yep. Sounds about right." He turned to Ann. "Now, are you ready to pack your bags and head north to the Baltic?"

"I am," answered Ann, "But on one condition."

Grady raised an eyebrow. "And what's that?"

"That I get to choose my crew chief." She turned to Ulrich and smiled. "That would be Ulrich Rohrbach. If he doesn't go, it's no deal."

Ulrich stared at Ann, smiling back, his mouth open a little, jaw working futilely to find words—but not very hard. He was too busy looking at her, Ann was delighted to see, like an infatuated puppy.

Grady cleared his throat. "Well, Mr. Rohrbach, how about it? Are you also willing to go to the New World and drill for oil without a rotary rig?"

Ulrich did not look away from Ann or even blink. "Where do I sign up?" he said.

Chapter 12

Luebeck, United States of Europe

Nodding to the after-hours Marine guard, Eddie entered the antechamber outside John Simpson's office. As he did, his stomach growled so loudly that he expected a Marine to enter behind him, sidearm drawn, scanning for whatever feral beast was making a noise akin to being simultaneously tortured and strangled.

And if being two hours overdue for supper wasn't enough, he'd just received yet another letter from Anne Cathrine. It was alternately sweet, steamy, and sullen at having to spend her nights watching her father pickle his royal brain with excesses of wine. She made it emphatically—indeed, graphically clear—just how much, and in what ways, she'd rather be spending those nights with Eddie, indulging in excesses of—

Nope, don't go there, Eddie. You have a job to do, which doesn't include learning to walk with a stiff prosthetic leg and an equally stiff—

The door opened. "Commander, there you are," said Simpson.

Yes, here I very much am. A bit too much of me,

in fact. Eddie cheated the folders he was carrying a few inches lower, shielding his groin from ready view. However, nothing slackened his line quite so quickly or profoundly as hearing the CO's voice, so he was safe by the time he had entered the room and saluted.

As soon as Simpson had returned the salute and invited him to sit, Eddie produced one of the folders—rough, ragged cardboard stock of the down-time "economy" variety—with a black square on the upper right-hand front flap. "News from the rotary drill project."

"Not good?"

"Disastrous, sir. The rig literally blew apart. But it wasn't a technical failure. One of the owners' inexperienced factors decided to show up for a surprise inspection and start the morning by playing platform chief."

"And how did that turn out?"

"Five dead, six wounded. The rig is a write-off. They're still trying to fish all the drill pipe out of the hole."

Simpson may have winced. "Well, so much for the overly ambitious hope that they'd have that drill working by the time we left, and be boring holes by fall."

"Yes, sir. But the Department of Economic Resources still wants to send the mainland prospecting team with our task force."

Simpson shrugged. "Well, that only makes sense, assuming the test rig was reasonably promising. That way, by the time they get a working rig ready, they'll know where to start drilling well holes."

"That's the ER Department's thinking on the matter, sir. They've shifted all the actual drilling crew and operators over to the Trinidad cable rig team."

"Which is just as well. That oil will be a lot easier to find."

"Yes sir, although there's a whole lot less of it."

Simpson looked up from the paperwork. "Commander, let's not go round on this again. First, Trinidad's oil will come to hand comparatively easily and it is sweet and light. Just what we need. And we're not equipped to ship more oil than they can produce, won't be for at least eighteen months. Second, and arguably more important, Trinidad has an additional strategic benefit of pulling our rivals' attentions away from our other operations."

Eddie knew it was time to offer his dutiful "Yes, sir"—which he did—and to move on. "All the regionally relevant maps, charts, graphs, and books that will comprise the mission's reference assets have been copied and are en route from Grantville. We still have two researchers combing through unindexed material for other useful information on the Caribbean, but it's been ten days since they found anything. And that was just some data on a species of flower."

"Hmmph. I suspect the focus in the Leeward Islands will be on agriculture, not horticulture."

"Yes, sir." Which was typical Simpson: he was the one who had insisted on extracting every iota of up-time information available on the West Indies, Spanish Main, and environs. And now he was turning his nose up at the tid-bits he had insisted on pursuing. *I suspect he's going to be a very cranky old man. Well, crankier.*

"Did you find any more data on native dialects in the Gulf region?"

Eddie shook his head. "No, sir." All they had turned

up were a few snippets of a local dialect alternately referred to as Atakapa or Ishak. And those snippets were so uncertain, they would be better described as "second-hand linguistic rumors" than "data."

"Provisioning and materiel almost ready?"

"Getting there, sir. Without the rotary drill equipment and pipe, we'll have a lot more room than we thought. But we're still taking on plenty of well casing for Trinidad. Each section is about the length, weight, and even girth of pine logs. So we got a lumber ship from the Danes to haul it."

Simpson frowned. "'Lumber ship?'"

"Yes, sir. Their sterns are modified. In place of the great cabin, they have an aft-access cargo bay, so the logs can be loaded straight in through the transom. Sort of like stacking rolls of carpet in the back of your van."

"Military stores?"

"Almost all are on site now, sir. We're still waiting on the molds and casts for the dual-use eight-inch shells. Which are working well in both the carronades and the long guns. All our radios are tested and in place, as is the land-station equipment. And the special-order spyglasses came in two days ago and passed the QC inspection."

"And the local binoculars?"

"There's an update on that in this morning's files, sir. The Dutch lens makers have demonstrated an acceptable working model to our acquisitions officer, but they haven't worked out a production method inexpensive enough for us to afford multiple purchases for each ship. My guess is that they'll have the bottlenecks licked by this time next year."

Simpson made a noise that sounded startlingly similar to a guard-dog's irritated growl. "Another key technology for which appropriations were not approved. Like the mitrailleuses."

Eddie sat up straight, genuinely alarmed. "Sir? They're not—not going to approve any mitrailleuses for the steamships? Why, that's—"

"Insane? Well, as it turns out, the Department of Economic Resources is not completely insane. Only half insane. Which is, in some ways, worse."

Eddie shook his head. "Sir, I don't understand: *half* insane?"

"Speaking in strictly quantitative terms, yes: half insane. Instead of approving one mitrailleuse for each quarter of the ship, they've approved exactly half that amount."

Eddie goggled. "A . . . a *half* a mitrailleuse for each quarter of the ship?" He tugged at his ginger-red forelock, doing the math and coming up with a mental diagram. "So only two? One on the forward port bow, the other on the starboard aft quarter?"

Simpson nodded. "That's about the shape of what the wiser heads in Grantville have envisioned." His voice was level and unemotional, but Eddie saw the sympathy in his eyes.

"But sir, how do you defend a ship against an all-point close assault with only two automatic weapons? If they come all around you in small boats—"

"Which they probably won't. As the holders of the purse strings were pleased to point out, yours is only a reconnaissance mission. So to speak. And you have no business going in harm's way, particularly at such close quarters. But if fate proves to take the unprecedented step of deciding to ignore all our reasonable expectations and plans"—Simpson's bitter, ironic grin made Eddie's stomach sink—"well, I just cut an order to Hockenjoss and Klott for a special antiboarding weapon. Two per ship, to take the place of the two missing mitrailleuses."

"Well, sir, I suppose that's better than nothing," Eddie allowed. And silently added, *but not by much, I bet.*

Simpson shrugged. "Certainly nothing very fancy or very complicated. Essentially I've asked them to build a pintle-mounted two-inch shotgun. Black powder breech-loader. It's already picked up a nickname: the Big Shot. It should help against boarders." He must have read the dismay in Eddie's face. "I know what you're thinking, Commander. That such a weapon will be useless against the small boats themselves. That was my first reaction, which the committee has now heard repeatedly and, on a few occasions, profanely. I'll keep fighting for the full mitrailleuse appropriation, but I think I'm going to have to spend all my clout just getting percussion locks standardized for the main guns."

Eddie nodded. "Yes, sir. Which is of course where your clout belongs. Those tubes are carrying the primary weight of our mission."

"Well said, Commander. And if you find yourself in a tight spot—well, to borrow a phrase from another service, improvise and overcome."

Eddie tried to be jocular, but could hear how hollow it sounded when he replied, "Oo-rah, sir."

Eddie's failed attempt at gallows humor seemed to summon a spasm of guilt to the admiral's face. It reminded Eddie of one of his father's post-binge reflux episodes. "It's bad enough that we're not getting all the resources we were promised, but having delayed your departure to wait for them was a bad decision. My bad decision. I should have insisted on keeping the mission lighter and going sooner. That would have given you more time in the Caribbean before hurricane season, less of a squadron to oversee—and fewer hangers-on, I might add."

Eddie shrugged. "Sir, your gamble to wait and get us more goodies may not have panned out, but that's in the nature of gambling, wouldn't you agree? If you had been right, we'd be leaving here with more combat power, and a mission which would have represented a much more complete test of the ships and systems you're planning to shift into standard production. And if the rotary drill had been ready, the cash back on the venture—and the need to rapidly expand our maritime capacity to capitalize on it—would have given you all the clout you needed for what you want. All the clout and more, I should say."

Simpson looked at Eddie squarely. The younger man wondered if that calm gaze was what the admiral's version of gratitude looked like. "You have a generous and forgiving spirit, Commander. I'm not sure I'd be so magnanimous, in your place. After all, it's not just you who now has less combat power, less time before the heavy weather sets in, and more official requirements added on while your departure was delayed. Your wife is now subject to the same vulnerabilities, too."

Eddie nodded. "And don't I know it, sir."

Simpson actually released a small smile. "You sound less than overjoyed to have your wife along for the ride, Commander. Not SOP for a newlywed."

"Sir, with all due respect, none of this is SOP for a newlywed. Am I glad that I won't spend a whole half year away from my beautiful wife? You bet. Does it make me crazy anxious that she, and her quasi-entourage, are heading into danger along with me? You bet. The latter kind of diminishes the, uh . . . hormonal happiness caused by the former."

Simpson chuckled. "You are developing a true gift for words, Commander. If I could spare you from the field, I'd make you our chief diplomatic liaison."

"Sir! It's unbecoming a senior officer to threaten his subordinates. I'll take cannon fire over cocktail parties any day!"

Simpson glanced down toward Eddie's false foot. "And this from a man who should know better."

"Sir, I do know better. I've experienced both, and I'll take the cannons."

"Why?"

"Permission to speak freely?"

"Granted."

"Because, sir, battles are short and all business, and cocktail parties are long and all bullshit."

Simpson seemed as surprised by his answering guffaw as Eddie was. "I take it, Commander, that you are not enamored of the, er, 'social consequences' of being accompanied by your wife?"

"Sir, I would be more enamored of taking a bath with a barracuda. Even though Anne Cathrine isn't a genuine princess, Daddy is sure acting like she is. I now have my very own traveling rump court. Well, it's not *my* court. I'm just a part of it. An increasingly lowly part of it."

Simpson frowned. "Yes, and from what I understand, Christian IV has saddled you with another senior naval officer, which bumps you yet another place down the chain of command."

"Oh, that's not even the worst part." Eddie tried not to succumb to the urge to whine, which was attempting to overwhelm the none-too-high walls of his Manly Reserve.

"Oh?" Simpson now seemed more amused that sympathetic.

"Admiral, you haven't heard the latest roster of my fellow-travelers. Essentially, Anne Cathrine, not being a genuine princess, doesn't warrant genuine ladies in waiting. So we get a collection of other problematic persons from, or associated with, the Danish court, plus naval wives who have been given land grants in the New World."

One of Simpson's eyebrows elevated slightly. "But Christian IV doesn't have any New World land to grant."

"Not yet."

Simpson frowned. "I see. So I'm guessing that, along with the not-quite royal contingent, we have a just barely official entourage of courtesans, councilors, and huscarles? Some of whom enjoy special appointments by, and are probably assigned to carry out undisclosed missions for, His Royal Danish Majesty?"

"Yep, pretty much, sir."

Simpson nodded. "Yes, leave it to him to sneak in something like this in exchange for the ships he's committing to the expedition. Given the condition in which we received those hulls, I'm not so sure he isn't getting the better end of the deal." Simpson fixed Eddie with a suddenly intent stare. "Has he either intimated or overtly instructed you to take any orders directly from him?"

"No, sir. Why?"

Simpson rubbed his chin. "Well, because technically he could try to work that angle."

"I'm not sure I follow, sir."

Simpson steepled his fingers. "In recognition of your marriage and service, Gustav made you Imperial Count of Wismar. That made you imperial nobility of the USE. Technically. And that made it easy—well, easier—for Christian to get the nobles of his *Riksradet* to accept your creation as a Danish noble, too."

Eddie blinked. "Sir, I'm not a Danish noble. Not really."

"No? If I'm not mistaken, one of Christian's wedding gifts to you was land, wasn't it?"

"Yes, sir. Some miserable little island in the Faroes. I think it has a whopping population of ten. That includes the goats."

Simpson did not smile. "And since you received the land as part of a royal patent, you were made a *herremand*, weren't you?"

"Uh—yes, sir. Something like that. I didn't pay too much attention."

"Well, you should have, Commander. You became Danish nobility when you accepted that land. And therefore, a direct vassal of King Christian IV. Who, unless I'm much mistaken, has bigger things in mind for you. In the meantime, we'd better inform the task force's captains that, in place of all that pipe they were going to be hauling, they're going to be billeting more troops. A lot more troops."

Eddie was relieved. The mission was no longer purely reconnaissance, although that was not common knowledge. Not even among all the members of the ER Department. "How many more sir, and where from?"

"Just under four hundred, Commander. And all from the Lowlands."

"So they're Dutch."

Simpson shook his head. "No. They're from the Brabant."

Eddie stared. "From the *Spanish* Lowlands?"

Simpson simply nodded.

"Sir—we're taking Spanish soldiers to fight for us in the Spanish-held New World?"

"Commander, here's what I know currently. The troops are being provided by the archduchess infanta Isabella. As I understand it, these troops will have sworn loyalty to her nephew Fernando the king in the Low Countries, but not her older nephew, Philip the king of Spain."

"But Fernando is Philip's younger brother, his vassal—"

"Precisely. And that's why we're going to stop our speculations right there, Commander. The story behind Fernando sending troops with us to assist Dutch colonial interests in the New World is one that is well above your pay grade at this early point in the process. I know that because it's above *my* pay grade. I am not yet on the political 'need to know' list. And I suspect the mystery will remain right up until the infanta's troops are being berthed aboard your flotilla. Which probably won't happen until the very last possible day."

Eddie shook his head. "Every day, this 'little reconnaissance mission' not only gets bigger and more complicated, it gets increasingly surreal." Eddie glanced at the map of the Caribbean that Simpson had produced from his own folders. "Hell, we can't even be sure that there are any remaining Dutch colonies for us to help. And vice versa."

Simpson spread his hands on his desk. "Well, we know that once the Dutch West India Company got their hands on the histories in Grantville, they got a two-year head start on their colonization of St. Eustatia in the Leeward Islands. By their own report, they redirected some of their best administrators there last year. Notably, Jan van Walbeeck, whom history tells us was very effective in improving the situation down in Recife."

Eddie shrugged. "And who returned to the Provinces from there just a week before Admiral Tromp arrived in Recife with the remains of the fleet that was shattered at the Battle of Dunkirk. Pity Tromp and Walbeeck couldn't have overlapped even a few days in Recife. If they had, we'd know a lot more about how the situation in the New World may be changing."

"Quite true. But at least we know that Tromp arrived in Recife, and was making plans to relocate, since the colonies in that part of South America were untenable after the destruction of the Dutch fleet at Dunkirk."

"Yes, sir, but relocate to *where*? The two or three friendly ships that have come from the New World since the middle of last year can't tell us. Even the *jacht* that Tromp himself sent last March only confirmed that he expected to commence relocating in April, but not where."

Simpson scoffed. "And can you blame him for not being specific? Imagine if the Spanish had stumbled across that ship, seized it, interrogated the captain. Then they'd know where to find him. From an operational perspective, every day that Tromp can work without Spanish detection is a found treasure. He will have to ferry a sizable population—well, 'contingent'—from Recife to whatever new site he's selected, house those people, find a reliable source of indigenous supplies, establish a patrol perimeter, fortifications. All without any help from back home. He has his work cut out for him, Commander."

"Agreed, sir. But the flip side is that while we're coming with the help he almost surely needs, we don't know where to deliver it to him."

"No, but we know the best places to look. Right now, there are three noteworthy Dutch colonies in the Caribbean and the northern littoral of South America. We know they've sent people and supplies to St. Eustatia. We know there's a small settlement on Tobago, just northeast of Trinidad. And we know that they sent an expedition under Marten Thijssen last year to take Curaçao."

"And that assumes Thijssen's mission was a success."

"Yes, it does. It also assumes that Tromp's stated intent to abandon Recife was not disinformation. But that seems very unlikely. Deceiving the Spanish on that point wouldn't buy him any durable advantage. In a few months' time, the Spanish would learn that he hadn't left, would blockade Recife, and grind him down. With the Dutch fleet in tatters, there's no relief force to be sent.

"So let's consider the three reasonable options. Curaçao is perilously close to the Spanish Main, just north of the path of the inbound treasure fleet. A great location from which to hunt the Spanish, but not a great location in which to hide from them. And the colony on Tobago is small. Too small: one hundred and fifty persons, at most."

Eddie nodded. "So, St. Eustatia."

Simpson nodded. "Exactly. St. Eustatia is in the middle of the Leeward Islands. So it's out of the way and not much visited by the Spanish. Yet history shows that, in time, 'Statia's central location could make it a powerful trading hub, once the traffic in the Caribbean picks up in intensity. It's also small enough to be defensible, but not so small as to be a rock from which there is no escape."

Eddie nodded. "Yes, Admiral, it all makes sense, but I'm still worried that even our last word of the Caribbean—from the Dutch fluyt *Koninck David*—still didn't include any mention of Tromp. Or much about St. Eustatia at all."

Simpson shrugged. "As I remember the report, the *Koninck David* left the Straits of Florida for its return to Europe in August. They wouldn't have been anywhere near 'Statia for half a year before that, in all likelihood. And although they didn't have any reassuring news for us, the American with them, young Phil Jenkins, also reported that the Spanish presence in the area was still pretty sparse. Which is historically consistent: until the Spanish were significantly challenged, they remained pretty close to their fortified ports and key colonies. With the abandoning of Recife, all the Dutch colonies are, practically speaking, off the beaten path. And St. Eustatia more than the other two."

"I agree that's where Admiral Tromp is likely to be, Admiral—if he's anywhere at all."

"What are you implying, Commander?"

Eddie produced one of the many history books he'd been poring over for the last several weeks. "I'm implying that in this period, the Spanish are realizing the need to establish the Armada de Barlovento, the squadron that enforces their territorial claim over the entirety of the Caribbean. If the ships that survived Dunkirk left Recife with even half of the ships that were already there, that's still a major force in the Caribbean. Too major for the Spanish to ignore, if they detect it."

"*If* they detect it—a very big *if*, Commander. But your point is well-taken. Even though our history books show that the Armada de Barlovento is fairly anemic right now, events since our arrival may have already led the Spanish to resharpen its teeth in this timeline. If so—well, then heed the Department of Economic Resource's exhortations, commander: remember that this is a recon mission only, and not to get embroiled in close range gun duels with the Spanish."

"Or pirates."

Simpson smiled. "Or them either." He stood. "Commander, I think that concludes the day's business. And unless I'm much mistaken, you have a lot of paperwork and correspondence ahead of you yet." He raised a salute.

Eddie jumped up and snapped a crisp response. "Yes, sir. Looks like I'll be burning the midnight oil. Again." And with that, he pivoted about on his false foot and made for the door, deciding that tonight he'd definitely need to use his remaining coffee ration. Definitely.

✧   ✧   ✧

Simpson's eyes remained on the door as it closed behind Eddie Cantrell and then strayed to the folder on his desk marked "Reconnaissance Flotilla X-Ray (Cantrell)." He resisted the urge to open it yet again and inspect its ever-changing roster of ships. Each new diplomatic, military, or resource wrinkle in the USE seemed to make themselves felt as revisions to the complement of hulls. And with every week that Flotilla X-Ray's departure had been delayed, its size and composition shifted.

Its original composition had been sufficient for its originally simple mission. And likewise, Eddie had been the only possible candidate for the flotilla's senior up-time officer. Indeed, he had as much naval combat experience as any other up-timer (with the exception of Simpson himself). However, that experience was paltry by comparison to the great majority of the flotilla's down-time captains and commanders, who had spent most of their lives at sea. Many began as common sailors working "before the mast," and during some parts of their careers just about all of them had traded broadsides with their sovereigns' foes. Although the down-time naval officers who had been training for the mission clearly respected Eddie for his combat experience and storied daring, they also were very much aware that he was a relative newcomer to their profession, and was almost completely unfamiliar with the nuances of the sailing vessels upon which they themselves had grown to manhood and in which they were infinitely more at home than any place ashore.

What Eddie had in lieu of their profound nautical skill—as much from his up-time reading and gaming as from recent training—was an innate sense of the tempo and requirements of a flotilla operating under steam power. He was the only officer in Flotilla X-Ray who had that almost instinctual insight. Even those down-time crewmen who had been intensely trained in the technical branches, and who had long ago outstripped him in the expertise specific to any given subsystem of Simpson's new navy, still lacked his totalized sense of how all those complex parts fit and flowed together, producing both incredible synergies of military power, but also incredible vulnerabilities to breakdowns in either machinery or logistics.

Simpson kept staring at the folder, kept resisting the impulse to open it and reassure himself that Eddie was being given an adequate force to complete his mission and to be able to overmaster or outrun any foes that might present themselves. After all, the admiral told himself, feeling sheepish as he echoed the Department of Economic Resources, it was a simple recon mission. There was nothing to worry about. So what if Reconnaissance Flotilla X-Ray was bound for the New World, beyond the limits of the USE's power to help, or even readily communicate with it? The flotilla was still fundamentally a shake-down cruise for the first production models of Simpson's first generation of steam-powered warships. They, usually with Eddie on-board, had been put through extensive sea-trials, and, except for a few quirks, had performed admirably—even superbly, if Simpson were to say so himself. They were good ships, and Eddie was a good, if young, officer.

Simpson studied the flaps of the folder, edges dirty with the wear of his worried fingers, of his impatient thumbs prying back the dull covers. Commander

Cantrell and the rest of the flotilla would simply conduct the preparatory operations in the Gulf and the Caribbean and then, when the time was right, Admiral John Chandler Simpson would bring over his new navy of mature, second generation ships, as shiny and lethal a weapon as this world had yet seen.

The consequent "pacification" of rivals in the New World would ready his blue water fleet for the more serious and definitive battles that it would almost certainly have to fight against one or more of the armadas of the Old World. It was impossible to foresee which nation, or collection thereof, would ultimately find the rise of the USE so intolerable a phenomenon that it would feel compelled to correct that trend in the most decisive manner possible: a no-holds-barred confrontation of navies. But in the dynamics of the rise and fall of nations, the uncertainties regarding such conflicts had never been *if* they would occur, but rather with whom, and when, and where.

That thought, however, made Simpson's eyes wander to the thinner folder lying alongside the one for Flotilla X-Ray. This one was marked with a white triangle: an intel synopsis, containing a review of pending threats that might require naval intervention, sooner or later. France, Spain, even the Ottomans, could conceivably stir up enough trouble to keep Simpson's larger, finished fleet from a timely deployment to the New World. However, none of those powers appeared to be disposed or deployed to do so.

But then again, John Chandler Simpson knew that appearances could be deceiving and that the only thing certain about the future was that there was never, ever, anything certain about it.

He pushed the folders away, rested his chin on his hand, stared at the door through which Eddie Cantrell had exited, and succumbed to his now-habitual array of worries—half of which were common to all commanders of young men regardless of the time or place of the conflict, and half of which were the dark legacy of every father who had ever sent a son to fight a war in a distant land.

Chapter 13

Brussels, The Spanish Low Countries

"So the Spanish tried to kill the pope? And *did* kill John O'Neill in Rome?"

Thomas Preston, oldest officer among the Irish Wild Geese who served in the Lowlands, and Maestro-de-campo of the eponymous Preston Tercio, stared back at the group that had summoned him and delivered this shocking news. Seated at the center was Fernando, king in the Low Countries and brother of Philip IV of Spain. To his right was Maria Anna of the House of Hapsburg, Fernando's wife and sister of Emperor Ferdinand of Austria. And sitting to one side, but in the largest, most magnificent chair of all of them, was the grand dame of European politics herself, the archduchess infanta Isabella, still an authority in the Lowlands and aunt of both Fernando and Philip. And therefore, Preston's employer for the last twenty years. Oh, and then there was Rubens, the artist and intelligencer, sitting far to one side of the power-holding troika that ruled here in Brussels.

Maria Anna leaned forward slightly. "Colonel Preston,

I assure you, my husband would not tell you such things unless they were true."

"Your Highness, I apologize. I did not intend that response as a sign of doubt, but of disbelief. It is shocking news, to say the least."

Fernando nodded. "To us, also, Colonel. And that is why we asked you to meet us alone. It may cause, er, unrest in the Irish *tercios*, if it comes to them as rumor. Coming from you, however, we might hope for a different reception."

Thomas Preston shifted in his suddenly-uncomfortable seat. "Your Highness, the reception might be *some*what different—but not as different as if it came from one of the Old Irish colonels."

Maria Anna's eyebrows raised in curiosity. "'Old' Irish?"

"Yes, Your Highness. My family name, as you are probably aware, is not an Irish name at all, but English. That makes us Prestons 'New' Irish, associated with the old, pre-Reformation landlords who eventually married into the Irish families. We are often wealthier than our Old Irish neighbors—which makes us suspect to begin with, I fear—but no amount of money will ever equate to having ancient Gaelic roots, to being one of the families whose names are routinely associated with the High Kingship's tanists—"

"The tanists?" Maria Anna echoed.

It was Isabella herself who answered. "The royal families of Ireland designate one of their number as chief among them. And it is usually from among these that, in elder times, the current king's successor—the tanist—was chosen."

"Ah," breathed Rubens, "so this is why Hugh O'Neill

the Elder was known as 'The O'Neill.' He was the chieftain of that dynasty and all those subordinate to it."

"That is my understanding, but I suspect that Colonel Preston would add details I have missed or misunderstood. Most pertinent to our concerns, though, is that there are—or were—only two scions of the royal houses remaining free, outside Ireland, who had clear entitlement to becoming tanists of the vacant throne: the recently deceased John O'Neill, the earl of Tyrone, and Hugh O'Donnell, the earl of Tyrconnell."

"*Attainted* Earls, My Grace," added Rubens.

"Yes, yes," she replied testily, "so the English have it. The same English who just happened to steal Ireland from its own people, and whose attainting of its few remaining nobles is merely the conclusive legalistic coda to their campaign of usurpation and rapine. It is not as if any legitimate monarch on the Continent, Catholic or Protestant, cares a whit for the juridical rationalizations of England's theft of a whole nation. But let us return to Colonel Preston's point. The Old Irish will, unfortunately, not hear this news as well from him as they would from one of the survivors of their royal families. But there is nothing to be done about that. The last O'Neill, who is not directly in the line of titular inheritance, is Owen Roe, and he now commands the pope's new bodyguard. The last O'Donnell is my godson, Hugh Albert, and he is . . ." She paused, either catching her breath or mastering a quaver in her voice: Preston could not determine which. ". . . is engaged in other matters and unable to return at present."

Preston sat straighter. Whereas John O'Neill had been insufferable and Owen Roe tolerable, Hugh

O'Donnell had been a good fellow: clever, a shrewd soldier, well-educated, well-spoken, and without regal airs. So why the hell wasn't he here? He'd disappeared in April, and now, when he was needed most—

"Colonel Preston," Fernando articulated carefully, as if aware that he would have to reacquire the mercenary's attention before continuing.

"Yes, Your Highness?"

"I should add that news of the earl of Tyrone's death, and the attempt on the pope's life, are only precursors to the primary reason I asked you to join us today."

"Precursors, Your Highness?"

"Yes. First, I welcome you to share your opinion on how your men will receive the news. This is material to the next matter we must discuss."

"Well, Your Majesty, I am not one to make predictions, especially not in regard to my own somewhat mercurial countrymen. But I feel sure of this: ever since news came that Urban had been forcibly removed—rather, 'chased out'—of the Holy See, and was being actively pursued by Borja's own cardinal-killing Spaniards, every one of my senior officers has expressed their support for Urban. When they learn that Borja and his Spanish army tried to murder the pope and killed John O'Neill while he was trying to rescue an up-timer and his pregnant wife . . . Well, let's say my biggest concern will be to make sure that they don't start picking fights with our 'comrades' in your own Spanish *tercios*."

Fernando raised a finger. "You happen to have used an interesting turn of phrase, Colonel Preston. In fact, those Spanish *tercios* are *not* mine, they are my brother's. They are on Spanish payroll, direct from Madrid."

Preston heard Fernando's tone shift, heard it move from the full-voiced, natural cadences of a frank conversation into one laced with slower, quieter insinuations. *Careful, now, Thomas. When a well-manicured Spanish gentleman starts addressing his topics on the slant, you can be sure there's a snake in the grass somewhere nearby.* "Yes, Your Highness," Preston agreed carefully, "the Spanish are paid directly from Spanish coffers. Unlike us."

Fernando smiled. "Precisely. Unlike you." And then he looked down the table at Rubens.

Which told Thomas Preston that now he was going to hear the real dirt, the snaky facts of real politick that Fernando could not afford to utter with his own lips. That way, if later asked to admit or deny having mentioned those facts, he could offer a technically truthful denial. Kings: even the best of them had a bit of viper's blood running in their veins. Thomas supposed they'd be dead, if they didn't.

Ruben moved his considerable bulk closer to the broad, gleaming table at which they all sat. "Colonel Preston, given recent events, we are concerned that this year, when the time comes for our hired troops to renew their oaths to Spain, that there may be, er, resistance in your ranks, particularly."

Preston waved a dismissive hand. "Then let's skip the renewal of the oath. After all, it has no explicit term limit. The renewal is symbolic."

"Yes, and it is a most important symbol. So, in order to preserve that symbol and yet also preserve the genuine loyalty of the four *tercios* of Wild Geese that are the ever-stalwart backbone and defenders of this realm, we have come up with a reasonable expedient: to simply change the oath."

"Change the oath?"

"Yes."

"In what way?"

"This year, when you take the oath, it will omit the reference to Archduchess Isabella as being Philip's vassal. You will take your oath to her as you have for twenty years, but without mentioning King Philip of Spain." Rubens paused, his eyes sought Preston's directly. "I presume you see the political practicality of this adjustment?"

Oh, I see it, painter. I see everything you hope I'll see without your having to say it. On the surface, the change of oath was just to minimize any possibility of disaffection or departure arising from any mention of direct fealty to the increasingly unpopular King of Spain. But, there was an underlying subtlety which, Preston was quite sure, was the real intent of the change of oath. *We'll only be swearing fealty to Isabella. And, unless I'm much mistaken, to her nephew.*

Rubens' next words confirmed his suspicions. "However, as a precaution, we will not point out the fact—which could be easily misconstrued, of course—that, in agreeing to renew your oaths to Her Grace the Infanta, that your service is most likely to be commanded by her nephew, whom she has been pleased to confirm as the senior power in her lands. So, although you now also serve the king in the Low Countries, that additional, extrapolative detail will remain unadvertised. For the moment."

Yes, for the moment. But Preston had been a pawn

on the chessboard where kings played their games for many decades and could see where this political compass was pointing. With the oaths of the Wild Geese transferred directly to Fernando, their obedience and their fates were locked to him, not to Spain. Yes, technically Fernando was still a vassal of Spain, but how long that would continue was debatable. And so, when and if the Lowlands became fully and officially separate from the throne in Madrid, the Irish *tercios* would follow suit. And they would indeed comprise the loyal core of its army, since Philip's *tercios* in the Lowlands would most assuredly not follow the same path. But, problematically, they would still be in the same country. Preston flinched at the thought of his *tercio* squaring off against their former Spanish counterparts. That would be a bloody, internecine business indeed—

"Is this change in the oath acceptable to you and your men, Colonel Preston?" Rubens asked. His small eyes did not blink.

"I will have to put it to them. However, given recent events, I think it will not only be acceptable but preferable. However, they will ask a question I cannot answer: how will they be paid? Already, the *reales* from Spain are few and far between. If it wasn't for the deal Hugh O'Donnell struck with the Frenchman Turenne, earlier this year, I don't know what we would have done for food these past three months. But that supply is almost over—and truth be told, I was never comfortable with the arrangement."

"And why is that?" Maria Anna asked.

"Because, your Highness, until France and Madrid cooperated at the Battle of Dunkirk, the French had been the enemies of this realm, ever threatening the southern borders of the Brabant. I should know; I spent many months in garrison there, over the years. And then suddenly we are at peace—but it's a peace which is already fraying. So in taking bread from Turenne, we took bread from a past, and very possibly future, adversary of this court. I was not comfortable condoning it, but I was less comfortable seeing my men's families starve. So when O'Donnell arranged it by serving Turenne along with sixty of the men of his *tercio*, I had little choice but to accept it. And, I must speak frankly, it brought trouble along with it."

"Oh?" asked Rubens. "What kind of trouble?"

"French trouble, Your Grace. Their agents have been lurking around our camps, letting it be known that the king of France is hiring mercenaries, and can pay them in hard coin, not cabbages and watered beer."

Rubens looked at the ruling troika. They just kept watching Preston. None of them blinked, but Maria Anna might have suppressed a small smile.

Rubens rotated one thumb around the other. "And have any of your men left our service for theirs?"

"No, but I worry that they may. I've heard rumors— rumors from this court—that some nobles here speak ill of us Wild Geese, say that we should be grateful for the scraps we're given, and that some of us are already taking service with the French."

"Yes," said Ruben, twirling his moustache, "we have heard the same thing. Largely, because we spread those rumors ourselves."

Preston gaped. "You what?"

Maria Anna leaned forward; Preston tried to ignore

the way it compressed her bosom. "Colonel, the privations of your people have never been intentional, but in the last two months, we discovered that they lent credence to the belief in Paris that our grasp upon your continued loyalty was weak, and that certain members of the Wild Geese were indeed finding it necessary to seek employment elsewhere. To be more specific, to seek employment with the French themselves."

Preston felt heat rise in his face. "Your Highness, one of us did. The very best of us, some might say. Hugh Albert O'Donnell may have fed us, but he did it by agreeing to serve Turenne. Turenne! He's Richelieu's hand-picked military favorite. If the earl of Tyrconnell will take service with the French, then why shouldn't they think more of us will follow? And sixty of us did, the ones who went with O'Donnell."

"And whose service there fed you," Isabella observed from behind gnarled knuckles folded before her on the table.

"Yes, Your Grace, but at what cost? Where was Hugh when the pope was threatened? Where does he tarry, now that he is the last earl of Ireland, the last hope of his people? Where has he been since late in April?"

"Evidently working for his employer," Rubens observed smoothly.

"Yes, evidently. Abandoning us to work for the French. Which makes him, for all intents and purposes, a traitor!"

Isabella was on her feet in a single motion, cane brandished in one hand, the other pointing in quavering fury at Preston—or maybe at the word "traitor," which seemed to hover invisible in the air. "You call Hugh Albert O'Donnell a traitor?" she cried.

Preston stood his ground. "Your Grace, if he serves your traditional enemy, that makes him—"

With a swiftness that belied her age, her infirmity, her arthritis and the gray habit of her order, she dashed her cane down upon the table: the heavy oak rod splintered with a crash. "A *traitor*?!" she shrieked, livid. "How dare you say—how dare you *think*—such a thing!"

The room was not merely silent, but frozen, all eyes on the trembling, imperial, terrible old woman who had risen up like a wrathful god from an elder age to silence them all with her fury and undiminished, magnificent passion.

Preston swallowed, but did not avert his eyes. "Your Grace, I mean no disrespect, but how are Lord O'Donnell's actions *not* those of a traitor? Before Philip set Borja upon Rome, before the pope was threatened and John O'Neill was slain, he turned back all his honors and Spanish titles and went to work for France. For France, Your Grace. Your enemy, Spain's enemy—and now, his employer. How is that *not* traitorous?"

"Colonel Preston, do you truly not see any other way to interpret Lord O'Donnell's actions?" When Preston shook his head, Isabella continued. "Hugh was the only one of you Wild Geese except Lord O'Neill who was made a naturalized Spanish citizen by the Crown, who became a knight, and a fellow of the court at Madrid. But then, when he saw that the same Crown never intended to make good its promises and debts to you and your countrymen, I understand that he came to your camp incognito, and explained his dilemma. Specifically, what response could he make if Philip had asked him, as an intimate of the court and loyal gentleman of Spain, to function as Madrid's special factotum and commander here? Which, given the current situation, could mean leading either his, or Spanish, *tercios* against those loyal to me, if Philip's displeasure with the Lowlands were to become so great. Was Lord O'Donnell to obey orders to attack me, or to attack you and his fellow countrymen, if that is how the loyalties of such a moment played out?"

Preston felt as though the chair he was seated in had been turned upside down. Or the world had. Or both.

"Think it through, Colonel. Lord O'Donnell had to step down from his post. And in doing so, it was incumbent upon him to return the beneficences he had received, and remove himself from Spanish territory. But not before he visited his men and yours, and enjoined you to think carefully to whom your allegiance would lie if faced with the eventualities that now seem to be hastening upon us. Philip is already attempting to compromise our non-Spanish *tercios*."

"Your Grace, all this I see plainly. But—France? Why not some other power? Why our old foe?"

Isabella reseated herself slowly. It was an almost leonine action, despite her age. "Because, it is through our old foe that he will orchestrate a solution to both your problem and our problem: money. Enough money for the Lowlands to survive without recourse to Madrid's coffers. Enough money for your families to eat, and your men to have ample coin in their pockets."

Preston knew the room wasn't spinning, but at the moment, it felt as though it was. "And how will

Hugh's service to France make possible this solution? And why has he not communicated this to us, as well as to you? My Grace, I mean no offense, but we are his countrymen: why has he not reassured us with the particulars of his plan?"

Isabella closed her eyes. "Because it is not *his* plan. It is ours. And I,"—she opened eyes suddenly bright and liquid, but from which she refused to let tears run down—"and I could not tell him of it."

"But why? If he doesn't know how serving the French will more profoundly serve us, then by what inducement has he left us to—?"

Maria Anna silenced him with a small, sly smile. "My good Colonel Preston, I counsel you not to let these unexplained—and apparently inexplicable—events perturb you. You will note they do not perturb us. Indeed, our plans are well set. But it is often necessary that a cog spinning in one part of a complex machine has no knowledge of how its peers are turning elsewhere in the same device."

Preston frowned at her words, heard two of Isabella's sentences once again in his head: *It is not his plan, it is ours. And I dare not tell him of it.* Implying that the truly ignorant cog in Maria Anna's machination was not Preston, but O'Donnell himself.

And he felt the oblique implication strike him so hard and so suddenly that the room seemed to tilt momentarily. Had O'Donnell's apparent defection been *planned*? Had he been maneuvered into it so that he was then a properly situated, yet unknowing, piece of some larger stratagem?

He looked quickly at Isabella, who was looking intently at him. He did not see canniness; he saw—

Love. Maternal love. Intense, irrational, desperate. But why would she do such a thing to O'Donnell, unless it was—?

To save him. Of course. Now it made sense. And suddenly Preston saw how, since the arrival of the up-timers and their library's revelation of the duplicity of the Spanish in regard to their Irish servitors, the grand dame of European statecraft had realized that in order for her cherished god-child to survive—and thrive—she would have to shift the game board so that he could weather the change in fortunes.

Yes, there was no doubt about it. It was clear enough that, in the days before the up-timers, she had, every step of the way, protected him, groomed him, got him a knighthood. Of course, then Father Florence Conry had almost ruined it all with his hare-brained proposal to invade Ireland. But whereas the priest had envisioned a force jointly led by the Earls O'Donnell and O'Neill and the predictable co-dominium that would arise in its wake, Madrid had embraced a different solution. Philip was no fool, and he had the benefit of the count-duke of Olivares' advice, to boot. So Philip had summoned young O'Donnell, knighted him in an order more prestigious than O'Neill's (which had been Isabella's intent), but then chose him to lead the Irish expedition alone. It was a politically prudent choice, one which Isabella had not expected, probably due to O'Donnell's youth and his clan's less storied name. But the Spanish king and his counselor had seen the qualities, and restraint, in the younger man that would make him both a more capable general of armies and a more capable revolutionary orator than his mercurial peer, O'Neill.

But, since the invasion never came off (largely derailed by Isabella herself, as Preston recalled), the only lasting effect of all this maneuvering was that it ensured that the already difficult relationship between O'Donnell and O'Neill became as bad and bitter as it could be. It hadn't helped that, in addition to simply choosing the younger over the older, Philip and Olivares had made their assessment of Hugh's superior qualities well known at court, and thereby, throughout Europe.

So Isabella had saved her godson from the disastrous invasion, just as she had taken pains to ensure that he was college-educated, naturalized, knighted, and furnished with a tremendously advantageous marriage. All done to both ensure his success, and ensure his survival. A target of English assassins since birth, the higher Hugh O'Donnell's station became, the more pause it gave to those who sent murderers across the Channel: were they plotting the death of a renegade member of the Irish royalty, or an immigrated Spanish gentleman? The former was an affair of no account, but the latter could easily become an international incident, and was therefore best avoided.

And having thus protected and provided for her charge, Isabella of the up-time history had died in 1633, presumably satisfied that she had seen him safely married with a title and land. But within the year, those plans had come undone, here as there. His wife having died without producing surviving issue, he lost more than his love; he lost the land and titles that had been her dowry. In that world, with his godmother dead, he had had little choice but to do what he might as the colonel of his own *tercio*. That he had recruited and commanded well there no less than here, that much was clear. But there, Fernando had evidently inherited Philip's utilitarian attitudes toward the Irish, and had spent them like water. Which was sadly prudent, Preston had to admit. After all, as the opportunity to reclaim Ireland became an ever-thinner tissue of lies, the Spanish masters of the Wild Geese feared that they would be increasingly susceptible to subornation by other, rival powers. And so the last of them were sent to Spain, and then to their destruction in putting down the Catalan revolt that began in 1640.

But what about in this altered world, where Hugh had no future with Spain and none in the Lowlands either, unless it officially broke with Madrid? What place for O'Donnell? Indeed, Preston realized with a sudden chill up his back, what place for the Wild Geese, for Ireland? And evidently, the old girl Isabella had hatched a scheme to correct some, maybe all, of these problems. But it was a scheme so deep, and probably so devious, that it had to be kept from one of its primary executors: Hugh Albert O'Donnell.

Isabella had obviously seen the understanding in Preston's eyes. "So you see, now."

The Irish colonel swallowed, nodded. "I believe I do, Your Grace. Just one question. Is there something my people, my Wild Geese, can do to help?"

"You already have."

Preston started. "I have?"

"Specifically, four hundred of the men of Lord O'Donnell's *tercio* have. They were not sent to garrison in Antwerp as you, and they, were originally told. They were sent there to board ships and have now joined a task force in order to fulfill their part in our plan."

Preston was too stunned to feel stunned. "And if they succeed?"

Fernando leaned forward. "If they succeed, our futures are secure. Both yours and ours. For many, many years to come."

"And if they fail?"

Isabella sat erect. "Colonel Preston, I am surprised at that question. Tell me, as the most senior officer of my Irish Wild Geese, how often have they ever failed me?"

"Only a very few times, Your Grace. But their determination in your service has a dark price, too."

"Which is?"

"That, rather than retreat, they die trying."

Isabella sat back heavily, looking every year of her age. She responded to Preston—"I know, Colonel, I know"—but her eyes were far away and seamed with worry.

Part Three

July 1635

What raging of the sea

Chapter 14

"Commander Cantrell, propellers are all-stop. Awaiting orders."

Eddie Cantrell looked to his left. The ship's nominal captain, Ove Gjedde, nodded faintly. It was his customary sign that his executive officer, Commander Cantrell, was free to give his orders autonomously. Eddie returned the nod, then aimed his voice back over his shoulder. "Secure propellers and prepare to lower the vent cover."

"Securing propellers, aye. Ready to lower prop vent cover, aye."

"And Mr. Svantner, send the word to cut steam. Let's save that coal."

"Aye, aye, sir. Cutting steam. Let free the reef bands, sir?"

Eddie looked at Gjedde again, who, by unspoken arrangement, reserved rigging and sail orders for himself. The sails had been reefed for the engine trials and with the engine no longer propelling the ship, it would soon begin to drift off course.

The weather-bitten Norwegian nodded once. Svantner saluted and went off briskly, shouting orders that were soon drowned out by the thundering rustle of the sails being freed and unfurled into the stiff wind blowing near the remote island of St. Kilda.

Well, technically speaking, they were just off the sheer and rocky north coast of the island of Hirta, largest and most populous islet of the St. Kilda archipelago. If you could call any landmass with fewer than two hundred people "populous." But even that small settlement was pretty impressive, given how far off St. Kilda was from—well, from everything. Over fifty miles from the northwesternmost island of the already-desolate Outer Hebrides, and almost 175 miles north of Ireland, Hirta and the rest of the islands of the group were, for all intents and purposes, as isolated as if they had been on the surface of another planet. And, since it was rumored that most of the inhabitants were still as influenced by druidic beliefs as by Christianity, it was not an exaggeration to say that, even though the natives of St. Kilda *did* dwell on the same planet, they certainly did inhabit a different world.

"Commander Cantrell, there you are! I'm sorry I'm late. I was detained below decks. Paying my respects to your lovely wife and her ladies."

Eddie swiveled around on his false heel. Time at sea had taught him, even with his excellent prosthetic leg, not to lose contact with the deck. "And you are"—he tried to recall the face of the man, couldn't, guessed from context—"Lieutenant Bjelke, I presume?"

The man approaching—tall, lithe, with a long nose and long hair that was several shades redder than Eddie's own—offered a military bow, and tottered a bit as the ship rolled through a higher swell. "That is correct, sir. I tried to present myself to you immediately upon coming aboard, but I found myself embarrassingly, er, indisposed."

Eddie smiled, noticed that Bjelke's pallor was not just the result of pale Nordic skin, but a manful, ongoing struggle against sea-sickness. "Is that why you did not attempt transfer to this ship until today, Mr. Bjelke? Waiting for good weather?"

Bjelke, although only twenty, returned the smile with a courtier's polish. Which was only logical: his father, Jens, had been the Norwegian chancellor for more than twenty years and was certainly one of the nation's wealthiest nobles. If one measured his stature in terms of influence rather than silver, he was arguably its most powerful lord, having been given the Hanseatic city of Bergen as his personal fief just last year. Henrik Bjelke had, therefore, grown up surrounded by wealth, influence, and ministers of etiquette.

Fortunately, his father was also a fair and industrious man, having studied widely abroad and now compiling the first dictionary of the Norwegian language. And Henrik, his second son, had apparently inherited his sire's talents and tastes for scholarship. Originally bound for the university in Padova, the arrival of Grantville had caught both Henrik's interest and imagination. Like many other adventurous sons (and no small number of daughters) of European noble houses, he had gone there to read in the up-time library, augmenting that education with classes and seminars at the nearby University of Jena. It was perhaps predictable that he was assigned as Eddie's adjutant and staff officer, as much because of Christian's keen interest in the young Norwegian as Bjelke's own unfulfilled desires to pursue a military career. He had ultimately done so quite successfully in the up-time world of Eddie's birth, rising to become the head of the Danish Admiralty.

However, Bjelke's familiarity with things nautical had been a later-life acquisition. For the moment, it was clearly a mighty struggle for him just to maintain the at-sea posture that was the down-time equivalent of "at ease" in the presence of a superior officer with whom one had familiarity (and with whom the difference in rank was not too profound). Eddie discovered he was inordinately cheered by Rik's unsteadiness. *At last! someone with even* less *shipboard experience than me!* He gestured to the rail.

Bjelke gratefully accompanied the young up-timer to the rail, but stared at it for a moment before putting his hand upon it. The "rail" was actually comprised of two distinct parts, one of iron, one of wood. The iron part consisted of two chains that ran where the bulkhead should be, each given greater rigidity by passing tautly through separate eyelets in vertical iron stanchions. Those stanchion were form-cut to fit neatly into brass-cupped holes along the bulwark line, and thus could be removed at will.

However, mounted atop those stanchions, and stabilizing themselves by a single descending picket that snugged into a low wooden brace affixed to the deck, was a light wooden rail. Each section of the rail was affixed to its fore and aft neighbors by a sleeve that surrounded a tongue-in-groove mating of the two separate pieces, held tight by a brass pin that passed through them both at that juncture. Henrik tentatively leaned his weight upon it. It was quite firm. "Ingenious," he murmured admiring the modular wooden rail sections and ignoring the chain-and-stanchion railing. "Your work, Commander?"

Eddie shrugged. "I had a hand in it."

Bjelke smiled slowly. "Modesty is rare in young commanders, my elders tell me, but is a most promising sign. I am fortunate to have you as a mentor, Commander Cantrell."

Eddie kept from raising an eyebrow. Well, Henrik Bjelke had certainly revealed more than a little about himself, and his role vis-a-vis Eddie, in those "innocent" comments. First, the young Norwegian obviously knew the ship upon which this vessel had been heavily based—the USS *Hartford* of the American Civil War—since he was not surprised by the presence of what would otherwise have been the wholly novel chain-and-stanchion railing arrangement, which reduced dangers from gunwale splinters and, in the case of close targets, could be quickly removed to extend the lower range of the deck guns' maximum arc of elevation. However, Bjelke had pointedly *not* been expecting the modular wooden rail inserts that Eddie had designed for greater deck safety when operating on the high seas. That bespoke a surprisingly detailed knowledge of the ship's design origins, even for a clever young man who'd spent more than a year in the library at Grantville.

Secondly, Bjelke confidently identified the innovation as Eddie's, which suggested that he'd been well-briefed about the technological gifts of the young American. Which went along with the implication that his elders considered Cantrell a most promising officer.

And that likely explained the third interesting bit of information: that Henrik Bjelke had not been encouraged to look at this assignment as merely a military posting, but as an apprenticeship of sorts.

And all those nuances, having a common emphasis on familiarization with up-timers and their knowledge, seemed to point in one direction: straight at His Royal Danish Majesty Christian IV.

Eddie had to hand it to his half-souse, half-genius regal father-in-law: USE emperor and Swedish sovereign Gustav Adolf might be running around physically conquering various tracts of Central Europe, but Christian had launched his own, highly successful campaign of collecting and captivating the hearts and minds of persons who were poised to become high-powered movers and shakers of the rising generation. His son Ulrik was betrothed to Gustav's young daughter. His daughter Anne Cathrine was married to the most high-profile war-hero-technowizard from now-legendary Grantville. And now, he had added sharp-witted Henrik Bjelke to the mix.

And that addition brought distinct value-added synergies to many of King Christian's prior social machinations. Bjelke's appointment no doubt bought the gratitude of various influential Norwegians, who had, so far, been the "forgotten poor cousin" of the reconstituted Union of Kalmar between Sweden and Denmark. Bjelke's appointment also provided Eddie with a gifted aide who was unusually familiar with up-time manners and technology, and who no doubt understood that this mentorship was an extraordinary opportunity to put himself on a political and military fast track.

Of course, thus indebted to Christian, it was also

to be expected that Henrik Bjelke, willing or not, would also serve as the Danish king's—well, not *spy*, exactly, but certainly his dedicated observer. And last, the bold Bjelke might just be valiant enough to help save Eddie's life at some point during the coming mission, thereby ensuring that Christian's daughter did not become a widow and that the familial connection to the up-timers remained intact. Alternatively, Bjelke, learning up-time ways and now having first-hand access to up-time technology, might also make a reasonable replacement husband for a widowed Anne Cathrine. Yup, the old Danish souse-genius had sure gamed out all the angles on this appointment.

About which Eddie reasoned he had best learn everything he could. "So what do they call you at home, Lieutenant Bjelke?"

"At—at home, Commander?"

"Yes. You know, the place you live." Although, Eddie realized a moment later, that the son of Jens Bjelke wouldn't have just one home. More like one home for every month of the year . . .

But that didn't impede the young Norwegian's understanding of Eddie's intent. "Ah, my familiar name! I'm Rik, sir. An amputated version of my proper name, so that I might not be confused with all the other Henriks in our family and social circles. Not very dignified, I'm afraid."

Eddie smiled. "Well, I'm not very dignified myself, so that suits me just fine, Rik. You got attached to the flotilla pretty much at the last second, I seem to recall."

Bjelke's gaze wavered. "Yes, sir. There were impediments to overcome."

"Impediments? Political?"

"Familial, I'm afraid. My father does not share in my enthusiasm for a military career."

Hm. Given the scanty biographical sources from up-time, that might actually be the truth, rather than a clever way of explaining away what might have been a maneuver by Christian IV to get Bjelke added to the flotilla without Simpson or Eddie having enough time to conduct research on his possible ties to the Danish court. What Christian had either not planned upon, or simply couldn't outflank, was the possibility that Simpson and Eddie had compiled dossiers on all possibly mission-relevant personnel without waiting for assignment rosters.

Which they had done. It had been time-consuming, but worth it. Although Eddie lacked any detailed information on many of the flotilla's senior officers and leaders, he had a thumbnail sketch for most of them. In fact, Ove Gjedde was the only notable exception.

Eddie nodded understanding at Bjelke's professed plight. "But your father finally listened to your appeals?"

Rik blushed profoundly, and Eddie could have hugged him: *and he blushes faster and redder than I do, too! Damn, even if he is a spy, it's almost worthwhile having him around so that another officer looks and acts even more like the boy next door than I do!* But Eddie kept his expression somber as Bjelke explained. "My father remained deaf to my appeals for military experience—but not to King Christian's."

Eddie was surprised and reassured by the frankness of that admission. He doubted Christian would have been happy with Bjelke drawing such a straight line between his own presence and the Danish king's desires. And while it was possible that this was disinformation meant to impart an aura of trustworthiness to Rik, a look at the younger man's face and genuine blush-response told Eddie otherwise. Bjelke was simply a polished, well-educated young man who was likely to prove courageous and capable in the years to come, but right now, was a youngling out on his first great adventure. If there was any duplicity in him at all, it would be minor, and contrary to his nature. Eddie could live with that. Easily.

"Well, Rik, however you got here, you're here. So, welcome aboard the *Intrepid*. First order of business is to make you at home."

"Thank you, sir. My man Nils has seen to my berthing and I must say it is a welcome change from the *Serendipity*. Those accommodations were most... uncomfortable."

"Well, I'm glad you like your stateroom"—*more like a long closet*, reflected Eddie—"but when I suggested we make you at home, I meant familiarization with the ship. Do you have any questions about the *Intrepid* that your briefers didn't answer for you?"

Rik brightened immediately; if he'd been a puppy, his ears would probably have snapped straight up. "A great many questions, Commander. Although not for want of my asking. Frankly, my briefers, as you call them, knew fewer particulars about your new ships than I did. I had studied the classes of American vessels that were the foundations of your designs, which they had not. And they could answer only a few questions about how they differed, other than the guns and the steam plants. Seeing them, it is clear that you have made other significant modifications."

Eddie nodded. "Yep, we had to. This class—the Quality I class—needs to be an even more stable firing platform than the original *Hartford* was."

"Because of the increased range and capability of her eight-inch pivot guns?"

Eddie shrugged. "That's a large part of it. But it gets more complicated. First, the *Hartford* had its broad side armament on the weather deck. We put ours below."

"Better performance in bad weather?"

"Well, that too, but it was actually the result of some complex design trade-offs. First, we wanted maximum clear traverse for the pivot guns. So that meant 'clearing the gun deck,' as much as we could. There was already a lot that *had* to go on up there. We needed our antipersonnel weapons on the weather deck so they could bear freely upon all quarters. And although we have a steam engine, that's for tactical use only. Strategically speaking, we're just a very fast sailed ship. Meaning we've got a full complement of rigging and sail-handlers on the weather deck as well. So, the only way we could clear the deck was to put the guns underneath.

"What we got out of that was a more commanding elevation for our naval rifles. But it also allowed us to bring a lot of the weight that was high up in the *Hartford* down in our design, thereby lowering the center of gravity."

"So, putting the broadside weapons on a lower deck also made the ship more stable."

"Exactly. But then, we didn't want to put our crew down in the bowels of the ship. So we had to put the crew quarters inboard on the gun deck. The only reason we were even able to consider doing that was because our broadside weapons are carronades. They're a lot shorter than cannons, and their carriages are wheeled so as to run back up inclined planes when they recoil."

"But that still wasn't enough, was it, sir?" Rik looked over the side at the noticeable slope that ran out from the rail down into the water. "So to get the rest of the room you needed for inboard crew berthing, you pushed your battery farther outboard by widening the beam of the gun deck."

Eddie nodded his approval. "Bravo Zulu, Mr. Bjelke."

"'Bravo Zulu?'"

Eddie smiled. "An up-time naval term. 'Well done.' Learned it from my mentor."

"Ah. That would be Admiral Simpson."

"The same. And so, yes, we widened the gun deck, which meant another change from the original *Hartford*. She had pretty much sheer sides, which is just what you'd want for a fast sloop. But when we designed the Quality I class, we realized that not only would adding that outward slope of the sides—or 'tumble home'—be a good thing to add in terms of deck width, but for stability in higher seas, thanks to how increased beam reduces roll."

Bjelke leaned out over the rail. His eyes followed the waterline from stem to stern. "Yes, these are the structural differences I saw, and at which I wondered. Thank you for explaining them, Commander." He pointed at the somewhat smaller steamship pulling past them at a distance of four hundred yards, her funnel smokeless, her sails wide and white in the wind. "I see the same design changes in the smaller ship—the Speed I class, I think?—but less pronounced."

Eddie nodded. "Yeah, we decided to keep her closer to the original lines of the sloop. So we put only one pivot gun on her, kept the tumble home shallower, and freeboard lower and the weather deck closer to the waterline. She sails sharper, faster, more responsively, and has three feet less draught."

"So better for sailing in shallows, up rivers, near reefs."

"Yes, and strategically speaking, our fastest ship. In a good breeze, she'll make eight knots, and she's rigged for a generous broad reach. Unless she's fully becalmed, she can make reasonable forward progress with wind from almost three-quarters of the compass, assuming she has the room to tack sharply."

"And yet you do not label her a steam-sloop, as was the ship that inspired her."

"You mean the *Kearsarge* from the Civil War?" Eddie shrugged. "Well, as I understand the Civil War nomenclature, if a ship had a fully covered gun deck, she wasn't a sloop. Even if she had a sloop's lines, she'd still be called frigate-built. Although frigate-built doesn't necessary imply a military ship."

Rik smiled ruefully. "I grew up on farms. Even though many of them were close to the water, I confess I do not have a mariner's vocabulary yet. I find these distinctions confusing. Because, if the reports I hear are true, you are not calling the other ship—the *Courser*, I believe?—a frigate, either."

"No, we're calling her class a 'destroyer' and the *Intrepid*'s class a 'cruiser.' As class names, they're not great solutions. But at least they're up-time terms that haven't been used to describe ships, yet, so they'll be distinctive and somewhat descriptive in terms of role.

If you're familiar with the up-time history of those classes of ships, that is. But anything else we tried to come up with ran afoul of the labeling confusion that already results from the current lack of international naming conventions.

"In fact, 'frigate' would have been the most confusing label we could have settled on. Ever since down-time naval architects started doing research in the Grantville library, most of the shipyards of Europe have started building new designs, the straight-sterned frigate chief among them. So if we called our new steam-ships frigates, they'd routinely get confused with the new sailed vessels currently under construction throughout Europe."

Bjelke nodded attentively, but Eddie saw that his focus was now split between their conversation and something located aft of their current place at the rail. As soon as Eddie noticed Rik's apparent distraction, the young Norwegian moved his eyes, ever so slightly, upward over his superior's shoulder and toward the new item of interest.

Eddie turned and saw, back by the entrance to the companionway leading down to the officer's quarters, that his wife—and her "ladies," as Bjelke styled them—had emerged to stand on the deck in a tight cluster. They were not an uncommon sight topside, but they usually reserved their appearances for fine weather, not overcast skies. However, despite the mild wind freshening from out of the southeast, they were all dressed for cold weather, apparently. Or were they? Eddie squinted, saw no coats or shawls, which made him only more confused. *So why the hell do they have kerchiefs covering their heads? And all three of them, no less. Damn, I've never seen a lady of the*

*aristocracy allow herself to look that, well, dowdy.
And now they've all adopted the same frumpy look?
What the heck is that abou—?*

"Commander, given the arrival of the ladies, perhaps it would be convenient for you if I were to take
my leave?"

Eddie nodded. "Probably so. Tell my wife that she
can"—and then a voice inside his head, the one that
was partially schooled in the etiquette of this age,
muttered, *No, Eddie, that won't do. Think how it
will look, how it will seem.*

Damn, ship protocol was tricky, and yet was still
kind of free-form in this era when navies weren't really
navies just yet, and had protocols for some things, but
not for others. For instance, take the simple desire to
have his wife join him alone at the rail. He couldn't
very well wave her over. That would be an obvious
blow to her stature, and mark him as an indecorous
boor, which would work against his accrual of respect
as well. But if he sent Bjelke over to summon her, that
would be like making the young Norwegian nobleman
his valet and also be entirely too formal, to say nothing of downright stupid-looking. Yet, if Eddie left the
rail to go over to Anne Cathrine, then it could be
difficult to extricate themselves from the presence of
their respective attendants—Bjelke and the ladies—if
they didn't *all* know how to take a hint—

Eddie discovered that, for the first time since he had
stepped on a deep water ship, he had a headache and
an incipient sense of seasickness. Which he allowed,
probably had nothing to do with the sea at all.

But Bjelke offered a slight bow to Eddie, and
inquired, "Might I—with your compliments—inform

the ladies and your wife that you are currently without any pressing duties? And that I would be happy to escort any and all of them wherever they might wish to go?"

And for the third time—*wasn't that some kind of spiritual sign, or something?*—Eddie felt a quick outrush of gratitude toward the young Norwegian. Bjelke's simple solution allowed the junior officer to decorously depart from his commander, greet the ladies, and inform them of the status of the ship's captain. Then Anne Cathrine could approach or not—with Bjelke and her ladies in tow or not—and this idiotic etiquette dance would be over and Eddie would have thus achieved the hardest nautical task of his day thus far: finding a way to converse with his wife, on deck and in private, for a scant few minutes.

Eddie nodded gratefully—hopefully not desperately—at Bjelke, who smiled and with a more pronounced bow, left to carry out his plan.

Which worked like a charm. He arrived at the ladies' group and presented himself. Cordial nods all around, a brief exchange, then he walked with Anne Cathrine halfway across the deck, and by some miracle of subtle body language, managed to successfully communicate to Eddie that he should meet them about halfway. Which done, effected a serene and stately rendezvous between man and wife as the crew watched through carefully averted eyes.

Bjelke nodded to both spouses and retraced his steps to the two remaining ladies. Eddie smiled at Anne Cathrine and as they walked back to the rail, the young American breathed a sign of relief. Another terrifying gauntlet had been run.

Chapter 15

St. Kilda archipelago, North Atlantic

Once they arrived at the rail, Anne Cathrine looked up at Eddie, face serious, but her eyes seemed to twinkle. "Hi," she said, not bothering to suppress the dimple that this use of Amideutsch quirked into being.

Commander Eddie Cantrell felt the protocol-induced queasiness in his stomach become a midair dance of happy butterflies. "Hi," he said. Or maybe he gushed: he wasn't really sure. He was never exactly sure of what came out of his mouth when he was around the singularly beautiful and stammer-worthy sex goddess that was his almost-seventeen-year-old wife.

But instead of indulging in any more of the small signs of endearment that they had evolved over the past year to communicate in a playful (or, better yet, racy!) secret banter when in somber and dignified social settings, Anne Cathrine bit her lower lip slightly. She looked out to sea, tugging fitfully at her head scarf. *What the hell is it with the head coverings, anyhow? It's nice weather, not really too windy, and—*

Anne Cathrine looked up at him again, smiling

through a slight frown. "So, how did your find your first conversation with Henrik Bjelke?"

Eddie almost started at her tone: measured, serious, possibly concerned. "Um . . . fine."

"I am glad, Eddie. Very glad."

"You sound as if you were worried."

"About Bjelke? No, not particularly. I very much doubt you have to worry about him. He is still an outsider at the Danish court, and too young to threaten you. Much."

"'Much?'" Eddie echoed. He hoped it hadn't come out as a surprised squeak.

Anne Cathrine turned very serious now, her very blue eyes upon him. "Dear Eddie, although this is a USE mission, conceived by the leaders of Grantville and given royal imprimatur by Gustav of Sweden, the majority of your commanders are Danish." She smiled. "Or hadn't you noticed?"

He grinned back. "Nope. Completely slipped past me. Past Admiral Simpson, too."

She lifted an eyebrow, curled a lip in a slow smile that Eddie associated with other places, other exchanges— *down, Eddie! down, boy!* Then she was looking out to sea, again. "Joking aside, Eddie, there are ambitious men in this flotilla, men whose personal interests may not be well-served if you are *too* successful."

"Me—successful? Wait a minute, it's not like I'm in charge of the flotilla. Heck, I'm something like the third rung down on the command ladder. Maybe less. It's hard to know how rank would play against nobility in this kind of situation. So it's not as if the success or failure of this mission is *mine*."

"Now it is you who must 'wait a minute,' Eddie.

You may not have the highest rank, but everyone in every ship—and back home—knows this mission to the New World was your idea. Yours. Admiral Simpson was intent on going to the New World, yes. Such plans were already afoot, yes. But it was you put forward the idea of making it a reconnaissance and a ruse all bound into one mission. If this stratagem works, you will receive credit as its architect. At the very least."

Eddie scratched the back of his head, remembered that gesture probably didn't radiate a dignified command presence, and snatched his hand back down to his side. "Yeah. Well. Okay. So who are all these Danish guys with hidden agendas?"

"First, my love, they might *not* have hidden agendas. That is the problem with hidden agendas: that they might or might not be there at all. Wouldn't you agree?"

"Well, sure."

"Excellent. So now, who first? Well, the commander of the task force, for one."

"Admiral Mund? He seems, um, barely communicative."

"And so he is, but that does not mean he is without ambition. He is a minor noble, although he does not flaunt his title. Which is probably just as well."

"Why?"

"Because he was granted a tract on Iceland." Anne Cathrine shivered. "It is not a very nice place to be a landholding noble."

"You mean, sort of like the Faroes?"

"Hush, Eddie! You must know that Father did not give you that land for any reason other than to furnish you with the highest title he might within the nobility of Denmark. And, I suspect, as an entrée to greater things."

"So I've suspected, also." He crossed his fingers, offered silent thanks to John Chandler Simpson.

She looked at him. "Then you are indeed learning the ways of these times, Eddie. Which is necessary, I am afraid. Now, the person you must be most careful of is Hannibal Sehested."

"You mean the guy who displaced the captain from his cabin on the *Patentia*? I met him at court, just this spring. Seems like a nice enough guy. Shrewd, though."

"He always has been a nice enough fellow in his behavior toward me, too, Eddie. But he is also, as you observe, shrewd, and history showed that he was shrewd enough to advance his fortunes in your up-time history's Danish government. Even though he made himself an enemy of the man who was to become its most influential member, Corfitz Ulfeldt."

"The guy who was a traitor, up-time?"

"Yes, the man who was to betray my father. And who would have married my sister Leonora in just over a year." Again, she looked over her shoulder at the shorter of her two "ladies," but this time the glance was both protective and melancholy. "Corfitz was already betrothed to her, you know. Had been since 1630."

"But . . . but she was only nine years old!"

Anne Cathrine nodded gravely. "Eight, actually. And here you see the fate of the daughters of kings who are not also full princesses. We are objects of exchange, no less than we are objects of Father's genuine love. He arranges marriages that ensure the nation of secure bonds between the king and his nobles, since familial ties to the throne are craved above all things by men of that class. And if, thanks to those ties between crown and *Riksradet*, we all live in a time of domestic harmony, prosperity, and peace, then would we king's daughters not be ungrateful if we failed to consider ourselves 'happy'?"

Eddie mulled that over. "That's what I call taking one for the team. And doing so for the rest of your life."

"If by that you mean it is a sacrifice, well—I think so, too. Although many thought me ungrateful for feeling that way."

"Well, they can go straight to—okay, I know that look: I'll calm down." *Hmmm: calming down—that reminds me.* Eddie turned so his back was to Ove Gjedde. "So, while we're dragging out the dirt on the Danish upper crust, tell me: what do you know about Captain Gjedde? He's the one guy that the admiral and I couldn't find anything useful about. Seems he led the expedition to set up your trade with India, but after that, not much."

Anne Cathrine frowned. "I am sad to say that I do not know much more of him than that. I do know that Father respects him, but—well, Captain Gjedde is not an exciting man. As you have remarked to me several times on our journey thus far. And he is still recovering from wounds he suffered in the Baltic War. From fighting against your Admiral Simpson's timberclads, if I recall correctly."

Oh. Well. He must really be a big fan of up-timers, then. Particularly the ones who had a direct hand in blasting his ship to matchsticks...

Evidently, Anne Cathrine could read the expression

on his face or was displaying an increasing talent for honest-to-God telepathy. "No, I do not think his reticence is caused by your being an American. He is more mature than that, and has seen his share of war. Like many older military men, he does not confuse the actions of following a king's order with the will of the men who must carry it out."

"Yeah, he looks old enough to have achieved that kind of perspective. What is he? Sixty, sixty-five years old?"

Anne Cathrine looked somber. "Forty-one."

"What?"

"He was always a somber, old-looking man, but his wounds from the Baltic—they drained him. He has not been at court since he suffered them, last year. But then again, he was never much at court. He doesn't enjoy it. And while Father respects his abilities, Captain Gjedde is not the kind of man that he takes a personal interest in. The captain excels at navigation and can predict the weather like a wizard from the old sagas. But he does it all quietly, calmly. Not the type of man to capture Father's often mercurial imagination."

"Not like young Lord Bjelke."

"No, indeed. And of course, Father's interest in Bjelke is also self-protective."

"How do you mean?"

"I mean that Henrik Bjelke was, historically, not always a supporter of my father or his policies. He could yet prove quite dangerous, I suppose."

"Really? Jeez, Rik seems like a pretty good guy, actually."

"Yes, Father thinks that as well. He just wants to

make sure that history does not repeat itself. And so he has involved Lord Bjelke in his plans for the New World." She looked over her shapely, and surprisingly broad, shoulder to where Henrik was escorting the ladies on what promised to be a quick looping promenade to the taffrail and back to the companionway. "In fact, I think Father put him aboard for a very special purpose."

"You mean, to watch me."

Anne Cathrine's eyes went back up to Eddie's and he felt wonder, appreciation, and perhaps the tiniest bit of sadness in them. "Ah, you are becoming adept at our down-timer machinations, Eddie—or at least, at perceiving them. Which, as I said, is a positive thing. But still, even so, I hope you will always be—I mean, I hope it won't make you—"

"Jaded? Subtle? Snakelike in my new and sinister cunning?"

Anne Cathrine tried to keep a straight face but couldn't. She laughed softly and swayed against his arm for the briefest of contacts. "You—how do you say it?—you 'keep it real,' Eddie. For which I am grateful. And which is one of the many reasons I love you so. But let us be serious for one moment more. Young Lord Bjelke's history and eventual friendship with Corfitz Ulfeldt, in your world, caught my father's attention. So I believe he wants Henrik indebted to him, and yes, hopes to gain a loyal observer in the fleet, as well. But I think Papa has another purpose, as well."

"Which is?"

"Marriage."

"Marriage? Of Bjelke? To whom?"

Anne Cathrine looked over her shoulder again. "To Sophie Rantzau. Or maybe my sister." She frowned as she watched the two ladies in question finish their circuit of the stern. "I cannot tell."

"Huh," Eddie observed eloquently. "Huh. A military mission to the New World as a means of kindling a strategically shrewd shipboard romance? Your dad sure sees some odd opportunities in some odd places. Why not just play matchmaker at court, where he can meddle with the young lovers personally? Which, let's be honest, is one of his favorite pastimes."

Anne Cathrine smiled and swatted him lightly. "For which you should be very grateful, husband. Otherwise, where would we be today, had he not played the part of Cupid?"

"Where would we be? Well, let's see. I'd still be rotting in the dungeon with a crappy peg leg on my stump, and you'd be married to Lord Dinesen, or some other wealthy noble."

"Yes, who would no doubt be three times my weight and four times my age. So, I'm not sure which of our two fates would be more grim."

"Yeah, well, when you put it that way—"

"Trust me, dear husband, that would literally have been my fate. The marriage you helped me avoid when you were my father's prisoner wasn't simply a staged engagement. My wedding to Dinesen was a very real possibility."

"No. Your father would never have made you marry that—"

"Eddie, you keep mistaking what loving parents of your time consider wise actions, and what loving parents of my time consider wise actions. I am a king's daughter, and so almost a princess in stature within my own country. But much less so elsewhere, because in marrying me, a foreign throne will not have gained any formal influence—or potential of inheritance—in the lands of my family.

"And so I was not to be married off to a crown prince of one of the other courts of Europe, but wedded to a Danish nobleman. And who among those men had enough wealth and influence to be a *de facto* dowry for my hand?" Her face hardened. "Old, ambitious men, most of whom spent their whole lives counting their money, counting their estates, counting the ways in which they might move one step higher in the nasty little games of social climbing that are their favorite sport." Eddie thought she was going to spit over the side in disgust.

But instead she rounded on him, her eyes bright and unwavering. "So you see, my darling Eddie, it is you who saved me, not the other way around." Her eyes searched his and he could almost feel heat coming out of them, and off of her. Her face and body were rigid with the intensity of passion that he loved to see, to feel, in her. When she got this way, she was just one moment away from grabbing and holding him fiercely, and what usually happened next—oh, what usually happened next!—

Didn't happen this time. Anne Cathrine seemed to remember her surroundings, looked away, readjusted her kerchief—*that damned kerchief! what the hell?*—and stared out to sea. She pointed at the *Courser*, now nearly two miles ahead of the *Intrepid* and widening the gap rapidly. "That is the smaller of your steamships, yes?"

Huh? She knows perfectly well that it is. But all he said was, "Yes, Anne Cathrine. That's our destroyer."

"A fierce name," she said with a tight, approving nod. "And that one gun in the middle of its deck, sitting in its own little castle, is the most dangerous of them all?"

He smiled. "That little castle is what we call a 'tub mount.' The round, rib-high wall protects the gun crew from enemy fire, shrapnel, fragments. As does the sloped gun shield. The rifle can bear through two hundred seventy degrees and fire several different kinds of shells to very great ranges."

"It is the same as these guns on your ship?" She pointed to the two naval rifles on the centerline of the *Intrepid*'s weather deck.

"Yes, but, umm...this isn't *my* ship, sweetheart. It's—"

"Yes, I know. It's Gjeddes'. But he has let you run it, with the exception of the sail-handling, since we left the dock."

Eddie shrugged. There was no arguing with the truth.

Anne Cathrine was pointing over the bow. "And that sail up ahead, that is the Dutch-built yacht?"

"Yes, the *Crown of Waves*. A good ship. She's out ahead of us as a picket."

"I thought you have provided us with balloons to look far ahead, so that pickets were no longer needed?"

He smiled. "Pickets are always needed, Anne Cathrine. Besides, we don't want to use the balloons if we don't need them, and if the winds get any stronger, an observer could get pretty roughed up, to say nothing of damage to the balloon itself."

"I see. And the other ship like your *Intrepid*—the *Resolve*—that's her, falling to the rear?"

"Yes."

She was silent for a long time. "Your ships are so big compared to ours. Even compared to the *Patentia*, the *Resolve* is easily half again as long and half again as high, except at the very rear. And still—"

"Yes?"

"Eddie, should your warships have so few guns? I know up-time-designed weapons are terribly powerful, but if they should fail to operate, or the enemy gets lucky shots into the gun deck—" She stopped, seeing his small smile.

"Trust me, Anne Cathrine, we have enough guns. More than enough. It's more important that our magazine is big enough to carry plenty of excellent ammunition to keep our excellent guns well supplied. Which is the case."

She nodded and turned her eyes to the ship lumbering along beside the *Patentia*. "Not a very handsome ship, the *Serendipity*."

Eddie let a little laugh slip out. "No, she's not much to look at." The *Serendipity* was a pot-bellied bulk hauler, with the lines of a bloated pink or fluyt. "But she's steady in a storm, and seven hundred fifty tons burthen. And we need that cargo capacity. So ugly or not, we're lucky to have her."

"Not as lucky as to have the *Tropic Surveyor*," countered Anne Cathrine with an appreciative smile and a chin raised in the direction of the last ship of the flotilla.

And Eddie had to admit that *Tropic Surveyor* was a handsome ship, her square-rigged fore- and mainmasts running with their sheets full. The large, three-masted bark had a fore-and-aft rigged mizzen and twelve almost uniform guns in each broadside battery. Her lines were unusually clean, reflecting the first influence of frigate-built designs upon traditional barks. Her master, a Swede by the name of Stiernsköld, was known to be a highly capable captain who, if he had any failing, tended toward quiet but determined boldness.

Anne Cathrine's attention had drifted back to the *Patentia*, however. "What are all those men doing on deck, and who are they?"

Eddie glanced over; he saw a growing number of men at the portside gunwales of the *Patentia*, many pointing at the island peaks to the south, some nodding, some shaking their heads. Eddie smiled. "Those are the Irish soldiers who came up from the Infanta Isabella of the Lowlands."

Anne Cathrine frowned. "I still do not understand how mercenaries who have been in Spanish service for generations—"

Eddie shook his head. "I don't understand it either. Not entirely." *And what little I do understand I can't share, honey. Sorry.*

"Do you at least know why they are on deck there— and look, more of them are gathering at the rail of the *Serendipity*! What are they *looking* at?"

The voice that answered was gravel-filtered and deep. "They think they are seeing their homeland."

Eddie and Anne Cathrine turned. Ove Gjedde was behind them, his eyes invisible in the squinting-folds of his weathered face. Neither had heard him approach.

"Their homeland?" Anne Cathrine repeated.

"Yes, my lady. Because the last week's wind has been fair, there has been some loose talk that we might sight the north Irish coast late today." He sucked at yellowed teeth. "That will not happen until tomorrow, sometime. But I am told that the Irish got word of these rumors. And as you may know, most of them have never seen Ireland, but were born in the Lowlands. Their eagerness is understandable." Gjedde made to move off once again.

Eddie offered a smart salute. "Thank you, Captain."

Gjedde returned a slight nod that was the down-time equivalent of a salute between officers of comparable rank, made a slightly deeper nod in Anne Cathrine's direction, and began slowly pacing forward along the starboard railing, hands behind his back.

Anne Cathrine stared after him. "He did not return the new naval salute, as per your admiral's regulations."

"But he does follow the rest of the regs. To the letter."

Anne Cathrine watched the spare man move away. "Captain Gjedde seems to grow more somber every time I meet him."

Eddie shifted his eyes sideways to his wife. "While we're on the topic of 'more somber' . . ."

Anne Cathrine glanced at him quickly, fiddled with her kerchief and tucked a stray strand of gold-red hair back under it. "I do not know what you mean."

"Sure you don't." If they had been alone, he would have put an arm around her waist and pulled her closer. "C'mon, Anne Cathrine, what gives? You're acting . . . oddly."

"I am not." At that particular moment she did not sound like her usual sixteen going on thirty-six. She just sounded like she was six.

Eddie smiled. "Uh, yes, you are. And what's with the head covering?"

Her hands flew up to her kerchief and she stepped away from him quickly. "Why? Has it come undone?" Satisfied that it was still firmly in place, she raised her chin and looked away. "There is nothing wrong. Nothing."

Huh. So there *was* a connection between his wife's hinky behavior and the kerchief. "Anne Cathrine, honey, don't worry. Tell me what's going on. Let me help."

She looked at him, her eyes suddenly glassy and bright, then glanced away quickly.

What? Has she lost most of her hair? Fallen victim to some strange depilatory disease particular to the high seas of the northern latitudes? "Anne Cathrine, whatever it is, it's going to be all right. Just tell me and—"

"Oh, Eddie—" She turned back to him and, oblivious to on-lookers, cast herself into his arms. "I'm sorry—so sorry."

"Sorry? About what?" He tried to ignore the fact that even through his deck coat and her garments, he could still feel his wife's very voluptuous and strong body along the length of his own. And in accordance with the orders given by the supreme authority of his ancient mammalian hindbrain, certain parts of him were taking notice and coming to general quarters. Well, more like standing at attention . . .

"Oh, Eddie, my hair! I should have seen to my packing, my preparations, myself. But in the rush to get everything aboard, and with all the last-minute changes—"

"What? Have you lost your hair? That's okay; we can—"

She pulled away from him. "Lost my hair?" She pulled herself erect. She might not have the title of a full princess, but she could sure put on a convincing show of being one. "Certainly not. But I—I neglected to oversee my servant's preparations. And now I, I..." She looked down at the deck, then reached up and tugged her kerchief sharply.

Eddie was prepared for anything: baldness, scrofulous patches, running sores, dandruff the size of postage stamps, medusan snakes—anything. Except for what was revealed.

Anne Cathrine's red hair came uncoiling from the bulky kerchief in a long, silk-shining wave that came down to the middle of her back. Eddie couldn't help himself: he gasped.

Seeing his expression, Anne Cathrine pouted. Her lower lip even quivered slightly. "I knew it."

"Knew what?" Eddie heard himself say. He was still busy staring at his wife's hair and trying to tell his lower jaw to raise and lock in place.

"Knew that you would be aghast to see my hair like this, without the curls. Oh, I tried, Eddie, I did. My servant forgot to pack the heating combs, and neither I nor Leonora—nor Sophie—know how to do our hair any other way. Commoners can make curls with wet rags, I'm told, so we tried that, but none of us did our own hair often." *Or at all*, Eddie added silently, now quite familiar with coiffuring dependencies of noble ladies. "I have been trying since we left to keep some curl in it, or at least a wave, but this morning, we all agreed there was nothing left to try."

"It's beautiful," Eddie croaked.

Her smile looked broken. "You are a wonderful

husband, to say that. But you can barely speak the words. I know the expectations of fashion, Eddie. And here you see the truth at last: I have straight, plain hair. No tumbling curls, not even a tiny ripple of a wave. Plain, straight hair."

He reached out and touched it. "Hair like fire and gold spun into silk," he breathed. "And in my time, that kind of hair was very much in fashion. Hell, I didn't think hair like this was ever *out* of fashion."

She blinked. "So—you like it? You like my hair this way?"

Eddie gulped. "Oh, yes. I like it. Very much. Very, very much." He roused himself out of his pre-carnal stupor. "But know this, Anne Cathrine, the hair is not important to me. What's *under* it is." He touched her cheek. "As important as the wide world."

Anne Cathrine's smile—shockingly white teeth—was sudden and wide. She caught his hand on her cheek and held it there. "Truly," she said, "I am the luckiest woman in the world."

"And a princess, to boot," Eddie added with a grin.

"A king's daughter," she corrected, and moved toward him again—

"Sail, sail on the port bow! Rounding the rocks, sirs. She's running before the wind!"

Chapter 16

St. Kilda archipelago, North Atlantic

Eddie transferred Anne Cathrine's hands from him to the rail—"Hold on, Anne Cathrine, and be ready to take the ladies below"—and made for the stairs to the observation deck atop the pilot house. "Orderly?"

"Yes, sir?"

"Glasses topside, please. And call Mr. Bjelke back on deck. Smartly."

"Yes, sir!" The response was already dwindling aft.

As Eddie made his way up the stairs—*damnit, can't this leg go any faster?*—he heard Gjedde's voice behind him. "No point in breaking your neck, Commander. Things do not happen quite so quickly in this century."

As Eddie thumped his prosthetic down upon the observation deck—another change from the *Hartford*—he turned to offer a smile to the older captain, whose mouth looked a little less rigid than usual. It might have even had a faint upward curl at one side. If he hadn't spent so much time with Simpson, he might have completely missed that hint of a smile. *So, Gjedde*

214

doesn't *hate me. Either that, or he's hoping I'll get offed in the next hour or so...*

Eddie went straight to the speaking tubes, popped back the covers, and toggled the telegraphic command circuit. "Circuit test," he shouted.

"Tests clear," came the muffled shout from under his feet where the intraship telegrapher was stationed.

The orderly bounded up the stairs, passing a new-pattern spyglass to Gjedde, and holding a case out toward Eddie, who snapped it open and lifted out the precious up-time binoculars. The signalman hustled past with a hastily muttered *"Verlot!"* and was immediately ready, pad to his right, left index finger poised on the telegrapher's key. "Comms manned, Captain Gjedde."

Gjedde shook his head. "You will make your reports to, and take your orders from, Commander Cantrell. He will direct this ship through her first combat."

Eddie turned, stunned, "What?"

Gjedde bowed. "Your command, Mr. Cantrell. Compliments of your father-in-law, Christian IV."

Why that old son of a— "Then Captain Gjedde, I say three times: I have the bridge. What's the word from the foretop crow's nest? What manner of ship, flying what colors?"

After a pause, the report came back. "A carrack sir. Old design. Spanish colors."

Spanish colors? Up here? What the hell were they—?

Apparently, telepathy was a strong trait in the Danish; now it was Gjedde who seemed to read his mind. "Not so unusual. They supply the Irish with guns and powder, from time to time. Sometimes the Scots, too. There is no shortage of rebels against English occupiers up here, and Spain is only too happy to provide them with assistance."

Eddie nodded. "I understand, but why ever they happen to be here, it seems that they've seen us. They ran between *Crown of Waves* and *Courser* like they were waiting for that opening. I suspect they saw our smoke, peeked around the northwestern point of Hirta—at Gob a Ghaill—saw our flotilla, measured the breeze, and realized their only way to avoid us was to run before the wind after our advance picket had passed them, but before our main van drew too close."

Gjedde nodded, the visible slivers of his eyes sharp. "*Ja*, that is how I see it, also."

"Very well. Signalman, relay this to intership telegrapher for immediate send. 'To Admiral Mund aboard *Resolve*. Message starts: Have spotted—"

"Sir," said the radioman, "incoming message from Admiral Mund."

Well, speak of the devil—"Read it as you get it, Rating."

"Admiral Mund commanding *Resolve* to Commander Cantrell, presumed to be in temporary command of *Intrepid*. Message begins: By joint order of Emperor Gustav Adolf and His Royal Highness Christian IV, I relinquish operational command of Reconnaissance Flotilla X-Ray to you for duration of first engagement. Stop. Awaiting instructions. Stop."

Oh, so all *the heads of state are seeing if I have the goods when the shit starts flying. Well, no reason not to give them a good show*—"Radioman, send the following under my command line. To Admiral Mund, on *Resolve*: message received and acknowledged. Stop. To all ships: general quarters. Stop." He turned to see

Bjelke pound up the stairs to the observation deck. Eddie gave him an order and a welcoming nod in the same instant: "Sound general quarters, Mr. Bjelke. Orderly, make sure our passengers understand that 'general quarters' means 'battle stations.' Only duty personnel on deck."

"And if they don't understand that, sir?"

"Then correct their misunderstanding. With main force, if necessary. No exceptions. Including my wife. Especially my wife. Is that clear, mister?"

"Very clear, *ja*, sir!" And again the young orderly was off, with a rising tide of coronets and drums carrying him on his way.

Bjelke returned to his side. Gjedde watched from the rear rail of the observation deck. Eddie thought for a moment, then turned to the signalman, "Forward mount, get me range, bearing, and speed of the Spaniard. Then send to *Crown of Waves* and *Courser*: I need their precise heading and speed."

"What are you thinking, Commander?" asked Bjelke.

"That whatever the Spanish do or do not understand from having seen us, we can't let them escape and report. Just knowing that a flotilla of USE ships is on a course that would suggest a New World destination is bad enough. Anything else could be disastrous. They might have seen the smoke and presumed that one of our ships was on fire, or that we have whalers with us who were putting blubber through some of the new shipboard try-works. But someone with better information on the USE's activities is likely to figure that this carrack spotted our steam warships. Word of this encounter can not—*not*—reach people with that kind of knowledge."

The radioman called out. "All messages acknowledged, except *Crown of Waves*. I think something is wrong with her radio-set, sir. Lots of lost characters. And they seem to be losing some of ours, too."

Well, now it's a real military engagement: we've got commo snafus. So without the radio—"Send to *Courser*: Radio on *Crown of Waves* inoperable. Stop. Your position gives best line of sight and shortest range. Stop. Relay command signals to *Crown of Waves* via semaphore and aldriss lamp. Stop. End of Message. New message to *Resolve* starts. Drop to rear of formation. Stop. Remain at one mile distance. Stop. Deploy balloon ASAP. Stop. Maintain close rear watch. Stop. Message ends."

Bjelke's left eyebrow raised. "Rear watch, sir? A trap? Up here?"

"Traps are most effective where they're least expected, wouldn't you agree, Lieutenant Bjelke?"

"Aye, sir."

"So we eliminate that admittedly slim possibility first, then take the next steps."

Gjedde folded his arms. "And what steps are those?"

"To box the Spaniard in. Radioman?"

"Just received acknowledgment from *Courser* now. Captain Haraldsen passes along word that Major Lawrence Quinn sends his compliments and will oversee technical coordination on that hull."

Eddie felt his heart rate diminish slightly. It was good to know the other—the only other—military up-timer in the flotilla was out there, lending a hand. The down-timers were competent, eager, and obedient, but sometimes, they just didn't get how all the parts of a steam-and-sail navy worked together. In all probability, the most important test during this shakedown cruise would not be of Simpson's new ships, but of the crews of his new navy. "Send Major Quinn my greetings and thanks. And have him relay this to the *Crown of Waves*: set course north by northwest, paralleling the Spaniard. Course for the *Courser*, the same."

"Speed, sir?"

"What God and sail-handlers will allow, radioman. We are not raising steam."

Bjelke made a sound of surprise. Eddie turned to look at him. "You can speak freely, Rik."

"Sir, I thought combat was exactly the time when you *would* order steam. Is that not one of the main purposes of this cruise, to see how the steam ships fare in actual combat, under power?"

"Normally, yes, but this time, I'm worried about detection. If this ship is not alone then, trap or no trap, raising steam means sending a message to any and all of the rest of an enemy formation about where and *what* we are."

The radioman cleared his throat politely. "Message from *Resolve*, Commander."

"What does Admiral Mund have to say?"

"Sir, he points out that in order to deploy the balloon, he will have to clear his stern of canvas. And if he does so, if he slacks the sails on the mizzen and swings wide the yard to clear the deck for air operations, he will slow down and fall further behind."

"Send that this is not an operational concern. He'll still have better speed than either *Patentia* and *Serendipity*, whom he must remain behind and protect. More importantly, please remind him that decreasing his ship's speed makes it a better platform for the balloon. When you're done sending that, send to the *Serendipity* and *Patentia* that they are to crowd sail. I don't want them lagging behind too far, and stretching out our formation. And have the *Tropic Surveyor* close on us as she is able, crossing our wake when we clear Gob a Ghiall."

"Aye, sir. Sending now."

Bjelke frowned. "You want the bark to the south of us, closer to the island?"

"Absolutely, Lieutenant. Because if the enemy has more ships behind that headland, I want to give them something to deal with while we bring round our rifles and teach them just how long our reach is."

Gjedde may have nodded. "And so, what will *Intrepid* be doing?"

Eddie smiled and, by way of answer, waved Svantner over. "Lieutenant, do we have solutions for range, bearing, and speed of the Spaniard?"

"Yes, sir. Mount One has rechecked first findings and confirms the following with highest confidence: the Spaniard is now just under a mile off, making two and a half knots and heading north by northwest true."

"*Crown of Waves* and *Courser*?"

"Now on parallel courses with the Spaniard, sir. *Crown* is making three knots and a bit, *Courser* is almost at six."

Eddie made a mental map plot. The Spanish carrack was in a tight spot. If she turned to either port or starboard, she'd be turning into the paths of faster, better-armed ships, and losing the wind in doing so. And since the ships boxing her in—*Crown of Waves* to the south, *Courser* to the north—could sail closer hauled and faster, their speed and maneuverability would be even less affected if they made a matching course change. He had the Spaniard straitjacketed. Now to shorten the chase—

"And our speed, Mr. Svantner?"

"Five knots, sir. We can make a bit more if we steer a half point to port, and put the wind just abaft the starboard beam."

"Do so, but keep me out of a direct stern chase. I don't want to shrink the target profile."

"Sir?"

"I don't want to have to shoot straight up that Spaniard's narrow ass; I want a little more of his side to aim at."

"Aye, aye, sir!"

"Mr. Bjelke, send the word to Mount One: stand ready."

"At once, Commander!"

Gjedde unfolded his arms as Bjelke hurried down the stairs. "About fifteen minutes then."

Eddie turned. "I beg your pardon, Captain?"

"Fifteen minutes before you start firing. The range will have dropped to under half a mile, by then."

Eddie smiled. "Less."

Gjedde narrowed his eyes. "How?"

Eddie felt his smile widen. "I would be delighted to demonstrate, sir."

Gjedde crossed his arms again and frowned. "Please do."

Eddie gave a partial salute and turned to his First Mate. "Mr. Svantner, has the Spaniard reacted to our course change yet?"

"A bit, sir. She shifted course slightly to the north, keeping us at distance."

"But closing on the *Courser*, yes?"

"A bit sir, yes."

"Then send to *Courser*: change heading one point to port. Full sheets on the spencer masts. Give that Spaniard a reason to run the other way."

"Aye, sir."

Eddie turned—and caught Gjedde smiling. His face became stony in an instant. "So. You'll scare him into tacking. Each turn of which costs him time and momentum."

Eddie shrugged. "It's what you taught me, second day on ship. Seems like the right plan, here."

Gjedde nodded. "Seems so."

The radioman uttered a confused grunt, checked an incoming message a second time. "Sir, signal from the *Courser*. But it doesn't make sense."

"Read it, radioman."

"From Major Quinn, technical advisor aboard *Courser*, to Commander Cantrell on *Intrepid*. Stop. Regarding course change. Stop. Aye, aye, Commander . . . Hornblower?" The radioman's voice had raised to an almost adolescent squeak. "Stop. Message ends. Sir, is Commander 'Hornblower' code, sir?"

Eddie smiled. "In a manner of speaking, rating. In a manner of speaking. Svantner?"

"Yes sir?"

"Tell me when that Spaniard starts to come around to port. As soon as he does, we'll crowd him from the south with the *Crown*."

Eddie checked his watch. *And in about ten minutes, we'll end the chase. For good.*

Nine minutes later, Commander Eddie Cantrell called for the range.

After a moment's delay, the intraship communications officer piped up, "Seven hundred yards, sir."

"Mount One, acquire the target."

The intraship piped up so quickly that Eddie suspected he was in constant conversation with the mount's commanding officer. "Acquiring, sir!"

"Send word to load with solid shot."

"Aye, sir." A pause. "Gunnery officer requests confirmation on that last order: *solid* shot?"

"Solid shot. Tell him we're not going to waste an explosive shell until we have a proven targeting solution."

"Solid shot, aye, sir. And Mount One reports a firing solution. Range now six-hundred-fifty yards."

Perfect. "Fire one round and continue tracking. Svantner, reef sails."

The wire-wound eight-inch naval rifle roared and flew back in its recoil carriage, smoke gouting out its barrel as a long, sustained plume. A moment later, a geyser of water shot up about thirty yards off the Spaniard's port quarter.

Eddie raised his glasses. He could see arms waving frantically on the deck of the carrack. While the Spanish had no idea exactly what kind of gun was shooting at them, it was a certainty that they knew it was like no gun they'd ever encountered before. And that it was also far more deadly.

"Reload," Eddie ordered as he felt the *Intrepid*'s forward progress diminish, its sails retracting upward, "and adjust. Watch the inclinometer."

From where he stood, Eddie could observe the gun's crew go into its routine like one well-oiled machine in service of another. The handle on the back of the gun was given a hard half turn and the interrupted-screw breech swung open, vapors coiling out and around the crew. The cry of "swab out!" brought forward a man holding what looked like, at this range, a gargantuan Q-tip. He ran it into and around the interior, ensuring no embers or sparks remained to predetonate the next charge. Meanwhile, a half-hoist brought up the next shell—akin to a short, somewhat pointed bullet eight inches at the base and sixteen inches long—and the loaders swung it out of the cradle and into the breech, where another man promptly pushed it in until it was snug. Powder bags were loaded in next and then the breech was sealed while the second gunner inserted a primer in the weapon's percussion lock.

"Loaded!"

"Primed! Hammer cocked and locked."

"New firing solution," called out the chief gunner. "Right two, up one!"

The second gunner hunkered down; he made a slight adjustment to a small vertical wheel on the side of the mount, and another to a small horizontal wheel. "Acquired!"

The intraship pipe at Eddie's elbow announced, "Mount One reports ready, Commander."

"At the discretion of the gunnery officer,"—*watch the inclinometer more closely!*—"fire."

There was a pause while the gunnery officer studied the levels that indicated roll, pitch, and yaw, and then he shouted, "Fire!"

The second gunner pulled the lanyard, and the long black tube roared again.

Eddie saw the shot go into the water only ten yards in front of the carrack's bow. And he also realized why the gunnery officer was always a fraction off on measuring the roll: because from his position on the deck, he could not watch the sea close to the *Intrepid*. Standing only seven feet higher, Eddie had a much better view. He could keep an eye on the inclinometer even as he read the proximal swells and troughs.

One of which was coming. The *Intrepid* came off the crest of a two-foot riser, slid down into a long trough—and Eddie knew the inclinometer was going to be perfectly level the moment before it was.

"Fire!" he yelled forward over the weather deck at the same moment that the inclinometer showed level.

The eight-inch rifle spoke a third time as Eddie jerked the binoculars back up to his eyes—

—Just in time to see the shell tear into the carrack, just aft of its bow on the starboard side. Planks and dusty smoke flew up and outward—and, puzzlingly, from the portside bow as well. Which, Eddie realized an instant later, had been caused by the round exiting the hull on the other side.

The Spanish ship reeled, first to port, then tottered back to starboard, the bow digging into the swells heavily. She wasn't taking water, but it was possible that her stem—the extension of the keel up into the curve of the prow—had been damaged and her forecastle was starting to collapse, riven by the tremendous force of the shell. As the smoke began to clear and the human damage was revealed—bodies scattered around the impact point, others hobbling away, several bobbing motionless in the cold northern waters—Eddie barked out his next order through a tightening throat. "Load explosive shell. Maintain tracking."

He waited through the thirty seconds of reloading. The *Intrepid* was now moving slowly, so her position was barely changing. And the carrack, which had already lost a great deal of her headway by being forced to tack back and forth in response to the harrying ships to either side, had been moving at barely one and a half knots before she was hit. And now, with her bow damaged and her crew panicking—

"Mount One reports ready."

Eddie kept his eyes just far enough from the binoculars to watch the inclinometer. "Fire," he ordered calmly.

Perhaps he had become so used to the sound and buffeting of the big guns that he didn't notice it. Or perhaps he was simply too fixated on the fate of the ship that he was about to kill. Either way, he could not afterwards remember hearing the report of his own gun. Instead, burned into his memory, in slow motion, was the impact of the shell upon the carrack.

There was a split-second precursor: a light puff of what looked like dust. That was the shell, slicing through the starboard corner of the stern so swiftly that it was inside the vessel's poop before the shock waves sent rail, transom, and deck planks flying in a wide, wild sphere of destruction.

But in the next blink of an eye, that was all wiped away by the titanic explosion that blasted out from the guts of the ship itself. The poop deck literally went up in a single piece, discorporating as it rose, bodies shooting toward the heaven that Eddie hoped was there to receive them. The mainmast, the rearmost on the two-masted carrack, went crashing forward, tearing the rigging down with her and stripping the yard clean off the foremast. Black smoke and flames spun up out of the jagged hole that had been the ship's stern, and the men on her decks were a moving arabesque of confused action. Some were trying to fight the fires, others were making for the rail, others were trying to give orders, several were trying to get her dinghy over to the port side. None of them were achieving their objective.

"Check fire," Eddie croaked. "Crowd sails and move to assist."

Ove Gjedde, as still and silent as a forgotten statue, now reanimated. Suddenly at Eddie's elbow, he asked, "Commander, you are planning to assist?"

Eddie stared at the men who were now in the water. Their cries were audible even at this distance. He nodded. "We have to."

Gjedde made a strangely constricted noise deep in his throat. "Commander, I do not wish to intrude upon your prerogatives—"

The radioman looked up. "Commander, message from *Resolve*. Coded urgent, sir."

"Read it, please."

"Aye, sir. Message begins. Admiral Mund of *Resolve* to Commander Cantrell of *Intrepid*. Stop. Balloon at three hundred feet has spotted three, possibly four ships fifteen miles south of Gob a Ghaill headland. Stop. Heading is due north. Stop. Currently making slightly less than three knots. Stop. Awaiting instructions. Stop. Message ends.'"

Eddie could sense Gjedde standing uncommonly close to him. *He wants me to break off, but that isn't right. We can save those men.* "Send this reply, my command line. Message starts: to Admiral Mund, *Resolve*. Stop. Lead flotilla north by northwest on heading parallel to *Crown of Waves* and *Courser*. Stop. *Intrepid* will effect rescue operations and follow all haste. Stop. Secure balloon immediately to minimize possibility of enemy sighting it. Stop. Message ends."

Gjedde was frowning. For some reason, Eddie imagined himself as Bilbo Baggins at one of those moments when he had pissed off Gandalf mightily. Avuncular Gjedde continued to stare at him, seemed to be weighing his next choice of words very carefully.

Finally he began, "Commander, this is not wise. I must point out—"

"Commander Cantrell," the radioman muttered, "another message from *Resolve*. Again, coded urgent."

Eddie held up a hand to pause Gjedde, nodded at the radioman. "Go ahead."

"Message starts. CO *Resolve* to acting CO *Intrepid*. Stop. First action is concluded. Stop. Command changes are now terminated. Stop. Secure from general quarters. Stop. Captain Gjedde resumes direct command immediately. Stop. Rescue operations hereby countermanded. Stop. Flotilla X-Ray immediately heads north by northwest true, at best speed of slowest ship. Stop. Compliments to Commander Cantrell for successful first engagement. Stop. Message ends."

Eddie was still watching the men struggling in the chill gray waters, saw that some of them seemed to be weakening already. Those who had been clustered around the dinghy got it into the water, where it promptly foundered. Probably some splinter or shrapnel had punched a hole in it and they had not noticed that damage in their frenzied attempt to escape their ship.

Which was a prudent course of action: the carrack, her stern savaged as if some kraken of the deep had taken a vicious bite out of it, was settling back upon her rudder, and listing slightly to starboard. At the rate she was going down, her decks would be awash within the hour. And her crew—

Gjedde put a hand on Eddie's arm, drew it and the binoculars it held down slowly. "There is nothing to be done, Commander. If we stayed to rescue those men, the Spanish would see us before we could get away again. We must break off now, at best speed, to remain undetected. You must know this."

Eddie didn't want to know it, but he did. "Perhaps they'll be picked up by the Spanish then."

Gjedde didn't blink. "You know better than that, too, Commander. They may see the smoke or they may not. If they do not, it is unlikely they would come close enough to see wreckage or hear cries for help. And even if they do, it will be fifteen hours from now. There will be no one for them to rescue and few enough bodies to see, should they chance to come so close to the site of our engagement."

Eddie looked over the bow. Only three hundred yards away, now, the Spanish were struggling in the water, and the first were already losing the battle to stay above the cold gray swells of the North Sea. He nodded. "Aye, aye, sir. You're the captain."

Gjedde's eyes fell from Eddie's. Suddenly, he looked even older. Then he turned on his heel and began giving orders. "Mr. Bjelke, secure from general quarters and give orders to unload battery and personal weapons. I want no unnecessary or accidental discharges as we run from the Spanish. Pilot, set us north by northwest true. Mr. Svantner, pass it along to crowd all sail. There will be no rescue operations."

As the crew of the *Intrepid* scrambled to set about their duties, Eddie noticed that the *Tropic Surveyor*, which had been traveling under full sail the whole time, was drawing abreast of them. Lining the starboard gunwales were more of the Irish mercenaries, who peered ahead at the wreckage and the ruined carrack.

The Spanish, seeing the ships approach, called out for quarter, for aid, for mercy for the love of god.

As the *Intrepid* passed them at two hundred yards off the portside, their cries were half swallowed by the sound of the wavelets against the ship's hull.

But the *Tropic Surveyor* passed them at a distance of only one hundred yards to her starboard side. The Spanish cried out to the men lining her rail, perhaps seeing the facial features and even the tartans and equipage they associated with their traditional Irish allies.

But the Irish made no sound, and watched, without expression or, apparently, any pity, as more of the Spanish began to sink down deeper into the low rolling swells of the North Sea.

Chapter 17

East of St. Christopher, Caribbean

Through the salt spray and dusty rose of early dawn, Hugh Albert O'Donnell compared Michael McCarthy, Jr.'s pinched, weather-seamed eyes with Aodh O'Rourke's pale-lipped scowl. The latter, staring at the balloon as it swelled up and off the poop deck, muttered, "You'd not get me to swing 'neath that bag o' gas." Then Hugh's lieutenant of eight years nodded to the up-timer beside him. "No offense to your handiwork, Don Michael."

"Don" Michael—whom Hugh had convinced, at no small expense of effort, to accept the honorific—simply shrugged. "No offense taken. I'm not riding in it myself. That's for young Mulryan, here."

Mulryan, an apple-faced lad with an unruly shock of red hair, nodded. "An' it's not so bad, O'Rourke. After the fourth or fifth time, yeh forget the height. Seems natural, 't does."

"To you, maybe," O'Rourke grumbled, and then moved aside as feet thumped up the stairs from the weather deck behind him.

Hugh swayed up from his easy seat on the taffrail

as Captain Paul Morraine rose into view. He was followed by a taller, thinner man whose arrival resulted in an almost uniform hardening of expressions and veiling of eyes: Morraine's immediate subordinate, First Mate George St. Georges, was not a favorite with the Irish, nor with his own crew. Only Michael's expression remained unaltered. The two senior officers of the *Fleur Sable* joined the group just as McGillicuddy, chief of the balloon's ground crew, set his legs firm and wide to help his men tug on the guidelines. Straining together, they drew more of the swelling envelope up toward them and away from the mizzenmast, the yard having been dropped to accommodate this process.

Morraine nodded at Hugh. "Lord O'Donnell."

Hugh nodded back. "You wish to have your mizzen back as soon as possible, Captain?"

The left corner of Morraine's mouth quirked. For him, this was the equivalent of a broad grin. "It is so obvious?"

Hugh smiled. "Well, yes. And sensible as well. But at a height of six hundred feet, we will see what lies before us and enter the channel between St. Christopher and St. Eustatia as fast and unseen as the wind that's rising behind us."

"Which I do not wish to miss, sir. Monsieur McCarthy tells me this is a swift procedure, yes?"

McCarthy shrugged, inspecting the billowing envelope. "It'll be aloft in fifteen minutes, up for ten, down in ten, deflated enough for you to remount your mizzenmast in another ten. So, forty-five minutes, barring mishaps."

Morraine nodded, nose into the wind. "Just in time, I would say. I want to be see the lights of Basseterre behind us by midnight."

St. Georges sniffed distastefully at the pitch-soaked combustibles already smoking in the hand burner that Tearlach Mulryan was readying. "I, for one, am worried that your observer will not see all the ships before us."

Mulryan raised a mildly contentious index finger. "Ah, but I will, sir. Six hundred feet altitude and this improved spyglass"—he tapped the brass tube in his rude "web gear"—"will show us the horizon out to thirty-three miles or so, and we'll see the top of most any masts at least ten miles farther out."

"So you have said." St. Georges sniffed again, this time at Mulryan's claim.

"And so we have seen in the trials we've conducted since leaving France," Morraine followed with a calm, if impatient glance at his XO. "However, we will want to keep your men below decks much of the time, now, Lord O'Donnell. In the event our reconnaissance is incomplete, or Fate forces an encounter upon us, it would not do to have a passing ship see our complement to be markedly greater than the expected crew of this vessel."

"Agreed, Captain. Point well taken. Besides, my men will be busy at their own tasks."

"Which shall be?"

"Sharpening their swords and cleaning their pieces."

Morraine's left eyebrow arched. "Indeed. I took the liberty of inspecting the armorer's locker after your men came aboard. All snaphaunces, even a few flintlocks. Expensive equipment, if I may say so."

"Say away, for it's true enough. But Lord Turenne agreed that it makes little sense to go to all the expense of mounting our expedition, and then arm the shore party with inferior firearms."

"It is as you say. But almost half were pistols and the new-style musketoons. Most uncommon."

"As uncommon as our task, Captain." Hugh leaned back against the taffrail. "We'll not spend much of our time at ranges greater than fifty yards, if my guess is right. So while we'll want the ability to pour in a few volleys, I expect we'll have little time or reason for serried ranks and maneuver. As I hear it, Pitch Lake itself is the only 'open field' we'll encounter. But there's plenty of bush to worm through. So I suspect most of the fighting will be quick and close."

Morraine nodded. "Reasonable. Let us hope you do not have much fighting to do, though. Sixty men is not many for such an enterprise, even on the sparsely populated islands of the New World."

O'Donnell nodded. "I agree." He smiled. "Perhaps you could convince Lord Turenne to send along a few more."

Morraine's lip almost quirked again. "Indeed. I shall mention it to him upon my return, perhaps over our first glass of wine."

Hugh nodded, let his grin become rueful. It was out of the realm of possibility that Morraine would actually ever meet Turenne, much less have the position or opportunity to suggest anything to the French general about operations here in the Caribbean. In addition to Turenne's being a phenomenally busy man, Morraine's appointment as the commander of the *Fleur Sable* had been a somewhat delicate business, handled by faceless bureaucrats at the unspoken but clear promptings of Turenne's immediate subordinates. To have gone about it more openly would have been seen as undermining the naval court which had been well-paid to dismiss Morraine as a scapegoat for a young and thoroughly incompetent executive officer who just happened to be the son of an unscrupulous duke. Consequently, it was necessary that Turenne should never have direct contact with Morraine, lest both of them come under the scrutiny of that same duke, who, like most powerful men guilty of suborning a court, would spare no effort to ensure that the lies he had paid to be called "the truth" would not be revealed or revisited.

Morraine's point about a scant sixty-man force was true enough. It left Hugh O'Donnell no margin for error, no extra resources with which to cope with surprises, reversals, or just plain bad luck. But the other Wild Geese who had been scheduled to follow him down from the Lowlands had never arrived. According to Turenne's last message, Fernando of the Lowlands had personally forbidden their departure, pending a reconsideration of their contracts and oaths to Spain. It all sounded a little suspicious to Hugh, but that was several months, and several thousand miles, behind him now. He would have to make do with the men and resources he had, and hope for the others to come along in due course.

Morraine's version of a smile had faded. He looked at the expanding balloon, then at the seas over the bow. "Well, Lord O'Donnell, I shall leave you and your, er, 'ground crew' to your business. The sooner you are done here, the sooner we can be under way and finish this dirty business."

Hugh kept even the faintest hint of resentment out of his voice. "Dirty business?"

Morraine paused. "Lord O'Donnell, I mean no

offense. As you, I am estranged from my country. And so I will not be happy until I may stand proud beneath French colors. I am no pirate."

"Indeed, and so you are not flying one of their dread flags."

"Nor am I flying the flag of France, Lord O'Donnell. And until I do, my loyalties and intentions must be considered suspect by all whom we encounter. So I leave you to your work, that we may both return to service beneath our nation's banners with all possible haste." He nodded a farewell.

As Hugh nodded in return, he considered Morraine's tight, craggy, and mostly immobile features. The Breton had a good record operating in the open waters off Penzance and Wight, and was patriotically eager to end his estrangement from the pleasure of Louis XIII. He was also clearly thrilled to have a cromster's deck under his feet. During her trials off Dunkirk, he had made eager use of her mizzen's lateen-rig, getting a feel for the *Fleur Sable*'s maneuverability. He had demonstrated a keen appreciation of her comparatively shallow draft, and enhanced (albeit not extreme) ability to tack against the wind—operational flexibilities he had not had much opportunity to enjoy while serving in His Majesty's lumbering battlewagons. Hugh just hoped that, like countless commanders before him, Morraine did not overindulge his new enthusiasms during combat. War was a messy business, best approached by leaving wide margins for error and the unexpected.

Morraine's swift descent from the poop deck prompted St. Georges into a hurried attempt to follow, which was suddenly blocked by the balloon's uncoiling guidelines. As he sought clear passage, further obstacles obtruded themselves. Spools of down-timer telegraph cable and McGillicuddy's thick, powerful legs threatened to tumble him. Aggrieved, the third son of a wealthy merchant glared archly at the Irish earl. "I must pass, Monsieur O'Donnell."

Hugh found the make-believe-officer too ridiculous to be a source of offense. St. Georges' class paranoia was as thick about him as the smell of his abysmal teeth. Every time he addressed O'Donnell as "Monsieur" instead of "Lord," he seemed poised to gloat over the slight. "I must pass," St. Georges repeated.

Hugh smiled wider. "And you have my leave to do so."

St. Georges stared down at the tangle of cables, grabbing ground-crew hands, and McGillicuddy's tree-trunk legs. Pointing at the latter, St. Georges raised his chin. "I know nothing of your Irish military *customs,* but in our service, this man must make way for me when I approach. You:"—he addressed the word sharply to McGillicuddy—"move! At once!"

Hugh had just decided that St. Georges was able to annoy him after all, when the aeronaut of the hour—lean and lively Tearlach Mulryan—jumped between them. He made his appeal with a lopsided grin. "Lieutenant St. Georges, the chief of our ground crew, McGillicuddy, regrets being unable to move aside, but he is hard at his duties. The equipment for the balloon is rather cumbersome and hard to control during deployment."

"Then he can at least show proper deference to his betters, and excuse himself."

"Sir, he does not understand French, and his English is imperfect. He is from a remote area of Ireland, and speaks little but Gaelic."

"Then use that tongue to acquaint him with my displeasure!"

Mulryan did so. McGillicuddy listened to young Tearlach's fluent stream of Gaelic gravely. Toward the end, the big crew chief brightened, looked up at St. Georges and smiled. *"Pog ma thoin,"* he offered sincerely.

"What did he say?"

"'A thousand pardons.'"

"That's better." St. Georges marched briskly off.

Hugh turned carefully astern, looked into the brightening east, and did not allow his expression to change.

Someone came to stand beside him: McCarthy. "Okay, what's the joke?"

"Joke?"

"Don't give me that. You're wearing your best poker-face and the ground crew is about to split a gut. What gives?"

"Mulryan translated *'pog ma thoin'* incorrectly."

"So it's not 'a thousand pardons?'"

"No. It's 'kiss my ass.' And by the way, McGillicuddy speaks perfect English."

Hugh glanced at Mike and saw the hint of a smile that matched his own. Then McCarthy shook his head and looked up at the dull blue-gray canvas swelling over their heads. "C'mon," he said, "let's go fly a balloon."

Hugh watched McCarthy snug Tearlach into the heavy flight harness. It was fundamentally just an extension of the gondola, which was itself little more than a tall apple basket. McCarthy, Mulryan, and the ground crew went through all the "preflight checks" that Hugh himself had memorized, having now watched the process a dozen times. But just as he expected to see the final, confirmatory thumbs-up, Michael tugged an old back-pack out of the port quarter tackle locker. From that bag, he produced a heavily modified and retrofitted metal contraption that might have started out as some species of up-timer lantern or field stove, now capped by a home-built nozzle-and-cone fixture. The only identifying mark was no help in discerning the purpose of the device. Near the base of the dark green metal tube, a legend was stamped in bold white block letters: "Coleman."

O'Rourke drew alongside Hugh and jutted his chin at the odd machine. "First time I've seen that tinker's nightmare."

"Me, too."

"And I've been on hand for almost all the development of the balloon, y' know."

"I know."

"And I don't think McCarthy shared this little toy with the French, m'lord."

"I think you're right," Hugh said slowly, watching as McCarthy tutored Mulryan in the simple operation of this new "toy," which, from McCarthy's overheard explanation, seemed to be an up-time auxiliary burner which could be used to extend flight time or gain further altitude.

McCarthy backed away from Mulryan and gave his customary benediction, which was, he had explained, a tradition among balloonists from his century: "Soft winds and gentle landings." And then he continued in a surprisingly fatherly tone. "Now don't be in too much of a rush. First, make a full three-hundred-sixty degree observation just to detect ships and other objects of interest. Then, conduct a close inspection of each before you signal its bearing, approximate range, and heading if she's under way. Then on to the next."

Tearlach was smiling indulgently at McCarthy's unaccustomed loquacity. "Yes, Don Michael, just the way you've told me. Twenty times, now."

"You ready, then?"

Hugh had the impression that Mulryan might have done anything to get away from stoic Michael McCarthy's unforeseen and unprecedented transmogrification into a nervous biddy. The former Louvain student nodded and smiled wider. The ground crew held tight the guidelines and then released their mooring locks with a sharp clack. Tearlach Mulryan started up gently, and then, with a whoop, surged aloft as the crew played out the lines.

Hugh stepped closer, craned his neck, and watched. "Well, Michael, in your parlance, the balloon is no longer in trials, but 'fully operational.' According to your history books, this is a historic first flight, is it not?"

Michael nodded. "First flight for an expressly military balloon, to my knowledge. Up-time or down-time." Then he looked almost sternly at Hugh. "And while we're on the topic of historic events, here's another: this journey to Trinidad will be your last 'flight' as an exile—the last flight that any Irish earl will ever have to undertake."

Hugh smiled at the optimistic resolve, but was a bit perplexed at the borderline ferocity with which Michael had uttered it. "From your lips to God's ear, my friend."

But Michael was looking at the balloon again. "First flight. And last flight. My word on it." He must have felt Hugh's curious stare, but he did not look over.

❖   ❖   ❖

Hugh stood, arms folded, intentionally radiating avuncular pleasure and approval, as Tearlach Mulryan finished delivering his ground report. The details conformed to what he had relayed from his floating perch using the dit-dah-dit agglomeration of dots and dashes that the up-timers called Morse Code. The channel between St. Eustatia and St. Christopher was all but empty. One vessel, probably a Dutch fluyt, was in the straits but while Mulryan watched, she had weighed anchor and was now hugging the coast westward. She would soon have sailed around, and tucked safely behind, the leeward headland, probably on her way to the relatively new Dutch settlement of Oranjestad. This meant Morraine could begin his approach, and with a strong wind over the starboard quarter, make the windward mouth of the channel before sundown. If the breeze held, Morraine declared he'd stay close to the north side of the channel, running dark along the craggy southern headland of St. Eustatia in order to make an unseen night passage. Barring unforeseen encounters or tricks of the wind, he surmised that, by the middle watch, he'd be raising a glass of cognac to toast the dwindling lights of Basseterre as he looked out his stern-facing cabin windows. Pleased with the prospect of so undetected a passage and such an enjoyable celebration of it, Morraine nodded appreciatively to McCarthy, and disappeared down the companionway into the bowels of the quarterdeck, calling for the navigator and pilot to join him at the chart-table in the wardroom.

Mulryan watched the captain and his all-French entourage depart, and then sidled over toward Hugh and Michael. "My lords," he said with a quick look over his shoulder, "I may have broken our hosts' trust."

Hugh carefully kept his posture unchanged, casual. "In what way, Mulryan?"

"M'lord, I, um, edited my report."

"Did you, now?"

"Yes, m'lord. There's one ship I did not mention. She's directly astern, maybe forty miles, due east. Not much smaller than us, judging from what little I could make of her masts."

"Saw them against the brightening sky?"

"Aye, but not well. I checked her again when the sun came up." He looked at the overcast skies. "So to speak."

"And tell me, Tearlach, why did you choose to 'forget' this piece of information that I'm sure would have been of considerable interest to Captain Morraine?"

"Because sir, unless I am very much mistaken, she was putting up a balloon, too. A white one. Like ours used to be."

Hugh kept himself from starting. "Was it the same design as ours?"

Mulryan grimaced. "M'lord, that new spyglass is a wonder, and my eyes are as good as any in County Mayo, but forty miles is a long way by any measure."

Hugh smiled. "True enough, Tearlach."

"But—another ship with a balloon? What do you think it is, Lord O'Donnell?"

Hugh was considering how best to tactfully phrase his speculations when Michael shared his own—bluntly. "That, young Mulryan, is our master's eye."

"Lord Turenne? He sent a ship after us?"

"He, or Richelieu, almost certainly," Hugh confirmed.

"It only makes sense that he'd want to keep an eye on what we do," Michael conceded. Then, with a smile, "If he can, that is."

Tearlach cocked his head. "What do you mean?"

"I mean that ship can't have seen us today. She was easy for us to spot, silhouetted against the dawn while putting up a white balloon. But, from her perspective, we were against the western predawn darkness, putting up a blue-gray balloon. She didn't see us."

Hugh rubbed his chin. "So that's why you had our balloon painted only after we left Dunkirk. You didn't want Turenne to know you'd camouflaged it."

"Right, and that's why we were four days out before I started running test ascents over three hundred feet. As far as Turenne knows, one hundred yards is as high as we're rated to go. He'll have tried pushing that limit a bit himself, but not as aggressively as we have."

"And he won't have that little toy you gave Tearlach right before he went up."

McCarthy nodded. "Yeah, the boost from the natural gas burner doesn't last long, but it does give you a little extra height. Or time. Which are the edges we need. And by tonight, we'll be so far off, that he won't have any chance to catch sight of us again. Now, 'scuse me. I'm gonna show Mulryan here how to take care of my 'toy.'" And he took the natural gas burner from Tearlach's hands and led the young aeronaut back to the poop deck.

As they left, O'Rourke sauntered over from the rail.

"Heard all that?" asked Hugh.

O'Rourke nodded. "Every word."

"And what do you think?"

"I think McCarthy is shrewd. Maybe too shrewd."

"What do you mean?"

"I know that look, Hugh O'Donnell. You've misgivings of your own."

"But I'll hear yours first, O'Rourke."

"As you wish. So, the ship on our tail couldn't see us today. Bravo. But hardly luck, eh?"

"What do you mean?"

"I mean that McCarthy has had every step of this game sussed out from the start. From before we left France, it seems."

"And that's bad?"

"Not in itself, no. But why didn't he bring us into his confidence on all this earlier? Because rest assured, he's been playing this game of chess five moves ahead of the opposition, he has."

"What do you mean?"

"I mean that he obviously foresaw that Turenne would send a ship after us. And so he saves some special tricks for our balloon, to make it more than a match for the one Turenne has. But in order to have those tricks at hand, he must have anticipated needing them much earlier. So, from the time he started working in Amiens, he must have been expecting that Turenne would be crafting a secret duplicate balloon off-site, even as he and Haas were constructing the original model."

"Strange, O'Rourke: having an ally with that kind of foresight sounds like a great advantage to me, not a source of worry."

"Aye, but that ally is an advantage only if he shares what he's seen from the peak of his lofty foresight, m'lord. And Don Michael, whatever his reasons might be, did not do so."

"So what are you saying? That he's not to be trusted?"

O'Rourke rubbed his thick nose with a flat, meaty thumb. "I wouldn't be saying so black a thing as that, m'lord. But if Don McCarthy is clever enough to keep important secrets from someone like General Turenne, then isn't it a possibility that he could be keeping important secrets from us, too?"

Hugh nodded and turned his gaze slowly to where Michael McCarthy was tutoring Mulryan, back at the taffrail. "Yes, O'Rourke, there is that possibility. There is definitely that possibility."

Chapter 18

San Juan, Puerto Rico

Barto—the only name he ever gave out because it was the only one he had ever had—ate the third slice of papaya greedily and washed it down with a mix of rum and soursop. The musky taste of the latter mixed well with the local spirit's strong cane flavor. Speaking around the mixture in his mouth, he addressed his host. "So you've business with me, eh? Can't remember when a man in silk trousers had business with me. Now, silk-trousered ladies, on the other hand—" Had Barto's senior "officers" been present, they would have no doubt laughed on cue.

But tonight, Barto had no audience. He was alone with his host, Don Eugenio de Covilla, who now seemed to be attempting to suppress a disgusted sneer, as he had throughout much of the meal. But Barto suspected that his host's duty to Spain and Philip came before indulging in displays of repugnance. "Señor Barto, I most certainly do have business to conduct with a man of your—experience."

Barto leaned back, belched, studied the Spaniard.

A minor functionary recently dispatched from Santo Domingo. A dandy who had probably been in fewer fights than Barto had warts (well, a lot fewer fights, by that count). But the Spaniard reeked of oils and silver, and while Barto had no need of the former, he had both a powerful need and lust for the latter.

Ironically, Barto's increased need of silver was a direct consequence of his corresponding increase in good fortune. His "free company" had grown prodigiously in just the past month. Three weeks ago, while drawing near shore at Neckere Island to take on water and any fruits they could find (scurvy having made yet another general appearance), Barto had come upon a sloop-rigged English packet in the throes of repressing a mutiny. Drawn by gunfire as a shark is drawn by blood, Barto quieted his men and commenced to run close against the far side of the headland at which the packet was moored. After putting his best boarders into his smaller boat—a shallow-hulled pinnace—he swept around the headland, the wind full at his back. He was on them in three minutes; the fight lasted less than half that time. He put the lawful owner, stalwart captain, and loyal crew to the sword—the whole lot weren't worth twenty *reales* in ransom—and put the mutineers to work cleaning the deck and transferring stores and cargoes between this new hull and Barto's two others. With the mutineers added to his ranks, he finally had enough men to consider plundering a larger town, maybe one of the small English settlements just recently established in the Bahamas, or the Dutch enclave that was rumored to have returned to Saba. Such a raid would only swell his coffers slightly, but would at least quiet his crews. They were already

restless and would soon make their displeasure known
to him—in a most pointed fashion, if need be. So,
since a full-scale raid would take more time to plan,
a smaller intermediary action was required to tide
them over and sate their appetites for both rum and
blood. A nuisance, reflected Barto, but it was all part
of a freebooter's life.

He belched again. "You invited me to dinner that
we might talk. So now I've eaten your dinner. What
have we to talk about?"

De Covilla smoothed his moustache. "The matter
is somewhat delicate, Señor Barto. Do I have your
word . . . hmmm, allow me to rephrase: is it understood between us that sharing this information would
attract the special disfavor of His Imperial Majesty
Philip of Spain?"

Barto smiled. He had thought that, having seized
four of Philip's ships, he had already attracted quite
as much of that imperial displeasure as anyone could
hope for. But apparently he had been mistaken. "I
understand. And I hope that His Majesty's representatives will realize that any past, er, indiscretions on my
part regarding his shipping were matters of mistaken
identity. Night actions, you see."

"Of course." De Covilla's smug smile indicated that
he knew Barto never attacked ships after sundown.
"Indeed, the representatives of my liege are not only
willing to pay handsomely in silver, but to provide
you with something else you might find of even more
durable value."

"Which is?"

"Which is a letter of marque."

Despite his attempt at bored nonchalance, this so

took Barto by surprise that he sat up. "A letter of marque, signed by—?"

"No less a personage than the captain-general of Santo Domingo, Don Bitrian de Viamonte."

Barto sneered. "Viamonte the Invalid? Really? He spent his years as governor of Cuba limping through the underbrush, building towers and forts to fend off, er, 'fortune-seekers' like myself. And now he is interested in hiring the very same free-spirited adventurers whom he meant to kill?" Barto snorted as he laughed into the dregs of his drink. "Perhaps de Viamonte's disabilities are not merely physical, hey?"

He had meant that insult to test de Covilla's mettle, to see if the young Spaniard had enough temper in him to burst through his almost effete courtly exterior. Barto was not disappointed. The well-groomed *hidalgo* rose slowly, hand on his rapier. "You will mind your tongue, Señor. The captain-general may suffer from infirmities that the Lord Himself saw fit to inflict upon his body, but perhaps that was to better stimulate the growth of his keen mind and indomitable will. He determined to reduce Cuba's vulnerability to pirates. He achieved that, and evidently you are not so bold as to have personally tested the walls and militias he raised for that purpose. Now he is set upon hiring men for a special mission. He directed me to seek appropriate persons among the self-styled 'brethren of the coast.' I started with you. However, I am under no compulsion to confer the contract upon you, specifically, and so, if you continue your insolence, I will take my *reales* elsewhere. And depending upon the severity of your further slurs, I may ask for the satisfaction of honor that must be demanded in response to your impugning the character and person of the captain-general. Am I clear?"

Barto smiled and lifted his cup. "Bravo. And I actually think you'd be foolish enough to play at swords with me, which you must know to be unwise. So you've a ready heart under that fine silken vest, I'll give you that. And so, to business."

Whatever de Covilla had been expecting, it hadn't been that. "Do you—do you *mock* me, Señor?" His hand turned slowly on the pommel of his rapier.

Barto made his best sour face. "Mock you? I am simply speaking to you plainly and man-to-man, not like some lace-loaded grandee at court. Let me make my words plainer. You'd be a fool to fight me, but you know it, and are still quite ready to cross swords on a matter of honor. You've got *cojones*, and that's what counts. Experience and age will furnish all the other necessary skills in good time. If you live that long. But that's not what we're here to talk about. So, I say again, to business."

De Covilla frowned, fiddled with his sword's hilt uncertainly, and then sat. "Very well, to business. I have offered silver and a letter of marque. Co-signed by the new governor of Cuba, no less: the field-marshal Don Francisco Riaño y Gamboa de Burgos. Whose name and martial reputation is known to you, I imagine."

In fact, Riaño y Gamboa's name was barely known to Barto, who had no idea what military glories might lurk hidden behind it. But de Covilla uttered it with the utterly reliable conviction of youthful loyalty, and so there might be enough truth in it to warrant credence.

But it wasn't the reputation of the governor or the money or the marque that commanded Barto's attention.

Rather, it was the attractiveness of the offer. Or rather, the *excessive* attractiveness of the offer, and the fact that the particulars were not presented up front.

Accordingly, the primary instinct of all successful pirates—wariness—arose in Barto, who frowned his mightiest frown. "Well, this is certainly a most intriguing offer. So far. But I have yet to learn what it is I must do for this handsome—eh, 'reward.'"

De Covilla sipped daintily at his glass of rioja. "It has come to our attention that a ship just recently arrived in the Caribbean will soon make landfall at Trinidad with the intent of taking, and holding, the land around Pitch Lake."

"What the hell for?"

"Does it matter? This banditry is an affront to Philip of Spain's exclusive dominion over the New World as per the Church's own *inter caetera*, and so, it must be prevented."

Barto rubbed his chin. "Very well, but if you know where this ship is bound, and you have Philip's express orders to destroy it, then why not deal with it yourself?"

De Covilla pushed at his goat stew with his fork. "I did not say the orders came from Philip himself, nor that the intelligence came from Europe. Not directly."

Barto leaned his large, hirsute forearms on the table. "Let us speak frankly. I stay alive in this business because I avoid jobs that stink like old fish, and this is starting to smell that way. Make clear the job, the information, and the sources, or I must decline."

De Covilla seemed surprised, but also pleased. "Very well. Last year, a Dutch captain who has apparently started a colony in Suriname—Jakob Schooneman, by name—brought a young American to conduct a brief reconnaissance of the area around Trinidad's Pitch Lake. After a variety of further trespassings and pillagings in His Imperial Majesty Philip's colonies, they both returned to Europe. Some time ago, that same ship, the *Koninck David*, returned and touched on the coast nearby San Juan, probably smuggling. That didn't stop some of her crew from wandering into town for a brief carouse, of course.

"When the *Koninck David*'s assistant purser was in his cups, he told one of our informants that he had overhead this same young American being closely interviewed in Bremen last winter by a good number of his countrymen and unprincipled adventurers. Whereupon a number of this group determined to send a warship to Trinidad to usurp the region around Pitch Lake in order to sell its petroleum riches to the USE. We learned roughly when the ship was due and also that it would not head directly to Trinidad, in order to avoid the heavily trafficked transatlantic route that leads directly into the Grenada Passage, just off Trinidad itself. But more than this we could not learn."

Barto leaned back, folded his arms. So, he was already entering into an ongoing plot rife with treachery, secrets, and informers. However, those were supposed to be his area of special expertise. Accordingly, it made him nervous when the Spanish—or anyone—displayed equal facility with them. Largely because it meant that he might be the one surprised, rather than the one springing the surprise. But balanced against those risks were the incredible benefits to be derived from taking this job, and succeeding. He pushed down his misgivings, and breathed out slowly as he made his response. "So have any of your informers told you how this expedition intends to take, and *hold*, a position on Trinidad? A single ship, even the largest, could not carry enough soldiers and supplies for a quick and lasting conquest."

"We have wondered this, also. But inasmuch as our forces are spread too thin to respond in a timely fashion, this may be precisely what these bandits are counting upon. They hope to have the time to fortify, consolidate, perhaps rally others to their banner while we collect the necessary forces, and authority, from Venezuela, Isla de Margarita and even our more distant colonial *audiencias*."

Barto rubbed his chin. "I have sailed near Trinidad in the past, but not recently. What are the conditions there?"

"They are most unfortunate, since our investiture of that island is indifferent at best. The governor is Cristoval de Aranda, who has held that post without any noteworthy distinction for four years. Indeed, his tenure is somewhat of an embarrassment to the Crown. He has been unable to substantively increase the size of his small colony, which is primarily engaged in the growing of tobacco. Which, it is reported, he then sells illegally to English and Dutch ships, rather than reserving it for the merchants of Spain."

Barto did not point out that it was well known throughout the Caribbean that Spanish ships almost never went to this all-but-forsaken possession of their empire, and that if Aranda didn't sell the tobacco to someone, he would soon be the governor of a ghost-town. Or maybe a graveyard, given the testy native populations on the island. Most of whom preferred any other European settlers over the Spanish. But Barto only nodded sympathetically.

"I suppose Aranda should not be made to bear all the blame himself," de Covilla temporized. "His fortifications are small, guns are few, and the size of his militia laughable. It may not total twenty men, all mustered. Indeed, when he was finally compelled to evict a pack of British interlopers from Punta de Galera on the northeast point of the island a few years ago, he had to appeal to the colony on Margarita Island to raise a sufficient force for the job. Pitiable. However,"—and here the young *hidalgo* fixed a surprisingly direct and forceful gaze upon his dinner guest—"I am told that you, Señor Barto, have a significant force at your disposal, that you are immediately available, and that you specialize in swift, direct, and—above all—final, action."

"That I do, Don de Covilla, that I do."

"Excellent, because that is precisely what will thwart the plans of this new group of interlopers. So, to the details: how many men can you bring with you to Trinidad?"

"It depends."

"'It depends?' Upon what?"

Barto leaned far back in his chair. "It depends upon how many *reales* you have to spend."

"I see. Well, how much would it cost to hire all of your men?"

Barto smiled. "All of your *reales.*"

Chapter 19

St. Eustatia, Caribbean

With the dawn silhouetting the culverins that jutted out aggressively over the ramparts of Fort Orange behind them, Maarten Tromp turned to look into St. Eustatia's wide leeward anchorage. Almost thirty-five hulls lay invisible there, except for the spars that stuck upward from them. *Like crosses in a water-covered graveyard,* he thought gloomily, *Which is what this harbor will become, if we—if I—fail to dance every one of the next steps correctly.*

Soft movement behind him meant the only other man in the skiff, besides the combination steersman and sail-handler, had approached. "Should we take you straight to the *Amelia*, Admiral?" asked Jakob Schooneman, captain of the Dutch fluyt *Koninck David*. A merchant, an adventurer, and now, quite obviously, a confidential agent for the United Provinces and possibly for the USE as well, Jakob Schooneman had been absent from the Caribbees for many months. He had made a northern passage back to the New World, touching at several places along the Atlantic coastline,

searching for other Dutch ships that could be spared
for Tromp's fleet: the last in this hemisphere flying
Dutch colors after the disastrous Battle of Dunkirk,
not quite two years earlier. Jakob Schooneman's success had been modest, at best.

Tromp nodded, not turning to face Jakob Schooneman, determined not to look him in the eyes until he
could be sure of what the captain would see in his
own. Tromp looked up at the sides of the hull now
looming out of the charcoal-blue mists: the *Amelia*, his
fifty-four-gun flagship, and one of the few to survive
the withdrawal from Dunkirk. He could still see her
as she was during that perilous October flight across
the Atlantic to Recife: her hull scarred and holed by
cannonballs, most of her spars and rigging incongru-
ously new because almost all of what they had sailed
into battle with had been shot away or so badly savaged
that they had to replace it as soon as they knew they
were free of Spanish pursuit. Only the stout mainmast
remained of the original spars, black with both age and
grim resolve. Or so Tromp liked to think.

When he could discern the faint outlines of her
closed gun-ports, he turned to the master of the
Koninck David. "Thank you for coming to see me
directly, Captain Schooneman. Your visit was most
informative."

"Glad to have been of service, Admiral."

"Which we are happy to return. The lighters will
be out with your provisions by noon. You are sure
that none of your men wish shore liberty?"

Jakob Schooneman smiled crookedly. "'Wish it?' They
most certainly do. I wish it myself. But circumstances
dictate otherwise, wouldn't you agree, Admiral Tromp?"

Tromp suppressed a sigh as he looked into the purple-gray western horizon. "Yes, they do." Now close abeam his flagship, Tromp called up to the anchor watch. The ship above him was silent for the moment it took for the watch officer to stick his head over the gunwale, squint down and determine that yes, it truly was the admiral arriving before the full rose of dawn was in the sky. Then the *Amelia*'s weather deck exploded into a cacophony of coronets and drums which rapidly propagated into the lower decks as well.

"Nothing like an unannounced inspection to set the men on their toes, eh, Admiral?"

"Indeed. And it is a serviceable pretext, today." An accommodation ladder was dropped down along the tumbledown of *Amelia*'s portside hull. In response, the skiff's tiller-man lashed his handle fast and grabbed up a pole to bump against the fifty-four-gunner's planking, keeping them off. Tromp put out his hand. "Fair weather and good fortune to you, Captain. You have need of both, it seems."

Jakob Schooneman's lopsided smile returned. "I shall not deny it. And you, Admiral, the same to you."

Tromp nodded, prepared to ascend, thought *Yes, I need fair weather and good fortune, too. For all our sakes.*

Tromp was surprised to see lanky Willem van der Zaan waiting for him at the forward companionway. It was Tromp's wont—indeed, most officers'—to first head aftwards for their berths. But here was Willi, waiting at the forecastle, his cuffs rolled up neatly and pinned, even.

Tromp managed not to smile at the fresh-faced youngster's quick nod and winning smile. "You are up early, Mr. van der Zaan. And more mysterious still, you knew to wait for me here, at the other end of the ship from my quarters. Have you been consorting with sorcerers?"

"No, Admiral. Just watchful."

"You saw me coming?"

"No, sir . . . but I was standing the last leg of the middle watch and saw the fluyt that came in slow and quiet from the north. At night. Passing other ships at anchorage without a hail."

Tromp stared at Willem. "Little Willi"—what a misnomer, now!—had not just grown in mind and body, but subtlety. A year ago, he might not have come to such a quick and certain surmise that the incoming ship's quiet approach signified an ally wishing to make a brief, surreptitious visit. Instead, he would have reflexively sounded an alarm signifying that pirates were upon them under cover of night. "You are very observant, Willi."

"I am the admiral's eager pupil, sir. If I'm not mistaken, that was the *Koninck David*, sir, wasn't it?"

"Mmm. And how did you know?"

"Captain Schooneman's rigging, sir. He's always ready to run as near to the wind as he can."

Because he's often working in dangerous waters, gathering, or carrying, confidential information. Tromp felt his smile slacken even as his pride in van der Zaan grew. *All of which you know, don't you, Willi? Knowledge is what brings childhood's end, and you are indeed Little Willi no longer. Which means that now, you will face the same duties—and dangers—as the rest of us. May*

God watch over you, dear boy, for from here on, my ability to do so will be greatly reduced.

They passed the galley. Urgent sounds of hurry that bordered on chaos spilled out.

"Early to be serving breakfast," observed Tromp.

"Turning out for the admiral," was the respectful correction offered by van der Zaan, as they passed. "I suspect the cook will be putting an extra few rashers of bacon on, today. Do you not wish to inspect?"

Tromp nodded. "Yes, but they are doing well to be about their business so smartly. I shall give them time to make good their special preparations." He turned to his young assistant. "Letting men succeed, particularly in a special task which they have taken up on their own initiative, builds their pride. Which builds their morale."

"Yes, Admiral," said Willi with a smile which also said, *As you have well and often taught me, and as I have well and fully learned.* After a moment, he added, almost cautiously, "You seem distracted, sir."

If you only knew. "Not at all, Mr. van der Zaan. I am simply quiet when I am most attentive."

"Ah. Yes, sir. Of course, sir."

Is that a way of saying, "Of course I will agree to your obvious lie, sir"? Well, no matter.

Willi followed Tromp to the next ladder down. "Where are we headed, sir?"

Tromp stopped, hands on either side of the almost vertical between-deck stairs that seamen called "ladders." He looked at the young man gravely; he knew that the moment he uttered their first inspection site, Willi would know what was in store, what kind of news had come in from the *Koninck David* in the small hours of the morning. "The bilges, young Willem. We are going to the bilges."

Willem van der Zaan's eyes widened. Because he had not forgotten—*how could he?*—Maarten Tromp's weekly litany about preparing for battle: "You check the ship from keel to foretop. You do it yourself. Meaning you start in the bilges."

"The bilges?" van der Zaan almost whispered, looking very much like Little Willi again.

Tromp just nodded and headed below.

Tromp was still trying to wipe the stink of the bilge water off his hands when he returned to the galley. The ship was in readiness—he had expected no less—and despite the long wait for action, she was well-caulked and her gear made fast with tight lashings and adequate dunnage. But the inescapable fact was that there was simply less gear than there should have been. Dry goods were low, as was cordage and canvas. They had managed to procure some through the intercession of Sir Thomas Warner, the English—*well, now state-less*—governor of nearby St. Christopher. But sails came at quite a price, since Warner got the canvas via the occasional traffic from Bermuda. Wherever possible, Tromp and his fleet of almost forty ships had adopted local expedients in place of Old World manufactures, but good, reliable chandlery—to say nothing of nails, tools, and metal fixtures of all kinds—was not being produced in the Caribbees, or anywhere in the New World, outside the greatest of the Spanish ports.

Even rags, Tromp reflected, continuing the futile task of cleaning his hands with a towel already inundated with bilge water, even rags were rare enough commodities, here. What weaving the locals did was crude, and not suitable to all purposes.

"Shall I fetch you another towel, sir?" Willi asked as he peered into the evidently expectant mess.

"No use, Willi. Let's not keep the cook waiting."

The watch officers had taken advantage of the admiral's inspection of *Amelia*'s orlop deck and stores to rouse the first watch out of hammocks and make for the galley, where the cook (one of the few that had all his limbs) had set about building his fires and preparing the food, all the while debating provisions with the purser, as usual. However, the moment the admiral entered, the men, regardless of rank or age, looked up expectantly, with the suppressed smiles of boys who've done their chores early and without being told to.

Tromp suppressed a smile himself, nodded to the cook. "Up early today, are we, Ewoud?"

Ewoud effected dour annoyance. "It is as the admiral says. These louts couldn't wait to fill their bellies today. Can't think why. Sir."

"No, me either," agreed Tromp, going along with the act. The men grinned. As had sailors from the dawn of time, they had a natural affinity for a quiet, firm commander who could enjoy and acknowledge a joke without becoming part of it himself. "What feast have you set on today?"

There was a quick exchange of glances—none too friendly—between the purser and the cook before the latter waved at the simmering pots with a hand that invited inspection. "Well sir, this morning I thought we'd depart from local fare, and—"

Tromp shook his head. "A nice gesture, Ewoud—and Mr. Brout," he added with a glance at the purser who had no doubt pushed Ewoud to use the Old World supplies, "but there are to be no exceptions while we are in port. Local foodstuffs only."

"But sir," Brout explained, hands opening into an appeal, "soon, even the peas will spoil if we do not—"

"Mr. Brout," Tromp let his voice go lower, less animated, and then turned to face the suddenly quiet purser, "I assure you, I have the spoilage dates of all our dry goods well in mind. And they do not worry me." *Particularly since, after today, we'll be finishing them up quickly enough.* "Do I make myself clear?"

Brout looked as though he might have soiled himself. "Yes, Admiral. Perfectly clear."

Ewoud was trying hard not to smile, and, satisfied, sent his young assistant—barely thirteen, from the look of him—scurrying to swap around the bags and casks of waiting food. "Tapioca and mango, then. Smoked boar for a little flavor." The mess-chiefs who'd come down from each group of mess-mates sighed. Tapioca and cassava crackers were the new staple of the Dutch navy. Such as it was.

Tromp looked over Ewoud's broad, sweat-glistening shoulders deeper into the galley and saw familiar bags and barrels with Dutch markings. *The last of the foodstuffs we sailed with, of the meals that we thought we'd eat until the day the sea swallowed us up instead.* Whether on the Dutch ships that had sailed into disaster at Dunkirk or on those moored in safety at Recife, there was little variation in the bill of fare that had been loaded into their holds before leaving the United Provinces of the Netherlands.

Each day had begun with bread and groat-porridge, and lunch had been less of the same, but usually with strips of dried meat and also a sizeable part of the daily portion of cheese. Sunday dinner meant half a pound of ham or a pound of spiced lamb or salted meat with beans. On Monday, Tuesday and Wednesday fish with peas or beans was on the menu. On Thursday it was a pound of beef or three ounces of pork and on Friday and Saturday it was fish again. But long before the food ran out, the beer was gone. Since it spoiled comparatively quickly, it was an early-journey drink.

Even before the disaster at Dunkirk, the admiralties of the United Provinces had also taken a page from the books of the up-timers, and citrus or other fruits had been part of the provisions on the way out, and then, were a high priority item to acquire as soon as landfall was made in the New World. Happily, that was easily accomplished. And if the transition from gin to rum had been strange, it was not unpleasant, and Tromp had to admit that it mixed with a wider variety of the local juices. Indeed, it turned a cup of soursop from a rather musky, acquired taste, into a delightful and reputedly healthful drink.

But what started as a few expedient replacements for Old World comestibles had now become a wholesale substitution of them, since the familiar foods of home had no way to reach them. It had been a month since Tromp had enjoyed bread made from anything other than cassava, and longer since he had any meat other than goat. But at least he had two full meals a day, which was more than could be said for the almost three thousand people who were his charges on St.

Eustatia. And now, he would have to dip deeply into already-scant stockpiles of durable food—

"Mr. Brout, you are to be given the first helping of breakfast."

"Why—yes, Admiral. Thank you."

"Do not thank me. It is so you may go ashore as soon as possible. You are to requisition as much salt fish, smoked goat, dried fruit, and hard-baked cassava loaves as you can find. Tapioca for porridge, and beans, too."

"I am to 'requisition' it, sir?"

"Yes. We will settle accounts later." *If we're alive to do it.* "You are to return by noon. The supplies are to be loaded by nightfall."

"Admiral, that leaves me little time to negotiate for a fair—"

"Mr. Brout, you do not have time to negotiate. You will see that the holds of our ships are provided with three months' rations, at a minimum. You are to begin by calling upon Governor Corselles. He will have my message by now, and will accompany you to ensure the compliance of your suppliers." *And to watch out for your own profiteering proclivities, Brout.*

Whose eyes were wide. "Yes, Admiral. If I may ask, are we soon to weigh anchor—?"

But Tromp was already out the door and into the narrow passageway. He was halfway up the ladder to the gun deck before the raucous buzz of hushed gossip surged out of the galley below him.

Willi, at Tromp's heels, laughed softly.

"Something amusing, Mr. van der Zaan?"

"Yes, sir. Very much, sir."

"And what is it?"

"How an admiral of so few and such quiet words can work up so many men so very quickly."

Tromp shrugged and turned that motion into an arm-boost that propelled him up onto the gun deck with satisfying suddenness. Men who were hunched in whispering clusters came to their feet quickly. Over his shoulder, he muttered, "A man who yells does so because he is unsure that he is in command. Remember that, Willi."

"I will, sir."

Tromp, walking with his hands behind his back, nodded acknowledgments to the respectful greetings he received from each knot of befuddled seamen. However, his primary attention was on the guns. The last of the culverins were gone, as he had ordered. In their place were cannon, although one of those was only a twenty-two-pounder, or "demi-cannon." But each deck's broadsides would be a great deal more uniform now: another up-timer optimization that tarrying at their Oranjestad anchorage had enabled. Gone was the mix of culverin and cannon of various throw-weights and the occasional saker, and with them, the variances of range and effectiveness that made naval gunnery even more of a gamble than it already was.

He popped a tompion out of a cannon's muzzle and felt around within the mouth of the barrel. He found it sufficiently dry, and with a paucity of pitting that testified to the routine nature of its care. Salt water was a hard and corrosive taskmaster.

Admirably anticipating his next point of inspection, a gunner came forward at a nod from his battery chief and made to open a ready powder bag. Tromp nodded approval and turned to young van der Zaan.

"Fetch Lieutenant Evertsen to find me here. He'll need to complete the inspection. Then make for the accommodation ladder."

"Why, sir? Are you expecting—?"

A single coronet announced a noteworthy arrival on the weather deck.

"Yes," Tromp answered, "I am expecting visitors. Now go."

Tromp looked up when, without warning, the door to his great cabin opened and Jan van Walbeeck entered. "You're late," the admiral muttered.

"I am more informed than I would have been had I hurried to be on time," retorted van Walbeeck with his trademark impish grin. He pulled up a chair and sat, heavy hands folded and cherubic smile sending creases across his expansive cheeks. Full-faced for a man of thirty-five, his jowls were apparently not subject to privations in the same way the rest of his now-lean body was. He, along with the other three thousand refugees from Recife, had narrowly avoided the specter of starvation over the past year. But somehow, van Walbeeck still had his large, florid jowls.

Tromp waited and then sighed. "Very well, I will ask: and what additional information did your tardiness vouchsafe?"

"I tarried on deck to exchange a few pleasantries with your first mate, Kees Evertsen. While there, a Bermuda sloop made port. Down from Bahamas, freighting our neighbors' sugar for relay to Bermuda. And as chance would have it, one of our most notable neighbors was on board."

Tromp frowned. By "neighbors," van Walbeeck

meant the English on St. Christopher's island, which was already visible as a dawn-lit land mass out the admiral's south-facing stern windows. A "notable visitor," meant the person was not of the very first order of importance, so it was not the governor, Sir Thomas Warner himself. Indeed, the "Sir" part of Warner's title was somewhat in doubt. Technically, shortly before the League of Ostend arose, Charles Stuart of England had ceded all his New World possessions to Richelieu. Or so the French maintained. And it was probably close to, or the very, fact. The English crown's protest over that interpretation was, to put it lightly, muted. However, the popular English outcry over losing its New World possessions had grown intense enough to propel the already paranoid Charles into a dubious course of instituting loyalty oaths and a standing, special court for the investigation and hearing of purported cases of sedition.

So was Thomas Warner's patent of nobility still effective, his governorship still legal? Not under the aegis of English law, but until someone took the island from him, the dispute was pointless. And given how these uncertain times required his full attention and involvement in the well-being of his now isolated colony, Tromp would have been surprised had he been the visitor to St. Eustatia. But there was another likely candidate. "Lieutenant Governor Jeafferson?"

"Bravo, Maarten! Your powers of deduction are undiminished. It was Jeafferson himself on the sloop, which must have left St. Christopher's in the dark of the night to be here so early. And you know what that means—"

Tromp sighed. Jan van Walbeeck was arguably the

single smartest, most capable man he had ever met, and he had met plenty of them. But his irrepressible ebullience—even at this hour of the morning—was sometimes a bit wearing for, well, normal people like himself. "Yes, Jan, I think I do. He's here to finalize and sign our five-year lease of the lands south of Sandy Point."

"Exactly. And thereby kill two birds with one stone: we get the arable land we need, and Thomas Warner gets the guards he wants. And frankly, we need to reduce the number of soldiers we have here on St. Eustatia."

Tromp laid aside his protractor and looked up from his charts. "And you feel certain this will not bring us into conflict with the French colony on the island?"

Van Walbeeck blew out his cheeks. "Who is certain of anything, Maarten? Indeed, who can say who will hold power over us, or these islands, when the lease is up in five years? But this much is true. The French had only one ship arrive last year, and that was before we arrived. As best we can tell, Warner's colony has grown to almost nine thousand, maybe more. The French have barely a tenth of that. So I think that it is unlikely there will be any trouble."

Tromp frowned. "So then, if that is true, I ask—as I have before—why is Warner so concerned with having our guards? What are we not seeing—and he not saying?"

Van Walbeeck nodded. "I think I have a little more perspective on that, now that our farmers and his farmers are talking with each other on a regular basis. Firstly, Warner has all his people gainfully employed, and most in food production of one sort or another.

Would that we could say the same. So the same people who man his militia are also the only ones available to oversee the workers and the plantations."

"You mean, guard and drive his slaves."

"Maarten, I know how you feel about slavery, and I share those feelings, but these are the conditions as we found them, and the best we can do is work to change them. And it won't be easy, given the tales our planters are telling his."

Tromp stared at his charts, at the outline of St. Christopher's. "I can only imagine. Our decision to prohibit slaveholding has not made me a popular man."

"You? *You?*" Jan leaned forward. "Maarten, you are not the president of the *Politieke Raad.* You don't have our planters screaming for your blood. Well, not so loudly as for mine, at any rate."

"And Corselles is still no help?"

"How can he be? I frankly feel sorry for the poor fellow. He arrived here with maybe two hundred and fifty souls, all of whom were assured that they will grow rich like the English planters. Which meant, in short hand, that they will own plantations and the slaves that allow the land to be worked at such a fabulous profit.

"And then, just a year after they arrive, we separately descend upon them like a horde of locusts, almost three thousand strong, ninety percent young or young-ish males, short on rations, and with our military leadership determined to eliminate slavery. Which was what pushed almost half of our farmers into league with their farmers."

Tromp nodded. "And this connects to Warner's want for our guards—how?"

Jan sighed. "Let us presume that he does indeed see that our survival may be the key to his, and vice versa. We are both without support from our homelands, albeit for very different reasons. But if we hang on to St. Eustatia long enough, we'll start seeing flags from our home ports. At that point, the advantage is ours. For Warner is a man without a country. So, while he still enjoys the advantage of being our breadbasket, he will naturally wish to enter into accords with us which will stand him in good stead when that balance of power shifts. And his power is in the food he makes, so he is not eager to have his overseers as his full-time militiamen. Food production will drop and with it, his fortunes."

Tromp looked up from the map. "That seems to track true, yes."

"Ah, but there's more, Maarten. He doesn't just want guards; he wants *our* guards. Dutch guards."

"Why? Are we Dutch especially good at guarding things? Even things that do not belong to us?"

"No, but our guards operate under the aegis of our flag. So if the French try cases with them—"

"Yes, of course. Then there is an international incident. And since Warner is no longer in charge of an 'English' colony, he has no such protection of his own."

"Precisely. The only thing that gives the French pause about running Warner off the island is the question of whether or not they can physically achieve it. But if his colony's guards are our men, with the flag of Orange flying above, the French risk a war. And if there is anything we have an overabundance of in this area, it is soldiers."

"Yes, but Warner seems to be acquiring their services

far earlier than he needs to. He has little to worry about from such a small French colony."

Van Walbeeck shook his head. "Except that the French colonists are not the direct threat. It is the dissent they have been successful at breeding among the English slaves, and some of the indentured workers from Ireland. And there is rumor that the French commander d'Esnambuc has been parleying with the natives as well. The Kalinago still want St. Christopher's back, you know."

Tromp stood. "Very well. So Warner wants our guards. When will the lease go into effect?"

"It will still be a few months, at least. Our people are eager to put the tracts around Sandy Point under cultivation, but it will take time to get them ready, to gather the equipment, to settle affairs here. And the same goes for determining which troops shall go."

Tromp shook his head. "Since we are so close—a morning's sail—there is no reason to make our forces on St. Christopher a fixed garrison. We shall rotate troops through the station, as we shall their commanders. I want our people to both know that island and to get a break from this one."

Van Walbeeck nodded enthusiastically. "Most prudent. And speaking of guards, I'm wondering if we shouldn't set up some special detachments of them here, too."

Tromp folded his arms. "You mean, here in Oranjestad? We already have greatly oversized guard complements on all our warehouses, on the batteries, the outposts, the—"

"We need them on the women, Maarten. Particularly the visiting English ladies."

"The ladies—?" And then Tromp understood. "Oh."

"Yes. 'Oh.' Maarten, there are fewer than four hundred women on St. Eustatia, out of almost three thousand persons, more if you count our shipboard crews. Most of the four hundred women are already married. And you have seen the effects, surely."

Tromp surely had. Brawls, drunken or otherwise, had been steadily increasing for six months. And however the causes and particulars varied, there was usually a common thread: it had started over a woman. It may have been that the woman in question had never spoken to, perhaps never even looked at, any of the combatants, but that hardly mattered. Like a bunch of young bucks in rutting season, any incident that could in any way be construed as a dispute over mating dominance resulted in locked horns. "What do you suggest?" he asked van Walbeeck.

"Cuthbert Pudsey."

"The English mercenary who's been in our ranks from Recife onward? A one man guard-detachment?"

"Maarten, do not be willfully obtuse. Of course not. Pudsey is to be the leader of, let us call it a 'flying squad' of escorts who will accompany any English ladies who come to call at Oranjestad. And given that it will be a merit-earned duty—"

"Yes. Perfect comportment and recommendations will be the prerequisite for being posted to that duty. With any brawling resulting in a six month disqualification from subsequent consideration. But really, Jan, you do not think our men would actually go so far as—?"

"Maarten, I will not balance the safety of the English ladies who visit—or perhaps, in the future, seek shelter with—us on my projections or hopes. We will assume the worst. And in the bargain, some lucky guards will come near enough to recall that ladies do, indeed, sweat—excuse me, *perspire*—in this weather. That they are not such perfect creatures, after all." Van Walbeeck squinted as the light rose sharply on the table before them. The sun had finally peeked around the steep slope of the volcanic cone that was known simply as The Quill, St. Eustatia's most prominent feature.

"Hmm. It is still the scent of a woman, Jan. And in circumstances such as ours, that will only quicken their starved ardor."

"No doubt, and no helping it. But charged with protecting the English ladies, I feel fairly certain that our guards would more willingly die defending them than protecting me."

"Far more willing," drawled Tromp,

"While you are around," smiled Walbeeck, "I shall never lose my soul to the sin of Pride. You are my guardian angel."

Tromp grunted as he felt the sunlight grow quick and warm on the side of his face. "A more improbable guardian angel there has never been."

"And yet here you sit, wearing a halo!" Walbeeck grinned, gesturing to the sun behind Tromp. "Now, have you decided to stop serving coffee on this sorry hull of yours?"

"Not yet," said Tromp, who almost smiled.

Two hours later, the coronet pealed again. Tromp frowned at Walbeeck's sudden and serious glance at the rum.

"Just one swallow. For perseverance in the face of immovable objects and irremediable ignorance."

"Jan, don't reinforce our enemies' characterization of us."

"Whatever do you mean?"

"You know perfectly well what I mean. Our resolve in battle is too often linked to our bolting shots of gin just before. 'Dutch courage,' they call it."

"Well, I could use a little of that courage right about now..."

The dreaded knock on the door was gentle enough but felt like a death knell to Tromp. "Enter," he said, trying to keep the sigh out of his voice. He flattered himself to imagine that he had succeeded.

The group that entered was not quite as ominously monolithic as he had feared. There were friendly faces among those crowding into the *Amelia's* suddenly claustrophobic great cabin. Servatius Carpentiere and "Phipps" Serooskereken had been part of the *Politieke Raad* at Recife, and early converts to the exigency-driven agricultural changes that they had brought to St. Eustatia. But Jehan de Bruyne, also a member of that body, had been diametrically opposed from the start, and remained so, now drawing support from original Oranjestad settlers Jan Haet and Hans Musen, whose expectations of quick wealth had been dashed by the arrival of Tromp's ships and slavery injunctions.

Respectful nods notwithstanding, Musen was quick to confirm both the purpose and tenor of this visit by the determinative civil bodies of the St. Eustatia colony. "Admiral Tromp, we are sorry to disturb you on this busy day—"

—not half as sorry as I am—

"—but we have just learned that you will be setting sail soon. Today, it is rumored."

Tromp shrugged. "There are always rumors. Please continue."

Musen looked annoyed. "Very well. Since no one seems to know, or is willing to say, when you might return, we must make an appeal now, relevant to upcoming matters of commercial importance."

Tromp had had cannon aimed at him with less certainty of fell purpose. "Yes?"

"Admiral, you have forbidden the acquisition of new slaves with which to work the plantations here on St. Eustatia—"

"—which we still protest!" Jan Haet put in archly.

"—but we presume that this would not apply to any farms established on land that is not Dutch-owned."

Tromp resisted the urge to grind his molars. *And damn me for a fool that I did not see this coming.* "Mr. Musen, allow me to prevent you from spending time here profitlessly. The rules that apply on St. Eustatia apply equally to any plantations you may put in place on St. Christopher's."

"But that is English land!" shouted Jan Haet.

"But under our dominion while we lease it!" retorted Phipps Serooskereken.

"Immaterial," countered Musen coolly. "The terms of use permitted on the tracts around Sandy Point were made quite explicitly by Lord Warner: use of slaves is expressly permitted."

Jan van Walbeeck smiled broadly, and perhaps a bit wickedly. "Then perhaps you are preparing to swear loyalty to Thomas Warner?"

The various combatants started at him.

"Because, logically, that is what you must intend."

Jan Haet, as ardent a Dutch nationalist as he was a

slaveholder, rose up to his full height of 5'5". "I intend
no such thing, and you know it, Jan van Walbeeck!"

"Do I? Here is what I know. Fact: Lord Warner
may no longer be a lord at all. England has renounced
claim to the land he holds and upon which his title is
based. Fact: your actions are not constrained by what
he permits, but by what this regional authority allows
you to do, as a Dutchman, in this place and time. And
you have been forbidden from acquiring more slaves.
So unless you wish to renounce your citizenship in the
United Provinces, what Thomas Warner permits you
to do is secondary to what your government permits.
And fact: swearing allegiance to Warner makes you
men without a country and therefore invalidates you
from working the leased land at Sandy Point, since
that agreement exists solely between the representatives of the United Provinces and Thomas Warner."
Jan Walbeeck smiled. "But of course, you can always
become citizens of Thomas Warner's nation. If he ever
declares one, that is."

Jehan de Bruyne had been frowning slightly at
the deck throughout the exchange. "I will ask you
to reconsider your ruling on slavery one last time,
Maarten. I am not sure you understand the degree of
dissatisfaction it is causing among our people."

*Oh, I understand Jehan. I even understand the
veiled threat in your calm tone.* Tromp folded his
hands. "Mijn heer de Bruyne, your own council,
the *Politieke Raad*, voted in support of this measure. And I remain unclear how you can conclude
that a slave population poses no credible threat to
our security here. You have only to look at Thomas
Warner's experience. In the last seven years, he has

had to struggle to maintain control over his colony. And why? Not threat from the Caribs: they no longer appear willing to try cases with him. No, his problems arise from resentment and rebelliousness among his slave population."

Musen sniffed. "That is because the French keep stirring the pot."

"That may even be true, Hans, but would we be immune to such trouble? The French see the English as interlopers; why should they see us any differently? Indeed, given the presence of our forces on the island, will they not consider us an even greater problem? Because once we arrive and provide both plantation and border security for Thomas Warner, they will have even less chance to displace him—and us. Unless, that is, we bring our own slaves, whom they would no doubt attempt to suborn as well."

Tromp leaned back and shook his head. "No. People who have no freedom have little to lose. When slaves are being worked to death, they understand quickly enough that soon they will also lose the last thing they value: their lives, and those of their families. At that point, it is only logical for them to risk the probable suicide of unarmed rebellion rather than continue toward the certain suicide of eventually dying of malnourished exhaustion in the fields."

Haet leaned in aggressively. "And then why are the Spanish so successful using slaves, Tromp? They seem to do well enough and get rich while doing it."

Tromp studied Haet calmly but very directly. "Because, mijn heer Haet, the Spanish are not hanging on by their fingernails, as we are. They are routinely resupplied, routinely reinforced, and routinely involved in ruthlessly squashing any hint of resistance in their subject populations."

"And the Dutch East India Company does no less. And thrives!" countered Haet.

Jan van Walbeeck spoke quietly and without any trace of his customary animation. "I have been to those colonies, Haet, have been among their slaves. Have seen, have *felt*, the hatred for us in their eyes, in their gestures, in their quiet, patient watching. Are those Pacific colonies profitable? Yes, most certainly. Are they safe? Only so long as you have guns trained on the slaves, Haet. And one day—and it will only take *one* day—we will be weak, or forgetful, and we will stumble. And they will slaughter us and drive us back into the seas which brought us like a curse to their shores."

Haet snorted. "So you prefer the natives to your own kind, van Walbeeck?"

"Haet, I don't have to prefer them in order to understand that their feelings about us enslaving them on their own land are identical to our feelings about the Spanish doing the same to us in the Netherlands. And you remember what we did to the Spanish when we finally got the chance."

Haet was going to speak, but swallowed whatever words he might have spoken.

Tromp exchanged glances with van Walbeeck. Good: the conversation had remained on a practical footing. The ethical discussions over slavery had long ago proven themselves to be emotional morasses which achieved nothing but the expenditure of countless, profitless, hours. And they invariably led to the slaveholding faction accusing their opponents of succumbing to up-time influence (often true) and, by extrapolation, being Grantville's lackeys (not at all true). Indeed, since adolescence, Tromp had been disquieted by the circuitous rationalizations his countrymen and others employed when resolving their Christian piety with their grasp upon the slaveholder's whip. But, as an admiral, his life had not had much direct involvement with such matters, or the resolution of such issues.

But here in a New World where the Dutch colonies were hanging on by a thread that only remained uncut because the Spanish had not yet discovered it, the domain of the military and the commercial had begun to overlap. With no help or even news coming from the United Provinces, all choices, all decisions made locally had a bearing upon all other local decisions. And so Tromp had been compelled to weigh both the practical and ethical burdens and benefits of slavery.

Van Walbeeck, having arrived in Oranjestad ahead of him, had been an invaluable interlocutor on the matter, and the smattering of copied up-time texts in his library had been the catalyst for their discussions and grist for much deep thought. Leaving Recife, Tromp had been leaning against slavery for practical reasons, which happily aligned with his largely unstudied ethical misgivings. But the past year at St. Eustatia had confirmed him in the belief that, just as he had felt it his duty to become a church deacon if he was to live a Christian life and not merely profess one, so too he could not truly call himself a Christian without also working to undo the institution of slavery.

Van Walbeeck turned mild eyes upon the gathered contingent of councilors. "Any other observations on the matter?"

The quiet, careful Servatius Carpentiere, shrugged. "There will be much unrest among the colonists, particularly since the *Politieke Raad* approved your recommendation to prohibit raising tobacco." His voice was apologetic. One of Tromp's most stalwart supporters, Carpentiere was raising an issue that clearly had been pressed upon him by the colonists, but would certainly play into the hands of the admiral's detractors.

Musen lost no time wielding it as a rhetorical weapon. "You see, Admiral? Your own hand-picked advisers from Recife foresee problems with your decisions. First you prohibit the further acquisition of slaves. Then you urge the growing of cane sugar, which involves immense amounts of labor, in place of tobacco, which is much easier to grow and harvest. And which was why most of us came to Oranjestad in the first place."

Tromp nodded. "Yes. That is true. And when you came, tell me: what did you plan to do with the tobacco?"

Haet, not seeing the trap, blurted out, "Why, sell it, of course!"

"Where?"

"Back in—" and he stopped.

Tromp just nodded again. "Exactly. 'Back in the Provinces.' Or 'Europe.' It hardly matters where, specifically. The problem is that those markets are an ocean away from us here, and our own ports are unreachable, due to the Spanish. What few ships remain sheltered in smaller harbor towns are merely jachts which have no reason to brave the swells of the Atlantic. And even if they knew we still existed here, ready to trade, what of it? Yes, jachts are fast, nimble ships. But useless for freighting smoke or anything else in bulk. So tell me, mijn heer Haet, given the changes since you arrived here, where, now, would you sell your tobacco?"

Musen smoothly changed the footing of his side's argument to a less disastrous posture. "Even if that were to be true, Admiral—cane sugar? The most labor-intensive crop in the New World?"

"And the only one for which we have any local use," replied van Walbeeck. "What else would you grow for high profit? Cotton? The labor is almost as bad as cane but, again, there's the same problem: where would you sell that cotton? The fact that drives all our choices is this, mijn heer Musen: we no longer have access to markets. Our ships cannot come here safely, and we cannot spare any to undertake the equally peril-ous voyage from here to Europe. And what's more, any regular commerce between us and our homeports would only tell the Spanish—or others—where to find us, where to hunt us down and exterminate us.

"So we grow sugar. We may eat it ourselves, and we may make rum—which has local value even to the natives, in these parts. And which we may further refine into disinfectants and a flammable fluid. And if we cannot grow so much because we have no slaves? Well, first, we have no shortage of able-bodies without tasks to occupy them. And so we will learn that you do not need slaves to grow cane, and thereby set the pattern for creating a durable local economy which is not based upon slavery."

Haet looked as though he might spit. "I did not come here to work like a dog in the fields. I came here to get rich."

Tromp nodded. "Yes. But apparently fate had other plans."

Jehan de Bruyne rubbed his chin. "Or perhaps it is Maarten Tromp that has had other plans."

Tromp kept his head and voice very still. "I assure you, mijn heer, that being defeated by treachery at Dunkirk, and seeing the Dutch fleet reduced to three dozen hulls, was not any plan of mine. And it is that outcome—that and no other—which forces these changes upon us. You wished to be rich? Fair enough. I wanted to return home, to my wife and children. As do many of us who fled to Recife." He stood. "What men want is of little matter to the will of God and the hand of fate. I suggest we focus on a new want that we should all share: the desire to stay alive long enough for our own countrymen to find and succor us. Because that outcome is by no means certain." *By no means, indeed.* "Now, mijn heeren, if we are quite done, I have arrangements to make for the fleet. About which you shall be informed shortly. Good day."

The envoys from both the *Politieke Raad* and the original colonists' Council nodded their way toward the door they had entered through. Van Walbeeck rose to go as well, but Tromp motioned him to stay in his seat with a down-waved palm.

When the rest had left, Jan cocked his head like a quizzical spaniel.

Tromp sighed. "Stay and hear what I tell the captains. Someone will need to report it to the *Raad* and Council. And the rest of the colonists, too."

Chapter 20

Maarten had expected the various captains he had summoned to arrive in bunches, being familiar with how the vagaries of currents and oarsmen made it nearly impossible to maintain perfect punctuality when calling a council aboard a single ship in the midst of a wide anchorage.

Nonetheless, just after the first bell of the afternoon watch, the coronet blew only two blasts, the second no more than a minute after the first. Five minutes later, the entire collection of summoned officers were asking Willem for admittance. As soon as the young officer put his head in the door, Tromp made a waving-in motion and spread out the charts he had prepared, the top one being a general map of the Caribbees and the Spanish Main. The precision of its outlines and scale marked it immediately and distinctively as a high quality copy of a map from Grantville.

Cornelis Jol—who was known to all his peers simply as Houtebeen, or Peg Leg—came stumping in first. Immediately after came the big Dane, Hjalmar van

Holst, with a broad smile on his face. Although two more dissimilar men would be hard to find, he and Tromp had taken an immediate liking to each other in the years before the disaster at Dunkirk. And that relationship had evolved into personal and political support of the admiral on more than one occasion over the year just past.

After that came his nominal superior, Dirck Simonszoon Uitgeest, who was considerably older and was as taciturn and spare as van Holst was gregarious and expansive. He, and one other attendee, young Pieter Floriszoon, had been in Recife when Tromp arrived. All the others—Klaus Oversteegen, Johan van Galen, and Hans Gerritsz—had escaped from the disaster at Dunkirk. Willem nodded the gentlemen in, then bowed to the admiral, halfway back out the door as he did so.

Tromp shook his head. "Willem. You are to join us and take notes. But fetch Kees, first. If something should happen to me, he must know the role the *Amelia* is to play in the action to come."

Willem looked like he had swallowed a pickled frog. "At once, Admiral," he croaked and rushed off to get Kees Evertsen.

There weren't quite enough chairs for everyone, but it didn't matter. Van Holst planted his feet, crossed his arms and looked ridiculously Norse and good-natured. Simonszoon had already slunk into a bench beneath the transom-spanning stern windows. There were seats enough for the others, but the room began to grow uncomfortably hot. That it was midday in the currently cloudless tropics did not help matters.

Tromp tugged his collar a bit wider and pointed at the map. "You've all seen one of these now, yes?"

Floriszoon leaned forward, admiring it. "No, Admiral. Not I. The precision is extraordinary."

"Yes. And quickly becoming universal. I would be surprised if the Spanish have not acquired their own copies. Although they are among the slowest to innovate in such ways. However, we must presume their charts are now as good as ours."

Van Galen looked eager. "So we sail against the Spanish? Finally?"

Tromp looked at Johan van Galen and reflected how the fleet's long period of inactivity made some men less aggressive, but made a few more so. For the latter, it was as if waiting to weigh anchor and sail into battle was some interminable itch that they simply could not scratch. "Some of us have been sailing against the Spanish all along. And their leader will begin by telling us of any changes he has encountered."

Peg Leg Jol thumped forward with a grin that he swept around at all the gathered captains, and hunched over the map with positively conspiratorial glee. The Spanish considered Jol an out-and-out pirate, and in that moment, Tromp had to work hard to remember that his countryman was, technically, still a "privateer."

"So, news from the Main, fellows. Hunting continues to be good there. Took a barca-longa just before coming up here. Shot it up too much so we had to give her to the sea, but there was a fine haul aboard."

"Gold?" asked van Holst loudly.

"Better than gold. Letters. She was a mail courier. From what we read, the Spanish are still spending the majority of their time arguing over regional responsibilities. The Cuban governor doesn't like footing the whole bill for general naval protection, the Armada de

Barlovento, against pirates and privateers throughout the Antilles, whereas the viceroy of New Spain is unwilling to spend on more than his own *garda costas*—half of whom seem to be freelancing as buccaneers as soon as the Silver Fleet finishes touching their respective parts of the Spanish Main every year."

"Anything about us?" asked Simonszoon quietly.

"Only mistakes. Their entire focus seems to be on Thijssen's seizure of Curaçao. There's a lot of speculation that we met him there after abandoning Recife. The governor of Venezuela has been trying to gather ships together to mount a counterattack, but his colleagues in the other coastal *audiencias* of the Viceroyalty of New Spain seem less than enthusiastic in helping him with that project. However, he has been gathering what forces he can in Puerto Cabello."

Klaus Oversteegen frowned. "Did you visit Curaçao yourself, then?"

Houtebeen Jol shook his round head. "No. Too close to the Spanish. But my sailing partner, Moses Cohen Henriques, roves nearer to their ports, since—having no Dutchmen aboard—even if they were captured, it wouldn't point the Spanish in our direction. He went as far as New Providence, where he made contact with Abraham Blauvelt, the famous 'explorer.'" Jol smiled. Blauvelt was not much less of a pirate that Houtebeen, truth be told. "So we got news from him, as well. All the attention of the Spanish Main, and even Havana, seems to be focused on Curaçao."

"That's good for us," observed Gerritsz soberly.

"Yes, but maybe not so good for Marten Thijssen," mused Jan van Walbeeck.

Tromp nodded. "True enough, but right now, we

cannot help him—cannot even send word—without tipping our hand and calling attention to ourselves here." *Although we may be doing so soon enough, anyway.*

Simonszoon shifted from a mostly supine to mostly upright position. "Maarten, this is all very interesting, but you didn't bring us here to listen to Houtebeen tell us what he's already jabbered about in my great cabin when he's in his cups."

Jol smiled at Dirck even as he frowned. Simonszoon smiled back.

In that brief moment of silence created by their gruff camaraderie, Tromp discovered, and not for the first time, how grateful he was to have these two snarling sea dogs in his command. Both privateers with more a decade of experience, they had been the ones least panicked by the fleet's relocation from Recife to its tenuous safe haven on St. Eustatia. They had long experience with the vicissitudes of fate that shaped the lives of seamen, and the changing menu of perils it offered as its daily fare. Where Tromp's other captains had wrung their hands anxiously, these two had reached out their hands for another cup of rum and exchanged tales of the earliest days of Dutch colonization (the Spanish rightly called it "invasion") when danger and uncertainty had been *truly* high. These days, they opined with slow, sage sips at their fermented cane juice, were just a bit unpredictable. Nothing to lose sleep over.

"Dirck's right," agreed van Galen. "We all know your purser has been in town from first light this morning, buying provisions for the fleet. And we've all seen a disproportionate amount of those supplies coming to the ships captained by the men in this

room. So where do we sail, Admiral? North again?
To take back St. Maarten?"

Tromp shook his head. "No. That would be the last
place I would sail, right now."

"Why? When the puny Armada de Barlovento came
nosing south from there last year, we boxed them in
and sank all four ships."

"Yes, thanks to the watch post the admiral set on
the high ground of Saba Island," Simonszoon pointed
out with a slow drawl that signified that van Galen's
simplistic view of that engagement was beginning to
annoy him.

Tromp waved away Dirck's compliment. "Simple
prudence. Any capable commander would have taken
that precaution. But Captain van Galen, have you
considered how very *lucky* we were that day?"

"Lucky? Admiral, it was your skill and our naval superiority that won the day. We started with eight ships to
their four and, thanks to the advance warning, had the
wind gauge on them before they knew we were sailing
the same ocean. And by the time they realized their
predicament, the other three of our ships appeared on
the leeward horizon, closing the trap. Those square-
rigged Spanish apple-barges never had a chance."

Tromp had to glance at Simonszoon to keep him
from commencing a low-voiced, laconical evisceration
of yet one more nautical fool he was not willing to
suffer gladly. "Mr. van Galen," Tromp said patiently,
"I mean, have you ever thought how lucky we were
after the battle?"

Van Galen blinked. "*After* the battle? How were
we lucky after the battle? We won a clear victory
and even—"

"You half-blind pup," whispered Simonszoon. "Have you never considered what must have happened on St. Maarten after those four ships failed to return?"

Van Galen's stunned silence—an expression of insult giving way to worried suspicion that he had missed a key piece of some naval puzzle—confirmed that he indeed had never considered such a thing.

Simonszoon acquainted him with the immensity of that oversight. "Then let me reprise the events on St. Maarten almost three or four weeks later, when, by any reasonable estimate, the Spanish on the island had to consider the under-equipped Armada de Barlovento to be missing. The commander there—Captain Cibrian de Lizarazu, if last word is accurate—no doubt picked up his goose quill pen and started a letter to his superior, one Captain-General Bitrian de Viamonte in Santo Domingo. In this letter, Lizarazu certainly reported the disappearance of the entirety of that puny Armada, and promised his continued vigilance for any sign of its return.

"But as months wore on, he could only report more silence, and ultimately he and Don de Viamonte considered the Armada de Barlovento lost and the matter closed. Except that then, we must assume that Don de Viamonte—whose physical infirmities and less than dazzling personality have never interfered with his ability to perform as one of Spain's most prudent regional administrators—no doubt sent word to Governor Gamboa in Cuba, along with a request to reconstitute the Barlovento. That worthy may or may not have initially agreed, but over time, it is hard to imagine that he would not ultimately concede to such an appeal. After all, how many times have four warships disappeared without a trace, unless they were engaged by a similar or greater force of adversaries? Pirates flee from strong adversaries, particularly a flotilla of them. So the thinking in Hispaniola and Cuba by early this year must have come round to entertaining the possibility that there is a rival power somewhere in the New World: a power that has reason to attack, and apparently seize or sink, four Spanish men-o'-war. And here's the lucky part, van Galen: they still haven't sent a reconstituted Barlovento south, to follow the path of the first. Because if they did, what's the first major island they'd come to after departing St. Maarten?"

Van Galen's eyes cheated sideways slightly to look at the outlines of Oranjestad.

"That's right, they'd come here. St. Eustatia. If the Spanish knew the problem was so close to their own holdings in Hispaniola and Puerto Rico, they'd waste no time exterminating us en masse. We're too close to the Flota's return route to Spain, too close to their silver pipeline. And too close to major ports that we could fall upon with little warning." Simonszoon leaned back, his dark eyes lusterless. "If you haven't given thought to all that, Captain van Galen, it's time you did. And while you do, consider this piece of extreme good luck: that Marten Thijssen's attack upon and investiture of Curaçao occurred, by blind chance, at precisely the right time to give the Spanish a completely plausible source for completely erroneous conjectures. Specifically, that the Barlovento must have run afoul of Thijssen's flotilla and been sunk. Otherwise, they'd have been looking out for another explanation. Meaning, us."

Pieter Floriszoon was still staring at the map. "Frankly, it seems impossible that they still don't know we are here. It has been a year since we arrived, almost three since Oranjestad was established, and they haven't once checked on what they claim to be their possession?"

Van Walbeeck shrugged. "This is not uncommon for the Spanish, Pieter. The Spanish haven't made landfall in the Leeward Antilles since they shattered the English and French colonies on St. Christopher's in 1629. They never even bothered to return to ensure that the English colonists who fled into the mountains didn't reestablish their settlement. Which they did. With a vengeance."

"Yet they must have word of the rebuilt colony. Its goods travel back to Europe, and its port is not unknown."

"Not unknown, yet almost never visited except by us. And the Spanish will hear less of those goods in Europe now. Charles the First has forsaken England's New World colonies and so has all but lost contact with his subjects—or former subjects—here. An English ship has no business in New World waters, these days. The French are said to be attempting to revivify their *Compagnie de Saint-Christophe* to grow their colony on St. Christopher, but seem to have a hard time attracting the focused attention of their primary patron, Richelieu. So, except for the two buccaneers we intercepted last winter, who visits these waters anymore?"

"And the Spanish are not curious after losing the three ships they sent south from St. Maarten earlier this year?"

"I am sure they are curious, but Thijssen's attack on Curaçao does offer a likely explanation. Far more so than the proposition that the last Dutch fleet in the world lies lurking, almost immobile, in the Leeward Islands. And when it comes to the losses of their individual ships to Houtebeen and our other raiders, common pirates are a far more likely explanation. Or an opportunistic attack by the god- and king-forsaken English who still endure on Bermuda, Barbados, New Providence, St. Christopher's and Antigua."

Simonszoon muttered, "Some are in the Bahamas, now. On Eleuthera, mostly, if the rumors are true."

Tromp nodded. "I am half-ready to believe those reports. Without regular resupply from home, the English on Bermuda have the same problem we do: too many people and too little cultivated land. Only their crisis is ten times greater. They outnumber us here by at least five-to-one, and Bermuda is not particularly arable. Or furnished with larger neighboring islands, as we are. So of course the English there must strike out toward better sources of sustenance."

"Meaning the Bahamas," observed Gerritsz.

"Yes, and Eleuthera is the outermost of the islands, with good bays, but not much frequented by the Spanish."

"Even the bastard buccaneers of Association Island don't sail that far out, usually," commented van Holst.

"No," van Walbeeck agreed. "But do not expect that the English are going to Eleuthera to find food, so much as establish a gathering point for it."

Van Holst frowned. "What do you mean?"

"Eleuthera is more pleasant than Bermuda, but still not a particularly good source of comestibles. The richer islands of the Bahamas are closer in to the continent. My guess is that the English—well, I suppose they are 'Bermudans,' now—plan on using Eleuthera as a staging area. Their ships will fan out into the better islands from there, and return there as well. Then a different set of ships will convey the foodstuffs they've gathered back to Bermuda."

Simonszoon rose into a sitting position. "Very well. So we have been very lucky, and the English have the same problems we do. But that tells me nothing about why there are dry goods getting jammed into every open space on my ship's orlop deck right now."

"No, it doesn't," Tromp admitted, "but it was imperative that we all have the best current knowledge about what we know or suspect conditions to be in the Caribbean."

"Why?"

"Because in the event that any of your ships must scatter away from each other to survive, you must be able to act independently and wisely to save your crews, your hulls, and hopefully, make it back here to St. Eustatia."

The quiet in the cabin became absolute.

Van Holst nodded. "To where are we sailing, Maarten?"

Tromp removed the top chart. Beneath it was another, this one of the Windward Antilles and Trinidad. He pointed at the latter's large, almost squarish mass. "There." He paused. "At first."

"What does that mean, 'at first'?" Simonszoon almost whispered.

"It means I have annoyingly incomplete information."

"Information that came in with Jakob Schooneman of the *Koninck David*, last night?"

"Yes. Here is what I know: a French ship was sighted

by the *Koninck David* some thirty miles southeast of this anchorage, heading due south. Cautiously."

"Cautiously? You mean it didn't want to be seen by us?"

"Perhaps. But more pertinently, it did not want to be seen by the ship it was apparently trailing, and so remained at a distance that allowed it to stay beneath the horizon from its prey."

Kees Evertsen frowned. "Admiral, it is rather difficult to shadow a ship once it is no longer visible. Hard to keep track of its course changes, I'm told."

Grins sprung up at Kees' profound understatement.

"That is true, Kees, but not if the following ship is flying an observation balloon."

Again, absolute silence. Several of the captains seemed to be trying to remember what that word even meant.

Simonszoon stood up, sauntered over to the map. "A balloon? How high?"

"Several hundred feet, at least, Dirck. Yet, at even fifteen miles, it would be less than a dot in the sky. You'd need to be looking at just the right spot, with a fine spyglass, to spot it."

Simonszoon nodded. "So even the tops of your masts could be well below the horizon and, with the balloon aloft, you could still keep your eyes on a ship ahead of you."

"Precisely."

"But why?" blurted van Holst loudly, "and how does Schooneman of the *Koninck David* know that both these ships are bound for Trinidad, which I presume must be why we are now going there?"

Tromp felt his teeth lock together. *How indeed does*

Jakob Schooneman know what he knows? Indeed, his reports are not made up of facts but intimations, as if he either knows he is missing important pieces of the underlying story, or has been forbidden from revealing them. "Hjalmar, you do know that the *Koninck David* is the first ship from home to find us here, do you not?"

"Yes, which is why I rather expected that you were gathering us: to announce that we would once again have the help and succor of the United Provinces arriving in the coming months."

"I wish that was the news that I have. And I suspect something like that may be forthcoming. But what you do not know is that when last the *Koninck David* was in these waters last year, mostly along the Spanish Main, she had an up-time passenger. One whose reports on the New World have apparently found interested ears back home."

The captains leaned in closer, like hounds on the scent.

"Among other things, Captain Schooneman bore a letter from Prince Hendrik's own chamberlain, indicating that the prince bade us listen carefully to the recommendations of the master of the *Koninck David*, who had been acquainted with His Highness's interests and ambitions as they related to pending events in the New World."

When it was clear that Tromp had finished, Gerritsz jumped to his feet. "'Pending events?'" he almost shouted. "What kind of oblique nonsense is that?"

Simonszoon cut a sharp glance at his colleague. "The kind of oblique nonsense that *remains* nonsense when heard by the wrong ears, Gerritsz. Ears that must not learn the secret intents and actions of our Provinces." Looking back at the map, Dirck put his hand beneath his chin. "And so, both Hendrik's 'interests' and this mysterious French ship lead Jakob Schooneman of the *Koninck David* to tell us that we must go to Trinidad?"

"Yes."

"But Schooneman won't offer any further explanation or speculation?"

Tromp shrugged. "When I asked him that very question, he simply responded, 'You know I was on Trinidad last year, don't you?' I replied in the affirmative. He explained that he had touched the coast at Pitch Lake to take on some of the tar, and that there had been no Spanish in sight. Not a single Spanish sail was spied in those waters, in fact. And then he mentioned that he had been made aware of an up-time book that indicated that beneath the tar, there were vast quantities of oil."

Simonszoon almost smiled, turned, and collapsed back into the bench, half supine again. The other captains stared around. "Oil?" asked Oversteegen at last.

"Oil," affirmed van Walbeeck. "Which is of interest to the up-timers, and to any nation that hopes to adopt their technology. It is the best source of energy for their engines, if I remember correctly."

"You do," nodded Tromp.

Kees matched the nod. "Well, that explains the French presence then. They clearly have ambitions to adopt up-time technology."

"Yes, it explains the French, but whose ship are they following?" van Holst asked. "Up-timers?"

"That's unknowable at this point," said van Galen

with a dismissive wave of his hand. "But we may be sure of one thing: it means that our presence here could be discovered soon. Within weeks, even."

Van Walbeeck perched his chin on his fist. "And how does the presence of the French ship return us to that concern?"

"Is it not obvious?" van Galen asked, either oblivious to or uncaring of the impatient glares his impolitic tone was earning. "This is the first French ship to even approach these waters since we arrived from Recife—or at least, since our arrival was known to the colonists on St. Christopher's."

"So?" asked Gerritsz testily.

"So what other friendly port does this Frenchman have in these waters? The French on Association Island are, from all accounts, lawless buccaneers. The so-called privateers who operate out of the tent-towns in the Bahamas and the Florida Keys are far away and would be more likely to seize the ship than help it." He thumped the table for emphasis. "No. When the French have concluded whatever skulduggery they are about, they will have to make landfall on St. Christopher's before departing the Caribbees. And from that moment, the candle that measures our remaining days of safety will begin burning down."

Simonszoon folded his arms. "Tell me, van Galen: have you received credible word that the French would send a fleet to expel us from St. Eustatia?"

"No," said van Galen, unperturbed by his senior's droll, facetious tone, "but why should the French not tell the Spanish that we are here? Or, better yet, use the threat of doing so to extort our cooperation?"

"Extortion to do what?" Van Walbeeck queried.

"Why, to help them drive Warner and his people from St. Christopher's. Knowing the French, I suspect they'd garnish the deal by offering to share the island with us. But I suspect they would only concede a tiny fraction of the lands they gained from displacing their hereditary English foes."

"Who, on St. Christopher's, no longer represent that hereditary foe."

"That's a mere detail. Hereditary foe or not, the French want St. Christopher's. And if this ship returns to Europe unable to effect that conquest now, they might be followed by a flotilla which can. Which would mean we'd have very large, and very dangerous, neighbors."

"So what do you recommend?" asked van Walbeeck.

"That we should be prepared to 'entertain' an offer to cooperate with the French in the matter of Warner and his people. If the French can take St. Christopher's without need of reinforcements, they might not summon a fleet. Not for a very long time."

Tromp simply kept staring at the map, and thought: *Van Galen is truly piratical. Not on the superficial level of operations like Jol. No, he is too comfortable with what makes a man a genuine sea wolf: a ready embrace of duplicity and stratagems based on guile and deceit. I wish I could leave him back here, but I've got to bring him along. He's just the type who, unwatched, might go looking for trouble, find it, and bring it right back to our doorstep. I just wish he didn't also have a very good point about the French ship.*

"That will be a matter for us to address when the time comes. And if it arises while we are still gone, then mijn heeren van Walbeeck and Jol will be available to make a suitable response."

Houtebeen Jol started. "You're leaving me behind? With the rest of the fleet? Maarten, surely you must—"

"Captain Jol. I am leaving you behind. But not with the fleet. That's not the place for you."

Jol's injured expression began to shift into a blend of shock and rage. "Why, I'm twice the captain of any—"

"Jol," Tromp said calmly, "I can't afford to tie you down to *any* fleet. Not the one I'm sailing with, and not the one I'm leaving here under the command of Joost Banckert. I need you to keep doing exactly what you're doing: being our ears and eyes in the wider Caribbean. Because, if any Spanish should happen to decide to venture in this general direction while we are gone—"

At which words, Peg Leg Jol held up a hand and nodded. "Yes, Maarten. I understand. I don't like it—but I understand."

Tromp hoped that Jol did understand the full import of his responsibility to St. Eustatia now. Yes, he had to keep Jol at his specialty—a rover—and had increased need of his ability to gather intelligence along the Spanish Main. But if Tromp failed, or worse yet, did not return, then the thin but crucial trickle of supplies that Jol's raiding provided would need to be expanded, and quickly. If the Dutch lost the ten fighting hulls that Tromp was taking south, the Dutch would, in the same act, have come to the attention of one or more foes. And sooner or later, that meant that the Spanish would seek the source of the destroyed ships, and attempt to reduce it by bombardment and blockade.

When it came to building up a reserve of munitions and supplies to endure such an eventuality, and yet to acquire them surreptitiously, Jol had no peer.

He was a master at finding single ships before they detected him, shadowing them, closing during the night (no mean feat, and he was its master) and then attacking them early and swiftly so that, by midday, he had the prize in hand. If the ship was in good enough shape and a good sailer, he brought her back with a prize crew if he had the men to spare and the distance was not too great. Otherwise, he took what he could, spars included, and scuttled her. No fires: that could draw attention.

Which was always, of course, his most important objective: to leave the Spanish unaware of his depredations. As far as the viceroy of New Spain and the governors of his various *audiencias* were concerned, these were ships that simply disappeared, as did so many others that sailed alone in the treacherous waters of the Caribbean.

The one difficulty with his operations had been prisoners. Not the presence of them—the Dutch only had three dozen under guard at Fort Oranjestad—but their paucity. Jol had taken eight large ships, so far. Almost all had crews that had been greater than twenty, some considerably more. And yet, only thirty-six prisoners. The Spaniards—indeed, everyone but the Dutch—had long considered Houtebeen Jol more of a pirate than a privateer, but even those detractors who labeled him El Pirata nonetheless grudgingly conceded that when it came to enemies and prisoners, Jol was a singularly humane and considerate fellow. And yet, only thirty-six prisoners.

In the past year, Houtebeen Jol's missions had not been for commercial gain; they had been for the survival of St. Eustatia. More than once, in the early days, widespread starvation had been narrowly averted by the timely return of Jol's twenty-two-gun *Otter*, loaded with Spanish foodstuffs but without a single Spanish prisoner aboard. What could explain such ominously suspicious circumstances? Jol, who had always been an almost insufferably merry fellow, had grown quieter over that year, and did not volunteer an explanation.

To his shame, Tromp had not asked for one. Because, after all, what was the point of doing so? Jol had known well enough that the thousands of newly arrived refugees on St. Eustatia could not feed themselves, let alone prisoners. Furthermore, each Spaniard taken prisoner was one more escape risk, one more chance that someone would alert the viceroys that there was a credible challenge to their power in the New World, but that it was fragile and vulnerable and could be eliminated by a single decisive blow.

Simonszoon had risen. "So, no pirates in our fleet." He poked his friend Peg Leg in the ribs to lighten the mood. "And the rest of us? We're the fleet?"

"You and a few other ships."

Van Holst crossed his arms. "Which others?"

"The *Neptunus*, the *Achilles*, and the *Kater*."

Pieter Floriszoon, who commanded the most heavily gunned of all the Dutch jachts, the *Eendracht*, nodded. "So I'm to be helping Captain Gijszoon of the *Kater*, then."

Tromp looked slowly sideways at Floriszoon. "No, he will be helping you."

For a moment, the young captain's face was blank as he worked through the unexpected inversion of syntax. Then his eyes went wide as the implication hit.

"But Admiral, Jochim Gijszoon is an old hand with coordinating the actions of jachts. The oldest, in fact."

"Which is precisely why I don't want him leading our scouting efforts. He is too valuable to put at the tip of the spear when we are maneuvering to secure the wind gauge." The gathered men nodded solemnly at this bit of wisdom that was only one half the real explanation, which they all implicitly understood from Tromp's indirect announcement of Floriszoon's promotion over Gijszoon.

Yes, Gijszoon was the oldest hand at leading the jachts, but was arguably slightly *too* old a hand. Years made some men more bold because they became more certain of themselves and their methods. Not so Jochim Gijszoon. Ever since the news of Dunkirk had arrived, he had acted like a man haunted. He had lost many—indeed, almost all—of his old friends that day, and although his seamanship and leadership skills were undiminished, he had become increasingly cautious, to the point where he was unwilling to take necessary, or at least, advisable and advantageous risks. And if that was an unfortunate trait in the captain of a slower, larger ship, it was a disastrous trait in the captain of the smaller, faster jachts, whose job it was to scout ahead, lure targets to the main body, and out-race adversaries to secure the wind gauge for the rest of their fleet when battle was finally to be joined. The light cavalry of the seas, leading the jachts was not a job for the faint of heart or the skittish, and unfortunately, Jochim Gijszoon had become both.

With characteristically unflappable focus on the practicalities of an upcoming mission, van Holst looked up from the map. "So. We do not know what we must do at Trinidad. But surely Schooneman shared some hint of the *means* whereby we may learn of the objectives that our ships are to pursue there?"

Tromp looked van Holst in the eye. "No. I do not have such information." He didn't give his captains time to formulate the questions he himself would already be asking—stridently—in their place. "I know how this sounds. I had the same reaction. But remember and consider the significance of this detail: the French are *not* making best speed to Trinidad, but are *trailing* another ship. Which sounds very much like Richelieu's *modus operandi*. Something is afoot which he wishes his men to observe, perhaps wishes them to take advantage of, but which he does not wish them to initiate themselves."

"Meaning what?"

"Meaning," Simonszoon put in, "that while Richelieu may be interested in Trinidad, Richelieu is not the primary actor. He is positioning himself to observe and react, not attack."

Van Holst threw out wide hands in exasperation. "But then whose flag *is* taking action on Trinidad? The Spanish already own it. The French are observing, not acting. The English aren't in the game anymore. Our forces are too crippled to make such a move. So who's left? Who is moving on Trinidad?"

"Who wants oil the most?" mused van Walbeeck.

The gathered captains exchanged glances as van Holst asserted. "The up-timers, the USE. As I conjectured."

"And you might well be correct. Let us not forget that this news comes to us via Jakob Schooneman, who has coordinated with the up-timers in the past. But all this is still just guesswork."

Gerritsz shook his head. "All this obfuscation worries me."

Tromp nodded. "Me too, Hans. However, we may be sure of this: whoever is taking action on Trinidad either prefers, or needs, our presence there. And unless Schooneman is lying, Prince Hendrik prefers, or needs, us to be there also. So we go." He leaned away from the chart-table. "Not so different from the missions of our forefathers, after all. Sail into the unknown, lay hold of the opportunities that chance puts before us. Except this time, it seems to be a matter of certainty, rather than chance, that such an opportunity exists on Trinidad."

"Yes," agreed van Holst, "but these 'opportunities' are not going to be wrested from feckless, ill-armed natives. We are set to beard the Spanish lion in its den. And that lion is likely to resist effectively and tenaciously."

"That, too, is true," Tromp agreed, and restrained a quick, unbidden impulse to glance at Little Willi. Protective instincts died hard, and right now, they were shouting loudly in Tromp's ear: *leave him behind, here in Oranjestad! Don't take him into battle! Don't bring another innocent with you, only to be gobbled up by death's greedy maw while you escape those fangs yet again!*

But Maarten Tromp knew that trying to shelter him was futile. Here, in the New World, the saying had it that *there is no peace beyond the Line*—the "Line" being the longitudinal divider known as the Tordesillas Line, west of which all territory was claimed by Spain. So there was no safe place for Willem van der Zaan in the Caribbean, and he might as well start learning the bloody trade into which he'd been born so that he had the best chance of surviving long and uncrippled. And at least he wouldn't be forced to do so under the command of a captain too rash, too timid, too uncertain to maximize the lad's chances of coming through that most difficult of all trials: the first battle. There, everything was new, and terrifying, and the novices died in windrows for one reason above all others: the shock that paralyzed them for one, fateful second. For in that second, as they stood gaping and horrified, they were easy targets for the grizzled veterans who knew that killing a neophyte now meant one less seasoned opponent to face later on.

Tromp looked around the room, where his own collection of grizzled veterans were already comparing notes on sailing conditions farther down the Caribbees and tactical contingencies for handling the different numbers and kinds of enemies they might face. They were, Tromp conceded, probably the very best grizzled veterans in the world.

But, even so, were they enough?

Chapter 21

Overlooking Pitch Lake, Trinidad

For the second time that day, Hugh came to the crest of the northern lip of the bowl-like depression that cradled their objective. And again, as he looked down upon it, he wondered: *I left kith and kin for* this?

Pitch Lake was wrinkled, its uneven folds sagging over upon folds in some places. It was as if an immense black peat bog had grown the hide of an elephant. The foliage around the bitumen expanse was low scrub, although on the modest northern overlook, it was mostly grass with a few trees bent sideways by the prevailing winds. The northern coast at their backs chased around to the west and then down south, the shore keeping a constant distance of about one-and-a-half miles from the tarry bowl. In the west, a forest rose up at about the halfway mark, whereas to the direct south and east, low grass and occasional trees crowded the lake more closely, rising into tall bushes and then true jungle canopy after only one hundred yards or so.

Hugh took in the total tactical picture. Good: this vantage point offered clear sightlines in all directions.

And since this overlook backed on the north shore—the deepest water and closest coastal approach to Pitch Lake—it confirmed Hugh's first instincts. "We build the stockade here," he announced with a nod.

Morraine came to stand next to him. "Very good," he said. "But then, you hardly need my approval."

Next to him, St. Georges had his mouth open to object—

Morraine held up a hand. "I am in command on the sea; Lord O'Donnell commands on the land. These matters are his affairs. At most, we can offer our opinion and advice."

"Both of which I welcome, Captain."

"For now, I have none." Morraine stepped back with a slight inclination of his head. "I will leave you to your command, Colonel."

"Very well." And as he turned to address the challenges of this venture, Hugh had an image of himself waving one last farewell to Anna's grave-swallowed coffin. There would be little time for dwelling upon the past, now. He turned to the business at hand.

"O'Rourke, establish four watch posts. One near the north coast, overlooking the anchorage. One at treetop to watch the west coast, one to watch the edge of the eastern forest, one at the south compass point of the lake. All in brush, all under cover, all in direct line of sight to this spot."

"Signaling mirrors?"

"Yes, and double muskets for all. Three day-watches. But we'll pull the outposts in at night."

"No night watch in the outposts?"

"O'Rourke, are you familiar with these jungles?"

"No, m'lord."

"Well, neither are the rest of us. But our enemies are quite familiar with the lay of this land, and so any men we leave out during the night will never see their killers coming. And we won't know our lads are gone until they fail to signal at the appointed time, or we're under attack by those who killed them. Now, let's get those outposts set up."

O'Rourke agreed with a frowning nod and swung away, roaring names as he went. "Brown, Garvey, Finan, O'Halloran, Hanley—"

Hugh turned to Michael, who was studying the area intently. "Michael, would you mind supervising my engineer, Doyle, as we lay out the camp?"

Michael shrugged. "Sure. It's always better to have something to do."

Hugh looked beyond Michael. "And Mulryan, you assist. You, too, have nothing else to do until your balloon comes ashore with the stores."

"Yes, m'lord. What's the layout?"

Hugh smiled at the young fellow's ready, unpretentious confidence. Mulryan had shown the same broad aptitudes at the University of Louvain, under the Franciscans. They had pleaded with the lad to consider a professorial vocation to show his love of Christ, but as soon as he had been old enough, Tearlach had signed on with O'Donnell to show his love of country, instead.

Hugh knelt to draw a rough map in the dirt. "We'll keep the defenses simple: square palisade, one hundred feet per side. If the available wood permits, ten foot high, but no less than seven. Green wood only. Two foot of soil buttressing the base on the inside. Platforms at corners, another at the center of each expanse, two at the gate—one to either side."

Doyle was adding details to Hugh's dusty top-down schematic. "Where do you want the gate, m'lord?"

"Center of the south wall, on a straight line to the lake. We'll be hauling pitch up here, before long. No reason to put curves in the pathway. Get up the walls before you start on the buildings, Doyle. We'll make do with tents until they're up."

Michael looked at the diagram. "Buildings?"

Hugh drew a square in the center of the north wall. "From the main gate, a lane goes straight though the middle of the compound and ends at the back wall. That's where we'll want a small warehouse with double doors."

Hugh's engineer frowned. "A warehouse? Not a shed?"

"No, Doyle. I know it's much work, but we've got to have a few hard points inside the compound. The storehouse will be one of them. Now, to the west, or left, of the storehouse, we put light sheds for storing and servicing the balloon. We keep those as far back from the gate as possible."

Mulryan frowned. "Pity we can't conduct all the balloon operations from inside the walls."

"The interior space needed for laying out the envelope before and after flights is a luxury we can't afford, Tearlach. It would double the perimeter, and therefore, the walls we have to build."

Michael nodded. "Yep, sure would. Go on."

"The blockhouse goes on the other side of the lane from the balloon sheds. So it's toward the northeast, or right rear, of the compound."

Doyle goggled. "A . . . blockhouse, m'lord? With respect, the time it will take—"

"I know, Doyle, so get to work on it right after the palisade. And double-time it, man. Do the block-house's inner walls first, but prepare the ground for a second course of timber four inches out from the first walls—"

"—the space between to be filled with rocks and mud?"

Hugh turned to look at McCarthy. "Have you been studying 'ancient fortification' techniques, Michael?"

"Some. That's going to take a long time to build."

"To completion, yes. For now, I just want the outer walls, a solid roof with a low waist-works, and an observation tower."

Doyle made his voice ridiculously respectful. "Is that *all*, m'lord?"

Hugh smiled. "We can leave the tower until last. We just need a light framework."

"Oh well, if that's all—"

"Doyle—"

"Pardons, m'lord. I'll just be checking now if I've any miracles left mixed in w' me pioneer tools."

"I'm sure you've got at least one in there."

"Without doubt, m'lord."

Hugh looked up as O'Rourke came back, florid, sweating heavily in his face. "Water, O'Rourke: drink lots of it. Starting right now. This isn't the Low Lands."

"With respect, m'lord, I've noticed."

"Then empty your canteen down your gullet. And after you do, get a water detail going."

O'Rourke nodded, then turned to McCarthy. "Don Michael, if I might look at your map, again?"

McCarthy handed him the map-tube, then kneeled

to look more closely at the evolving layout of the stockade. "And what are you going to put on the south side of the compound, near the gate?"

"Tents for the men, huts when we get the chance to build them."

McCarthy scratched tentatively at the diagram. "I wonder: can I get a small work detail from the ship's crew? Just for a day or two?"

Hugh leaned closer to Michael, keeping his voice low. "That's problematic. As it is, it's awkward, having to keep St. Georges and his half-dozen men here. The fiction that they are our guests is unconvincing, at best." Then Hugh conceived of a strangely pleasant solution to the dilemma. "Michael, perhaps you can use St. Georges and his men, instead of a separate work detail."

McCarthy's answering smile was not pleasant. "Perhaps I can."

"And now I must ask—what do you need them for?"

Michael shrugged. "I've asked Morraine to demount two of his eight-pound sakers for the fort. I need to wheel them in, emplace them."

Hugh frowned. "To cover the land approaches, or the sea?"

McCarthy smiled. "Neither. Actually, what I had in mi—"

"M'lord," a new voice interrupted.

Hugh looked up. It was Kevin O'Bannon, softest foot in the regiment, and one of its best shots as well. He and a team of four had put ashore in a cat-boat at dawn, two miles east of Pitch Lake. Their mission had been to sniff out the natives who might be in the area and, according to most reports, kept a fairly constant eye out for trespassers. Hugh stood. "Good to see you back, O'Bannon. Your report?"

O'Bannon scratched his ear. "Sir, I—"

"A problem? Fast, man: tell me."

"No, m'lord. Not a problem. Not one damned problem. The opposite, in fact."

Hugh had been ready to hear, and respond to, any contingency—except this. "What do you mean?"

"No sign of natives, m'lord. At least nothing recent. We found one campsite, about a mile to the east. There were the remains of a small fire that had to be at least two weeks old, maybe a month."

Hugh frowned and considered. This was either very good news, or very bad news. If the natives had—due to disease, disinterest, or disputes—abandoned their unofficial coast watch of this area, then their absence was a stroke of extraordinary good luck. But if the absence was intentional, it might indicate that the *Fleur Sable* had been seen approaching. Which, given her nighttime approach and dark running, would be hard to imagine. The other possibility, but even harder to imagine, was that their arrival had been anticipated, and the natives were merely hanging back for now. But either way—

Hugh clapped O'Bannon on the shoulder. "Good news or no, mystery or no, you've done fine work and we proceed as if you had seen the Arawaks in the flesh. Set watches and patrols as already assigned. If they're waiting for us to relax our vigilance, they'll have a long wait." He turned to Doyle. "Get your timber from the forest on the western shore, but all from the landward side."

"—because by taking trees from the landward side, passing boats won't see any changes to the forest there."

Hugh nodded appreciatively at Mulryan's foresight. "And so you also know when we'll use the balloon?"

Tearlach nodded. "At night only."

Doyle gaped. "And what are you to be seein' at night? Banshees? The moon?"

Hugh shook his head. "Actually, Doyle, we'll never go aloft when the moon is up. We could be spotted, then. But on the nights we do go up, we'll be looking for lights. On the water, lights show us the positions of ships, and on land, lights mark the presence of natives or Spaniards. Either way, there's a good chance we'll have warning the night before we have any daytime visitors."

Hugh looked around the group, waited. "Well? Am I going to have to build it all myself?" With the exception of Michael, the command staff fragmented outward, each fragment heading for a different cluster of waiting soldiers.

Michael watched them go, watched the different groups set about their assigned tasks. "They love you, you know," he said at last. "All of them."

Hugh looked away, to hide the emotion he felt welling up behind his eyes.

Part Four

August 1635

In noble eminence enthroned

Chapter 22

Eddie Cantrell was about to put down the water jug,
then thought the better of his manners and tilted it
toward his guest. Larry Quinn nodded, hand out to
receive the pitcher as the younger man reached it
across the slightly swaying table.

"It doesn't taste half bad," Quinn commented.
"Particularly for desalinated water."

"The condensers are doing pretty well," Eddie
admitted. "Which is good: the Caribbean is not a
great place to run out of feed water."

Larry poured out a half glass of water. "Ironic. At
sea, steam engines are just as vulnerable as humans."

"What do you mean?"

Larry leaned back in his chair and screwed his
eyes closed as he apparently strove to find a distant
memory. Which turned out to be a line of poetry:
"'Water, water, everywhere, and not a drop to drink.'"

"Uh . . . Wordsworth?"

"Right poetic church, wrong poetic pew. Coleridge.
'Rime of the Ancient Mariner.'"

Eddie tried not to look crestfallen. He was supposed to be the book hound, not Quinn. But then again, although Quinn had read less deeply, he had read more broadly. In a bookstore, Quinn had been a wanderer, a browser, whereas Eddie's attention had been largely confined to the fantasy and science fiction shelves, with frequent forays into military history and relevant technology.

Apparently, Eddie's attempt to conceal his disappointment was not successful, although Quinn misread the cause. "Hey, so there's a little metallic taste to the water. I've had worse on camping trips. And lots worse when I went on maneuvers with the Reserves back in West Virginia. Overall, these ships are functioning just great. You should be really proud."

Now Eddie tried not to sulk. "I'll be a lot more proud when we get the bugs ironed out."

"Bugs? Like what?"

"Like the lower compression ratios we're getting out of the engines. That and the handmade brass fittings and pipe joints all mean less speed because we can't push the engines as hard. And those condensers you're raving about, yeah, they work, but they're finicky. And we've got higher-than-anticipated gear wear on every system that uses down-time alloys. I mean, the local fabricators have made huge, huge strides, but—well, let me put it this way: this may look like a nineteenth-century ship, but there's still a lot of semi-improved seventeenth-century technology under the hood."

Larry knocked back the last of the water, which was in marginally better supply upon the *Intrepid* than it was upon the *Courser*, the ship he had been assigned to. "Eddie, my boy," he said with a big-brotherly grin, "you worry too much. Which, truth be told, is probably why you're so good at this job."

"If I'm so good at this job, then why did we almost botch a balloon recon op again? We rehearsed it so many times on the crossing, but as soon as we get close to the Caribbean and the men see a sail—"

Larry put down his cup with a resounding, but not quite startling, clack. "Look, Eddie. There are going to be teething problems with everything on these ships. Everything. That's why they call it a shakedown cruise." He smiled. "It's a shakedown cruise for you, too. And you did just fine today. I watched you handle each new wrinkle like a pro. Not as calmly as an old pro, mind you—" his smile broadened. "—but a pro, nonetheless. You saw how the change in the wind was going to produce updrafts that would also push the balloon in the direction of that Spanish ship right about the same time they came around toward our heading."

"And they may have seen us, you know."

"Hmm, really? The only reason *we* knew they were out there was because we had a sky-guy up in your balloon, sending down Morse code updates of what he could see well over the horizon. So the Spanish *couldn't* see our ships, and would have to be wizards to see our blue-gray balloon. And when you had us tack away to get leeward of them, that gave us all the speed we needed to slip off to the south. It also helped that you hauled in the balloon to counter the updraft, and got your pilot to keep his hands off the burner, even when he was sure the bag was going to deflate and plunge into the sea." Larry poured out another two fingers of the mechanically purified water and toasted his companion. "You were a steely-eyed rocket man—well, balloon man—today, Commander Cantrell. We got away and got our balloon under the horizon in plenty of time."

Eddie scratched his ear. "Thanks, but that's not what bothered me, Larry. It was the retrieval. It took twice as long as it should have. Damn it, I can't keep my fantail cleared that long if we're going straight from being a balloon ops platform into a combat platform."

"I think you're still overestimating the speed with which naval combat takes place in this century, Eddie."

"With respect, I don't think I am. Or, to put it another way, if my deck evolutions can't take place faster and more smoothly than today, we are undercutting our great advantage: tactical speed. Yeah, we can run rings around other sailed ships, but I can't start running those rings until my decks are clear for sailing operations and all my yards are free. Every minute I lose bringing them about to catch a breeze because I'm still reeling in and deflating a balloon is me pissing away my greatest advantage and giving my adversary a slightly more level playing field."

"Yup," smiled Larry, "you are absolutely perfect for this job. A born leader and man of action when you're on deck, and a born worrier before and after. Simpson would bust his vest buttons with pride if he could see you now."

Eddie smiled. "Ah, go to hell, Larry."

"Why, that's pretty much exactly where I'm heading this very afternoon. Louisiana in early summer? Southwest bayou country? Oh yes, hell. Which, in this case, is not blessed with a dry heat."

Eddie nodded and felt suddenly very alone. Larry

was the only other up-timer in the fleet, unless you counted Ann Koudsi, who he never saw anyway. She had remained in the *Patentia* for the whole Atlantic crossing, along with her drilling equipment and crew.

But Larry had been a pal and a confidante on the way over the Atlantic. They had compared notes on their respective ships—Eddie was always looking for failure patterns in the new machinery common to both hulls—and the incredibly polyglot population of the flotilla. They had joked, as only they could, about how the D-Day invasion must have been a bit like this, where there had been units of various nationalities mixed into the forces of Operation Overlord. Here, Danes vied with Swedes for the most common demographic of crewmen, but there was no shortage of Germans in the ships' troops and technical services, a few Dutch military types who remained closeted on the *Tropic Surveyor*, and last but certainly not least, the almost four hundred Irish mercenaries who still claimed to belong to a *tercio* based in the Spanish Lowlands. Had the mission planners been able to include a few Mongolians, Micronesians, and Kalahari bushmen, it would have started resembling a floating version of the UN.

But beyond the perspectives and routines the two up-time officers had in common—and the shared knowledge of why Quinn was along, and where the *Courser* was ultimately bound—Eddie had found a genuine chum in Larry. Quinn was only a little bit older, and so became something of a big brother as Eddie struggled with the uncertainties and insecurities that come with a first command. Eddie had, prior to departing Luebeck, girded his loins to face these personal demons in silence and alone. That was part of command image, after all. But Larry had been a sympathetic ear, and his tales—many funny, several scandalous—about his time in the Army and Reserves, had reassured Eddie that he was not alone. Not alone as a new commander—Larry had been there before—or as an up-timer. Because, no matter how (often fiendishly) smart and insightful down-timers were, there was just no way for them to understand what it felt like to lead an expedition back to the continent and land that had comprised the country of one's birth some three and a half centuries in the future. He had been glad for the fellowship of another inadvertent time traveler and had not looked forward to the day when he would lose it.

But that day was today, and that time was now. Larry stood up, looked out the fairly humble stern windows of the *Intrepid*. "Well, it's about time for me to begin my role as master but not commander of the *Courser*. I wonder how the good Captain Haraldsen is going to like that bit of news."

"Since they're sealed orders with Gustav's signature and signet stamp on them, I doubt Olle will debate them much."

"Oh, it's not a debate I'm worried about," Larry said as he made sure all the items on his web-gear were snug and secure. "I'm worried that Olle, who's been a fine fellow up to now, might get his nose out of joint and dig his heels in at some point. I'd hate to have to pull rank formally and in front of the crew. I don't want to put him in that kind of situation, but I need to know he's going to take orders without delay. Being on our own, and far away from any friendlies, means we've got zero margin for error."

Eddie nodded, rose, and managed not to blink when Larry came to attention and snapped a salute, albeit with a shit-eating grin on his face. "Commander, request permission to debark and commence independent operations."

Eddie returned the salute. "Permission granted, and Godspeed, Major. And...I'll miss you, Larry."

Quinn, who had finished the salute and was already halfway to the door, looked back. "Now that's just an out-and-out lie, Eddie. You've got a twenty-four/seven job on your hands here, as well as a drop-dead gorgeous young tigress-wife who's sure to keep you busy the rest of the time."

"Yeah, well, even so, don't be a stranger. You miss a check-in and I will keelhaul your ass when you bring it back."

"Daily squelch-break, and a quick sitrep every third day, for as long as we're in range. My word on it, Commander."

"Do you think the crew has figured out where you're going?"

"Hell, I think the only ones who even know we're about to split off are the ones we told at the start of the voyage: Haraldsen and his XO. And I don't think it's dawned on Haraldsen yet that he can't remain in command of the mission because he doesn't have the right skill set to carry it out."

"It should be an interesting couple of hours when you get back and break the news, Larry."

"That it should. Take care, Eddie."

With a single long stride, Larry Quinn was out the door.

❖   ❖   ❖

From Anne Cathrine's slightly padded chair in her sitting room (merely two lieutenants' cabins with the paneled partition removed), she watched as Larry Quinn swung energetically down the accommodation ladder to the yawl-rigged skerry that had brought him over from the *Courser*. His visit had been relatively short, and she watched him go with mixed feelings.

On the one hand, it was irksome that her husband clearly shared secrets with his fellow up-timer to which she was not privy. Not that this had been a surprise. Shortly after her marriage to Eddie, older ladies of the court had counseled her not to let such inevitable professional confidences bother her. After all, her husband was a military man with ties to three separate polities, now—Denmark, the USE, and the singular institution of Grantville—and was sure to traffic in secrets which he might not share with anyone, even (some said, *particularly*) his wife. But, despite the ostensible wisdom of those words, Anne Cathrine had never been willing to blithely concede the wider world of power and secrets to men—not even her darling Eddie!—and her father's use of daughters as marriage-primed pawns in his political chess games had only confirmed her in that resolve.

In the case of this voyage, the only impediment to her enjoying full access to her husband's professional life was one Lawrence Quinn: a slightly older up-timer whose mild-mannered self-assurance made him a Man Worthy of Notice for her two ladies, and even for the reclusive Edel Mund, the stolid wife of the flotilla's stolid naval commander, Pros Mund. Quinn's allure had no doubt been further spiced by the aura of mystery surrounding his slightly smaller

ship, the destroyer *Courser*. It was quite clear to Anne
Cathrine, having grown up in the courts of the high
and the powerful, that this ship and its crew had
either been, or would be, given special orders. There
was no other explanation for the strange exclusion of
the vessel from the intership contacts that had been
commonplace among all the others in better weather.
Even the rumored differences in *Courser*'s crewing
and supplies were not mentioned, let alone detailed,
in the routine intership communiqués. That way, no
conjectures could be made as to her final destination
and purpose. The only thing Anne Cathrine was sure
of was that, sooner or later, the crew of the *Courser*
would set off upon a task both hazardous and secret.

And so Anne Cathrine had consoled herself that,
ultimately, Lawrence Quinn would depart, and she
would have her husband's first and last confidence
in all things, and so, be fully satisfied once again.
Except, as she watched Larry's skerry whisked away
by a beam-reaching breeze back toward the *Courser*,
she discovered that now that his moment of departure
was imminent, she regretted it.

Partially, this was because she had come to like the
American, despite his annoying claim upon an exclusive
confidentiality with her Eddie. Quinn was easygoing,
affable, courteous without being affected, and seemed
genuinely concerned for her beloved Eddie's well-being.
She was quite sure that the older up-timer had, on
more than one occasion, offered her husband sage
council on how to handle some of the junior officers
who chafed at being subordinate to him, since they
were not only older than he was, but had lived upon
the waves since the age of twelve. While not openly

insubordinate, those officers had tested the willingness and ease with which he exercised his authority. Larry had steered Eddie through those first encounters, helping him avoid the predictable extremes: resorting to barking orders and standing on rank alone (the mark of an insecure officer) or pretending not to notice the slights, thereby avoiding any corrective action at all (the mark of an even more insecure officer). Anne Cathrine had no doubt that Eddie would have found his footing as an officer and commander soon enough, but with Larry's extra guidance, her husband's missteps had been very few, and those but very slight. The net result was that, by the time the flotilla had crossed the Atlantic, Eddie was both well liked and well respected by not only the crew of the *Intrepid*, but the entirety of the complement of Reconnaissance Flotilla X-Ray.

But there was another reason she now regretted Quinn's departure. She realized, for the first time, that it would probably make her husband feel lonely and perhaps a bit sad, and she chided herself for not having foreseen that before this moment. Up-timers were truly alone in this world, which was, for them (she still suspected) a primitive, ignorant, and often squalid place.

"Sister, you are scowling like Vibeka Kruse herself, just now." The voice, of her younger sister Leonora, was jocular and wrung a smile from Anne Cathrine in spite of the dark thoughts that Larry Quinn's departure had spawned. Vibeka Kruse had been her father's somewhat plain mistress for some years, whose virulent hatred for the children of his prior marriages was a matter of common knowledge, if not public display.

"I would rather you compare me to the Gorgon," Anne Cathrine replied in the same tone. "What is more ugly than a predatory woman whose hunt has been frustrated by the family of her carnal prey?"

But instead of smiling at the rejoinder, Leonora's eyes grew quite large and round and drifted ever so slightly in the direction of the third woman in the room.

She, the tall and stately Sophie Caisdatter Rantzau, did not *seem* to notice the remark. Perhaps she was too engrossed in her up-time collection of Donne's verse. At least, Anne Cathrine hoped so, because she understood Leonora's meaningful semi-glance in an instant. Sophie was, herself, the offspring of one such beautiful yet Gorgonic woman, whose pursuit of male prey had been frustrated by his powerful family. In fact, it was King Christian IV of Denmark who had "rescued" his besotted eldest son from the scheming of Sophie's own mother: Anne Lykke. She had entranced Prince Christian when she appeared in court but a year or so after her first husband's death in 1623. Christian IV had ultimately imprisoned her, which incensed even neutral nobles against him: the king had no legal right to imprison either a nobleman or noblewoman without specific criminal charges. Christian IV responded with an (unfortunately characteristic) outré counterattack. He charged Anne Lykke with sorcery, claiming she had hired a reputed witch by the name of Lamme Heine to strike down the king once he became an obstacle to her amorous designs upon the crown prince. The resulting furor in the *Riksradet* was as vitriolic and bitter as only truly stupid disputes can be, but left Anne Lykke with a reputation of being a "dangerous woman."

However absurd the scandal, though, even Sophie had suffered from it. Hence her presence on this voyage as a person wanting an increase in royal pleasure. Anne Cathrine, who would have liked to have kicked herself for her impolitic remark about Gorgons and unscrupulous women, looked cautiously sideways at Sophie Rantzau.

Sophie sighed and, not looking up from her reading, remarked, "Rest assured, I am not my mother, much less an admirer of her tactics. She is so—" Sophie tossed a long-fingered hand into the air, fingers miming her mental search for the proper word.

"—so strong-willed?" supplied Leonora tactfully.

The fingers stopped. Sophie allowed a slow smile to accompany her response and looked up. "It is said that there is a fine line between being strong-willed and willful. Wherever that line is, you will find my mother well on the other side of it."

Anne Cathrine beamed, both in relief and a sudden rush of appreciation for Sophie, who was the oldest of the three of them at the advanced age of nineteen. They had been cordial and carefully convivial during the crossing, and the sisters had endeavored to make her feel welcome, but the pre-extant gaps between them—of both social station and family feuds—had been an unaddressed and therefore unresolved factor. After all, Christian IV had not only imprisoned Sophie's mother, but threatened her with a capital crime, and then grudgingly released her on the condition of house arrest. It was perhaps a trifle optimistic to assume that she would welcome friendship from that same king's own daughters.

But in this unlooked-for instant, Sophie Caisdatter

Rantzau showed herself to be her father's child in temperament, even though she was her mother's daughter in looks. Cai Rantzau—sheriff of Copenhagen and an eminently trustworthy and even-tempered man—had been admired not merely for his abilities, but for his wry sense of humor. And that sense of humor was now evident in the charmingly crooked smile with which Sophie regarded the two sisters.

Anne Cathrine giggled and put her hand out to touch the much taller woman's arm. "I am so glad you are here with us, away from all—that."

"Yes. It is good to be away from all—that." And Sophie closed her eyes, looking simultaneously pained and relieved.

Anne Cathrine looked at ever-politic Leonora, who showed no sign of inquiring into Sophie's reaction. So Anne Cathrine herself plunged onward despite the risks, as was her wont. "Good Sophie, you repeat my words in a most unusual tone and with a most unusual expression. If you are disposed to share the cause of—"

"I shall do so, my lady Anne Cathrine." Sophie opened gray eyes that were calm and grave. "But, if it please you, not this day."

Anne Cathrine swatted Sophie's arm. "Here, now. This is the last time you will call me Lady Anne Cathrine. I am simply Anne Cathrine, she is simply Leonora, and you will tell us of your woes if, when, and as you choose. Agreed?"

The wry smile was back on Sophie's face. "I would not think of disagreeing. Thank you—Anne Cathrine. Being able to have a conversation as frank as this— well, it is among the reasons I am most grateful to be away from all 'that,' from the endless intrigues that swirl in and around your royal father's court."

Anne Cathrine tilted forward with a conspiratorial whisper. "Me, too, Sophie: me, too." But as she leaned back again, Anne Cathrine found herself longing for that court's plush chairs, even though the last time she had sat in one had been emotionally uncomfortable...

Four days before boarding the *Patentia* for her pending rendezvous with Eddie and his up-time-crafted ships, Anne Cathrine's royal father had summoned her to see him in the middle of the day. Which meant that although their meeting would be private, it was also motivated by official business. She had sat—indeed, had sunken into—her wonderfully soft chair while her father outlined his plans for her, for the New World, for Denmark's place in the USE, and how this journey to the New World would advance all of them.

"That is all very fine, Father," Anne Cathrine had said after listening to the lengthy and surprisingly coherent presentation. "But I must ask: why are you telling me all this? Full and open disclosure has not been one of your notable traits, to date."

"Ungrateful child! You cut your royal father to the quick!"

"Possibly. Yet I note you did not deny the truth of my observation."

Christian's answering smile was as sly and long as those he usually wore when he was inebriated and thinking himself surpassingly clever. "Daughter, you make me proud. Your wit is barely less than my little sage Leonora's, and you have five times the courage of any of my other offspring."

"You mean, your female offspring."

A dull look seemed to reduce the intense focus of Christian's eyes for a moment. "I said what I said. I see no need to modify it."

To which Anne Cathrine made no response. The conversation would not proceed well if the king began to brood upon his own regretful implication that she had more nerve and brains than his namesake, the crown prince Christian.

Fortunately, her father was not one to let a silence drag on. Indeed, he was not one to allow a silence to take place at all, and this time was no different. "However accurate—or not!—your initial observation may be, my Anne Cathrine, it is necessary that, on this occasion, you are made aware of all my plans in regard to what Admiral Simpson calls Reconnaissance Flotilla X-Ray."

She nodded, but thought: *Not true, Father. You haven't told me who else is charged with overseeing your interests, who might emerge to express your royal ultimatums when we find ourselves in the Caribbees, nor how, nor when. You have only told me what I need to know so that I will not be surprised and so that I cannot unwittingly foil your plans. But you have told me nothing with which I can help Eddie be on guard for your picked men in our little fleet.* But Anne Cathrine only said, "What makes this full disclosure so necessary, Father?"

"Because I know what you want, Anne Cathrine, even though you've not asked for it."

"And what is it you think I want, Father?"

"Why, to be made a duchess. Or, more to the point, to have Eddie made a duke."

Anne Cathrine was again impressed by how shrewd

her father remained, despite all the alcohol he consumed. "And this voyage to the New World is necessary to that eventuality...how?"

"Daughter, certainly you must see it for yourself. If I am to pass over some of my own children to award this honor to your husband—"

—and to thus confer upon me enough power so, come what may, I will not be treated merely as a "king's daughter," but akin to an actual princess—

"—then Eddie must prove himself worthy, and mightily so, in my service."

Anne Cathrine smiled. "Is not his present service to the USE also, in part, service to the Union of Kalmar, and hence, service to you?"

"Well, it is...and yet, it is not. I am one of the monarchs of the multinational hodgepodge over which Gustav presides. But to follow the orders of the USE, and to serve its interest...well, it cannot be equated with service to me, to this crown, directly. If Eddie makes 'prudent' choices when the right opportunities arise, then we may construe his service with Flotilla X-Ray as service to us. Perhaps his actions will show he is worthy of being made a duke. And perhaps you can encourage him in this regard. If so—then, we shall see."

Anne Cathrine rose stiffly. "So we shall," She bowed and turned toward the door. She was amazed, for a fleeting moment, that familial extortion so obvious as that now being plied by her father did not actually have a physical stench.

Christian's voice implored her spine. "Daughter!" His tone softened when she halted and turned back to face him. "Now do not become cross with me."

"Then do not demean my husband."

Christian's eyes seemed to grow more shiny. He straightened in his chair and his voice was loud and sharp. "You dare scold me?"

"I do not. But I do dare to defend my husband when he is held to be deficient in deeds of valor and conquest that, quite obviously, he has already performed. And I observe that the standard to which you propose to hold him is already far greater than what you expected of most of the men to whom you have forced my sisters to become betrothed. How very lucky I was that a landless up-timer fell into our hands. Otherwise, I might have wound up a consort—or should I say mattress?—for that hero of whore- and counting-houses, Friherr Dinesen."

Christian grew very pale, then very red, then returned to normal color. "Anne Cathrine . . ."

At that moment, Vibeka Kruse drifted past the open door. Her idle stroll and excessively sunny smile were akin to an open admission that she had been listening from the hall. Christian nodded at her, rolled his eyes once she had passed, and his gaze swept across the single, small portrait of Kristen Munk—Anne Cathrine's mother—that he allowed to remain in the palace. He smiled sourly as his eyes came away from the picture of the woman for whom his desire had led to an ill-considered morganatic marriage. Anne Cathrine raised an eyebrow, staring at him.

Christian's sour smile became wry. "I was preparing to lecture you, once again, on how—for royalty and their offspring—marriage is not reserved for love, but for duty. But I am afraid my own behavior would hardly support my case."

Anne Cathrine allowed herself a smile that was almost a copy of her father's but said nothing.

"So I allow you this: young Commander Cantrell is everything I could hope for in a son-in-law save in one way. His birth."

"He is not of low birth.. Such a concept is meaningless to up-timers."

Christian nodded. "True enough. Which is—and I will deny this if you ever repeat it—a political trait of theirs I admire, in many ways.

"But our exigencies are dynastic, not democratic; our concerns realistic, not idealistic. There are only so many titles I may grant, particularly hereditary ones, before I begin to dilute the significance of those titles by making them too commonplace."

"That is what Eddie calls 'inflation.'"

"Yes. And I do not argue that he is bold and brave and clever and unswervingly loyal to those whom he has sworn allegiance. But beloved daughter, remember this: he demonstrated all those qualities not while in my service, but while in service against me. Against us. Let him match—even faintly—those deeds while in my service, or showing similar regard for Denmark's interests, and then I can make him what you wish. Indeed, I will seem at once magnanimous and just, raising him up as a hero, unprejudiced by the fact that half of his heroism was exercised against me."

Leonora's low-voiced comment brought Anne Cathrine back to the present. "The *Courser* is departing already." Her sister nodded toward the single porthole in the ladies' sitting cabin.

Anne Cathrine blinked, still slightly disoriented by the rapid shift from memories of Denmark eight weeks ago to the rolling currents of the New World. Sure enough, the *Courser* had most of its canvas in the wind, and was already skimming swiftly southwest, angling away from the rest of Flotilla X-Ray's increasingly southeasterly course.

"Where do you think they are going?" asked Leonora, who had effectively memorized several atlases worth of New World maps.

Anne Cathrine was debating how best to reply when Sophie Rantzau said, "Someplace dangerous, Leonora. Of that I feel certain."

"Yes," Anne Cathrine breathed into the silence that followed Sophie's oracular pronouncement. "Someplace very dangerous indeed."

Chapter 23

Pitch Lake, Fort St. Patrick, Trinidad

Tearlach Mulryan stared down past the spyglass that hung at his chest, and saw the tiny outline of their stockade, which McGillicuddy had dubbed "Fort St. Patrick." The glimmer of lights—the low, steady fires of dry branches dipped in pitch—just managed to pick out the corners of the smaller, dark square that was the recently completed blockhouse. The storehouse, although barely more than a large, sturdy shack, was also completed. Every other faint outline was a tent. Mulryan smiled, glad not to be sleeping in one of those canvas shelters, because, floating four hundred feet above the ground, he was kept wonderfully cool by occasional gusts of the less humid night air. Down on the ground, his comrades sweltered and sought refuge from the incessant attention of an infinitude of mosquitoes.

Beyond the rough darkness of the land beneath him was the smooth, inky darkness of the sea. And the only sounds besides the wind were the distant cries of high-flying birds. That and the surf, Mulryan amended, as he heard the distant sigh of waves rubbing their backs against the steeper slope of the north beach, as well as the faint swells that ran whispering in over the tidal flats that scalloped outwards from the west beach—

His reveries came to an abrupt end: the west beach had lights beyond it. A quick check through the spyglass revealed that it was not one, but three separate lights, probably no more than twenty miles away. That put them much closer than the normal maritime traffic, which traveled primarily from east to west, following the prevailing winds and making for destinations farther along the South American coast. But more significantly, these three lights were all on parallel courses, bound directly for the west shore. Their slow but steady progress indicated that they were probably fore-and-aft rigged vessels, tacking tight against the wind.

Mulryan resisted the powerful impulse to signal his ground crew for a fast descent. Instead he followed the special orders—*protocols*, Don Michael called them—that had been established for handling this eventuality.

Tearlach looked down, and carefully noted the arrangement of the time-marking lanterns on the balloon's servicing pad. As he watched, the quarter-keeping lantern was moved from the 1:15 position to the 1:30 position. Time of observation was fixed. He tapped it down to the ground crew, who now knew that something was afoot. He signaled bearing, course, approximate distance, and best guess at speed. And then he lifted the spyglass back up to his eye and commenced the first of several slow sweeps of the horizon, each one of which would be a concentric circle that overlapped the prior one by about twenty-five percent, all spiraling in to a close observation of the immediate environs of Fort St. Patrick. But before he finished even the first full sweep, Mulryan spotted another light, this one solitary and farther off, perhaps thirty miles to the east. Whether or not that ship was underway, and what its heading might be, were impossible to determine at this range. Meaning that it could very well be nothing more than a typical merchant vessel, moving slowly or at anchor for the night.

But somehow, Tearlach Mulryan suspected that this was not an evening for coincidences, and as he clicked the Morse code data string pertaining to this second sighting, he thought, *And what are you doing waiting out there, my lovely? Have we seen you and your balloon before, or are you a new partner in our dance?* Mulryan felt very sure that he'd know the answer by this time tomorrow.

Presuming, of course, that he was still alive.

Barto stabbed a finger down at the left edge of the crudely rendered map of Pitch Lake and its environs. "We land our real raiding party here on the western coast, in force and in secret. The rest of our men remain aboard while all ships hug the shore, beating northward, still using the coastal trees for cover."

"The water is very shallow dere," observed Riijs, the most quiet of Barto's company and unquestionably the most dangerous. A multiple murderer who had fled Frisia, he killed with a quiet efficiency and calm that defied the assignation of any suitable *nom de guerre*. He was just called Riijs—and he preferred not being called at all. "Is it safe passage? And will we not be seen, staying so close?"

Barto looked at Berrick, the Englishman; who shook

his hoary head. "I sailed wif them whut sailed wif Raleigh, and they told me that the draft is enough for hulls such as ours. And the trees will hide ye fine. One needn't dally in the breakers to stay in their blind spot, 'cause the high land near the lake is none too high. They can't see over the treetops for miles out."

"And if dey have a watch post dere, on de western coast?" Riijs' voice lacked any discernible intonation.

Barto shrugged. "Then you signal us and we move quickly to deeper water, around the headland, and engage their ship near the north beach. You comb and clear the woods along the west beach, and wait for our diversion. But remember: you don't charge the rise"—for it could not reasonably be called a "hill"—"until you hear our guns."

"So, we use de same signal either way: your first cannonade. And either way, you follow de same plan for engaging de enemy ship."

"Aye. But if we can move slowly and unseen, all the better. Best if you can advance to the eastern edge of the west woods undetected. It's more than half a mile to the high ground, so you can't charge it all the way. And the more time they have to see you—"

"*Ja*. I know. De more of us will die. But I am more worried by dis: do you really tink dey will be so stupid as to focus all dere attention on de north shore when our ships show up dere?"

Barto smiled. "I'll make sure of it. The pinnace and the packet will be loaded with almost eighty men, and will seem to make briskly for the beach. Of course, our foe's 'daunting ship and superb seamanship' will scare us off. And so we'll appear to delay the landing of what will certainly look like our main raiding force."

Riijs was the only one who did not smile at the elegance of the ruse. "It is a gut plan. Let us hope our enemy does not also have a gut plan."

Barto smiled at his coolly homicidal lieutenant. "You worry too much, Riijs."

Who nodded. "*Ja.* Dat is true."

Hugh looked up at Mulryan, who was on the blockhouse roof, standing atop a hastily erected ten-foot platform, spyglass aimed at the western woods. O'Donnell shouted up through the brisk morning breeze, "Are their small boats still heading for the west shore?"

"The treetop outpost signals that the raiders are approaching the tidal flats now. A pinnace and packet. They're full to the gunwales."

Hugh nodded to his command staff. "Aye, that's their main attack force, sneaking up on our 'blind side.'" He shouted up to Mulryan. "Is O'Bannon in position yet?"

"Yes, m'lord. Just got the signal this second."

"Good. Signal back that message is received, and our treetop watchers are to withdraw and fall back to join O'Bannon's team at the first ambush site."

St. Georges, who had missed the predawn preparations, stuck his face into the ring of officers around Hugh. "What do you mean, 'first ambush site?'"

"Good of you to join us, Lieutenant. O'Bannon, my best scout, left before dawn with his original landing team plus a few other men. They've taken up positions at the edge of a clearing near the northern tip of the woods."

St. Georges, still bleary-eyed and endued with a faint vinous reek, pulled his uniform collar straighter. "Why there?"

"Because when we finally put our balloon up, that's where our visitors will no doubt send some marksmen—probably their best, with rifled pieces—to snipe at it. Once they've positioned themselves in the clearing and they've begun to fire, O'Bannon will take them by surprise." Again, Hugh shouted up to Mulryan, "Tearlach, has Morraine acknowledged your earlier signals?"

"Yes, Lord O'Donnell."

"Then down you come, and at the double-quick."

St. Georges looked meaningfully back at the balloon sheds but saw only the beginnings of activity there. "I see you are not ready to put Mulryan aloft. Would not his observation be invaluable at this time?"

"Not as valuable as his becoming a decoy a little later on."

"A decoy? How?"

"I'm not going to put Mulryan up in the balloon until our visitors to the west have all landed, and settled themselves into the woods. Or until they start getting too close to O'Bannon. Whichever occurs first."

"Why wait so long?"

"Because I want the attackers to think their attempt to surprise us has worked. The farther they proceed with whatever plans they've made based on that assumption, the more likely we can turn the tables on them later on."

"I see," said St. Georges.

Hugh doubted he did, based on the Frenchman's hesitation and muted voice. "But once they see the balloon, they'll know that we have them under observation, and they will have to begin improvising. Their first step will be to snipe at the balloon. And that's when O'Bannon will give them their first surprise."

"And when they pursue him?"

"He'll run back fifty yards, through a maze of preset snares, turn and wait."

"And ambush the dogs again when they become entangled. Ingenious," conceded St. Georges.

Ignoring the faintly supercilious tone, Hugh finished the tactical overview. "O'Bannon will do this twice, if he can, and then fall back out of the woods and around to the brush just off the north beach. And I'm hoping that a lot of our visitors on the west shore will chase him."

St. Georges nodded. "Because the more of them that are chasing him—"

Hugh nodded back. "—the fewer of them they'll have to attack the stockade. Either way, O'Bannon and his men will take up concealed, prepared positions just a hundred yards northwest of the stockade. If he's not busy defending himself from following forces, he'll wait there as a reserve, or will harry any attempt to land to our north. Although I don't think they're going to try a landing on the north coast."

"Why?"

"First, it's a little too obvious. Second, the water is deeper there and they have to come closer to put men ashore. Third, I believe Captain Morraine and *Fleur Sable* will make it too costly for them."

That brought a genuine, and somewhat fierce, smile to St. Georges' face. "*Oui, vraiment.*"

O'Rourke frowned down at the map that Hugh had hastily sketched in the dirt as he spoke. "So how many do you think they're landing in the west woods?"

"I wish I knew, but I expect no less than one hundred, perhaps as many as one-hundred-twenty. That assumes they need to keep running crews and some boarding parties on all three ships."

O'Rourke emitted a low whistle. "Steep odds. There are only sixty of us—sixty-six, counting Lieutenant St. Georges and his men. It could become a desperate affair, fighting against those numbers—"

Hugh smiled. "Yes, but their advantage in numbers will also be their undoing."

"How so?"

"They will want to use that advantage to make a quick, decisive attack. Which is why they're positioning themselves to approach under cover, and then charge the fort *en masse*."

"That's just what I'm afraid of."

"Ah, but that's just what I want. O'Rourke, you're to take forty men and get into concealed positions at the edge of the eastern forest. All except for your five best marksmen and three of the green lads to work as reloaders. They're to be prone and concealed out in the brush, forward of the forest."

"I'm taking forty of our sixty men? That leaves you—what?—four for running the balloon, six for O'Bannon's team in the west wood, and ten for the fort itself?"

"Yes."

"And then what? Am I to twiddle my thumbs while these dogs swarm around the fortress gates?"

"At first, yes."

"They'll break in!"

"Of course. That's what I want."

"Are ye daft—m'lord?"

"No, old friend, I am not. When the raiders get the gate open, that's when your marksmen go to work. They'll be bunched up, so whittle them down, drive them inside the stockade for cover—and then charge for all you're worth. Leave your long pieces back with your marksmen. The rest of you close and engage with musketoons, pistols, even swords if it gets that tight. But I don't think it will."

"No? And why not?"

"Because when they finally open the gate—"

Barto, watching the almost empty pinnace exit the shallows, glimpsed movement over the trees lining the shore to the west of Pitch Lake. As he watched, a swollen, inverted teardrop shape rose up higher than the palms. Berrick pointed to it with an inarticulate stutter that always afflicted him during combat.

Barto sucked the salt wind through his irregular and incomplete teeth. "I see it, fool. But what is it?"

"I d-d-don't know, b-but th-there's a m-m-man in a b-basket b-b-b-beneath it."

And so there was. Hanging near the tapering base of the upward-falling blue-gray teardrop was a single figure. Its hands and arms raised towards its face, and Barto saw a split-second glint of sharply reflected sunlight.

"Bastards! They're watching us from that—thing. With a spyglass."

"B-b-but what is it?"

"What does that matter? They can see us from it and, no doubt, signal their forces on the ground. Damn it, we have to move now—and fast!" Turning to his mate, he ordered, "Signal the pinnace to run large and catch up with us. We've got to put a boarding party on her, but we'll have to do it on the move, rather than pausing at the northern headland."

❖   ❖   ❖

Riijs stared up through the trees at the strange, tapering globe, which rose slowly, like—like what? Where had he seen this kind of lazy, steady ascent? And then he knew: it was akin to the way that heavy embers, or whole leaves, rose up out of a fire. But this distended sack, and the single man slung beneath it, kept rising and would soon be high overhead. He looked through the trees and out to sea. The pinnace was just dropping from sight around the headland to the north, trying to catch Barto's sloop. Well, the man hanging under that swollen sphere had doubtless seen those ships, so that part of their attack was no longer a surprise. But had the observer been aloft in time to see Riijs' landing force?

His uncertainty was not resolved by the runner who came bounding through the brush toward him, breathless. "News from the eastern edge of the woods," the man panted.

"*Ja.* Say."

"As we thought, there is a stockade on the rise to the north. But if they had outposts, they have pulled them in."

"Do you tink dey saw us?"

"No sign of it from the fort. But who knows what they might see from that," and he glanced through the forest canopy, up to the strange, skyward-receding orb.

Riijs thought. The floating sky-ship created another problem: as commander, where should he position himself? At the edge of the forest with the waiting assault forces, or back here to oversee the marksmen who he would instruct to bring down the sky-ship as soon as Barto's guns fired? Or should his marksmen go to work even before Barto's signal? If the airborne observer had already caught a glimpse of Riijs' main attack force, the element of surprise might be slipping through their fingers, even now—

Riijs focused outward once again; the runner, who had been standing there the whole time, seemed to reappear in front of him. "Go back to de edge of de forest wit deese orders: 'wait for my command to charge.' I will move to a position two hundred yards back from de line. Go." He looked round at the marksmen and loaders he had gathered to him. "All of you: go to de clearing we saw. Load wit small balls and use silk. You will need much range. Wait for my order to start shooting. And you:"—he pointed to one of the loaders—"come wit me. When I tell you to go, you will run back to deese men wit orders to fire on de ting in de sky." Riijs waved for his personal guards to form on him, and then followed after the first runner at a brisk walk, and wondered, "When will Barto fire those damned guns?" To which there was only one sure answer: the sooner, the better.

Chapter 24

Pitch Lake, Trinidad

Barto signaled for his packet to move closer to shore as they came around the headland—and found the enemy ship already bearing down upon them.

And it was a cromster, damn it. But an older one: her mizzenmast was lateen- rather than yawl-rigged. And from the look of how that rigging was dressed—

"Boys, I think we have some navy-trained fool captaining that ship."

"Fool or no, he's got twenty-eight guns to our sixteen," offered Dorsey, the chief gunner. "Probably heavier ones, too."

"Which he's been taught to use in set-piece broadsides, I'll wager. Out in deep water." *In deep water, where the great ships lumber like corpulent applebarges*—and then Barto saw how he was going to win this battle. "Gianetti, hard a-starboard. Berrick, signal the rest to follow us in."

Gianetti, back at the whipstaff, was wide-eyed. "Starboard? You mean—?"

"Take us into the shallows, Gianetti, as close as you can. And Dorsey?"

"Aye?"

"Give him a portside volley as we come over."

"At this range? Even with shot, we'll fall short by—call it two hundred yards."

"Good."

"You want to waste powder *and* make him think we don't know how to shoot?"

Barto turned to smile at his gunnery chief. "Yes, Dorsey, that's *exactly* what I want him to think."

Riijs heard the distant cannonade and turned to the second runner. "Run hard, back to de marksmen. Tell dem to shoot dat sky-ting and de man beneath it. Remember: silk on de musket balls, a half-measure more of powder. Go." Then, Riijs resumed moving toward his front line but did so at a slow walk. He would not be comfortable until he heard his marksmen firing at the observer watching his forces from the sky. . . .

Morraine felt the *Fleur Sable* lose headway as the wind spilled from his square-rigged sails, and then regain a half-measure of it as the breeze began filling out his lateen.

"Captain, he runs before us," called his pilot.

Morraine nodded, watching the pirate sloop and her two smaller sister ships—the latter packed with troops—run in closer against the shore. They were far in and had to be in danger of running aground. He had a deeper draft and could not follow them very far into the shallows, but he didn't need to do so. He only needed to come close enough to bring all his guns to bear. "Two points more to port, pilot. Crowd them in against the land."

"Captain, we have lost much of the wind, and if we go much closer—"

Morraine slapped the rail impatiently. "Obey, blast your eyes. We have not lost all the wind. We have the mizzen"—he jerked his chin at the billowing lateen sail—"and that will allow us to sail clear again. We are not attempting to board, merely coming over to bring our portside battery to bear."

"Yes, Captain." The pilot made his reply through a nervous swallowing noise.

Morraine looked overhead. The breeze was steady into the lateen. So what if it caught a bit less wind than a more modern fore-and-aft rig? It was not so *very* different. He had put *Fleur Sable* through her paces and she was a well-sprung hull, sprightly and responsive compared to the contemptible monsters he had commanded before. With this hull, surely it was possible to get in a little closer and put a solid broadside into the sloop before turning out to deeper water.

Morraine glanced up. The lateen sail's leading edge began to sag and flutter faintly. But surely such a simple maneuver as he intended was still possible.

Behind Riijs, the chaos started, at it usually did, all at once. From back in the clearing where his marksmen were now sniping at the sky-thing, the intermittent sounds of gunfire redoubled and became a fierce exchange. Riijs, now three hundred yards behind his main force, debated: ignore the sudden appearance of enemy troops behind him and start the charge, or set things to right in his rear area first? There were no lieutenants he could trust with either task. The skirmish behind him was unexpected and could be a trap. Charging the enemy stockade, while simpler, was a sprint into the unknown.

Riijs slapped his oldest bodyguard, Hernandez, on the shoulder, said, "Go bring twenty men from de front line." Then he turned and started sprinting to the rear. First things first.

The gunfire started and stopped a few times as he ran. Then it ceased, just as the runner he had sent back originally burst out of the brush in front of him—and almost got a ball through his head.

"Report," said Riijs, who lowered his snaphaunce pistol and resumed moving to the rear at a trot.

"An ambush. They were waiting—"

"I know dat. How many are dere, what are dey doing, how have we responded?"

"Riijs, we do not know how many there are. There could be twenty shooting occasionally. There could be five, reloading quickly and always moving. Our marksmen are dead—"

But of course they are—

"—and the rest of us have taken cover."

Riijs needed no further report. He had arrived at the rear of the defensive line his remaining men had set up on the safe side of the clearing. The senior among them, a mestizo who went by the strange name of Madre, pointed across the sun-flecked stretch of grass and scrub. "They pulled back. We sent four to follow. They're going to—"

Deeper in the trees that fringed the far side of the clearing, there was a sudden crash, a shout that turned into a scream, a single shot. Silence. Then three ragged pirate voices began shouting and cursing.

Riijs nodded. "Traps. Our enemies planned all dis.

Dey reasoned we would sneak in from de west coast, which means dey must have seen us coming ashore. And now dey want us to waste more time here. Which we will not do." As Hernandez arrived with the twenty men Riijs had requested, he looked down at Madre. "Use deese men to hold dis position. Do not follow de enemy further into de bush. Secure your flanks. I will start de attack on de stockade as soon as I reach our front line. Do not follow us. You must make sure dat deese enemy snipers do not threaten our rear."

Madre nodded and looked across the clearing again. "And what about the four—eh, three men we sent after them?"

A second scream and a shot. Silence.

Riijs shrugged. "Dey were dead men de moment you sent dem." He turned and began sprinting back to the main force.

Hugh, standing at his signaling position on the roof of the blockhouse, estimated that it had been a full two minutes since he had heard the rattle of musketry in the west forest. From the sound of it, the pirates had taken the bait once, but had not followed on into the second set of snares. Well, so far, things were going much better than capricious fate usually allowed. He put two fingers to his mouth and whistled twice. Out beyond the western wall of the stockade, in the center of the ballooning field, McGillicuddy's thick outline stopped moving, then his head came around. Hugh pointed up, and then made three down-pulling motions. McGillicuddy nodded and turned to his ground crew, who began hauling in the balloon's guide wires at the double-quick. Yes, Hugh reflected, everything seemed to be going almost suspiciously well, both on land and at sea. He turned to check on Morraine's pursuit of the pirates—

—and saw *Fleur Sable* angling landwards, saw the three pirate ships running before her, saw the mottled aqua moiré of shallows that the pirates had obviously navigated before, and into which Morraine had no business venturing. Not that he'd run aground: he had room enough to come over and avoid that, but if the lateen was out of position to tack back across the wind...

"Captain Morraine!" The cry of the leadsman, sounding line high in his hand, was shrill and anxious.

"Yes, yes, I see. Harder to port, Pilot."

Who complied, and then looked up. The lateen sail sagged to half her fullness. Morraine felt his heart quicken.

"Captain!" The leadsman, staring down into the water directly beneath the starboard bow, sounded even more panicked.

Morraine bit his lip, looked down amidships toward his gunnery officer. "Camignon?"

The gunnery officer snapped straight. "Yes, Captain?"

"How much of our portside battery bears on the sloop?"

"Nine guns, Captain. But we are losing the angle."

Which matched Morraine's own assessment: the sloop was running out of his field of fire faster than *Fleur Sable* was turning to track him. "Pilot, hard a-port. Camignon, stand ready! Steady, steady..." Morraine watched the firing angle improve, but then, as his lateen sail luffed and lost more wind, the rate of turn diminished, and the angle began widening out again. "Fire!"

But even as Morraine gave the order, the pirate sloop heeled over hard to port herself, swinging her bow sharply away from land and aiming it directly at *Fleur Sable*. This put the sloop head-on to Camignon's guns, and thus shrank her target profile by two-thirds. Of the nine balls that came roaring out from the port side of Morraine's cromster, three went past the sloop on her port side, four overshot her on the starboard. The other two smashed into her, blasting a deck gun overboard, clipping a sail free, and gouging a smoking pit into the middle of her weather deck. But the extraordinarily maneuverable pirate resumed her portside turn, tacking through the wind smartly to come all the way about. Her course now fully reversed, she headed back to cross in front of the almost completely becalmed *Fleur Sable*.

Like little curs following a wolf, the packet, and then the pinnace, turned about also—but they came straight back out toward the *Fleur Sable*. Morraine saw the men rising up on those crowded decks, boarding hooks held at the ready.

Mon Dieu, those brutes are not a second landing force. They are boarding parties. Which meant, Morraine realized, that he had done exactly what the pirate captain had wanted, and expected, him to do. The low-hulled packet would be under Morraine's guns before they could be reloaded and the sloop would have just slipped past on his port bow. Only the pinnace was far enough out that his guns could—

Then the pinnace heeled over, her five small port-side demi-culverins tilted up by her movement. As she began to right herself, the guns fired in volley.

A second before Morraine's eyes told him what was inbound, his ears detected the unmistakable, ferocious

moaning of chain-shot, headed straight up into his
drooping sails.

Riijs, nearing the end of his long sprint, vomited in
midstride: his breakfast came out in a side-streaming
rush, and then he was among the rearmost men of the
attack force. He looked up and down the tree line,
estimating rather than counting. He was about a dozen
shy of a full company. Not a lot, but it would have to do.
"Stand," he shouted. They rose, the assorted firearms of
their bloody trade bristling upward and outward like a
ragged hedge. "Ready and—at de trot—forward."

Half a step behind Riijs, who loosened his brace
of pistols and drew his cutlass an inch from its scabbard, the eighty-seven remaining buccaneers of the
Frisian's main attack force began loping northeast
toward the stockade.

Barto, eyes never leaving the cromster, shouted
back at his sailmaster. "Spill the mainsail, man; bring
to as we cross his bows." Then, to Dorsey: "Has the
starboard battery been reloaded as I ordered?"

Dorsey nodded with a gap-toothed grin. "The garbage is ready to go, Cap'n."

Gianetti, who was young for a pilot and new to The
Life, called forward through the wind. "'Garbage?'"

Barto shouted over his shoulder. "Do you know
what we pirates do with broken nails, old fishhooks,
rusted grommets?"

Gianetti, confused by the question, blinked. "No,"
he shouted back.

Barto turned, smiled. "Then just watch this."

❖   ❖   ❖

Morraine peered through the tangle of his shredded sails, dangling yards, and tilting masts to try to keep track of the sloop's progress. She had slowed just before she went athwart his hawse. Camignon's voice reached him through the ruin and sting of impending defeat. "Half the portside battery is reloaded and bears."

Morraine glanced quickly to his left; the pinnace was trying to bring its bow around to point at the *Fleur Sable*'s waist, but a quirk of the wind had slowed her. "Fire all, Camignon!"

Seven guns of the *Fleur Sable* spoke. Wood and smoke jetted up from the pinnace, which listed precipitously. Her jigger down, she slowed further, but then the wind freshened and she sped away after the sloop, her deck littered with bodies. Morraine felt a quick surge of hope; he looked forward again—just in time to see the sloop's midship gunwales swing into sight over his starboard bow and the pirate gunners lowering matches to fuses.

"Down!" Morraine shouted, and rather than flattening himself against the poop deck, he vaulted the rail and dropped into the quarterdeck's companionway. As he landed there, the discharges of eight cannon came roaring up the length of his spar deck. He had expected grape: he was not prepared for sangrenel. The uneven bits of metal screamed like enraged hornets, then growled and hissed and spat as they splintered, ripped, and chewed their way into and through everything that was upright on the main deck of the *Fleur Sable*.

It was over in a fraction of a second. Morraine rose quickly, wondering if maybe, just maybe, some straggler of that swarm of slaughtering scrap-iron might kill him, too. But he had to live to see the aftermath. Gunners who had been on the far side of their cannons had survived, as well as those few sharpshooters still up in the rigging. Behind him he heard feeble movement and a moan on the poop deck. But everywhere else, men were screaming, spurting blood from impossibly irregular gashes, whereas those who had been caught in the very center of the cone of death lay in mangled heaps, moving weakly as their blood poured out of scores of hideous wounds.

Morraine caught it all in a single glimpse. The very next second, the sloop's starboard bow swung about to roughly kiss his own and pirates swarmed onto his low fo'c'sle. A moment later, boarding hooks snapped down over his portside gunwales, and like a hoard of spiders, the brutes from the packet flowed up and onto his main deck, killing any who had strength enough to stand.

For Morraine, the situation was as easy to read as a book, which, in this case, was clearly a tragedy: his ship was lost. As he drew both his pistols, he watched half of the scant remains of his deck crew blasted aside by blunderbusses and run through by cutlasses. His own two shots, although each dropped one of the boarders, only served to infuriate and attract the attention of the ravening horde that is a pirate crew intent on slaughter. Six, maybe eight of the unwashed, bangled buccaneers came roaring at him, and Morraine realized that he had only one way to still snatch victory from the jaws of this defeat.

A ball splintered the heavy door frame as he turned and sped for the stairs to the gun deck. Yes, victory could still be his.

If he followed the example of Pyrrhus.

✧   ✧   ✧

Hugh waved St. Georges and his men back from the gates. "No, damn it, get on the platforms. Don't waste time bracing the doors. They won't hold anyway. They're not *meant* to."

"But *monsieur*, these timbers will buy us precious time as we—"

"St. Georges, do as I say or I will shoot you where you stand." Hugh produced his most coveted pistol, a double-barreled flintlock, to give substance to his threat.

St. Georges nodded to his six French marines. Each team of three dropped the heavy timber they had been preparing to wedge in behind the gates. "I must point out that, in civilized countries, the conventions of siege craft—"

"*Get on the wall,* St. Georges. Let's see if you can shoot as well as you talk."

With a curt nod, St. Georges dispatched his two three-man teams, one to each platform on either side of the gate. They joined the ten Irish soldiers of fortune already working there, each of whom slowly but steadily fired and reloaded a long-barreled rifle, electing not to touch an impressive array of preloaded smoothbores, all ready to hand. The marines, following the example of the Irish, did not disturb their own racks of preloaded weapons, but used their regular muskets to fire occasional, careful shots at the distant pirates.

Riijs considered his options. His men were tired from the trot, and most had drained their water skins at least an hour before. The sun was climbing higher and the volume of fire from the fort had picked up. At two hundred yards, this had been deemed a safe range at which to rest and reorganize, but some of the marksmen on the walls were evidently quite accomplished. One of his force had been killed, two incapacitated, and many unnerved by balls that came much closer than they should have. *The defenders have plenty of powder and, if I give them enough time, they have enough marksmen to either chase us back or whittle us down. No,* decided Riijs, standing up and earning a near miss for his trouble, *the time has come.* "All stand." He was answered by the rustle and clattering of eighty-four raiders rising to their feet. Many stared at the two hundred yards of open ground and then at Riijs. Mortal uncertainty—and the contemplation of mutiny—glimmered in the eyes of several.

Riijs brought up his pistol and aimed it at the dense jungle to the south. "You plan to hide dere? The Arawaks will kill you by sundown. And if our boats are sunk, you are stuck on dis island. So. You have one safe place to go:"—he swung around and aimed at the stockade—"dat fort. Everyplace else is death."

Those pirates who had wavered swallowed, nodded.

Riijs nodded back, then shouted. "Musketeers, halt at seventy yards and volley to cover our final approach. Every one else, we charge all de way. Axe-men and maul-men, stay near de front: you'll deal with de gate. Ready? Now—"

"They're charging!" Hugh called down to the wall. But the men there had seen it for themselves. They immediately shouldered their current weapons for one last shot at range. Their rifles spoke; a few of the onrushing figures sprawled. Then they set to cocking the hammers on all the waiting pieces.

At seventy yards, Hugh saw the pirates with longer weapons slow and bring their pieces up. "Down!" he shouted. All but one Frenchman responded promptly.

The pirates' loose volley was still impressive. Balls zipped overhead, splintered timbers, and one found its way through the slowest Frenchman's forehead. He pitched back off the platform as limp and lifeless as a sack of stones.

Only one or two of the pirates were hanging back and reloading. Hugh yelled down to his men, "Stand and fire at will."

The defenders needed little encouragement. With a horde of ruthless attackers at fifty yards or less, the Irish and the French quickly found targets, fired, dropped the spent musket, grabbed the next. At about twenty yards, a few of the pirate muskets spoke again, joined increasingly by pistols and blunderbusses as the distance narrowed. The defenders started feeling the firepower of the attackers. Another Frenchman went down. An Irishman, soft-voiced Murphy, toppled off the platform, an arterial wound spraying like a bright red roostertail as he fell. Others were wounded.

St. Georges, wild-eyed, spun to look up at Hugh. "Monsieur, do you lack the courage to defend your own walls?"

Hugh gritted his teeth and ignored the question. "Abandon the platforms, St. Georges. Fall back to the barricades to either side of the lane. As we discussed."

"Abandon the—?"

"Off the walls, damn you!"

"But without us to fire down upon them, the brutes will surely get in."

"Damn it, do as I say."

St. Georges spat conspicuously but complied. Hugh would worry about offended honor later. For now, he was counting how many men he had lost, and let his eye wander back to the storehouse, where McGillicuddy stood waiting in front of the doors.

Axes started thudding into the gates, followed closely by the dull thump of mauls. From Hugh's vantage point it was difficult to tell just how many pirates were clumped together there, or were surprised to discover that the gates were built more lightly than the walls of the stockade, being fashioned of wide-set trunks that were both thin and dry. The light, gapped construction had been an essential part of Don Michael's tactical contribution to Hugh's overall defensive strategy—a tactic which Michael had insisted on withholding from the French. When asked why, he simply answered, "I don't trust 'em to protect us, so why should I trust 'em to follow our plans or keep our secrets?" Hugh had publicly expressed nothing but confidence in the up-timer's daring tactic, but had nursed his own unspoken doubts about it. Which rose up once again: *Michael, if your plan doesn't work, they are going to rush over us like a wave over ants—*

The sound of thumping and hacking doubled. "Get your men back and under cover!" Hugh shouted down toward St. Georges, who made a wan attempt to comply.

Your funeral, thought Hugh, who turned toward McGillicuddy and raised his fist high. McGillicuddy nodded, raised his own fist, signaling he was ready. Hugh dropped his hand.

McGillicuddy heaved at the left-side door of the storehouse. It swung open, revealing the French eight-pounder that Michael had positioned there, muzzle trained directly at the gate. "Fire," shouted McGillicuddy.

The roar of the saker was underscored by a faint rush of what sounded like immense, growling bees. The bow-wave of the double-loaded grapeshot went straight thought the lightly constructed gate, splintering almost half of it and summoning forth a chorus of shrieks and screams that, though inarticulate, conveyed one fact very clearly:

Many of the remaining pirates had just been wounded or killed.

Riijs wiped blood from the side of his face, checked, found that it was not his own but had instead come sheeting over him when the maul-man who had been hammering at the gate's right-side hinge-points had his left lung blown free of his body. Riijs—who had been standing farther to the right and was thus sheltered by the stockade wall—had escaped death by mere inches. Which did not impress him in the slightest.

Instead, he counted his men as he moved toward the gate. He had lost about fifteen dead and wounded reaching the stockade. This blast of grapeshot had cost him almost twenty more, most of whom were incapacitated or killed outright. Grapeshot rarely inflicted flesh-wounds, after all. That left him a force of about fifty, too many of whom were wavering. But judging from the enemy's sudden abandonment of the walls, Riijs had the sneaking suspicion that—

"Dere are less of dem than we thought. Hernandez, you keep five men out here to watch our backs. De rest of you: through de gate and follow me!"

❖   ❖   ❖

Morraine used the butt of his pistol to club the pirate who had discovered him on the gun deck. The man fell, but with a long moan. The other pirates, who were slipping in through the gun ports, heard, looked, saw, and started back toward the captain.

Morraine finished staving in the top of the powder keg, laid his pistol down upon it sideways, so that its action touched the loose gunpowder just beneath the copper lip of the cask. He cocked the flintlock's hammer—

—just as he felt something cool slide into the center of his back. Before he could blink, a pirate's cutlass-point came out the front of his doublet, coated in his own blood.

But you are too late, Morraine thought. His lip quirked, and he pulled the trigger of his double-primed flintlock.

Barto had just jumped onto the foredeck of the crippled cromster when, beneath the main deck, and just abaft the mainmast, he heard a loud, hoarse explosion, more like a large grenade than a gun, but clearly greater than either.

In the first split second after the sound, Barto realized he had heard it once before, but could not immediately place it.

In the next split second, he remembered how, when pouring a close broadside into the first galleon he had ever attacked, he hit the ship's magazine, which did not, as tales tell, go up all at once. Rather, there was a loud but muted blast that announced the first fateful ignition of a keg of powder—

And in the last split second, Barto connected the

present sound with that earlier one—and thus knew that, truly, this was his last split second.

A louder, timber-ripping roar blasted deck planks upward as the full contents of the *Fleur Sable*'s magazine detonated.

Chapter 25

Pitch Lake, Trinidad

Behind Hugh, there was a shuddering blast that sent a tremor even through the timbers of the blockhouse's roof. He turned and saw, half a mile out to sea, tiny specks flying up in the air, smoke and flame billowing after them, chasing them into the sky. Staying low, Hugh scrambled across the roof to the northern waist-works and peeked over—just in time to see the back half of the pirate packet sink like a stone: her bow was entirely gone. As was the *Fleur Sable*. The sloop listed, engulfed in flames, and then, the ready powder for her deck guns started going off. Like explosive hammer blows, the loose charges tore apart her spar deck, section by section, until, after the fifth blast, some ember or burning chunk must have sleeted down into the reserve munitions she kept below. With a final concussive roar that rivaled the *Fleur Sable*'s, the pirate sloop disintegrated outwards in a fury of self-annihilation.

Riijs heard the two titanic blasts as he and a dozen of his men shouldered open the tattered gate, guns in hand, looking for targets—

—and found themselves facing a dandy in the uniform of a French naval officer, four of that nation's marines standing nervously behind him, apparently uncertain whether they should raise their muskets or not.

Riijs raised his gun. This was going to be easier than he thought.

The dandy stepped forward from behind a rude barricade of wooden crates. "Monsieur, my sword."

And, as if he were on some battlefield where such things actually occurred—which Riijs secretly doubted—the Frenchman drew and proffered his sword.

Riijs stared at it, saw, from the corner of his eye, some other soldiers—mercenaries from the look of them—clambering up on a platform set against the stockade's inner, eastern face. They glanced up toward the compound's central building—a fair approximation of a blockhouse—and then, after waiting a moment for some signal that evidently did not come, went over the wall.

Before Hugh could finish recrossing the blockhouse roof back to his signaling position at the south-facing waist-works, he saw that two of his men had scrambled up one of the platforms on the east wall, and now vaulted the top of the stockade. Deserters? From *his* ranks? No. Not unless—

Frowning, dreading the worst, he rushed to see what was happening near the gate—

Riijs stared at the Frenchman's sword, took it. Now what?

The dandy did not keep him waiting. "Naturally,

we would have fought on as honor demands, but our commander, he is an Irish incompetent and all but opened our gates to you. Now he is nowhere to be seen. So shall we arrange a ransom?"

"A ransom?"

"But of course. It is the civilized option, no?"

Ransom? To Riijs, this young Frenchman didn't look or act like any prince. "Who's your father?" he asked.

The dandy actually made a little bow. "I am the son of Geoffrey St. Georges of Rheims."

"And is he a duke? A count?"

"No, my father is a wealthy merchant."

"Den his son is a dead man."

Before the dandy could blink, Riijs shot him through the forehead.

Hugh saw the shot as he arrived back at the roof's southern waist-work. The French marines, stunned, raised their muskets. One was fast enough to get off a shot before they went down under a hail of pistol fire.

But not as much pistol fire as Hugh had expected. Indeed, he saw very few ready pistols still dangling from the pirates' sweaty neck-lanyards. And with St. Georges gone, there was nothing obstructing the line of sight between the storehouse and the raiders...

O'Rourke crawled forward from the fringe-scrub of the east woods, and tapped Fitzwilliam on the boot. He pointed out the half dozen pirates clustered around the stockade's gate. "Nice and steady now."

Fitzwilliam raised his very long flintlock. A moment passed. Another. Then he fired and immediately reached toward the loader for another of the weapons.

One of the handful of figures by the gate fell to his knees with a yell that came quite clearly over the one-hundred-thirty yards.

The rest of the Irish marksmen began to fire their long, rifled weapons. Another pirate went down. The others crouched and milled uncertainly.

O'Rourke turned back toward his other thirty men, their faces dim within the edge of the forest. Dim except for their bright, eager eyes.

"So lads, here we go. And no wastin' breath shouting 'O'Donnell Abu.' We'll chant it loud once these bastards are dead. So—up now!"

Despite the forty-odd pirates near the gate, Hugh stood up and looked back toward the storehouse.

McGillicuddy reappeared in the doorway.

Hugh raised his hand just as a loud, enraged shout warned of a figure on the roof of the blockhouse.

McGillicuddy raised his hand also.

Down below, a piece fired; a bullet clipped the wooden waist-works five inches to Hugh's left just as he brought his hand down.

McGillicuddy did likewise as he pushed open the storehouse's right-hand door—and revealed Michael's second French saker.

The crew didn't wait for the command: the weapon roared. The carnage around the gate was immediate and horrific.

Hugh gave the "lock up" sign to McGillicuddy. The crews reached out and pulled the two storehouse doors closed. Hugh ducked back down, scurried to the stairs, and descended them three at a time.

Michael was waiting at the base of the stairs, watching

the blockhouse's open doorway from across its wide ground-floor room. "What the hell has gone wrong?"

"I went wrong."

"You?"

"Yes. I took a moment to check on Morraine. Who is dead." Hugh began checking and cocking his pistols.

"And let me guess, while you were gone—"

"St. Georges also went wrong, yes." Hugh looked ruefully at the open doorway. Doyle had intended to hang the door this afternoon. Too late now.

"Okay, so St. Georges messed up. No surprise. But where are his men, and yours?" McCarthy matched Hugh's worried glance at the doorway to the compound. "I kept waiting for all of them to fall back in here and—"

"They're not coming. They're dead or gone. It's just us, now."

"Us?"

"No time to talk, Michael. We've got to hold out until O'Rourke gets here. I'll cover the door."

"Well, then I'm coming along to—"

"No. You fetch the musketoon we gave you and go to the roof. Cover the door, but don't shoot too soon. Let them bunch up."

"I'm a newbie, not an idiot," Michael grumbled, and he was gone.

Hugh drew and hefted two pistols. So now it was a race between how fast the pirates could overwhelm them and how fast O'Rourke's men could get inside the compound.

Had Hugh been a betting man, he wouldn't have wasted any money betting on himself.

❖   ❖   ❖

Riijs picked himself up off the ground, found he was one of the lucky ones who had, again, survived the grapeshot unscathed, and counted the rest. He was down to twenty-five men. But half of them were either glancing or drifting back out the gate: *fools, turning back with safety finally at hand*.

However, it seemed that their flight might be short lived. Judging from shouts outside the stockade, the group he'd left with Hernandez was evidently under attack and preparing to fall back *inside* the walls. Which probably meant a threat from the east wood—

But there was no time to think about that now. The first order of business was to take the blockhouse. The gate hung in ruins, so the stockade walls would not keep out a new threat. He had to commandeer the one remaining strongpoint. Which meant no time for better tactics, no time to reload. Just—

"Rush de blockhouse! Now!"

Hugh got to the blockhouse's reinforced doorway just as the irregular wave of pirates drew within ten feet of it, cutlasses drawn. Firing and pulling one pistol after another, Hugh dropped the first three while standing his ground but had to retreat back inside the doorway to get the next one—who sagged but did not go down. Hugh pulled his double-barreled flintlock as the rest, clumping together in their rush, came tight around the door. And Hugh thought, *Now, Michael, now!*

As if on cue, there was a thunderous roar, akin to a shotgun, overhead. Two more pirates at the rear of the press went down, cursing.

But the rest surged forward. Hugh fired his flintlock's

two barrels in rapid succession, and drew his saber just in time to parry the first blow from a pirate cutlass.

Once forced back from the door, Hugh had no time to plan, no time to feint, no time to trick his foes: they were all around him. He yanked out his main-gauche and was immediately glad for it. His attackers hemmed him in so tightly that he had almost no time to attack, only parry—and be grateful for every second that he remained alive. Most of the pirates were passable swordsmen, but their shorter weapons were at a disadvantage in this relatively open space. However, two of their number—and in particular, a tall, very pale, very blond, and very calm fellow—were quite good, much better than what Hugh usually encountered on European battlefields. Nevertheless, in the first ten seconds, Hugh had managed to wound two and sever another's windpipe with an unexpected backhand cut. In return, he had acquired a deep slice in his right thigh, a flesh-wound in his left arm, and a growing need to know the answer to one key question:

Where the hell *is O'Rourke?*

The blond pirate, evidently the leader, must have seen Hugh's reflexive glance toward the blockhouse door. He launched a back cut that was actually a feint, taking Hugh off balance just as the true strike came in. Hugh got his main-gauche up in time to block the pirate's cutlass, but not solidly: his long-quilloned parrying dagger rang, spun out of his left hand and skittered across the floor. The blond fellow smiled: removing the main-gauche had obviously been his intent. As he came in again, two of the others followed, coordinating their attacks with their leader's—

The report of a gun, unusually loud and piercing,

stopped the swordplay as abruptly as if it had stopped time itself. The blond man sagged and crumpled to the floor—revealing Michael at the base of the steps, legs braced, both hands wrapped tightly around the little gun that his father had given him. Which now spoke again and again. Six more times it fired; three more pirates went down. The last four tried bolting out the door, but Hugh was faster. He ran two through from behind, and cut down another that turned to parry. The fourth and last, falling over the bodies piled in the narrow doorway, begged for mercy that Hugh chose not to show.

When he came back into the blockhouse, he discovered that Michael was trimming the straps on his up-time backpack. Hugh leaned against the wall; he wanted to laugh, both with relief and amusement at Michael's rather bizarre choice of post-combat activity. "Going on a trip?"

Michael looked up, no smile on his face. "Uh, yeah. I've got to go. Now."

Hugh laughed, then stopped, seeing Michael's unchanged expression. "You're serious."

"Yep. Listen, you've done a great job, Hugh. Turenne is going to be very pleased, and I suspect his ship will be along soon to help you."

Hugh frowned. "You 'suspect'? You must *know*. How else were you planning to depart?"

"Well—there's another ship."

"Another—?" And then Hugh stopped and felt cold spread outward from his spine. "Another ship. The ship that Mulryan spotted farther to the east, last night."

Michael nodded. "Dutch. The *Koninck David*, under Jakob Schooneman."

"And why do you only tell me this *now*...?" But he saw the reason before Michael could respond. "This expedition has all been an elaborate ploy, hasn't it?"

"No, the deal with Turenne is real. Sort of. He's already got his balloon and he'll get his oil—*if* Richelieu's agents make you the best deal for it. Just as we agreed."

"Then why this skulduggery, Michael? Why not stay and—?"

"Because that's not part of the plan."

Hugh narrowed his eyes. "Whose plan?"

"Mine. And the USE's."

"So you are their agent. And now that this site has been wrested from the Spanish, will I be expected to turn it over to Gustav Adolf, or directly to you Americans?"

"No, absolutely not. It's yours."

"It's Turenne's."

"It is if he decides to make the best offer. And if you decide to sell it to him. You might want to wait a day or two, see if a better offer comes along."

Hugh frowned. "Turenne paid for this mission. All of it."

"Look, Hugh, right now you own this piece of real estate. Or rather, your 'corporation' does. But tell me, what will you do if Turenne's boss Richelieu won't offer a fair price?"

And Hugh once again suddenly found himself hobbled by his personal Achilles' heel: his reflexive tendency to put faith in self-professed allies and their promises. "I do not know what I would do. I suppose I would have to trust in Turenne's influence."

"Turenne's influence is at Richelieu's pleasure. Here's

another poser for you: what if Richelieu decides he's not interested at all? What then?"

Hugh had no answer. "Then, I suppose, we are all lost."

"You suppose wrong. There are other people interested in making you an offer if Richelieu's falls through. Remember, Hugh, you own this land. Capturing it was your mission, and you've succeeded."

Hugh scoffed. "Succeeded? Michael, have you been paying attention over the past few weeks? Our 'secret' approach to Pitch Lake was obviously disclosed to our foes. Within two weeks of arriving here, we have been attacked. And although the enemy we fought was only a pirate band, we can rest assured that they learned of us from a greater power. I'm betting on Spain. Which must therefore know of our landing and, as soon as sufficient force has been gathered, will come and obliterate us. Against which we have little defense, since all of Morraine's crew is surely dead, and our only ship is lost. And you call this a success?"

But in staring long at Michael's gray eyes, Hugh saw that his arguments had made no impact. So how would this debacle still be a success for Michael and the USE? And then, he knew. "You want them to come here, don't you? All of them, and in force: the Spanish, the French, and the Dutch. Our attempt to seize Pitch Lake highlights its strategic importance. And you amplified that impression with your great show of stealth. The balloon was the masterstroke. Who would employ so special and secret a device if the stakes were not correspondingly high? And besides, it was a piece of technological bait that Turenne could neither resist nor ignore. But in reality, it was all just theater, staged to make this miserable patch of tar a seemingly irresistible object, and to draw the attention and the forces of the great powers here." He thought, then smiled. "So if you Americans want everyone's attention focused here, it only stands to reason that your real interest was to distract them, so that they will be less likely to notice when you advance on your true objective here in the New World—"

Mike suddenly grew very pale, and his gray eyes jumped sideways. "I've gotta go."

Hugh leaned back again. "You might as well admit that my conjecture is correct. The change in your color has told me as much." He glanced to confirm that Mike had indeed packed away his pistol and then smoothly brought out the boot dagger he kept as a final hold-out. "And now, having discerned your true objective, I have become a danger to its attainment. So logically, you will wish to move against me."

Michael's pallor was dramatically superseded by a bright, angry flush, and his eyes narrowed. "Damn it, Hugh, that's the first stupid thing you've said."

"How so?"

"Because part of what makes you so valuable is how damned smart you are. Which means it was always probable that you would figure this out, anyway. It's a risk that was considered, and was deemed acceptable."

"But now that I know—"

"—'Know' what? What do you really 'know'? That the Americans might be up to something in South America or Mexico or the Caribbean? If I had a dollar for every one of those rumors, I'd be a rich man. All you 'know' is that we wanted this to happen."

"And probably, in the long run, hope to own Trinidad yourselves."

But Mike was shaking his head. "No. That's not the point of this."

"Then what is?"

Michael looked away for a moment, seemed to listen—probably for O'Rourke's approach—then he met Hugh's eyes again. "Now listen carefully, Hugh. Right here, right now, you're in charge of Pitch Lake. You make the decisions. And as long as you hold this ground, you have leverage. You have something—at last—with which to bargain, something that will actually make nations pay attention to your cause and keep their promises."

Hugh blinked. He had been a captain of soldiers since before he truly needed to shave, so he was well acquainted with faces of men whose passionate determination was not only grim, but vengeful. And that expression was now set deep into the lines of Michael Jr.'s suddenly aged face. To which he addressed the question, "Why?"

"'Why' what?"

"Why do this for me? Without promise of alliance?"

Michael's eyes did not waver. "You've said it yourself: you, your family, and your nation have had a belly full of broken promises. You've been bled white by the people who strung you along on easy assurances of aid and alliance. And as the years went by, they simply turned you—all of you—into their pet war-dogs." Mike suddenly grew very red again. "No more. Not one bit more. Take this place. Bargain with it. Bargain hard. Recruit any Dutch who hate the Spanish: there are plenty. Recruit the English, who have been forsaken by their own king. Recruit the privateers who thought themselves patriots, but found themselves disowned by their own nations. It won't take many desperate men to hold this place. And if you deal fair with the natives, they'll deal fair with you."

"And how do you know that?"

"Because our Dutch friends in Suriname have been in contact with the Nepoia tribes here on Trinidad for half a year. The Nepoia's own displaced tribal king Hyarima has given Jakob Schooneman his word that he will receive your envoys and deal fair with you. With you alone, Hugh O'Donnell. Think it through, man: why do you think the Arawaks were not here when you landed? Because our Dutch partners convinced Hyarima to make war on the Arawaks, and draw them away from peripheral areas like Pitch Lake. Hyarima and the rest of the Nepoia tribes want to throw off the Spanish control of their towns, and take their lands back from the Arawaks. Armed with trade muskets from the *Koninck David*, I suspect they're making some progress, too."

Hugh wished there was a chair to collapse into. "And so I am to simply sell Pitch Lake to the highest bidder?"

Mike shrugged. "That's up to you. If Richelieu makes the best offer, it seems like you owe him the right of first refusal. But whatever you do, remember this: sitting on oil means you're sitting on both great peril and great promise. For yourself and your country. And by your country, I don't just mean the Spanish Lowlands. I mean Ireland."

Hugh felt himself suddenly, inexplicably moved. McCarthy's often veiled eyes seemed not only open, but pleading. And he felt his face smile crookedly, despite his resolve not to. "You have some of the bardic tongue of your forebears, Michael McCarthy. I shall heed your words, and watch my step."

Michael nodded, walked to the doorway, stopped, and handed Hugh a heavy cloth bag. "In case some of your enemies require a little extra persuasion," he explained, and was out the door at a trot.

Hugh heard Michael's hastening boots diminuendo toward the north end of the stockade. He heard O'Rourke's loud and worried approach from the south. He looked at the bodies littering the floor of the blockhouse. And then he looked in the leaden bag.

In an ungracious lump at the bottom he saw Michael's holstered .45, four magazines, and several boxes of ammunition. He hoped he would not need them.

But Hugh O'Donnell conceded that, before too many days had passed, he probably would.

Mike McCarthy, Jr., found Hyarima's hand-picked Nepoia scouts waiting for him just outside the stockade when he reached the platform at the center of the north wall. They tossed up a hooked line. Mike snugged the hook between two of the palisade's timbers and went down, hand over hand.

Staying on east-bound game-paths, they made good time, first moving within the tree line that paralleled the north coast, and then directly alongside the shore itself.

After approximately twenty minutes of brisk walking, Mike caught sight of a lugger beached in a small cove up ahead. The crew, two Dutch seamen, saw them coming, and stood up slowly, casually—

—the same way Ed Piazza had stood up when Mike had entered his office in Grantville almost a year ago to present him with The Plan. . . .

✧   ✧   ✧

Mike and Ed had made small talk for a few minutes on that day, and then got down to discussing Mike's proposal. McCarthy pointed out that, with the situation changing across Europe, Simpson and Stearns must already be thinking in terms of a journey to develop and tap into some of the singular resources of the New World. "But I know that's not happening too soon," qualified Mike, "at least, not until Simpson's done building his expeditionary force."

Ed kept his posture and his face relaxed, but his voice betrayed him. In a tighter, slightly nasal accent, Ed repeated, "Not until Simpson's done *what*?"

Mike leaned back. "When I was up north on the Baltic coast a few months back, I saw the kind of ships he's building. High weather designs. More than you need if you were just going to sail around the Baltic. I also noticed his mast arrangements, as well as the smaller hulls he's been procuring. Handy, shallow-draft, fore-and-aft rigged boats. Again, not for the Baltic."

"Perfect for the Med, however."

"Sure, they'd work in the Med, except we have no reason to go there and any operations would have to start with a very high-profile run through Gibraltar. That's not been the USE's *modus operandi*, to date. But the Caribbean—and the Gulf—is open access, and more importantly, it has something the Med doesn't."

"Oh? Like what?" Ed seemed to be trying to hide a smile now.

"Coastal oil. In a variety of places."

"True enough. And does your crystal ball reveal our hypothetical destinations there?"

"Nope, and I don't want to know. Because then

I'd know too much, and you wouldn't let me leave Grantville, much less go on a Caribbean cruise."

"True enough. For now. But how can you help me if you don't even know where we're—hypothetically— going?"

"Well, part of the trouble with any move into the Caribbean and the Gulf is that there's a good bit of traffic there already. And most of it belongs either to potential rivals or outright enemies, both of whom would like nothing better than to get wind of what you're doing, and either give you hell while you're doing it or make it entirely impossible."

"Okay, so how can you fix that?"

In response, Mike made his "Pitch Lake pitch," including the use of the balloon. Ending with, "And that's why Pitch Lake is the perfect stalking horse for your *real* operation."

"A 'stalking horse'?"

"Sure. Look, all your rivals already know that Pitch Lake exists, so you're not giving away any intelligence, right? And because it's a source of easy oil, it's going to be a pretty appealing piece of real estate, once they start thinking about it a little more. There's minimum difficulty accessing the crude, and they can boil and process a lot of what they need right out of the seeps in the lake itself."

"Go on."

"So if any colonial power in the Caribbean makes a grab for it, the others will probably wake up and follow. They all understand the importance of oil. Hell, Turenne chose to raid the field at Wietze not just to put it out of commission, but to acquire technical intelligence on oil production. So the French are thinking about using oil, which means they're thinking about getting it. And the rest can't be too far behind."

Ed tapped his goose quill lightly on the paper in front of him. "Hypothetically speaking, it might be very helpful to create a diversion in Trinidad. But we're spread so thin as it is, that—"

"I didn't say anything about *our* taking Trinidad, did I?"

Ed stopped tapping the pen. "Why, no—no, you didn't." And he smiled. "Turenne?"

"Yep, Turenne. Indirectly, that is. You give him the opportunity to grab Pitch Lake and get a leg-up on hot air ballooning all in one fell swoop, and he'll take the bait. Even if he suspects he's being played. But he won't have the authority to seize a Spanish possession himself, so he'd have to bankroll a 'free company' of independent speculators. From whom France can then buy the property they've 'acquired.'"

Ed frowned. "That's a pretty small legal fig leaf."

"It's a giant palm frond compared to the legal contortions the Dutch and the Brits have undertaken to justify some of their 'rightful conquests.' But that's okay, because the more ambiguous the French claim is, the more contention there will be. Meaning France will have to send some local forces quickly to protect her ownership. Spain will attempt a swift reconquest, so they'll need to use local forces, too."

Ed's frown had not disappeared. "I'm not sure the news that Pitch Lake is up for grabs will make its way to Havana and Cartagena as quickly as you're hoping, Mike."

"Then we help it along by leaking it selectively. Some of the Dutch traders that young Phil Jenkins traveled with last year could spread a few rumors in the right ports, at the right time. And the resulting clustering effect around Trinidad should reduce the general traffic in the other parts of the Caribbean. Which gives Admiral Simpson, or whoever he sends, a freer hand and more open waters to make a run to—well, to wherever they're going."

"Mike, I won't deny it: your plan has some promise. But there's one hitch."

"What's that?"

"Hugh O'Donnell. His willing cooperation is central to your plan's success."

"Absolutely."

"Well, from what I know of him, this isn't exactly his style. Ethically speaking, that is. What you're contemplating is just half a step shy of outright land-piracy. If that much. What if O'Donnell decides he just doesn't want to play?"

"He'll play. He *has* to, Ed. He's learned some difficult things about his future. So he needs to make a change, a big change."

"Okay, but how do we, um . . . 'guide' him into believing that leading an overseas land-grab is the right way to go about making this kind of change?"

"By using a carrot and a stick."

"Huh. I can see the carrot: money, power, and influence are all needful things for an estranged earl. But the stick?"

Mike rubbed his nose, looked away. This was the part he loathed. "Once Hugh leaves Spanish employ, we could lead him to believe that he needs a new patron. Really quickly."

"And how do we do that?"

"Hugh grew up knowing that his godmother, Archduchess Isabella, was shielding him from English assassins. One of The O'Neill's young sons, Brian, was strangled in Brussels about eighteen years ago when his keepers got careless one evening."

"Okay, but O'Donnell is no boy. He won't scare easily."

"No, but if he thinks his presence poses a threat to those he cares about, he'll want to put some hefty distance between himself and them. And that, of course, will give him a strong incentive to snap up any reasonable opportunity to pursue his goals overseas. At least for a while."

"Okay, I'll buy that. It fits his character. But how do you propose to convince him that he's got this kind of immediate bull's-eye painted on his back?"

Mike squared his shoulders. "We hire the necessary agents through our contacts in the underworld and stage an abduction attempt."

"We have 'contacts' in the underworld?"

"Ed, as I understand it, the Abrabanels and their partners not only know whose closets contain which skeletons, but also which confidential agents were responsible for making the skeletons in the first place."

"Ahem . . . okay, I'm still listening."

"So, we go through those 'channels' to recruit a pair of apparent kidnappers."

"And what would their orders be?"

"Simple: to make a 'gentle' attempt to capture the man wearing the earl of Tyrconnell's cloak. Which I'll make sure that *I* have on when they come calling."

"You? Why should you be the shill for your own con game, Mike?"

Michael felt like vomiting. "Because Hugh has

adopted Dad and me like we're family. If one or both of us are threatened because of him—"

Ed nodded. "Then he'll feel guilt and be more tractable, easy to guide, particularly overseas where you'd both be out of harm's way. Okay, but how do we keep you and Hugh safe during this sham abduction? What if the kidnappers get a little too, um, enthusiastic when they try to grab you, or resist O'Donnell?"

"We tell our hirelings to use minimal force, and that if they kill or even wound either the mark or his friends, they get no pay."

"Won't that make the kidnappers suspicious?"

Mike shook his head. "Not if we make it clear that the point of the kidnapping is extortion. When the objective is to acquire surreptitious leverage over people, you can't kill the hostage, or their family, or their friends. Any 'professional' will understand that. So we explain that if the abduction is too difficult to manage safely, it's enough that they give the mark a good scare."

Ed smiled, stood. "Y'know, Mike, this plan might work. I'll think it over and send word in a couple of days." He put out his hand—

Now Michael found himself staring at a different hand—that of a Dutch sailor who was offering to help him into the lugger. Michael took the hand and let himself be guided over the side of the boat. He wondered at the sudden weakness in his limbs, wondered at the wetness on his cheeks, wondered how he had been able to betray O'Donnell, and wondered why the rationalizations he had repeated to himself every day since leaving Ed's office just didn't make the self-loathing go away.

But here—surrounded by Nepoias and common Dutch seamen who probably didn't understand one word of English—he could whisper the real, gut-level, impolitic truth of why he had so profoundly and horribly manipulated the life of Hugh Albert O'Donnell:

"He's their only hope," Mike confessed to the shining waters in a murmur that barely got past the thick ache in his throat. "His family, his men, his country: they'll be dying even sooner, now—unless Hugh can get enough leverage to save them."

But if the Nepoias or the Dutchmen had even heard Michael, they gave no sign. Instead, without a word, they swung the lugger's prow around and began a swift run across the bright blue bay toward the waiting *Koninck David*, and ultimately, a rendezvous with the allies Hugh didn't even know he had.

For McCarthy, the presence of the *Koninck David* was a message in itself, the text of which read: *we have found Tromp's fleet and they are coming.* And if the fates were kind, Tromp's ships would already have linked up with Simpson's advance recon flotilla, which was carrying a letter from the infanta Isabella to Hugh. That probably lengthy missive was all at once a plea, an explanation, and an apology from the one person in power that the attainted earl truly trusted. But Michael was uncertain that any of Hugh's trust would survive a reading of that letter's explication of the many half-truths, deceptions, and wiles that had made possible his seizure of Trinidad.

Michael McCarthy felt his throat tighten again. He stared at the sun's reflection upon the scudding wavelets, letting that light burn into his brain, burn away the guilt, help him to think of nothing.

Chapter 26

Off Saba, Lesser Antilles

Of all the officers and ground crew gathered at the *Intrepid*'s mizzen, only Ove Gjedde seemed immune to yawns. Staring up where the balloon tether disappeared into the predawn dark, Eddie Cantrell was not the only one who yearned for the comfort of his bunk, but he may have yearned for it more than most. Of them all, only he had a wife in his bed, a wife who often awakened right about now. It would not have been accurate to say that she then arose, but rather, that she drowsily greeted the day and her husband—amorously—before catching another two or three hours of post-coital slumber.

But instead of that wonderful conjugal greeting, Eddie was waiting to see what came sparking down the telegraph wire that was secured to the balloon's mooring cable. Which, he decided, was a pretty lousy trade. At least some of his command staff, such as Rik Bjelke, were still catching shut-eye. On Eddie's orders, no less.

Mutiny was apparently in the early morning breeze, though: Rik Bjelke appeared in the companionway that led down to the staterooms. "Captain, Commander: any news?"

Eddie tried to frown. "Nothing except a discussion about how long you're going to be thrown in the brig. What are you doing out of your bunk, mister?"

Rik was smiles and apologies as he made his way over to Eddie and Gjedde. "My pardons, sirs, but I could not sleep. Not even with an extra swallow of brandy. Too eager to hear the news, I suppose."

Which, Eddie conceded, was certainly understandable, but wasn't any help. "Mr. Bjelke, I appreciate your interest in the results of our reconnaissance, but as the day wears on, I need someone at the con who was not already awake at the end of the middle watch. That was supposed to be you."

Rik glanced up into the darkness sheepishly. "Yes, sir. My apologies. I could go below, try to drink more brandy." Gjedde's mouth twitched to resist the emergence of a smile.

Eddie sighed. "Well, I'd rather have you tired than drunk, Rik. You might as well stay on deck until we get word."

"Which should be soon," Gjedde said with a look eastward. The rim of the world was no longer satin black, but dark, downy gray.

Rik's glance traveled from the balloon cable to the reefed sails. "Where are we, just now?"

Eddie felt the wind rise to about two knots, then settle again, and he wondered what their observer in the balloon was experiencing. "St. Eustatia is about twenty-eight miles south-by-southeast. Saba is about fifteen miles south-by-southwest. At about five-hundred-fifty feet altitude, our observer reported seeing multiple light sources in what should be Oranjestad. That's probably good news. The number of original settlers wouldn't generate enough light—or the right type—to be visible at 0400 hours."

"That's wonderful!" Bjelke exclaimed. "So Tromp is there!"

Gjedde's voice was much cooler than the breeze. "Or the Spanish. In which case, Oranjestad has been conquered and we must reformulate our plans."

As if to rebuff the gloom of the Norwegian's caveat, the first bright rim of the sun pushed over the wine-dark horizon. Far above them, the gray-blue canopy of the balloon seemed to materialize out of the diffusing darkness, catching the first feeble rays a moment before they also glowed faintly against the spars and gunwales of the *Intrepid*.

Eddie knew there wasn't light enough for the observer to see clearly yet—that would take a little longer—but he still found himself listening for the first chattering of the telegraph that would announce the fateful report from aloft.

Rik's hands were moving nervously. A glance from Gjedde had the young man fold them quickly behind his back. "So," Bjelke said in a tone that suggested he was casting about for a subject, "evidently no encounters with the Spanish when we passed Saint Maarten?"

"None," answered Eddie. "Captain Gjedde timed our pass perfectly." Which, despite sounding like hyperbole, was a simple statement of fact. True to his intent and his word, Ove Gjedde, piloting for the fleet at Mund's insistence, had slowed Reconnaissance Flotilla X-Ray's approach into the Caribbees so that at 9 PM, they were approximately fourteen miles northwest of St.

Maarten. Crowding sail once the last light was out of the western sky, the flotilla ran past the Spanish-held island at a distance of ten miles, each darkened vessel running but one small light well beneath the weather deck of its starboard quarter. Traveling in a westward-staggered echelon, the ships of Reconnaissance Flotilla X-Ray thus presented the potential Spanish watch posts to their east with their lightless portside hulls. The piloting task was not difficult for the ships that followed the path blazed by Gjedde. Each one only needed to keep the starboard-quarter light of the ship in front of them one point off their own port bow.

However, that meant that the success of the passage had been wholly dependent upon Gjedde's ability to maneuver southward into lightless seas on a fairly precise and constant heading. Nonetheless, over the course of the six hours it had taken to sail to their current position on a close reach, the grizzled captain had given fewer than ten commands in accomplishing this feat. This did not count the occasional corrective grunt or gesture when the prevailing winds from the east edged northward and threatened them with the prospect of having to run close hauled.

Eddie discovered that, like everyone else, he was staring up the increasingly visible cable toward the balloon overhead, as if the observer might shout something down. Instead, the telegraph finally began to clatter in the below-decks communications center, too fast and muted for Eddie to make out the message.

The clattering did not last long, which was either a very good, or a very bad, sign. The comm officer's young assistant came up the steep stairs that seamen called a "ladder" two steps at a time and handed a slip to Ove Gjedde. Whose slow, expressionless perusal of it was quite maddening.

Eddie resolved to show no more emotion or anticipation than Gjedde and so, when the older captain proffered the slip to him, he shrugged. "I'm sure Mr. Bjelke would enjoy summarizing it for us." Judging from Rik's nervous foot movements and florid face, this was a very safe conjecture.

Gjedde's lips twitched as he handed it off to his young fellow-Norwegian.

Rik's eyes raced across the lines as he breathlessly summarized. "Approximately thirty hulls observed in Oranjestad Bay. Many have outlines discernible as jachts and fluyts. Although it is difficult to see sufficient details, a large encampment is noted surrounding the town. Its layout is not consistent with a military bivouac." He looked up. "Tromp and the refugees from Recife. It has to be—doesn't it?"

Eddie was surprised by Gjedde's sharp nod. "Unquestionably. But not because of the encampment. The whole colony could have surrendered, after all. And they'd still be living in camp conditions, anyhow."

"Then how are you so sure it is Tromp?" Bjelke asked.

By way of answer, Gjedde glanced sideways at Eddie. Who, although new in his mastery of things maritime, had a life-long interest in and aptitude for things military and strategic. "The types of ships reported, Rik, particularly the jachts. They wouldn't be present if the Spanish took Oranjestad."

Gjedde completed the explanation. "Dutch jachts are among the fastest and most maneuverable boats in the world, Mr. Bjelke, and they certainly hold that pride of place here in the Caribbean, along with the smaller sloops patterned after the Bermudan kind. So if the Spanish fought Tromp, or attacked Oranjestad, they could not have captured so many of them. They, at least, would make good their escapes. Yet there they are, present in the bay. And the fluyts are the further assurance of Tromp's presence and continued control. The Dutch who first settled St. Eustatia had, at most, but two or three such vessels at their disposal. And I suspect if the Spanish had taken such ships along with the town, they would have used those same vessels to deport the colonists to Cuba." He scowled. "It is Spanish mercy, you see. Instead of killing colonists who have violated Madrid's popish *inter caetera* right to all lands west of the Tordesillas line, they take those trespassers to Cuba, where they can be more charitably kept in chains and worked to death. That's what happened to the first Dutch colony on Saba, if I recall the reports properly."

"So, what now?" asked Rik.

Again Gjedde turned to Eddie. "At this point, I believe we are to turn to you for special instructions, Commander."

Cantrell shrugged. "Not exactly, but I'll need to be on hand for the initial contact and negotiations when we reach Oranjestad." *Because there are some parts of this operation that remain very much need-to-know, and therefore, are topics for one-on-one conversations with the folks at the very apex of Oranjestad's military food chain.* "Runner,"—he turned to the boy who'd brought the message—"return to the communications center and inform the duty officer to send to the *Crown of Waves* that she is to pick up the waiting diplomatic parties on *Resolve* and *Patentia* and rendezvous with us. She will then precede the *Intrepid* by three miles as both ships press on to Oranjestad at best speed. The rest of the flotilla will follow."

Oranjestad Bay, St. Eustatia

It was just after 9:30 that a skerry launched from a Dutch jacht drew alongside *Crown of Waves*, which was running with the tompions still in her cannon's muzzles. Of the four men in the small boat, two reached up to take hold of the short boarding stairs that had been put over the side. Once on deck, they stared at the group gathered before them—Eddie, Pros Mund, and the personal secretary of Hannibal Sehested—and then up at the ensign-staff just behind the Danish jacht's taffrail, where no less than four flags were flying: those of the United States of Europe, of the Union of Kalmar, Gustav Adolf's house standard of Vasa, and a diplomatic pennant of Prince Frederik Hendrik of Orange.

The older of the two gestured around at the *Crown*'s weather deck. "This is a Dutch ship, but you are not dressed as Dutchmen, nor do I know any of you."

Eddie looked to Pros Mund. Who, in keeping with his taciturn nature, simply nodded and spoke in passable Dutch. "You are correct in all these observations." He switched to Amideutsch. "One of my officers will explain." He folded his arms and then nodded at Eddie.

Well, that was gracious. Eddie simply smiled and put out a hand. "I am Commander Edward Cantrell of the United States of Europe. From Grantville."

Their visitors' eyebrows rose markedly at the word "Grantville." The older of the two extended a hand. "We are pleased to see you, Commander. Very pleased. I am Philip Serooskereken and this is Matieu Rijckewaert. We welcome you to Oranjestad." He smiled. And he waited.

Which was, Eddie reflected, perfectly understandable. Living in the unremitting fear of Spanish discovery, two ships—one of which is the immense and oddly shaped *Intrepid*—arrive out of nowhere, running a bewildering array of flags that had no reason to be on the same ship, and one of which was the ensign of their own Prince of Orange. What, then, were these ships? Harbingers of strange news from home? An elaborate ruse that bordered on the surreal? Or—the most nail-biting alternative of all—the arrival of long-prayed-for succor from home and/or allies? Well, no reason to keep them wondering. "Mr. Serooskereken, I believe that Admiral Tromp is, well, not exactly expecting us, but had reason to hope for our arrival. It is imperative that we meet with him at once to discuss—"

But Serooskereken was shaking his head. "I am sorry, but I must inform you that the admiral is not in port—"

Not in port? Damn it, what's happened?

"—but that Councilor van Walbeeck may be able to answer your questions, and may have also been told to expect you."

So van Walbeeck made it here alive, and it sounds like he's serving as Oranjestad's senior political leader. That's good. But still— "Excellent. We look forward to meeting with Councilor van Walbeeck, but I wonder if you could tell me where the admiral has traveled to, and with how many ships?"

Serooskereken's experience as a political figure was becoming increasingly evident. He redirected Eddie's inquiry with an easy gesture and relaxed smile. "I suspect Councilor van Walbeeck will be eager to discuss these and many other matters with you. In the meantime, let us arrange for the berthing of your two ships at adequate anchorages and then depart for—"

"With respect, Councilor Serooskereken, we'll need to arrange for seven berths, not two. The rest of our flotilla should be here by three o'clock or so."

Serooskereken's eyes widened, as did his smile. "Seven ships? Well, that is very good news indeed, Commander. The mate in the skerry can arrange the anchorages with your chief pilot, I'm sure. In the meantime, allow me to offer you the hospitality of Oranjestad." His smile buckled. "Such as it is."

Eddie glanced over the man's shoulder. Now less than a mile off their port bow, the tent-city that had burgeoned into existence around the skirts of the original colony's few permanent buildings was starkly visible. While it was neither ramshackle nor particularly dirty, it was strikingly crowded and makeshift.

And suddenly, Eddie was seeing the tent-city that had gathered around Grantville mere months after it had fallen into this world. Refugees had heard of the miraculous town from the future, a self-proclaimed safe-haven for victims of the intensifying Thirty Years' War that up-timer intervention ultimately diffused into a much less sweeping and destabilizing set of conflicts. The promise of food and warmth, as well as an absolute guarantee of religious toleration, had attracted the tired, the poor, and the huddling, hungry masses like moths to a single, distant flame of hope. Yes, Eddie was well-acquainted with the realities of tent-cities, even in one that seemed to be nestled in an island paradise: the smells, the near-despair, the staring eyes and hollow cheeks—

"We look forward to sharing some refreshment with you," he assured Serooskereken brightly. "And of course, you won't mind us bringing some gifts from back home. And some supplies we were tasked to carry for you."

The Dutch councilor looked like he might faint from delight. "No. We would not mind. Not at all."

"Then while you work out the berthing for our ships, we'll signal to our larger vessel to meet us ashore with the gifts and some of the supplies. The balance of the shipment is being carried on our other ships. So if you could arrange for a few lighters—"

"They will be waiting at the anchorages," Serooskereken assured Eddie with an eager nod, and then he followed Pros Mund's gesture toward the *Crown of Waves*' pilot. After a bemused glance at Eddie, the nominative admiral of Reconnaissance Flotilla X-Ray stalked toward the bows, hands behind his back.

Sehested's secretary, who was also the coordinating purser for the flotilla, turned a bright smile on Eddie as soon as both Mund and Serooskereken were out of easy earshot. His eyes were panicked, however. "Commander, I am, er, dismayed. I was not aware that we are carrying gifts for Oranjestad. And I would certainly have noticed it on our cargo manifests if the flotilla's collective lading included any general supplies for—"

Eddie turned an equally bright smile on Lord Sehested's secretary and made his eyes very hard.

"You are mistaken. We are carrying both gifts and supplies for this colony. The gifts are coming from the officers' messes on this ship, and the *Intrepid*. Collect all their discretionary provisions and deliver them to Councilor van Walbeeck. He has a reputation for being evenhanded and honest. You will do the same with all the comestibles of the officers' messes on the other ships when they arrive at anchorage."

"But—!"

"I'm not done. You will then off-load thirty percent of the reserve rations on board the *Patentia* and the *Serendipity* as general supplies, again delivered to the attention and discretion of van Walbeeck. He'll know where it's needed most."

"Sir, I must protest. I cannot be held accountable for mission provisioning if our own dried and durable foodstuffs are so severely diminished at the outset of our—"

"We already have replacement provisioning waiting for us on Trinidad, acquired from the Nepoia tribes. So we will be fully restocked within a fortnight." *Please, please let me be telling the truth.*

The secretary was momentarily mollified but retained an erect posture of prim disapproval. "Very well, sir, but surely, given the ladies aboard the *Intrepid*, and the noble personages aboard the *Patentia*, you cannot mean that their messes are to be *completely* transferred to—"

"I said clean them out, and that is precisely what I mean. And not another question about it."

"And if your wife protests?"

"She won't." *She's made of sterner stuff than you, evidently.*

"And if any of the nobles, such as Lord Sehested, should complain?"

"Then they can come see me."

The master purser's voice took on a sinuous quality. "Lord Sehested might expect you to be responsive to his desires to exclude his mess from these unexpected depletions."

"Unfortunate. Because if he does complain, the only response he can reasonably expect from me is 'too bad.'" *And maybe "go to hell" and a punch in the nose if he insists too often or too loudly.*

"Sir, my duties bind me to convey your exact words to Lord Sehested. Are you aware of that?"

"Aware of it? I'm counting on it." *I hope I'm not buying a political battle over a few hogsheads of dried beef, but if Sehested turns out to be a self-indulgent grandee who expects life in the field to resemble life at court, then we might as well have it out now. I can't afford to have class-privilege crap popping up if we face some real hardships.*

"Commander Cantrell!" called Serooskereken as he returned from the jacht's taffrail. "I have arranged the anchorage and we are ready to depart. When would it be convenient for your party to join us ashore?"

Eddie glanced at the signalman who was sending prearranged messages via semaphore to the *Intrepid*, then smiled at the Dutch councilor. "How about right now?"

Chapter 27

Oranjestad Bay, St. Eustatia

Anne Cathrine looked up at the humble battlements of Fort Oranjestad and saw Eddie's silhouette as he strolled there with the other civil and military commanders. She repressed—barely—a surge of offended pride: *I should be up there, too.*

And if it hadn't been for the Swedes on the mission, she might very well have been. But the suspicions that had kept her from joining Eddie as he worked on the fleet in Luebeck had followed her, albeit indirectly, into the flotilla itself. Although reunited with her husband, there were still meetings from which she was excluded, plans to which she was not made privy. Most of that was due to the hard-line Swedes who had insisted that their nation's long-range plans were no business of the Danish royal family, not until tests and time had demonstrated that Copenhagen's commitment to the forcibly reconstituted Union of Kalmar was genuine and robust. Gustav Adolf could certainly have overridden those exclusionary stipulations, but Anne Cathrine had to concede that it was a wise king who chose his domestic battles with care, and the Swedish monarch had evidently allowed his hard-liners this minor victory. After all, it cost him little and made them feel useful.

But Anne Cathrine could not overlook the lesser source of her exclusions from Eddie's business: Eddie himself. In fairness to Eddie, she knew that he would have trusted her with the hidden details of their mission. But the captains and kings who had come to control the shape and fate of his stratagems were not similarly minded. As Eddie had apologetically explained to her, knowledge of various elements of their mission to the New World were on a "need-to-know" basis: a peculiar, hyphenated phrase that had the pragmatic, engineered sound typical of so many other up-time political and military expressions. Eddie assured her that even he, himself, was not fully briefed on all elements of the voyage: he was carrying a set of sealed orders and letters about which he knew next to nothing, to be delivered to a person he had never met.

"Step careful, m'lady," prompted a voice at her elbow. Anne Cathrine looked over at the escort that had been assigned to her and her two companions: a group of Dutch soldiers led by an Englishman named Cuthbert Pudsey, who jerked his own eyes downward hastily. It was to his credit that he had been tutored not to steer a noblewoman by the elbow, but at this moment, it might have been helpful if he had been a bit less proficient in etiquette. Anne Cathrine followed his eyes downward—just in time to see her foot descending toward a low pile of goat dung. Unable to stop her momentum, she hitched up her skirts and cleared it in one graceful hop, much to the delight of

a boy who stood waiting beside the odiferous muck
with a crude wooden shovel.

She nodded thanks to Pudsey. "Happily, it seems
no one else shall have to hazard the same obstacle I
did." She glanced meaningfully back at the boy who
was already scooping up the dung.

Pudsey frowned in momentary confusion. Then his
face brightened. "M'lady, it please ye, but cleaning
the street is the lesser part of his work." When Anne
Cathrine's face registered no more understanding
than Leonora's or Sophie's behind her, he explicated.
"We're careful using wood, on a small island such as
this, ladies, and we've not had new axes for more'n a
year. So, when a fire is wanted for something other
than cooking—" He let the sentence hang unfinished.

Anne Cathrine nodded. *Well, that explains the
smell.* Following Pudsey's guiding gesture, she continued walking toward a small paddock that backed
upon the windward wall of the fort. A tent, arrayed
pavilion-style, was pitched therein, under which a most
ancient fellow sat on an upended cask, hands on his
knees. As the ladies approached, he tilted his head
back and squinted, as if the ten yards separating him
from them were in fact ten miles. As Anne Cathrine
neared, he labored to rise.

As one, the three women rushed toward the old man,
exhorting him to remain seated. He—a wrinkled, sun-
browned raisin—did not heed them, but rose, and spoke
in fluent Dutch. "Ladies, I am told you have just come
ashore from the ships recently arrived in our bay, and
that you are persons attached to the Danish court." He
actually bowed. "Greetings and felicitations to you all.
I am your servant, Ambrósio Fernandes Brandão, and

have been asked by our illustrious senior Councilor, Jan van Walbeeck to answer what questions you might have about this place and our condition here."

Before Anne Cathrine could think how to best reply to this grandiloquent greeting, quiet Leonora stepped forward with unusual eagerness. "You are that Ambrósio Brandão who authored the *Dialogues of the Greatness of Brazil?*"

Anne Cathrine suspected that very little rattled or surprised the wizened, white-locked sage, but this inquiry had precisely that effect. He swayed a bit and smiled, showing that a full two-thirds of his teeth remained in his head. "I am he, but how—how do you know my name?"

Leonora had, over the years, been introduced to many of the crowned heads of Europe and, in her words, an "interminable" number of their direct off-spring. Never had Anne Cathrine heard her one-quarter as excited as she was now. "Dr. Brandão—for you are also a physician, if I recall correctly—your work on the flora and fauna and natural sciences of Brazil is one of the primary reasons I commenced learning Dutch. I wished to read your work myself one day. All who have read it speak most highly of not only its unusual eloquence, but its exacting observations."

Brandão gabbled like a startled turkey for a moment. Anne Cathrine could barely suppress her smile. *Hardly the mien of a dignified sage. And here is my own beloved sister acting like—what is Eddie's term?—a geek. Or maybe her behavior is better defined by the expression "fan-girl"—except, to be categorized as such, she must emit a sound akin to "squee." Which she has not done. Yet.*

Brandão had recovered enough to ask leave to sit. The three young women nearly fell over each other helping him to re-perch upon his empty, up-ended cask. "My dear Princess Leonora—"

"Doctor, please. I am but a king's daughter, and to you, Leonora."

"Then my dear Leonora, I am at a loss for words. So you have read the *Dialogues* in Dutch?"

Leonora's large brown eyes stared at the ground. "I must confess I have not." Her eyes came back up quickly. "But not for lack of interest. I had no opportunity. Father was uncertain whether I would derive sufficient benefit from the book, and so did not instruct his purchasers in Amsterdam to acquire it. And then the war intervened, so—" Leonora held up her hands in a display of futility.

"I see. I wonder that your royal father was so dubious about your interest in the *Dialogues*. They are not so very difficult, and you must be fourteen, now, yes?"

"Well, yes, but my interest in your book is not a new phenomenon."

"No? When did you conceive of a desire to read it?"

"When I was seven," Leonora answered promptly. And in such a matter-of-fact tone that it was quite clear that there was not the faintest bit of pride or ego behind her reply.

"Ah, er, I see," replied Brandão, whose brief glance at Anne Cathrine was filled with incredulity and no small measure of alarm at Leonora's intellectual precocity. All Anne Cathrine could do was smile and shrug. Which seemed to settle the old man into accepting that the young woman before him was exactly what she seemed: one of the most extraordinarily gifted intellects he had ever encountered. "Well, Princes—my dear Leonora, I suspect that the book exists in Councilor van Walbeeck's personal library, and I would be surprised if he would not consent to lend it to you. But there will be much time to see to that. Let me first discharge my duty as your guide to this place." He glanced more inclusively at all three women. "Surely, you must have some questions?"

Anne Cathrine nodded. "More than we may ask in any one sitting, Doctor. But you might start by telling us how you—I mean, *all* of you—came to be here. We heard rumor that Admiral Tromp had reached Recife, but with only a handful of ships. However, now we find you here with a veritable fleet."

Brandão nodded. "A quick telling will do much injury to the tale, but for now, that is all that time permits. It happened thusly: the ship that brought me back to Recife from Europe in 1633 was the same one which, departing but three weeks later, carried Councilor van Walbeeck back to the Dutch Republic to report on conditions in Brazil, along with the governor of Dutch Brazil, Dierick van Waerdenburgh. Their crossing had an unexpectedly eventful conclusion: they ran into the blockade the Spanish imposed after winning the Battle of Dunkirk, ultimately finding safe harbor in some small port town on the Frisian Islands."

Brandão shrugged. "So, ironically, van Walbeeck and Admiral Tromp passed each other on the high seas, the latter arriving in Recife mere weeks after the former departed. The two working together would probably have quelled much of the dispute and debate that arose over leaving Recife."

Anne Cathrine shook her head. "But was the decision

to abandon the colony not obvious? How was Recife to survive, after the rest of the Dutch fleet was sunk at the Battle of Dunkirk? It was an isolated enclave on a Portuguese coast."

"Lady Anne Cathrine, your ready wisdom would have been an aid in those councils. Our position was made more dire by the colony's inability to support itself. As had been the case since its founding, almost ninety percent of the non-native population of Recife was military. It was profitable in that it exported sugar, but it could not feed itself, and depended upon the Provinces for all its staples.

"But men who have sacrificed much, including the comfort of their homeland, to pursue the goal of becoming wealthy landowners in the New World are not easily convinced to abandon that which they have gained at so dear a cost. Admiral Tromp was hard put to build a consensus to forsake Recife, was harder put still to formulate a plan whereby he was able to evacuate the almost 2700 souls that required relocation. I doubt he would have been able to do it without help from two key persons: a local farm owner named Calabar and the pirate Moses Cohen Henriques."

Leonora leaned forward. "A pirate named 'Moses Cohen'? He is a convert—a *converso*—from Judaism?"

Brandão nodded. "As am I: a *murrano*. Specifically, a Portuguese of Sephardic birth. He is actually somewhat renowned."

The voice that amplified the old doctor's assertion was thoroughly unexpected. "Henriques was instrumental in ensuring Piet Hein's victory and seizure of the Spanish treasure fleet at the Battle of Matanzas

Bay seven years ago," supplied Sophie Rantzau. The corner of her mouth curved slightly as all the eyes in the group turned towards her in surprise. "I do take up the occasional pamphlet or book," she explained. "And, Dr. Brandão, I take it that Henriques was an acquaintance of yours?"

The octogenarian nodded. "It is as you conjecture, Lady Sophie. It was through me that his initial participation was coordinated with Admiral Tromp's commanders in Recife. Moses has—well, *had*—an island that he used as a base off the Brazilian coast. This became a staging area for the evacuation, allowing us to make preparations beyond the gaze of the uninformed persons of Recife, as well as the eyes of whatever informers certainly lurked there. Meanwhile, Calabar's knowledge of the region around Recife guided the maneuvers that both misled the Portuguese at their citadel of Bom St. Jesus and the surrounding native tribes as to our ultimate intents."

"Still," put in Pudsey from behind the ladies, "it were a most delicate dance, right before we left. Tromp offered the *creoles*—who would have refused to go, anyway—double wages to build another fort, further up the bay. When they finished it the day before the evacuation began, it became their prison for a few weeks. Got 'em neatly out from underfoot, it did, and no one harmed in the doing of it. But it were a delicately dance, as I say."

Brandão nodded. "Delicate and complex. Because of the size of the population and the materials needed for resettlement, the relocation was too great to effect all at once. So it was conducted in stages. A small number of troops and the majority of the strictly civilian colonists—including my own Sephardic community, which enjoyed freedom of worship in Recife—were taken by a limited number of ships here to St. Eustatia.

"Meanwhile, under the guise of a quarantine, access to Recife from the countryside was restricted for some time. By then, the rest of the population—the soldiers and, in many cases, their families—were evacuated as well. Slightly more than three hundred souls chose to expand the Dutch colony already present on Tobago. That left almost two thousand persons, mostly soldiers, to be carried by approximately thirty-five ships, all the way from Recife to here. It was a journey of some privation. It consumed all but a small measure of our dried foods."

"How did you live, afterward?" Anne Cathrine wondered. "Did many starve?"

"No, not outright, Lady Anne Cathrine. But the first months were not kind to the very young, the very elderly, or the ailing. Nearly a hundred such persons perished in those first weeks. Sadly, since the Dutch have long experience in the vagaries of colonial life, they were prepared for such an outcome, and consequently, that grim cost did not have the additional sting of being a surprise.

"It would have been much worse, had Tromp not had the foresight to send us civilians on ahead, in enough time to get in most of a growing season before the balance of the evacuees arrived. After we early arrivals had acquainted the colony that was already here with the size of the resettlement that was pending,"—Anne Cathrine noted wince-spawned wrinkles shoot across Brandão's forehead as he tactfully skirted how the refugees had effectively usurped control of the original Oranjestad colony—"we both put new land under tillage and made contact with Governor Warner of St. Christopher to secure the necessary sustenance. Even so, food was, and remains, in short supply." The doctor smiled. "You will find few rotund Dutch gentlemen here, I am afraid. But we manage."

Sophie looked solemnly over the tents that radiated outward from the permanent structures of Oranjestad in mostly even rows. "Still, there must be considerable difficulties. Wastes, for one."

Cuthbert Pudsey rubbed his chin. "We are, eh, encouraged to stroll into the surf when nature calls loudest, m'lady. Not all do, but there's a fine for, eh, being repeatedly uncooperative."

Sophie nodded. "And fresh water?"

Brandão shook his head. "It is still rationed, almost as closely as our foodstuffs, Lady Sophie. Thanks to our many strong-backed soldiers, we were able to build cisterns quickly. But after one season spent in tents during the storm season, their labor was shifted to building permanent shelters as soon as our water supplies were even marginally sufficient." His face fell. "Unfortunately, the temperament that leads a man to become a soldier for coin is often quite unsuited for tasks such as building and farming. Tensions—of all sorts—remain high."

Anne Cathrine heard a host of unspoken problems hovering behind the doctor's conclusion, given weight by Pudsey's own grumble at what he clearly considered an immense understatement of the present challenges. Anne Cathrine looked out over the tents, then back at the bay, where Reconnaissance Flotilla X-Ray had arrived, the comparative immensity of *Intrepid* and

Resolve creating a strange shrinkage in the apparent size of the other vessels. She focused particularly on the *Intrepid*, where her comfortable stateroom and bed (an actual bed aboard ship!) waited for her at the end of the day. Was it wrong to be glad for the clean linens and comfortable pillows of that bed? Was it wrong for her to have been the slightest bit annoyed when the *Intrepid*'s purser arrived, hat in hand, to explain that the choice delicacies in the officers' mess and the ladies' own private larder were being appropriated "to help the colonists"?

She was not sure if those selfish twinges made her a lesser person. For all she knew, Eddie himself had felt something similar when he had ordered the transfer of all those fine foods. But that hadn't stopped him from doing so immediately, reflexively. She looked up at the battlements. Eddie's silhouette had moved farther down the wall of the fort and was distinguishable from the others only because of his slight limp. She frowned; that meant he was deathly tired. But that would not stop her Eddie: it never did, any more than considerations of wealth or class or race or sex or religion did. Which might be, she thought with an almost girlish flutter behind her breastbone, why she adored him so very much.

Chapter 28

Fort Oranjestad, St. Eustatia

Eddie Cantrell nodded farewell to Hannibal Sehested as the group that was leaving to take stock of conditions in Oranjestad began retracing their steps to the stairs down from the ramparts.

The initial gathering had been a large one. Every commander and councilor and aristocrat from both the flotilla and St. Eustatia had met to share schnapps, stories, and get the measure of each other. Now, the councilors and aristocrats were finally departing, led by Phipps Serooskereken. Trailing in his wake, Hannibal Sehested, Rik Bjelke, and the original governor of the colony, Pieter van Corselles, exchanged comments on the relations with the English of St. Christopher's and Nevis. Following behind were three councilors who seemed to be Tromp supporters—Calendrini, Carpentiere, and Van der Haghen—and an equal number who glared balefully whenever the admiral or his policies were mentioned: De Bruyn, Haet, and Musen. However, the six of them had been on good behavior and mostly stayed on neutral conversational ground: the stories of their escape from Recife.

Which, from the sound of it, had been a pretty dicey proposition. Tromp and the rest of the military were in agreement that, in the wake of the disastrous Battle of Dunkirk, there was nothing to prevent a repeat of the earlier attempt to starve Recife into submission, originally carried out by the victor of Dunkirk, Admiral Oquendo, in 1631. Even back then, it had been the sheerest luck that the patrolling jacht *Katte* had spotted the Spanish, who—again, luckily—stopped over at Salvador after being sighted. And even if the Dutch and Recife were that lucky again, could they afford a reprise of the ferocious and costly naval battle which followed? Because even if the Dutch once again repulsed the Spanish, how would they replace lost ships? And how swiftly and well could they repair the damaged ones? It was akin to the final siege of a nation's last uncaptured city: with no hope of relief remaining, the outcome was a foregone conclusion. The only variable was how long and grim the eventual defeat would be.

So, before the Spanish arrived with news of destroying the Dutch fleet at Dunkirk, Tromp—on the advice of the mixed-race *criollo* named Calabar—carried out a sharp, successful assault against the Portuguese stronghold of Bom de Jesus. That apparent bid to expand the Dutch colony prompted discussions of a five year truce as the Portuguese and their native auxiliaries licked their wounds and plotted how best to use the time.

Of course, that Portuguese fixation upon securing and getting a truce was precisely the misdirection Tromp had intended to engender. Long before the local enemy commander, Duarte de Albuquerque, had recovered enough to contemplate breaking the truce,

Tromp had abandoned Recife and embarked upon the exodus that ultimately brought most of the colony safe to its new home on St. Eustatias.

Eddie had found the tales and anecdotes of that exodus interesting and informative, and would have listened with reasonable avidity on some other occasion. But right now, he had a mission to move forward, and he had not been able to do so until now. There were details that he could not share with anyone but the two persons currently at the top of the colony's chain of command: Jan van Walbeeck and Vice Admiral Joost van Trappen Banckert. And those were the two locals who had elected not to accompany the general tour, and now stood with Eddie and Pros Mund, surveying the wide anchorage of Oranjestad Bay.

Mund broke the silence. "Must we continue to stand here? I would prefer walking."

Van Walbeeck offered a small smile. "With your indulgence, let us remain a few moments longer. It is good we are seen here together. Once we walk further leeward, where the walls are over the shore, the people have no view of us."

Unlike the Dutch adventurers of the New World, who usually had to combine an aptitude for statecraft with military acumen, Mund's perspective was purely that of a wartime captain. "And how does this help you and your colony, van Walbeeck?"

"In several ways," the genial Dutchman replied. "First, to be seen together in public means that we have no major quarrels that must be kept hidden."

"But we have no such quarrels," Mund interrupted testily.

"Of course not," van Walbeeck soothed. "But there

are doomsayers in every crowd, Admiral Mund. And they would seize upon a wholly closeted meeting as a means of concealing our differences. Our appearing publicly here—and the others from your flotilla now touring the town with our councilors—will silence those cynics, or at least show their anxieties to be groundless."

Mund made a noise that was half grunt, half sigh. He had little patience for civilian perceptions or judgments of what he believed were purely military affairs.

"Besides," van Walbeeck continued, "Commander Cantrell wisely asked that we find a private place to discuss more sensitive matters. With the lookout discharged temporarily from this post, I can think of no place simultaneously so proximal and yet so private. Now, your questions?"

Eddie was about to commence his inquiries about Tromp and his squadron, but Mund jumped in first. "What do you know of Thijssen and Curaçao? Is he secure there?"

Van Walbeeck seemed as surprised as Eddie at the query. If Joost Banckert was surprised—by this or anything, ever—he had the poker-playing face to conceal it completely. "Marten Thijssen has indeed driven the Spanish from Curaçao and has set about building a fort overlooking the natural harbor at St. Anna Bay. More than this we do not know. Word of this came to Cornelis Jol by way of the privateer Moses Cohen Henriques."

"Privateer?" Mund scowled. "I have heard the word 'pirate' assigned to him. He has no letter of marque, certainly."

"That may have been true before the evacuation of

Recife, but Admiral Tromp thought it wise to provide him with the appropriate papers."

Mund darkened and his jaw worked angrily—but before he could speak, Banckert added a blunt declaration. "Tromp was right to do so. I fully support his decision. I would have done so myself, had I been in his shoes."

Mund shot a fierce look at Banckert, but did not make whatever comment he had been about to utter. Which would probably have been an untactful comment about the suitability of Henriques for their letter of marque, given how piratical the Dutch were themselves.

Eddie sought, and found, a topic which redirected the discussion just enough to get off this possible point of contention, but not so much that the other men would feel themselves being steered toward safer conversational waters. "You sound concerned about Thijssen, Councilor van Walbeeck. Do you foresee problems?"

"I am concerned that the plan to take Curaçao was, well, ill-advised."

Mund's curiosity swept aside his irritation. "How so?"

Van Walbeeck shrugged. "The notion of seizing Curaçao predated the Battle of Dunkirk. I was in Recife when the discussions began and so only became acquainted with them upon my return home, but the Nineteen Heeren of the West India Company had determined that, given its natural harbor and location, Curaçao would be an excellent advance base from which to harry Spanish shipping along the Main."

"You disagreed?" Mund pressed.

"I wondered if that motivation remained prudent," van Walbeeck amended smoothly. "Remember, the mission to take it was not launched until late spring of last year. The ships were collected from scattered berthings as far as the Baltic, given the Spanish blockade of Amsterdam. How, I asked, were we to resupply Thijssen? Who could provide him support, here in the New World?" Van Walbeeck smiled. "And for having the temerity to ask that latter question, the Nineteen decided I should also become my own answer to it. Without having any certainty that Maarten—Admiral Tromp—would come to St. Eustatia, it was decided that I should come to the colony here at the head of a small group of additional settlers and reinforcements, as the United Provinces' on-site coordinator."

Banckert added, "'Coordinator' is a fancy Company word for the fellow who must make sure that all our New World possessions support each other when threatened. Easier said than done."

The long-suffering smile on van Walbeeck's face suggested the veracity of his countryman's observation. "At any rate, my concerns were waved aside. The Nineteen wanted Curaçao, and with the news that we had lost St. Maarten as well, they reasoned that there was even more reason to go ahead with their plans."

Eddie shook his head. "I don't understand how losing St. Maarten makes Curaçao a more urgent target."

"Salt pans," Banckert answered flatly. "That was one of the great values of St. Maarten: flats in which to salt fish or even meats for shipment around the Caribbees. When we lost St. Maarten, the Company turned its eyes toward the only other flats we might take: those at Curaçao."

"But they refused to seriously address the risks of doing so," van Walbeeck resumed. "With our naval forces so crippled and constrained, it seemed likely to me that the Spanish would become more aggressive, here in the New World. With a reduced need to patrol the route of their silver fleet against our raiders, they may now have enough surplus forces to mount an assault against Thijssen. Indeed, my greatest worry was always that his raiding along Tierra Firma would become *too* successful, and I fear that may have occurred. Cornelis Jol brought word that the governors along the Spanish Main have been gathering a small armadilla in Puerto Cabello. It is hard to imagine what they intend for such a force, other than an attack on Curaçao."

Eddie knew that timing made his next speculation unlikely, but it would serve to shift the conversation where it really needed to go. "Perhaps they intend to send it to Trinidad?"

Van Walbeeck glanced sideways at Eddie and his smile became sly. "Ah. Trinidad. An island of which we have had some mention recently. From the fluyt *Koninck David* and her master, Jakob Schooneman. An acquaintance of yours, perhaps?"

Try "an agent of ours." And now, of your own Prince Hendrik, as well. "A shared asset," as Nasi likes to say: he's read too many up-time spy novels. "Captain Schooneman is known to us, yes."

"And so you feel that the Spanish strength building at Puerto Cabello may be intended for Trinidad. Why?" Van Walbeeck's eyes were bright, very alert.

"Oh, I don't know," drawled Eddie. "Maybe Captain Schooneman might have an answer. Where is he, anyway?"

Van Walbeeck laughed and clapped a friendly

hand down on Eddie's shoulder. "Well done, young Commander: you sent the ball right back to me. So, enough dancing, yes? You guess that Tromp is headed to Trinidad in the wake of Jakob Schooneman himself and you are correct. Now you tell me: why? The message that Schooneman brought was, to understate the matter, surpassingly cryptic."

Eddie shrugged. "You've probably already guessed the reason: oil."

Banckert nodded once, sharply. "Yes, we guessed that. It was the obvious answer to 'why' you would go to Trinidad. But how do you plan to take it? And I am not referring to overcoming the Spanish on the island. They are so weak there that it could be years before they were aware of an intrusion. I am interested to learn what you plan to do about the competition?"

Eddie felt his brain screech to a stop, head in a new, unpleasant direction. "What competition?"

"Several weeks ago, we had report of a French ship passing St. Christopher's, trailing what was thought to be a balloon. It was following an earlier ship that Schooneman told us was bound for Trinidad. That first ship would have arrived there weeks ago, presuming the winds were at all favorable."

The ship carrying Mike McCarthy and O'Donnell went through almost a month ago? And was followed by a French ship with its own balloon? Which, given its presence in these particular waters, was probably the ship Richelieu was sure to send. Which would mean that the whole timing of the operation—the leak to the Spanish about an upcoming incursion at Trinidad, McCarthy and O'Donnell's arrival there—was all running ahead of schedule...

"I was unaware the, er, competition would be so—prompt," Eddie gabbled. "Accordingly, we will need you to make all possible haste sending more lighters to our ships. We've got to complete unloading your provisions, as well as some special radio gear which we'll use when we return here. In the meantime, I need you to detail exactly when Admiral Tromp left for Trinidad, with what ships, and the sailing characteristics and armaments of those vessels. And, as soon as we've finished with all that, we've got to set out after Admiral Tromp with our fastest ships. Preferably before sundown." Eddie felt Mund's eyes on him, wondering, frowning. *Because now you can smell that even you, the commander of the flotilla, are not privy to all that will be revealed once we get to Trinidad. And you won't like that one damned bit.*

Van Walbeeck looked as alarmed as Eddie felt. "Commander Cantrell, surely we have the time to complete discussing these matters in a more leisurely mann—?"

"Councilor van Walbeeck, I would very much enjoy an extended conversation, but every hour I delay the flotilla's departure increases the chance that we won't arrive at Trinidad in time."

Banckert blinked. "In time for what? To get your oil?"

"No. To save our men."

Part Five

September 1635

A universal wolf

Chapter 29

Fort St. Patrick, Trinidad

Hugh Albert O'Donnell stared down from the top story of the fort's blockhouse at the French skiff that was approaching the shallows of the north shore. The rowers, six to a side, leaned into their task with a will while, toward the stern, a well-equipped soldier and a man in a shiny silk waist-coat sat calmly riding through the swells. The dandy in the bright clothes, Hugh thought, would be the mouth of Richelieu.

That dandy had taken his time about arranging for his visit. The French ship had arrived three days after Michael McCarthy, Jr., had gone over the wall to rendezvous with the Dutch fluyt *Koninck David*. For several full days, the French sat approximately two miles off-shore, doing nothing but putting up their balloon. Hugh had been tempted to show he and his lads could still do the same, but he let good planning trump pride. *Better they think we lost our balloon on the* Fleur Sable. *No reason to let them know anything about what we do or don't have.*

The regrettably cautious and cynical character of that

thought had become an increasingly significant part of O'Donnell's attitude toward his backer's agents. After all, why had the French waited so long to send a boat ashore? What had they been looking for? Signs that it was, indeed, O'Donnell and his men in possession of Pitch Lake, rather than the Spanish or their servitors? He'd wanted to believe the French were simply being that cautious, but it made less sense with each passing hour. On the second day, O'Donnell had all but ten of his men march beyond the wall, form up in ranks, and fire a well-timed salute with their pieces, synchronized with discharges from both cannons. Yet the Frenchman had remained motionless in the waters of the Gulf of Paria, waiting and watching—for what?

Hugh and O'Rourke had come to the same conclusion before they voiced it to each other. The French were looking to assess how weak they were, if there were any signs of desperation, of food or water shortage, of medical want. Which meant that the captain of the ship was thinking far more about the Wild Geese's bargaining position than he was about their well-being. Perhaps Michael McCarthy, Jr., was right: perhaps the French would have to be dealt with at arm's length, after all,

In a way, however, the French indolence was a blessing in disguise. Given the ruthless pragmatism that probably motivated their delay, Hugh had used the time to strengthen his own negotiating position. He set his men about further grooming the fort and ordering their logistics. The bodies of those few pirates that had not fled into the forests were located and stripped for gear before being carried down into the waters off Point Galba a few hundred yards to the west. The current's acceleration around that slight promontory carried off the bodies, which there had been insufficient tools or time to bury. Alternately, a mass pyre would have alerted the Arawaks to their ongoing presence near Pitch Lake. Leaving the bodies open to the air would have created an equally compelling signal—a steady, sky-climbing gyre of vultures—while simultaneously inviting disease and vermin into the area.

While the powder for the two French sakers was not sufficient for an extended duel with nearby ships, it did provide an excellent magazine for their small arms. That was expanded handsomely when the powder horns taken from the pirate corpses were added in: the attackers had not had much opportunity to fire at the Wild Geese. A few volleys during the charge to the fort had accounted for the majority of their powder expenditures. The rest of the grim battlefield harvest produced a plenitude of weapons, tools, boots, belts, and other useful gear, all in good condition or better. Contrary to apocryphal tales of the slovenly nature of pirates, Hugh and his men discovered the more nuanced truth behind those legends. On the one hand, pirates did indeed have little care for objects or tasks that were not directly involved in the furtherance of their livelihood. Regrettably, this included personal hygiene and cleanliness. According to several of the Wild Geese who had spent some time as hog butchers, their porcine stock-in-trade had been far less odiferous and dirty than the pirate bodies they released into the surf. However, when it came to their weapons and equipment, it seemed that freebooters were, if anything, freakishly fastidious. Their weapons were in good to excellent condition, as were their tools, powder horns, sewing kits, and other accoutrements.

As Wild Geese's armory and other stockpiles grew, Hugh saw to it that their fort did, as well. Under Doyle, the Irish mercenaries had improved the walls, finished the blockhouse, built reasonable huts to function as barracks, and sunk one nighttime privy within the walls and two daytime privies without. Torn clothing was mended. Game traps were set and fishing parties established. Ripening fruit trees were found and fresh water supplies were located and surrounded with snares that would ostensibly show if the Arawaks had ventured near them. And daily drill and training kept the men mindful of and ready to perform their first function: soldiering.

So by the time the French sent their first boat ashore, inquiring if the comte Tyrconnell would find it convenient to receive a visit from Cardinal Richelieu's personal representative, Sieur Jean du Plessis d'Ossonville, Fort Patrick and its men had been growing stronger and more fit, rather than weakening. The mild annoyance and dismay on the face of du Plessis' messenger suggested that his master had been hoping for the reverse.

That had been yesterday. And now, sweeping a feathered hat back on to his balding head, du Plessis himself had at last arrived to visit, make an offer for Pitch Lake, and in so doing, very possibly determine the fate of hundreds, even thousands, of expatriate Irish families in the Spanish Lowlands. Hugh could imagine Michael McCarthy's sardonic comment on the upcoming meeting, could almost hear it as if the up-timer had been there himself: "No pressure; no worries." O'Donnell started down to meet du Plessis.

They arrived at the gate at more or less the same time, Hugh smiling and walking toward his guest, hand out. Technically, du Plessis' knightly title was as minor as they came, but Hugh had little patience for the formalities of rank and class outside of court. Besides, any man or woman who elected to face the dangers of the New World to make their fortune shared a kind of aristocracy of spirit, of courage, so far as he was concerned.

But du Plessis apparently had a different sense of social stratification and a keen sense that while Hugh might have the far greater title, he commanded far fewer resources. The Frenchman stood very straight, put out his hand very far, and announced himself, "I am Sir Jean du Plessis d'Ossonville, senior factor for the *Compagnie des Îles de l'Amérique* in this place, and personally appointed by his Eminence, Cardinal Richelieu. And you are?"

The tone was distant, faintly dismissive, not quite condescending. Not quite. *And besides, am I supposed to believe you don't know who I am, that you weren't given a description of me?* No, Hugh decided, this meeting was probably not going to evolve toward an amicable agreement between partners, not judging from du Plessis almost defiant greeting.

"I am, as I suppose you conjecture, Lord Hugh Albert O'Donnell, Earl of Tyrconnell. Please come in where we may speak more easily."

Du Plessis nodded serenely and entered the block-house, but was surprised when O'Rourke started following them up the stairs to the second floor. "And your man—he is to hear our discussion?"

"My 'man' is Aodh O'Rourke, whose counsel and

loyalty have ever been among the greatest gifts with which God has elected to grace my life. And your companion—?"

"Shall remain down here," du Plessis concluded, with a glance at the well-armed soldier, who did not meet his superior's eyes but came to a stop at the base of the stairs. Hugh continued leading the way up.

Once seated and refusing refreshment of any kind, du Plessis leaned back in one of the two rude chairs available, one hand rising to prop upon his hip. He waited, his chin slightly higher than it really ought to have been. And he waited some more, looking out a window instead of at his hosts. He might have been sitting for a portrait.

Hugh could almost feel heat radiating from the silently fuming O'Rourke behind him. But instead of becoming aggravated himself, O'Donnell simply leaned back, sipped at his water and thought at his guest: *I've no need to start this conversation, my dandy French friend, but you are under orders to do so. We'll see how long it takes you to give up this silly game you're playing.*

It took about half a minute for du Plessis to realize that he could not keep affecting bored toleration as he waited upon an inquiry from, and therefore the implicit supplication of, the other party. Flipping an irritated wrist, he gestured beyond the walls of the blockhouse. "So it seems you have taken Pitch Lake, after all, Monsi—er, Comte Tyrconnell. But with more loss than expected, I observe."

Hugh shook his head. "There was never any discussion about the possible level of casualties, Sir du Plessis. There was no basis for such discussion, since we had no idea what we might find upon our arrival, or afterwards."

"Perhaps I mis-state, your Lordship. I was referring more to the imbalance of casualties. I find no surviving Frenchmen here, but few enough of your own men seem to be missing."

Hugh managed not to bridle at the implication of favoritism, also managed not to point to the blatant incompetence and cowardice of St. Georges, and the probably marginal incompetence of Morraine in maneuvering too close to the shallows. "That is because all but a handful of your men were aboard the *Fleur Sable* when she was destroyed. And I emphasize: destroyed. She was evidently struck in her magazine, or suffered some similar fate. None of which I could change or ameliorate, I'm afraid."

Du Plessis seemed irritated that his first attempt to secure superior footing in the prenegotiation grappling phase had been unsuccessful. "Perhaps that is true, my lord—"

O'Rourke snapped a correction before Hugh could stop him. "You need not wonder if the Earl of Tyrconnell's words are *perhaps* true. He tells no lies."

Du Plessis stopped; he looked simultaneously outraged at O'Rourke for interrupting, but also suddenly alarmed at having been caught up on what could easily become a point of honor. He had little choice but to start over with an apology. "My regrets. I simply meant to say that even if we presume that the Earl of Tyrconnell's overview of the battle and its vagaries are complete, it does not alter the simple fact that, for the French Crown, this has been an expensive expedition. Much more expensive than anticipated."

Hugh leaned forward over the table. "Many things here were not as anticipated. Such as the attack itself. We were barely here two weeks before we saw their sails approaching. And it was not a matter of chance that they clashed with us here. They came knowing, or speculating, enough about our positions to approach us under the cover of the western wood while they feinted at making their primary landing on the shore just north of here."

"And so? I am sorry that fate was unkind to your adventure, but, to borrow your own words, it was hardly in France's power to change or ameliorate that."

Touché—almost. "Sir du Plessis, I must reemphasize that it seems unlikely that we were the victims of unkind fate. Rather, given how closely the pirate attack followed our arrival, one must also suspect a more logical cause: incaution on the part of those who knew of our mission. Or, more extremely, betrayal."

Du Plessis forgot to keep his hand on his hip. "Lord O'Donnell, do you suggest that Lord Turenne himself would stoop so low as to—?"

Hugh waved a hand. "I suggest nothing of the sort. Lord Turenne is an honorable man, and too intelligent to play at such self-defeating idiocies, besides. No, whoever hired the brigands that came with the intent of driving us off—for surely, the pirates themselves would have conjectured that we lacked any riches worth plundering—was willing to work with a crude and unpredictable implement to smash us out of the way. But many more people in France knew of our destination than people in my employ. Indeed, before boarding the *Fleur Sable*, only three persons knew we were bound for Trinidad."

Du Plessis was mollified but still vexed. "First, Lord O'Donnell, your implication still does great disservice to your backers, implying, as it does, that we are incapable of controlling the actions of our own servitors—"

Of course—because bribery is unknown in La Belle France. Despite the fact that it's a way of life from Rheims to Marseille.

"Furthermore, the information of your anticipated arrival here could have trickled down through channels unknown to either of us. Conversations overheard through doors, or in places thought private, are all too often how foreign agents discover secrets. And last, why should the three members of your own party be above suspicion in this regard?"

Hugh resisted the bitter smile he felt trying to bend his mouth. "Because, Sir du Plessis, all three of those persons were in direct mortal peril as a result of the pirate attack: myself, my aide-de-camp O'Rourke, and Michael McCarthy, Jr., the up-timer."

Du Plessis acted as though Hugh had given him a trump card. "And up-timers are of course known for their ready embrace of, and loyalty to, actions undertaken by the French crown."

Hugh decided not to make an issue of du Plessis' richly sarcastic tone, but also could feel that his patience was becoming perilously thin. "Perhaps not, but Don McCarthy's risk was as great as mine. He and I were trapped in this blockhouse, fighting off more than a dozen of the pirates ourselves, at the end. It was a close thing."

"An altogether *too* close thing," grumbled O'Rourke from behind.

But in that brief moment, Hugh had to ask himself: *and how, really, do I know that Michael, or his superiors, were not in fact the ones who ensured that our enemies knew of our arrival here? Perhaps the risk he took by my side was simply part of his mission, too. But why? Why inform our enemies? It tempted failure and death. And all for what?*

But there was no time to scrutinize that possibility any further. "Sir du Plessis, I do not bring up the apparent betrayal of our mission here to cast aspersions upon France. I do so to demonstrate why considerations of expense or casualties did not enter into my initial discussions with Lord Turenne. We understood this mission was rife with uncertainties. However, despite the unpleasant surprises we have encountered, we have taken this place as agreed. Accordingly, we should be happy to learn the terms you bring from His Eminence, Cardinal Richelieu."

Du Plessis' hand went back to his hip. "With all humility, Lord O'Donnell, the terms you are to be offered for this land were not fixed by His Eminence, but presented to me as a range of options that I was at liberty to adjust, according to the situation I found upon arrival. I have surveyed this fort and its environs from our balloon for several days. My visit here has confirmed what we detected. Consequently, here are the terms that seem just, and even generous, for France to offer in exchange for this plot of ground." He held out a slip of paper in O'Rourke's direction.

From the shift of his aide-de-camp's feet, and then the tone of his voice, Hugh was relatively sure that O'Rourke had adopted a broad, arms-folded stance. "*Your* man is downstairs, Sir du Plessis. We can summon him up here, if you need him to deliver your mail."

Du Plessis became very red, then his chin went back. He rose, hand still on hip, approached the driftwood-table behind which Hugh was sitting and dropped the paper on it before returning to his seat.

Hugh raised an eyebrow, picked up and unfolded the parchment sheet—

Jean du Plessis d'Ossonville resisted the urge to produce a handkerchief to dab the sweat from his brown. Weeks of pursuing careful relations with the Caribs of Guadeloupe had not been half so unnerving as walking into this lion's den of desperate Irishmen. It would have been a great deal easier had he and his fellow-factor for the *Compagnie des Îles de l'Amérique*, Charles Liénard de l'Olive, not needed to shift some of the silver originally intended for the Wild Geese into their own overtaxed coffers. But that would hardly matter to Richelieu if they were able to report success on both islands without incurring any additional expense. And His Eminence certainly wanted to lay hold of both the islands, but presumably for very different reasons. Du Plessis could well imagine what those different reasons might be, but Richelieu was not, to put it lightly, in the habit of informing minor nobles of his long-range plans. However, it was quite clear from the color building in the earl of Tyrconnell's face that he would soon make his feelings and opinions on the offer for Trinidad quite clear indeed.

The Irishman did not disappoint du Plessis' expectations. "Surely this is a joke. And a very bad one."

"Surely, it is not, Lord O'Donnell."

"In that event, it is an insult."

"I regret that you elect to conceive it so, my lord. We consider it a most generous offer: half a year's pay, in advance, for all those men and their families who leave the Spanish Lowlands and come over the border to serve under French colors."

"Sir du Plessis, that would not even be a particularly attractive hiring incentive, particularly not to long-service mercenaries such as the Wild Geese. Yet that is all you are willing to offer for the mercenary contract you offer us *and* for the technical help that built your balloon *and* the successful completion of this mission to Trinidad? I fail to understand how you can make this offer to us intending it to be anything *but* an insult."

"Allow me to share what *I* understand, my good Earl of Tyrconnell. I understand that you have a great many mouths to feed in and around Brussels. I furthermore understand that Cardinal Richelieu, in consideration of the service you have performed here on Trinidad, has elected to both feed them and to pay your men at their present rate. And he is willing to relay your first half-year's payroll to you here and now, in this place, as a sign of his goodwill, and as an indication that you will never need to wait upon the prompt satisfaction of his payrolls. Unlike the case with your *tercio*'s present employer."

Du Plessis saw that this line of debate was angering the semi-civilized Irishman even more—which meant, in all probability, that his remarks were cutting deep because they were landing upon the tender bruises of unpleasant truths. Perhaps, though, he should have increased the amount of the bribe, or "special service commission," that he had explicitly set aside for O'Donnell himself in the written offer. But, being inherently unprincipled, high-ranking sell-swords often became greedier for bigger bribes once their appetites were whetted, so it probably would not have made a difference. Besides, it was too late to adjust that number now. The offer had been made, and due to the presence of the colonel's aide-de-camp, the thinly disguised bribe could not be confidentially renegotiated or even remarked upon. Well, that was the Irishman's loss and the *Compagnie des Îles de l'Amérique*'s gain.

The Irish earl, like a tiresome dog with a well-worn bone, seemed insistent upon returning to the terms of the settlement. "Assuming, for one improbable second, that you and His Eminence are serious in making this offer, it ignores a number of problematic realities. Such as this: what if no more of my men are allowed to leave their employ in the Spanish Lowlands? What then?"

"Then that is most unfortunate for them, but I do not see how you could reasonably hold us accountable for the actions of another sovereign lord." Du Plessis congratulated himself on the smoothness with which he had furnished that rebuttal. He had foreseen this objection, had planned and even scripted the best way to deflect it.

And if his planning continued to prove itself adequate, it seemed likely that he and his partner Charles Liénard de l'Olive would manage to stretch Richelieu's somewhat scant fiscal underwriting to secure two islands for the price of one and thereby specially acquaint His Eminence with their shrewd resourcefulness. Liénard, a French settler on St. Christopher's, had brought du Plessis a fair stratagem for investing Guadeloupe with a French colony last year. His timing had been auspicious: not only were du Plessis' failing family fortunes reaching an alarming nadir, but Richelieu had just sent word to those interested that he was rejuvenating the mostly mismanaged and moribund *Compagnie de Saint-Christophe*. Never having met its mandate to seed other French colonies in the Caribbean, Richelieu had charged one of his councilors, Francois Fouquet, to reinvent the enterprise as the *Compagnie des Îles de l'Amérique*.

Ironically, most of the new investment money had gone to Pierre Bélain d'Esnambuc, who was still tussling with the English for control of St. Christopher's. Most of the remaining silver was earmarked for the purchase of a base on Trinidad from a group of Irish adventurers who had surreptitiously seized it for the Crown of France, or from any non-Spanish who might have ousted them from the place. It mattered little to Richelieu and Fouquet who was paid for that slip of Trinidadian coast.

Indeed, Liénard's and du Plessis' own venture in Guadeloupe was of such decidedly tertiary interest to the cardinal that he had only agreed to their request to retain one of the two ships with which they had journeyed to the New World because they had agreed to go to settle matters at Trinidad, and leave the other ship and most of the professional troops there.

But Richelieu's and Fouquet's eyes and hands were far away from the strings of the purse that they had entrusted to du Plessis. Who realized swiftly enough, that, if the holders of Trinidad—Irish or otherwise—could be made to accept less money, then the livres saved thereby could be used to ensure more reasonable funding for the colonization of Guadeloupe. And surely no one would notice if a few hundred more found their way back to France to defray some of the more onerous debts looming over the good name of the family du Plessis.

However, the attainted, therefore landless, and therefore relatively powerless earl of Tyrconnell was determined to keep quibbling over the terms of the exchange. "Sir du Plessis, in all our discussions with Lord Turenne, we were assured of a fair price for our success here and for helping to make the balloon which you have been using. But what you have offered is not a fair price at all; it does not even include any pay for the time that my men have spent upon this mission. Frankly, no sovereign would dare make such an offer in Europe, lest word begin to spread among mercenaries to avoid service with that crown."

"But we are not in Europe, my lord." Du Plessis was no longer able to resist tugging a handkerchief out of his sleeve and dabbing at his damp brow. "And just as we did not stipulate what number of casualties we considered reasonable, you did not stipulate what sum of silver seemed fair. What I have offered is, I repeat, what we think is both fair and generous." Seeing that the Irishman was becoming more, rather than less, determined in his intransigence, du Plessis deemed it time to reveal the threat he had been hiding. It would have been more convenient if the benighted bog-hopper had inferred its possibility from the conversation, but that was not to be expected with single-minded sword-swingers such as he. "I feel that I must point out, my good Earl of Tyrconnell, that my mere presence alone is a sign of reciprocal good faith. A most profound sign of it, in fact. One that is worthy of your gratitude, I should think."

O'Donnell looked stunned and du Plessis managed not to scowl or sigh. *Really? Can this mercenary truly be so dense? Are they not all schooled in guile and duplicity from the cradle?* "It has perhaps escaped your attention, my lord, that, for half this sum—indeed, much less, I suspect—we could find another pirate band much like the one which nearly overwhelmed you here. And we could offer them a contract akin to the one which you conjecture brought that first group to these shores: seize Pitch Lake. They would be glad for the coin and, were we to recruit among the *boucaniers* of Tortuga or their kin in the Bahamas, we could garnish that offer with letters of marque, and pardons for any offenses committed in France or its possessions." Du Plessis looked out the window at the long, low breakers. "It would delay us for two, maybe three, months, but we would have what we wish and for a much lower price than we are offering you now. So perhaps your gratitude might be improved by considering my offer in the context of that alternative. Which I remain willing to forego."

O'Donnell's sharp reply caused him to start. "No, my gratitude is not improved. Not at all." Thus far, the displaced earl had seemed a bit slow to utter conversational ripostes. But the crisp decisiveness in this counter made du Plessis wonder: *did I mistake "measured responses" for "slow" ones?*

The colonel's next comments made that conjecture seem all too likely. "Sir du Plessis, it was understood that Cardinal Richelieu's agents would have the right to make the first offer for Trinidad, and if it was at all fair, that we were honor-bound to accept it. However, while we might argue long and inconclusively as to whether your offer is in any way 'fair,' here is something that is simply *not* a matter of debate: Lord Turenne never implied that he would wrest this hard-won ground from us by force if we did not take whatever offer was made to us. Indeed, if that were the case, then the entire notion of this 'negotiation' is simply a sad charade. Out of respect for Lord Turenne's intents, I will allow you the opportunity to withdraw your current offer, and present a new one—one which does not include any odious bribery, by the way."

Du Plessis rose. Well, the Irishman was clearly as stubborn as the rest of his recidivistic race, and, in addition to being impervious to reason, was beginning to demonstrate a distressing gift for both logic and eloquence at exactly the wrong moment. Time to let the desperate nature of his circumstances do the arguing that would ultimately bring him round to accepting du Plessis' terms. The Frenchman tucked his handkerchief back inside the margin of his cuff as he said, "Lord O'Donnell, my first offer is my only offer. I will return tomorrow to hear your response to it. I bid you good day."

And, without waiting for leave to do so, du Plessis started down the stairs but a bit more quickly than usual. He was still not entirely certain that the troglodyte named O'Rourke, or even the earl himself, might not throw a knife into his departing back.

However, just as du Plessis arrived on the ground floor and called the guard to his side with a gesture not unlike that he used to summon his hounds, an unusually-dressed man of middle age, and with the flat-footed gait of a rank commoner, entered the block-house with several of the Irish mercenaries around him. At first it seemed that he was another visitor, arriving under guard, but then du Plessis noticed the smiles on the faces of the Wild Geese, the gentle banter with which they engaged the newcomer, and he understood: this was the American, the up-timer who had built the balloon for Turenne.

Du Plessis drew up to his full height, which was still two inches less than the American's, and attempted to look down his nose at the workman. "So, monsieur, perhaps you will be able to prevail upon your lord to accept my offer. I suppose you have some measure of influence with him?"

The American stopped, stared at du Plessis and then barked out a laugh. "Some measure, maybe," he chuckled. "But thanks for telling me he's turned you down. Now I know where I stand when I give him *my* offer." The American actually winked as he brushed past du Plessis and started up the stairs two risers at a time. "And you might want to stick around to hear the outcome. It could save you the problem of making another trip here and mussing up your waistcoat."

Michael McCarthy, Jr., knew that, the moment his head rose above the second story's floorboards and he saw Hugh, he'd be able to tell if his friend had decided to disown him or not.

If anything, it didn't even take that moment. Hugh was on his feet, beaming, by the time McCarthy's brow had cleared the planks that hemmed in the stairs. "Michael! Are you well? This is strange timing indeed." Hugh paused as a rueful smile crept across his face. "Or is it?"

Mike stared around the mostly finished second story approvingly. "If you mean, was I watching today's proceedings from some hiding place, no." He turned toward Hugh. "As for how I'm doing, I'm passable. You?"

Hugh nodded, put out his hand. "I am well enough. Better for seeing you, I think."

Damn it, that smile and frankness of his is like a magic spell; no wonder so many Irish mercenaries followed him to their death, up-time. "It's good to be seen," Mike admitted as he shook Hugh's hand, nodded at O'Rourke, who nodded back with a careful, but hopeful, smile. "Look, I don't mean to interrupt, but—"

"Not like you're interrupting anything, Don Michael," grumbled O'Rourke. "The Frenchman bearing Richelieu's terms was pretty much done buggering us, I think."

Mike winced. "That bad?"

"Worse," O'Rourke snarled, "but I'm too much a gentleman to give a full description of the reaming."

Hugh glanced over his shoulder, his attempt to muster an expression of disapproval completely undermined by his amused grin. "Always the way with words, eh, O'Rourke?" He fixed his attention back on McCarthy. "But he has the right of it, Michael. As you may have anticipated."

Mike rubbed his chin. "Yeah, that French guy didn't look too happy, coming down the stairs. I kinda reckoned you hadn't reached a meeting of the minds."

"To say nothing of suitable terms. But that is a

different topic, for a different time. I am delighted to see you Michael, but surprised. I had suspected you would be well on the way to—well, wherever you were going."

Carefully now, Mike. "Actually, Hugh, I'm here for the same reason that he is."

Hugh leaned back slightly. "You are here to—to make an offer for Pitch Lake? *You?*"

Mike waved a hand testily. "Yeah—I mean, no, not me personally. I mean, yeah, I'm the guy sitting here in front of you but I'm not—" *Sheesh: this is harder than getting shot at.* "Look, Hugh, I thought I was done here, that somebody else was going to do all the fancy talking. At least, that was the plan. But from what I can tell, the guys making those plans got their schedules fouled up, and now, the ones who were going to present the deal to you are still en route."

Hugh did not blink, did not even nod. "And how do you know all this?"

Mike shrugged. "We have a radio on the *Koninck David.* Starting last night, it started going haywire. Fragments of transmissions, but nothing very clear. Then just before dawn, we got a clear signal."

He pointed northward. "Hugh, right now, there is a fleet sailing this way. One of the ships was designed by up-timers. It's powered by steam and it has a large radio. They'd been trying to reach me on the *Koninck David* for days because they were worried that you'd have to make a decision before they could get their deal in front of you. So when we were finally able to exchange messages early this morning, they asked me to convey the broad outlines of what they are willing to offer for Pitch Lake. And here I am."

"And this offer, it is from the USE and Gustav, after all?"

"In part. But it is equally from Prince Hendrik of the United Provinces and from your former employer, Fernando, King in the Spanish Lowlands."

Even the indomitable O'Rourke goggled openly at this constellation of improbably cooperative political luminaries. Hugh leaned forward after a long moment of silence. "The USE, the United Provinces, and the Spanish Lowlands—all in agreement, and working together?"

"Yes. Although it shouldn't come as a *complete* surprise, Hugh. C'mon, how many times now has your godmother had up-time visitors? Seems like there are always a few of us in her court, to say nothing of our books. And we did make sure that Fernando got his Austrian bride safe and sound out of Germany, courtesy of one of our aircraft. And we've been working to help the Provinces against Spain itself—not the Lowlands, but Spain—in all sorts of subtle ways. This is no different. Well, except that it's a whole lot less subtle."

"I should say so," agreed Hugh, who still did not blink. "I am not surprised at the cooperation between the USE and the United Provinces. They have many common interests, and share many of the same predilections. For technology, for instance. But the Spanish Lowlands—"

"Maybe you were too close to the changes there to see them clearly," Mike offered. "Or maybe not. Who was it, less than half a year ago, who told the leaders of all the Wild Geese *tercios* that they might soon have to choose between loyalty to Philip of Spain and Fernando of the Lowlands?"

Hugh became a bit pale. "Yes, I said that."

"Well, follow it to its logical conclusion. If Fernando ultimately parts company from Madrid, how will he survive? Who might be his new friends? Certainly no one allied with Spain. Certainly not the French, who'd like to extend their borders north of Brussels. The English are in disarray, Austria is a shadow of its former self."

"And so Fernando and my godmother are willing to ally with Protestants?"

"Why?" asked Mike around a smile that assured Hugh he knew better. "That bother you?"

"Certainly not, Michael. You know I have become quite sympathetic to Grantville's enlightened policy of religious freedom. But my godmother and her nephew—"

"Are not so different from yourself, Hugh," Michael interrupted with a grin. "Unlike the fossils creaking around the court in Madrid, they understand that the times, they are a-changing. And is the USE a 'protestant' union? Hell, if it was, I—and the millions of other Catholics, from rulers to peasants—would be in a pretty tough situation. But we're not. Because what unites the USE is not a common faith, but rational political agreements. And, slowly but surely, shared values. Such as religious toleration."

Mike waved in the approximate direction of Europe. "Fernando sees this clearly, although I'm pretty sure it was your godmother who pointed it out to him. Hell, she can see new trends and changes coming before anyone else in Europe, so far as I can tell. She had been cooking up a scheme like this on her own when some of us from Grantville approached her with an idea about how to kill a bunch of birds with one strategic stone: seizing Trinidad."

Hugh nodded. "So. This has my godmother's blessing, you claim."

"Hugh, you don't have to believe me. There's a sealed letter from her being carried on one of our ships, the *Intrepid*. I'm sure it will explain the underlying tangle of statecraft spider webs better than I could given a year's time."

Hugh rose and came around to sit on the desk directly in front of Mike. "The desirability of the oil is easy to understand. But I do not understand how all the other objectives can be met simply by taking Trinidad."

"You will when you hear the offer."

"Which is?"

Mike drew in a deep breath: *all or nothing, now.* "Trinidad, and its oil production, is to be a shared venture. The split is: fifty percent belongs to the USE. Twenty-four percent belongs to the United Provinces, and twenty-four percent to the Spanish Lowlands."

Hugh frowned. "That's only ninety-eight percent. What happens to the last two percent?"

Mike felt how crooked and desperate his smile was. "Can't you guess?" *Don't you know this is why I pushed and pulled you and the Wild Geese into this crazy scheme—just like your godmother did?*

Mike saw understanding illuminate Hugh's face like the iconic light bulb snapping on. "It is for us. For the Wild Geese."

Mike nodded, explained slowly. "Two percent of all production and proceeds from oil operations on the island of Trinidad will be placed on account for the

Irish expatriate community in the Lowlands. That, by extension, puts it at the disposal of the last free and legitimate leadership of Ireland, Hugh."

"We'll have much to discuss with the earl of Ulster, I can see," O'Rourke said sourly from behind the desk.

Mike looked away, having heard the latest grim news regarding John O'Neill. "Maybe not," Mike muttered evasively. "Look, however the details swing, this is a lot of money, Hugh. Do you know how much a gallon of oil—just unrefined oil—sells for right now?"

Hugh shook his head.

"About twenty guilders per unrefined barrel of crude. And the price continues to rise. And will for the foreseeable future. We are sitting less than five miles from where, in my world, some of the earliest, smallest sweet crude gushers produced one hundred barrels a day. Within a few years, there should be a dozen other wells, at least. And many of those will be producing more. Much more."

Hugh's mental math was quite good: the earl's eyes opened wide. "And for how long may we enjoy this entitlement?"

"It is permanent. And can you guess what Fernando has sworn to do when he gets his first proceeds from the speculators, long before the first oil gets back to Europe?"

"Buy an army with which to resist his brother's *tercios*?"

"No, Hugh. He's going to pay all of what's owed the Wild Geese, and fifty percent more, in honor and appreciation of your loyal service. And then he wants *you* to buy that army for him—you and Colonel Preston, working together."

O'Rourke came forward and leaned against the table. "Don McCarthy, this sounds so blasted fine that I know it *can't* be true. As you must fear yourself."

Mike frowned. "What do you mean?"

O'Rourke spread his hands. "So I'll assume that there's a piece of paper somewhere that asserts we are part owners of the oil concession here on Trinidad. And similarly, that the king of the Lowlands has gone on record saying that we are his chosen troops, and that he shall settle all our back pay and then some." O'Rourke shook his head. "But none of it will come to pass, because of the people upon whom it depends: high and mighty lords and ladies that can't even agree whose carriage comes first in a progress, let alone share ownership of something which is, as you yourself said, a strategic piece of real estate. They'll be bickering before the first oil comes out of the ground. And so none of it will ever get to market."

Mike shook his head. "That's a reasonable fear, O'Rourke. But those same lords and ladies foresaw that same problem. And that's why the ownership of the oil is structured as it is."

"Eh?" said O'Rourke.

Hugh saw it, nodded. "That's why the USE owns half of the oil. It can force cooperation among the other partners."

"Or can simply have its own way, I fear," added O'Rourke.

"No, not entirely," said Hugh, suddenly staring at Mike, who realized that the Irishman was starting to realize just how much the up-timer sitting in front of him must have been involved in the formation of this arrangement. "If all the other parties—the

Spanish Lowlands, the United Provinces, and we Wild Geese—are all in agreement against the will of the USE, there will be no majority. It will be fifty percent against fifty percent."

"Ah, that's fine, it is," O'Rourke growled. "Deadlocked. Just like clan politics back in Ireland. Everyone with a voice, and so nothing can be agreed upon."

Hugh shook his head. Mike wondered if he had already foreseen the answer to the question he was going to ask: "How is a deadlock prevented, Michael?"

"Majority vote among the four shareholding directors, one from each of the groups. One vote, one director."

O'Rourke persisted in his sour tone. "And so, two votes for each side of any dispute, and again, a deadlock."

"No," corrected Hugh. "Almost certainly not, because it would take the combined shares of all three of the minority shareholding groups to create the first deadlock. Logically, then, their three directors would outvote the USE director three to one, in that circumstance."

Mike nodded. "That's the idea. And stability in the Netherlands is maintained by a similar device. If the United Provinces and the Lowlands resume hostilities with each other, or ally with an enemy of the other, or undertake any one of a list of actions which have been decreed impermissible, then oil proceeds are not distributed to either party but are held in trust until such time as they resolve those differences."

O'Rourke couldn't help smiling. "So each has a pistol to the other's head, both fired by the same trigger. Heh. That might even work. For a while."

Mike smiled. "Nothing is permanent. But if this lasts even five years, the Lowlands and Provinces will have rebuilt themselves and made great progress toward forging a single nation, the USE will have a ready supply of oil flowing, and you, Lord O'Donnell, will have well-paid men, a war-chest, and new allies with which to seek justice for Ireland."

"And Spain will be thirsting for all our blood," finished O'Rourke.

Hugh chuckled. "And just how is that any different from the situation as it stands right now, old friend?" He stood. "No, I think we've just heard the offer we're going to take." He put out his hand to Mike. "And something tells me that the man whose hand I am shaking to seal our commitment was involved in crafting some of its stipulations."

Mike didn't look away, but he couldn't lie. "There were a lot of cooks consulted in the making of this crazy stew," he allowed.

Hugh held his hand, his eyes, a moment longer than necessary. "I'm sure there were, Don Michael McCarthy. And I thank you for being one of them, and for remembering Ireland when the final recipe was decided upon. Now," he said, withdrawing his hand, and striding towards the stairs, "I think we can deliver our final answer to our French guest."

O'Rourke, who'd wandered over to the window, whistled sharply. "I suspect our Gallic friend may have already deduced our response. Come and see."

Hugh and Mike joined O'Rourke at the window. Just below their vantage point, Jean du Plessis was standing on the platform that lined the north wall of Fort St. Patrick, staring out to sea. The three men followed his gaze to the horizon.

Half a dozen ships were emerging out of the heat-misty horizon: two Dutch jachts leading a brace of

man-o-wars with forty or more guns. More ghostlike
sails seemed to be approaching from farther back in
the indistinct distance behind them.

Mike nodded. "Unless I'm much mistaken, that would
be Admiral Maarten Tromp of the United Provinces."

Du Plessis must have heard the comment; he turned
sharply, eyes as cold as a promise of murder. "So, Lord
O'Donnell, this is how you deal in good faith? How
convenient for you that your new owners have already
arrived."

O'Rourke smiled wolfishly down at du Plessis.
"Correction, sir. Those are not the 'owners.' They are
the 'co-owners.' Now run along; from what I recall,
your fleet betrayed Tromp's at Dunkirk. But if you
prefer, you could stay a while and test the limits of
the admiral's forgiving nature."

Du Plessis was off the platform and headed for the
gate before Mike had finished chuckling.

Chapter 30

Fort St. Patrick, Trinidad

After putting his three announcements before the group, Lieutenant Commander Eddie Cantrell looked for surprise or alarm on the faces of the down-timers and saw little. The news that Cardinal Borja of Spain had driven Urban VIII off the *cathedra* in the Holy See was not news to anyone but Tromp. Hugh O'Donnell and Aodh O'Rourke had heard of the events in Rome before departing Europe. And Tromp didn't seem to care very much. Mike McCarthy, Jr., had heard what Hugh and O'Rourke had, and Ann Koudsi had enjoyed the same access to recent events that Eddie himself had, traveling with the flotilla.

The announcement of John O'Neill's death affected only one person very strongly: O'Rourke. He leaned protectively toward the earl of Tyrconnell and actually glanced around as if checking for inbound assassins from every point of the compass. O'Donnell, now the last legitimate royal heir of Ireland, simply looked saddened. Hugh's reaction was somewhat surprising to Eddie. All reports indicated that there had been no love lost between the two earls. But the same sources had indicated that whereas they were rivals for preeminence in the eyes of the Irish, John also had a number of purely personal grudges against his royal cousin. O'Neill had long nursed a profound jealousy for Hugh, who had completed his degree at Louvain University and had been well liked for his wit and charm. John O'Neill, on the other hand, had inherited his illustrious father's temper and self-seeking instincts, without a corresponding measure of his brilliance and personal magnetism. In some ways, Eddie had to admit, Ed Piazza's analysis—that with the passing of O'Neill, Irish politics became a great deal clearer and less tangled—was probably correct. Tromp's careful face showed no reaction to the news of John O'Neill's death: a prudent reaction from a Dutchman sitting in council with representatives of the Wild Geese and the court in Brussels which they served. The only diplomatically safe reaction was polite and respectful silence, a behavior at which Admiral Maarten Tromp excelled.

However, Tromp's composure was quite undone when Eddie announced the outline of the deal that Mike McCarthy, Jr., had struck with Hugh O'Donnell and his Wild Geese. He started visibly at the news of the accord between the United Provinces and the Spanish Lowlands portions of the newly reunited Netherlands that both made the joint oil-development possible and was in turn made feasible by the common interests thus forged. However, he did not interrupt, and as Eddie continued to detail the agreement's particulars and the various checks and balances built into it, he nodded once or twice.

Well, thought Eddie, *so far so good. Which is better than I was hoping for. Sitting down with major leaders of the contending forces in the Lowlands could have gone sideways at the double-quick. And never mind that one of them is among the most famous admirals in history, and the other is the last heir to the Irish throne and godson of Archduchess Isabella. Which reminds me—* "Lord O'Donnell, I was asked to bring you a sealed letter. From your godmother, the archduchess infanta Isabella." He produced the wax-sealed tube and proffered it to the earl of Tyrconnell.

O'Donnell smiled—*such a bright and guileless smile!*—and took it carefully from Eddie's hands. "I very much appreciate your carrying this letter to me, Commander. Or, if the Wild Geese aboard your ship have told me correctly, should I say Lord Cantrell?"

Eddie felt himself blush, wishing he could wave away the color as easily as he could wave away the title. "I'm just Eddie. That title doesn't mean all that much, I'm afraid."

Hugh cocked an eyebrow. "You own land? You currently enjoy the use of it?"

Eddie nodded. "Yes, to both."

Hugh smiled again. "Then your title is more real than mine—Eddie. My lands are attainted. I am nobility in name only."

O'Rourke's brow had lowered. "There's many as would contest that, m'Lord O'Donnell. With flags waving and swords high."

The attainted earl of Tyrconnell nodded at O'Rourke's somber interjection. "We can safely leave that aside for now. And we can still hope that the swords will not be necessary." His expression transformed into a quizzical grin. "There's one more bit of news—or perhaps 'insight' is the better word—that I'm eager to have, Eddie: just how is it that the pirates seemed to know to come find us here? And so quickly? From the time we entered the Caribbees, we didn't see any other ship except for du Plessis', following us. So it's difficult to imagine how they learned of our presence here. Without some help, that is."

Eddie nodded. He'd been told that the Irish earl was shrewd, so he had half-expected this. "You are right, Hugh. The pirates—or more accurately, the Spanish—had help learning about your mission here. They had to, or they might not have come in time."

O'Rourke leaned forward. "Might not have come *in time?*"

Eddie nodded. "That right, Sergeant O'Rourke. In addition to getting oil from Trinidad, this mission had another purpose: it's a draw play."

"A 'draw play'?" Tromp echoed uncertainly.

"My apologies, Admiral Tromp. An up-time term—a sports term, actually. A draw play is an operation designed to pull an adversary's attention and units to a specific part of the playing field. In this case, that was Trinidad."

Hugh was frowning, rubbing his chin. "Why so?"

Eddie hoped that the two-thirds truth he was telling would be convincing enough on its own. "To draw in any units that the Spanish had in the area so they could be eliminated, either by the *Fleur Sable*, or, if absolutely necessary, by our follow-up force. It was imperative to get them to commit, and lose, any nearby units early on. The strategic logic was that this would leave them unable to even reconnoiter the area before our main forces and drillers arrived, much less make another bid to take it back. That should have taken the Spanish several months, by which time we'd have been well-established here."

Mike was frowning. "I note you said 'should have' taken the Spanish several months. Which makes me suspect that not everything has been going to plan."

Eddie shrugged. "Well, it hasn't."

O'Rourke's brow had beetled down once again. "And why not?"

Eddie put out a hand by way of appeal, wondered how he'd introduce the ticklish answer to that question, but Maarten Tromp saved him the trouble. "I am the answer. I am why things are not going according to plan."

All eyes were on the ever-composed Dutchman. "How could you be responsible for derailing plans of which you were unaware?" asked Ann Koudsi.

"Well, strictly speaking, I did nothing to derail the plans, but my actions and those of Admiral Thijssen have no doubt made the Spanish more easily provoked, and more decisive in response, than they were a year ago.

"Specifically, Admiral Thijssen took Curaçao from the Spanish in September of last year, although I suspect word of it did not reach any of the *audiencias* on Tierra Firma—excuse me; you call it the Spanish Main—for some months. At almost the same time, I abandoned Recife and relocated to St. Eustatia. From whence, shortly after, we were compelled to intercept the Armada de Barlovento when it ventured south from St. Maarten." He shrugged. "I suspect they had emerged in search of us, never guessing we were just one island further south in the Leewards."

Hugh nodded. "The Spanish conjectured you had reinforced Curaçao, that your actions and Thijssen's were coordinated."

Tromp nodded. "Exactly. Ironic, since we initially had no idea of each other's whereabouts or circumstances. But consequently, the Spanish evidently began considering the necessity of a mission to unseat Thijssen. Which meant that, by the time you and your men arrived here, Colonel O'Donnell, they had coincidentally brought additional forces down closer to Tierra Firma, including detachments from Havana and Santo Domingo. So Commander Cantrell's plan to draw off and destroy the usually paltry forces with which the Spanish patrol this area has fallen afoul of the Spanish decision to build up a greater power here to unseat Thijssen. Consequently, the first Spanish response to your attack on Trinidad"—he nodded at Hugh—"was to recruit a band of cutthroats. Otherwise, they would have had to draw ships from the flotilla they were gathering to oust Thijssen, which would have delayed those plans."

"And when the pirates didn't return with news of success," Mike nodded, "the people who hired them are now getting *really* worried."

Tromp nodded. "Yes. As we sailed here from St. Eustatia, we met one of our privateers, Moses Cohen Henriques, who touches along the Spanish Main both to gather information and raid, intermittently. Evidently, the Spanish are now delaying whatever plans they might have been evolving to attack Curaçao and are coming here instead." Tromp's smile was crooked. "In a way, I suppose you could say that, due to our activities here in the New World, Commander Cantrell's plan to attract Spanish attention has worked all too well."

Hugh nodded. "So, practically, what does this mean to us here? How many Spanish ships, how many troops, and when can we expect them to attack?"

Damn, thought Eddie, *I wish I could be so calm when asking questions like those.*

Tromp nodded. "We do not have anything approaching complete information, but between our own rovers, such at Cornelis Jol, and privateers such as Moses Henriques, here is what we have heard. The Spanish have three separate fleets converging on Trinidad: one from Havana, one from Santo Domingo, one from Cartagena. Their greatest difficulty will be effective rendezvous. That did not particularly matter when they were gathering to strike at Curaçao. They were simply gathering slowly in Puerto Cabello, waiting for their numbers to be complete. Now, because they have no specific intelligence on us, they must be ready to contend with a strong force that might meet them anywhere near Trinidad. And because they must act quickly, they cannot afford the luxury of rendezvousing in a single port anymore. They must attempt to arrive in this area, probably in the lee of Grenada, at approximately the same time and then order themselves for battle. This means they will have pickets out well ahead of their formation, searching for each other. And for us, as well.

"The Cuban fleet will take some time to get here, even though they have been underway for some weeks. Crossing the open water of the Caribbean from the north is a fickle business, as the prevailing winds will be coming abeam whereas the galleons want a following wind to make reasonable speed. The fleet from Santo Domingo is closer, but again, operating with many of the same constraints. However, they may catch a few more favorable winds by moving southward within the fifty miles of the lee-side of Lesser Antilles. The ships from Cartagena will be having the hardest time of it, tacking constantly to keep from being caught in the eye of the east wind."

Seeing the perplexed look on Ann's and Mike's faces, he explained. "'In the eye' means to be sailing straight into the wind. If you do so, you'll find yourself held fast, or 'in irons,' as we say, without any reasonable chance to make headway. This is a constant problem for ships sailing eastward along the Spanish Main, since both the current and prevailing winds are strongly westward, and Cartagena is a long way off. On the other hand, it is quite possible that the ships from Cartagena and other *audiencias* along the Main may have already been gathering closer to Curaçao, and so could be starting their journey from much closer than the fleets from Cuba or Hispaniola."

Tromp stood and gestured toward the map spread out on the table in the captain's combination ward-and chart-room. "It will be some weeks, we believe, before they arrive. And we do not have enough ships to maintain a line of pickets, searching for them. We will need to rely on our three balloons: Admiral Mund's flotilla has two, and Colonel O'Donnell still has his one. Those, along with our excellent glasses, should give us reasonable warning. However, it means keeping most of our ships on station near the Grenada Passage, if we are to intercept them at the time and place of our choosing. So we will presume that we are relatively safe for at least one more week and keep all but two of our ships in close anchorage here in Trinidad to take on supplies and prepare. After that week, we will need to put to sea and seek an anchorage near the Dragon's Mouth, where the Gulf of Paria meets the waters of the Grenada Passage."

Hugh smiled patiently. "And how many ships, guns, and troops do they have? You will forgive me for being so numerically-minded, Admiral Tromp."

Tromp almost smiled in return. "I share your fixation, Colonel, for those numbers will largely determine our fate. Informers who were in Hispaniola three months ago saw nine suitable ships being readied. I think we may assume that these were the captain-general of Hispaniola's contribution to the intended move against Curaçao. I think we may also reasonably assume that most, or all, will have received word to make way against us, instead.

"We have little other than guesswork concerning the other two fleets. However, when Havana has contributed to a larger effort in the Caribbees, it is usually half again as sizable as what emerges from Santo Domingo. Mind you, this is the very crudest of estimates, and may bear little resemblance to what is actually occurring. However, my captains all agree that it would be unusual if, in this particular circumstance, they did not send at least a dozen. They also note, with some alarm, that Havana's ways were more active in the last year than they have been in the preceding five. The new governor of Cuba seems to have received permission from Madrid to recommence his former prodigious rate of ship-building."

"That is not good news," O'Rourke observed softly.

"No, indeed," Tromp agreed. "And as for Cartagena, or more properly, the contributions drawn from along the length of the Spanish Main, we have no basis for estimate. The last time there was a significant problem here, Cartagena was able to muster sixteen ships, not counting lighter *garda costa* hulls, pickets and auxiliaries. However, that was a gathering performed on very short notice. They may have assembled far more, this time."

"So we can expect somewhere between twenty and forty ships, give or take a lot," Mike summarized sardonically.

Tromp did smile this time. "Your numbers are every bit as precise as our own, mijn heer McCarthy. As far as troop totals, this is unknowable. They may hope to rely mostly upon local natives with whom they have alliances, or they may be carrying a thousand seasoned Spanish troops. But I rather doubt the latter."

"Why?" asked Ann.

Hugh looked at Tromp for permission to field the question, who nodded his leave. "Logistics, Lady Ann. These three flotillas have something in common: they must spend a long time at sea to reach us. That means a great deal of food. The more men they bring, the more food, water and other perishables they must carry. Logically, if any of these fleets are furnished with significant numbers of troops, it would be the one from Cartagena. That one can at least touch at various points along the Spanish Main for reprovisioning."

Tromp nodded, seeming to be pleased. Eddie noted that the admiral had a ready and catholic appreciation for competence, wherever he found it. Including, in this case, a commander who, under prior circumstances, would have been his enemy. "The colonel could not be more correct," Tromp averred. "Fortunately, the troops found along the Spanish Main are not the best-trained nor best-equipped of Madrid's New World army. Such as it is." Tromp hastened to provide an explanation for his apparent derogation of Spanish soldiery. "Do not misunderstand me. The Spanish troops we might face are likely to be quite competent, but they will not be trained in drill and field maneuvers as you would encounter in Europe. Here, in a land of jungles, swamps, and grasslands, where most of the opponents are native tribes or perhaps a company of pirates, there are no reasons to keep *tercios* in camps, ready to take the field against organized armies. The New World's wars are skirmishes in remote areas or on the outskirts of towns. Or, occasionally, small cities. There is no maneuvering of serried ranks, no sweeping cavalry attacks against exposed flanks, no clashes of thousands of armored men under the gaze of generals on two opposed ridges. Here, men fight in the bushes, at close range, with little warning of the combat to come, and no expectation of quarter if they lose. The Spanish formations of the New World have adapted to this style of warfare. So while they are not much use in set-piece battles, and are indifferent artillerymen at best, they are as deadly and ruthless a foe as this environment can make them. And you will find, I fear, that this environment is a harsh teacher, indeed."

Eddie distractedly rubbed his palm over the butt of his holstered HP-35's worn grip. *Sounds like it's Vietnam all over again for you, pal.*

"So, other than waiting for them to show up, do we have a plan?" Mike didn't sound annoyed so much as faintly anxious.

es," Tromp said with a decisive nod. "First, we believe that the Spanish have no idea that the up-time designed steamships exist, much less what attributes they might have. Our plan is to allow the Spanish to believe they have a reasonable chance to gain the weather gauge on our fleet. Only then will we use the steam power at our disposal to show them the error of their assessment and to secure the weather gauge for ourselves."

O'Rourke's eyebrows canted skeptically. "You are saying they may be bringing an average of thirty ships to face our—what?—twelve? Admiral Tromp, I know you have seen the full armament of a war galleon up close, but are you sure your memory is furnishing you with an accurate recollection of their firepower, just now?"

Tromp glanced at Eddie, who leaned forward, smiling. "Sergeant O'Rourke, I have a question for you: have you ever seen an eight-inch breech-loading naval rifle in action?"

"Be damned, but I'm not even sure what sort of iron-mongery that might be."

"Well, at some point in the coming weeks, I suspect you'll get a chance to see it in action. I think our naval strategy will start making a lot of sense, then. But in the meantime, we've got some unconventional ground operations in mind, as well."

Hugh had not missed Eddie's leading tone. "For which my Wild Geese might be particularly well suited?"

"They just might be," admitted Eddie, "and as you're probably aware, we brought many more of the men of your *tercio* over with the flotilla."

"Yes, I had the opportunity to chat with a few when we came aboard." And he shot Eddie a most unusual look, a smile that was almost mischievous, as if it concealed a shared secret...

Eddie managed not to start, hoped he hadn't flushed: *damn it, he's halfway to figuring out Quinn's part of our mission! His own troops probably fell over themselves rushing to tell him that we had a third steamship in the flotilla—the* Courser—*which split off from us just before we entered the Caribbean. And Hugh's already guessed what that means: the real reason we're pulling all the attention here to Trinidad is so the* Courser *can fulfill its undisclosed mission with a minimal chance of observation by, or chance encounter with, the Spanish. A mission that no one's talking about, or even alluding to...*

But Hugh was evidently going to let him off that hook. The Irish earl kept on the primary topic of conversation. "So what kind of unconventional action are we talking about, Eddie?"

Eddie leaned in. "Let's call it a special mission, and leave it at that for now. We'll go over the details after we've wrapped up this general meeting, okay?"

"Very well." Hugh's eyes drifted along the map to a point well west of Trinidad. "I must ask: what of Curaçao? Can we not involve the Dutch forces there in our plans, Admiral Tromp?"

"I wish we could," mused Tromp with a frown. "But we have yet to establish contact with whatever colony Thijssen has planted there, and he did not have many ships or men to begin with. Perhaps we will send an envoy, in the months to come, urging him to join with us—"

Rourke's smile was small, sad, sympathetic: "But you don't think such a suggestion will set him a-hurrying in our direction."

Tromp shook his head. "No, I don't think it would. And that is unfortunate, for he is too far exposed for his own sake. And for ours."

Ann frowned. "What do you mean?"

Tromp gestured toward the green line of Trinidad's shore, visible out the portside windows. "We are soon to deposit you and your, er, drilling crews, on a very large island, Ms. Koudsi. "We need Thijssen's force here, securing you, the land, and the oil. But I doubt he will quit Curaçao, and I fear that decision may prove his undoing."

Eddie leaned forward, glanced toward Ann. "Speaking of oil, perhaps you'll brief everyone about what you're expecting to be doing for the next half year or so, Ann, and why it could make this a very valuable piece of real estate."

Ann nodded; she leaned her lips against her folded hands, apparently thinking how best to make a simple, cogent explanation out of a very complicated and multifaceted operation. "First," she almost mumbled, "we have several huge advantages drilling for oil here on Trinidad. Probably the greatest of those advantages is how much we know from up-time sources about the early oil industry here. We know, roughly, where the first successful wells were sunk to within two square miles, and we know the sorts of geological formations the prospectors were looking for. So the hardest part of our surveying work is already done."

"Second, the number of wells sunk in relatively close proximity to each other was high, so we don't

have to start drilling exactly where the first successful up-time prospectors did. As long as we're in the
right area, we should hit oil after a few tries, at most.

"Third, Trinidadian oil is not only sweet and light,
but very close to the surface. None of the first wells
required more than two hundred and fifty feet of
drilling; some required little more than one hundred
and fifty. And that's all easily within the depth range
of our cable-drilling rigs. We also know that a lot of
them were gushers, so we know to go slow and be
prepared. That way, we'll suffer less damage and lose
less oil. A lot less."

Eddie nodded. "And when do you expect to start
drilling?"

Ann grinned crookedly at him. "As soon as your
boats finish ferrying my gear to the colonel's fort, and
as soon as we get the 'all clear' to start surveying. As
I understand it, it's not safe for us to go wandering
around inland, yet."

"Not yet," nodded Eddie, "and I suspect the colonel
will need to provide you with security contingents,
even so."

"Then how will it ever be secure enough to drill
in any of the sites we find?"

Eddie nodded. "When you've got a high-confidence
find, we'll throw up a security cordon around it. If it's
further off, we'll need to patrol an eventual access road
as well. Which is why we've asked you to concentrate
your initial surveying close to Pitch Lake. It's off the
beaten-track of the Arawaks, and with any luck, we
won't even need an access road."

Ann shrugged. "I'll do my best. We do know there
were some wells sunk in sight of Pitch Lake itself.

But that's a lot different from being able to deliver one on the first shot, and by request."

Tromp was shaking his head. "No one expects that, Ms. Koudsi. Nothing of the kind. We understand that you might need many tries and much time before finding oil. Which is why we are trying to formalize an active alliance with the Nepoia tribes. If that can be accomplished, our work here will be much easier."

"And how have those efforts been coming along?" Ann's keen interest vied with her obvious anxiety as she inquired.

"Pretty well," Eddie answered, "but we've had a hard time setting up a meeting with their cacique, Hyarima. He's in the field carrying the fight to the Arawaks right now. But he's interested in meeting his new neighbors." Eddie glanced at Hugh. "Particularly you."

Hugh raised an eyebrow. "I am honored. But I suspect that I, too, will be too busy for that meeting." He smiled. "Speaking of which, when do you need us to start on that special mission?"

Eddie grinned sheepishly, shrugged. "Actually, it would be best if your Wild Geese could leave today, Colonel. Before which, I'll want a few words with you in private."

Hugh smiled knowingly. "Of course, Commander. Well, O'Rourke, I see we shall be working for our share of the profits along with everyone else. No more lolly-gagging about for us!"

O'Rourke glanced at his earl sourly. "Sure and I'll be missing my life of tropical leisure, m'lord."

Eddie nodded agreeably, but thought: *O'Rourke, you might soon mean those ironic words seriously enough. Particularly given where you and the earl are heading.*

For Hugh O'Donnell, the end of the private meeting with Eddie Cantrell did not mark the end of business. Emerging from the aft companionway, Hugh had found his sergeant pacing the deck of the *Intrepid* like a caged bear. He had immediately summoned all the Wild Geese that were aboard, who swarmed their two senior officers, as eager as puppies to go ashore and mingle with their comrades manning the walls of Fort St. Patrick.

But that was not to be for the half being retained as ship's troops. And of those, forty were hastily transferred to the Dutch yacht *Eendracht*, which was to weigh anchor at dusk and commence carrying Hugh and his men to their distant objective. But before then, Hugh and O'Rourke had much to do in little time: familiarizing the recently arrived officers of the *tercio* with the routines and particularities of Fort St. Patrick; supervising the transfer and placement of a small battery of demi-culverins ashore; and calming Doubting Thomas Doyle who was lamenting the impossibility of completing all the inevitable new construction projects in the time required.

They finished their work ashore just in time to wave farewell to the *Koninck David* and the *Crown of Waves* as those two ships set sail back north. Michael McCarthy was at the taffrail, waving back at them. Word had it that he was bound for 'Statia to perform yet another piece of up-time technological wizardry. Exactly what he was to conjure up remained unknown to all but Tromp and Cantrell, and they were not sharing that information. *More secrets*, thought Hugh. *Nothing but, here in the New World.*

And Hugh was not innocent of secrecy, himself—not until he could share his destination with his men, which for security's sake he could not reveal until they drew close to it. Nonetheless, they would be training for their upcoming operation as they traveled west along the Spanish Main on a course known only to the Dutch captain, his mate, and his pilot. The prerequisite level of mutual trust between the commanders made for a markedly strange situation, reflected Hugh, since he had fought the Dutch since he could hold a sword.

But this first joint enterprise of forces from the newly cooperative Lowlands also presented a wholly unlooked for silver lining in the form of the young and wonderfully alert young captain of the jacht *Eendracht*, Pieter Floriszoon. Good-natured and every bit as weary of religious bigotry as Hugh himself, they quickly worked out their respective command prerogatives—Floriszoon commanded on the water, Hugh on land—and got under way. The prevailing winds were handy, coming from the east abeam the starboard gunwale, and Floriszoon accurately predicted no more than five hours sailing to traverse the Gulf of Paria to the near side of Dragon's Mouth, where they would make anchorage in a protected cove.

Shortly after dark, the *Eendracht* dropped anchor at the appointed place and Hugh went below to take a congenial meal with the almost fifty Wild Geese who were aboard. In addition to the forty troops that had been drawn from the *Intrepid*, ten specialists had been hand-picked from the original group at Fort St. Patrick, all of whom spent the evening telling the new arrivals heavily embellished tales of their time at Pitch Lake.

As the rations of grog were being ladled out, Hugh had noticed O'Rourke getting ready to break away from the below-decks camaraderie. No doubt to button-hole Hugh so that they could finally compare notes on the day's events. There had certainly been plenty of food for thought in the news they had heard, and careful counsel was in order. But, with an unvoiced apology to his old friend, Hugh slipped off alone to examine the day's last potential source of surprises and secrets: the letter from his godmother.

Had Hugh read it before the pirate attack, its contents would have flabbergasted him. She revealed that, for almost half a year, she had foreseen the inevitable effect that Fernando's increasing distance from his brother Philip of Spain would have on her godson, that he would be placed in an impossible position if he remained in Philip's service. Consequently, she had set about her slow campaign to properly position him to be in the right time and right place to take advantage of the changes that were coming.

Her indirect encouragements to meet the up-timers; her back-channel negotiations with that group's President Piazza to maneuver Hugh into a partnership with Michael McCarthy; the up-time brokered agreement between Fernando and Hendrik to share the responsibilities and profits that might arise from tapping oil in Trinidad; the inclusion of the Wild Geese as a smaller but fully entitled partner in that larger deal: what would have shocked him a month ago now seemed like an embarrassingly obvious answer to the apparent coincidences of the past half year. Even so, the amount of invisible negotiation and creation of common points of interest that Isabella had brokered, groomed, and achieved was formidable. It might yet prove to be her finest coup in a career chock-full of diplomatic tours-de-force.

But Hugh could see another level that few, if any, other observers would have detected: that the foundation and driving force behind her grand accomplishment had been her love for Hugh, her largely hidden determination that his legacy, and potential, should be married to resources that might enable him to realize and capitalize upon both. McCarthy's passion for Ireland had been the crucial catalyst she had been seeking, the means of bringing together a strange, wholly unofficial, yet powerful political bond between the interests and persons of the Spanish Lowlands and the interests and persons of the USE.

After reading the letter twice, Hugh spent some minutes just looking at it, cherishing his godmother's familiar, bold hand and the wry wit that lurked behind so many of her comments and observations. For the briefest moment, he seemed to feel her fingers touch his face like a ghost's, reaching all the way from the other side of the ocean.

It took a while to get to sleep. The water was calm, but his mind was filled with surges of other faces and facts: John O'Neill dead, Urban VIII missing, Prince Frederik Hendrik an ally, and a cascade of silver for his Wild Geese and their families. And upon him, the title of the last legitimate earl of Ireland. He wasn't sure whether to feel it as a great weight or a great joke, being such a tremendous reversal from the life he had lived and expected. He was still trying to decide which reaction was more appropriate when the gentle movement of the *Eendracht* finally rocked him to sleep.

Ann Koudsi had been rocked to sleep a lot more energetically than Hugh O'Donnell. In a manner of speaking. When she awoke in her cabin in the middle of the night, it took her a moment to reorient herself. First, because it was her own cabin on land—part of the newly built housing for the drilling team on Trinidad—not the even tinier cabin she'd shared with another woman on the *Patentia*. And second, because she hadn't shared a bed with anyone in . . .

A long, long time. Since the Ring of Fire, in fact—as if the simple act of sexual intercourse would somehow have finalized the disappearance of the world she'd once known and loved.

Now, lifted up on one elbow and gazing down at the recumbent form of Ulrich Rohrbach, she realized just how foolish she'd been. The truth was, no matter how fond she'd been of her up-time existence, it was a pale shadow compared to her new life. She knew she'd never have experienced such adventures, nor had such awesome responsibilities thrust upon her. Never been so challenged—and never shown herself how well she could and would rise to those challenges.

And she'd never have had a lover like Ulrich. A man who admired and respected her as much as he did, without being intimidated by her. Because, despite his lack of formal education and his modest birth, he'd absorbed the up-time belief in self-betterment and applied it with a determination that bordered on ferocity.

There'd been no chance to further their relationship while they'd been on the *Patentia*. There'd been no privacy, for starters. Perhaps more importantly—this was hard to pin down, exactly—Ann herself hadn't felt quite ready. So long as they were in transit from the old world to the new, she'd somehow felt as if her life was still suspended.

No longer. They'd reached their destination—for the moment, at least—and her fate was back in her own hands. This was their first night on Trinidad since the cabin was finally declared ready and they could transfer off the ship. And she'd made the most of it, by God!

For the first time since the Ring of Fire, she was finally able to fully accept and welcome her new life. O brave new world.

Ulrich shifted slightly on the bed. And, then, began to snore.

All right, fine. Some things stayed the same. But it was still a brave new world.

Chapter 31

Entry to Galveston Bay, Texas

Major Larry Quinn glanced over his shoulder at the darkening southern horizon. Even at this range, he could see actinic flashes inside the low line of gray clouds that were beginning to rise up through the hazy air mass above them. He glanced back up the tumblehome of the *Courser*, trying not to sound either anxious or annoyed as he said, "Any time now, Karl."

Karl Klemm swayed down another step of the netting that had been played over the side of the destroyer, then glanced at his feet before starting downward again. This time, however, his foot remained in midair, thrashing about in search of the next foothold, which the gentle sway of the ship had snatched away.

In the boat, two of the elite soldiers of Grantville's increasingly proprietary Hibernian Mercenary Battalion, Volker and Wright, exchanged world-weary glances. Wright looked at Larry. "Major Quinn, should we lend Mr. Klemm a hand in—?"

Larry shook his head and said quietly but firmly, "No. He can handle it." *And hopefully he'll do so before the month is out,* the up-timer added silently. Because with a hurricane coming straight up out of the Gulf of Mexico, and the *Courser* waiting for them to lead it to safe anchorage, every minute counted.

But it was also important that Klemm, the only man on the *Courser* who had not started out by embracing a life of risk on either battlefields or the high seas, should learn to master the skills and attitudes necessary to survive beyond the margins of civilization.

Klemm eyed the six feet remaining to the deck of the small, up-time motor boat bouncing against the fenders separating it from *Courser*'s hull. Larry saw the assessing stare, and shook his head. "No jumping, Karl. That's a good way to twist an ankle, and you have to stay mobile."

Karl glanced at Larry, nodded tightly, gritted his teeth and put another foot down, then again, and finally, half-stepped and half tumbled into the cockpit of the bright red 1988 180 Sportsman. He straightened, panting slightly, and looked Larry in the eye. "Apologies, Major. I will work hard to improve my climbing."

Larry nodded for the lines to be cast off and the fenders pulled in, then glanced sideways at the young Bavarian. "You seemed a good enough climber when we were touring various rock formations with Ms. Aossey. Hell, you were as good scrambling up a rock face as I was."

Karl looked about the controls of the motorboat, alert, as if reading the function of each lever and button. "With respect, Major, cliffs do not move as you climb them. So it seems strange to me to try to put my foot where the netting *will* be, rather than where it was when I last looked down."

Quinn smiled. "Fair enough."

"Major," said the middle aged sailor perched on the bow of the motor boat, "we are ready."

Karl looked at Larry. "Shall I help the leadsman with—?"

"No, Karl. You stay here. I want you to learn how to pilot this boat."

Karl's eyes were wide—with apprehension or avidity, Larry wasn't quite sure. "Me?"

"Yes. You have a knack for machines and we'll need at least two people to pilot it when we make our way back up the coast to the Mermentau River. Besides, this boat can be a little finicky."

Klemm stared at the unfamiliar word. "'Finicky?'"

Evidently that colloquialism hadn't made the jump into Amideutsch. At least not yet. "Finicky is, er, sensitive, twitchy. Like a nervous cat."

"Ah. Delicate controls. I shall watch closely."

Quinn eased the throttle forward and turned the wheel to the right. The slow, clockwork mutter of the outboard rose into a ragged purr and the Sportsman sheered away from the hull of the *Courser* at a leisurely pace. Before them, the blue-green waters that marked the narrow entry into Galveston Bay roiled, mildly agitated as they moved over and among that gap's notoriously migratory sandbars. "Leadsman," cried Larry into the wind, "reading."

"Not quite three fathoms, sir."

Damn it, that was close. The *Courser* drew almost two fathoms without her drop-keel down, and because she was heavily loaded for a long mission away from resupply, she was probably drawing a full thirteen feet. That left only four feet between her keel and the muddy sands that she would need to traverse. Larry eased the throttle back. Frequent depth readings were going to be needed in order to make sure they didn't miss a submerged bank or other protrusion that might snag the *Courser* and leave her trapped before the slashing jaws of a rapidly approaching hurricane. "Keep singing out those marks," he shouted toward the bow as he glanced at Volker and Wright.

The two soldiers kept an easy hold on their rifles— down-time copies of the Winchester 1895 chambered for .40-72—one scanning the low, sandy end of the Bolivar Peninsula on the northeastern side of the channel, the other alert for movement on Galveston Island's higher southwestern shore. The glass-smooth water and the lack of birds confirmed what the barometer had started predicting two days ago and what the dark line of clouds on the south now promised: that the approaching storm was certain to be quite ferocious.

"Fourteen feet," called the leadsman grimly. "Silty and thick."

Another one foot rise. Much more, and the *Courser* would have no safe harbor. This was what Admiral Simpson had called the worst-case scenario of the mission: that, arriving along the Gulf coast during hurricane season, the *Courser* could find itself unable to make a run into a good high-weather anchorage. Her ultimate objective, the Mermentau River, was known to be shallow, and the harbors at Port Arthur and the Calcasieu Channel did not exist in this world. Without dredging, they were barely half the depth required. Until one reached the mouth of the Mississippi, the tidal flats were precisely that: very flat, and very shallow. No ports worth the name. And while the

Courser could lie off the Mermentau easily and safely enough in most weather, she was at severe risk if she stuck to the open water in the teeth of a hurricane.

The only option had been Galveston Bay, a full one hundred miles west of the Mermentau. Fortunately, they had heeded the barometer's warnings and taken no chances, bypassing the Mermentau and making straight for Galveston.

But making straight for Galveston was not synonymous with racing into her bay. Although the channel ranged from one and a half to two miles wide, the shifting silt and sand made the actual pathway something of a slalom course. And in an era without dredging or regularly updated depth charts, the trick to finding safe harbor depended upon trail-blazing the sinuous path of the greater depths.

Consequently, at the start of the first watch, Larry had given orders that the Sportsman 180 should be uncovered, which was achieved by disassembling its disposable warehouse-cocoon on the ship's main deck. Captain Haraldsen, who had finally begun to forgive Larry for taking over the mission when the *Courser* parted from the rest of the flotilla, had been unable to suppress his pointed interest in the up-time boat as, board by board, it was revealed and then made ready for lowering over the stern by a hastily erected pair of davits. Now, Larry just hoped they had put her in the water soon enough. "Give me another reading."

The leadsman shook his head. "Steady at fourteen. Might have risen another inch."

Not good. Quinn looked back at the *Courser*. Haraldsen himself was waiting patiently in the bows, spyglass ready to distinguish any hand signal that might come from the motorboat. Because if the channel continued to rise, the best the *Courser* could do was anchor herself in the mouth of the channel and hope that the path of the storm was such that the headlands broke the worst rush of wind and water, rather than focused it upon her. Still, even that was better than catching the storm out in the Gulf and being pushed up against the land without any control. But being carried out of the center of the channel by a storm surge might be almost as bad, leaving the ship stranded in a position from which they would not be able to get it back into the receded waters. That would mean the end of their mission, and quite possibly, the end of their lives—

"Three fathoms full, again, Major!" cried the leadsman. "And dropping fast. We must have been moving over a silt shelf."

Quinn nodded. "Good, but we're not safe yet. We've got about another mile of channel to go, and we haven't encountered the narrower sand bars." *Assuming there are any narrower sand bars, that is.* Working from a few nineteenth- and twentieth-century accounts that had been located in the Grantville Library didn't exactly provide them with an extensive maritime gazetteer of Galveston Bay. For all anyone knew, the sandbars might have been a later phenomenon or one with a long periodic arc.

But whatever the case, they were well over a mile into the channel, which meant they had reached the point where it had been determined it was worthwhile bringing the *Courser* in for anchorage, even if she could go no farther. "Wright," Quinn called over his shoulder. "Signal to Captain Haraldsen that he should start following along in our wake. Precisely in our wake.

Otherwise he is at risk of running aground from bars that we're not detecting farther to the east or west."

"Yes, sir," Wright said, standing and making the appropriate hand signals back to the *Courser*.

"Leadsman," called Quinn. "Reading."

"Three fathoms full and less silt. Feels like we're past the muck."

Larry nodded, pushed the throttle forward. "Okay then, we're picking up the pace. The sooner we blaze a trail to get the *Courser* into the bay, the better the anchorage she might find." The Sportcraft 180's engine sound grew throatier. The prop dug at the water harder, putting a thready vibration through the deck. The leadsman called out largely unchanging reports.

Quinn felt Karl's eyes watching his hands upon the controls. "Catching on?"

Klemm nodded. "Yes. It seems simple in principle. But, like many such things, I suspect it is more difficult than it looks."

"A little," Quinn admitted with a smile. "But once the hurricane has passed us and we're ready to head back to the Mermentau River, you'll get some time behind the wheel. We'll share the piloting when we head back. By the time we're ready to motor into the bayous, you'll be an old hand."

Karl looked skeptical. "If you say so, Major. But the close margins of inland waterways will be a more difficult task, no?"

Quinn frowned. "Different, more than difficult. On open water, you've got to watch the risers and the chop, particularly in a light boat like this one. And you've got to read the skies well, so you can run to an inlet, a bay, or even a beach if heavy weather is on the way. Inland, the worry is that you'll put a hole in her hull, run aground in the shallows, or get snarled in vegetation. Either way, the best rules for a new boater are to look sharp and go slow. That way, you'll last long enough to become an old boater."

The leadsman called more loudly. "Sand bar. Up to fifteen and rising toward port."

Quinn turned the prow slightly starboard, eased the throttle back. "Now?"

"Holding steady. Now dropping. Sixteen."

Quinn held the wheel motionless, maintained speed. "Now?"

"Steady at sixteen."

Quinn called over his shoulder. "Volker, toss back a weighted buoy where we turned."

Karl watched the small float, trailing a bottom-weighted rope, soar through the air, land with a splash well back in their wake. "Let us hope the bar does not rise in this new direction, as well."

Larry nodded. If it did rise up higher, they'd have to backtrack, keep trying different directions until they found one that would get them all the way into the bay. But they didn't have the time for that kind of trial-and-error anymore. He looked back at the southern horizon. The sky was hazy as high up as he could see, and the dark storm bank had risen to show more of itself over the rim of the world. It would be on them in two hours, maybe less.

The leadsman's next shout sounded like a sigh of relief projected through a bullhorn. "Seventeen. No, eighteen. And widening out on all sides. You can cut back to port again, I think."

Which would be a good thing, since their current

heading would have fetched them up against the scree and rubble shore of Point Bolivar in another few hundred yards. Quinn swung the motorboat slowly back to port.

"Steady marks, Major. And we're just about out of the channel."

Quinn eased the throttle forward again, discovered that Volker was trying to catch his eye. "Herr Major," he said, just loud enough to be heard over the engine, "who or what are Wright and I watching for?"

"Most likely natives. Possibly Spanish, but our histories say they were pretty hesitant to make landfall along here."

"Because of the sandbars?"

"Possibly. But probably more because of the Atakapas."

Volker smiled. "So the natives don't much like the Spanish?"

"Oh, they do," Wright observed sardonically. "For dinner."

At first, Volker was perplexed. Then his eyes widened. "They are cannibals?"

Quinn was wondering how best to defuse any surge in anxiety over the rumored culinary habits of the natives, but Karl beat him to it. "Actually, Herr Volker, that is a matter of some debate. There was little mention of them in the books in Grantville. However, while most accounts do suggest that they ate their foes ritualistically, it seems that the only Europeans they ever defined as 'foes' were the Spanish."

"Why?" asked Wright.

Quinn shared the last of the scant knowledge that had been gleaned on the Atakapas. "Apparently, the Spanish enslaved and tortured the first groups of

Atakapas they came across. And it seems the Atakapas have long memories. At least that's what the history books say."

"The very *few* history books," Wright amended soberly, "based on scant travelers' tales, from the sound of it. Let's hope they're right."

"Well, Mr. Wright, we'll be the first to find out." Quinn watched the last of the headlands that formed the two sides of the channel fall away behind them, Galveston Bay spreading out around them. "Mr. Volker," he called back, "signal to the *Courser* that we've marked their passage, and are now going to scout anchorages." Quinn moved the throttle farther forward and felt the nose of the boat begin to rise as their speed increased.

Larry stole a rearward glance. The hurricane had changed again. Taller, darker, and, given the rate of visual change, moving directly toward them at one hell of a clip. Safe anchorage or not, they'd also need a good measure of luck to come through the storm in one piece.

He turned to survey the wide bay before him and saw little in the way of making their own luck. One of the problems with Galveston Bay was how very flat its sheltering islands were. They were simply sand spits, really, studded with a few rocks here and there. The only feature that rose up to any height was Pelican Island, immediately to their west, which meant it was back across the sand bars they'd just avoided.

Quinn kept a worried frown off his face, as he called forward to the leadsman. "I'm going to take us a little farther east, to see if we can find some deep water in the lee of the Port Bolivar headland."

The leadsman simply stared at the water there, which was entirely too calm and not particularly dark, and then stared back at Quinn.

Who thought: *yeah, I know. Doesn't look promising. Problem is that* nothing *looks promising. Most of all that damned storm.*

Karl was close at Larry's elbow. "Major, without depth charts, how shall we know where best to make a quick search for an anchorage?"

Quinn sent an entirely artificial grin at the young German. "We make our best guess and take our chances." *And right now, our chances aren't looking too good...*

Part Six

October 1635

What plagues and what portents

Chapter 32

Outside Puerto Cabello, Venezuela

Hugh O'Donnell turned, listened, went into a crouch, and motioned the thirty men following him to do the same. Behind them, a faint voice cried out in Spanish, but only to silence a barking dog. Then, all was quiet again in the lightless, mostly abandoned village of Borburata, just five hundred yards behind them.

"Have we been seen, m'lord?" asked one of his senior ensigns, Daniel O'Cahan.

Hugh glanced up at the sky. Stars stared back down, impassive. Too clear for his liking. He'd waited for a near-moonless night, but could only pray for clouds, which had not materialized. "No, Daniel, I think not. The skiffs put us in better than four hundred yards northwest of the furthest huts, which the Dutch say are deserted. And they should know. They've raided here a bit."

The ever-laconic Jimmy Murrow glanced back at the faint outlines of tilted thatched roofs, many half-collapsed.

"What's to be had, I wonder?"

"Not much anymore. Less than a hundred souls there. Quiet now. There will be coast watchers ahead."

As if to confirm Hugh's warning, O'Bannon slipped out of the bushes lining the thin strand. "Two coast-watchers, m'lord. About two hundred yards further on."

"About what we thought, then. Where's Purcell? Is he keeping an eye on them?"

O'Bannon's face was unreadable in the dark. "In a manner of speakin'. I should have said there *were* two coast watchers."

O'Donnell nodded. Purcell was as quiet as a cat, handy with a dagger, and disturbingly eager to use both skills. Which he had done tonight. Hugh would rather not have commanded such men as Purcell, but such fine moral scruples were luxuries a colonel could not afford. Having a diverse collection of tactical tools at one's disposal, no matter how devious and dark some of those tools might be, meant more success and fewer lost men. Better a stain on his honor that no one else perceived than a few more trusting *cultchies* buried in a foreign field.

Or in this case, possibly more than a few. It would be nothing short of disastrous if the Spanish had any warning of their approach over the thin arm of land that framed in the northern side of Puerto Cabello's protected anchorage, and was only two hundred fifty yards wide at its narrowest point. If detected, it was quite possible that they'd fail to reach the inner harbor at all, and quite unlikely that they'd capture the ship they had seen sitting almost astride the channel into it. And since the Dutch commander of the up-time-inspired steam pinnace that was set to rendezvous with them had no way of knowing if they were repulsed, or where to retrieve them if they were, it was all too likely that any determined Spanish pursuit would end in the wholesale slaughter of Hugh's detachment.

O'Donnell nodded at O'Bannon, his senior lieutenant in this group. "Any other pickets that you could see?"

O'Bannon shook his head. "No, m'lord. Looks clear all the way down to the inner harbor. Nothing on this arm of land until you reach the guardhouse and the open battery we spotted overlooking the narrows."

Which, for all intents and purposes, meant they could make their way down to the shore of the inner harbor unobserved. The narrows were more than six hundred yards west of their destination, with a small rocky promontory blocking the sight line between them.

O'Cahan didn't sound convinced, though. "Can the Spanish really be that lax? Natives could be just as quiet as and deadly as Purcell, and the jungles are thick wid 'em."

O'Bannon smiled at the cautious new ensign, who was clearly eager to show that he was competent and alert to all dangers. "Not so many natives about as you'd think, Daniel. They stay well back from the bigger towns unless they mean to burn 'em to the ground. And the Spanish aren't worried about their neighbors sneaking in from here on the north beach, because there's naught they can do. So the natives take the northern arm of the inner harbor. Then what? Are they going to swim out into the anchorage and threaten the Spanish ships?"

"No," muttered Jimmy Murrow, "because they're not such bleedin' goms as we are."

"Are you saying you've reservations about our plans, Mr. Murrow?" Hugh asked coolly.

Murrow made a sound as if he was swallowing his shoe. Sideways. "None 't all, m'lord."

"Mm. Didn't think so. You'll be wanting that length of bamboo handy about now, I'd think. And you too, O'Cahan. In a few minutes, it will be time for your midnight swims."

Aodh O'Rourke brought up his pepperbox revolver as the bushes rustled in front of him. "Advance and be recognized."

A swarthy, much-scarred man of medium height and build emerged from between two giant fronds. "It's Calabar," he said quietly. "What are you doing this far forward on the path?"

"Being where I'm not supposed to be," O'Rourke answered, waving to the men behind him to rise and prepare to move.

"And why is that?" asked Calabar, who eased the hammer forward again on his flintlock pistol.

"Because if any of the Spanish bastards had caught you and indulged their taste for torture, I didn't want to be where you'd have told them we were."

Calabar's voice was quiet, distant. "I'd not have told them anything. Not unto death."

"Which is as may be, friend, but I'll not be trusting the lives of twenty mothers' sons to any man's resolve when his captors start playing mumblety-peg with his fingernails. Or his manhood."

Calabar's shadow shrugged. "Very well. The path ahead is overgrown. It is not much used, possibly only by hunters."

"I thought Puerto Cabello was mostly home to fishermen," put in Malachi O'Mara, O'Rourke's second in command, from behind.

Calabar's voice was half-droll, half-annoyed. "As I said, the path is not much used. Are your men ready?"

O'Rourke nodded. "The oil and charges are ready, and the men are arrayed in their pairs."

"You've reapplied mud?"

"We've done as you instructed."

"And look like a horde of Moors, to boot," mumbled Patrick Keenan, from farther back in the column.

"You mind yourself, you blue-eyed Moor," scolded O'Rourke, who kept his focus on Calabar. "Have you seen the warehouses?"

The half-Portuguese *mameluco* from Brazil's Pernambuco coast shrugged. "Their roofs, only. I did not wish to go closer. But they are where Moses Henriques reported them to be."

"And you trust this pirate-friend of yours?"

Again, Calabar paused before speaking. "He is my friend, and I saved his life near Recife, so yes, I trust him. And he is a pirate, but a selective one. He rarely takes a ship lest she be Portuguese or Spanish. Most importantly, no one knows this coast half as well as he does. His men were in Puerto Cabello only two weeks ago and saw war materiel being moved into the warehouses, saw the guards standing watch night and day, saw that most of the crews were being kept aboard their ships, not billeted in town."

O'Rourke nodded. "Meaning the Spanish are presuming they could receive orders to weigh anchor any day. Very well; we'll trust your Hebrew pirate friend." He turned to his men. "Blades, not pistols, until we leave the jungle. If we bump into patrols, we take them quietly. Once at the outskirts of the town, it will be guns and fast feet, lads. We'll not have much time."

Maintaining a tight crouch, Hugh crept down to the water's edge, with Murrow and O'Cahan beside him. O'Bannon had already taken a few men to keep watch over their right flank, just in case a patrol meandered out of the guard post farther to the northwest. He scanned the inner-harbor as the two young men, the best swimmers in his two companies, reblacked their faces and checked their bamboo breathing tubes. In the briefing for the mission, Cantrell had kept calling them snorkels and seemed to presume they were easier to use than past experience had proven them to be.

O'Donnell had used them once, himself, years ago during the siege at Bruges. It was not unknown to use breathing tubes to cross shallow moats, but it was a risky undertaking. Moats were usually barely a step above open sewers in terms of cleanliness, and using the breathing tubes meant swimming in an awkward position: half on one's back, almost. Which made strong swimmers the users of choice.

That was even more true on this mission, where they would be towing lightly weighted lines out to the *patache* that was almost sitting astride the inner mouth of the channel that communicated between the outer and inner bay. Two days of observation—by a team deposited under cover of a cloudless night on the uninhabited lump of rock and brush named Isla Goaiguaza—had confirmed that the ship was approximately half-crewed, and kept ready to sail at a moment's notice. This was not an uncommon practice among

the Spanish, particularly at the smaller ports along
the Tierra Firma. More yachtlike in design than any
other Spanish ship, the *patache* was capable of sailing
close to the wind and was often fitted with oars, as
well. Consequently, it would be optimally responsive
to any attempt to enter a protected anchorage such
as Puerto Cabello's. That she hadn't the weight of
shot or of men to fight off a concerted attack was
hardly a concern. At the very least, she would buy
the greater ships in the harbor time to ready their
guns and sails, whether the threat was from a boat
full of boarders or a fire ship.

"So, m'lord, do we know whether we're to seize
her or sink her?"

O'Donnell nodded as his two swimmers checked the
pitch seals on the sewn top-folds of their oilskin bags.
"Yes. We seize her. Her sails are reefed but ready and
we've got the right wind, coming from the northeast.
That's directly abeam, so we should be able to get up
the channel at a good speed. Seven knots from the
sails alone, if Captain Floriszoon guesses right and
his prize crew is up to handling the rigging a-right."

"And when we go past the guns at the mouth of
the channel?"

It was a good thing that the observers on Isla Goaiguaza had been furnished with new, up-time-modeled
10x magnification spyglasses. "Our fellows sitting out
in the bay got a good look at those guns. Small demi-
culverins, at best, so probably ten-pound balls. Not
enough to do heavy damage unless they have plenty of
time to fire at us. Our real worry is from the guns in
the battery across the bay. They have full cannon over
there, according to the Dutch and their pirate-friends.

But as long as the *patache* is being contested, I'm wagering they won't fire upon their own men. Besides, with any luck, the men of the battery will be more than a little distracted by other events."

"Such as?" prompted Murrow with a hastily appended, "m'lord."

Hugh smiled. "We'll leave that to O'Rourke. He excels at mischief, you know."

"So he does, Colonel," conceded Murrow. "But once we start the fireworks on board the *patache*, that's likely to draw their attention even so. And so I'm wondering: just how fast can we get up that anchor?"

O'Cahan's rolled eyes caught the faint lights glimmering across the water from Puerto Cabello. "We're not going to raise the anchor, eejit. We're going to cut it."

"And just how are we going to do that?"

"Ships have axes on 'em, y' great gom. For just such occasions."

"And if this ship doesn't have one, or we can't find it?"

"That's why one of our lads is bringing over a small saw."

"Oh." Murrow had stripped down to a loin-clout, with his waterproof pack and the weighted line lashed to the belt that held it up. "And the prize crew? How do we know those damned Dutchmen will get here in time? How do they even know when it's time to come?"

Hugh interrupted with a voice signifying that the discussion was over. "Because, Murrow, we've fireworks and a whistle with us, and the steam pinnace is waiting to detect either, just a mile off the mouth of the channel."

Murrow seemed surprised. "You trust that fire-breathing brass beast? Look how long it took the Dutch to get it to work, Colonel!"

"That's because they were being careful, Murrow, just as they were during all the practice runs we made as we traveled along the Main from Trinidad. Without the steam engine's power, we'd be entirely at the mercy of the wind. This way, even if the wind dies or turns on us, we can still make three knots out of the channel. And if the breeze stays will us, we could do close to ten."

O'Cahan nodded. "It's a well-conceived plan, m'lord— but, well, what if you and the lads don't take the ship?"

Hugh looked squarely at O'Cahan. "You know the answer to that, Daniel. That's why you have the augurs. And the scuttling charges."

"Aye, sir, but we've not had an opportunity to test the charges, lest we waste them. And how do we let you know to go over the side, once they're planted?"

Hugh nodded. "Wish I had those answers, Daniel. It's the best system we could devise. The charges are well-wrapped, and the primers are lit by percussion cap. So as long as you don't dislodge the arming system inside the oilskin, the fuse should light and burn down. The tamping is crude, but should at least buckle a light hull such as the *patache*'s. The two together should breach it. And as for warning us?" Hugh shrugged. "If it goes as badly as all that, I doubt they'll be many of us left to warn. And mind you, no heroics. You stay under the curve of the hull, out of sight. And if you hear the signal, you scuttle the *patache* and leave. And no looking back. That is an order. Do you understand?"

"Yes, m'lord. I expect we'll be putting out the second set of tow-lines for O'Rourke, instead."

"So do I. Now, into the water, lads. Tell me, how quietly can you swim?"

Murrow looked dubious. "As long as I keep my feet from floating up, I thought I'd not make any noise swimming underwater, m'lord."

"Well, I'll let you know afterward. Or I suspect the Spanish on the *patache* might let you know first."

Murrow's eyes were large as he waded into the rippleless water. "I'll mind my feet, Colonel."

"Yes. You do that."

Calabar held up a hand, waving O'Rourke's column down into the ferns at the edge of the jungle. Gesturing for the sergeant to come forward, Calabar pointed toward low, squarish outlines that were located halfway between their position and the sparse lights of Puerto Cabello, only six hundred yards to their northwest. "The warehouses. Simple frame construction. Recent. Almost certainly to house fleet stores."

O'Rourke scanned the bay. Ten large ships pushed their masts toward the stars. Half again as many smaller hulls rode at anchor around them. "That's not the whole fleet from Cartagena, is it?"

Calabar shook his head. "No. They're not all here yet. Those are probably from Maracaibo or Coro. The galleons—any square-rigged ship—has a hard time heading east along Tierra Firma. The current and winds are both against them, and they can't tack well." Calabar considered. "But the Cartagena fleet can't be too far off. A week or two at the most."

O'Rourke nodded. "Which of the warehouses are our main targets?"

Calabar shrugged. "All are worth destroying. Most only contain food and casks of water and wine, but after all, a fleet without provisions is hardly a fleet. However, if you mean powder and shot..." Calabar pointed at a smaller warehouse of superior construction, located at the center of the larger ones. Whereas the patrols moved in a leisurely pattern between the other buildings, the guards around the munitions warehouse circled it endlessly, and in pairs. And they were armored. Of course.

O'Rourke turned to the men behind him. "Listen closely, lads. When we get close to the powder and shot stores, we're going to have to fight genuine Spanish regulars: breastplates and morions all. So don't load lead bullets. Iron's what we need. Double shot for the musketoons and balls for the pepperboxes." He looked across the ground to the warehouses. "Assume they'll hear us coming at about one hundred yards, see us at about seventy or so, if we're running."

"We could crawl to the warehouses," Calabar offered.

"We could, but it's too easy for us to get spread out that way. When we attack, we have to be close enough so that our numbers sweep them aside and give us a direct line to the munitions. So we crawl the first twenty-five yards, then up and crouched approach until we're spotted. Then kneel, fire a round, and charge."

Calabar nodded. "Let us do so, then. Spread your men along the edge of the jungle. I have been here once before, so I shall lead the way."

Chapter 33

Puerto Cabello, Venezuela

Hugh O'Donnell was a fair swimmer but was not enamored of being fully submerged. Particularly on a nearly lightless night. So despite the steady flow of air down the bamboo breathing tube, and the fact that it assured him of remaining within eighteen inches of the surface, he was nonetheless eager to get his head above water as soon as he reached the end of the weighted cord that O'Cahan had secured to the *patache*'s rudder by looping it over the pintle-and-gudgeon joint that was closest to the waterline.

Hugh knew his eagerness to resurface was a danger insofar as he would disturb the water with a sudden breach, so he forced himself to take a final breath through the tube, remove it from his mouth, draw it straight down, and float up slowly.

The stars and faint sounds seemed to rush in at him after towing himself with one hand along one hundred yards of submerged line. The lack of current in the inner harbor had made corrections of balance negligible, particularly since this water was calmer than any of the bays or inlets in which they had practiced during their journey along the Spanish Main. Now out of the silent darkness, he strained his ears and eyes to assess the situation.

Looking back toward the shore, and only because he knew to look for them, he spotted two irregular lines of small bumps protruding above the smooth surface of the inner harbor: the last of his thirty men finishing their submerged approach to the *patache*. He moved forward, keeping a steadying hand on the undercurve of the hull until he could glimpse the waist of the *low-slung ship*. In the water along her side were a cluster of what looked like oversized coconuts—his men's heads—bobbing underneath the shelflike outboard channel that held the chainplates at bottom of each ratline in place. They had approached along the second line, looped over the rigging cleats beneath the channel, and were now concealed from overhead detection as long as they stayed put and hugged the ship's waterline.

A slight disturbance in the water beside him caused Hugh to turn. O'Cahan rose up so slowly that he barely sent out a ripple. He cut his eyes southward, toward the town and the main battery. He tilted his head slowly, quizzically.

Hugh understood O'Cahan's silent question: Should he start across the rest of the channel, running yet another tow-line to the opposite shore for O'Rourke's men? It was a reasonable question. Yes, Hugh's detachment was supposed to wait for the unmistakable sounds of O'Rourke's attack before they took their own next steps, but more time had passed than should have. Still, if anything had gone wrong, there would have been the sound of more distant gunfire. So in all probability, it made sense to have O'Cahan start his swim now, giving him more time. On the other hand, if the attempt to board the *patache* went very badly, very quickly, Hugh would want the young ensign on hand with his augur and scuttling charge in order to—

From well south of the center of Puerto Cabello, there was a sputter of gunfire: sharp, distinctive reports of the new pepperbox revolvers and the brash roars of the double-barreled musketoons of the Wild Geese. The answering fire was irregular and vaguely flatulent in quality. Evidently, some of the Spaniards here were still armed with venerable arquebuses.

Hugh smiled and nodded vigorously at O'Cahan, who drew a deep breath and sank back down into the dark water. O'Donnell started counting heads, listening to the first concerned mutters of the Spanish anchor watch less than six feet overhead, and heard their feet moving toward the opposite, port side of the ship, closer to the sounds of combat. *So far, so good...*

O'Rourke cocked back the hammer on the third of the five chambers in his pepperbox, drew down on the charging Spanish sergeant, cheated a little low, and kept the cutlass in his left hand ready on his shoulder. At about three paces, he squeezed the trigger.

Aodh O'Rourke was a good shot to begin with, and the excellent Brussels-based workmanship of the pepperboxes made them quite reliable and consistent in their performance. Add to that his long experience in combat and the incredible proximity, and the outcome was hardly surprising. One of the two double-shotted iron balls punched through the bottom rim of the

Spaniard's breastplate, the other disappeared through the jerkin that began at the top of his groin.

The man stumbled and almost fell, his blood already running down his legs in black rivulets: the color of nighttime death, when you could see it at all. But Spanish regulars were tough soldiers and even their softest sergeants were still the consistency of cured leather, both inside and out. Teeth shining in a grimace against the pain of raising his rapier and straightening up, the veteran tried finishing his charge.

But O'Rourke knew a dead man walking when he saw one. He gauged the vastly decreased reflexes and flexibility of his armor-sluggish opponent and brought the cutlass off his shoulder in a chop aimed at the head of the stricken Spaniard. Who parried through his grimace—

—But missed the subtle hints that the simple diagonal cut was merely a feint. O'Rourke waited until his opponent had committed to the parry, then shifted the body-crossing trajectory of his blade into more of a downward, outside sweep. The rapier made a light, ringing contact with the cutlass just before a twist of O'Rourke's wrist jinked it over into the side of the Spaniard's right knee.

The veteran fell one way, his rapier the other. With his right leg already half-covered by a glistening tide of blackness, the sergeant spat a defiant curse at O'Rourke. O'Rourke had no time for the foolishness of trading insults on a battlefield, and was equally unwilling to spend a bullet to end either the man's invective or his life. He ran on, shouting for his men to light the fuses and get to the harbor channel. *Besides, it's not as if that old soldier is going to be able to achieve anything while he's busy bleeding to death.*

The munitions warehouse's dedicated patrol had fallen to the pistols and musketoons of the Wild Geese. But in actuality, the attack was the easy part of the mission. It was the escape that worried O'Rourke. Once they were done with the warehouses, they had to run to the inner harbor, skirting the town. They didn't have the time to stop, reload, and conduct a moving gun-duel with randomly appearing Spaniards. But that also meant that those randomly appearing Spaniards would be more likely to kill his men.

As if to underscore the dangerous tendency to expend too many of the charges already loaded in their weapons, one of O'Mara's men, Edmund Butler, used a second round from his pistol to kill the last and badly wounded guard covering the door to the warehouse. "Mind your ready ammunition, Butler," O'Rourke grunted, "There was but one sword-stroke between that man and his Maker. Loftus, Ealam, get those doors open. O'Hagan, you have the charge ready?"

As the doors to the munitions warehouse creaked open, O'Hagan replied, "Ready. De Burgo, get up here with that oil. And—watch out! To yer left!"

De Burgo fumbled the oil, reaching for his pistol. The bag fell, ruptured, and sent a thick petroleum reek up around them.

O'Rourke cursed. "Peter's Holy nut sack, O'Hagan, can't you tell a stray cat from a Spanish soldier? Damn it, a waste of oil and a waste of time, both." He scanned the frenetically running figures of his command, most routing the remaining Spaniards beyond the northern limit of the warehouses. "Sheridan?"

The soldier in question, who had reached the next warehouse, turned round, then ducked as a musket ball clipped the building's corner. "Yes, Sergeant?"

"Get over here with your oil. We need it for this warehouse."

"Yes, sir." He reported as he came. "Ensign O'Mara's having a problem, sir. Both of his sappers' fuses are ruined."

"Ruined?"

"Aye, sir. Probably mud. Soaked through the bags when we were lying in the jungle."

Well isn't that just feckin' perfect. "Right. Butler, make yourself useful for a change. Run to O'Mara, tell him that in place of the fuses, he's to use a trail of oil, touched by a trail of powder."

"But, Sergeant, that could—"

"O'Mara's putting flame to food and wine, not powder. His men will get away in time. Now, no more thinking, Butler: ye're not very good at it. Get on with you."

Butler shrugged, trotted out the door—and went down with a bullet through the gut. Sheridan saw the lagging Spaniard who'd fired the shot, popped a round after the retreating silhouette, missed.

O'Rourke bellowed. "No time for that, Sheridan. Your job is in here. Spread your oil. De Burgo, you take Butler's message to O'Mara. And you'd best do it on the double-quick or you'll be a pin cushion for Spanish rapiers."

O'Hagan sidled up to his sergeant. "What about Butler, though? Do we carry him? 'Cause it's sure he can't walk."

O'Rourke hated what he said—and would have to

do—next, more than any other part of soldiering. "It's sure he won't *live*, O'Hagan, not with that wound. Get about planting your charge. I'll see to poor Butler."

Hugh waited for the first of the warehouse explosions before signaling Purcell and then O'Bannon to board the *patache*. Purcell climbed up toward the stern along the aft-anchor line with a steadying hold on the tiller-chains, and O'Bannon slid up over the chainplates and laid hold of the dead-eyes at the amidships ratlines. The rest of the men stayed below the curve of the hull, waiting for their team leaders to affix and toss netting over the side, by which they would ostensibly swarm aboard the deck of the Spanish ship.

A hoarse curse overhead drew O'Donnell's attention to Purcell. The infallible and silent climber was twisting his left hand around vigorously, as if it had been suddenly caught in a trap. Which wasn't far off from what had happened. A slight shift of the rudder had tightened the chain, snagging his left index finger. With another curse, the *tercio*'s best climber toppled and fell into the water with a noisy splash.

O'Bannon's silhouette froze. O'Donnell waved up toward the deck, hoping that the scout's extraordinary eyes could make out the gesture. Evidently they did, because O'Bannon was up and over the gunwale in a blink, snagging the net on one of the cleats as he went.

Rapid footfalls padded on the low quarterdeck overhead—right as Purcell came up gasping. O'Donnell ripped open his oilskin pouch and pulled out Michael McCarthy's .45 just as two muskets fired down into the water and cries of alarm came from the ship's stern. Purcell, hit, grunted, twisted, and rolled to one side.

Hugh tugged himself to the aft end of the rudder with one quick jerk of his left arm; he pinned himself against it as he raised the up-time pistol and snapped off its safey. He brought its sights in line with the stern and the two Spanish guards he saw there, one of whom was reloading, the other of whom had drawn a hanger and was calling for help. Remembering to pause between shots long enough for the barrel to drift down toward his target again, O'Donnell started firing.

Disobeying every rule he'd ever heard or been schooled in regarding such weapons, Hugh did not even bother to count the rounds. He had learned that in a crisis, the initiative lost by striving for perfect execution—even if that only took one second—was often the difference between defeat and victory. In this case, precise shooting and conserving ammunition were simply not priorities. Clearing the stern and terrifying the Spanish with a startling volume of fire were.

And his split-second decision seemed sound. His first two shots missed, but the third punched a red hole straight through the musketeer's sternum. The other Spaniard, who'd been facing the other way, spun around just in time to be missed twice and hit once. He staggered back out of sight. And Hugh realized that he'd been counting his shots, after all. Having started with one round already in the chamber, that left him two more before he was dry.

Letting the weapon hang on its lanyard, he reached down toward the faces clustered around the stern. "Bill Kelly, where's that hand-spike your were carrying? Good. O'Bregan, fetch that coir netting out of the drink and be ready to throw it up to me. The rest of you, weapons in hand."

O'Donnell, driving the hand spike into the pintle-and-gudgeon joint halfway up the rudder, pulled himself halfway to the taffrail. He clutched at the top of the stern-window shutters for fingertip-purchase while he freed the handspike and swung it over to dig into the edge of the transom, just seven feet over the water-line. From there he'd have to pull himself toward the deck, since jumping wouldn't be much help: one foot was dangling in midair and the other was precariously balanced upon the rudder. If a new bunch of Spanish found him now—

A sudden eruption of gunfire from amidships signaled that the remainder of the *patache*'s anchor watch had discovered O'Bannon's boarding party. But only one pepperbox revolver was speaking in response to what sounded like several Spanish pistols. Cries and readied steel rang along the length of the ship and more shouts were audible beneath the weather deck. The rest of the crew was starting to react and would be coming topside.

Hugh paused long enough for a half-second of precaution to push through his impulse to act immediately. "Grenades!" he hissed down below. "Who's got 'em out?"

Three men answered tentatively. "But no way to light the fuses, m'lord."

"Pepperboxes?"

Half a dozen replied, even more tentatively. "Can't tell if they're too wet, Colonel," said one. "Looks like the bags leaked."

"Never mind that. Odds are one works. One man fires a gun, the next man holds the fuse of his grenade against the nipple vent. If you get it lit, lob it over the taffrail. Now, damn it!"

Two pepperbox hammers fell before the third one fired, but the grenade's fuse fizzed and died. And now Spanish voices were coming up on deck, and a few were growing louder behind the shuttered stern windows only three feet away from Hugh's midriff.

Another dry snap of a pistol's hammer, then another full discharge, followed immediately by the lively hiss of a lit fuse. The grenade arced past Hugh's head toward the deck, just as he heard the weather braces getting yanked out from behind the shutters of the stern windows. He muttered to the men beneath him in Gaelic, "The two of you with working pistols: aim at the windows. Sweep 'em clean."

The windows opened at the same moment that another grenade sputtered into life, and the one that had been lobbed on the deck went off. The Spanish musketeers who appeared in the stern windows—two black muzzles running out—fell back under a fusillade of fire from not just two, but three of the pepperbox pistols. A moan up on the quarterdeck suggested that the first grenade had at least wounded someone.

Hugh rapped out new orders. "Half of you, in the stern windows and hit them along the lower deck." The second grenade went off. "O'Bregan toss me the netting. Follow with the rest as soon as I've secured it."

Without pausing to consider the possibilities or consequences of failure, O'Donnell simultaneously pushed and pulled himself toward the *patache*'s low-slung quarterdeck, scrabbled madly for a handhold, almost fell, but got three fingers over the taffrail. That gave him enough leverage to get his second hand on it as well. Fear and natural strength helped him heave his whole body up and over it in a single powerful yank.

Hitting the quarterdeck at an angle, he rolled toward one of the flag lockers; he saw a ferocious melee amidships and saw heads turning in his direction.

He leaped up, looped the netting twice about the handspike, and snagged its sharp hook around one of the taffrail's balusters. As he tossed the netting out over the transom so it spread down to his waiting men, Hugh caught up the .45 in his other hand, and turned.

Two sword-armed Spaniards were already pounding up the four shallow stairs that separated the main deck from the quarterdeck. But behind them, another one was raising a matchlock pistol.

Hugh drew a careful bead on the pistoleer, let the up-time barrel drop a little, and squeezed the trigger slowly. The .45's sharp roar stopped the two approaching swordsmen for a moment, their eyes wide. The pistoleer grabbed his left thigh with one hand, but fired his matchlock with the other. The resulting stagger spoiled whatever reasonable aim he might have achieved; the ball whined off into the dark, well over Hugh's head.

The two Spanish swordsmen resumed their charge. Hugh gave ground, drawing—and hating—the short cutlass, and hearing the first of his men's hands scrabbling at the taffrail.

Rather than fire immediately, Hugh waited for the two Spaniards to finish closing. He noted the quick exchange of glances that meant they would try to time their blows to be simultaneous, eliminating any reasonable chance for him to parry both. But that wasn't what Hugh had in mind. As they lunged forward, weapons back to strike, Hugh swung the cutlass in his left hand to deflect the blow of the smaller of the two at the same moment that he raised the .45 and fired its last round straight into the chest of the much larger man at a range of three feet. Not because he was more fearful of the larger man—they were often the less nimble, and so, less dangerous, swordsmen—but because he was a considerably bigger target. And Hugh dared not miss, not now.

He didn't. Although the bullet was low and off center to the right, the large man gasped, his overhand slice becoming a wavering and easily dodged swat. The fellow on the left, who was clearly the better swordsman, feinted rather than striking directly. But Hugh's long professional training, even with so cumbersome and inelegant a tool as a cutlass, allowed him to roll his wrist in a tight, defensive *moulinet* and almost trap the real blow between his sword's blade and abbreviated top quillon.

The Spaniard cursed, yanked his weapon back, then started and stared over Hugh's shoulder. A pepperbox roared once alongside O'Donnell's left ear. Three wide red holes, made by .30 caliber lead balls, appeared just below the swordsman's right clavicle. He staggered back and immediately disappeared under a rush of torsos and cutlass-wielding arms: the first wave of Wild Geese had arrived over the taffrail. Hugh drew in a deep breath. *Time to spend a second assessing the situation.*

The fight amidships was a desperate brawl of flashing blades but only occasional gun discharges. Which meant that more of the oilskin bags had leaked, ruining the powder of the pepperbox revolvers that normally gave his men a decisive edge in firepower.

Even so, those few that still functioned were doing so decisively. The Wild Geese just arrived from the Lowlands had long trained for this kind of contingency and used the five chambers of each heavy unipiece cylinder sparingly. No fusillades, therefore, but when one of their own number was flanked or threatened by multiple opponents, the triple-charged weapons intervened, eliminating an enemy and thereby allowing the superior swordsmanship of the Irish mercenaries to carry the day. Hugh could see that the Spanish had already become so fearful of the weapons that they held back from assaulting too directly, and thus were not gaining the ground that their superior numbers should have made possible.

But that would not last for long. And judging from the deck-muted discharges and grenade blasts underfoot, the Spanish would soon be pouring up on the weather deck with increasing speed, running from the Wild Geese who'd entered by way of the stern windows. And those growing numbers were already exacting a toll, despite the intercession of the occasional pepperbox. At least half a dozen of the Wild Geese who'd boarded behind O'Bannon were down, and many of those still fighting were doing so with gashed arms, legs, or freshly missing fingers. The Spanish had to be broken, and there was only one sure way to do it.

Hugh gave orders to his boarders as he ejected the spent magazine from the Colt and pulled a fresh one out of the oilskin bag. "Those with working pistols, you've five seconds to load fresh cylinders. The rest: ready grenades with short fuses, to throw at my signal. Or, if you've only a cutlass, charge as soon as we start forward."

Two more of the Wild Geese in the amidships melee staggered and fell, one clutching the Spanish rapier that was still lodged in his chest.

"Ready, men," Hugh cried. "Follow me!"

Hugh sped down the four stairs just as several of the Spaniards on the main deck saw him and made to charge. But they drew up sharply as he shouted. "Now, at the walk—fire!"

Two, and then a third, pepperbox started blasting away, each discharge sending three of the lead balls into the densely packed Spaniards. Several slumped over, others clutched suddenly bleeding limbs. Half a dozen Wild Geese with nothing but cutlasses charged past Hugh and headlong into the flank of the Spanish, who turned to meet them.

But Hugh kept walking forward, .45 raised level with his eye, watching the Spanish, picking out the leaders. At seven paces, and seeing the onslaught against O'Bannon's Wild Geese faltering as the Spanish began shifting to deal with the new threat from the quarterdeck, he brought up his second hand to stabilize the gun. He stopped, chose a tightly grouped cluster of likely targets, and started squeezing off rounds from the up-time weapon with the steadiness and finality of a metronome.

The mass of Spaniards recoiled from the sharp, percussive roars of the .45 and from the falling bodies that were closest to its chosen field of fire. And then three at the back of their ranks broke for the bow at a run.

That was what Hugh had been watching, and waiting, for. "Grenades! Into the crowd at the portside gunwale!"

As Hugh reloaded, and the Spanish roiled in a confusion of men trying to flee, men trying to fight, and men trying to choose between those options, two grenades arced into the largely undecided rear ranks of those lately come sailors who had yet to add their numbers to the fight against O'Bannon's boarders. Several leaped away from the sparking bombs, two diving over the gunwale itself. The first went off at the same moment that Hugh brought up the reloaded .45 and fired through the magazine in one long rush, straight into the milling crowd.

As often happens in battle, the Spanish broke all at once, the way deer do when a hunter approaches too closely. Without any apparent coordination other than an instinctual sense of the disintegrating morale of their fellow creatures, they scattered wildly. Some went over the gunwales, while others ran to the bow and swung down the lines in the water. Two tried escaping below decks along the forward companionway, only to be bowled over by a panicked group streaming upward, who, to a man, joined the rout over the side and into the water.

As the press of the melee broke, it also revealed many of the half-naked Wild Geese who lay dead or writhing on the deck of the *patache*. Hugh forced himself to look beyond them to O'Bannon, and shout, "No time for the wounded, now. We need to get the signal rockets and the whistles. Until those Dutchmen tow us from under the Spanish guns, we're none of us sure of living out the hour."

O'Rourke ducked as a Spaniard swayed around the corner of the harbormaster's ramshackle cottage and fired. The ball bit into the dirt five feet ahead of him. *Thank God that bastard is drunk, and he won't reload in time, so no need to stop and cut him down.*

Half-reminding himself, he shouted to his much-reduced unit, "Sprint for the harbor, lads. Look for the lines just in the water at the foot of the wharf. Bag your guns when you've shot 'em dry. We're running, not fighting, now!"

At that moment, the rolling, intermittent explosions from the warehouses behind them were almost drowned out by a sharp and sustained sputter of gunfire from the middle of the inner harbor. And through the many hoarse discharges of down-time weapons, Aodh O'Rourke heard the distinct, reverberant reports of Hugh's .45 automatic.

He'd been prepared to shout an alert to his men, but they didn't need it. As if it had been a supper-bell rung for hungry hounds, the surviving Wild Geese fixed on the sound of that gunfire and sprinted toward it, their flagging endurance suddenly refreshed, their trajectories homing on the same relative compass point. *Good—*

—or maybe not so good, O'Rourke amended. Passing within ten yards of the eastern end of the low, rude rampart of Puerto Cabello's harbor battery, he could hear urgent shouts in Spanish. And they were loud enough to be easily understandable:

"The *patache* is under attack, too? Is it a diversion?"

"Fool: if it was a diversion, she would have been attacked before the warehouses, not after."

And a third voice: "So they mean to escape on her?"

"Madness. There cannot be enough of them to take her and sail her."

"Not take her? Dolt, those aren't ordinary guns. Hear them? Again?" Hugh's .45 now emitted a slow, sustained pulse of thunder,

"What is it?"

"I don't know. Maybe a new gun made by up-timers or their allies."

"Up-timers? Here? But—"

"Idiot. We must act, not debate. Bring the guns to bear on the *patache*! Quickly!"

"The *patache*? But she is our own—!"

"The *patache* is lost," confirmed an older, calmer voice. As if to prove that assertion, the .45 tore through the other sounds of combat with a fast staccato flurry, counterpointed by the dull crump of black-powder grenades. "Pass the word to the barracks: the raiders are running. Cease hunting them in the streets. Man the battery, instead. Stand to guns one and two. Others will be brought to bear as new crews arrive. Hurry."

"Yes, Lieutenant."

Well, that ties it. Seems I'll be disobeying my own orders to make for the water. But I could do with a little company. O'Rourke scanned the closest silhouettes of his fleeing men. "Hsst! Hssssssst! O'Hagan, De Burgo!"

"Sergeant?"

"Aye?"

"To me. Here, in the shadow of this shed. You've cylinders left for your pistols, yeh?"

A moment of silence. Then nods, and De Burgo's slow bass, "But we're to be running, heading for—"

"Not us three. Not yet. Fresh cylinders, lads. Either of you have grenades?"

Both nodded. "Never had the need or chance to use 'em," appended O'Hagan.

"That's because it was possible we might need them for what we're going to do now."

"Which is?"

"We're going to sow some grapes of wrath in behind that open battery to the west of us. Each of you light a slow match and follow me."

Hugh heard as much as saw the approach of the Dutch pinnace that had been fitted with a downtime steam engine. The demi-culverins at the mouth of the channel spotted her as well. Two spoke, put plumes in the water, almost fifty yards behind her. Either they were very poor gunners, or, more likely, not used to shooting at that fast a target so close to shore. Unburdened except for her operators and the prize-crew for the *patache*, the pinnace was making at least six knots.

Hugh shouted toward O'Bregan in the bows. "Found an axe?"

"No, m'lord. This ship is a pigsty. Nothing's placed proper. We're almost through the anchor line with the saw, though."

"Keep at it. O'Bannon?"

"Sir?"

"Losses?"

"Nine dead. Three more will be by dawn. Half a dozen wounded."

Hugh's stomach sank. That was half of the men who'd boarded. He kept to the tasks at hand. "Set the rest to get the nets into the water over the port quarter. That's where O'Rourke's men will be coming in along the lines that O'Hagan and Murrow swam over to the opposite shore."

"Right away, m'lord."

Hugh nodded, looked around, saw his men at their tasks, wanted to busy himself alongside them, but stayed that impulse. A commander's job was to stay alert, to watch for the next threat or task, not to become embroiled in the ones already being handled. He stared out toward the low ramparts of the inner harbor's battery, the walls of which screened most of Puerto Cabello from view. No sign of O'Rourke's men yet, of their own bamboo breathing tubes bobbing across the hundred and twenty yards of glass-smooth bay water between the *patache* and the guns that could sink her. There were lights, and now drums and coronets, on the Spanish ships deeper in the harbor, but that was of no consequence. They were too far off to see what was happening, and so could not be sure of a course of action. They would learn too late, and still be too far off, to respond.

But the battery: even on a mostly lightless night, they would have seen and heard the savage gunfight on the *patache*. And when it ended without a reassuring flurry of coronets and responses to the fort's many hails, they would know the outcome of that fight as surely as had they been standing on the deck themselves: the *patache* was now an enemy vessel.

Their only hesitation might be to avoid sinking her where she sat astride the inner mouth of the channel. But once they saw, and heard, the approaching steam pinnace above the flash, glare, and roaring of the sabotaged warehouses, it was a certainty they'd respond.

And perhaps they were doing so already. There was a blast near the ramparts. But as the sound died away, and shouting rose up from the dim outline of the battery's covering walls, Hugh realized that it hadn't been the roar of a cannon, or even a range-finding musket shot. It had been a black powder grenade.

Which was to say, it was O'Rourke.

O'Hagan finally reached the ready powder for the middle gun of the battery, grenade fussing fulminatively in his left hand as he cleared a path with the pepperbox in his right. One of the gunners sheltering behind the next cannon popped up and fired a miquelet-lock pistol at him. O'Rourke snapped up his pepperbox, but was too late. The man had already ducked back down.

O'Hagan had stumbled, but, limping, finished his rush up the stairs. He pried the loose cover off a readied powder keg, dumped the grenade in and then prepared to jump down from the battery platform to the ground. And, as O'Rourke had expected, the same gunner at the neighboring gun popped up again, furnished with a fresh pistol. O'Rourke fired twice; the second round hit the man, who disappeared with a yelp. Not dead, but he and any proximal friends were now probably disinclined from trying to fight back anytime soon. And when the seven-second fuse on O'Hagan's grenade had burned down, thoughts of counterattack would almost surely be swept away by a panicked impulse toward self-preservation.

O'Rourke counted through two of the seconds, jerked his head at the gimping O'Hagan, and shouted toward De Burgo, "Help him! Get to the water!" O'Rourke counted another two seconds, then ducked and ran himself, jumping over and around the half-dozen bodies that marked the path by which they'd entered the rear of the battery.

It hadn't been that hard to do, actually. With the noise of the warehouses exploding, the panicked shouting, and the Spanish presumption that the raiders were all in flight, O'Rourke and his two troopers hadn't encountered any guards until they were down in the marshalling area of the battery itself. There'd been powder enough there, too, but most of it was still in tightly sealed barrels that they wouldn't be able to get open in time, not before the gun crews and soldiers would see what they were up to and swarm them. By sheer numbers, if nothing else.

So instead, O'Rourke and his men blended into the chaos as best they could, responding to a few casual inquiries in perfect Spanish as they approached the stairs to the gun platform. There, in the lantern light, their identities became suspect and the shooting had started.

But it had not been random gunplay. Even De Burgo understood, without having to be reminded, that their targets were the soldiers guarding the battery, not the gunners. So when the pepperboxes started snapping quickly, the gun wielding, morion-helmeted Spaniards were the first to go down, not even understanding who was attacking them. The gunners fled behind their pieces. O'Rourke and De Burgo kept their heads down while O'Hagan charged up the stairs to one of the gun's ready powder supply, lighting his long-fused grenade . . .

. . . Which went off as O'Rourke cleared the waist-high covering wall at the east end of the battery. "Down!" he shouted, and saw De Burgo carrying O'Hagan to the ground with him.

An eyeblink after the grenade, the powder went off with a roar and a flash. Pieces of wood, mortar, stone, maybe metal struck the other side of the screening wall and went hissing over it. Then another blast, and another—

Panicked screams of women and children and no small number of men began rising up from the town itself. O'Rourke gauged the distance to the water: twenty yards, maybe twenty-five. If any Spanish happened by while they tried to find the lines...

"De Burgo, run down and find the lines. I'll cover you. Signal when you've found 'em. I'll bring O'Hagan and we'll go swimming. Well, towing."

O'Hagan muttered. "Feck, O'Rourke, I'm no cripple. I can—"

"You can be shutting up now, you eejit. You'll get us all killed, hobbling down to the beach on your own like a creaky old gaffer. De Burgo, what are you waiting for? Dawn?"

De Burgo's large dark mass rolled up off the sand flats and loped down toward the water. O'Rourke moved toward O'Hagan at the crouch, turned, kept an eye on the town, and suppressed a sigh. He had one round left in the cylinder. *Better than nothing*, he temporized. *But not by much*.

A Spanish soldier appeared around the far end of the battery, shaken, shouting to locate survivors, ducking when still more powder went off, blowing a sheet of angry white-yellow flame high into the night sky.

Damn it, he'll see me in this light, thought O'Rourke, who doubted he'd make the shot at this range. Another ten paces, though—

"Wait here," he ordered O'Hagan in English, and scrambled up, running toward the soldier, yelling, "Help me! Help me!" in Spanish.

The Spaniard had apparently just noticed O'Rourke peripherally, but approached so openly, and with explosions still roaring behind him and just overhead, the man ducked, his weapon forgotten in his hands. He ran toward the Irishman. "What? What help do you need?" he shouted back.

You just gave it to me by running closer, O'Rourke thought with a twinge of regret. He raised the pepperbox and fired.

The Spaniard stopped as if stunned, then staggered as he saw fire-reflecting blood begin leaking out of the hole in the front of his buff coat. With a groan he sagged down to his knees, eyes pinching tight against a sudden wave of pain.

O'Rourke turned, ran back to O'Hagan, and saw as he did so that De Burgo had found the weighted lines that O'Cahan and Murrow had put here and by which the rest of his raiders were no doubt making their way to the *patache*. O'Hagan hobbled up. The sand covering his right thigh was dark and slick with blood. "Let's get you home, you clumsy oaf," O'Rourke muttered as, shouldering up O'Hagan on the right side, he led them down to the edge of the inner harbor.

De Burgo had already stripped out of his clothes and had his breathing tube out. "Need a hand?" he cried out in English.

O'Rourke shook his head angrily. *A fool for crying out, a double fool for doing it in a foreign tongue—*

O'Rourke never heard the shots: they were drowned out by a new set of roars from the battery as more ready powder went up. One Spanish ball cut off the lobe of O'Hagan's left ear, two more drilled into the water beside him. Others whined overhead and one struck De Burgo in the shoulder. The big man cursed and staggered before a defiant instinct brought him back upright—and into the path of two more balls that caught him in the midsection.

As the already-dead Irishman sank down into the water, O'Rourke found the line and got O'Hagan's hands on it. As he kicked his shoes off, he felt a sensation like a wide, hot poker go through the large expanse of stocky muscle at the back of his left thigh. *Damn it*, O'Rourke thought, losing hold of his breathing tube as he stumbled. The length of bamboo disappeared into the fire-reflecting water. *Well, it's up and down to breathe for me, or I'm musket-fodder for sure.*

O'Hagan stared at him around his own breathing tube, frowning at the dark stain in the water around O'Rourke's right leg.

"Get going, O'Hagan. You're blocking the line."

O'Hagan shrugged and sank under the water until only two inches of his breathing tube remained, moving slowly but steadily out toward the inner mouth of the channel and the *patache* that sat astride it.

O'Rourke towed himself a yard, drew in a deep breath, dove down sideways and kept pulling himself along the lightly weighted line, hand over hand.

There was a muted bacon-frying sound around him, and something hot bumped off his abdomen: a musket ball, flattened and slowed by the three feet of water under which O'Rourke was sheltered.

Well, lucky me. And all I have to do is stay *lucky all the way to the* patache.

A pity that I've never been a lucky man.

❖ ❖ ❖

Hugh watched as the Dutch sailors swarmed over the port bow and O'Bregan and Kelly tossed the severed anchor cable to the pinnace's crew. Along with mooring hawsers and lines from the bowsprit, it would serve as a makeshift tow-cable at least until they got out of the channel and away from the Spanish guns. There, a proper towing rig could be improvised on the move. No one was sanguine about stopping to square away the pinnace as a proper tug, not while within reach of possible Spanish pursuers.

O'Cahan, still dripping from helping O'Rourke's wounded raiders out of the water, passed by. Hugh hailed him. "How many made it back?"

"A baker's dozen, m'lord, including that Calabar fellow. Half are wounded."

"O'Rourke?"

O'Cahan shook his head. "No sign of him. Last seen scooting over to make the mischief we saw in the battery. But there's hope yet, sir."

O'Donnell smiled sadly. "There's always hope, with O'Rourke. We might find him rowing out to us on a raft of palm trees in a day or so." He said it more for O'Cahan's benefit than to assert any serious hope of O'Rourke's survival.

But O'Cahan must have detected his commander's suppressed tone of grief. "I'm not just blathering fairy-wishes, m'lord. We've still got weight on one of the lines to the far shore. Probably the weight of one or two men. Hard to tell. But it could be O'Rourke, that stubborn tinker's mule."

Hugh nodded, trying not to get overly hopeful. "It just might be."

O'Cahan sucked breath in meditatively. "My only

worry, Colonel, is in waiting for them. We shouldn't spend any longer here than we have to."

"I agree. Get two men and start reeling in the line. If they're not on board by the time the Dutchmen are ready to move"—which, would not be long, judging from their competent progress rigging the tow-lines and raising the *patache*'s fore-and-aft main-sail—"then secure it to the pinnace."

O'Cahan gaped then smiled. "We *tow* them out, Colonel?"

"Why not?" O'Donnell smiled back. "I think we can be certain that they'll be hanging on for dear life. Literally."

"Aye, sir. I'll pass the words and gather the men to start reeling them in. Any other orders?"

Hugh nodded. "One, Mr. O'Cahan. Detail two men to take our dead below deck. The Spanish, too."

O'Cahan seemed startled. "As you say, sir. But, as regards the Spanish, I'm sure the fish are hungry tonight, sir."

O'Donnell stared at O'Cahan. "They always are, Daniel. But they've been fed enough this night." Hugh glanced over the deck littered with the bodies of his men, envisioned the others they'd left behind. "More than enough."

Chapter 34

Anne Cathrine wiped her hands on her apron and stared distractedly as a larger-than-necessary party of Dutch soldiers-become-workmen wheeled half a dozen large boxes out of the fort's landward sally port. They were all stamped in unusually regular block letters and she had to think hard for several seconds in order to decipher the up-time legends: *primary transmitter components; secondary transmitter components; transformers; wiring, non-antenna.* The boxes had been among the first unloaded from the ships of Reconnaissance Flotilla X-Ray, and had been handled with more care than a cargo of silk, fine crystal and irreplaceable gems.

Because, according to Eddie, their contents were every bit as valuable and irreplaceable. A radio, using spokelike lines of transceiving wires elevated on The Quill's volcanic northeast slopes, would be capable of reaching Vlissingen in the United Provinces. The communications would not work routinely, and not enable them to have what Eddie called "voice-grade exchange." But even if a single, two-hundred word message took three days of constant, repetitive signaling or listening to send or compile, it hardly mattered. The fastest other means of exchanging information was by swift ship, and even the swiftest could rarely make an Atlantic crossing in as little as forty-five days. Sixty was more typical. With this powerful new radio, strategic updates could be exchanged promptly, and calls for assistance could reach their allies within the same week, rather than (hopefully) the same season.

Anne Cathrine realized that the soldier-workmen were loitering around their boxes. Unusual behavior, since she had observed that most of the Dutch preferred to finish work quickly and efficiently once they started it. And then she realized that, quite slyly, they were all stealing looks at her.

She felt heat rise up in her face, accompanied by a wild mix of outrage, shame, and, worst of all, flattered vanity. At the same moment, a long hand came down upon her shoulder gently. Sophie Rantzau stood just behind her, staring at the men with unblinking gray eyes. After a moment, they gave up their pretense of lounging about and returned to their chores. The youngest, a fellow whose blond hair was almost white, actually flushed, bowed an apology, and set his shoulder to one of the crates with repentant vigor.

"Well," observed Sophie mildly, "at least one of them has some breeding. Or shame."

Anne Cathrine glanced at the young woman's face— Sophie was just two years her senior—and marveled at the gravity in it, the composure. She wondered if anything of mundane origin could ruffle that smooth brow, those chiseled features. And for the briefest moment, she felt envy. Not the petty, childish envy of a young woman craving the looks or possessions or popularity of another. Rather, her envy was one with her admiration for Sophie's apparently effortless transcendence beyond such trifles. At times, her demeanor reminded Anne Cathrine of the tales she'd heard in childhood of the Norns: tall, mystical fate-maidens who were woven in and out of the pagan mythology of the Scandinavian countries in the way that ligaments connected bones and tissue. They connected past and present, action and outcome, free choice and fate in ways that were both various and mysterious, always transmitting and influencing earthly and heavenly power, but never holding it themselves.

She realized that Sophie was looking at her, one eyebrow raised. "You are lost in thought frequently today, Anne Cathrine. Tell me, does the appearance of the radio equipment mean that you have had word of your husband? That he might be returning?"

Anne Cathrine turned back into the full shade of the tent in which Ambrósio Brandão first received the sick of the colony. "No, quite the opposite. He is remaining in the south. And again, he may not say why, or where." She clenched her apron so hard that her fingers became white.

Leonora, watching Brandão examine a young child with a fever, glanced over, her brow dipped in concern.

Sophie nodded gravely. "It would prey upon any woman's soul, since we know that secrecy and hazardous enterprises go hand in hand. But be calmed: your husband is with good men and loyal guards. His steamships are the finest in the world and may strike their foes with impunity."

Anne Cathrine frowned. "Yes, but it will not always

be thus, for the war machines of one nation quickly become the war machines of all others."

"Truly spoken," Sophie agreed. "But leave that worry for the future that shall bring it. For now, the unique power of his ships means that there is *less* cause for worry."

It was a logical argument, and comforting in its way, but Anne Cathrine, much as she hated to admit it, was not a creature of logic first and foremost. She was a creature of passion. She was not concerned with reasons or rationalizations. She just wanted Eddie. She wanted him in her cabin, in her arms, in her bed, and in her, and in that order. And she wanted it—wanted it all—right now. "I think I should return to work," she muttered hoarsely, with a quick smile at Sophie, but without eye contact. She did not want her Norn-friend to look into her eyes and see her shallowness, her illogic, and the primal heat that old-wives' tales warned went along all too often with her red-gold hair.

Drawing alongside Brandão, she heard him finishing his examination of a young child no more than four years old, of mixed Amerind and African parentage. "The low fever and the location of the transient pains are consistent with both yellow fever and the dengue. Malaria or a systemic viral infection—influenza, I think you call it—is not out of the question, but unlikely. The location of her aches is overwhelmingly associated with the first two illnesses, and none of the secondary signs of malaria are present."

Anne Cathrine looked at the child's light brown back, patient and calm under Brandão's expert hands, and felt a terrible, gnawing compulsion to run soothing palms along it, to bring a moment's comfort, if nothing else.

Leonora, eyes alert and incisive, watched Brandão's fingers as they gently mixed calming touches with an almost unnoticeable palpation of the lymph nodes of the neck and armpits. "How long," she asked, "until we know which manner of disease is causing the symptoms?" In her sister's tone, Anne Cathrine could hear the intensity and discipline of a budding physician, but also found it oddly detached and disturbing.

Brandão shrugged. "A day, maybe two. Watch for the growth of a rash"—he let his hands tarry at two points on the girl's back—"here, and here, almost like measles. That is a discriminating symptom of dengue. In the meantime, this child must be kept quiet and resting. If this is a hemorrhagic fever, then we do not wish to tax the body, or cause a rise in what the up-timers call 'blood pressure.' This precaution is not decisively efficacious at reducing the possibilities of internal hemorrhage, but is the best alternative at our disposal. Also, this child is to be given—by which I mean, compelled to drink—a cup of water every hour. At the very least. Dehydration is a prime concern, regardless of which malady is at work, here."

From behind, Sophie's voice calmly pointed out, "One cup every hour is three times the adult ration, Doctor. Will Councilor Corselles allow it?"

"I expect so, but it hardly matters. If Corselles forbids it, I will appeal to van Walbeeck and he will approve it. From his time in the East Indies, and then Recife, he knows what an outbreak of a serious disease can do to a colony's morale. He will not take chances here. He will allow us to retain the child in quarantine and use what resources we need to effect a cure."

"Some of the landowners," said Sophie in a quiet, and almost dangerous tone, "voiced their opinion that the surest means to protect the colony is to place the child in an oubliette until she dies."

"Idiots," Brandão declared in a low mutter. "Unless this is influenza, which I very much doubt, they should be fearful of mosquitoes, not this child. That is how yellow fever, dengue, and malaria are spread. And in caring for the child, we may also watch the development of the symptoms to make a more certain diagnosis and provide care appropriately." He turned around to face Anne Cathrine and Sophie. "This is why I returned to the New World, you know."

Anne Cathrine nodded. "To treat the sick."

"Well, yes, that too," Brandão allowed. "But it is the education, the teaching, that I meant to do. The up-timer information and methods change everything, even without all the wonderful devices that they used in their scientific achievements. Surely, married to a man such as your husband is said to be, you must see this even more regularly than I."

Anne Cathrine found it hard to think about Eddie without getting distracted by sensations that were decidedly not logical or learned in nature. "I am uncertain what you mean, Doctor. Perhaps you would explain further?"

"Well," smiled Brandão, "I suppose it *is* different in your husband's areas of expertise, where his knowledge is made manifest through engineers. In the case of medicine, the phenomenon is subtler, albeit no less profound. Indeed, I hazard to say that it is *more* profound, particularly when it comes to the identification, management, and treatment of epidemics.

"Consider the case of this child, and how the library at Grantville has revolutionized how we may approach her illness. Ten years ago, when faced with such maladies in the Pernambuco, we had Dutch physicians, Portuguese physicians, *murranos* like myself, and persons with lesser medical experience whose journeys took them through Recife. Each one of us spoke Latin, but yet, we had no common compendium of epidemiology. And we simply accepted that state of affairs as inevitable. We did not see that we were milling about our own tower of Babel, each of us having different names for the same disease. And just as often, we were unable to agree on distinctions between diseases. For instance, some persons among us insisted that all tropical hemorrhagic fevers were simply different expressions of the same underlying disease. Most held that diseases such as cholera were spread by miasmas operating at the will of God, while a few of us held with Italian physicians that the means of contagion were natural and not simply spread by airs polluted by rotting matter."

He shook his head. "Then, Lady Anne Cathrine, your husband's town appears. There, not only in learned texts in its library, but in the 'home health' pamphlets possessed by even the least educated families, our theories were shamed, shown to be a mixture of bad guesswork and superstition. And the impact upon us down-time physicians was not restricted to such concepts as germ theory and variable vectors of infection, but also by the sheer uniformity of the observations, of the nomenclatures, of the methodologies. It was no longer necessary to guess what caused a disease. It was an established fact, often illustrated by pictures taken through these extraordinary devices you call microscopes. It was no longer necessary to strive across barriers of different language and experience to determine if, in fact, we were speaking about the same diseases. Now all the diseases had names in Latin arising from a single classification scheme applied to their causal microorganisms, and all of which were described according to a proven range of diagnostic and symptomatic variables. In short, physicians were suddenly able to speak a common tongue, wherever they might be, whatever their experience had shown them."

He rubbed the child's back as might a loving grandfather. "And so I knew I had to come back to the New World, where we have brought so many of our diseases. And which has so many diseases that are completely unknown to us. It was incumbent upon me to share the particular features of the many maladies, and also the standardized means of identifying them, of discerning and conducting treatment, of assessing and thereby preventing further spread."

He leaned back and patted the child gently between her shoulder blades. The four-year-old rolled over; her large brown eyes scanned all of them gravely, possibly apprehensively. *Poor child,* Anna realized, *she's probably never been this close to this many white people this long without being ordered about, or, quite possibly, beaten.* Anne Cathrine had noticed that, despite their wonderfully civilized and learned accomplishments in most other areas, many of the Dutch landowners showed a marked disregard for the welfare of the poor creatures whom they compelled to work their upstart cane plantations. "Doctor Brandão, this child, is she a slave?"

"Yes, she is. One of the few who came with us from Recife."

Leonora's careful eyes rolled round to study Brandão. "But we have been told that there is no slavery permitted on this island."

Brandão smiled. "I have observed that, here on St. Eustatia, different persons give different answers when asked about the existence or absence of manumission. The most precise description is, I believe, that there is no *new* slavery permitted. Mostly."

"That is not a very precise definition, Doctor," Sophie observed dryly.

"No," sighed Brandão, "but it is the only one that fits our current situation."

"I was under the impression," Anne Cathrine said impatiently, "that Admiral Tromp and Jan van Walbeeck both disapprove of slavery."

"They do."

"Then this is a very strange way of demonstrating their disapproval."

Brandão shook his head. "Despite all the soldiers here, this is not simply an armed camp. There was a civilian authority in Oranjestad before we arrived, just as we brought one with us from Recife. And the question of who holds the greatest power is, often, less than clear."

"So the Dutch colonists have resisted Admiral Tromp's wishes in this matter?" Leonora asked slowly.

"That would be overstating the case in several particulars," Brandão explained through a sigh. "First, not all the colonists support slaveholding. That sentiment predominates only among the landowners. Second, they are not so much resisting the dictates of Tromp and van Walbeeck as they are finding ways to subvert or avoid them.

"Before leaving from Recife, Maarten Tromp unsuccessfully attempted to leave the slaves in that colony behind. But many feared life under Portuguese taskmasters, and in the case of many *mamelucos*, their actual status was ambiguous. Some were bondsmen, some were slaves, and some fell in between: persons whose bond-price had grown so many times greater over successive generations that there was no hope of ever buying their way out of servitude."

"So slaves in everything but name," Sophie observed. Anne Cathrine started at her tone. Although it conveyed anger, it had gone from cool to cold.

Brandão helped the little girl to sit up. Anne Cathrine crouched down, ladled a cup of water out of the covered drinking pail, and poured it into a cup made of a coconut shell. The Jewish doctor nodded his thanks, passed it to the girl, and sighed as he continued his story. "Upon arriving here, the problem became even more complicated. The local workforce was predominantly African slaves, many brought over immediately after the first settlement, some purchased from the English and French on St. Christopher's. And the cash crop was tobacco. So when Tromp arrived he had many battles to fight. He was arriving with a military and refugee group almost ten times the size of the original colony, was making the island a more noticeable and urgent target for the Spanish, and needed to compel the local landowners to change their crop from the tobacco they no longer had a way to sell to the cane sugar that was at least practical and a reasonable commodity even among the settlements of the New World."

Anne Cathrine saw the problem immediately. "Of course. He had to choose between the changes he wanted to make and the changes he *had* to make."

Brandão nodded. "Precisely. He already was in a position where he was, de facto, usurping political and military control without the colony's consent and dictating policy to people who'd come to the New World seeking the freedom to do and work as they pleased."

"Which included owning slaves who would never have such freedoms," Sophie added darkly.

"Ironically, yes. However, it was painfully obvious to Tromp that, on top of all those impositions, he could not presume to change anything else, lest the original colonists rebel. Which would, of course, have been the end of everything. If the landowners from Oranjestad did not cooperate with those from Recife, and if both did not work together to grow the needed foodstuffs for almost three thousand people, the colony would have been as thoroughly destroyed as had the Spanish bombarded it for a week."

Leonora nodded. "And so this is what you mean by no 'new' slaves are permitted. Only those who were already in the two colonies before Tromp arrived are allowed."

Brandão shrugged, took the empty water cup from the young girl, whom he eased back down toward her sleeping palette with his palms. "If it were only so simple as that, Leonora."

"It *should* be as simple as that," Anne Cathrine snapped. "I am sorry, Doctor," she apologized hastily. "My impatience is not with you, but with your implication that there are still other 'exceptions' to Admiral Tromp's rule against slaveholding."

"And you are as forgiven for your impatience as you are correct in foreseeing such connivance. Shortly after Admiral Tromp arrived and his perspectives on slavery became known, the original landowners sent their ship over to Africa yet again."

"To gather more slaves, in defiance of Admiral Tromp's law?"

Brandão shook a gnarled old finger. "Ah, their disregard for his policy was not so straightforward. You see, among their many other accomplishments, the Dutch are masters of circumlocution and legalistic distinctions so fine that a gnat could not perch upon their edge without falling off."

"How can this matter? When is a slave anything other than a slave?"

The old *murrano* physician smiled ruefully. "When there is a document stating that he is not. Consider: the fluyt sent by the Dutch landowners arrives on the western coast of Africa. Ghana, let us presume. Slaves are brought to her master. He says, 'Actually, I am not interested in buying slaves. I am here to purchase the work contracts of bondsmen. I am here to find indentured servants who must work at whatever their master directs, under whatever conditions, for ten years, at which point they may buy their freedom. That is, if they have been able to save enough to do so.'"

"But that is absurd," Leonora exclaimed. "Given the conditions under which they work, any such person would be lucky merely to be alive after ten years. It is unthinkable that they would have the time or opportunity to set aside valuables equal to the price of their bond."

"Naturally. But by *law*, they are not slaves. And

Admiral Tromp and Jan van Walbeeck will be hard put to challenge this casuistry successfully. Oh, it does give them the ability to prevent or at least ameliorate the worst offenses of slavery: murder, rape, seizure or outright prohibition of personal goods. These new workers will enjoy the basic protections of our laws. But being signed over into indentured servitude by their African bondholders dodges the technicality of slavery, even though their lives will be little different."

Anne Cathrine stood. "And Admiral Tromp and van Walbeeck will tolerate this subversion of their clear intent?"

Brandão rose, crooked and bent, alongside her. "In the short term, they have little choice but to turn a blind eye. But if, as seems likely, the appearance of your flotilla is the harbinger of more ships flying friendly flags, and bringing aid against both the threats of hunger and of the Spanish, then I suspect Tromp and van Walbeeck will no longer pay so high a price for the cooperation of the landowners and their farms. And that—" Brandão said with a pat on her firm arm—"would be a very good thing indeed. Now, enough speculating. We have serious work before us. One fellow gave himself quite a gash while shoveling manure and is predictably infected. Then there are two Dutch imbeciles who tried to teach themselves spear fishing yesterday and believed that, since they were in the water the whole time, they were protected from the effects of the sun. After that, we will see how much pure ethanol our apparatus has distilled today and shall check on our stores of—"

As Leonora followed Brandão into an adjoining tent, Anne Cathrine felt a hand on her shoulder delay her from following immediately. She turned and saw Sophie's serious Norn-eyes gazing down at her again. "It is not every king's daughter, princess or otherwise, who conceives of a dislike for slavery. Too many see all but their highest-ranked subjects as nothing more than their thralls. And so, their minds and hearts are more than halfway reconciled to slavery as permissable, even desirable." Her gaze wavered, the first time Anne Cathrine had ever seen it do so. "Whatever unfortunate exchanges there have been between our families, I am proud to call you friend. And happy to think that our king has raised a person of such charity and integrity." Sophie nodded and followed the path Leonora had taken into the adjoining tent.

It took Anne Cathrine a full three seconds to recover from her surprise. She made to exit after the others but then remembered the lambent brown eyes that had looked at her so solemnly minutes before. She turned. The small girl now lay on her side, a light blanket pooled around her waist, her jet-black hair slightly tangled from the sweat of her fever, her thumb half in her mouth as she shivered despite the warmth of the day.

Anne Cathrine kneeled down and drew the blanket up a bit higher. As she placed a hand upon the child's cheek, she felt a tear run down her own. But she did not know why.

Chapter 35

Oranjestad, St. Eustatia

Mike McCarthy, Jr., was puzzled by his escort from Oranjestad's small pier, Reverend Johannes Theodorus Polhemius. A man who seemed to alternate between shy silence and garrulous excesses of expostulation, he'd provided the up-timer with the complete dossiers of the eight workers who had volunteered to "learn about radios from the ground up" over the course of their work for Mike.

Two were sailors by trade; six were soldiers. From Polhemius' anxious yet highly generalized accolades about two of the latter, he suspected that pair were simply in it for the extra money. It was also possible they were motivated by boredom, wanting something better to do than waiting around to get a job they liked (going out as part of a ship's contingent) or a job they hated (farming as a contract laborer down on St. Christopher's). But the other six all seemed to genuinely have the blood of gadget-tinkerers running in their veins. One had been a watchmaker's apprentice before declining family fortunes sent him off to sea.

534

Another had been a sapper in the Provinces before journeying to the New World. A third had most recently finished refurbishing various items of ships' chandlery that some half-piratical character named "Peg Leg Jol" had brought back to Oranjestad after raiding a small Spanish port down along Tierra Firma.

He also heard a good deal about their behavior, and piety or implied lack thereof, sobriety or implied lack thereof, and work ethic, which most of them seemed to have in fair measure or even excess. And he also had to fend off Polhemius' numerous invitations to a late breakfast of cassava bread and fish. Happily, he'd dined aboard the *Koninck David* this morning with Captain Schooneman, enjoying the comparative delicacies of turtle and sweet potatoes served with a side of fried plantains.

As they walked through what was still mostly the tent-city of Oranjestad, families stopped to stare at Mike's clothes. Although he didn't have much left in the way of up-time duds, he had brought a western-style brimmed hat to shield against the tropical sun, as well as a bandana. That, and his lack of facial hair drew enough attention that he asked Polhemius, "Reverend, my clothes aren't *that* strange. Why are all these people staring at me like I'm from another planet?"

Still walking briskly, Polhemius turned to stare at him and almost tripped over his own feet doing so; he was a markedly ungraceful man. "But you *are* from another planet, mijn heer McCarthy. A planet almost four hundred years away from ours, in time. They are staring at you not because your clothes are strange to them, but because they know what they signify:

that you are an up-timer. Please remember, they have heard of your people, but have never met one. They commenced their journey here less than six months after your town appeared in Germany." He rubbed his large, sunburned nose. "And they know that the, the *steam*-ships are designed by your people, as well as the radio you will be commencing to build today."

"Well, I'm not really *building* the radio—" Mike started, and then gave up. He was building this radio the way a kid builds a model airplane: assembling parts somebody else fabricated, according to painstaking instructions. Oh, sure, he understood the majority of the physics and mechanical properties of the transceiver, but he was mostly an engine and body-work guy. Drive-trains and differentials: that was his comfort-zone. Sending sparks halfway across the world? Well, he just hoped he didn't have to resort to improvisation . . .

Polhemius looked concerned. "You're not building the radio? But I thought—"

"Well, yeah, I'm building it in the sense that I'm putting it together. But it's not like I'm its inventor."

"Perhaps not, but that hardly matters. The aim of the entire project, to be able to send signals home instantly, is as other-worldly as you up-timers are. Or so it seems to all of us."

Mike heard the words "all of us," and frowned. "Reverend Polhemius, just how many people know what I'm going to be working on over the next few months?"

"The radio? Oh, a great many, I should say."

Well, damn. That wasn't part of the original game plan. "Reverend, I'm a little confused. I was told that we'd try to keep the radio a bit of a secret, at least for a while."

Polhemius frowned. "Ah. Yes. I see. But, as it turned out, we were faced with a dilemma when trying to find you helpers for the construction phase. As our leased plots on St. Christopher's have now become available for tillage, the demand for farm-workers has gone up. Also, we are sending more troops there to protect those farms, along with the English possessions. So, in order to be sure that you would get the kind of workers you needed for this task, we had to explain enough of what it entailed to pique the interest of those with the correct aptitudes. Otherwise—" The reverend held up his hands in a gesture of futility.

"Yeah. Okay, I get it." *Which doesn't make it any better, though. The sooner the town knows, the sooner informers hear. That's just the way of the world. So our secret international radio advantage isn't going to be secret for very long.*

They had arrived at the eastern edge of the tent city where an intermittent arc of shallow ditches had been scraped out of the sandy soil. Bamboo spikes lined their outer berm like irregular, narrow fangs. "Expecting trouble?" Mike asked Polhemius.

The reverend shrugged. "We are in the Caribbees, mijn heer McCarthy. It is always prudent to expect trouble. I remind you that many of the Caribs whom Warner and the Frenchman d'Esnambuc drove from St. Christopher's less than ten years ago still consider these islands rightfully theirs and would be happy for any opportunity to reassert that claim. In the bloodiest possible fashion. The brutes."

McCarthy managed to stifle his impulse to point out the reverend's rather profound double standard regarding barbarous behavior. In his world-view, it was

apparently acceptable for white settlers to dispossess
the natives of their own land via massacre, but it was
"brutish" for those same natives to consider reversing
the situation with identical methods. He also suppressed
verbalizing his less arch curiosity regarding how the
reverend would feel in the natives' place, about being
on the losing end of the stick with which the Europeans had beaten the prime lesson of all colonialism
into the Caribs' heads: that might makes right, not
uncounted generations of habitation and ownership.
Of course, it could also be averred that, in the case
of the Caribs, it was simply a matter of what goes
around, comes around. According to the history books,
the Caribs had been the local colonizers less than half
a millennium ago, driving the comparatively peaceful
Taino out of the Windward and then Leeward Isles in
a slow but inexorable campaign of northward expansion-
by-genocide. Not for the first time, Mike wondered if
maybe that's all history was; a succession of bullies
and thieves, each one dressing up their own conquests
in veils of fancy rhetoric and moral speechifying.

Polhemius had signaled to eight young men lounging
near the only permanent structure near the eastern
skirts of Oranjestad: a shack fashioned from discarded
planking and spar fragments. They rose, revealing a
collection of stenciled crates behind them. "These are
the fellows I was telling you about," he said by way
of introduction as the group drew closer.

Mike scanned them and, by posture alone, identified
the two who were coming along simply for the money
and what they presumed would be light labor. While
not so rude as to look obviously bored, they were
not attentive, scanning the outskirts of the tent-city

for objects of interest. First among which were young women, origins and status notwithstanding. Mike managed not to smile. *Okay, guys, I've had overgrown boys like you walk into my shop, looking for a job. Let's see if you're up for it, because I'd rather have two positions that still need to be filled rather than two positions filled by young punks who won't give me a solid day's work.* "You, and you. Yeah, you. Both of you. Have you worked on ships?"

After overcoming their surprise at being singled out, and gruffly, the two started explaining that they were not sailors, of course. But that they had lent a hand while aboard. Here and there. Not so much as to mean that they knew how to work on ships, but—

"That's enough," Mike interrupted brusquely. "So you've climbed masts, worked out on the ends of yards."

They both started babbling out further qualifying statements—

"I said that's enough. You two are lucky, because you get to start work without having to spend today learning about a bunch of dull radio components and wire-splicing, here in the shade. Instead, your job is to go to the eastern side of The Quill and survey its slopes for tall trees. Specifically, you are to locate and tag every tree that's at least thirty feet tall in the northeast quadrant of the slopes. Double tag any trees that have plump, straight trunks up to fifteen feet. There won't be many too close to the level ground, since the wind off the Atlantic pushes most of them over sideways. But as you get higher up, the jungle itself provides a partial windbreak, so you'll find more of them as you climb higher." Mike tossed a bag of white, ribbonlike rags at them. "There are your tags."

One of the pair simply looked at him, unspeaking. The other held the bag, looking helpless. "Hammer?" he asked. "Nails?"

"No nails," Mike announced with a single shake of his head. "Too scarce to use on something like this. And besides, we don't want to kill the same trees we're going to use to mount our antenna lines. Now, get moving. You've got a good walk ahead of you, and a lot of work when you get there."

"We're not going to learn about radios?" said the one who had been speechless. He sounded as if Father Christmas had put coal in his stocking.

"You are learning about radios," Mike said with a smile. "From the ground up. Literally. Now git." He turned to the other six young men.

Except that there were now seven men, and the seventh wasn't as young as the others. He was leaning in the now-open doorway of the shack. He nodded at Mike, a broad easy smile pasted on his big, blunt peasant features. But his eyes were bright and alert, and Mike immediately recalled similar faces from his thirty-five years working on cars and in other mechanical industries. This was the face of the guy all the bosses underestimated, the guy they pegged as being "slow," but who turned out to be the sharpest knife in the drawer, and the guy who not only got his own work done on the shop floor but managed to drag a small passel of prior slackers along with him into genuine productivity. Mike smiled back. "Hey old-timer," he said to the thirty-something fellow. "Glad you could join us."

The man laughed—a deep, easy rumble—and nodded. "Hah. *Ja*, old-timer; that's me. Been a second-mate for almost ten years, now. About time I try something new. Maybe skill with radios will get me that overdue promotion to first mate. Or, if not, maybe I'll work for you, hey? Lots of sailors around, these days, but not many people who know radios."

Mike nodded. "True enough. I'm Mike—"

The man bowed a bit. "Oh, we know who you are, Mr. Michael McCarthy. We've been waiting for you to build this radio."

"'We?'"

The man scratched at his thick, and decidedly unruly, brown hair. "*Ja.* Me and the young fellows, here."

Mike nodded, beginning to understand. "So, you were responsible for choosing who was going to be on this job?" He glanced sideways at Polhemius, who nodded almost nervously.

"Yes," the reverend answered, "that is correct. Mr. Kortenaer expressed interest in your project and was also accustomed to dealing with lively young men, such as were needed."

McCarthy saw Kortenaer's eyes twinkle and he suppressed a new smile. *So, the good Reverend Polhemius isn't comfortable providing leadership to a bunch of young roughnecks. They probably don't pray and clean their fingernails often enough for his comfort. So he pulls an older version of them from before the mast to choose and baby-sit them. Which is just as well. Now I don't have to find a foreman, because I've already got one.* "Well, now that you've been kind enough to finish making all the introductions, Reverend Polhemius, I think I'm ready to get to work." Mike put out his hand. "Thanks so much, and I'm sure I'll see you soon again."

Polhemius, who was possibly aware that he was

being politely but swiftly brushed off, shook hands while uttering a few abbreviated pleasantries and then strode back toward the western side of the town and his small wood-framed church. Mike watched him go. He turned to Kortenaer, who'd come to stand beside him. "So, if you're going to be my foreman"—the man's smile was as honest as it was sudden and broad—"I need to know your whole name. So I can know who I'm cussing at, you understand."

The answer rode atop a faint chuckle. "I am Egbert Bartholomeuszoon Kortenaer. 'Bert' for short. Now, how shall we start?"

Mike thought. "First we check the components and the wires, and make sure they all made the trip safely. If we're going to have any technical problems, I need to know right away."

"To send home for new parts?"

"Well, that eventually, but mostly to see if we can jury-rig something until then. We need this radio for local strategic coordination, including finding out what happened to a ship of ours."

"The other steamship?" Bert asked. Then, seeing the surprised look on Mike's face, added, "It cannot surprise you too much that we heard. Your crews drink with our crews, and try to impress the ladies of Oranjestad with their choicest rumors."

Mike shrugged. "Yeah. We should have heard from the other steamship, the *Courser*, on our own ships' radios by now. Even if it was just some chopped up Morse code, we should have heard them trying to make contact."

"But all has been silence?"

"Yeah. For weeks, now. So I need to know if we're

going to have any mechanical problems up front. In practical terms, that means I need your guys to open the crates carefully and unpack them carefully. One at a time. I don't want the components to touch the ground, so have them put on a table."

"No table. All our new wood goes into building and ship repair," Bert said with a shake of his head. "But—" He turned to the men and ordered them to uncrate a spool of wire first. "Put the wire on a canvas drop cloth. Then, break its crate apart—carefully. Keep each side intact."

"Why, Heer Kortenaer?" asked the very blond and very young one of the group.

"Because you're going to use those crate-sides to make tabletops. The bases will be wormed casks from the ships. I knew there'd be a reason to keep them, and here it is. Then, unload the contents of the next crate, the one with components, upon that table."

"And make another table out of that next crate?"

"There's a bright lad. Now get about it." He turned back to Mike. "What next, Heer McCarthy?"

"Next, you learn to call me Mike. After that, you tell me the most important thing any job-boss needs to know."

"And what is that, Mike?"

"Well, there's a saying that we don't fail because of what we don't know. We fail because of *things that we don't know* we don't know. Understand?"

Bert smiled. "I don't know. But at least I know that I don't know."

"That's the ticket. Now, what problems are lurking around that a dumb-ass up-timer like me has no clue about?"

Bert's smile faded. "It is not that you have no clue about them, Hee—er, Mike. It is that the clues, the signs, of the problems are being kept from you."

Mike repressed a sigh. He'd hoped that his fishing expedition for unseen troubles would be fruitless, but he'd also been sensible enough to know the odds of that were low. And that's just how it was playing out. "Okay, Bert, what local problems could get in the way of setting up the radio?"

As the six young Dutchmen started lifting spools of precious wire onto old canvas, Bert considered Mike's request with a deepening frown. "Well, you will find out quickly enough, I suspect, that not everyone in Oranjestad considers your arrival an event for celebration."

"Oh? Who have I managed to piss off, already?"

"No, no, I am not referring to your coming, personally, Mike. I mean the arrival of the Reconnaissance Flotilla and what it signifies."

"You mean, that the USE is getting involved in Dutch affairs?"

"Oh, not that so much. We're probably just about the most grateful Dutchmen in the world when it comes to receiving help from unexpected benefactors. No, it is about this agreement that has been reached with the Spanish Lowlands. There are some who just won't have it, no matter how beneficial it might be."

Well, that *cat came out of the bag pretty quickly, too.* "Bert, do you have any idea just how the news of the oil deal and the Lowlands' participation already arrived in Oranjestad?"

Kortenaer shook his head. "No, but word of it was running up and down the tent-lines like a brush fire last night. I suspect someone who'd overheard discussions at Trinidad went on liberty from the *Crown of Waves* or *Koninck David* when you arrived just after sundown and offered to trade tales for grog... Well, you know how these things happen."

Don't I just, though. "And so who in Oranjestad has decided they'd rather stay at war with Fernando than get oil-rich?"

Bert shrugged. "The same settlers who came here wanting to grow tobacco, own slaves, and get away from Catholics. I mean no offense, Mike. These are their sentiments, not mine."

Mike nodded. "Understood. But aren't these settlers very much in the minority, here?"

"It is true they number but a few hundred of all who are here, but they are the ones who own most of the land, who were granted the charter to St. Eustatia. Although the soldiers and sailors and tradesmen are almost ninety percent of the population, they haven't the money, the possessions, or the backing of the Dutch West India company."

"Well, from what I hear, the Nineteen Heeren who call the shots of the Company were pretty enthusiastic about the oil trade when Prince Hendrik shared word of it with them a few months ago. Everyone in the New World is trying to grow tobacco and sugar, but right now, we've got the monopoly on oil, and it's worth far more, pound for pound. And it requires far less labor, cheap or otherwise. So the representatives of the Dutch West India Company were very vocal supporters of the oil co-dominium from the start."

"Well," said Bert thoughtfully, "that is good news, and that is bad news."

"And that is as cryptic a sentence as I've heard you speak, Bert. What's it mean?"

"It means that, in the long run, the Company will get what it wants, which is also what makes most sense. But the bad news is that I know these men on St. Eustatia, and their friends and sons who are now working leased plots on St. Christopher. They are almost all staunch Calvinists of the most orthodox type, men who will not abide Catholics. And they will not want to be made less powerful, less important, by the development of oil on another island." He toed the dirt irritably. "Understand, Mike. These are men who *like* owning slaves, who feel powerful commanding them to work in the fields, and commanding the women to—well, you know."

Mike found that he was grinding his teeth. "Oh, I know, Bert, I know. And I guess they know I'm dead set against letting that kind of shit start here, all over again."

Bert started at Mike's tone more than his words. "I—I do not know if they know your personal feelings about slavery, Mike. But it has been made clear, from what little we have heard about the up-timers, that despite your diverse faiths and beliefs, you all hate slavery. I suspect they will not be surprised to find an enemy in you, Mike."

Mike could feel the better half of his nature ready to drop the tasks and tools of setting up an intercontinental radio. Instead, he discovered that he was already thinking of the ways in which he could take the fight to the bastards who got a thrill out of raping slave women while their two-year-olds hid under the bed, eyes wide at the brutality, terror, and humiliation of the violation taking place only a foot over their heads. But he scooped up that rage, crammed it forcefully into a mental vault and reluctantly sealed it, promising the growing fury within, *you've got to wait a bit. Just a bit. First we build a radio. Then we get lots of ships and guns over here. And then . . . Oh, and then—*

"Mike, are you quite well?"

"Me? Never better, Bert. I love having something to work toward, and you've just given me another very fine purpose to get this radio up and running as quickly as possible. About which: as soon as we've finished identifying the trees we're going to use, we'll need to get a much bigger work crew together to affix the wires to run down and outward from The Quill's cone in rays spreading toward the northeast. So here's what I want to know: is it any more expensive to, well, lease a slave or bondsman from one of the landowners than it is to hire one of these soldiers or sailors?"

Bert frowned. "It is not so much a matter of cost. It is that the slaves and bondsmen can be made to do work that none of the colonists will agree to do. Working in cane fields is hard. Very hard."

Mike nodded. "I know. But I've heard rumors that right now, the landowners aren't making as much from their cane crops as they'd like. They don't have any way to ship it back to Europe, yet, and they can only use it as a barter good, here in the Caribbees. So wouldn't it be profitable for them to lease out slave labor for silver?"

Bert shrugged. "Yes, but why should you do so? We have many soldiers who can help us as part of their military orders, working in shifts."

"True. But we'll get them on short, rotating assignments, I'm told. But if we have a large core of steady workers—such as leased slaves—they'll quickly get a higher level of expertise at the job. And then rotating laborers from the military becomes more effective more rapidly."

Bert's smile crept back on his face. "But that's not the only reason, is it, Mike? You want to speak to the slaves, away from their masters, don't you? Before their masters come to realize how you feel about slavery?"

Mike smiled back. "That obvious, huh? But yeah, that's just what I mean to do. Maybe we can get a few hired over from St. Christopher's, as well."

Bert's smile faded. "I think you mean to do a good thing, Mike, but I'm worried it could hurt the very people you mean to help. I counsel you to consider this: let us say you move the slaves to assert themselves. And so they refuse to work. Whatever else may happen, we will all starve. So perhaps, at first, you could simply work in the same direction as Tromp and van Walbeeck."

"Which means what?"

"They are trying to get the slaves converted into bondsmen. I know, I know: there is still great inequity in being a bondsman. But any more rapid transition will destroy the colony. On the other hand, if this colony becomes a place where outright slavery ceases to exist, then escapees from the Spanish colonies, and those of other nations, will flock here. They will come for the same reason we did: to have a chance, no matter how distant and uncertain, to live a better life than the one we knew at home."

"And how is the life of a bondsman that much better than that of a slave?"

"It is, if it follows the model that Tromp and van Walbeeck are trying to get the councilors to accept. In which the slaves and current bondsmen shall all earn their complete freedom with five years of bonded work."

"And then what, Bert? Without any possessions, without any land of their own, they'll be desperate. They'll have no options, no means of providing for their own needs. Which means they'll massacre us to take what they must, or we'll massacre them to keep it."

"Or," temporized Bert calmly, "like peasants have since the beginning of time, they will continue to work the same land, but now will keep a share of what they grow. And that shall be the beginning of their wealth."

Mike started. Bert was of course not aware of it, but in suggesting serfdom, he was rebirthing the basic principles of sharecropping, and Mike knew full well the abuses to which that grim institution was subject. But, on the other hand, it was a hell of a lot better than slavery, and was probably the most progressive policy that the local freemen would accept. With the great majority of them being tradition-minded political moderates, they would reflexively reject an immediate conferral of full equality. But this was a middle course they could probably get behind. Meaning that this was probably the shape of the near future. The hard-liners wouldn't like it one bit, but wouldn't be able to get enough support from fence-sitters to keep their slaves from becoming bondsmen. At best, they'd be able to haggle about the details of the agreement.

Mike looked at Bert, looked at the second crate of radio components being delicately unloaded, looked up at the slopes of The Quill, and conceded that, in this New World, the challenges were never simple, the solutions never perfect, and the need for flexibility never-ending. "Okay," he muttered. "We'll take the gradualist approach. Now, which landowners are hurting enough financially to rent us some well-spoken and charismatic slaves?"

Chapter 36

Chaguamara Peninsula, Trinidad

Even after the partition separating Eddie's cabin from
the *Intrepid*'s wardroom had been removed, the space
around the chart-table still felt crowded. Pros Mund
was next to the map-table with his executive officer,
Haakon. Immediately across from them was Tromp,
who had brought his own first mate, a bright young
fellow named Evertsen. And of course both Gjedde and
Bjelke were there from *Intrepid*. Arrayed back in
a second rank along the walls were Simonszoon, von
Holst, and van Galen and the pilots of their ships,
who'd need at least as good an awareness of the situation and planned maneuver as the captains themselves.

A pewter pitcher of water made its way slowly
around the circle of men, several of whom muttered
about preferring grog, and one who wondered, aloud,
if there was any food to be had. Eddie wondered if he
should get an orderly to meet those needs, but found
Gjedde glancing at him. The old Norwegian shook his
head faintly and returned his attention to the map.

That, Eddie allowed with an imaginary slap to his

own face, was a prompt he shouldn't have needed. It had been unnerving, learning that the final commanders' conference was to be on his—well, Gjedde's—ship, but that didn't mean he had to worry about catering the event. It was a working gathering, not a social occasion. The captains should certainly have been able to feed themselves before they traveled to the *Intrepid* in their individual skiffs.

And it wasn't as if meeting on the *Intrepid* was any kind of unusual honor. The decision had been based solely on the consideration that it was the one location that could not offend or call into question the comparative status of any of the senior officers. It was a lot of rubbish, Eddie thought, but the same kind of seniority and rank issues had persisted down through to the up-time navy of his own nation, so he really shouldn't have expected any different, or any better, here.

Tromp was, by any reasonable measure, the senior commander, and brought the greatest number of ships to the fleet that was currently raising its anchors from the twelve-fathom depths of northwest Trinidad's Scotland Bay. However, Pros Mund was senior among the USE commanders, and although only two ships of his flotilla were present, the *Intrepid* and the *Resolve,* they were arguably far more powerful than all the Dutch ships combined. This was further complicated by the ticklish fact that the most knowledgeable person about the details of how the new cooperative oil ventures between the Provinces and the USE did or did not influence military cooperation in the protection of those ventures was none other than Eddie himself. Eddie calculated that, in anything like a chain of command, he was probably somewhere about fifth or sixth, with Gjedde, Simonszoon, and the *Tropic Surveyor*'s Stiernsköld coming after the uncertain Tromp-Mund dyad.

In short, notions of seniority were completely scrambled and everyone knew it. But they were also too polite to say anything for fear of starting a disagreement that might result in an inability to pursue a coherent response to the Spanish threat that had finally arrived this morning. And no one had to dance more carefully than Eddie. On the one hand, he had to be careful not to step on any superior-ranking toes; but, on the other, was the only person who really understood the technological opportunities—and also, limitations—of the up-time designed steamships that were the lynchpin of their plans.

Happily, Tromp had proven to be a calm, almost ego-less commander whose quiet graciousness had become familiar to Eddie over the course of several shared dinners on both the *Amelia* and the *Intrepid*. And if Pros Mund was, by comparison, standoffish and cheerless, he was patient and prudent enough to realize that Tromp had to insist upon equal command dignities. The Danish admiral certainly cared more about the quality of their plans and leadership than any folderol about seniority and rank, but it was also true that he had to protect his staff, to ensure that his captains were not made to answer to a commander they had never met, let alone (in most cases) heard of. Consequently, Eddie had led both admirals toward a strategy that made a virtue out of being allies whose relationship was as new and unspecified as their chain of command was undetermined.

Eddie pointed to the map, which illustrated yet another reason why this final council of war had been called aboard the *Intrepid*. Not only was it "neutral ground" in that it was not on either Tromp's or Mund's respective flagships, but it put the best up-time maps, clocks, and drafting equipment at the disposal of the entire command staff. Resting his finger next to a red pin stuck fifteen miles northwest of the island of Grenada, Eddie looked around the room. "So this is where the Spanish were when the first sighting was made by our balloon, land-moored at Prickly Point on Grenada, one hour ago. Since then, twenty-six ships have been spotted, of which five are *pataches*. Their main van was making about two knots."

Simonszoon frowned. "Then they're not taking full advantage of the leeward breeze. I saw the morning weather reports from your radiomen who are with the balloon's ground team: almost fourteen knots south by southwest. Perfect for the Spanish square-riggers, coming just one point off their port quarter. Even their high-hulled scows should be able to make four knots with that God-given breeze."

Eddie nodded. "That's right, but they've got the *pataches* out in front of them, looking for any forces we might have in the region. That means their main body has to slow down, let their fore-and-aft-rigged scouts run ahead and around, come close enough to send signals, then work their way out again."

Tromp nodded. "That is good in that it gives us more time, which we will want since we have to tack to windward to meet them. But it is not good insofar as it suggests that the Spanish are being cautious, rather than rushing in hastily."

Mund shrugged. "So we will need to follow what Commander Cantrell calls plan Beta. We will need to conceal our true intents longer, which will require more careful coordination as we approach the Spaniards."

Simonszoon rested his finger at the southern tip of Grenada. "It also means we shall need regular reports from your balloon, here. They will be able to keep the Spanish under observation as we maneuver to make contact with them in the place and in the formation we have decided upon. The balloon will need to keep us updated so that we may adjust to any course or formation changes *they* might make."

Eddie smiled. He liked working with Dirck Simonszoon, whose laconic wit was a screen behind which he hid an agile and incisive tactical mind. More than any of the down-timers he'd met thus far, Simonszoon appreciated how the adroit use of balloons and radios made it possible to both deceive an approaching foe and maneuver for advantage. That was why it was his ship, the comparatively fleet-footed forty-four-gun *Achilles*, that was to be towed by the flotilla's one available steam pinnace to keep up with the *Resolve* and *Intrepid*. Once the allied fleet came in sight of the Spanish, these three ships would push forward as a flying wing stretching north from the eastern flank of Tromp's main body of Dutch ships. "That's absolutely correct, Dirck. We need those airborne eyes as we close to contact. Which is why I've already ordered the balloon to land, for now."

Simonszoon frowned, then nodded. "Yes, because of their limited ability to keep heating the air in the envelope."

"That, and because as the Spanish get close to

rounding Grenada, which we guess will be happening in about four hours, they'd be far more likely to spot our balloon. If it was still up in the sky, that is. Two hours after they draw past Grenada, we'll send it aloft again. They'll be less likely to spot it astern to the north when all their lookouts are concentrating on finding us to the south, east, and west."

Von Holst sounded concerned. "But during those six hours when the balloon is on the ground, how shall we know if they change course?"

It was Tromp who pointed almost fifty miles northwest of their position in Scotland Bay. "Because Gijszoon is out there, with the yacht *Kater* and his own balloon."

"What?" van Galen almost shouted. "You told us he was—!"

"I said nothing specific about his whereabouts, merely that he was on patrol. Which he was, working from out beyond the north tip of the Paria peninsula. He's been sheltering in the Cove of Palmar behind Punta Mejillores and then patrolling approximately thirty-five miles north. With the balloon we gave him, that allowed him to spot either a Spanish fleet coming from the Greater Antilles directly across the open waters of the Caribbean, or for the Cartagena fleet to the west. And as he had a reaching wind both coming out of and going back to his anchorage, he had great flexibility of movement.

"As for the Spanish who have now appeared, they will not see him at his patrol point unless they change course to the southwest or west. But Gijszoon will see that change first and let us know."

"So if we receive no radio signals from Gijszoon,

we know that they are still rounding Grenada and heading in their last known direction," von Holst concluded with a nod.

Van Galen was frowning, though. "Unless they decide to turn around and run home, head back up the Leeward side of the Lesser Antilles."

Mund frowned at van Galen's frown. "Yes, but this would not concern us. If the Spanish turn back, the wind will be in their faces. They'll either be in irons, or sailing very close-hauled. And being close-hauled on those big square-rigged galleons, they would be lucky to make headway faster than one knot. Within ten hours we would know that they had turned about, and we would be upon them in two days, at the most."

"Yes, but only your two steam ships could catch them so quickly," van Galen protested doggedly. "And how do we know your ships are as powerful as he claims—" a head jerked insolently in Eddie's direction—"or that you won't take all the spoils?"

"First," Mund answered with slow, crisp syllables, "Commander Cantrell is not the only one who has seen or been aboard these steamships when they are in action. Consequently, you have my personal assurance that he has not, in the slightest particular, exaggerated their capabilities. Second, it is utterly illogical that we would or could 'take all the spoils,' as you put it, Captain van Galen. If by spoils you mean gold or silver, then you are here fighting the wrong battle, both because treasure is not our objective, and because these are not treasure ships. If, on the other hand, you are calling the ships themselves the 'spoils,' consider the complements of my flotilla. I might be able to crew a captured galleon or two as prize hulls, but not all of them. There would be 'spoils' enough for all, in that event."

Tromp turned a slightly testy eye upon van Galen, and asked quietly, "Does this answer your concerns, Johan?"

The Dutch captain glowered at the map and folded his arms. "Yes. For now."

Tromp turned to Eddie. "So this means we will not have *Kater* and Gijszoon rendezvousing with us?"

Eddie crinkled his mouth apologetically. "It's not likely, Admiral. If our guesses are right, we'll be meeting the Spanish only a few hours before dusk, about eleven hours from now. But it will be six hours until we are certain that the Spanish are doing what we expect: to crowd sail once they enter the Grenada Passage and try to slip into the Gulf of Paria via the Dragon's Mouth just after nightfall. That means *Kater* would have only five hours to sail into the eye of the wind and cover almost thirty miles to reach your van. I know that Joachim Gijszoon is a fine sailor, but—"

"But he will not make six knots an hour if he must constantly be tacking through a wind from the northeast. And finding a steady heading in the Grenada Passage can be tricky, particularly right where the Leeward breeze meets the prevailing westward wind that blows along Tierra Firma." Tromp shook his head. "You are right, Eddie, we may not count on Gijszoon's ship. Which means my van will have no jachts."

"Which leads me to ask," von Holst asked, "where is Pieter Floriszoon, the *Eendracht*, and those Irish Wild Geese?"

Tromp shrugged. "Probably tacking against that same westward wind. They could have been here, at the very earliest, a few days ago. They could easily be another week in reaching us. Either way, the Spanish are here now, so we should move with all haste. Are there any other changes to plan Beta?" His glance started on Pros Mund, bounced to Eddie—and stayed there.

Eddie shook his head. "No, Admiral. Just remember that no matter what the Spanish do when they come at your van, keep your hulls in formation, and be the first to show the world what well-gunned ships can do when engaging the enemy in a line. Just like you did in my world."

"So you tell me. In your up-time world, I introduced this tactic in 1640, yes?"

"Correct, sir. At the Battle of the Downs. Which will now never happen. Here, they'll say that the first use of the naval 'line of battle' doctrine was in 1635 at the Battle of Grenada Passage."

"Yes. Assuming we win it," added Gjedde darkly as he glanced out the portside window into a sudden shaft of bright yellow light. He rose, his slate-on-granite voice already rising into cries to unreef the sails and ready the commanders' skiffs.

With the sun now fully up, the time had come for the fleet to get under way.

Grenada Passage, Caribbean Sea

By two PM, Eddie no longer needed the radio relays from the balloon at Prickly Point to tell him where the Spanish were. He could see them himself.

And evidently, vice versa. The lighter *pataches* had already begun angling off to the flanks of the Spanish van, which had altered course perhaps one point in a more southerly direction, making straight for the seven Dutch sails they first saw there. When, a quarter of an hour later, they evidently saw the other three sails of the second group of ships following perhaps a mile behind the main van, their *pataches* began coming forward more aggressively, no doubt in an attempt to get a better look at what this second formation might be. But the main body made no further course change.

And, Eddie allowed, why would it have? From the initial Spanish perspective, their fleet was facing seven Dutch ships that had fewer guns, but were better sailors. But with twenty-one galleons or smaller galleoncetes, they outnumbered the Dutch three to one in large ships, and had the wind right where they wanted it: running fresh and steady over their port quarter. If anything, the Spanish might wonder why the Dutch were willing to maneuver toward contact under such unfavorable conditions. But they would reasonably conjecture that, given their intrusion near Pitch Lake, the Dutch were desperate to keep the Spanish ships from reaching the Dragon's Mouth, and thereby entering the Gulf of Paria. Because once there, the Spanish were too numerous for the smaller Dutch fleet to contain. While the galleons kept the Dutch ships occupied, a squadron of the smaller galleoncetes could easily break off and disrupt or destroy their incursion upon Trinidadian soil. And so, the defiance of the Spanish *inter caetera* would be at an end.

But now the time had come to change the playing board in a way that the Spanish could not anticipate, and, more importantly, would not strategically understand. Not this first time, anyway, Eddie reminded himself. He turned toward Ove Gjedde, who was already looking at him. "With your permission, sir."

"Commander Cantrell, you have the con. I will mind the sails. As usual."

"Very good, sir. I say three times, I have the con. Now, a question, sir: can you get me six knots by canvas alone in this breeze?"

Gjedde looked at Eddie as if the up-timer had insulted him. "You know very well that I can, Mr. Cantrell."

"Then, as soon as we've got the steam-pinnace fired up, I'll be asking you for those six knots." He turned away, raised his voice. "Mr. Svantner?"

"Sir?"

"Ring down to the engine room. Ready the bitumen-treated wood for the burner. No coal yet, but they are to keep it handy."

"Just warming the boiler, sir?"

"Precisely. Mr. Bjelke?"

From Eddie's left elbow, Rik's voice was tense and slightly higher-pitched than usual. "Sir?"

"Send by semaphore to the pinnace towing *Achilles* that she is to make full steam as soon as possible and fall in behind us. She is to alert us at once if she cannot sustain six knots. Helmsman?"

"Yes, Capt—Commander Cantrell?"

"You'll be following the wind as Captain Gjedde tells you, but bring our heading due north."

"Sir, that will have us angling away from Admiral Tromp's ships."

"It will, Helmsman," Eddie affirmed with a smile. "It will indeed."

❖   ❖   ❖

Lieutenant Admiral Fadrique Álvarez de Toledo y Mendoza glanced sideways while Captain General of the Armada Jorge de Cárdenas y Manrique de Lara's attention was upon the latest report from the crow's nest. And Fadrique wondered, *how did it ever come to this?*

Honored just last January by Philip IV, he had then been dismissed in near-disgrace mere months later by Olivares for being too popular at court and also too outspoken about the danger to the viceroyalties of the New World. Happily, the need for capable admirals in the field was greater than the power of Olivares' displeasure in court. September brought news that he had been reappointed to a military command, largely thanks to his brother who commanded the galleys of the Mediterranean. Taking leave of his wife and children to oversee the re-expansion of the Armada de Barlovento, he quit his villa just ahead of the diphtheria outbreak that, he learned shortly after, had claimed him in the "up-time" world of the heathen Americans.

However, that good luck did not follow him to the New World. Upon arriving, he discovered that the Armada de Barlovento, shrunken to three or four worm-eaten hulls, had disappeared and evidently no longer existed. Worse yet, in reply to the governor of Cuba's plea for an overall naval commander to coordinate activities in the Caribbean, such as finding and eliminating the resurgent fleet of the blasted Dutchman Tromp, Olivares' advisory council, the *Junta de Guerra de Indias* sent none other than the largely ineffective de Cárdenas y Manrique de Lara to do the job. *It should have been* me *they chose to hunt down the Dutch, damn them.* Me! *I've won more battles against them than Jorge has ever fought.* But of course, Fadrique knew precisely why he had been made merely the commander of the decrepit (and now extinct) Armada de Barlovento and why de Cárdenas y Manrique de Lara had been placed over all naval matters in the New World: favor at court.

Jorge wasn't particularly gifted overseeing naval operations, but he was an inspired navigator of the ebbs and flows of the prevailing tides of popularity in Madrid. And so here he was, four years Fadrique's junior, and not even vaguely his peer in matters military, but still in charge of the largest single offensive reprisal that Spain had mounted in the Caribbean in years. It was possibly the largest since Fadrique's own successes in driving the English and French from their settlements in St. Christopher's and Nevis only six years earlier. But the brazen violators of His Imperial Majesty's exclusive right to settlements west of the Tordesilla line had returned as soon as Fadrique's galleons had disappeared over the horizon. Just as Fadrique had said they would. And just as he had warned Olivares—*the whoreson!*—the same thing had occurred in similarly isolated possessions throughout the Caribbean. Chasing and imprisoning violators was not enough. Deporting them to mines or fields in Cuba or Tierra Firma was not enough. Nor even was extermination. Only by settling and holding the land itself could the Spanish Crown be sure that godless trespassers would not sneak in to usurp it. And of course Olivares had not wanted such talk bruited about, because that level of commitment, that strategy of certain success, also cost more money. Or it meant giving the viceroys and governors of the New World increased authority to raise their own navies and armies, which meant, once again, pulling some measure of power out of Olivares' grasping hands. And that was simply not going to happen, not until some crisis forced that simpering bootlicker to take action.

"Well, Fadrique," de Cárdenas y Manrique de Lara mused, "the reports are confirmed. Two large ships to the east of the Dutch van are now advancing well north of their line. A third is following them. That one may be afire, since it is putting out some smoke."

It was no less than de Toledo has seen through his own spyglass. "That smoke makes little sense. There was no sound of a prior battle as we approached."

"Perhaps they are still recuperating after an earlier encounter with our fleet from Cartagena. That would explain both the smoke of the one ship, and their diminished numbers. This is certainly far fewer ships than Tromp was said to have at Recife."

Fadrique kept any hint of impatience out of his reply. "Perhaps. But none of our *pataches* have located the *patache*-pickets of the Cartagena fleet, Captain-General, not even those which we sent down here so that they might watch for their arrival and report back. Also, the Dutch numbers may not signify prior losses, but current caution. If Tromp is still in the Caribbean, he has been here for better than a year. If seems certain he must have a base somewhere, possibly Curaçao. If so, he must leave much of his fleet behind to protect that base."

De Cárdenas y Manrique de Lara flipped a dismissing wrist at the objections. "Well, then, the smoke could signify a fire-ship. The Dutch are outnumbered and may hope to scatter us, lest we gather too tightly upon any of their number."

De Toledo nodded, answered, "Perhaps," and thought, *Are you mad, or simply stupid?* Fadrique continued carefully. "However, a fire ship puts out more smoke, and blacker. And it is best used in a bay or channel, where maneuver is limited or difficult." *Besides, you ass-kisser, you can see through your own glass that the smoking ship is fully and handsomely rigged, and therefore, well-crewed. Fireships are manned by skeleton crews so they may be abandoned at the last second, in haste.*

De Cárdenas y Manrique de Lara merely pouted. "You may be right, Don Álvarez, but I shall suspend judgment. In the meantime, why do you think these two great ships—built along *fragata* lines, no less—are coming out in front and to the flank of the main Dutch body?"

Álvarez de Toledo shrugged. "The wind is from the northeast. They are to our east, heading north. They hope to get the weather-gauge on us. And, making better than five knots, they are likely to accomplish that."

"But to what end, Fadrique? They are but three ships, and one is burning. And see, the large ones have few ports for cannon. Not even sixteen on the port side that we can see." He rapped the rail along the port quarter decisively. "They must be large merchants, some new kind of argosy, trying to slip past us rather than try cases against our twenty-six-gun broadsides!"

"'Slip past us'?" echoed Fadrique. "How? If they get the weather gauge, they must sail to the west—*toward us*—unless they wish to find themselves tacking in baffling winds, or even caught in irons."

"And so they may, Fadrique. Really, I am surprised

you do not perceive their ploy. They shall try to outsail us, to get north of our van. Meanwhile, the regular Dutch ships will slow down, baiting us to use our following wind to descend upon them. I suspect they will turn their tails and run to the Dragon's Mouth, then. And when we crowd even more sail to catch them, these great argosies shall come about to put the wind over their starboard beams and run westward, hugging close against Grenada and escaping behind us."

Fadrique nodded. "I hadn't thought of that." That was because it was the most absurd collection of inanities he'd ever heard. Whatever these large ships were, they were not "argosies." Their hulls were too long and narrow to be effective cargo ships. Besides, their rigging was different and their lines were— strange. And why would they be taking a burning, but apparently conventional, ship with them? Something was not right here . . .

"Well, Fadrique, whatever these large ships are, and whatever their intents, we have all the speed, and all the hulls, we need to ruin their strategy."

"Certainly, sir. However, I—"

But before de Toledo could offer his tactical counsel, de Cárdenas y Manrique de Lara was declaiming his own. "So then, you shall give the Dutch what they want. You shall take half our ships and strike south at the Dutch van. I suspect they will not give you battle, but if they do, press close and smash them, Fadrique. Seize any that you may, but I am not overly concerned with prizes. I want these Dutch interlopers swept from the waves, and if that necessitates blasting them into driftwood rather than risking a boarding, so be it.

"Meanwhile, I shall take the other half of our ships due east to cut off the three fleeing ships. I shall send the *patache*s slightly northward, to deny them any chance of working around to the leeward side of Grenada. And the rest of our ships will bring cannon to bear against the argosies, which may well be too large to sink quickly. But that will be acceptable. I have a powerful curiosity to see what special cargoes they must be carrying, to abandon their own fleet in so desperate a fashion."

De Toledo was glad to wait through de Cárdenas y Manrique de Lara's lecture of the day's intended tactics. It gave him a few extra moments to distance himself from the absurdity of his commanding officer's assessments and plans. "Captain-General de Cárdenas y Manrique de Lara, are you certain that splitting our forces is wise? The large ships are unusually fast, and it is entirely possible that they might turn toward us, and—"

"And what, Fadrique? Challenge our twenty-six-gun broadsides with their fourteen-gun impotence? Will they hope to swarm us, board us, being outnumbered better than four to one? They mean to flee, Fadrique, of that much you may be sure. And you may also be sure of this: I shall stop them. Now, return to your ship at once. We are drawing close enough to ready the guns, and you must lead your half of this fleet south against the Dutch." And with that, Captain-General Jorge de Cárdenas y Manrique de Lara turned away from his subordinate, signaling that their conversation was over.

Chapter 37

Grenada Passage, Caribbean Sea

At one-mile range, and with the sun starting down toward the horizon, Eddie turned to Svantner to confirm—one more time—the weather conditions he'd been watching so closely. "Mr. Svantner, wind, currents, and sea?"

Svantner didn't even have to inquire. He'd arranged runners to give him updates every two minutes. "Sir, wind is running in from the east-northeast at a steady twelve knots. That is only one point off the direction of the current. Seas are reasonably calm: one-foot waves, sometimes one and a quarter, sir. Conditions remain steady, wind shifting only a point or so from the prevailing direction."

Eddie nodded. He called down to the intraship comm officer beneath his collapsible "flying bridge." "Range and bearing of the enemy's lead ship?"

"Mount One is calling it 1600 yards to the lead packet—er, *patache*—sir, bearing 285 degrees. About 1900 yards to the first galleon behind her, bearing directly abeam at 270 degrees."

Eddie nodded, as much to himself as to the men around him. "Right." He looked up at the *Intrepid*'s funnel. For the last ten minutes, a thin, whitish smoke had been rising out of it. "Rik, have they warmed up the engines and boilers?"

"Yes, sir. They've used about half the wood."

"Tell them to shift to coal. Captain Gjedde, we'll be moving to steam as soon as our boilers are up to pressure. Tell the men aloft to expect her to get lively."

"They are ready, Commander Cantrell."

They ought to be, given how often we've briefed them. "Radioman, instruct the *Achilles* that she is to signal the pinnace to cut her loose and sheer off." Over the muted "Aye, sir," from below the deck, Eddie asked, "Rik? Do I have steam enough for ten knots?"

"The chief engineer says you do, Commander."

"Then ahead three-quarters." *And let's give those Spaniards something to gawk at.*

While still more than a mile away from the Dutch ships, Fadrique de Toledo was distracted by a cry from the lookout in the mizzen's crow's nest. He turned and saw a single gout of smoke coming up from the center of each of the big ships as they started drawing northward at an almost inconceivable rate—and sailing broad-hauled, at best.

And then he understood what he was seeing, and what the smoke had to signify. He had heard reports of the American armored river ships that had destroyed the Danish fleet last year. And had heard rumors that the up-timers were building ocean-going craft with the same motive power—steam—somewhere on the Baltic. Luebeck, probably. He had discounted those rumors as just more of the fear-mongering that surrounded the up-timers, who, if you were to listen to half the tales, could achieve any technological marvel they chose give a few weeks and a few tons of steel.

But these had to be those ships. Logically, their steam power was the source of both the smoke and their sudden burst of speed, which was even now making paltry nonsense of Jorge de Cárdenas y Manrique de Lara's attempt to cut them off. The up-time ships had already raced well north of his lumbering galleons, and were already starting to turn westward into a broad reach with the wind slightly abaft the beam: the very fastest position for ships with such uncommonly maneuverable and versatile rigging and spars. Although the range was too great for Fadrique to be sure, the ships' great speed actually seemed to make them more stable, cutting through the almost imperceptible swells with the ease and speed of a razor-sharp hand-plane cutting smooth the edge of a slightly frayed plank.

"Sir!" called the first mate of Álvarez's ship, the *Nuestra Señora de los Reyes*, "The chief gunners wish to know how to position their pieces. At what range do you plan to come about to commence firing upon the Dutch ships?"

Staring through his spyglass, de Toledo responded, "I shall know the answer to that question in ten minutes time, Roderigo." *Because what happens next to the north—to our rear—will decide what I do about the enemies in front of me...*

"Eight hundred yards to the first Spaniard," cried the intraship comm rating from beneath Eddie's feet.

"Very good." Eddie glanced at *Resolve*, about nine hundred yards off the starboard beam and trailing by perhaps one hundred yards. Which was according to plan. Although Pros Mund was clear about his precedence in the chain of command, he was quite content to let his young up-time commander establish the pace of operations, set an example by acting first, and arguably, become a likely scapegoat if things did not go as planned.

But judging from the way the Spanish were reacting, it seemed that those plans were unfolding as envisioned. They were heading straight at the *Intrepid* and *Resolve* in a kind of elongated pack, the five heaviest galleons clumped relatively close to the rear of their van, three slightly lighter ones arrayed in a more open formation to the front. Tactically, it was a reasonable enough arrangement. Notionally, the three lighter ships were to constrain the maneuver of the two up-time cruisers, and ultimately pin them in place by engaging them. That would give the big galleons enough time to approach and gang up on the two ships in whatever fashion seemed most advantageous, surrounding them and battering them beneath the waves or into submission at murderously close range.

Eddie lowered his binoculars and watched the high-pooped Spanish ships persist in lumbering toward him in a close-reach, even though they had lost the weather gauge. And again, why wouldn't they, given their presumedly decisive superiority in guns and numbers? It was typical of battles in the decades before the advent of line-tactics. Ships more or less headed towards each other in much the same way that opposing rugby teams formed a scrum. They rushed together, usually trying to achieve some initial positional advantage that was quickly forgotten as the battle became the maritime equivalent of a dog-piling brawl. If the speed and responsiveness of the contending ships were more or less equal, it was typical that neither managed to attain the upper hand. What resulted resembled, to Eddie's sensibilities, a demolition derby where the contestants had big cannons and attempted to board, rather than ram, each other. However, the devolution into this boxing-match in a broom closet was not a consequence of choice, so much as it reflected a kind of grim necessity. In addition to the difficulty of maintaining control over widely arrayed fleets, it was also unusual for ships to attempt to fire their broadside armament beyond two hundred yards because of both the poor accuracy and drastic reduction in striking power of balls fired at those ranges. Besides, trained gunnery crews were fortunate to get one shot off every two minutes, in part because the guns were so irregular and cumbersome, and in part because the use of bagged powder was, for reasons both traditional and technical, not much practiced yet. So wise captains of the 1630's tended to hold their fire until the ships were "at pistol shot"—meaning one hundred yards, give or take—before they really began firing in earnest.

And even so, despite what seemed the murderously close range and immense cannons of those exchanges, most combats between ships were ultimately decided by musketry and boarding actions. Comparatively few vessels sank outright during battle, although many were so badly battered that they had to be scuttled. Too unreliable because of the damage to both their hulls and spars, heavily damaged vessels were frequently more impediments than they were prizes. Unable to keep up with the truly functional ships, and likely to capsize in even moderately high seas, many a riddled hull was finally surrendered to the sea bottom by those who had taken her at no small cost in powder and blood.

And here were the Spanish, following all the best practices of their day. Which was not in itself scorn-worthy. Even if their galleons were considerably smaller than the two up-time cruisers, they were far more numerous, sported far more and bigger guns, and could still effect boarding actions, given the great height of their poop decks, which the Spanish still conceived as "war-towers."

The only thing that bemused Eddie was that, despite the sudden and unprecedented burst of speed displayed by the two USE cruisers, the Spanish had not changed their formation. Perhaps they were still trying to decide what to do, or perhaps, given how unfavorable the wind was now, they simply intended to keep making whatever headway they could, with the intent of coming about to deliver a broadside once the big enemy ships got close enough.

But that was not going to happen today. Nor was Eddie going to steam into the middle of the Spanish van to invite the accretion of yet another maritime scrum. He leaned toward the speaking tube that led down to engineering. "More steam, please. Comm rating?"

"Yes, sir?"

"Signal *Resolve* that we are commencing evolution Delta. Report when they reply and comply."

"Yes, sir!"

"Mr. Svantner?"

"Aye, sir?"

"Bring us two points to port, and ahead three-quarters."

The intership radioman called up from below. "Sir? Admiral Mund has received, understood, and is carrying out evolution Delta."

"Excellent. Rik?"

"Sir?"

"Instruct Mount One to bear upon the second Spaniard, the more southerly one. I want a firing solution within the minute."

"The southerly one, sir?"

"Yes. Of the two, she's at longer range and we're turning to cross her at an angle. Mund will be doing the same to the northern, closer Spaniard. I want him to have the easier target."

"You are most considerate, sir."

I am most practical. Mund has worked his gunnery crews as well as he knows how, but he's just learning himself. Intrepid's accuracy is almost ten percent better, particularly with the deck guns.

Rik followed up his comment with a report. "Mount One indicates they have a solution." He smiled. "The gunnery chief expresses his hope that the commander does not believe that it takes him a whole minute to acquire a target, sir."

"I'm quite aware of that, Rik. But today I need the solutions to be correct, and triple checked, rather than quick. There's a morale war we're waging here, as well, although the Spanish don't know it yet."

"And what morale war is that, Commander?" asked Gjedde from his left side.

Eddie looked over. "The war to break their spirit by convincing them that they are facing a foe so precise and lethal that it makes no sense to stand against him. I don't want a lot of misses, today. And we've got the right weather for shooting. Pretty calm seas, with both wind and current following, now that we've got the weather gauge on them. So there's minimal chop, and what little there is, we're counteracting with our propulsion: we're cutting through those little waves without a bump. All good news for our gunners. And all bad news for the Spanish. And by the time we've fired three rounds, I want them thinking that retreat or surrender are their only reasonable options."

Rik stepped back into the group at the front of the flying bridge. "Mount One reports a triple-checked firing solution, sir. Range is six-hundred-eighty yards. The Spaniard is trying to turn into us, but she's still close-hauled and sluggish. We'll have a target that's in three-quarter profile."

"Very good. Confirm that Mount One is loaded with solid shot and tell them to stand by. Has Mount Two signaled she can bear on the target, as well?"

"Just a few moments ago, sir. They're getting a solution, now. Range is now just over six hundred yards, sir."

Eddie sighed softly. *Which means it's showtime. This is what we trained for. And this is where we see if all our fine technology will perform, and if Admiral Simpson really knew what he was doing when he put me in charge of all this high-octane machinery and all these brave men.* And, somewhere behind that self-focused anxiety, Eddie remained aware that, today, success for him would ineluctably mean death for dozens, probably hundreds, of Spanish sailors and soldiers.

"Mount One reports ready and tracking, Commander." Rik's voice was a little tense, was clearly the verbal equivalent of a light jog to his elbow.

Eddie exhaled. "Mount One may fire at will. Mount Two?"

"Has a solution, now, Commander."

But Eddie was watching Mount One's chief gunner, now perched on a removable observer's pulpit, attached to the side-gunshield of the eight-inch naval rifle. Watching both the swells and the interferometer from that greater height, he leaned forward, like a hunter about to spring after prey—

His order to fire was immediately drowned out by the roar of the naval rifle. With well-trained speed, the gun crew had the breech open, and were already swabbing it.

Eddie saw this only peripherally. His eyes were on the galleon only five-hundred-fifty yards off his starboard bow, where a tall plume jetted upward about ten yards short and to the left side of the enemy ship.

The gun-chief's fulminations in Swedish and German, at himself and his men, were quite audible all the way back on the bridge. In point of fact, it had been an excellent first shot, and Eddie found himself strangely relaxed as he gave the next order to Rik almost casually over his shoulder. "Mount Two, fire when ready."

Mount One was loading another round when the *Intrepid*'s second eight-inch naval rifle roared from abaft the bridge and sent its solid shell through the foremainsail of the galleon, only three yards above the deck.

"Mount One is to fire when ready. Mount Two is to load explosive shell, adjust, and fire."

"Yes, sir!" Rik almost shouted, as Eddie looked

down at his watch. Thirty-one seconds since Mount One had fired. Any moment now, she should be—

Mount One thundered again, smoke geysering out toward the galleon.

The shell went into the Spaniard's hull just two yards under the gunwale amidships, but the extent and nature of the damage was not immediately visible as dust, splinters, and debris vomited outward in a wedge-shaped cloud. By the time it had settled, there was more smoke rising up from the deck of the Spaniard. Clearly, the shell had hit something substantial and easily flammable on that first gun deck. Otherwise, the eight-inch shell would quite possibly have exited the hull on the other side.

With the smoke of the impact clearing, the full scope of the damage was now evident. An immense hole with a saw-toothed periphery had been ripped out of the galleon's side. One gun and its crew were nowhere to be seen. The piece adjoining it was over on its side and figures struggled and flopped fitfully in the distant gloom of that savaged center gun deck.

"Mount One is asking if it should load explosive, Commander," Rik asked.

"Tell them to stand by, and continue tracking. The next shell from Mount Two could end the engagement."

"Aye, sir," acknowledged Rik, just as Mount Two thundered behind them.

Eddie prepared himself for the resulting impact by visualizing the effect of the explosive shell on the carrack he had sunk off St. Hirta island, months ago. He had been careful to recall every detail of that explosion, of the discorporating ship, of the shattered bodies, so that he would be prepared for this moment.

But he wasn't. The shell tore into the ship just where the stairs that led down from the poop deck met the maindeck. Entering at a slight angle, it sent splintered wood and gunnery gear in all directions. A flash of powder—probably a readied fusing-quill—touched off as the shell passed deeper into the ship.

In the next moment, the forward frame of the poop deck seemed to blast outward, flame and smoke vomiting through rents made by the murderous pressure that now shot outward and upward through its riven timbers. Fragments—of chandlery, stored spars, cooking pots—ripped skyward through the pilot's post atop the poop deck. The mizzenmast went over, taking out the port quarter rail and several of the mainsail's stays.

The human costs were hard to make out at five-hundred-fifty yards range, but Eddie hesitated before raising the 10x binoculars to his eyes. He knew he needed to assess the enemy ship's state of readiness, but was not eager to see the carnage at a corrected equivalent of fifty-five yards.

Thankfully, the wounded and dead were all below the screening sides of the gunwale. Most of the fever-pitch activity about the deck was concerned with providing aid to the wounded or dragging the fallen out of the way. A swarm of sail-handlers were streaming aft, some reinforcing the mainsails' remaining stays, others starting aloft to rig new lines. Harder to see, on the port side of the spar deck, hurrying men with axes and buckets were wreathed in a steadily growing plume of smoke from below decks. It was unclear if they, or the fire they were fighting, were going to be the winners in their desperate contest. Along the gun decks, blood-smeared gunners heaved splintered wood, ruined tools, and no small number of bodies out the two gaping holes in her starboard side.

Meaning that, although the ship was stricken, she was still capable of putting herself in order for combat. And the troops aboard her, their morions and pieces bobbing as they crowded toward the starboard side, were clearly still spoiling for a fight. Whatever criticisms you might lay at the foot of Spanish soldiers and sailors, you couldn't fault them for a lack of courage. But unfortunately, that meant that Eddie had to give an order he'd hoped to avoid.

Perhaps Rik was reading his mind again. "Do we take them under fire once more, Commander?"

"Yes, Rik, but not with the deck-guns. I want Mounts One and Two to commence tracking our next target." Eddie pointed to the next ship on the extreme southern side of the Spanish formation, which the *Intrepid* would pass still farther to the south, thereby fulfilling its mission as the lower pincer of evolution Delta.

"So, a broadside from the carronades to sink the Spaniard, then?"

"Well, I'd be happy not to sink her, Rik. Remember, the Dutch have a lot more crew than they have hulls. Any Spaniard we can take as a prize is an addition to our fleet. So, solid shot in the carronades. Tell Svantner to bring us one point to starboard and hold her steady. Get me to within four hundred yards of the Spaniard so the battery has a decent shot."

Rik nodded as he cut hand signals in Svantner's direction. "Very good, sir. But four hundred yards won't score nearly as many hits as if we press in to three hundred."

Eddie smiled. "Yeah, as I taught you, Rik. But we

can't spare the time to maneuver closer. And actually, I'm counting on a few extra misses at four hundred yards. Firing at three hundred yards would be overkill."

"Would be what?"

"I'll explain later. Pass the word."

Rik was already sending the orders to the gun deck.

Admiral Pros Mund watched eagerly, greedily, and, he had to admit, with a measure of envy, as *Intrepid* steamed swiftly around the extreme southern flank of the Spanish, quickly found the range of the closest ship, and, after two misses, put two shells into the hull's center of mass. An impressive feat of gunnery, even given the current favorable conditions.

But now it is my turn, to defeat my foes and please my king. Unbidden, he recalled the image of Edel's strong but aloof profile, staring hatefully at the snowy lumps and naked peaks of the Icelandic coast, and thought: *and if Christian is pleased enough, then maybe I can also bring her to a place where she will smile once again.*

Resolve, engines vibrating beneath Pros Mund's feet, had worked her way beyond the north extents of the approaching Spanish van. The only exception were the three *pataches* that had almost comically attempted to deny the steamship the weather gauge. Their captains, either showing that they had better sense or better speed than those aboard the galleons, ultimately scattered like so many cream-winged pigeons as the tremendous speed of the up-time ship left them struggling to react swiftly enough. Stranded between and behind the now fully opened pincers formed by the *Intrepid* running along the southern edge of the Spanish van and the *Resolve* skimming along its northern edge, the Spanish *patache*s were now circling, as if uncertain what to do. With the wind turning so it was more from the north, flight to the northeast along the comparatively treacherous windward side of the Lesser Antilles was becoming increasingly problematic. The wind could, instead, catch them in irons, or buffet them back toward their own fleet, or down upon the *Achilles*. But she was a big ship, outgunning them by at least two to one, and more than that by far in weight of shot per broadside. In the time it took for them to get the weather gauge on her, night would be falling and the steamships might be back. On reflection, Pros admitted, it was easy to understand why the *patache*s were biding their time, waiting for some indication of which course of action might prove most prudent.

Haakon, Mund's first mate, approached and bowed. "Admiral Mund, we are at four hundred yards, as you instructed. Orders?"

Mund nodded. "Do Mounts One and Two have the gauge—er, have firing solutions for the Spaniard?"

"Yes, sir."

"They are loaded with solid shot?"

"Yes, sir."

"Then tell them to fire at once and await reloading orders."

"Yes, sir." Mere moments later, both of his ship's great guns spoke. Two geysers appeared in front of the enemy ship, bracketing it to left and right.

"Load solid shot, adjust, fire when ready," he shouted to the orderly, who relayed the orders into the speaking tubes.

On the Spanish ships, musketeers were beginning to ascend into the rigging, finding comparatively stable spots higher up on the ratlines.

Mount One spoke shortly before Mount Two, and put a shell into the low-slung bow of the Spanish galleon, the bowsprit coming down with a crash, stripping off stays and planking that trailed, foaming, in the water along her port side. The shell from Mount Two fell short rather than long this time, but only by fifteen yards.

"Load with explosive shell," Mund said, and told himself he did not feel a thrill to give that order. "And fire at will."

Mount One spoke first, again, and put her shell into the Spaniard's fo'c'sle. Planks, rails, bodies flew up in a blast of dust and smoke, snapping two bow stays of the foremast as the ship veered sharply to port. A moment later, the second shell sliced into the ship's deck just a few feet to the port side of the mainmast, penetrating both the spar and the layered hardwoods of the shaft in which it was set. The explosion was sharp and fierce. Deckplanks sprayed in all directions as the thunderclap of smoke and woodchips sent the mainmast several yards into the air, stripping free of its stays and shrouds, the main topgallant snapping away from the main spar of the mast, sails flying wildly about as if signaling distress. That cyclone of splintering spars severed another foremast stay and the fore topgallant teetered and shook, a telltale sign that the entire mast was in jeopardy.

"She's all but dead in the water," exulted Haakon as they passed abreast of the crippled galleon, "A broadside to finish her off?"

"No, we move to the next target." Mund gestured to the next Spanish ship, a smaller galleoncete, another five hundred yards farther west. "Our job is to work along both sides of their van, crippling ships so that we and the Dutch may take them as prizes later. This ship has only the use of her mizzen, and has fires to control, beside. She will not escape, and cannot maneuver to return fire. If she tries, the Dutch will cross her bow and sweep her decks with grape." *Although* I *want to take her, blast them.* I *want—*I *need—the honors, the favor, of my king.* "Order more steam, and as soon as we have it, ahead full."

"Sir?" Haakon asked carefully. "We are already at the speed that was set—by you—for this phase of plan Beta."

"Plans change, Haakon." Mund drew his sword and nodded to the ensign of the Wild Geese whom he'd put in charge of his boarding team. "The sun is going down and we can have a more decisive victory if we hurry. And perhaps we can yet board a rich prize for the glory of our king." Mund's small, rare smile caused his subordinate to blink in surprise. "We have only begun to hunt, Haakon."

Chapter 38

Grenada Passage, Caribbean Sea

Fadrique Álvarez de Toledo had seen enough to know that the day was lost, and that the most valuable thing he could do now was to save what was left of His Imperial Majesty's fleet and report the presence of these extraordinarily swift and lethal up-time ships to the governor of Havana. If he was able to pull away in good enough order and his ships were not scattered by fleeing into the approaching night, he would dispatch a *patache* to inform Cartagena, as well. But those lazy Tierra Firma bastards had not even been reliable enough to show up for this fight. Although, seen objectively, it was probably a fortunate thing that they hadn't.

Whatever guns were on those two up-time ships, they were like nothing he'd ever seen or even heard rumors of, with the exception of last year's shelling of Hamburg. There, the up-time ironclads had reduced the heavy walls of that city to pulverized gravel in a matter of hours. And if these guns were not quite as devastating in their effects as rumor had described

those long cannons, they were accurate and lethal at
ranges that made the ships carrying them almost completely unapproachable. Fadrique had watched as the
two long, fast ships split apart, bracketing and running
along the northern and southern fringes of Jorge de
Cárdenas y Manrique de Lara's van of eight galleons.
In minutes, and firing from almost six hundred yards,
the two ships had, with less than half a dozen shots
each, disabled the two leading galleons. And unless
he was much mistaken, several of those shells had
carried explosives within them, almost like mortars.
Then the southernmost up-time ship had unloaded a
broadside into its target from the almost unthinkable
range of four hundred yards. More unthinkable still
was the accuracy and effects of the enemy carronades.
The galleon had literally reeled under the force of the
blast; its mainmast fell immediately, and an already
thin trail of smoke became thicker and darker. Now,
as the shadows were starting to lengthen, that hull,
the *San Salvador*, was listing severely to starboard and
putting out increasing volumes of smoke.

And as if to prove that these results were the rule
rather than the exception when fighting against these
up-time ships, they had now completed savaging the
next two galleons along their path. Once again, they
had used the long guns that were mounted high
on their weather decks and that had sharp reports,
almost like thunderclaps, when they discharged. On
this occasion, it was the northernmost of the up-time
ships which then fired a *coup de grace* broadside,
apparently of exploding shells.

It was hard to discern the range at which the
up-time ship had unleashed that broadside. Álvarez

de Toledo hypothesized it might have been as little as two hundred yards since its smaller target, the galleoncete *La Concepcion*, had fired back, probably more in defiance than out of any reasonable hope of scoring a hit. And it was impossible to know exactly how many hits had been scored upon the galleoncete or where. But to Fadrique's trained ear, it did indeed sound as if all the shells of that broadside were tipped with explosives. Because after the thunderous crashing and eruptions of smoke were over, *La Concepcion* was still there, meaning it wasn't her magazine that had been struck, despite the sound. But she was fiercely aflame from stem to stern and settling rapidly into the water, listing to port. If Fadrique had still been a betting man, he'd have predicted she'd burn to the waterline by ten o'clock and would roll and go down at about midnight.

But if he had any say in the matter, neither he nor any of his ships would be here to see either of those moonlit events. He swung his glass around to gauge the range to the Dutch: five hundred yards. If he turned to port and came about one-hundred-eighty degrees, he would put more distance between his ships and theirs before heading due west to catch the following wind and so, escape with all haste. He would use that wind to run overnight and regather his ships come dawn. If there was no sign of pursuit, he could then start working his way across the great central expanse of the Caribbean, tacking to make northern progress toward Santiago, the closest place of Spanish strength.

But that portside turn would take him through the very eye of the wind, and his galleons were finicky when tacking. They lost way so quickly that there was always the chance that, if the breeze died as they began to turn into it, that they might not tack across but struggle through baffling winds or, worse yet, get caught in irons. In which case the Dutch, whose ships could sail closer hauled, would catch them astern.

But the alternative, a hard turn to starboard, had its own risks. Yes, it put the wind behind him almost immediately since he only had to make a ninety degree turn, but he was still sailing obliquely toward the northbound Dutch. And at this range—

—well, at this range, he hadn't the time for indecision. "Roderigo, tell the pilot hard a starboard as tight as she'll take it."

"Admiral!" cried Roderigo, "that could bring us within two hundred yards of the Dutch guns, closer if they read our intent correctly."

"We've no choice. Do as I say, and signal the other ships to do so at once as well."

"Yes, sir. I shall—"

There was a cry from the foretop crow's next. "Smoke! Smoke off the starboard bow! And sails!"

De Toledo cursed, swung up his spyglass, and felt a bitter cold in his belly that threatened to unman him. Sharply outlined against the western horizon was a single, thin, but rapidly advancing plume of smoke and the sails of three sizable fore-and-aft rigged vessels: outsized jachts or *pataches*. Bigger than his *pataches*, at any rate. And that smoke could only mean one thing.

"Sir," Roderigo asked hoarsely, "what is it? What are they?"

"The third side of the trap," Fadrique answered bitterly. "And that smoke is yet another of these blasted up-time steam ships. I cannot tell how big it is—those ships are too far off—but it hardly matters. If we turn due west to catch the wind, they shall cut us off. They can sail closer to the wind and are heading northward, across our line of withdrawal."

"So what do we—?"

"We still come about hard to starboard, but we keep turning. Take us through a one-hundred-thirty-five degree turn, so that our final bearing is north by northwest. That and due north are the only open sides of this box ambush they've sprung upon us. And of the two, the northwest allows us to keep the wind over our starboard quarter. We should be able to outrun them. Maybe. Pass the order."

"Yes, sir." Roderigo tarried a moment, concern in his dark brown eyes. "And the rest of our fleet? What of them?"

De Toledo looked behind to the northeast. The southernmost of the up-timer ships was starting to fire on a third galleon, while the northernmost steamship was leaping ahead even faster, bearing down directly upon its third target, de Cárdenas' own flagship, the *San Miguel*. The up-time ship's angle of approach suggested an intent to board. "Roderigo," Fadrique breathed heavily in answer, "the rest of our fleet is already lost. Now let us go, and hope we can avoid being crippled by the Dutch guns as we make our escape."

"Commander Cantrell, a message from Admiral Tromp!" the voice from below decks was surprised but pleased.

"Read it off, rating."

The rating complied. "Message begins. Tromp commanding *Amelia* to Commanders *Resolve* and *Intrepid*. Stop. Radio signal from Gijszoon. Stop. Has rendezvoused with *Eendracht*, steam pinnace, and prize *patache*. Stop. Currently twelve miles west of my van. Stop. Maneuvering to deny Spanish escape to west. Stop. Spanish ships coming about to flee. Stop. Have taken two under fire, attempting to intercept. Stop. May be delayed reaching your area of engagement to help with crewing of prizes. Stop. Will update on pursuit of Spanish soonest. Stop. Message ends."

"Well, Floriszoon and the earl of Tyrconnell showing up now: that's a pleasant surprise!" exclaimed Rik brightly.

Gjedde nodded. "Yes, but that's not." He pointed almost due north as *Intrepid*'s Mount Two roared and put a final shell into the third galleon's sterncastle, flame and smoke gushing out all her shattering windows as the explosive shell went off deep inside her.

Eddie followed Gjedde's finger past the devastated galleon and suppressed a gasp. Even from this distance, it was clear that *Resolve* had not merely closed to broadside range with one of the largest galleons, but could only mean to board her. "My God, what is Mund doing? We agreed that neither of us would—"

Gjedde shook his head; he looked sad but oddly unsurprised. "Pros Mund is the admiral. He is the one person who may elect not to follow the orders that were agreed upon."

"But then why didn't he radio, let us know—?"

"Commander Cantrell," Gjedde said sadly, slowly. "Let us move to the next ship, and try to signal

Admiral Mund. And let us shift two points to star-board as we do so."

"Tuck more tightly to the north? Why? Do you want to start boarding galleons now, as well?"

"No, Commander Cantrell. I want to be closer to *Resolve.* In case something goes wrong."

You mean, "more wrong," thought Eddie, but instead he shouted, "Mr. Svantner! Two points to starboard and give me some more steam. We may be changing our plans."

Pros Mund's heart leaped up as the great galleon's mainmast came down. The long pennant that announced it as the flagship of the fleet's admiral went over the side with the topmain spar and disappeared into the wreckage-strewn waters.

After finding the range, his deck gunners had put three solid and three explosive shells into the galleon, which he had feared might sink her. But the towering Spanish ship with a looming broadside of twenty-six-, forty-two- and thirty-six-pounders proved that sheer mass was a quality unto itself. The heavy timbers of the craft were rent in many places, putting out smoke from several, but it remained seaworthy and upright.

The same could not be claimed for a great many of her crew, however. Her top decks were a writhing mass of sailhandlers attempting to save the fore and mizzen, seamen struggling to douse fires, muske-teers trying to find enough calm among the chaos to keep a bead on the approaching up-time ship, and a foot-tangling mass of dead and wounded comrades. Along the gun decks, four of the guns had spoken in response, but at slightly better than one-hundred-fifty yards, only one had scored a hit. It was respectable shooting, actually, but futile. The ball had rebounded from the *Resolve*'s stout reinforced timbers, its only effect having been to leave a significant dent in them.

"One hundred and twenty yards!" cried Haakon from the deck.

"Helm," shouted Mund, "one point to starboard. Haakon, as soon as we're alongside the Spaniard, fire portside battery. Mitrailleuses,"—Mund had moved both to the same side of the ship for this very reason—"prepare to concentrate fire upon the enemy's quarterdeck."

The *Resolve* straightened from her starboard correction, and the portside carronades, all fourteen of them, roared, sending jets of smoke toward the Spaniard that quickly diffused, forming a single, cloudy smear that veiled the other ship.

But even through those drifts of gunpowder-fog, Mund could see that eight of his fourteen eight-inch carronades had struck the galleon, including one of the three he had loaded with explosive shell. The ruin along the first gun deck was unlike anything he'd seen before. Half the strakes were broken at least two places and the interior explosion ejected a spray of gear, balls, and bodies from deep within the Spaniard. The scene on the deck was more frenzied still, with the new casualties and growing panic undermining the ongoing attempts to put the ship a-right for combat. And now that the smoke was clearing, he could see that the quarterdeck, the logical location of both the admiral and a guard of his best marksmen, was returning to order noticeably faster than the rest of the weather deck. That was almost surely a sign that effective commands were still being issued and followed, there.

Haakon was shouting a warning at the same moment that Pros Mund pointed his drawn sword at the Spaniard's quarterdeck and shouted, "Mitrailleuses, fire on the quarterdeck!"

The .50 caliber multibarreled guns began firing rapidly. The two weapons emitted a rippling roar and their stream of projectiles played in tight arcs back and forth across the galleon's quarterdeck.

Mund discovered that he had stopped exhaling in mid-breath. He had seen carnage aplenty in his years before the mast: waves of musketry sweeping decks; cannon balls blasting through bulkheads, sending forth a wide spray of daggerlike splinters that sliced men to ribbons. But nothing prepared him for this: the methodical and relentless cone of death that walked back and forth upon the Spaniard's high quarterdeck with terrible precision and even more terrible lethality. Probably two-thirds of the rounds fired passed high, splintered rails, or chewed at the hull's side, but the one third that did hit dropped men in windrows and shattered every object they hit. The tiller was riven, the compass stand blasted, lights shattered, flag boxes riddled. The bullets not only went through the breast plates of the crowded soldiers, but out the back as well, still carrying enough force to slay men behind the first. But unlike the broad sprays of blood he associated with wide, slow-moving musket balls, these bullets simply rose a brief, maroon-colored puff, or left no external sign whatsoever—and seemed all the more haunting, for that. It was as if the bullets themselves were too focused on killing to make any sign that they had done so, were too busy finding another life to extinguish or limb to maim.

Mund was still staring at the abattoir that had been the crowded poop of the Spaniard when the questioning cry came from the rear mitrailleuse mount. "Do we reload, Admiral?"

"Yes," barked Mund, rousing from his fixated daze and leaping down the steps of the running bridge to join the boarders sheltering behind the portside gunwales. Most were Irish, who he had always heard were a rather loud and raucous lot. But now, as they waited to join the combat, they were among the most silent and ferociously focused troops he had ever seen. "Three points port," he shouted over his shoulder at the pilot. "Bring us alongside her to board." Mund envisioned Edel smiling again, smiling as they neared a new land grant, this one back home in Denmark, maybe along the coast near Skaelskor...

"Admiral!" shouted Haakon again.

Edel and her elusive smile had been swept away by Haakon's cry. "Damn it, man, what is amiss?" he asked sharply, scanning the Spaniard for signs of trouble.

His eyes gave him the answer the same moment Haakon did. "Swivel guns up along the bow, Admiral. Get down—!"

It hardly seemed fair, Mund reflected, as he saw a half-dozen Spaniards swinging their hastily remounted small guns in the direction of his boarders. *Resolve*'s first hits upon the Spaniard had been in her forecastle, had started a fire there and left bodies draped over her gunwale and caught in her spritsail sheets. But Spanish professionalism was not to be underestimated. Even before they brought the fires under control, some of the troops at her waist had evidently discerned that the sides of the up-time ship were too high to allow them to engage her weather deck from their own. So they had sought a better vantage point by relocating to the greater altitude of the fo'c'sle and poop. So a good number of the midship's swivel guns—a mix of falconets, patereroes, morterettes, and espingoles—had been moved to yokes on the bow. It was not part of a subtle scheme to initiate counterfire from a part of the galleon that its attackers might reasonably conclude was no longer in the fight. Rather, it was a product of dumb luck and the training and dogged resolve of professional soldiers who insisted on finding a way to strike back, even when higher orders were no longer forthcoming.

Mund turned to order his own swivel guns on the starboard side, the two-inch "Big Shots" of down-time manufacture, to fire upon their Spanish equivalents. As he did, the morion-helmeted Spanish leaned over their pieces and discharged them in a ragged volley. Pros Mund saw Haakon diving for cover, thought that he should have done so himself before shouting his most recent order, felt a rapid patter of dull thumps in his chest, saw Edel's disapproving frown—

And then he saw nothing at all.

Eddie Cantrell's foul-mouthed alcoholic father had always been outraged when any of his children emulated his colorful use of language. He had communicated that displeasure with either a tongue- or a belt-lashing. So Eddie had come to adulthood with a reflexive tendency to avoid cursing. However, when the *Resolve* sent a second broadside into the ship she had closed with, he let out an oath between clenched teeth.

Although his eyes were still locked to his binoculars,

he could hear Gjedde shift alongside him, imagined the Norwegian staring at him. "Is Mund boarding her?"

"No," Eddie grumbled, "he's destroyed her."

As if on cue, the broadside—evidently all explosive shells—went off within the galleon, which seemed to fly apart. The last two masts went down, the mizzen cartwheeling into the water. The sterncastle and forecastle both seemed to detonate from within, planks, window frames, bodies flying outward in a shower of general destruction—

The magazine went up with a roar like two fast thunderclaps. The flash it made was reminiscent of the nighttime battleship gunnery duels that Eddie had seen on the newsreel footage included in countless documentaries on the History Channel. It wasn't just one great light, but a kind of quick-strobe effect of overlapping explosions. An all-obscuring blanket of white smoke fumed outward furiously, catching the slightly roseate light of the descending sun as it did.

Rik swallowed nervously. "How close was *Resolve* when—?"

Eddie sighed. "One hundred yards, maybe a little more. They're safe, but will be catching some of the debris on their deck. Damn it, I wonder what happened, why Mund decided to—?"

"Commander Cantrell," the intraship comm rating called up. "Mounts One and Two report they continue to track our target and are loaded with explosive. Awaiting your orders."

Eddie suppressed yet another sigh and swung his glasses toward the fourth galleon on his target list. She was coming about and starting to make some headway in her attempt to run to the northwest. Not that it mattered. The best she could do was three knots, if she was lucky. *Intrepid* was already doing ten and Eddie could call for more, if needed. "Range?" Eddie asked lazily. Strange how the combat gunnery that had been a nail-biting novelty forty minutes ago had become a comparatively dull routine.

"Five hundred fifty yards, sir."

"Fire at will. Reload and maintain tracking but check fire."

Although Eddie was eager to see *Resolve* emerge from the now-thinning smoke of the vaporized galleon, he forced himself to watch his guns' effects upon their present target. One shell struck the fo'c'sle, penetrating deeply before exploding. Timbers and smoke roiled outward, a cannon upended and disappeared off the opposite side of the shattered weather deck. The second shell passed into the stern windows of the galleon and went off after a beat. It made a muffled noise, and smoke started trailing out the ruined captain's cabin about the same moment that the ship's rudder seemed to loosen and the breeze in the sails tugged the ship into a more westerly course.

"She's sailing before the wind now, rudderless," commented Gjedde. "The shell probably exploded somewhere near her whipstaff or tiller-chains."

Rik nodded, turned toward Eddie. "Shall we come close enough to let the carronades fire some canister-shot into her sails?"

Eddie shrugged. "Even if we didn't, she can't steer, so she's going nowhere fast. But we might as well slow her down a little, even so." He aimed his next query down at the comm ratings working beneath below deck. "Any word from *Resolve* yet?"

"No, sir."

"Then hail them, ask for an update."

Gjedde nodded at the last ship of the Spanish fleet's eastern van. "What about her? I suspect we'll only have to put a few shells into her at range, and ask her to strike colors."

"Because of what she's seen us do to her sister ships?" asked Rik.

Eddie saw what Gjedde was getting at, shook his head. "No, because she's not *really* a sister ship. Look at her waterline, the slope of her tumblehome, the more widely spaced gun ports. She's not a galleon but a nao, a trading ship that the Spanish sometimes rearm for combat."

"She looks quite similar to the galleons," Rik observed with a dubious frown.

Gjedde nodded. "Because there's little difference when the Spanish lay down a galleon from when they lay down a nao. In an emergency, they can reequip her, as I'm sure they've done now. But she'll have a crew more accustomed to trade and running from enemy ships, rather than fighting and heading toward them. She knows she can't outrun us before dark. And, as you said, she knows what our guns can do." He folded his arms. "Since she's already running, I'd say she's half-ready to surrender. Just give her master a good excuse—two shells from the rifles—and I suspect she will strike her colors."

"Commander Cantrell," the intership radioman called up, "I have a report from the *Resolve*. From First Mate Haakon."

Eddie, Gjedde, and Rik exchanged rueful glances. "Please read the message, rating."

"Message begins. *Resolve* to *Intrepid*: Admiral Mund killed by enemy fire. Stop. First Mate Haakon in temporary command. Stop. Unaffected by explosion of galleon. Stop. Minor casualties among deck personnel from enemy swivel guns. Stop. Awaiting orders. Stop. Message ends."

The news was somewhat worse than it might have been, but it was hardly a surprise. The three officers stood quietly on the flying bridge for several long seconds. Then Eddie turned to Gjedde. "I believe this means you are now in command of our ships, Captain Gjedde. Do we continue with the second half of our plan, to chase the Spaniards' southern van?"

"We can overtake them within the hour," Rik added. He sounded eager.

Gjedde stared at the setting sun for several more seconds. "We could, but we shall not. There will not be enough light left to use our guns for very long, and to chase them will take us far away from Tromp's van. Furthermore, the *Resolve* just lost her captain who is also the only senior officer with extensive training in all the technological innovations on the ship. The section heads are all competent, but Haakon was a late addition to the command staff and did not receive enough training across these various areas of new expertise. So even if we had more light, we may not count upon the *Resolve* to perform as she might under better circumstances."

Eddie leaned back and let Rik lead the charge for action, watching Gjedde's response. "So shall we engage the *pataches*, then? They are slipping away to the south, just a few miles to port."

Again Gjedde shook his head. "They are maneuvering southwest because they are fleeing. I suspect they hope to slip between our steamships and Tromp's van, and thence, escape west into the open waters of the Caribbean, following in the wake of the Spanish southern van. They are smaller and more maneuverable, and so are much harder to hit. And there is nothing to be gained in chasing them into the dark. We have enough work ahead of us just to regroup, take what prizes we may, sink what we may not, and decide upon our next course of action."

"Not back to Trinidad as we planned, then?" Rik sounded perplexed.

Gjedde shook his head. "Not all of us."

Eddie was careful to make his observation oblique enough to avoid sounding like criticism. "With respect, Captain, we have over a hundred Wild Geese, twenty other ship's troops, and an oil-prospecting team on Trinidad. It seems we have some difficult choices to make, weighing adequate defense for them against our obvious need to tow our prizes back to St. Eustatia for refit."

Gjedde stared at Eddie but nodded. "Just so. And that is why we may not take as many prizes as we wish. As you say, we must balance how many of the spoils we may take from this battle against how much it costs us to take them at all. And I assure you, Commander, I will not leave Trinidad poorly defended. But we must make a quick run to St. Eustatia if we are to meet Trinidad's special needs, just as we must provide for the new requirements of our fleet."

"You mean, we need to bring Ann Koudsi and the drillers the gear they need to start sinking some holes?"

"That, and we need to inaugurate a new class of officers and seamen, Commander."

Eddie nodded. "Of course. There are a lot of extra sailors waiting in St. Eustatia who could be reassigned as crew for the prize vessels we take here."

Gjedde's brow seemed to wrinkle. "Yes, but that was not what I was thinking of, primarily."

"Oh, Captain? Then what new class of officers and seamen are you talking about, sir?"

"The ones you are going to train, Commander. Between these new guns, the cruisers, the steam pinnaces, the balloons, and the radios, we are now fighting a very new kind of war. And you are the person who is going to teach a new cadre of officers how to fight it. Now, Commander Cantrell, I believe we have a nao to frighten into submission before we may set about regrouping and taking our prizes."

Chapter 39

Le Grand Cul-de-Sac Marin, Guadeloupe

Jacques Dyel du Parque glanced over his shoulder out into the bay known as Le Grand Cul-de-Sac Marin, where the Dieppe-built bark *Bretagne* rode at anchor. He wished he was still on it, and bound back to Martinique. Possibly all the way back to France. He hadn't yet decided the limits (if any) of his aversion to the Leeward Islands.

His uncle, however, had no such reluctance or regrets, having made his admittedly inconstant fortunes here in the New World, and, most particularly, on St. Christopher's. Which, Jacques readily admitted, was a pleasant enough place, but seemed doomed to be overrun by the English, their Irish bondsmen, and now the Dutch. It was only a matter of time before the island's French colony would be taken over, either by martial conquest or marital cooption.

So, in an act of prudence that was also an attempt at creating a legacy (his uncle, Pierre Bélain sieur d'Esnambuc, had not married and so Jacques had come to understand that he was to be the beneficiary of his intermittent and inchoate patriarchal impulses), Jacques found himself the lieutenant governor of the two-month old colony on the island of Martinique. Which was neither as friendly to husbandry nor as hospitable as St. Christopher's, and furthermore, was the home of natives whose receptivity was, at best, uncertain. However, Uncle Pierre had met with the rather daunting Caribs on his way to fetching Jacques, and reported that the proposal he had made to them in that meeting had significantly improved the local cacique's opinion of their French neighbors/invaders. Jacques remained unsure which term better represented the native attitude toward the pale-skinned visitors, and suspected the Caribs themselves remained undecided.

After sending a skiff to fetch Jacques from his glorified shack in Fort St. Pierre, d'Esnambuc had set course directly for Guadeloupe, inquiring affectionately after his nephew's health and spirits and then immediately closeting himself with the Carib warrior who had accompanied him from Martinique. From the few words he had exchanged with his uncle since then, this fellow, Youacou, was a person of some diplomatic significance by dint of his relations. While not a cacique himself, he was well-placed for Uncle Pierre's immediate purposes. On the one hand, Youacou's maternal aunt had married a renowned hunter from the Caribs of Guadeloupe. On the other hand, Youacou's second-cousin-once-removed had been killed by Thomas Warner on St. Christopher's in 1626, at the genocidal massacre that had since acquired the eponymous label the Battle of Bloody Point. Jacques had not wanted to embarrass his uncle by inquiring how it was that Youacou had been convinced that Thomas Warner alone had been responsible for the death of his second-cousin-once-removed, since d'Esnambuc had fought alongside the English in that battle and, according to stories told by his uncle's long-standing assistants, the battle had fundamentally been fought at his urging. Warner had, it was whispered, been exceedingly reluctant to interpret deteriorating relations with the Caribs as an inevitable prelude to slaughter.

But Jacques had no opportunity to ask such ticklish questions. It was almost as if his uncle was trying to avoid him, or at least to have any sustained conversation with him while they were aboard the *Bretagne*. But now they were ashore, and Youacou had disappeared into the bushes, just as two of d'Esnambuc's men started down the beach to make contact with the French settlers here, who, having arrived almost four months ago, were still living in tents. Just around the next headland, the smoke from their cooking fires rose lazily up toward the cotton-ball clouds.

"Uncle," Jacques began mildly, "I do not know if this is a better time for us to converse?"

D'Esnambuc turned with a genuine smile. "It is, my boy. I am sorry I have had to hold you at arm's length since I spirited you away from your duties on Martinique, but it was essential that you not know just why you were being brought here."

"That sounds quite mysterious, Uncle."

"Not so much mysterious as delicate, Jacques. You remember that I spoke to you of the two men that Richelieu's agent, Fouquet, sent here to colonize Guadeloupe?"

"Yes. One was a former colonist under you at St. Christopher's: Charles Liénard de l'Olive. A bold man, you said, but not particularly politic."

"Precisely my words, I believe. Well, during his partner's absence, it seems he has further mismanaged his supplies and his relations with the Caribs of this island. I suspect he shall be raiding them for food before the year is out."

Jacques frowned. "But does this not match your expectations and hopes?" D'Esnambuc had not welcomed Fouquet's diversion of finances and assistance to the strange pair who had undertaken the settlement of Guadeloupe, and had refused their first requests for aid two months ago.

"It matches my expectations, but my hopes have changed, Jacques." He glanced at their guards, who were patrolling beyond the thin line of palm trees in whose shadows they waited. He lowered his tone so that it almost blended with the sound of the surf. "With the Dutch arriving in such great numbers on St. Eustatia, and now collaborating so freely and extensively with Warner's colony, my hopes that his settlement would wither for lack of support from England are dashed. Indeed, he now has such multitudes of workers and troops at his disposal that it is sheer inertia that keeps him from pushing us off the island altogether."

Jacques wondered if the principle of honoring one's agreements might not also work as a constraint upon the Englishman, but suspected his adventurer-uncle might not appreciate that perspective. "And our changed fortunes on St. Christopher's change your attitudes toward this Guadeloupe settlement in what way?"

"In every possible way, my boy, considering their most recent letter to me. A little less than a fortnight ago, a packet came to Basseterre in St. Christopher's. Despite much circumlocution, the letter's author, Jean du Plessis d'Ossonville, revealed that he had failed in a mission given to him by Richelieu. He was to have purchased a tract of land on Trinidad that had been seized by a group of 'adventurers' who were known—favorably—to the cardinal's allies in France."

Jacques frowned. "Will the Spanish care for such fine legal distinctions? It will not matter to them whether the land in question passed through independent hands before coming into Richelieu's grasp."

"Just as it shall not matter to the crown of France that Spain is offended. The law here in the New World, my boy, is that there is no peace beyond the Line. And even so, we did not field our flag against Spain's to come by the property. Beyond that, everything is a pesky detail of interest only to ministers-without-portfolio and historians."

Jacques shrugged. There was no arguing that almost certainly correct point. "So du Plessis failed to purchase this land on Trinidad. How does this impact our fortunes on St. Christopher's?"

Muttering, "Ah, my boy, my boy," d'Esnambuc ruffled his twenty-year-old nephew's head. Jacques put up with such inappropriately juvenile displays of affection in small part because the man expressing them had also undertaken to furnish him with a potential for wealth far beyond anything his rather neglectful father had assayed. But more so because he knew his Uncle Pierre loved him genuinely and that was worth more than all the islands and livres in the world to Jacques.

"Ah, my boy," d'Esnambuc repeated. "You have a good soul, bless you. Perhaps your prayers will redeem my sins, when I'm gone. But for now, listen and learn.

From reading between the lines in du Plessis' letter, I am quite sure that he got greedy in his negotiations with these adventurers on Trinidad. From what de l'Olive told me of him, the fellow is clever and a shrewd bargainer. But I suspect in this case, he bargained a bit too hard. He forgot that in any negotiations, whether with priests or pirates, the objective is to shear the sheep, not skin them. For if they feel the edge of the shears, even if you have them bound to your will in that moment, they will remember that injury and look to repay it to you four-fold."

Jacques wondered if Uncle Pierre was always so prudent as his advice suggested and wondered how many shear-shaped scars Thomas Warner and the other English leaders of St. Christopher bore and still reflected upon with ill-feeling.

If d'Esnambuc perceived a disjuncture between his advice and practice, he did not evince it. "So, in his most recent letter, du Plessis once again requested aid. But this time, he is not only offering to pay for the food that his intemperate partner de l'Olive has now mismanaged into nonexistence, but is offering twice the highest rate I have seen. In livres, mind you."

"So, he is willing to spend the money that was entrusted to him to purchase this land in Trinidad— embezzle it, essentially—to save his failing colony here."

"Exactly."

"So, do you mean to help them?"

"Yes, but not as they asked or expect. There is a reason I did not try to establish a colony here on Guadeloupe, Jacques, despite the fine waters of its own basse-terre and reasonable promise of husbandry."

"The Caribs."

His uncle nodded. "I have fought them once before and am in no rush to do so again. And here they are far more numerous than on Martinique. I would not have planted you in that place, my boy, unless I felt sure we could make it safe. But this place?" Pierre waved a hand dismissively toward the south. "They are thick in those volcanic valleys, and they will remain so."

Jacques frowned. "So, du Plessis and de l'Olive are worried that they must have a success to show Richelieu that will induce him to pardon their failure at Trinidad, and now, are failing here as well. And the natives are populous upon these islands and unremittingly hostile. And the English have new friends—the Dutch, no less—on St. Eustatia and so our days on St. Christopher may be numbered." He shook his head. "Yet you report all these things as if they are harbingers of some great venture that may be undertaken. I do not see it."

D'Esnambuc smiled. "As I said, you have a good heart. Now, be schooled by your uncle who shall have all his successes in this world, not the next, I am quite sure. With the arrival of the Dutch, the Caribs know that their designs to retake St. Christopher's are all but dashed. And we, being pushed out like them, find ourselves sharing islands with them. And the current representatives of France on Guadeloupe are becoming more unwelcome by the day, for the natives know what the five hundred settlers under du Plessis and de l'Olive will do once their food runs out. They will raid their primitive neighbors and take what they need. And then, as it was on St. Christopher's, it will be war to the knife. So, logically, the natives are considering taking that fateful step first. And quite soon. But the Caribs know all too well what our weapons do, how many dozens of young warriors they will lose for every one of us firing from behind the walls of our forts.

"But in this moment, the interests of both parties, Frenchman and Carib, are strangely aligned. We have a common enemy in Warner, for with the Dutch on his side, he ruins both our designs on St. Christopher's. And since he now holds Nevis and Antigua as well, and the Dutch are crawling upon St. Eustatia like maggots on a dead cat in summer, we must all come to the same conclusion independently: that time is running out. And the only way we can change that is by combining our strength."

Jacques nodded, impressed and slightly horrified by the plan implied by his uncle's analysis. "So. You approached the Caribs of Martinique and offered them an alliance in exchange for—what? The English parts of St. Christopher's?"

D'Esnambuc nodded. "For them, and for the Caribs of Guadeloupe, if they both join us in driving the English and the Dutch out. And nothing if only one aids us."

"Whereby you hope the Caribs of Martinique will press the much larger tribes of Guadeloupe to cooperate."

Uncle Pierre shrugged. "It should not be so difficult. The great cacique slain almost ten years ago on St. Christopher's—Tegreman—has much family on Martinique, including a well-respected cousin. His sister's daughter is married to the young son of the cacique here on Guadeloupe. So through those relations, we shall bring the stick of family pressure to bear upon the Caribs, even while we dangle the carrot of reclaiming two islands under their noses."

"And how do du Plessis and de l'Olive fit into this?"

D'Esnambuc pointed at the headland, from whence their scouts were already returning, waving to signal that a safe approach could now be made. "There are at least four hundred desperate Frenchmen over that rise of land. All are armed. All can teach natives how to use firearms. And all that can be done here, and on Martinique, far away from the watchful eyes of Warner and his Dutch friends."

Jacques tilted his head in uncertainty. "But Uncle, training natives to use weapons: what is the point? Where would we get so many extra weapons, and powder, and shot? And with what funds?"

"The 'where' is handily answered by having high friends in low places. You may recall that we have traded more than once with the *boucaniers* who range this far from Jamaica and Tortuga. I have had occasion to be in contact with them recently. They can provide us with almost one hundred fifty pieces, mostly old Spanish matchlocks, and no small amount of powder and shot. And all they want in return is silver."

Jacques nodded. "Which will come from the unspent purse that Richelieu sent along for the purchase of Trinidad."

"Which du Plessis and de l'Olive may eventually report purchased his Gray Eminence sole European possession of the richest of all the islands, St. Christopher, to say nothing of Nevis and Antigua, and bought goodwill and a cohabiting entente between us and the Caribs of Guadeloupe and Martinique."

D'Esnambuc rose, carefully picked up his snaphaunce

pistols from the canvas in which he had wrapped them as they sat, and started toward the scouts returning from the headland.

Jacques, following, shook sand from his own piece, and wondered aloud. "But how will we share so many islands with the Caribs? It is not feasible, in the long run, since we must turn their jungles and grasslands into cane and cotton fields. How will we resolve that problem?"

D'Esnambuc turned, smiled crookedly, shrugged and shook the pistols he held in his hands. "With these," he answered. "Now, let's meet these two fools from Dieppe."

Jacques had to admit that his uncle's uncharitable characterization of the two governors of the Guadeloupe settlement was, nonetheless, accurate. De l'Olive was a great fool, as could be determined within two minutes of meeting him. Bombastic, self-important, and with a heightened sensitivity to both real and imagined social slights, he was a man perpetually prepared to do battle with anyone and anything, and not for any particularly good reason. He was a fixture of French provincial farce come to life.

Du Plessis was the more educated and measured of the two, whose one crucial failing made him a lesser fool, but arguably a more dangerous one. Although intelligent and shrewd, he believed himself to be far more intelligent and shrewd than he actually was. Jacques was fairly certain that, if one was able to peruse a dossier of his past blunders, one of which had reportedly landed his family in debt and near-disgrace, they would all reveal a common thread. Namely, that du Plessis was ever and again snatching a baffling defeat from the jaws of almost certain victory. He was that species of man who would fail, time after time, and remain mystified how it could occur to one so mentally gifted and incisive as himself. And so he would ultimately bring ruin upon all unlucky enough to cast their fortunes in along with his.

This was clearly the case unfolding here in Guadeloupe. The squalor, short-tempers, and thin, hungry faces of the sprawling, unclean tent-city that was His Majesty's colony of Grande Terre read like a still-life of imminent disaster. And the look on du Plessis' face as he heard Pierre Bélain d'Esnambuc calmly and patiently unfold his bold plan was that of a man who was so distracted by his "inexplicable" failure at reversing the catastrophe rising around him, that he could neither admit to, nor even fully perceive, the brilliance of the seasoned adventurer who had come to offer him an alternative that reconfigured so many of their enemies and obstructions into assets.

Strangely, it was de l'Olive who embraced d'Esnambuc's strategies first, possibly out of an old instinct for following his former and usually successful leader. Or possibly because the hinge upon which the plan turned was all-out war. His first and last comment on it was as self-defining a statement as Jacques had ever heard come from a human. "I like a plan that allows me to cut through our problems with a sweep of my sword. I'm with you, on this!"

D'Esnambuc nodded, pleased, turned toward du Plessis. "And you, Jean, how about you?"

"Eh? I suppose it is quite prudent, quite well reasoned out. Actually. But I am unsure how Touman, the local cacique, will react to it."

"We'll know soon enough."

Du Plessis frowned. "I do not understand."

Uncle Pierre shrugged. "I sent Youacou, a Carib warrior from Martinique, ahead to invite him to a meeting."

"Here? In my camp?"

"Where else should one leader meet another? And he has my guarantee of safe-conduct, so you'd best tell your guards to be particularly polite when they receive him."

Du Plessis and de l'Olive exchanged looks, then de l'Olive nodded to one of the three lieutenants they had present. That bearded fellow left the rude table made of planking and headed for the sentry post that watched over the approaches from the southern, volcanic lobe of the island.

"Excellent," d'Esnambuc nodded. "He will be here soon, so I must make haste to explain the other reason why we must not delay in carrying out this plan. There is a new threat to our interests here in the New World."

Du Plessis perked up. "You are referring to the up-timers, of course."

For the first time in years, Jacques saw his uncle genuinely start in surprise. "You know?"

"I know one of them had managed to sway the mercenary colonel on Trinidad away from doing business with the agents of France. I know that he seemed to be in league with the Dutch. And I know if I see one such instance of cooperation, there must be others."

"There are indeed other instances of cooperation," d'Esnambuc affirmed with a vigorous nod. "According to the merchants in my own town of Basseterre who trade regularly with the English, two large up-time ships powered by steam made port in Oranjestad some weeks ago, then left. They came with other ships, about half a dozen, that had all been sent under the aegis of the USE or the Union of Kalmar, and they have delivered much needed stores to the Dutch."

Du Plessis seemed to grow pale. "If they manage to reinforce the Dutch position on St. Eustatia—"

D'Esnambuc nodded slowly, his gaze compelling the other Frenchman not to look away. "Then we are done. Beyond all hope. We already see that the Dutch are making common cause with the disowned English of St. Christopher, Barbados, the Bahamas, Bermuda. If the USE has decided to pursue interests along with them in the New World—"

"They have," du Plessis stated flatly. "That was why Richelieu was interested in the land in Trinidad."

Jacques understood du Plessis' reference immediately. Being the most recent arrival in the New World and the youngest of the Frenchmen present, he had had both the opportunity and inclination to immerse himself in matters pertaining to the up-timers and their technology. "Of course. They are after Pitch Lake. It is bitumen, and nearby, there is almost always oil. That is how most of their vehicles run, you see. It is the key to the operation of so many of their machines."

Du Plessis was nodding. Uncle Pierre was simply smiling, delighted and discernibly proud at his nephew's knowledgeable addition to the conversation. "Young Monsieur du Parquet knows whereof he speaks. Trust me, d'Esnambuc: the up-time presence here is not fleeting. They mean to have that oil. And that means they must establish a nearby stronghold in the New World. And where better than here in the middle of the Leeward islands, by expanding upon an already-extant port?"

Uncle Pierre nodded vigorously. "Yes, so we must destroy that port, that facility, before they can develop it. And I think you are very right that they mean to develop it as a military base, as well."

"Why?" asked de l'Olive suspiciously.

D'Esnambuc leaned back and folded his hands. To Jacques, his uncle suddenly looked like an improbably well-armed and vigorous school-master. "There is an up-timer on St. Eustatia now who has commenced a most unusual project. He is stringing what seem to be some kinds of cables high in the trees on the northeastern side of the volcanic mountain called The Quill. Specifically, on the slopes that face back toward Europe. I do not know what it portends, but an unusual amount of manpower, both free-man and slave, has been dedicated to the project. It also seems to involve the construction of a siz-able steam engine that spins metal wheels, which resemble the blades of windmills trapped within a broad hub."

Jacques folded his hands and nodded. "They are building a radio, I think. A very powerful one. That steam plant you have heard about is to furnish power for it. A generator, I believe they call it. When the steam blasts through the tubes containing those wheels, their spinning generates electricity. I think. But for a radio to require that much electricity, it must be very powerful. And if those wires on The Quill are some kind of antenna—a metal grid which gathers or spreads radio signals—then this radio is not only meant to receive those signals over great distances, but send them as well."

"How great a distance?" Uncle Pierre asked quietly.

Jacques shrugged. "I do not know. My reading about their technology was more broad than deep. I do not know what the limit of such a radio might be."

"Perhaps not," said d'Esnambuc in a quiet, determined tone that sent a chill down Jacques' spine, "but I can find out. And I'll need to do it soon. This same American is making other problems for us."

"How so?" asked de l'Olive.

"He is apparently talking to the slaves working for him about ways in which they might acquire the means to buy their freedom. Likewise, he is speaking to the Dutch townsfolk about the greater safety and ease of having a colony of freemen and bondsmen, rather than spending every waking hour ensuring that their slaves do not flee or revolt."

"And the Dutch are listening to this nonsense?" de l'Olive snorted.

"Some. Perhaps enough. At any rate, no one is silencing this American. Even though he is not making any public speeches or the like, he is becoming famous for his casual conversations about such matters. Or, in the eyes of some, he is becoming infamous. When the landowners heard about these 'conversations,' most of them stopped leasing him slaves to help with the construction of whatever it is he is building on the windward side of The Quill."

Du Plessis frowned. "That should have put an end to his project, right there."

"It should have, but it did not. Tromp apparently found townsmen willing to add to the daily rate of the slaves' leases. The landowners, between their prior agreement and the lure of all that money, could hardly continue to refuse. And the slaves, of course, repeat the American's seditious ideas and exhortations back among their own people."

De l'Olive grumbled. "That's the end of your long-standing scheme for inciting a slave revolt, Captain d'Esnambuc. I remember how diligent you were in trying to bring one off from the time we returned after the Spanish chased us off in '29."

"Yes," d'Esnambuc agreed sourly. "If the Dutch convert their slaves to bondsmen, and they hold to their word, it is difficult to see how we will stimulate an effective revolt. Indeed, St. Eustatia may become a destination for escaped slaves and *encomienda* laborers from all around the Caribbean. And I suspect that Warner would adopt the same policy quickly enough, if he saw it succeeding. So this may well be our last opportunity to not only protect our colony on St. Christopher's, but arrest a trend that could create problems for the *Compagnie des Îles de l'Amérique* throughout the Lesser Antilles."

"Agreed," announced du Plessis, with a slap at his knee. "I think our plan must take precedence over all other efforts, at this point." Jacques was bemused to note how his uncle's plan had become a collective stratagem, in which du Plessis was now not only invested, but ready to claim a share of the authorship.

His uncle was too pragmatic a man to allow any impatience or resentment show, if he felt it. D'Esnambuc simply nodded and pointed his chin slightly southward. "And here comes our company, gentlemen. I believe that is cacique Touman and his entourage. And although it may irk you, I recommend you stand to receive him. Willing cooperation of the Caribs is, after all, the lynchpin of 'our' plan."

❖   ❖   ❖

Jacques found himself quickly admiring Touman, who sat among both proven and potential enemies without any sign of fear or anxiety. He expressed no happiness, was indeed, quite grave, but was in no way rude. His inquiries were focused and well-considered. When he occasionally sensed that he was being given half-truths, he bluntly asked for a more complete explanation of the issue or item in question. Jacques wondered if his own countrymen would have been so collected and serious and yet polite if the circumstances were reversed, and he frankly doubted it. He knew that he would not have been.

At the end of half an hour, Touman nodded and surveyed the faces of the Frenchmen. He ended on d'Esnambuc and said, "You are bold, to contact my relatives on Madinina, which you call Martinique. And to come before me here on Karukera."

"And why is that, Cacique Touman?"

"Because you are he who slew Tegreman and took Liamuiga — St. Christopher's—from my people, the Kalinago. Had you not come to Youacou on Madinina first, and with only a small guard, I would not have heard the sounds of your tongue, but given orders that it be ripped from your head."

"Cacique Touman," d'Esnambuc said with a sigh. "You are a warrior so you understand that in war, events transpire that we do not intend. The terrible killing of the Kalinago on the island we call St. Christopher's was one such event. Had it not been for the fear in Warner's breast—that, having started slaying your people we would not be safe unless we left none alive—there would have been far less blood spilt. And among the blood that would not have been spilt was Tegreman's own. He was a leader and a straight-standing man. We did not always agree, and did not always part happy with each other, but men do so without killing each other. It should have been thus with him."

Touman stared with narrowed eyes at d'Esnambuc while the other Frenchmen held their breath as if witnessing a duel between well matched pistoleers. "So with these words, do you claim that your hand was not the one which slew Tegreman?"

"I do claim that," d'Esnambuc replied quickly, truthfully.

"And you claim that your tongue did not give the command that others should kill him?"

"I claim that as well," Uncle Pierre lied just as quickly and convincingly.

Touman continued to look at d'Esnambuc for the better part of a minute, as if trying to read him the way his people read the clouds and wavelets for favorable signs to cross the great expanses between the islands of the Caribbean. At last, he looked away and spoke. "I shall speak plainly. I do not agree to become a part of these plans gladly. My people, the Kalinago, have had little luck trusting the word of pale men from over the sea, regardless of how they differ from each other in their language and dress and customs.

"But this I know: you speak the truth of the changing times in these islands. Although my people no longer do so openly, we visit our islands, even those you hold most strongly. We know the truth of what you say, that many ships and many Dutch came to Aloi, which you call St. Eustatia. And we have heard reports from our distant cousins of great ships that burn fires on their deck as they move more swiftly than the strongest men may row. I had wondered if these tales were true, but I doubt them no longer."

He met the eyes of each of the four white men once and then spoke again. "If you shall provide us with guns as you say, then the Kalinago people shall make this war with you against the English and Dutch of Liamuiga and Aloi. Afterward, we shall live there with you in peace and mutual protection, staying within the borders we have agreed upon today, which shall not change."

D'Esnambuc nodded. "We shall provide the guns as we have promised. You shall have thirty today and your warriors may have instruction in them before leaving."

"And these guns are ours to take?"

"They are. Within two weeks, we shall have at least one hundred more. We hope to have two hundred more. All these guns shall be yours also. We only ask that you do not use them, nor change them, when away from us. We must conserve the powder and shot to train you, and if any part of the mechanisms are changed, the guns may not function as well, or at all."

"I understand. I wonder if *you* understand."

"I do not know what you mean, Cacique Touman."

"Can you not? Whether or not I have heard lies, sitting in council with you this day, you have given me guns, and the promise of many more. Which means you have given me the power to make men from over the sea keep their promises. It does not matter whether it is you, or the Spanish, or these men you say have come from another world of future spirits. We shall not tolerate lies any more.

"Furthermore, we have seen that you do not know the ways of these islands. Without our help, you would soon starve. We will provide what food we may, and trade with our cousins to the south for more. But now you will know—*all* will know"—he shook the matchlock he'd been given lightly—"that nothing may be taken from us, or gained by threatening us. Those who depend upon our food will eat so long as they keep their promises. This I resolve. And so, I am finished." Touman stood. "My people will return tomorrow with food, and to learn more of how to use the guns you have given us. I hope this day marks the start of better times between our people." He nodded, turned, and left. Youacou remained behind for a moment, nodded, and left also.

When both were well gone, de l'Olive rounded on d'Esnambuc. "But Captain! You always said that we must never furnish the savages with guns. You always said if they—"

D'Esnambuc interrupted with a quiet voice that silenced his old follower more surely than a shout would have. "Yes, I did say that. And those were different times. Times when we did not need savages as allies. Times when the Dutch were not selling trade muskets near the Orinoco. But I am unworried."

Du Plessis frowned. "Why?"

"Did you not notice what Touman failed to ask for?"

Jacques nodded. "Metal for casting musket balls and the casting tools. And assurances of a constant supply of powder. They know what guns do, but do not yet have a full understanding of the other items they must possess and the skills they must master, if they are to continue using them."

"Just so, my nephew," Uncle Pierre said.

"But they will learn of these needs," du Plessis sputtered. "They will figure it out within the first few days and—"

"And we shall never let them want for powder or shot. Not now, not until that day comes when French ships sail untroubled from St. Eustatia to Guadeloupe and these lands are brimming with our colonists."

"And then?" asked Jacques, dreading the terrible answer that was sure to be uttered by the uncle he loved so much.

"And then," d'Esnambuc replied in a tone that sounded like an apology, "a day will come when our ships will ensure that the Caribs cannot leave our islands to trade for powder with anyone else. And so, the powder will go away. And so will they."

Part Seven

November 1635

Office, and custom, in all line of order.

Chapter 40

*Three miles east by southeast
of Pitch Lake, Trinidad*

Ann Koudsi took off toward the number three hole at a dead run even before the first deep-toned alarm rang out. Her rig workers called the hoop of brass which made the sound a gong, but she thought it sounded more like a cowbell. However, she'd known a full three seconds beforehand that something must be happening, either good or bad, because the relentless percussive slamming of the cable drill rig stopped suddenly, and long before the scheduled personnel break and maintenance check.

As she emerged from the tree line into the small clearing where they'd first found the oil seeps, she scanned the crazed activity around the well. Ulrich was at the center of it, gesturing wildly, his German crew scattering to perform tasks that seemed to take them in every direction.

"Good news or bad?" Ann shouted as she came to a panting halt a dozen yards away.

"Both! Get back, Ann. Please!"

Instead, she rushed across the rest of the distance. She had decided, some months ago, that while she was not interested in taking stupid risks, she wasn't about to allow Ulrich to take any she wouldn't also. It would be bad enough to go on living without him. To know that she had seen to her own safety instead of being there to help, and maybe save, him would be simply unbearable.

"Ann—!"

"Save it. We'll argue later. What's up with number three?"

But even as she asked it, her nose told her the answer: a faint spoiled eggs smell. "Gas?"

"Yes, but then it stopped. And the last shavings that we took up were these." He pointed backward into a bucket. At a glance, she knew: they were near oil. Very near.

That was when the hole emitted what sounded like a muddy burp. It ended in a stuttering hiss that faded away.

She looked overhead. The cable was mostly out, spooling up onto a drum being cranked by two of the largest roughnecks. Two more waited to swing the drill bit up out of the casing and clear of the hole. "How far down are you?"

"One hundred eighty-seven feet. We were going slowly, just as you recommended. You were right about this one, Ann."

"Yeah," she said, purposely trying to sound as sour as the old eggs smell around her, "we'll see about that." She didn't want to get her hopes up, not when there was so much riding on—

"Pans are in place; catch tubes laid!" one of the workers shouted before backing away at a reverse trot.

"Ann," Ulrich insisted, "we can't do any more here. Let's get back, wait and see if—"

The platform vibrated slightly for a second. Out of the hole came a sound like a whale having a titanic episode of indigestion, punctuated by occasional flatulence.

Ann and Ulrich grabbed each other at the same instant and started running. A moment later, surging up from the ground behind them came a sound like a prolonged, slow burp, ending in a sigh—*okay, so not a gusher*—which chased them off the platform with a light, misty shower of fine gray-and-black goo. The oil smell was unmistakable.

Ulrich, his white teeth incredibly bright in the midst of his smudged face, turned to her in the boyish glee that so endeared him to her. "You've done it, Ann! You've—"

"*We've* done it. We. Us. And keep running. Never trust an oil well until you've capped it, and I'm not getting near that one for at least an hour." But as they ran farther up the trail, back into the comparative safety of the tree line, she could not suppress the surge of elation that arose with the word: *Oil! We've struck oil!*

Santo Domingo, Hispaniola

Fadrique Álvarez de Toledo y Mendoza pushed away the cup of decidedly inferior rioja but schooled himself not to allow the gesture to become so forceful as to signal displeasure. After all, he was a guest in the modest palace of Santo Domingo's captain-general, and the fellow, while lacking the body of a soldier, seemed to have the heart of one, since what he was suggesting was tantamount to political suicide. And given how petty and vicious Olivares was becoming these days, it was not beyond imagining that poor crippled Don Juan Bitrian de Viamonte y Navarra would receive a summons to Spain that would mark the end of his titles and honor and money. And a semi-invalid such as he might not survive very long without the ease and medicines his position made available to him. So, it might reasonably be said that de Viamonte was risking his life as much as any other man who decided to serve Spain's best interests, even if that meant dangerously bending or misconstruing the intent of Olivares' many dicta. And as for inferior rioja? Since Fadrique's duties seemed certain to keep him in the New World for the foreseeable future, he might as well accustom his palate to what was available this far from the vineyards of home.

The other man at the table was a youngish fellow, one Don Eugenio de Covilla, who had introduced himself as the confidential liaison between Captain-General de Viamonte and the redoubtable governor of Cuba, His Excellency Francisco Riaño y Gamboa, a hard-bitten old soldier whose physical and mental toughness were legendary. Gamboa had proven the truth of those legends even before he had fully arrived at his new assignment in Cuba. His ship having capsized off the coast of Mariel, the white-locked septuagenarian swam ashore with nothing but his royal patents and sodden clothes. And in the year that he'd been at his new post, he had made significant changes, as well as significant enemies. A field marshal prior to becoming the governor of arguably the most important Spanish city and island in the New World, he was aggressive in combating corruption and was not willing to look the other way when Spanish merchants conducted their (admittedly far more profitable) trade with the itinerant merchantmen of other nations, or with the so-called Brethren of the Coast. But, popular or not, given the alarming reports now emerging from the Lesser Antilles all the way down to the eastern edge of Tierra Firma, seventy-year-old Gamboa was precisely the sturdy warhorse needed to take on the Dutch and their new allies.

Whether de Covilla would represent Gamboa's wishes as forcefully as the Cuban governor himself was another question entirely. Frankly, Fadrique did not envy the young *hidalgo* his job. Being the mouthpiece for the blunt, and even impolitic, Gamboa meant he would frequently become a most unwelcome messenger in the palaces of men who stood far above him in both rank and access to courtier's ears back in Madrid.

Fadrique stared down the table at Captain-General de Viamonte, who was finishing his wine, probably at the order of doctors. His withered arm was tucked against his far side and largely out of sight, but his patchy hair and labored breathing were unfortunately beyond concealment. It was obvious looking at the man why he had been bounced out of the governorship in Havana to make way for Gamboa, but the doing had not been the old general's, who was said to have a high regard for de Viamonte's quiet competence. Rather, Fadrique's present host had been undermined at court by the Marquis of Cadereyta, Don Lope Díez de Aux de Armendáriz, who, prior to his recent ascension as the new viceroy of New Spain, had been a skilled captain-general and admiral of the flotas that went to and from Seville. He had couched his public disapproval of de Viamonte in terms of the man's conventional and uninspired policies, of not having the dynamism necessary to a position as trying and so wanting bold action as the governorship of Cuba. Privately, he made no secret of loathing the infirmity and inwardness of de Viamonte, and so, was only more resentful of the man's quiet resistance to de Armendáriz's attempts at bullying concessions out of him regarding the equipage and provisioning of his various flotas, and Havana's defenses.

Fadrique shifted in his chair impatiently. "So, then, what news, Don de Viamonte?"

"I will learn it along with you, my good Don de Toledo. De Covilla here is just off the advice *patache* this morning and we have not had the time to talk."

Fadrique turned to the young fellow, who nodded his respect again, as he had upon meeting Fadrique. He glanced back at the captain-general. "Then, sir, with your leave—"

"By all means, Eugenio. Please share the messages from His Excellency Governor Gamboa."

De Covilla smoothed his vest, put aside his wine, and folded his hands. "First, he sends his compliments and greetings to you, Don de Viamonte, and especially commends your speedy and bold decision to send three ships as couriers to Spain as soon as you received news of the battle in the Grenada Passage."

Bold indeed, Fadrique reaffirmed silently. Olivares was renowned for confusing those who alerted him to bad news with being the causes of that news. De Viamonte might have a frail body, but he had courage enough for any five men to send prompt news without flinching or second thoughts. A pity that Spain tended to push aside or pillory those loyal and imprudent enough to do their duty even when it was sure to anger Olivares.

De Covilla had not paused. "He also confers his approval of your initiative to restore the shipyards here in Santo Domingo to full production capacity. He has followed your example and given identical orders to the shipyards on Cuba. He has also exhorted, in the strongest possible language, that the new viceroy of New Spain, Don Lope Díez de Aux de Armendáriz, and the viceroy of Peru, Don Luis Jerónimo Fernández de Cabrera Bobadilla Cerda y Mendoza, follow similar programs of reinstating their shipbuilding industries at their maximum level of production."

Fadrique tried not to look dubious or disgusted. Armendáriz, while capable, was also known to be self-interested, secretive, and, it was rumored, perverse in his affiliations and actions. He might trouble himself to become part of the solution to the growing Protestant threat in the New World, but he was just as likely to allow the regions most directly influenced to bear the brunt of the expenses. The only reason to have strong hopes otherwise was that Armendáriz, a *criollo* from Quito, had made his name in the world by commanding the flotas. He, as well as any man alive, was likely to fully understand just how disastrous any loss in control or security of the sea-lanes would be to the fate of all of Spain's New World possessions. And whereas Peru's Don de Cabrera was a reliable fellow, he was stuck on the other side of South America: a strange place from which to govern the affairs of Cartagena and the majority of Tierra Firma, but that was Spanish governance for you. Getting a timely message to him, and getting his authorizing response, would be the biggest problem, and represented a considerable delay.

"Last, he agrees with you that, as practicable, we should identify all recent wrecks in shallow waters and commence salvage operations at once. He has already contracted two masters of intercoastal trading ships to undertake this activity."

Álvarez de Toledo leaned forward. "What is this? You are sending diving bells down to wrecks, now? For coin to pay for the shipbuilding?"

But Don Juan Bitrian de Viamonte shook his high-domed head. "No, Don Álvarez, for cannons, balls, and if they are still serviceable, the very nails themselves." He continued when Fadrique's expression showed his increasing perplexity. "Don Álvarez, we may lose men to accident and high weather during salvage operations, yes. But, God save me that I must say so, we have no shortage of men. However, what of the ironmongery with which we must build and outfit the ships that we are even now commissioning in our yards? And of the armaments which we must provide for them?" He shook his head sadly. "These objects are our new wealth, my dear Álvarez de Toledo. For we have no capacity to make such objects ourselves, and if Olivares does not send them to us in considerable bulk, all our efforts to build a fleet here shall come to naught. We have no choice but to find and refurbish that which we have already lost once."

Fadrique nodded, realized his eyes had opened wide, and simply did not care that his admiration for the wizened little man was so frank. By God, if one of every ten Spaniards had both his clear mind and gigantic *cojones*, their empire would cover every inch of the globe. "As you say, these are our new wealth, Don de Viamonte."

De Covilla had turned his body as well as his head to face Fadrique. "His Excellency Francisco Riaño y Gamboa is glad to welcome you to the New World and of course wishes it might have been under better circumstances. However, he is extremely glad that you were present to manage the scope of the difficulties that befell our fleet in the Grenada Passage, commends you for your prudence in saving as many ships as you did, and for taking steps to distribute intelligence of our new enemies not only to himself and Don de Viamonte, but to Governor de Murga in Cartagena."

"His Excellency is a kind man, to thank me for losing a battle."

"He does not see it so, Don Álvarez de Toledo. However, he anticipated that you might be just so harsh with yourself. So he bade me communicate to you how he perceived the outcome of the most recent battle. It may be that the unfortunate Admiral de Cárdenas split your fleet in the face of the enemy for the wrong reasons—for how often is such a stratagem a good one?—but the governor observed that it was nonetheless a fortunate choice. Because had all of your fleet engaged the USE steamships, far fewer of our ships would have returned home. Conversely, had you all sailed together against the Dutch, it seems most certain that the outcome would have been worse still. The USE steamships are, by your report, so swift that they would have taken your fleet in the flank, which, constrained by having engaged the Dutch van, would have been destroyed in bunches. It is difficult to see, therefore, any other course than the one you chose once Admiral de Cárdenas had fallen: to salvage what you might, and quickly.

"So, in consideration of that wisdom, and your many past successes, His Excellency wishes you to know most explicitly that you have his full confidence. And furthermore, that you have full authority to do whatever is necessary to rebuild the Armada de Barlovento, which we must now presume is truly and permanently lost, and to fashion a strategy which allows us to defeat our new foes. His Excellency the Governor is keenly interested in any actions you take in these regards, and asks to be informed of them at once, Admiral, so he may mobilize any local support your initiatives might require."

Fadrique hadn't heard the last part of de Covilla's courtly summary of Gamboa's message. "Did you call me 'Admiral?'"

De Covilla smiled and nodded. "The governor has so ordered your promotion to full admiral, to replace the fallen de Cárdenas. He emphasized, several times, that he was most glad to have you close at hand for this important duty." De Covilla paused and met Fadrique's gaze steadily. "Most especially glad."

Ah, so a special nod from the old boy in Havana. Fadrique interpreted the subtext of Gamboa's repeated emphasis on both his gratitude and relief, which translated roughly as: *Thank God we are no longer saddled with a* poseur *such as de Cárdenas. Now we professional soldiers can get to work.*

De Covilla's next comment also confirmed Fadrique's assessment that Gamboa's natural impulse was to take decisive, practical steps against the new threat. "His

Excellency has also taken it upon himself, and his own authority, to directly call upon the other ship-building towns of the New World to contribute their efforts to build a more credible local fleet." *Going over the head of the viceroys to get fast action? Gamboa's sense of urgency is obviously much greater than his reluctance to make powerful new enemies.* "Accordingly, His Excellency has dispatched advice *pataches* and barca-longas to deliver his vigorous encouragements and exhortations *directly* to the mayors and shipyard masters at Salvaleón de Higüy, San Juan, San Germán, Veracruz, Campeche, Jamaica, Cartagena, Maracaibo, and Caracas. He welcomes Admiral Álvarez de Toledo to add to that list, or make specific recommendations, of course."

Fadrique nodded. "In Maracaibo and Campeche, you must restrict the shipbuilding to small hulls with shallow draughts. Maracaibo has shifting sandbars and Campeche's harbor is too shallow for big ships. And I suggest one further proviso. When we are building warships, we must begin to increasingly adopt the frigate designs that the Swedes and Dutch have been producing for almost two years now."

"I beg your pardon, did you say *fragata*?"

"I did not. I do *not* mean our small versions of these craft, but the larger brig- and barquentine-sized hulls that have no perceptible quarterdeck and but a single gun deck. They should be of about one hundred tonneladas and between twenty and thirty guns, total."

De Covilla frowned. "That may not be received well in Seville, Don Álvarez de Toledo. While the smaller *fragatas* are not so large nor a sizable investment, the class of ship you are asking for will be almost as long and expensive to build as a small galleon. And our craftsmen are not familiar with the design. They would need to be taught."

"In Havana, they are familiar enough with similar designs. And in the other yards, they may be taught. Let us be plain about what Olivares and the Royal Council of the Indies are interested in: getting gold and silver from the New World. To do that, they want to ensure that we have enough high-pooped, heavy-hulled galleons to wallow safely up and down the waves of the Atlantic and so bring the treasure to Seville. That has been a reasonable strategy. Until now."

Fadrique leaned forward. "Formerly, it did not matter if our ships were less maneuverable than theirs, were slow as scows if they lacked a following wind, had quarterdecks so high that they are a constant drag upon the hull as it strives forward against the sea and the air. We had the advantage of numbers, of size, of immense steady platforms from which to fire our immense cannons, and of those high fore and aft castles crowded with our infantry. Our galleons were forts upon the sea, and none could assail them with impunity."

De Toledo jabbed his finger down into the tabletop, the sharp *clack!* drawing attention to the moment. "But now, size is no longer decisive. Even without the up-time ships to support them, the Dutch and the Swedes are producing ships—frigates—with sleeker lines, mixed rigging, a long, low profile, and heavier guns. They are not capable of absorbing as much damage as our galleons, but being swift, they are hit far less often. And, again because they are swift, our advantage in numbers is no longer decisive. They can outmaneuver us and herd us into clusters, bringing almost their full force to bear upon each isolated group in turn. And so, through cunning maneuver, they may contrive to outnumber us at every point of contact, even though we may outnumber them, total hulls to total hulls."

"Well," soothed de Covilla, "regardless of how many changes Count-Duke Olivares is willing to approve, I suspect that he will not bridle at their mere suggestion. Don Lope Díez de Aux de Armendáriz, Viceroy of New Spain, who departed shortly after I arrived in Havana, took the opportunity to recount, at length and in detail, the mood in the Council of the Indies earlier this year. I am pleased to say it is most aggressive in regard to the foreign violation of our *inter caetera* rights in general, and to the Dutch seizure of Curaçao in particular."

"Indeed," de Viamonte murmured. "Please do recount the viceroy's words in as great a detail as you might recall." The captain-general's tone suggested he was not looking for information or revelations so much as he was searching for a weakness, a gaffe, a misstep on the part of de Armendáriz.

De Covilla heard the tone as well; he inclined his head to study some notes he had brought with him. "According to Don Lope Díez de Aux de Armendáriz, he was invited to observe the proceedings of a 'granda junta' of the council. It was attended by the councils of State and War, as well, and was presided over by none other than Don Gaspar de Guzmán y Pimentel Ribera y Velasco de Tovar, comte d'Olivares et duc de Sanlucar la Mayor, himself.

"The count-duke initiated the proceedings by explaining, at some length, that the Dutch capture of Curaçao might endanger, or at least delay, the sailing of this year's treasure fleet, if Thijssen proved highly active in raiding along Tierra Firma. That has not materialized, although the new threats we have discovered more than compensate for the dangers and losses with which Thijssen failed to present us. However, regardless of whatever might have transpired this year, Count-Duke Olivares averred that a Dutch presence at Curaçao was inevitably a springboard for further Dutch raiding along Tierra Firma and further island seizures in the Caribbean. He called for many forms of assistance, including Portuguese ships added to our own, but in particular, maintained that the Armada de Barlovento, or Windward fleet, needed dramatic expansion. The four galleons he believed her to possess at that time were to be increased to eighteen within two years' time."

"So perhaps he is already planning to authorize a full renewal of shipbuilding here in the New World?" Fadrique inquired hopefully.

"Frankly, the viceroy made it sound more as though the count-duke saw this increased need for hulls as a windfall for the yards in Vizcaya. However, given the recent losses here in the New World, I suspect that, for now at least, any increase in the size of our fleet will be a welcome development in his eyes, regardless of where the ships are built."

"So you think he will be, er, open-minded, about the special measures we have taken to address the current crisis?"

"He might well be. The count-duke was quite explicit about the finality of the war he wished prosecuted against those who trespass upon His Majesty's lands, or who threaten their safety. He repeatedly referred to the Dutch as faithless rebels and heretics and, because they were, that they should be slaughtered when captured."

De Viamonte's eyes widened slightly. "And both the Council of the Indies and the Council of War permitted that policy?"

De Covilla nodded slightly. "Don Lope Díez de Aux de Armendáriz did mention that there was worry in the chamber that the Dutch would simply retaliate by massacring the crews of Spanish vessels they intercepted in the Caribbean. Olivares was unmoved, and simply reiterated his insistence that Dutch prisoners be killed in any way expedient, at any time it was convenient for Spanish commanders to do so."

Fadrique could not keep himself from blinking in surprise. "This is not well-considered," he murmured. Which was hardly a surprise in and of itself. Olivares had become increasingly injudicious in recent years, and anything remotely touching upon the Dutch and the interminable problems spawned by the wars in, or troubles pertaining to, the Spanish presence in the Lowlands, excited him to excesses of anger and ready vengeance. "But I think it makes it all the more wise that his Excellency Captain-General Gamboa took such extraordinary steps in establishing our own fleet, here in the New World."

"And why is that, Don Álvarez de Toledo?"

"Because," Fadrique said, drawing his wine a bit closer, "if we do not take matters into our own hands, and find answers that we may vouchsafe with own labor and treasure, then Olivares will do what he's best at: increase our taxes to pay for our own defensive fleet. Which he will likely have built in Spain, where it is easier for him to 'manage' the funds."

Álvarez de Toledo sneered openly. "The last time he increased taxes in the New World, I think he almost doubled the New Spain *alcabala* sales tariff. It was an unmitigated disaster. The money went to Spain, and in exchange, we received an undersized shipment of new weapons and ships, along with a veritable army of the count-duke's current flatterers and sycophants. And from what I could tell, it was their especial job to oversee the utilization and distribution of the scant and shoddy resources Olivares had sent, along with ensuring that the collection of the additional tariff continued." Fadrique had meant to take a sip of his wine, but now gulped at it angrily and set it down with a loud clack. "We cannot afford the pointless cost of Olivares' infinitude of sinecures in our coming struggle against the Dutch and their new allies. And we must prosecute that war sooner, rather than later."

"Why?" wondered de Viamonte, frowning.

"Because they will waste no time attacking us again. We suffered the losses, not they. We have slower communications, if we may conjecture that they are making some use of radio. And yet we have a much greater area and more far-flung units to coordinate than they do. Our size has often made us powerful, but against these adversaries, I fear it simply makes us ponderous. This is why we must have faster ships."

Don de Viamonte smiled wistfully. "And up-time radios, too, perhaps?"

"You may have meant that as an irony, Captain-General, but I am deadly serious when I say I would give ten galleons for five radios and their operators." Fadrique spread his hands. "Our empire's size is, in many ways, a disadvantage, if we cannot coordinate its far-flung locales and assets properly. Imagine twenty oxen, tied together in no particular fashion by a clutter of ropes. Their immense power is useless because it is not focused. Now imagine only four oxen in paired yokes, all following the same lead-line. They provide much less raw power, yes, but they can get many times more work done, because they are all pulling in the same direction, all answering to one will and voice. This is precisely the difference between us and our foes. With their steam speed and radios, their much smaller numbers will defeat us almost every time."

"Then what is to be done?"

Could he really not see? "Build faster ships. Get radios. Find alternatives to reduce or eliminate our handicaps. Ensure that we have strong, consistent, central leadership. And remain mindful that they hope to strike us severe blows—mortal, if possible—before we can find their primary base. For once we do, we may bring all our force to bear upon what must be a fairly weak port. Their largest colony, Recife, they abandoned. How much could they have built since? A few ramparts, a few dozen houses? They have no Havanas, no Cartagenas, and they know that we are well aware of that. So they will attack us as quickly as they might, to preemptively protect whatever base and settlement they are operating out of."

"And where do you think that might be, Admiral?" de Covilla asked, leaning forward intently. "Curaçao?"

Fadrique shrugged. "That is a logical location, but I am not convinced it is correct. Not at all."

De Viamonte emphasized his single-syllable question by attenuating it. "Why?"

"Because if it is Tromp who engaged us at the

Grenada Passage, and I think it was, then Curaçao is exactly where we would expect to find him, after he abandoned Recife. But siting himself so close to so many of our cities along Tierra Firma, it would be almost an invitation to us to attempt to mass against him, to beat him back into that island's well-protected harbor, no matter the cost. And then we would land our troops at all points of its tiny coastline and destroy him and his colony like burning a badger in its hole. Clearly, they cannot have any significant fortifications thrown up yet, nor supplies to resist a siege, so no matter how numerous his soldiers might be, they would ultimately succumb."

De Viamonte mused before answering. "So he would go someplace he is not likely to be found?"

"Quite possibly. Tell me, when was the last time you sent a patrol to see what was going on in the islands we do not visit frequently?"

De Viamonte's voice was reedy. "Alas, before it disappeared last year, that was a significant part of the Armada de Barlovento's mission. So it remains unaccomplished."

"Hmm. I wonder. Perhaps that part of their mission, is, in fact, the one thing that they *did* accomplish."

The captain-general, who had modest reserves of stamina at best, looked more weary by the minute. "I do not understand."

"Let us consider what we last knew about the Armada de Barlovento, and what is unusual about its disappearance." Fadrique folded his hands and leaned forward. "First, is it not strange that *all* four ships of the Armada de Barlovento should disappear? Even in a terrible defeat, usually one or two hulls escape, live to tell the tale. And that is usually what occurs because you typically meet an enemy without warning, in a place neither of you had thought to meet another ship at all."

"So, you suspect an ambush?"

"Of a sort. Let us suppose that, rather than joining Thijssen in Curaçao, Tromp chose instead a safe port where he hoped to hide, a place farther from the regular route of our flotas."

Fadrique saw de Covilla's eyes widen slightly. A smart lad, evidently. "Tromp would keep a watch on the approaches to such a port, with his own ships ready to trap any others that discovered his anchorage so they could not escape to report."

"Precisely. Now there is no guarantee that this is why all four ships are missing. Storms claim whole fleets, on occasion, and we have little news of it if the high weather comes and goes where our flag does not regularly fly."

De Viamonte shook his head. "So how would you propose to determine if our ships were the victims of an ambush, and furthermore, where Tromp's secret anchorage might be? The Caribbean is a wide sea, and, if your earlier comments about an impending Dutch attack are correct, we may not have enough time to send *pataches* to its far corners."

De Covilla cleared his throat. "There may be another way. Though I am loath to suggest it."

Fadrique frowned. "Come now, young fellow, it is the honor of Spain and our king we are trying to save, here."

"It is the honor of Spain and our king that I mean to protect by *not* suggesting what I just conceived, Don Álvarez de Toledo."

Fadrique narrowed his eyes, nodded. "I think I understand what expedient you may be considering, and your repugnance of it. But you are right: it answers our need. And may show the way forward to meet other challenges, as well."

De Viamonte, who was usually a most astute man, sounded very puzzled and slightly annoyed. "I should be most grateful if you two gentlemen would stop speaking in a code known to you alone, apparently. What solution have you conceived that might answer our need for scouting more widely, Eugenio?"

"Don de Viamonte, I am ashamed to say it, but in the time that I coordinated the activities of the raiders commanded by the bandit Barto, I learned that others of his ilk, the so called Free Companions, range far and wide. Which we knew, of course. But it is also true that there are havens, also suspected by us, where they convene. In these places, they trade their ill-gotten goods, ply themselves with drink, satiate their appetite for women, and share their tales, many of which are fanciful fabrications, but many of which are true. Many of which would therefore include recent intelligences on the ships and powers of rivals and nations. Which might very well include word of the Dutch."

De Viamonte leaned back, his nostrils pinching tight as if he were smelling the reek of such a den of debauchery. But he stiffened and nodded. "You are right, of course. In both regards. It is a vile alternative. And it is also the only one which may provide us the necessary information in time. You have my leave to send agents amongst them, and to let it be known that we would deign to speak with them in our ports. Where we will trade hard silver for information. Although, I fear that many will come to tell us lies we cannot disprove and depart with silver we cannot withhold."

"Not if we make it worth their while to tell the truth," mumbled Fadrique.

"And how should we do that, sir?"

"By offering them ten times as much if they sail with us to plunder the Dutch in their ports and take their fine ships."

"We should *recruit* them?" de Viamonte almost gasped.

"From what young Don de Covilla has said, it sounds as though you already have, once. But if we need to act quickly—and we do—and we need to have eyes, ears, and eventually guns in many places at the same time—which we will—then I fail to see how we can exclude this expedient."

"And we are to let them plunder the Dutch settlements?"

"Is that so much worse than following Olivares' orders to exterminate the Dutch wherever we find them? The pirates may choose to show them mercy, or not. We, on the other hand—" Fadrique let the sentence dangle unfinished, felt sure that a noble soul like de Viamonte's would choose an alternative that afforded some hope for civilians to survive over the ineluctable alternative of being their black-hooded executioner.

De Viamonte did not disappoint him. "But we will still need to control these 'free companions,' somehow."

"They were manageable when promised letters of marque," de Covilla pointed out.

"And so we legitimize their barbarism," the captain-general spat.

"As Olivares has legitimized ours," observed Fadrique.

De Viamonte seemed to hug his withered arm close, shivered as though suffering a chill. "This war will come to no good end," he predicted.

"That is most likely," agreed Fadrique Álvarez de Toledo.

Chapter 41

Oranjestad, St. Eustatia

The rude-planked coffin, draped by a Danish pennant, was lifted out of the skiff by six Danes from the crew of the *Serendipity*. With Gjedde in front and Eddie Cantrell following behind, they made their way slowly past the assembled on-lookers, who numbered close to two hundred, and toward Edel Mund. She stood straight and stiff and very alone at the foot of the west-facing walls of Fort Oranjestad. They marched directly toward her and the Dutch soldiers flanking her on either side.

As the casket arrived before her, the procession stopped. The Dutch troopers raised their already-drawn swords, a wave of silver streaks catching the gold of the late morning sun even as they glinted silver. Then the six men carrying the casket marched through a slow pivot of ninety degrees and paused in that profile position, motionless before Pros Mund's pale widow. After a thirty count, and at Gjedde's gesture, they resumed their slow march, Eddie lagging so that dry-eyed Edel Mund could fall in directly behind the coffin as it made its stately way to the town's humble church.

Maarten Tromp had considered offering his services as a deacon to Reverend Polhemius but had ultimately decided against it. There were too many ways such an act could be misinterpreted: as being intrusive, as a Dutchman taking a place that should logically belong to a Dane with a similar calling, as having the humility of the act perceived as ingenuine. Any and all of which would only call attention away from the man who was rightly the center of reflection, appreciation, and mourning in this, his last hour among the persons he had left behind.

Edel and a few crewmembers made their way into the church, followed by a large number of ladies led by the three who had come from Christian IV's own court: his two daughters and the tall Sophie Rantzau. At the same moment, Tromp noticed Jan van Walbeeck sidling up to him where they stood under a pavilion outside the church, along with the others who had come to pay their respects to a man they had hardly known.

Van Walbeeck looked about surreptitiously. "You've chosen an auspicious spot for the ceremony, Maarten."

"Have I? The shade is no better or worse here than anywhere else."

"True enough. But I mean that we are standing so far to the rear that we may speak—quietly, of course—without being overheard."

Tromp glared at van Walbeeck. "Jan, I know you are not a conventionally devout man, but this is—well, it is disrespectful to the deceased and our Lord, alike."

Jan winced, shrugged. "I suppose that is true. But

I also suppose we may have no other time to discuss matters relevant to the meeting later this afternoon."

Maarten sighed, unhappy. Because, as usual, Jan van Walbeeck was right. Having arrived in port in the late hours of the middle watch, the ships that had returned from Trinidad remained steadily busy until well after breakfast. The few wounded were transferred ashore; the Spanish prize hulls were brought to secure anchorages near the beaches at which they might be safely careened. Secure arrangements ashore were worked out for the half dozen Spanish prisoners they had retained for purposes of debriefing. And of course, the burial of Reconnaissance Flotilla X-Ray's slain commander had to be hastily arranged.

And so, when Maarten Tromp exited the ketch that brought the senior officers to shore in the wake of the funeral skiff, that was the first he had seen of Jan van Walbeeck since departing Oranjestad for Trinidad.

As Polhemius' almost quavering voice called the mourners to their first devotions, the two Dutchmen folded their hands solemnly and leaned toward each other. Van Walbeeck started their whispered exchange. "I notice that Houtebeen Jol is not here. Have you done away with him, or has that great heathen foresworn even his face-saving attendance at funerals and weddings?"

"Neither. And I could ask you the same thing about Joost van Banckert's absence, which is stranger still, since he is a reasonably pious man."

"That he is, but we must have someone ready aboard a flagship to lead the fleet if the Spanish should discover us this hour."

Tromp allowed that this was quite true and quite prudent. "Jol is actually doing much the same thing."

"Protecting us from possible attack?"

"No, but readying his new ship and squadron to weigh anchor and make for Trinidad."

"So soon?"

"I wish it could have been sooner. We could only leave three ships there: *Achilles*, *Vereenigte Provintien*, and *Amsterdam*."

"And is Simonszoon in charge down there?"

"I couldn't spare him. I had to leave the Trinidad squadron in the hands of Hjalmar von Holst. A solid man, and clever enough, but not as brilliant and, er, unconventional, as Simonszoon."

"And so now you are sending that old pirate, Jol."

"Yes. He'll take over command from von Holst, who will be an excellent second-in-command. And Houtebeen will be bringing more ships with him to strengthen our Trinidad squadron: *Sampson*, *Overijssel*, *Thetis*, the fluyt *Koninck David*, and the jachts *Leeuwinne* and *Noordsterre*. They are escorting the Danish transport *Patentia*, which is carrying the balance of the oil drilling gear, along with that clean-lined bark of theirs, the *Tropic Surveyor*."

"Quite a formidable fleet."

Tromp forgot himself and grunted diffidently. Two Dutch women turned and stared at him. He smiled apologetically, took another half step back. Van Walbeeck followed, smiling. "So, *not* a formidable fleet, then?"

"Not if de Murga in Cartagena manages to wring any significant cooperation from the other *audiencias* along Tierra Firma. If he does, he could raise a considerable armada, easily twice the size of what we will have in Trinidad."

Tromp could tell from van Walbeeck's long, silent consideration of this information that he was trying to conceal both his surprise and reservations. His voice was measured and tactful when he finally commented, "Hm. Jol is a good man, but I am still puzzled that you haven't sent Dirck, and more ships, to guard the oil."

Tromp nodded as much of an agreement as their presence at a public funeral allowed. "I can see why you might be puzzled. But no one knows that coast like Peg Leg Jol. And he has the trust of a number of vehemently anti-Spanish reivers that prowl those waters. Not that he or I would ever trust them as dedicated allies, but they are free enough with information if they think sharing it will hurt the Spanish. So Jol's relationship with them gives us a means of remaining at least partially apprised of what our enemy is up to. Quite possibly, they might give us advance word of any move against Trinidad or Curaçao." Tromp paused. "But, that's only half the reason I'm sending Houtebeen down there."

"Or perhaps you mean to say, 'keeping Simonszoon up here'?"

Tromp smiled. "There's no fooling you, Jan. Yes. I want, *need*, to keep Simonszoon up here. For the good of the fleet. By which I mean the whole fleet, ours and that of our allies."

"I don't understand," van Walbeeck whispered as, in response to an invocation from Polhemius, the mourners lowered their heads in silent prayer.

Tromp did not explain until the reverend resumed the liturgy. "With Pros Mund dead, and seeing that we need to find a way for our very different forces to work together more effectively, we must rethink both our command structures and tactical doctrines. To make our combined fleet a unified implement of naval warfare, we must carefully assess how to amplify its tremendous advantages and reduce its unusual weaknesses. And at the center of all those efforts is Eddie, er, Commander Cantrell. He understands our down-time principles of naval warfare well enough, but more importantly, he is the only one who understands the up-time technologies and doctrines thoroughly. He must be the liaison, and translator, even, between our two different naval traditions."

Van Walbeeck only looked more confused. "And so? For this he needs Simonszoon alongside him?"

"In fact, yes, he does."

"Again, I do not understand."

Tromp smiled. "That is because, after your years before the mast, you became a governor, not an admiral. It is all well and good to say that Eddie must bring these two doctrines of warfare, and training, together into a functional whole, but it is quite another thing to achieve it. Think of who his students will be: young captains commanding ships or ambitious first mates. All of them will be more senior than he is and are unlikely to be able to get past the galling fact that the twenty-three-year-old teaching them has one tenth their combat experience and one-one-hundredth of their sailing experience. How effective do you expect his 'instruction' will be to such a class as that?"

Van Walbeeck nodded. "Ah. Now I see. So Dirck Simonszoon, the most laconic and facetious of all our captains, shall be present in the class as well, showing Eddie deference and paying serious heed to his instruction. And thereby, setting an example the others will tend to follow. An excellent plan. But I have one question about Dirck: *will* he show Cantrell that deference?"

"Strangely, I am quite certain he will. You know Dirck almost as well as I do, and you've seen what makes him bristle, and what doesn't. He is temperamentally incapable of suffering fools. And the more such a fool tries to justify or defend his foolishness, the more arch and combative Dirck becomes." Tromp shifted his stance, changed his hands so that his left was now folded over his right. The first notes of a hymn wafted out of the church and were taken up irregularly by those gathered outside. "But Dirck took to young Cantrell right away. I suppose Dirck's temperament is like a coin, furnished with two opposite sides. Whereas he is harshly impatient with people he considers slow-witted, he seems charmed and protective of those he considers quite clever. And you have seen for yourself that young Cantrell is quite clever, indeed."

"And refreshingly modest, too," van Walbeeck added. "So, with Dirck sitting as a respectful pupil in young Cantrell's classes, our young officers transfer the respect they feel for the revered and feared Captain Simonszoon to Eddie himself, and so, they will not challenge him. Which we cannot afford them to do."

"Eddie cannot afford it either," Tromp added quickly, "since he will almost certainly now be first among the Danish and USE commanders that remain."

"What of Gjedde?"

Tromp frowned, thinking. "Both by temperament and orders, I suspect that Gjedde is here as both a mentor and a hand on the reins with which the Danish throne means to govern the progress of Cantrell. Gjedde himself has never sought war-time commands, and is quite vocal about preferring exploration. He will, I think, maintain his current position as Eddie's titular superior, but will not exert that authority except where the young commander may be making a misstep."

Van Walbeeck's sigh suggested he was not fully convinced of the workability of such a scheme. "And what of the other USE captains and junior officers in his flotilla? Will they be so willing to serve under so young a commander?"

"That," replied Maarten Tromp with his own sigh as Polhemius called for the concluding hymn, "is something over which I have no control, Jan. Now let us be first in line to offer our condolences to Lady Mund. That will allow us to be first to leave, and so, the first to arrive for the general meeting."

After looking around at the commanders and councilors who had been called to the meeting, Pieter van Corselles, the original governor of the first Oranjestad colony (and who had since been side-shifted into the post of Superintendent for the Dutch West India Company), shook his head in disbelief. "So after a year of hiding, now we are to make ourselves known? By launching an attack against the Spanish? From here?"

"That is correct, Superintendent Corselles." Jan van Walbeeck said with a mild nod.

"But it will bring them here in droves! It will mean our certain destruction!"

"Actually, if we do *not* attack the Spanish, it will mean our certain destruction. If we do not seek them out and cripple their main fleet, then they will eventually find and engage us here. That is not merely tactically unwise, it is strategically unacceptable."

"I do not disagree with your conclusion," Hannibal Sehested commented, "but I would welcome an explication of your reasoning in the matter."

Tromp nodded. "Certainly. Although I should begin by saying that the two senior commanders in each of our fleets—myself and Adrian Banckert for us, and Captain Gjedde and Commander Cantrell for you—are unanimous that we have no reasonable alternative." Tromp stood and put his finger on the up-time map of the Caribbean, planting it firmly upon St. Eustatia. "Note our position. We are near what you might call the pelagic elbow of the Caribbean. From here, the Greater Antilles stretch westward to Cuba, and the Lesser Antilles drop all the way down to Grenada. Until now, our island has been a relatively remote and, to the Spanish, uninteresting location. Prior to the four ships they sent south from St. Maarten's last year, they had not bothered to examine any of the Lesser Antilles islands since Fadrique Álvarez de Toledo led forty ships on a campaign of expulsion and extermination from St. Croix southward in 1629, thereby enforcing Spain's *inter caetera* claim to all lands west of the Tordesillas Line."

Tromp moved his finger to Puerto Rico, then Hispaniola, and finally Cuba. "Perhaps all these nearby places of considerable Spanish power embolden them to think that no one is mighty enough, or,"—he smiled—"idiotic enough to decamp so close to them, here in the northern extents of the Lesser Antilles." His finger drew an arc from Saba, through St. Eustatia and St. Christopher down to Nevis. "And yet, here we all are."

"All us idiots," Simonszoon growled. He almost grinned when his comment elicited a few equally sardonic laughs.

Tromp merely smiled. "Whether it is foolishness or fate that has brought us here is, for the moment, a debate we need not have. Rather, we must ask: after their defeat at the Grenada Passage, what will the Spanish do now?"

Chapter 42

Fort Oranjestad, St. Eustatia

Corselles, who was neither a seaman nor a soldier, gestured to the great blue expanse of the map on the table. "Why, it is obvious what the Spanish will do next. They will look for us all over. Relentlessly. Our only consolation is that finding us could take many months, maybe another year."

Tromp shook his head. "No. It will not."

"But why?"

Eddie leaned forward. "Because the Spanish that got away from the Grenada Passage brought back information that will help their bosses in Havana and Santo Domingo know where, and where not, to look for the ships that beat them up."

"What information would that be?" asked Sehested, studying the map as if seeing it anew.

Eddie shrugged. "Well, for starters, the mere fact that two immense USE steam cruisers were in the fight means a new team has slipped into the Caribbean. And given that our ships would have come out of the Baltic, they've probably got a pretty good guess at our course across the Atlantic. They will correctly guess that we entered the local swimming pool someplace very near that island-elbow Admiral Tromp was pointing out a minute ago.

"Which means that, unless we happened to stumble across Admiral Tromp's ships right before the battle, and by accident, we were already operating in coordination with a Dutch fleet. And I'm pretty sure they'll know the Dutch fleet they tangled with is not Thijssen's fleet from Curaçao, but the one that abandoned Recife."

"And how would they know that?" Corselles wondered in an almost desperate tone.

"First, the number of ships. As I understand it, Thijssen took Curaçao with just four, and that was the last expedition the United Provinces were able to mount. Next, how would Thijssen, sitting at the middle of the Spanish Main, have learned that we were going to be at Trinidad? And what reason would he have to come out and meet up with us? And how did all that happen just in time to catch a southbound Spanish fleet that he had no reason to suspect was headed toward Tierra Firma?" Eddie leaned back and shook his head. "As the guys in Havana start to put together those facts, and consider the other reports they must be receiving, they're going to become increasingly convinced that it couldn't have been Thijssen they met in the Grenada Passage."

"What other reports?" Sehested asked.

"Well, take the report that they'll get regarding the earl of Tyrconnell's raid on Puerto Cabello. The Spanish strategists would have to be pretty stupid not to interpret it as precisely what it was: a preemptive raid. By destroying their warehouses, we took out the provisioning for any fleet coming from Cartagena, thereby preventing it from joining the other fleet that was responding to our attack upon Trinidad. That is proof positive that there was widespread prior coordination between our forces before we engaged the Spanish off Grenada. Which in turn suggests that the attack on Trinidad was not simply a rogue event, but part of a much larger, well-considered operation."

Sehested nodded. "Which would logically mean, to them, that the wheels of this plan had been turning for half a year beforehand. Longer, since they must logically presume that our flotilla left Europe with the intent of arriving here at just the right time."

Eddie returned the nod. "Exactly. And how would Thijssen, whose base on Curacao is almost halfway to Cartagena, be able to get word of, and coordinate with, such a plan that far in advance? So, once they realize it wasn't him, they figure it can only be Admiral Tromp, who's been off their radar for more than a year. And when they start thinking about it, they'll start to make some pretty predictable conjectures. Such as: 'Well, if that was Tromp in the Grenada Passage, then those couldn't have been all of his ships. Which means he has a base somewhere. Where he's been hiding out for a whole year. And if he's feeding even half of the people he evacuated from Recife, then he can't be in some uncharted Brazilian cove because they'd have starved to death by now. And he can't be anywhere on the Spanish Main because our garda-costa and trade traffic along there would have encountered him months ago, at the latest.' And so their eyes drift to a part of the map where there are islands with rapid access to European supply, have a history of excellent fertility, where they know there are still some non-Spanish settlements, and where they know the Dutch tried starting some of their own." Eddie dropped his finger so that it touched St. Eustatia and Saba.

"And then they start wondering about the four ships that went missing—and which you sank—just off Saba late last year. And so, they will eventually realize that all the hypothetical smoking guns are, in fact, pointing right about here." He pushed his finger into the map again. "Oh, they won't figure it out that quickly, because the information will come in dribs and drabs, and they will have to exchange emissaries and letters and speculations and share any reconnaissance results they get. But make no mistake, thir light ships will come here looking. And when they do, one of two things will happen. They'll either see us before we see them and live to report. Or we'll see them first, catch them, and sink them without a trace. But even so, that still sends a kind of message." He leaned back. "The first rule of reconnaissance is that if your scout doesn't come back to report, the odds are good that he found something. So then you send three scouts in a group to visit the area where the first scout disappeared. And when they don't come back, well—" Eddie ended with his hands upraised, the conclusion so obvious that he didn't need to articulate it. "Which is pretty much what they already saw happen with the four ships they sent south from St. Maarten."

"Very well, so the Spanish will find us," Corselles agreed with a nervous nod. "But how will attacking them now save us? They are located all across that map, with many places of power. Once they know of us, they will drive us into the sea. Effortlessly."

Van Walbeeck folded his hands. "Pieter, the Spanish are not the monolithic force they may often seem. I have made a close study of their structures of government here in the New World, much of it revealed by research available at Grantville, paradoxically. Here is what I may tell you. In addition to great difficulties and loss of time in communicating with each other across such vast distances, the viceroyalties and governorships and *audiencias* are often rivals, striving to advance themselves at the expense of their neighbors. Knowing this, we may reasonably project the following:

"The greatest single power, the Viceroyalty of New Spain, is centered in Mexico. She is not particularly concerned with affairs in the Caribbean except and unless they impact her single overriding concern: the safety and reliability of the flota as her means of shipping gold and silver to Spain, and receiving supplies in return. She is slow to move and often sees Tierra Firma as a nuisance. Conversely, she traditionally perceives Havana as a competitor for preeminence and royal favor, since that city is the great shipbuilder and maritime defender of the region. But let us skip to a consideration of the Spanish power that is more likely to be concerned with maritime incursions: Cartagena, the closest naval power of any size."

"Not Caracas, and the *audiencias* of Venezuela?"

Van Walbeeck interlaced his fingers. "I do not think so, simply because what little strength she has is continually focused upon her contention with mainland natives. However, although Cartagena will be the most concerned when it comes to our invasion of Trinidad, she may well be fickle or undependable in her responses to the implication of our broader presence in the Caribbean."

"Why?" asked Rik Bjelke, who had remained almost motionless beside Sehested until now. "I thought the governor there—er, de Murga?—was a most active man."

"He is, but he answers to the viceroy of Peru."

Rik seemed puzzled. "But Peru is—"

"On the other side of South America, yes. It is a curious arrangement, an artifact of historical flukes and no small amount of sinecure. However that may be, this will work to slow and limit Cartagena's response. And in turn, that means she will concentrate her forces strictly upon that which threatens her interests most directly: Trinidad. This was confirmed by the surviving captains of the vessels we took as prizes there, several of whom were brought here for further questioning."

Corselles' eyes became grim. "And the rest of the prisoners?"

Tromp waved a dismissive hand. "Back at Trinidad. On one of what are called the Five Islands, just a few miles offshore from Port-of-Spain. They are quite secure."

"Because the island is so remote?"

"That, and because the Nepoia natives have decided to watch it quite carefully. They are most determined not to allow any new Spanish to set foot on Trinidad."

"So," Sehested said, returning to the main topic, "you do not expect either New Spain's or Cartagena's fleets to aid any efforts made against us here, in the northern extents of the Lesser Antilles."

"Correct. For both of them, we can only be reached by a very long sail against the prevailing winds or currents. And for now, at least, we represent no threat to their livelihoods. However, in the case of Cuba and the islands that are her immediate satellites"—Tromp ran

his finger to Havana and drifted it slowly eastward to
touch Jamaica, Hispaniola, and Puerto Rico—"we must
expect an aggressive response. We threaten them in a
variety of ways, not the least of which is our ability
to sail north and attempt to intercept the flota as it
returns to Spain with the silver that keeps Madrid's
bloated economy afloat."

"So, you are saying we need to mount a campaign
against the entirety of the Greater Antilles?" Corselles
looked as incredulous and horrified as he sounded.

Tromp moved toward the map again, shaking his
head. "Not at all. We know where they will gather
their strength for a strike against us. It is also the
same port to which most of the fleet we defeated
undoubtedly fled." He jabbed down at the south coast
of Hispaniola. "Here. Santo Domingo."

Sehested stroked his goatee meditatively. "Why
there?"

"Cuba is too far. Puerto Rico is too undeveloped,
particularly on her south coast, and her north coast
often has unfavorable winds. But Hispaniola is well-
developed, has several large towns, and Santo Domingo
has shipyards and quite respectable fortifications.
Furthermore, although the prevailing winds there
are contrary, they are milder than the breezes that
come straight off the Atlantic on the northern coast,
and her anchorage could easily accommodate a fleet
as large as sixty, perhaps seventy hulls."

"And how far between Santo Domingo and St.
Eustatia?"

"Approximately four hundred and fifty miles. Let us
assume contrary conditions, with a forward progress of
one knot. A fleet, sailing steadily, would still reach us

in no more than three weeks. Let us say four weeks, if they touched at Puerto Rico and refrained from sailing on moonless nights. Let us say five weeks if they encounter high weather."

"But that is after they find us, and decide to gather a fleet to send against us," Corselles said hopefully.

Simonszoon shrugged. "Yes, but finding us might not take more than two weeks."

"But at one knot—"

"Superintendent Corselles," Simonszoon interrupted sharply, "you have no doubt noticed that our jachts travel much more speedily than our fluyts, particularly when the weather is unfavorable?"

Corselles looked indignant, but too intimidated to speak. He simply nodded.

"Well, the Spanish *pataches* are akin to our jachts. Not so fast, not so agile, but they tack well and would be here in a week's time, easily. They could make it back to Santo Domingo in half that. So although it might take them six weeks to send a fleet here, their scouts could arrive much sooner than that."

"So we are to strike Santo Domingo," Sehested murmured. "To disable them before they may exterminate us."

"That is the gist of it," Tromp said with a nod.

"And how do you propose to protect Oranjestad, while you are off on this mission?" Corselles' eyes were large and bright. Eddie wondered if the man might be verging toward a breakdown. He hadn't been so anxious when the flotilla first arrived, but it almost seemed that, with relief and resupply finally at hand, his spirit was not pliable enough to face new risks and uncertainties. "And if we manage to defeat their fleet, won't the Spanish simply build another? How does this strategy furnish us with a lasting solution?"

Gjedde looked up. His voice sounded rough from disuse. "It is not a lasting solution. Nothing is. That is in the nature of contending nations. This stratagem answers the immediate threat and buys us time. But that time could be decisive. With the agreement forged between your Provinces and Brussels, you will soon have the renewed support of your homeland. The USE and my sovereign have established interests here, as well. You are no longer alone. Be consoled in this. It is a far brighter outlook than you had three months ago." He folded his hands and lowered his chin again.

Sehested nodded at this interjection and turned to Tromp. "However, there is another, more pressing danger in this stratagem. It means dividing our collective forces into three groups, does it not?"

Tromp sighed. "Yes. It is, unfortunately, unavoidable. We may not leave our forces and interests on Trinidad unguarded. Nor may we leave St. Eustatia without defenses. But we must carry the attack to Santo Domingo unless we are content to wait here until they overwhelm us, even with the up-time steamships."

Corselles' eyes had grown even larger. "So even your ships could not destroy all the Spanish hulls that might try attacking us here?"

Eddie shook his head. "No. They can't be every place at once, and we have a lot of strategic vulnerabilities that a knowledgeable enemy could exploit. The Spanish probably wouldn't even come straight at us. They might realize that our greatest vulnerability on this island is actually food, and so go after St. Christopher's instead, where we get our bulk provisioning. And then what do we do? Keep one steamship here, and send one there? And if they get a toehold on St. Christopher's, they can land troops there, and then try to get them across the channel at night. It's only eight miles, shore to shore." Eddie leaned back. "Look, if the Spanish are at all smart, they'll learn from the mistakes they're sure to make, and which—being Spain—they can easily afford. And once they've learned those lessons, then, even if they can't beat our steamships, they'll outflank us and take us on land. It might be a long fight for them, and it would be costly, but in the end, the only thing the Spanish wouldn't have beaten into submission are those two steam cruisers. And if those two ships have burned up their full supply of coal running back and forth, putting out fires—well, the wind can give us trouble just like anyone else. And we can run out of ammo just like anyone else, too."

"So you're saying your ships *aren't* magic?" Simonszoon leaned over to smile at Eddie.

Eddie smiled back. "Damn," he play-acted, "I guess I let that secret slip." He shook his head seriously. "The fact of the matter is that our steamships are fundamentally offensive platforms. They are at their best when they are on the attack, not defense. And that means, among other things, that the attack on Santo Domingo is going to require more than just warships. We're going to need to bring a number of Dutch fluyts along with us. We're going to need to bring a lot of troops and a lot of supplies, because we can't just beat their fleet. We have to hit the city itself so hard that they can't use it any more. If we accomplish that, then their next closest reasonable base is on Cuba. That means that the next time they try to mount an offensive campaign against us here, they would have to project that force almost twice as far. That means a lot more ships, a lot more money, a lot more men to feed for a lot more weeks. And for us, that means a lot more time before they can mount that kind of offensive. And that's what we're playing for here: enough time for our side to send what we need to prevail."

Corselles looked slightly less nervous. "Very well, but do you really need the fluyts? I have seen these immense ships of yours, riding at anchor. Can they not carry proportionately greater numbers of our troops, of the needed supplies?"

Eddie smiled, shook his head. "Oddly, no. For those of you who have not been below decks on one of our steamships, you would probably find it a strange sight. In the place of throngs of men, there is a lot of machinery and even more supplies. We shoot much faster and so use far more ammunition. The steam engines must be fired by coal, or at least wood, which must be kept dry and handy in special fuel bunkers. We have radios, intraship speaking tubes, special areas and companionways reserved for the exchange of stores or for access to secondary systems, such as our condensers."

"Your what?"

"Condensers, Superintendent Corselles. We use them to convert sea water to fresh water."

"So you may enjoy a refreshing drink whenever you choose, on your voyages?" Corselles tone hadn't been derisive, but nor had it been entirely jocular. The laughter that rose up was genuine, but slightly strained.

Eddie joined in, chuckling. "Well, that is a side benefit, Superintendent Corselles. But the real reason we have the condensers is because you can't run steam engines on salt water. You have to have fresh water. But if you can tell me where to find some bubbling island springs in the middle of the Atlantic, maybe we can leave those condensers behind to help you with your water shortages here on St. Eustatia."

A little polite laughter followed Eddie's reply, but most importantly, he could see in the faces at the table, even Corselles', that he had made his two points. First, that fresh water was an operational necessity not an indulgence, and, second, that it was inadvisable to make jokes based on superficial assumptions.

Tromp leaned his fists on the table. "Although we will be meeting often as we move our plans for the attack on Santo Domingo forward, we do have one last matter that must be addressed now. Speaking as the nominal commander of our allied fleet, we must find a new captain for the *Resolve*, and this means selecting a person who will learn the technologies of the ship, and its operation, quickly and well. The late Admiral Mund was schooled in this extensively at Luebeck, and personally witnessed much of *Resolve*'s final construction. We cannot hope to duplicate that level of familiarity here, but we must have a captain. We must also have a larger staff of technical specialists, led by the *Intrepid*'s executive officer Henrik Bjelke, ready to take the ship into battle. So, after polling my command staff, I consulted with the two senior officers of the USE and Danish flotilla, and we are unanimously resolved that the new captain should be Dirck Simonszoon."

Simonszoon groaned. "Oh, by all that's holy, Maarten. How could you do this to me?"

Tromp smiled. "I've seen you eyeing those guns, those engines, Dirck. And your sailing skill will be key, as well, since *Resolve* only uses her steam engines when she's in combat."

Simonszoon shook his head. "First you took me off my yacht, and put me on a great scow of a warship. And now I am to move from commanding a mere giant to a full-blown leviathan? And with a mere Danish pup to tell me how to run the machines?"

Bjelke, who was not yet accustomed to Simonszoon's broad gibes, started.

Tromp only smiled more widely. "Dirck, you know very well that Rik has the necessary skills for both roles, since you've told me so yourself. Multiple times."

Rik looked as suddenly pleased as he had been suddenly dismayed. Simonszoon only looked annoyed at having had his better nature and opinions publicly revealed. "I was lying. And what of the matter of authority?"

"What do you mean?" asked Joost van Banckert.

"I mean that with Gjedde and Cantrell on *Intrepid*, that puts both of the senior USE commanders on one ship, and none on the *Resolve*. How is that wise? And furthermore, by what authority am I to be in charge there? I am not a part of that flotilla. I serve Maarten Harpertszoon Tromp and the United Provinces, and in that order."

Sehested smoothed his mustache. "I fear the command situation is even more complicated than that, Captain Simonszoon. In the command ranks of our flotilla, Captain Gjedde is now the first senior officer.

But arguably, Tryggve Stiernsköld, as a Swedish post captain, is next, and *then* Commander Cantrell. By all rights, therefore, it should be Captain Stiernsköld who is the master of the second steam cruiser."

Eddie scanned the faces, ended upon Stiernsköld's; he was fairly sure what he read there, and that he had an accurate measure of that taciturn yet straightforward man. "Captain Stiernsköld, tell me, do you feel comfortable commanding one of the steam cruisers?"

Stiernsköld shook his head. "No," he said flatly.

Sehested started, stared between the two men as if seeking prior collusion and frowned when he saw there was none.

"Captain Stiernsköld," Eddie continued, "do you think you ever *will* be comfortable commanding one?"

The Swede nodded. "Most certainly. Once I have received adequate training. But I have not. I am told I was included in the flotilla for my abilities with fast, mixed rig sailing vessels, such as the *Tropic Surveyor*. As you no doubt know, Commander Cantrell, I was only briefed on the steamships' capabilities so that I knew what they might do and how best to coordinate with them. I received no training in their operation."

Sehested leaned back, nodded. "Very well. You have made your point, Commander Cantrell, and most convincingly. I withdraw my reservations over the proper chain of command in the ships of the flotilla. But I still cannot countenance a foreign captain—even one so skilled and friendly to our cause as Captain Simonszoon—to be the master of *Resolve*."

Eddie rubbed his nose and schooled his voice to be apologetic yet firm. "Unfortunately, Lord Sehested, that objection is a bit beside the point."

"I beg your pardon?"

"Lord Sehested, so we all understand your position with complete clarity, who appointed you to the flotilla?"

Sehested's frown intensified as he spoke, seemed to be veering toward umbrage. "You know very well that it was your own father-in-law, Christian IV, who asked me to accompany this mission."

"Yes, but on what authority did he make that assignment?"

Sehested opened his mouth but shut it again, his eyes narrowing slightly. Clearly, he saw where this was heading. "He was exercising his prerogative as one of the sovereigns of the Union of Kalmar."

"Yes. Which is not a member of the United States of Europe, nor are any of its constituent powers. Now, the steam cruisers: to whom do they belong?"

"The United States of Europe—whose monarch is Gustav Adolf, who is also *primus inter pares* among the monarchs of the Union of Kalmar."

"That is very true. But it is also quite a separate matter. Gustav Adolf may indeed dictate the actions of the USE in his role as its monarch, but not in his role as the king of Sweden or as the first-among-equals from the Union of Kalmar. Consequently, unless my understanding of the prerogatives that attach to these separate roles is in error, none of the Danish, or even Swedish, members of the flotilla may speak for, or presume authority possessed by, the USE. That would fall to individuals who are nationals of the USE, or who have been directly and explicitly named by Gustav Adolf of Sweden to be operating in its service."

"Such as yourself," van Walbeeck concluded, a slight grin hidden behind his hand, "on both counts."

Eddie shrugged. "It does so happen that I am the senior ranking representative of the USE with the flotilla." *A position which Simpson made absolutely sure of, bless his crusty and irascible hide. It was as if he saw this wrestling match coming from the very moment I proposed the mission.* "Consequently, while it was agreed, from the outset, that I could not hold a field rank equivalent to the many senior Danish and Swedish commanders in the flotilla, my equal share of authority regarding the management and strategy of the flotilla was—and remains—undiminished." He turned to Simonszoon, whose usually veiled eyes were wide in frank admiration. *Didn't think I had the stones for this sort of down-and-dirty politicking, eh, Dirck? Well, guess what: neither did I.* Eddie didn't miss a beat. "Captain Dirck Simonszoon, as a sign of the amity and alliance between our nations here in the New World, might I ask you to accept the temporary command of the USS *Resolve* as a special commission?"

"Commander—Sir! It would be my honor, if my admiral may spare me from the Dutch fleet."

Tromp smiled. "You have my leave and encouragement to accept Commander Cantrell's offer, Captain. Make the Provinces proud."

Simonszoon scoffed. "And when have I done any less?"

Van Walbeeck grinned. "Do you mean on the deck of a ship, or in a grog shop?"

Dirck pointedly did not glance down the table at Jan, but rather, tugged at his collar. "It's getting hot in here. Let's finish this damned meeting."

Chapter 43

Oranjestad, St. Eustatia

The one large wooden building in Oranjestad—an all-purpose *gemeentehuis*, indoor market, and dance hall—was already starting to fill with eager guests. The somber mood of the late morning funeral that had been conducted not twenty yards away had dissipated completely. That was hardly a surprise: Pros Mund had stepped ashore all of one time, and the whispering behind cupped hands opined that his wife was at best a recluse and at worst an emotionless and aloof exemplar of all that was deplorable in aristocrats.

"A welcome occasion, a party," Tromp observed as he remained well to the back of the slightly elevated platform at the rear of the building.

"A novel occasion," van Walbeeck corrected. "This is the first true party we've had."

Tromp, who had spent many weeks on patrol, and the rest of the time too busy to partake, or even become passingly familiar, with the social life of Oranjestad, started. "Can that—can that be?"

"It most certainly can, Maarten. What did you think?

That while you were slaving away for the good of the colony, the rest of us were dancing and drinking?"

"No, no, but I—"

Jan laughed someplace down in his belly, and put a hand on his friend's shoulder. "You are always so delightfully earnest, Maarten. I know you were well aware that our colonists have not had a lightsome time, this past year. But I do suspect that you might have imagined that, out here in the town, the rituals of life managed to go on as before, albeit much diminished."

Tromp reflected. "I suppose I did. I suppose I wanted to imagine it that way. Because if there was some semblance of normal existence, it meant that I—we—were providing for the colonists sufficiently."

Jan squeezed his shoulder. "Well, see now? All your hard work is finally rewarded: a party!"

"Yes," Tromp grumbled, "mostly victualed from the larders of Danes."

"Well, how should it be otherwise? It is a presentation of their king's daughters to the society of Oranjestad. Such as it is."

"We have 'society' in a town that has not had a single party in a year?"

"Of course we do."

"And how do you tell the members of society apart from everyone else?"

"Quite simply, Maarten. The members of Oranjestad society still have real shoes."

Tromp stared sidelong at Jan, saw his smile, and could not resist joining him in a brief chuckle. "It is good to have a moment to leave business behind, my friend."

"It would be," Jan admitted in a slightly more somber tone.

Tromp resolved not to frown. "And what is it now?"

"I have had word from Michael McCarthy. He believes the radio will be ready tonight."

"Tonight? So he will not be here?"

Jan shook his head. "No. And I suspect he is secretly relieved at the coincidence. He sent his formal regrets to Lord Sehested, who seemed relieved to receive them, as I understand it."

"Sehested doesn't like McCarthy?"

"Oh, no. Nothing of the sort. But I suspect he may plan to use this social event as an opportunity to do a bit of politicking. And radio messages to and from Europe would only get in the way. Particularly since those communications would involve contact with uptime authorities."

"Ah," Tromp exhaled, seeing where Jan was leading. "So you think Sehested wanted Eddie on his own, tonight, and without recourse to his leaders?"

"The possibility has crossed my mind. However, one thing is certain: before this party begins, you and I must decide who we shall continue to meet with openly as we frame our plans for Santo Domingo, and who we must exclude."

Tromp nodded. "Because we must restrict spreading word about the radio, which will be an integral part of those plans."

"That, and general prudence against setting loose lips flapping here in our own town. Consider Corselles. He has no role in deciding upon how we shall attack Santo Domingo. However, were he to be kept apprised, he would, alas, be quite capable of giving away subtle strategic details without even knowing he was doing so. And there are other avenues by which necessarily secret information might become widely known. For instance, ship's captains often drink to excess just as much as their sailors do."

"Jan, are you referring to—?"

Walbeeck held up a hand. "I am not mentioning individuals because I am not thinking of individuals. I simply note that, the more persons who are involved in the early planning of our attack, the more chances we have of enemies getting wind of its particulars."

Tromp sighed. "It is sad, but prudent. Besides, there is entirely too much dissent among our own landowners. They have regular contact with our captains, our pursers."

Van Walbeeck shook his head. "And what of our tradesmen and workers who go back and forth from St. Christopher's? They seem to do a more lively trade in rumors and gossip than anything else. And the French there, those who mix in with the English, will carry those rumors down into their capital at Basseterre. And we know that both governors, Warner no less than d'Esnambuc, both turn a blind eye toward trade with the pirates of Jamaica and Tortuga."

"So who is our inner council of war, then? Just the two of us?"

"Well, Maarten, truth be told, I'm none too sure about your reliability, either."

"Very funny, Jan. Who else? Eddie, obviously. Banckert."

"Even though you have to leave him behind in Oranjestad, again?"

"Absolutely. Joost must know what we are doing, and when, and why, if he is to be able to react to unforeseen crises or changes."

"Fair enough, Maarten. Anyone else?"

"I do not think we can include Eddie without including Gjedde. It would be too profound a slight to the senior officer of our allies. And besides, Gjedde doesn't speak much, but when he does, it's always worth listening to."

Van Walbeeck nodded vigorously. "Agreed. Simonszoon?"

"I think we must, and he's not much more talkative than Gjedde, usually."

"What about the ground commanders? Once we get to Santo Domingo, they will need to know everything."

"Yes, but at this stage, they do not need to know anything. As we begin studying the maps we have of Santo Domingo, and gathering reports on its walls and troops, then we will bring them in. Although—"

"Yes?"

"I wish we had the earl of Tyrconnell here. He is a clever fellow, quite experienced, and well educated. More importantly, he has spent his life in Spanish service and knows the smallest details of their protocols."

"Having taken a few Spanish ships and towns ourselves, we are hardly ignorant in such matters, Maarten."

"True, but we still remain outsiders to that knowledge. It is not *instinctive* to us. Conversely, the earl of Tyrconnell was a well-placed insider, trained in Spanish service, including artillery. Besides, he is a prudent man who has spent a lifetime learning how to hold his tongue and be cautious. He had little choice, since the English have wanted his head, and do so more than ever, now."

"Ah. Because he is the last earl of Ireland. Tell me, why is he not here?"

Tromp shrugged. "Because he is doing other important work that only he may do."

"And what, and where, is that?"

"O'Donnell and Pieter Floriszoon split off from our fleet when we drew near Montserrat."

"Why there?"

"The population is overwhelmingly comprised of Irish catholic refugees from Nevis. Apparently they fled after a religious disagreement several years back. He is hoping to rally the support of the settlement there, possibly even draw some new recruits to his colors."

"Well, it still sounds as though he had some help with that. Without Floriszoon's *Eendracht*, he would have had to ask the recruits to swim back here."

"Not entirely true. He is half owner of the *patache* his men took in Puerto Cabello. We own the other half."

"And so is the earl a proficient seaman, among his other wonderful traits?"

"No, although Floriszoon tells me he has the right instincts for it. And whereas our fellows are teaching the Irish how to be sailors, the Wild Geese are imparting some lessons in weapon-handling and even the finer arts of boarding a ship."

"They are teaching *us* how to board ships?"

"Many of them spent time as ship's troops. The Spanish train their lead-rank boarders quite specially it seems. O'Donnell and Floriszoon are sharing that knowledge and between them, they seem to be making a good team."

"Yes," agreed Jan, "it's all needful skills they are exchanging."

Tromp shook his head. "I mean more than that, and more than the greater and improbable combination of our Dutch sea dogs and O'Donnell's Wild Geese. I'm referring to the pairing of O'Donnell with Floriszoon *personally*, the fact that they get along well, that they have worked together. That is a serendipitous first bridge between Amsterdam and Brussels in this new Netherlands in which we now exist."

"In what way?"

Sometimes, Jan van Walbeeck's fine intellectual insights blinded him to more visceral human truths. Not often, but this was one of those moments. "Jan, O'Donnell and Floriszoon are both young men, both educated, both tired of the religious bigotry that fueled the wars that defined their lives and those of their forebears. We are fortunate that both are philosophical enough in their respective faiths to find ample room for toleration of the other." Tromp leaned back. "I would not interrupt the solidification of that friendship even if it cost me a ship and twenty good guns. Because the cooperation—*willing* cooperation— between the Brabant and our United Provinces, of linking our fates and fortunes as a single nation means more in the long run than any single battle. And it will be fortunate and wise to have men of intelligence and experience who may be liaisons between those two dominions at moments of friction. Men such as O'Donnell and Floriszoon. Much may be done if the leaders of our new country are operating in concert. Much may be lost if they are not. And men such as these two young captains may be just the insurance the Netherlands needs to maintain enough unity of purpose and mutual understanding to survive the first years of genuine integration. Allies are far more difficult to manage than enemies, after all."

"How timely an axiom," murmured van Walbeeck. "Here comes another one of those potentially difficult allies, now."

Hannibal Sehested, attired in understated splendor that flattered the event without quite making him conspicuous, approached with a broad smile. "Gentlemen," he said in passable Dutch, "how do you fare this evening?"

They bowed, Jan replying as he did so. "Quite well, Sir Sehested, and our thanks for your sovereign's generosity, that we might make merry while making the formal acquaintance of his lovely daughters."

He bowed in return. "I wish the evening could do both better honor to the ladies, and to you, our hosts in this far land. And it saddens me that fate had us choose the date that should turn out to be the same as marks our mourning of Admiral Mund."

"Indeed," agreed Tromp solemnly. "I did not know him well, but he seemed prudent and concerned for the safety of his men." Tromp spotted Eddie entering the building from the rear door, scanning faces as he began roving along the edges of the early-comers. "Ah, Commander Cantrell, do join us." *And save me from this eager young Danish diplomat.*

Eddie, looking very distracted, stopped, nodded and wandered over, remembering to bow instead of shaking hands at the very last second. "Nice to see you all, gentlemen. I wonder if you have seen my lovely wife?"

"I am afraid not, Lord Cantrell, although with half an hour left before her entrance, I would not expect to find her here," Sehested replied. "But this is an excellent vantage point to scan for her, if she makes an early appearance. And as you do, you might perhaps share your insights on our fallen hero, Admiral Mund."

Eddie sounded confused, looked suddenly cautious. "Uh—insights? I can't really say I knew him that well."

"No, of course not. Pros Mund was a private man. And so, the causes of his actions were not always fully understood by those who witnessed them. Indeed, I had not foreseen that he would be such an indomitable lion once combat was joined. But he was bold indeed, taking so many prizes."

Tromp suppressed a sigh. Now Sehested's motivation for this conversation was becoming clear: to further "discuss" the matter of the Spanish prize ships. Which had caused some debate in the wake of the battle.

Of the twenty-six Spanish ships that were present for the Battle of the Grenada Passage, three had been sunk outright. Five more were so badly damaged by the guns of the USE steam cruisers that they had necessarily been scuttled. Three had to be abandoned before guns or other valuable items could be recovered from them. The fires had been too dangerous and widespread to risk coming alongside. Four had been taken as prizes, although only one—a refitted nao that had struck her colors when the *Intrepid* bore down upon her—was fundamentally undamaged. Of the other three, one—a galleoncete that Tromp's own Dutch ships had been raked with fire and disabled before she could flee with the rest of the Spaniards' southern van—was still capable of independent maneuver. The other two, galleons much pummeled by the two USE steam cruisers, had suffered immense damage to their spars, and, in one case, the rudder and tiller mechanism.

An even split of the prizes was deemed fair in the immediate aftermath of the battle, the Dutch claiming a galleon and the galleoncete that they had taken themselves, while the USE and Danish contingent had settled for the nao and a galleon.

However, upon radioing a report of this ahead to Oranjestad when they finally came into range, Hannibal Sehested had initiated a swift, if polite, challenge to that apportionment of spoils. Specifically, the Danish diplomat had argued that the steam cruisers had performed the greatest deeds of the day, and so, had earned more than half of the prizes. When there was some resistance to this by Tromp, Sehested countered by pointing to the bravery and sacrifice of Mund as a further reason that it was the contribution of the Danes (he began omitting references to the USE at this point) which had made the victory possible at all. Accordingly, they should at least be given the two largest warships— the galleons—instead of accepting the ponderous and decidedly mercantile nao as one of their prizes.

It was uncertain how the debate would ultimately have resolved, had not Ove Gjedde finally, and reluctantly, become involved. He pointed out that the galleons were not particularly useful to his own Danish fleet as warships. In the current circumstances, they were too slow and incorrectly rigged for military operations in the Caribbean, and two galleons would have been difficult to crew, when the flotilla already had enough guns and hulls to man. However, in claiming the nao, Gjedde pointed out that Denmark had also received first choice of her intact stores and cargo, and that being a high weather ship, like a galleon, she would be well-suited to convoying those spoils home to Copenhagen. Sehested was at pains to graciously accept this perspective (which matched the original division of prize hulls) and thanked Gjedde for his "subtle wisdom" in making these choices on behalf of Sehested and King Christian IV. Or, as Simonszoon had commented, for having shown that the Danish diplomat had as much knowledge about ships as a boar had about bathtubs.

But here was Sehested mentioning the prize hulls yet again. Tromp hoped that the Dane would not be so crude as to use his role as the magnanimous provider of tonight's food and drink as a means of exerting pressure to yet again revisit the twice-approved division of spoils.

But that did not seem to be the Danish diplomat's intent after all. "I understand that other bold actions were undertaken beforehand to secure our alliance's resounding victory. I refer, of course to the daring raid upon Puerto Cabello. I had hoped to meet that commander, the Irish earl, here at the party but I am informed that he did not return with your fleet. Is that correct?"

"It is, Sir Sehested. He and one of our captains, Pieter Floriszoon, diverted to Montserrat. They had refugees to deposit there, and it was also thought best to also acquaint that island's settlers with the earl of Tyrconnell *bona fides*."

"Ah, yes," Sehested said with a nod. "It is populated by Irish Catholics, is it not?"

"Yes," affirmed van Walbeeck, "and it is our hope that they might proclaim loyalty to the earl. Which, given his service to Brussels, would mean adding another safe haven for the ships of the Netherlands."

He nodded at Eddie. "If we were to be able to count upon Montserrat as another island allied to our cause, along with those inhabited by the English, we would be most excellently situated, having control over all the northern Lesser Antilles. With the exception of our old colony on St. Maarten, that is."

"That would be an excellent development," agreed Sehested, "and it is fortuitous that you should mention St. Maarten. That island is of particular interest to his royal Danish Majesty, Christian the Fourth."

"Indeed? Is he interested in its salt-flats? At some point we hope to return there to reestablish our salt-fish production. Would he wish to join us in this?" asked van Walbeeck.

"No," Sehested said calmly. "He wishes to take and claim the island for Denmark, in recognition of his contributions to the defeat of the Spanish throughout the Caribbean and the rescue of your colony here in particular. Of course, his Majesty would be happy to grant the right to reopen the commercial operations you call 'factories' without tariff or other fee to his Dutch friends, and would be particularly gratified to materially aid those who lost their business interests in the place when the Spanish evicted you last year."

Tromp was stunned but, being a fairly quiet man, knew that his stunned silence was not particularly noticeable. Garrulous van Walbeeck's speechlessness, on the other hand, was a marked contrast with his usual demeanor. His cheeks puffing, he reddened slightly and finally sputtered. "This—this is most unexpected, Sir Sehested."

Eddie Cantrell's arch stare suggested that he had not expected it, either. "Excuse me, Sir Sehested."

"Yes, Sir Cantrell?"

"Is this according to the will of the Union of Kalmar? Which is to say, does Gustav know anything about this—request?"

"No, he has not been apprised of this *requirement*. But after all, your royal father-in-law is a sovereign. In all that the term signifies and entails. This falls well outside the peripheries of consultation between the different monarchs who are bound together in the Union of Kalmar."

"Yes. I see. Please excuse me a moment."

"Do you have a pressing matter, Lord Cantrell? You shall figure prominently as we continue this discussion, I assure you."

Eddie smiled—a bit too brightly, Tromp thought. "I'm sure I do, but as the spouse of one of this evening's guests of honor, I have a little of my own coordinating to do before the festivities begin. Excuse me. I won't be long."

Tromp had to consciously stop himself from calling— "No! Don't leave!"—after Eddie as Hannibal Sehested began discussing the optimal timetable for retaking St. Maarten from the Spanish.

Chapter 44

Oranjestad, St. Eustatia

Anne Cathrine rolled her eyes as, yet again, there was a knock on the door. "We are hurrying as quickly as we may, Matilde," she called patiently and, she hoped, sweetly to the young Dutch girl who had been working as messenger and girl Friday for the three young Danish ladies. Who were deeply involved in making their toilet and the dress preparations necessitated by their imminent presentation to Oranjestad society.

The voice that responded was not Matilde's. "Uh, it's me, Eddie."

"What? Eddie? Husband—dear—I am, that is, we are—" Anne Cathrine glanced at shy, half-dressed Leonora and Sophie Rantzau's calm, casual nudity—"we are indisposed. Most decidedly indisposed."

"Oh. Still? Um, honey, are you still indisposed, too?"

"I am dressed, if that is what you are asking." Anne Cathrine had to remind herself not to sound coyly seductive. Which is how she usually responded whenever Eddie had occasion to ask her about her state of dress.

"Yeah, that's exactly what I'm asking. Because—"

"Yes?" Anne Cathrine stood. The tone in Eddie's voice was uncommonly serious. "Is something wrong, Eddie?"

"Well, yeah. Someone's making trouble at your party. Already."

Anne Cathrine, without having any idea who might make trouble at a party that would not yet start for twenty minutes or how they would do so, gathered her considerable skirts and began walking to the door. "Who is making this trouble? Have you told Sehested about this?"

"Oh, he knows. Actually, he's helping the trouble-maker."

"What? Who is this troublemaker?"

"Unless I'm very much mistaken, it's your father."

"*What?*"

"Honey, come on out and walk with me. I'll explain on the way to the main conference room in the fort. I've already sent Matilde to get Sehested and the others."

By the time Eddie reached the wide, shuttered room on the second story of the fort's expansive blockhouse, Tromp, Sehested and van Walbeeck were all there. Sehested rose, smiling, "So, we are to have a meeting to settle this matter now? That is quite agreeable to—"

And then he saw Anne Cathrine enter from behind Eddie, who was holding the door for her. She was not smiling. "L-Lady Anne Cathrine," he stuttered. "This is a most awkward surprise."

"Yes," she replied archly. "I rather imagine it must be."

Eddie could hardly keep from beaming as he thought at her, *you go, girl!*

Sehested spread wide, temporizing hands. "Lady Anne Cathrine, I am dismayed that you were summoned away from a party being held in your honor. Of course, it is also for Lady Leonora as well, and it is a privilege to introduce Mistress Rantzau along with you. But you are the oldest king's daughter, and so—"

"And so it is my duty to be present when the king of Denmark's affairs of state are to be discussed. My husband was quite right to summon me, and I will be pleased to have you present this *requirement* that my royal father has evidently instructed you to impose upon our Dutch allies."

Unless Eddie was very much mistaken, Jan van Walbeeck was ready to explode in amusement and enthusiasm for the spirited and capable young Danishwoman who had, uninvited, swept to the seat at the head of the conference table. Tromp himself hastened to hold her chair, which she acknowledged with a smile as radiant as the rising sun.

The men sat, and she nodded at Sehested.

He shifted slightly in his seat and gazed down at the table. "Lady Anne Cathrine, I must point out that, while I am delighted that you take such keen interest in your father's royal desires and political actions, he did not ask you to represent him here in the New World."

"He did not need to. I am his daughter. I do not need to be told that I should pay close heed to my father's interests. And to my husband's as well, since you told him that this conversation would concern him, too."

"And so it does. But that is predominantly a military matter. And as a king's daughter—"

Anne Cathrine's green eyes were bright and wide, as if daring Sehested to take one step further down the inevitable path he intended: to point out that since she was not a princess, she had no material interest in the royal family's possessions or affairs. She was not in line of succession herself, nor was she a full royal sibling to any of Christian's potential successors.

But on the other hand, she was now sitting at the head of the table, her father's very fiery and competent daughter, with her up-time, Danish-titled husband to one side, and the senior Dutch admiral and administrator in the New World seated on the other side. Sehested's eyes rose from the tabletop, scanning their faces, and Eddie knew what he was looking for: the faintest hint of uncertainty or anxiety. *He's playing poker. He's trying to see whether we're bluffing or whether we will see his bid and call.*

Sehested was no fool, and was evidently good enough at poker to see that the other players were not going to fold, but would see this hand all the way to the bitter end. Which meant that, even if he was perfectly within his legal rights to exclude Anne Cathrine from the conversation, and even the room, he would have destroyed his credibility with the three men sitting around her, to say nothing of his relationship with her. And, princess or not, she had her father's ear and she would clearly not be an advocate for Sehested's interests in court. On the contrary, she might become an implacable and quite effective foe. So Sehested shrugged. "As a king's daughter, you are welcome to hear of your father's wishes. They were given to me as a contingency that might require execution, based upon what we might find upon arriving in the New World, and what actions we might be called upon to undertake once here. However, while I would be saddened to displease you in any way, you must of course realize that, as the agent of your father's will, I may not alter my duty to suit your own wishes."

Chin high, Anne Cathrine nodded. "You would be a poor representative of his interests, if you did. Please continue."

"As you wish, Lady Anne Cathrine." Sehested turned his gaze to Tromp and van Walbeeck. "I hope you gentlemen will not think ill of me if I am quite candid."

"We would prefer that," Tromp said quietly.

"Very well. His Majesty King Christian IV is concerned, and somewhat dismayed, that no provision has been made to reward Denmark for her participation in this mission to the New World. She is not party to the joint ownership of the oil drilling ventures in Trinidad, has been promised no land rights on any of the islands there or here in the Lesser Antilles, and most recently was even denied what seemed a just share of the treasure gained in the recent battle of the Grenada Passage even though her ships were responsible for crippling or sinking all but one of the Spanish vessels that were defeated."

Eddie frowned. "Sir Sehested, you are incorrect in one particular. *Intrepid* and *Resolve* are not Danish ships. They are USE warships."

"Yes. And seventy percent of their crews are Danish."

"Provided to the USE through the kind agencies of Gustav Adolf as first sovereign of the Union of Kalmar, not directly by King Christian IV."

"Your father-in-law the king sees the matter differently. However, that is ultimately of no account, here. His requirements are not contingent upon whatever gratitude these Dutch gentlemen might feel for his contributions to this alliance, although he would have preferred that those finer sentiments had been strong enough to induce them to offer voluntarily that upon which I must now insist. Namely, that the island of St. Maarten be taken with all practicable haste in the name of King Christian IV of Denmark."

Tromp shook his head, more in bemused confusion than negation. "And we are supposed to do that *for* you?"

"Several support ships and troops are all we require. As for the act of claiming, that will be done by our senior representative and the leader of the expedition to St. Maarten."

Eddie frowned. "I don't think Captain Gjedde will wish to—"

"Lord Cantrell, it is you who are the senior representative."

"*Me?*"

"Of course. Oh, you are not the ranking military commander, but you are a noble of Denmark. You are the husband of the king's daughter. And, as your king, Christian IV is happy to pass to you the honor and duty of taking and claiming St. Maarten in his name."

Eddie was about to wax prolific and even profane on what he thought of being bushwhacked to be the executor of that honor and duty, when he peripherally detected a stiffening in Anne Cathrine. He paused, not looking at her because that could signal weakness or lack of resolve to Sehested. But what might have caused Anne Cathrine to sit up a little straighter, lose her relaxed, confident posture?

The answer came to him immediately. *Oh. Sure. Because she's now skewered along with me on her*

Daddy's two-pronged loyalty test. Prong One: is Eddie loyal enough to take up this duty, which would mean that I'm putting my duties as an honorary Danish citizen before any possible objections that might arise from the USE? But if I defy the order and flunk my test, then King Daddy's Prong Two activates: will Anne Cathrine be more loyal to her father, or her husband?

Eddie frowned. He'd learned, from both life and countless strategy games, that if an adversary confronts you with a choice, your best chance at winning lies in breaking outside that either-or paradigm. In short, you need to come up with a choice of your own. And Eddie saw a way to do that, and save everyone's reputation and honor, if only they were open-minded enough to play along for the first few steps—

He turned away from Sehested and faced Maarten Tromp. "Admiral, I am put in the uncomfortable position of having to request your assistance in taking St. Maarten as a Danish expedition. With apologies in advance, may I humbly ask for your cooperation in this matter? I assure you, it will earn tremendous gratitude from the highest authorities whom I serve."

Tromp frowned. "It seems that your highest authority believes our instincts for gratitude are sorely wanting, so I am not sure how our cooperation will improve your royal-father-in-law's opinion of us."

Eddie shook his head. "Allow me to clarify. King Christian IV of Denmark is not the highest authority I serve." He detected flinches from either elbow, one from Anne Cathrine and one from Sehested. "I am an officer in the service of the USE and its commander-in-chief, Gustav Adolf of Sweden, who is its monarch. While I suspect he would frown upon the requirement being exerted by his royal cousin's proxy-agent, Sir Sehested, I suspect he would be more concerned with ensuring that our fleet continues to be a functional combat force."

Tromp's eyes narrowed. "Yes. I see what you mean."

"Well, I don't!" van Walbeeck exclaimed. "How does this issue affect the operational status of our combined fleet?"

Eddie shrugged. "As Sir Sehested pointed out, almost seventy percent of the flotilla's crews are Danish. They were trained and furnished to the Union of Kalmar and hence to the USE thanks to my father-in-law's keen interest in technology and training his subjects in its uses. But, unlike me, their first authority is King Christian IV, and I suspect they will listen to a known junior councilor of his court,"—Eddie glanced at wide-eyed Sehested—"before they listen to me. At least in matters of national loyalty, and of discerning which banner they must serve and obey first: that of Denmark, the Union of Kalmar, or the USE. But perhaps Sir Sehested will shed some light on the crux of this matter by answering a simple question: if I were to refuse to carry out King Christian IV's directive, would he, in turn, order the Danish members of my crews to stand down from their duties until I complied?" Eddie turned to look at Sehested and felt his wife lean closer to him.

Hannibal Sehested gestured vaguely at the fleet anchored beyond the shuttered blockhouse windows. "I am the agent of my sovereign's will and so, would be compelled to do as you say. If pressed." He looked at Eddie, and then Anne Cathrine, and lastly at Tromp, very intently. "And I assure you, I truly pray you will not press me to do such a thing." His eyes pleaded more desperately than his words.

So, Hannibal wasn't such a bad guy after all. He was just a man doing his job, and not liking it too much, right now. Denmark had ties with all the allies who were literally or figuratively present in the room. As part of the Union of Kalmar, it was de facto allied to the USE. His king's daughter was not merely married to but genuinely and thoroughly smitten with an up-timer and his people's ways. And there had long been amity and exchange between Copenhagen and Amsterdam. Sehested would clearly not enjoy being placed in a position where he was an agent of potential discord among those forces, all allied in their mission against Spanish domination in the New World.

Eddie nodded. "I understand your duty," he said to Hannibal. "However, in order to fulfill my duties to all parties, I must also predict that ordering our Danish crewmen to stand down would potentially jeopardize our alliance with the Netherlands, with which the USE is now involved in a crucial co-ownership of New World oil supplies." Eddie turned to Tromp. "Am I right in assuming that the United Provinces would be disinclined to comply with King Christian IV's requirement if they are not offered at least a token of appreciation for their willingness to overlook the highly irregular and manipulative manner whereby the requirement was issued to them?"

Van Walbeeck was not able to hide his sly smile as he bumped his elbow into Tromp's. The admiral cut his eyes at his friend and murmured, "Apparently, a token of appreciation would ensure our compliance."

"Very well," said Eddie, who at last stole a second to look at his bride—and nearly lost his composure. Anne Cathrine was smiling at him with an admiring, horny ferocity that made it necessary for Eddie to shoo away visions of her ravishing him here on the tabletop right after she peremptorily dismissed the other three men from the room. He swallowed and pulled his eyes away. "So, er, given that King Christian IV has charged me with accomplishing the task of retaking St. Maarten, and insofar as it requires Dutch cooperation to do so, I hereby secure the willing aid of the United Provinces by ensuring them that, in recognition of their cooperation and amity to help Denmark accomplish that which she could not accomplish alone, that her captains and commercial factors shall enjoy full and tariff-free access to St. Maarten, in perpetuity. This includes all harbor facilities, all trade, and free and equal access to the salt pans of the island in the interest of resuming their former salt-fish production there." He turned back to Tromp and van Walbeeck. "Is this acceptable to the representatives of the United Provinces, presuming we do not undertake operations until some time next year?"

Tromp, eyes still narrowed, smiled and nodded slowly as if watching a pupil solve a problem several steps more advanced than he should have been ready to address. "It is most acceptable, Commander Cantrell. It will be my personal pleasure to work with you in securing St. Maarten for the Danish crown in 1636, given its generous assurance that the United Provinces shall have free and equal use of its facilities in perpetuity."

Eddie looked over at Hannibal. "Do you have any questions, concerns, or objections to this arrangement, Sir Sehested?"

And Sehested, knowing full well that if he objected, King Christian could conceivably blame him for the failure to snatch the island, shook his head and smiled.

"No, Lord Cantrell, I have nothing to add or object. I think we may consider our business here concluded. Lady Anne Cathrine, I believe it is time for you to meet your sister and make your entrance to the party. And here, providentially, are your two hosts whose duty it is to escort you into the building."

Tromp and van Walbeeck rose, each offering an arm to Anne Cathrine. She rose with their completely unnecessary assistance and led the way to the exit. Tromp did not just smile but grinned at Eddie as he passed. A step behind, van Walbeeck jiggled the up-timer's elbow conspiratorially. "After the party—some schnapps, perhaps?" Eddie nodded diffidently, was too busy watching his wife—

—Who, as she exited the room, turned her head briefly in his direction and sent him a look that sent all thoughts of schnapps out of the up-timer's head. Eddie knew just what he was doing after the party tonight, and it didn't involve sitting around tossing back shots with a genial, middle-aged Dutchman.

When the trio had left, Sehested rose, his hand out. "Lord Cantrell, well done."

Well done? He took and shook Hannibal's hand. "No hard feelings, then?"

Sehested looked slightly perplexed, slightly confused. "If I understand your idiom, no: no 'hard feelings.' In fact, your solution is a great burden lifted from me. I was unsure if the Dutch could be brought around to help us take an island upon which, to some degree, they have best claim. You found a solution that your father-in-law did not foresee." He stopped, considered. "Or perhaps that was his purpose."

"What do you mean?"

"I harbor a suspicion, Lord Cantrell, that King Christian occasionally sets us tasks for which he has no solution in mind, simply to test our determination, our resourcefulness, our ingenuity. If I am right in this conjecture, then I suspect he will be happier with *how* you achieved this than he is with the achievement itself." Hannibal smiled. "And as for me, I am happy to be sharing this strange adventure with a fellow who at once respects royal authority, yet is no fawning slave to its every whim. To attempt one of your stranger up-time idioms, would it be correct to say that I 'like your spunk'?"

Eddie laughed aloud. "I guess it would, although I haven't heard that expression in quite a while."

"It is out-dated then?"

"Given that it's 1635, I don't see how anything from my time could be called 'out-dated.' And hell, if it is, who cares? And by the way, call me Eddie, from now on."

"Very well, Eddie. And you should call me Hannibal. And we must hurry if we are to be on time. I suspect you will not want to miss your wife's grand entrance."

Michael McCarthy, Jr., pushed through the old sail-cloth that was the curtain that screened off the recovery cots from the dispensary. Aodh O'Rourke's alert eyes were already on him as he entered. "Damn it," Mike grumbled, "are you still laying about?"

"It's a vacation I'm having, Don Michael. Don't be spoiling it."

"Huh. Some vacation. Almost lost your leg to that damn infection that set in on the way back here. I'm guessing it took a few gallons of one hundred proof cane spirits to save it."

O'Rourke grumbled, licking his lips at the words "cane spirits." "Hrm. Then t'was a bad waste of good rum."

Michael stared at him. "You'd have rather had the rum than kept your leg?"

O'Rourke frowned.

"Well?" Mike pressed.

"Never rush a man when he's making a difficult choice, Don Michael. I'll cogitate on it a bit and get back to you. Now what brings you here, anyway? I would have expected you'd be making merry at the party I'm hearing."

"Me? At the party? Hell, I'd rather be hung by my thumbs."

"Which I'm sure some of the landowners would be happy to arrange. So you've just dropped by to check in on my sorry self again?"

Mike shrugged. Evidently Dr. Brandão's three noble Danish nurses had updated O'Rourke regarding the visitors he'd had when still lost in a febrile, trackless delirium. "Yeah. Maybe. But I had to come out this way, anyhow."

"Ah, you're making me feel so special, y'are. And what has you coming to the fort in the middle of the night, or near thereto?"

"First message from Europe just came in. Took three days to get it."

"Three days? I saw the radio we had on the *Een-dracht*. Those boyos sent messages in a few minutes. At most."

McCarthy nodded. "That's because they were transmitting over short ranges. When we try to get or receive a signal from over the Atlantic, there's a lot of signal loss and unreliability, and there are certain times of the day when you can send more easily than others. We're working through all that now. So we had to tell the folks in Vlissingen to keep repeating the message. And they did. Over and over and over. But finally, we got the last pieces filled in about an hour ago. Then we were able to run it against the code-book. And here I am with the message."

"Well, good on yeh, Don Michael, for getting that beast up and running. And that steam engine you brought to make the power for it: working as well as you hoped?"

"It is now. Took effort and then some to get it to run on either wood or petroleum by-products."

"On what?"

"Er, the less valuable parts of the oil that we'll be getting from Trinidad."

"So they're producing oil? Already?"

"No, but the bitumen of Pitch Lake can be separated into different components. Some of them make a reasonable fuel on their own, some work best when you use them to inundate wood. That radio itself was the real trick to get running. The Alexanderson alternator that makes it possible is pretty big and pretty delicate. Well, delicate enough that it's a little grumpy after having made an Atlantic crossing in a small ship like the *Intrepid*."

O'Rourke raised an eyebrow. "The *Intrepid* is *small*? Then just how big were your up-time ships?"

"We'll talk about that some other time. Like maybe after half of the farm owners are done trying to kill me."

"It's come to blows, then, has it? I've heard a bit about that ruckus you've started."

Mike shrugged. "Well, no, it hasn't come to blows. But I'm pretty sure some of the landowners would be eager to finish me off in a *single* blow. They're not interested in fisticuffs, O'Rourke. Every slaveholder on this island pretty much hates my guts enough to want to wear them for suspenders."

O'Rourke folded his hands meditatively over his broad, flat belly. "We've a saying in Ireland about such situations."

"To listen to my dad, the Irish have a saying for *every* situation."

"So we do. It's the hallmark of wisdom, don't you know. But here's the saying anyway, you ungrateful pretend-Irishman: 'it's a compliment to be both hated and feared by all the scoundrels in one's own town.' So, it was your rabble-rousing rhetoric that's brought things to their current state?"

"Oh, they probably could have lived with it if it was just coming from me. But, having been the first go-between for Eddie, and Hugh, and Tromp, I had access to the admiral's ear. And van Walbeeck's. And we had conversations about how different colonial powers in the up-time history weaned themselves away from slavery. And they started to put those methods into practice here."

"Hrrmmm," O'Rourke subvocalized. "I'm not surprised to hear it. Maarten Tromp's a man of principle, he is."

"You know him?" McCarthy said, surprised. "How?"

"Well, after the wound from Puerto Cabello turned ugly, that heathen Tromp came by to stare at me a bit on my sickbed aboard the *Intrepid*."

"'Heathen?'"

"Well, he's not a Catholic, is he?" Seeing the bemused look on McCarthy's face, O'Rourke scowled. "Ah, that's right. You up-timers are above petty differences such as the path a man must go to see the face of God."

"We're not above it. We just don't kill each other about it."

"Yes. Well. So the heathen Tromp came to see me and inquire after my health on a few occasions—although, I must allow, he's a most civilized and pleasant heathen, and sure it will be a shame that he's to burn in hell."

"Er. Yes. So you were already familiar with his attitudes about slavery?"

"And tyranny in general, for that matter. As I said, a most principled man."

McCarthy nodded. "Yeah. But he knew he wouldn't be able to sell his reforms based on principles. He persuaded most of the council here by walking them through the up-time historical models I showed him. However the models differ, they all show pretty clearly that any economy dependent on slave-labor is extremely vulnerable to all kinds of disruptions. Van Walbeeck pushed them further along by outlining what he had seen himself while in the East Indies, how every slave population *always* becomes a breeding ground for crippling rebellions. So between those arguments, Tromp got the council to support his directive to recategorize all slaves as bondsmen."

"Changing a term doesn't change whether a man is treated like a slave."

"No, but it does change whether he is property, whether he can be bought and sold. And as Tromp intended, that was just the edge of the wedge to make further changes. The council just recently agreed that all bondsmen will earn their freedom five years from now, or, for those who come later, after five years of service. Next, I think he's going to try put in a rule that new laborers who arrive in the colony against their will or wholly indigent can't be swept into the current debt-peonage system, but must be allowed to enter as regular indentured servants."

O'Rourke smiled. "That must make you even *more* popular with the local men of substance, then."

Mike smiled back. "You have no idea. I'm accused of corrupting Tromp and van Walbeeck, possibly using up-time sorcery to inveigle them to rot the colony from within by welcoming natives, Africans, and Jews. And of course, the arch-Calvinists among them are happy to point to my Roman Catholic background as proof that I am a malevolent being."

"Are you a Catholic, then? I couldn't tell."

"Well, *they* are sure I am," Michael replied, ignoring the veiled remonstration, "since I visited you a couple of times when you were still delirious. And brought some extra food to the other Wild Geese who were recuperating from their wounds, here."

"Ah, you consort with low companions, you do, Michael McCarthy. I knew there was a reason I liked you. Now, do you happen to have some of those infection-killing cane spirits about you? I'm asking for purely medicinal reasons, of course."

"Of course." McCarthy unsuccessfully tried to keep the smile off his face as he rose. "I'll see what I can do."

Part Eight

December 1635

Commotion of the winds

Part Eight

Chapter 45

Santo Domingo, Hispaniola

The sound of a military campaign in preparation was loud beyond the large window that overlooked the veranda of Captain-General Juan Bitrian de Viamonte y Navarra's villa. Nestled tight around the precincts of Santo Domingo was an armed camp almost half again as large as the city proper.

Standing at the window, Fadrique Álvarez de Toledo nodded at the activities among the tents of his troops, and the swift skiffs carrying messages between the ships in the bay. "Our preparations here are well in hand. What of our Free Companies, Captain Equiluz?"

Antonio de la Plaza Eguiluz, at last returned to civilization after many weeks of making contact with cut-throats and *boucaniers* from Jamaica to Tortuga, nodded. "I come from meeting with their gathered forces, near Isla Vaca, far to our west."

"Why there?" asked Eugenio de Covilla as he patted the grease of the roast boar medallions off his lips.

Equiluz shrugged. "It was a reasonable midpoint between the two greatest concentrations of raid—er,

705

Free Companies. A large number make their hidden homes along the coasts of Jamaica, while the more numerous ones frequent the northwest coast of Hispaniola in general and Tortuga in particular. They are none too trusting of each other and so wished a neutral midpoint in which to work out any, er, differences that might exist among their officers. Besides, a *boucanier* of some education from England claimed that one of his country's most famous pirates, who may still be born this year, found it an excellent place in which to gather forces prior to a raid, or to which to retire in the wake of one."

"Who is this newborn heathen reiver?" asked Fadrique.

"I think they called him Harry or Henry Morgan. I did not pay particular mind to the reference. At any rate, the ships of the Free Companies are mostly as we expected: sloops, barca-longas, *piraguas*, a few of our own *pataches*, a few Dutch jachts, and a few more of the same craft built to accommodate the English or 'Bermudan' style of rigging."

"Nothing too large, then," de Viamonte summarized.

"That is so, Your Excellency. And that is what I believe we desired, is it not?"

"It most certainly is," Fadrique said, putting his hand on his hip and feeling notably less flesh between his knuckle and hip-bone than he had only eight weeks ago. Being in the field again gave him purpose and vitality, which reduced his need for the rich food and strong drink with which he had formerly dulled the aching wounds that Olivares' displeasure had inflicted upon him. "The Free Companies are the weaker half of our trap, true, but their speed and maneuverability are essential. They must be able to reach broadly and turn quickly. If each hull has no more than a dozen guns, it is still of little matter. Their numbers are important, however." He turned a questioning eye upon Equiluz.

"We can count on a dozen who are reliable enough to actually sail along with our main fleet, as we discussed, Admiral. I have offered letters of marque to another forty-three, most of whom are likely to accept."

"Excellent. How have you arranged for them to be paid for these, eh, special services to His Majesty, Philip of Spain?"

"As agreed, Admiral, they were given one part in twenty of the promised *reales* when they signed to our colors. When I meet with those who have agreed to sail with our main fleet four days hence off Isla Beata, one hundred miles to the west, they shall be given a further nine parts of the twenty. The balance shall be paid upon completion of their task."

"And how do we know these dogs will not simply fly upon receiving a full half of their payment at Isla Beata, having incurred no risk?" De Viamonte tossed aside his napkin angrily. He despised pirates and every minute spent discussing their necessary recruitment and management made him increasingly ill-tempered.

Fadrique interceded, knowing the captain-general would not dare to vent his spleen on an equal. "My dear de Viamonte, it is a surety that some of these dogs will do just as you fear. It is in the nature of soldiers of fortune and adventurers everywhere. However, we cannot ask for a perfect solution, merely one that provides us with the forces to defend the interests of our King and Country. Of the one in five or one in ten that desert without providing the contracted service? We shall put a heavy bounty on their heads. And those of their brethren who survive this battle shall be put on their trail like so many hounds on the scent of a fox." He smiled. "They know each others' dens so much better than we do, and the pursuers will be aware that, if they hurry, they will not only get the bounty, but the silver the blackguards stole from us. And so, by the hands of thieves, we will yet see justice served, Captain-General de Viamonte."

De Viamonte, considering this, smiled tightly and toasted the proposal with a lifted glass of rioja. "I suppose one can ask no more of justice than this: that if it must be imperfect, at least it should be poetic. And our main fleet is now complete?"

Fadrique nodded. "It is. The last eight warships arrived from Santiago de Cuba yestereve at dusk. We now have thirty-five men-of-war and fourteen smaller supply ships. Add to that our dozen *pataches.* And add the dozen Free Company ships that Captain Equiluz will be paying, just before he leads the rest of the dogs off on their southeasterly course. All together, we shall number just over seventy ships."

"Let us not forget the nine naos that shall transport the troops," de Viamonte added.

"I've not forgotten them, but I will not load and bring them with us until our battle fleet has met and defeated the foe."

"Which we have at last found, I hear." De Viamonte turned toward de Covilla. "You are sure that last night's reports are accurate, Eugenio?"

"They are, Admiral. The *patache Tres Santi* encountered a Dutch yacht scouting the Anegada Passage just four days ago. The gin-swillers broke away as soon as they discovered that they had been spotted."

"This is thin evidence upon which to project the presence of a larger 'target,' Don Álvarez de Toledo," observed de Viamonte.

"On its own, yes," Fadrique agreed, "but this sighting was precisely what we were watching for, given what the Free Companies have told us."

Eguiluz nodded. "I took pains to gather intelligence from pirate captains while they were still at remove from each other, and therefore, were unable to coordinate their stories. Yet their reports usually overlapped in all the crucial particulars: that the English colony is back on St. Christopher's and stronger than before. That a French colony is also there, but more anemic in its growth and vitality. That both engage in occasional trade with the Free Companies, particularly those on the north coasts of this very island."

De Viamonte sounded cross. "Here on Hispaniola? Why?"

"It seems, Your Excellency, that when Don Álvarez de Toledo extirpated the colonies on St. Christopher's in 1629, he took many hundreds of prisoners, particularly the English who stayed to fight at their coastal fort after the French abandoned them and fled into the mountains. Those English prisoners were put to work in *haciendas* on this very island, and many subsequently escaped to join the *boucaniers* of Tortuga. In consequence, they still have friends, or at least acquaintances, among the English of St. Christopher, and make use of those prior associations when engaging in trade. It is they who were most recently at the island, trading old muskets to the French, as I understand it. And it is they who report that the Dutch presence on St. Eustatia grew dramatically since last year."

"And that," concluded de Toledo, "is why the single jacht we saw scouting the Anegada Passage tells me we shall soon have the target we want: the Dutch fleet. Probably led by these two up-time steam ships."

"All that derived from spotting a single jacht?" de Viamonte wondered.

Fadrique nodded. "Yes. A jacht that, according to Don Equiluz, was tacking more than she needed to, which meant she was not heading to a destination so much as searching for something."

"But for what?" de Viamonte asked.

"For us, Your Excellency," de Covilla supplied deferentially. "If I understand the admiral correctly, he deduces from the maneuvering of the jacht that it is sweeping the waters, seeking enemy sails in the Anegada Passage. That is the best place to catch a fair wind to move down along the leeward side of the Lesser Antilles, in the general direction of St. Eustatia. In short, our adversaries are trying to learn if our strength is in port, or on the water headed for them."

"Which is more crucial for them to ascertain than it is for us," Fadrique added. "They have but one base. They cannot afford to sally out in search of our fleet, only to sail past and miss us as we are bound for their home port with the power to utterly destroy it."

De Viamonte nodded. "I see. Well, I suppose being charged with defending ports for so long has made me unaccustomed to think along such risky lines. But you make a sound case for perceiving this yacht as a probable confirmation of what the Free Companies have told Don Equiluz. But tell me"—he turned to the young captain—"should we not suspect that the Companions with ties to St. Christopher will in fact impart warnings of our current actions to their associates there?"

Equiluz nodded somberly. "I had the same misgivings, Your Excellency. That is why I did not extend offers of letters of marque to such men, nor did I even mention our plans. I simply paid them for the information they provided. Even so, I suspect that, before too many months elapse, our recruitment of the other pirates will become known to them, as will its purpose, and so, they shall realize why we were asking the questions we did. However, by then, the actions we plan to undertake against this new Dutch threat will have long been completed." He held up a palm. "There was, unfortunately, no way to solicit information from the Free Companions without, indirectly, releasing some to them as well."

De Viamonte nodded indulgently. "This is in the very nature of asking a question, good Don Equiluz. You always inform the one to whom you address a question that the answer is in some way important to you." He set down his glass. "So it seems our plans are coming together as hoped. The enemy's strength is tentatively located on St. Eustatia and seems to be readying itself, or has begun, to head toward us. Which means that you must commence your difficult tasks of coordination, gentlemen. What you propose is fairly ambitious."

"It is," Fadrique admitted, "but we have the resources to carry it out. Our main fleet has all the warships we could ask for. Our Free Companions have swift, maneuverable ships, and have been furnished with mirror-backed heliographs for signaling and maintaining formation during the night, and lensed reflectors for doing so during fair days."

"And if the weather turns foul, you still believe that will be to our advantage?"

Fadrique felt his lips become rigid, straight. "Captain-General de Viamonte, after what I saw those steamship deck guns do at the Grenada Passage, I may absolutely assure you of this: any engagement in which their accuracy is undermined is to our advantage. Our numbers will prevail, but only if we survive long enough so that they may be brought to bear upon our foe."

"Yes, of course," agreed de Viamonte. "But with so much depending upon a fairly complex plan, I could wish that we had had more time to address all relevant the preparations, particularly with the Free Companies."

"More time is always good," Fadrique agreed openly, but thought, *except that now, with their radios, these up-time supplied bastards have an advantage over us. The clock and the calendar are always their friends and never ours. So our one alternative is to press matters wherever we may. Wherever we determine they wish they had more time, that is precisely where we must act with utter swiftness, even if our plans are not well or fully set.* "But fear not, Captain-General de Viamonte, we are in adequate readiness. And our Free Companies are already straining at their leashes to set upon the Dutch. So the time is ripe to set them in motion."

No matter how hateful the doing of it might be.

Chapter 46

Fifteen Miles East of St. Croix, Caribbean

The soft knock on the cabin door was recognizable as Svantner's. "Come in, Arne!" Eddie called out, picking up his next report.

The lanky Swede slipped into the cabin. "You asked to be notified as soon as the *Zuidsterre*'s sighting was confirmed."

"So, the Spanish have come out to play. Do we have a count?"

Svantner nodded. "Sixty sail, sir. Maybe a few more toward the back of their van. Hard to tell, even from the balloon." He sounded admirably calm, given that it meant the Allied fleet was outnumbered, three to one. Even counting the supply fluyts that were to be kept far away from any combat, lest the troops and ammunition and extra coal on them be lost. But, odds notwithstanding, it was a good thing that both Eddie and Tromp had pushed relentlessly for getting their own fleet under way as soon as possible. Had they put it off another five days, they'd have been meeting these Spanish in sight of Oranjestad itself.

Eddie nodded at Svantner's report. "So it's as Tromp expected. The Santo Domingo fleet has been reinforced from Cuba. Heavily."

"Maybe not, sir. A lot of the ships are smaller than we expected. A lot more *pataches* or other fore-and-aft rigged craft, sir."

That made Eddie pause. "Hmm. Less weight of shot, but more maneuverability. And harder for us to hit." Of course, it was entirely possible that the Spanish had simply scraped together whatever hulls they had available to throw at the new Caribbean threat that had announced itself at the Battle of Grenada Passage. But it was also possible that the composition of this Spanish fleet was not a matter of chance, but careful design... "Arne, signal Dirck and Admiral Tromp that we need to keep a close eye on how the Spanish maneuver."

"What, specifically, are you recommending they watch for, Commander?"

Eddie shrugged. "I wish I knew. But typical Spanish doctrine would have them line up a wall of galleons against us. Either they don't have them to spare, or they're trying something different. And since they've changed the balance of their fleet toward lighter, handier hulls and fore-and-aft rigs, I'm thinking that their tactics are going to emphasize maneuver more than usual."

Svantner shrugged. "They might, but I don't see how they could get the weather gauge on us, sir. We're running before the breeze coming steady from east by northeast. And we'll be north of St. Croix before they reach us, so it's not as though they've got enough room to turn our flank unless we let them."

"All true, Arne. But they know all that, too, and they've known we're coming for at least a week now, what with our yachts playing hide-and-seek with their *pataches* and piraguas in the seas between us. So whatever they've got in mind, they've taken all that into account. Which means either I'm missing something, or they are. Or these are the only ships they've got available near Santo Domingo."

"Probably the latter, sir."

Which was both a reasonable and a comforting conjecture. Which was why Eddie refused to accept it, refused to be lulled into a dangerous complacency by hearing what he *wanted* to hear. "You might be right, Arne, but until we know that's the case, we're going to behave as if it isn't. How long until we reach them?"

"If we push on, we'd make contact at night, sir. Some time during the middle watch."

Eddie started. "What? How strong is the wind?"

"Up to thirteen knots sir. Seas are rising toward three-foot swells."

Too fast an approach and increasingly choppy seas: no good. "Send to the admiral that I recommend we half reef the sails and close slowly. I think our best scenario would be to have the Spanish at about five miles come tomorrow morning. We can use the rest of today's light to tighten up our formation so we've got minimal dispersion to correct at dawn. And we won't put the steam pinnaces in the water until we see first light and determine how high the seas are going to be."

"Very good, sir. Anything else?"

"Yes, Svantner. I want you to bodily throw the chief engineer in the brig."

Svantner blinked. "Sir?"

"I'm kidding, of course." *Well,* mostly *kidding.* "But I swear that if Pabst sends one more of his 'black gang' up here with a panicked request to test the new treated wood before we enter combat, I will cook him in his own precious boiler."

Svantner stared at the deck. "Well, sir, to be honest, a lot of the engineering crew aren't entirely sure why we're carrying a fuel that seems to be—well, an added fire risk."

"Okay, Arne. Then I'll explain it to you, if you promise to go down there and explain it to them."

"Aye, aye, sir," Svantner said sheepishly.

"To start with, where can we get more coal?"

"Uh...nowhere. Not without going back to Europe."

"Precisely. There's plenty of it here in the New World. Coming from a coal-mining town originally, I can assure you of that. But no one's tapped into it yet. And it could be quite a while before they do. So we either burn the coal we brought with us, or the wood that comes to hand."

"Yes, sir. Which is why we haven't burned coal since the Battle of Grenada Passage."

"Right. So, now: burning wood. You've seen how fast we go through it, particularly if we're trying to get the boiler up to full pressure."

Svantner nodded. "Yes, sir. It's gone in no time."

"But if we soak the wood in petroleum by-products, the ones we separated from the bitumen we took from Pitch Lake, then we get some of the benefits of oil burning, even though our engine is designed to burn solids."

Svantner nodded. "Yes, sir. I understand all that.

I suspect they do down in engineering, too. But it will still burn quickly, and these oil-soaked, one-inch cubes are not only as dirty as sin, but leave a flammable residue on whatever they touch. In short, what's the benefit?"

"Saving coal by getting the engines to operating heat before we start shoveling it in. Svantner, tell me, have you seen the oil-treated cubes burn?"

The Swede nodded. "Yes, sir. Like the fires of hell itself."

"Exactly. Now, let's say we're closing with the enemy and must get our engines up to speed, but we don't know exactly when we'll need to commence tactical maneuvers. That means we have to get the boilers up to a useful temperature quickly, but don't want to burn any of our irreplaceable coal doing so, or holding them in preheated readiness."

The figurative light came on over Svantner's head. "So the oil in the wood cubes gives us that fast, high heat before we start shoveling in the coal." He nodded again. "Thank you, sir. But Pabst is still worried about the wastes, is concerned it might leave a heavier residue that could smother the draught to the burners."

Eddie nodded. "That's a good thought, but we've separated out the impurities from the bitumen pretty well. So the treated wood should burn just as cleanly as regular wood. In addition, we've chosen woods that burn to a finer ash—a powder, really—that should actually make less trouble than coal dust." He smiled. "Do you think that will make Pabst—and you—rest a little more easily?"

Svantner stared quickly at the deck again. "My apologies, sir. I didn't mean to—I wouldn't dream of—"

"Arne, you needed to voice a concern that impacts the safe and effective operation of this ship, for which you are the executive officer. You'd be derelict in your duty if you didn't bring the matter up with me. You've done your job, and done it well and respectfully. Now, if there's nothing else—?"

"Sir, there is one other thing. Do you think the Spanish know that our steamships burn coal, predominantly?"

Eddie frowned. "I'd expect they do. It would be strange if none of their personnel weren't familiar with at least that aspect of our steam technology."

"Then I was wondering: are you using this wood to mislead them, to make them think we're burning more coal than we are? When I saw the treated wood burning, just before we left Oranjestad, I noticed that the color of that smoke was close to what one sees with the coal."

Eddie made sure he didn't grin anywhere near as widely as he wanted to: Svantner was proving to be more shrewd than he originally seemed. "Well done, XO. That is exactly what I hope they'll think. If they're watching the clock, waiting for us to run out of coal or to start getting stingy with it, they'll be working from the mistaken assumption that we started using it much earlier than we actually did. And every time they make that kind of wrong guess, it puts us in the position of be able to hand them another nasty surprise."

Svantner nodded, chimed in with the mantra he'd learned recently. "Because the side that has to guess, and keeps guessing wrong, loses the initiative. They are playing by the rules set by the opposition."

Eddie nodded, pleased. "And we want them playing by our rules, Mr. Svantner. Until they've lost the game and go home. Assuming there are any left to do so."

Seventeen miles south of Cerro Indio, Isla de Vieques

Admiral Fadrique Álvarez de Toledo lowered his spyglass and spoke over his right shoulder. "Time for you to be getting back to your ship, Captain de Covilla. It seems the Dutch and their heathen friends have taken the bait."

"They are steaming towards us already?" De Covilla sounded alarmed.

Fadrique laughed. "Hardly. They seem to be slowing, probably reefing their sails, from what our pickets report." Which meant that, given the many relays it had taken the report to reach them, from the lead scout-*patache* all the way back to their position toward the rear of the van, the change in the allied fleet had probably been observed twenty minutes ago.

"Then how would that indicate they are taking our bait, Admiral?" De Covilla sounded perplexed.

"As I observed off Grenada, they will wish to conserve their fuel, and also to take us at distance with their deck guns. They would achieve neither if they pushed on now." He gestured behind at the sun which would be kissing the horizon in an hour. "Instead, they would reach us in darkness, a time that all but eliminates the superiority of their gunnery and they would have burned much coal to do so. No, they will approach slowly through the night and leap upon us in the morning, using full sail to overtake our fleet before shifting to their steam power to outmaneuver us tactically."

"Except we will not be where they expect," smiled de Covilla.

Fadrique nodded. "Sailing before the wind all night, we will be ten miles farther to the west, compelling them to chase us. Naturally, they will be frustrated, and will find the poorer sailing speed of the Dutch warships, and particularly their supply ships, to be particularly annoying."

"Perhaps they will abandon the slower moving ships, then."

"We could hope for that, but I doubt it. I have not seen that species of rashness in their commanders, to date. But I suspect that, in straining to catch us, they may not maintain the formation they intend. And that will be serviceable enough. Assuming that all our own plans are in order. About which: have we had another signal from Equiluz?"

"Yes, Admiral. He reports the easternmost scout of his privateers have sighted the western mountains of St. Croix."

"Are our privateers in good formation, reasonably tight?"

"That final part of Equiluz's message failed, sir. As the sun sank, his reflector became dim, then unreadable. We will need to wait until nightfall for our far southern pickets to see his heliograph."

If we see it at all, Fadrique grumbled mentally. This had always been the part of the plan about which he had harbored the greatest misgivings: that an armadilla of pirates-made-privateers, maneuvering independently, and with only one Spanish ship to oversee their compliance, would in fact be where they were needed, when the time came. St. Croix had been the visual anchor point for that southern detachment's furthest eastern picket, and had obviously served that purpose well. Navigating to a position in unmarked, open waters would have been an unreasonable expectation. But if the weather turned, or a mist rolled in—"The weather, Captain de Covilla: what do our scouts report from the east?"

"Clear skies of a pink tint, Admiral. We should have good visibility to receive new messages, at least unto the middle watch."

"Excellent. When you return to your ship, remember to send word that the sappers on board the *San Augustin* must finish distributing the pole-petards to the *piraguas* by midnight. It will take time to rig them on their booms and run the fuses through the pitch-sealed tubes."

"I shall do so immediately upon my return, Admiral. However, I must report that the crews of the *piraguas* are still none too confident that the spikes will hold the petards to a hull, no matter how forcefully they are rammed home."

Fadrique shrugged. "In all honesty, de Covilla, I share their uncertainty. But their duty is to Spain and her God-loving king, so we shall hope that divine grace shall vouchsafe either safety for their bodies or salvation for their souls. A commander in war-time may hope for little else when he sends so many men in harm's way." *Although, truth be told, the men in those petard-carrying* piraguas *will be consorting with more bodily harm than I would happily embrace.*

"Now, be on your way, de Covilla, unless you have some other question."

"Just one, Admiral. How can we be sure that the enemy does not have a second contingent of ships, one which might be coming around St. Croix from the south? If so, they would find our southern privateer armadilla and quite ruin our stratagem."

"Yes, they would, but you are watching for spectres of your own fears, my dear young captain. Be assured, the Dutch fleet in front of us is all they can spare to hunt us. Indeed, they have sortied more ships than I expected. But if we further assume they sent at least ten or a dozen hulls to protect their new assets on Trinidad, then they can barely have enough ships left to guard their probable base on St. Eustatia. So, to send yet *another* flotilla southward around St. Croix would necessitate reducing their home guard. And I'm sure the Dutch would not do anything to jeopardize the only safe anchorage they have. I'm sure they left it in well-armed and highly-vigilant hands."

Capisterre Bay, St. Christopher's

Pierre d'Esnambuc shook hands with cacique Touman and strolled over to where Jacques Dyel du Parque waited nervously, staring out over the bay into the darkling east. He looked at his nephew's still-wrapped sleeping roll. "You should get some sleep, my boy," the older man murmured.

"I will soon," Jacques lied. "I wish you did not have to go."

D'Esnambuc sat next to his nephew. "I wish that

as well. But I must lead the ships from Dieppe Bay south tomorrow. There is no captain skilled enough that I may delegate the responsibility of overseeing the attack upon the English upon him. And we must not fail in that mission." He put a hand on his nephew's arm. Jacques tried very hard to suppress the shiver there. "And you must not fail either, Nephew. But if anything unexpected should occur, stay close to du Plessis."

"Du Plessis? I thought you said that de l'Olive was more trustworthy, and certainly more loyal to you. And so, more loyal to me."

"That is true. But de l'Olive is also a hothead and will not think to flee until it is too late. Du Plessis has the one virtue of all cowards: they are quick to their heels. And if he must fly, he will want to rescue you as a means of currying favor with, and forgiveness from, me. And he will be right in expecting that I shall be grateful that he looked out for you."

Jacques shivered even more. "I will not disappoint you, Uncle Pierre."

"I know you shall not, dear boy. But do not get carried away and think you must be a captain in this fight. That is not your role. Your role is far more important, for I have many captains, but only one of our number understands enough about up-time machinery to accurately assess it, divine its purposes, and to inflict enough damage upon it to terminate its functions without utterly destroying it."

"Do you really think Richelieu will be so pleased by having a radio here in the New World? Even though he does not have a matching radio of power in France?"

"'Pleased?'" D'Esnambuc laughed aloud. "Jacques, if what the disgruntled, and now well-bribed, land-holders of St. Eustatia have communicated to us is true, the Gray Eminence would rather get his hands on such a radio than any two islands. Because if this radio may do all the things you have told me, then he will understand readily enough that with it, he might take those two islands and many more besides. Think of the coordination that would be possible, the swift confirmation of successes or failures, the proper deployment of forces to where they are needed in a timely fashion and in the right numbers." D'Esnambuc shook his well-shaped head. "You have not lived before the mast and on the battlefield, Nephew—may you never have to do either!—but I have, and I may assure you of this: the radio would dramatically shrink the uncertainty, the confusion, and above all, the titanic waste of such adventures. If Richelieu learns that we have such a powerful device in our possession, it means he will send ships and troops to protect it, experts to repair it." D'Esnambuc thumped the ground in both triumph and annoyance. "The neglect of this colony, of all our island colonies, will be over. Our colonies shall be transformed from a dabbling in New World fortunes to a locus of new and essential power. Our fortunes, and your future, will be assured, my boy."

"In the meantime," Jacques wondered aloud, "how will we manage all of them?"

For a moment, d'Esnambuc seemed to stare at the one hundred scruffy Frenchmen who had traveled along with the almost nine hundred Carib warriors to this sparsely settled coastline near St. Christopher's northern tip. Then he followed further along his nephew's gaze

to the natives. Uncle Pierre smiled, almost apologetically. "Oh, them. I do not see much trouble in the
initial years, Jacques. We shall do just as we have
promised the Caribs. And when the Spanish come—
and be assured, they will—we shall be glad of the
Caribs' friendship. They know these waters better than
anyone else, and are excellent scouts. Their small boats
may see our tall ships far off, and yet remain unseen
themselves. With them, and perhaps with several of
these balloons du Plessis has used, we shall see the
Spanish coming from afar, and the natives will join
us in fighting them off, harrying any troops they land,
raiding whatever cachements they establish ashore.
And later, when things are secure—well, I suspect
that will be beyond my time, Jacques. But more to
the point, it is not a matter that needs resolving this
day or tomorrow, whereas we already have enough
work for those scant hours, wouldn't you agree? Now,
remember, if either du Plessis or de l'Olive resists
getting under way before midnight, you must support
Touman against them. The cacique is not lazy, and he
understands best how long it will take to cross the
passage and make an unobserved predawn landing on
the windward side of St. Eustatia. Our countrymen
will not be mindful of such details that the natives
shall rightly deem critical. For instance, the Caribs
will want to allow an hour to hide their boats on that
part of the shore where the trees come down close to
the water. You have seen well enough that such cover
is sparse on the windward side of these islands, and
the few trees that grow there are stunted and bent
by the constant breeze. The natives understand the
need to conceal their boats, and appreciate the time

it will take to achieve that. They must be in charge of the maritime portion of your journey, and its timing. However, once you are ashore, Touman knows he must defer to du Plessis and to you.

"Caribs, or as they style themselves, the Kalinago, will be good in battle. But their real value to you will be as scouts. Give them time to thoroughly assess The Quill and all that is going on upon it. The wait shall be worth your while, I am sure, and you should easily be in your positions by dawn.

"Once the attack begins, you know what to urge, even if du Plessis forgets or believes he has devised— God help us!—a superior plan. The Kalinagos are to skirmish and their bowmen are to work from forest ambush wherever possible. That said, do not depend over-much upon the musketeers, either ours or theirs. Bring them up like artillery when you run into concentrated defense, then let the Kalinago lead the attack once again. And once you reach Oranjestad, you need only get far enough into it to allow the torch to be your final weapon."

As his uncle squeezed his shoulder affectionately and rose to leave, Jacques realized that there was one topic that had never come up in all the discussion of the attack and its details. "What of prisoners, Uncle Pierre? What should we do with them?"

In the growing darkness, d'Esnambuc's face was a black outline. "They would be a great inconvenience," he said slowly. "I recommend you defer to Touman and the Kalinago regarding the disposition of any persons who surrender."

"But Uncle—"

"Defer to the Kalinago. And do not stay to watch."

Chapter 47

Off Bloody Point, St. Christopher's

The late autumn sun was now southerly enough that, at dawn, it did not rise over the high, green spine of St. Christopher's mountains, but over the flat uplands just north of the French town of Basseterre. Pieter Floriszoon screened his eyes with his hands and looked back at Hugh Albert O'Donnell. "Seems rather quiet, don't you think?"

Hugh shrugged, smiled. "Having never been here, I wouldn't know."

"Well, in my time, I've rarely seen so few boats out fishing. Is it some holiday?"

"None that I'm aware of." Hugh felt the strong tugging pressure fade out of the *patache*'s whipstaff and heard and saw the mainsail begin to luff slightly. "Wind is shifting," he commented.

"So it is," grinned Pieter, who folded his arms and smiled.

Hugh rolled his eyes. This was not a tricky wind, but Floriszoon was probably trying to see if navigating so close to land spooked the Irishman. But as the wind from the northeast shifted to north by northeast, and he went from close reaching to close hauled, it was a simple matter of turning one point to port to bring the wind back into the mainsail and return to close reaching.

The flutter of the mainsail's luffing subsided and the *patache* resumed a brisk northwesterly pace, aimed directly at the headland known as Bloody Point.

Malachi O'Mara approached from where his Dutch tutor in sail-handling had just relieved him. "My lord, you look a bit of a pirate this morning, you do."

"Mind your tongue, O'Mara, or you'll find out what it's really like to be keelhauled."

"Yes sir!" He approached and watched Hugh's work with the whipstaff meditatively, clearly paying not a jot of real attention to it.

O'Donnell knew a purposeful loiter when he saw one. "Out with it then, O'Mara. For whom are you playing the part of an emissary, this morning?"

"Why, my lord, I wouldn't dream of—"

"We never dream of things we do routinely. So out with it, I say."

"As you say, m'lord. There's some concern among the new lads from Montserrat that maybe we should have gone to Nevis first, after all. Showing up on Governor Warner's doorstep might be seen as being a bit bold."

"They feel that, do they?"

"Well, yes, sir. Respectfully, sir."

"I appreciate their respectful concerns. You may convey to them my resolve to proceed as planned. Governor Warner is not so grand and well-established a lord as he once was. He's been cut loose by his king. So I suppose you might say, having both lost our titles, mine was greater and older than his and I've no reason not to pay him a visit and my compliments directly. Besides, it was he who accepted their deportation to the Irish colony on Montserrat. It is he who would have to repeal it, at least enough so that they might trade freely here once again without any prejudice or suspicion of being agents for the French."

"Or for them to recruit for you among the relatives and friends they left behind?" Floriszoon all but winked at Hugh.

"Just so," the attainted earl replied. "You say his plantation is beyond that headland?"

Floriszoon nodded. "Yes, a mile or so north of Bloody Point. And what town he has is there, as well. The English are far more populous, but also more spread out. They have no single settlements as large as Dieppe Bay or Basseterre. Although now that we Dutch have sent over so many soldiers, I wonder if—"

From beyond the headland, thunder rolled. In a clear sky.

"Cannon?" O'Mara wondered aloud.

"And not just one, so not a signal or a hail," Hugh glanced back over his shoulder. Floriszoon's own ship, the well-gunned *Eendracht*, was only one hundred yards off their port quarter. "Pieter," muttered Hugh, "I'm not liking this."

Floriszoon nodded. "None of the usual French ships in Basseterre Bay, no fishing boats out. But would the French really be bold enough to—?"

"If our fleet has left to take the fight to the Spanish, they might have drawn off quite a few of your Dutch soldiers, most of whom are scattered about the countryside anyhow, aren't they?"

"Yes, but given a little time, they would be able to gather and—"

"There may not be any time, not if French mean to eliminate the leadership of the English colony first. Which they would do by attacking Bloody Point. Jeafferson lives around here as well, doesn't he?"

Pieter Floriszoon nodded. "We should come about into the wind and into irons, wait for the *Eendracht* to lay to so I can transfer and—"

"Pieter, if the French are shelling Warner's estate and the town"—another cannonade confirmed that— "then we don't have the time to stop and put things in order. We must deal with the situation as we find it. Immediately."

"Hugh, we don't know what we'll see when we come around Bloody Point."

"No, but we know one thing: they won't be expecting us. And we have almost one hundred twenty troops between our two ships, and forty-four guns of respectable size."

"And they may have more. Of both."

"Yes, but they don't have the element of surprise. And if they're shelling, they'll be stopped, possibly at anchor." Hugh turned another two points to port. The sails billowed out as the ship came into a broad reach. "And we have speed a-plenty."

"Your man O'Mara is right," Pieter grumbled as he motioned for the pilot to take the whipstaff and gestured for the captain of the deck battery to join him on the shallow poop deck.

"O'Mara is right? About what?"

"You *are* a bit of a pirate, aren't you?"

❖   ❖   ❖

The *patache* that Hugh and Pieter had named the *Orthros*—since, being jointly owned by Dutch Protestants and Irish Catholics, it seemed fitting to name it after a two-headed hell-hound—came round Bloody Point at seven knots. One mile ahead, and motionless in the water, was a French bark of approximately thirty-two guns. Another similar ship was largely obscured behind her, perhaps eight hundred yards farther north. The morning breeze was blowing westward and so was pushing the smoke of their bombardment back in their faces. Since the French were no longer firing concentrated broadsides, but allowing their pieces to speak at will, the noise was ragged but unrelenting.

"Fat, deaf, and looking the wrong way," summarized Floriszoon as *Eendracht* came around the point behind the *Orthros*.

"For now, let's leave them that way," Hugh muttered as he finished giving orders to his boarders: almost all the Wild Geese and new recruits from Montserrat were aboard the *patache*.

"We'll never reach them undetected, you know."

"I know, Pieter. But tell me, when they see us, what will they do?"

Floriszoon considered. "Crowd canvas and turn to port. Try to get around so their unused battery is facing us. Give us a broadside."

"Yes, but how much speed will they have?"

Floriszoon scoffed. "Given what little time they'll have to react, not even half a knot. Probably not a quarter."

"So once they commit to a portside turn—"

Pieter's eyes studied the position of the closest French ship, and then went wide. "You're not a pirate.

You're a madman, to even think of risking a last-second shift to—"

"But would it work, given our speed and maneuverability?"

"Damn, it might. But it will be a rough ride. And a hell of a stop."

Hugh smiled. "Then let's not scare ourselves by wondering about it. Make for her stern and get me in position."

The *Orthros* was only four hundred yards astern of the Frenchman when the lookout in the bark's main crow's nest spotted the two fore-and-aft rigged vessels bearing down on them, the first one's decks fairly bristling with troops. Panicked yells ran the length of the Frenchman, and, as expected, her sails unfurled in such haste that one end of her foremain tangled in its reef-points and had to be shaken out. With only its mizzen fore-and-aft rigged, and almost in irons at that, the ship struggled to bring its fresh, unfired batteries around to face south toward the approaching ships.

But at three hundred yards, the faster of the two—the Dutch yacht—turned another point to port, catching the breeze full a-beam. Accelerating, she heeled over, angling off to the northwest, and away from her partner. On that new course, she'd enter the Frenchman's field of fire that much sooner. The Spanish-made *patache* held course, but with barely half as many guns as the jacht, was certainly the lesser of the two evils bearing down upon the Frenchman.

When they were at two hundred yards, the bark had begun to catch the wind. Her mizzen started filling slowly, allowing her rate of turn to accelerate. Gunners began muscling their pieces into position. Below decks and above, the crews from the landside pieces left off their shore bombardment and crewed the half-manned portside guns. By that time, the jacht had straightened out again, soon to pass almost directly parallel to the Frenchman, whereas the *patache* showed an almost dull-witted obstinacy, maintaining a course that now had her prow aimed at the bark's port quarter. Had she had a ram, it might have made some kind of sense.

At one hundred yards, three guns of the Frenchman's portside battery spoke, seeking the range. Two white geysers erupted behind the flying jacht and one hundred fifty yards beyond it. The bark slowed its turn, preparing to unleash a broadside at the Dutchman when she closed another thirty or forty yards, which would be in less than twenty seconds.

That was the same moment that the *patache* cut dramatically to starboard. That maneuver spilled some wind out of her sails—she came into a close reach—but she had barely lost momentum by the time she crossed behind the bark. As she did so, she swung hard back to port—putting her on a course to sideswipe the French ship.

Shouted warnings about a collision were lost in the roar of the bark's port side broadside, which discharged just as the jacht heeled harder to port once again, catching the breeze full a-beam and speeding directly away from the Frenchman, showing the enemy battery her narrow stern. Bracketed by geysers, one ball crashed into her deck, mauling a gun and its crew.

But on the starboard side of the Frenchman, the

patache closed rapidly, only eight yards separating the two craft. One cannon from the Frenchman's shore-aimed battery discharged at the speeding craft but soared over the heads of the cold-eyed boarders waiting beneath its gunwale.

A Dutch-accented voice shouted from the *patache's* stern—"brace yourselves"—just before the ship turned one more point to port and put her bow into the side of the Frenchman's hull.

Wood screamed, flew up as stripped off strakes and splinters. The lighter Spanish-designed ship rebounded slightly, but her angle of impact had been shallow, so she came back easily with her remaining momentum. The second impact was lighter, so light that the men on her decks were able to remain standing and fling grappling hooks over the Frenchman's shattered gunwale.

Not expecting to fight another ship, the bark had no marksmen in her rigging when the other ships were spotted. The first ones to respond were just climbing up, and so were blown down by massed musketry from the *patache's* deck. Similarly, as the French deckhands leapt to swing their swivel guns about, they found the Spanish ship's patereroes already trained upon them and firing. The would-be counterattackers were blasted away from their pieces, trailing spatters of blood.

The boarders swarmed onto the bark's deck, where the hastily organizing resistance met with a terrible surprise: their attackers were armed with pistols that fired repeatedly. A vanguard of ten Wild Geese led the rest of the troops over the Frenchman's gunwale, their pepperbox revolvers killing a few of the defenders, wounding many. More significantly, that sudden wave of fire surprised and quickly broke the morale of most of the survivors. Fleeing to the poop and the fo'c'sle respectively, the French had given up the midship weather deck before any officers had been able to organize a stand. The rest of the Wild Geese poured over, sniping at any defenders who raised a musket in opposition to the more indifferently armed Montserrat recruits who spread like a tide across the deck, wielding everything from daggers to cutlasses to old Spanish matchlocks. A few went down, but each one who fell was hastily replaced by three others, and more Wild Geese came on along with them, carrying musketoons, fresh pistols, and competent orders for the new recruits.

Meanwhile, the jacht had moved well out of range, and made swiftly for the farther French ship. Seeing the fate of her sister, and unsure of how many more enemy hulls might appear, that ship was crowding sail and making for open water. There, she could take advantage of putting the wind behind her square-rigged mainmast even as she put her stern to a following sea.

With most of the first Frenchman's surviving crew trapped on the gun deck and unable to move up the companionways for fear of the revolvers and cutlasses covering the stairs, the remaining officers and sail handlers huddled behind what cover they could find at either end of the ship. And in their silent, collective consternation of wondering how best to fight back, one of the tallest boarders stepped forward, raised a sword toward the captain on the poop deck and shouted:

"I am Hugh O'Donnell, Earl of Tyrconnell, and on my word, I promise you this: I will have your honorable parole or I will have your heads. The choice is yours."

In the profound quiet that was the immediate

answer to his ultimatum, a single man stood on the poop deck. "Monsieur, that choice is no choice. You have our parole."

Hugh watched the second French ship fade into the distance and counted the dead being laid out on the deck. Six of the new recruits from Montserrat had already earned the bitter coin of service to their homeland's last earl, along with two of the Wild Geese. A dozen more of his men were wounded, but only one so severely that he was in any immediate danger. "What now?" asked Pieter Floriszoon who was still flushed and seemed eager to find yet another ship to fight. Hugh wondered who, truly, was the pirate at heart. "I go to St. Eustatia. At once."

"What? But they put troops ashore here, and Warner could be—"

"You will take care of that, and protect this place. We cannot be sure the other ship will not return, and we have no way of knowing if others might not be on the way. You will stay here, with this ship as a prize and with yourself on *Eendracht*."

"And you? You're going to St. Eustatia alone?"

Hugh smiled as he looked back over his shoulder at the men on the *Orthros*. The recruits from Montserrat lofted the French muskets and cutlasses with which they had re-armed themselves. "I think I have company enough. But I'll want your second pilot for the helm. We don't want a ham-handed beginner like myself at the whipstaff, or it will be all of us who'll need rescuing."

"Truly spoken," grinned Pieter. "You can leave the wounded here—"

Hugh shook his head. "Your Dutch doctors are best, and you've told me you have a Jewish surgeon in Oranjestad. If we succeed, they'll want to be close to that care. If we don't succeed—" He shrugged. "There won't be much hope for any of us, perhaps."

"Yes, perhaps. Which is the why you should not go alone. If these French officers are telling us the truth, that there is an attack under way on St. Eustatia, it could be twice as large as they're claiming."

Hugh stopped and held Pieter's gaze. "True, but if the French return here and overwhelm the defense we leave behind, then the English are defeated. And that means you'll all starve on St. Eustatia. So, either way, we must have a force in both places. And *this* is where ships are needed most, not at Oranjestad where your defense fleet is at anchor."

Floriszoon chewed his lower lip slightly and looked away. "Well, when you put it that way—"

Hugh put his hand on the Dutchman's shoulder. "Lend me some of your ship's troops, now. You should be able to scrape together some of your Dutch plantation guards once you put a skiff ashore. But I'll have more want of foot soldiers, I suspect."

Floriszoon nodded. "How many do you think you'll need."

"Thirty more?"

"Take fifty. And then get going. If there's anything I can't stand, it's watching a lazy Irishman loiter about."

Chapter 48

Off Vieques, Caribbean Sea

Eddie Cantrell lowered his binoculars and frowned.

Ove Gjedde's soft-voiced observation was annoying, mostly because it was perfectly accurate. "It is unlikely anything will change so dramatically that you need to examine the enemy every two minutes. They continue to run. We continue to chase. It has been thus since dawn. And the range is closing steadily."

"Yes, steadily. But not fast enough."

Gjedde shrugged at the receding Spanish sails that dominated the western horizon. "Like us, they have fair winds and following seas. Nothing could be better for their galleons. With the exception of our steamships, none of our hulls are much faster than theirs."

Eddie nodded, turned about and raised his binoculars to better see the allied fleet behind. Led by the steam-tugged *Amelia* and *Gelderland*, eight more Dutch warships had crowded sail to keep up with the USE steamships: *Hollandsche Tuijn, Zeeland, Neptunus, Utrecht, Prins Hendrik, Eenhoorn, Omlandia, Wappen von Rotterdam.* They were among the lighter and swifter Dutch hulls, none carrying more than thirty-eight pieces, but even so, their speed was not much greater than that of the Spanish galleons. Van Galen had loudly protested the decision to send almost all the bigger ships south with Peg Leg Jol to Trinidad, or to be kept as a home guard at Oranjestad, but now, Eddie's foresight was making itself felt as a lived reality. Once the Spanish saw the smoke from the steamships, he'd predicted they might not come straight to grips but do everything they could to maneuver for advantage. However, while the *Intrepid* and *Resolve* would be able to quite literally run rings around the Spanish heavies, it would be unwise to fully break formation to do so, not until the enemy was firmly engaged.

Van Galen had scoffed at this doctrine as overly cautious; he even came close to suggesting it was cowardice, at one point. But Eddie had maintained that the fleet sent to Santo Domingo had more need of speed and maneuverability than weight of shot. The steamships provided overmastering firepower on their own, but that would do little good if they raced far ahead of the rest of the fleet. So with the exception of the *Amelia* and the *Hollandsche Tuijn*, the other warships of this fleet had been selected for their operational flexibility. So had the five jachts that worked as both pickets and escorts for the four troop- and supply-laden fluyts that wallowed along with the *Serendipity* at the rear.

And yet, despite all those precautions, the fleet's van had begun to stretch out as the swift lead elements pressed to engage the rear of the Spanish formation. It would have been easy enough to achieve with the steamships alone, but whereas many of the Dutch presumed that the steamships would be able to destroy anything that came close, Eddie eyed the unprecedented number of enemy fore-and-aft rigged ships with concern. They, too, were swift and highly maneuverable, several looking to be highly streamlined jachts. With the seas' rising, he could envision being unable to bring his guns to bear upon enough of those hulls swiftly enough to prevent being swarmed by the survivors. So whereas van Galen wished to charge straight ahead, confident that the Spanish would scatter and their galleons would flare and die as one after the other came under the eight-inch guns of the onrushing USE ships, Eddie was uncertain of such an outcome. And so far, Tromp and Gjedde had heeded his uncertainty. But, judging from the signals being flagged between the following ships, the impatience among the fleet's captains was growing.

Beneath him, down at the inter-ship comms position, Eddie heard the wireless start clattering. There were only four radios in the fleet—on *Intrepid*, *Resolve*, *Amelia*, and the yacht *Zuidsterre*—and messages would not be coming from the latter, since she was not in the command loop and placed well back in the formation. Which meant communiqués were coming exclusively from Tromp or Simonszoon. Which meant, in all probability, another debate.

The runner pounded up the stairs. "Signal from the *Amelia*, Commander!"

Eddie nodded the boy to give the message to his XO. "Summarize it if you would, Svantner."

"Yes, sir," said the Swede, taking the sheet out of the runner's hand and gesturing for him to wait for a reply. "Admiral Tromp is asking you to respond to Captain Simonszoon's respectful observation that with the enemy at only three miles range, we could increase steam and engage them within the hour. We still have better than four hours of daylight left. Without going so far as pursuing the Spanish into the dark, we could inflict considerable casualties upon them and yet be safely regrouped by nightfall." Svantner looked up slowly, deferentially. No doubt he'd been thinking the same thing. And wondering why they weren't doing it.

And why weren't they? Because Eddie Cantrell had misgivings. Nothing more specific than that: simply misgivings. *Doesn't exactly constitute a sophisticated tactical reason,* he admitted to himself. *But damn it, sometimes being in command means knowing when to play a hunch. Okay, so I'm the details-and-data guy in this crowd. So I'm the tech-wizard. And so they all think I don't really have the belly for a close-in fight. And who knows? Maybe they're right. But damn it, that's not what's holding me back.*

He glanced forward at the Spanish sails again. There had to be damn near sixty of them, and there were probably more farther on. If they'd been able to run up a balloon, they'd have been able to get a look at the seas for thirty-five miles in every direction, which would have been comforting to Eddie. But with the wind gusting erratically, and given that any ship conducting balloon ops lost the use of her mizzenmast, and thus, lost speed, the fleet had to rely upon their last long-range observations, now almost sixty hours old.

But even if the visible sixty sails represented all the Spanish ships between here and Santo Domingo,

Eddie still kept coming back to one distressing fact, which he murmured loud enough for Ove Gjedde to hear. "These Spanish must know what happened at the Battle of Grenada Passage. They must know what our steamships can do. So, whatever else they intend, they are not going to come about and sail straight into our guns and their own certain death."

"No," agreed Gjedde in a slightly puzzled tone. "That is why they are fleeing."

"Are they fleeing, do you think?" Eddie raised his eyes to his binoculars again. "I'm not so sure."

Gjedde was silent for a long moment. "They are making good speed away from us."

"Yes. But tell me, Captain, you've seen adversaries fleeing before. Do these Spanish look to be in as much of a hurry as they should be if their objective is to break contact, to get away?"

Gjedde's next silence was even longer. "No," he admitted. "And it is puzzling. But still, whatever their reasons for such a measured withdrawal before us, what risk do we take by closing briefly, sinking several, and regrouping before dusk? Because you must directly answer that very question for Tromp, and soon."

Eddie nodded, and thought, *yeah, but if I give the answer I want to give—"Hell, no: we stay in formation, damn it!"—then Tromp's either got to support me against all the other commanders, or ignore me and give them their way. So, the smart move is to give advice that will calm his officers a bit, while also reigning in any excessive overconfidence. Which isn't the best military advice, but the reality of command is that sometimes, the human factors can be just as decisive as the strategic ones.*

"Here's my answer, runner," he said. "Insert stops where needed. To Admiral Tromp. I recommend that *Resolve* move ahead to engage enemy ships at range. Recommend one thousand yards as closest approach. *Intrepid* will remain five hundred yards astern of *Resolve*'s port quarter to cover her flank against any lighter ships that may maneuver to close with her from that side. I presume that will be where they wish to do so, keeping the open waters of the Caribbean to their southerly backs. Recommend that both ships drop back again at four PM to facilitate dusk rendezvous with the rest of the fleet. Very Respectfully, Commander E. Cantrell. Please read that back."

The runner did. Eddie waved him on his way, felt the frown return to his face.

Gjedde nodded. "That was wise."

Eddie shrugged. *Yeah, wise. But it's also stupid. I can feel in my bones that it's not the right move. Now, if only I knew why...*

Tromp agreed with Eddie's plan, with the exception that he authorized *Resolve* to approach the rear of the Spanish van to a range of eight hundred yards. Apparently, though, he had to exert more than a little of his special authority to make his commanders fall in line with the rest of Eddie's recommendations. Van Galen was particularly resistant, and the semaphore exchanges between his ship and Tromp's *Amelia*, visible through Eddie's fine binoculars even as the main van dropped farther behind, were spirited. In the final analysis, Tromp prevailed upon the inevitable math of the strategic situation. Given that the Dutch ships were slightly faster than the Spanish, they were sure to fully overtake their enemies long before reaching Santo Domingo. In reply to van Galen's point that, with a full head of steam, the USE ships could overtake and destroy them today, Tromp serenely replied that, since it was already noon, waiting another eighteen hours to press home the final attack would make no difference.

The wind was such that the Dutch fleet would be within a mile of the Spaniards' sterns by nine o'clock the next morning. And if the enemy should happen to come about in the middle of the night, their square rigged galleons would be putting their bowsprits into the eye of the wind and so, be in irons. Unable to close or maneuver, they would be lucky to blunder within sighting distance, much less shooting range, of a target. Furthermore, if the Spanish hoped to continue making maximum headway as a fleet even after the sun had set, their stern lights would show any course changes they might make. If, instead, they doused those lights, they would be hopelessly scattered by the first rose of dawn. In short, there was no rush. One way or the other, the Dutch fleet would be upon the enemy tomorrow. Which meant that Commander Cantrell's recommendations for a more measured approach did not threaten the surety of a decisive engagement with the fleeing foe, and so had the virtue of prudence against unforeseen events. Van Galen's flags ceased to signal except to acknowledge receipt of the admiral's last message.

By that time, Simonszoon had raced ahead, prompting Eddie to wonder just how much coal the senior Dutch captain had already burned throughout the day. Perhaps infatuated with the new technology at his disposal, Simonszoon's *Resolve* had been putting out more smoke than the *Intrepid* and had been less assiduous about courting the winds. But there was no way to ask Dirck if he'd been careless about his fuel levels without also insulting him and possibly souring what was both a growing friendship and crucial ally among the command ranks. Besides, there was no longer any time to do so.

By one o'clock in the afternoon, the *Resolve* had closed to within eighteen hundred yards of the rearmost galleon in the Spanish formation, The lighter *patache*s and almost piratical-looking yachts scattered away from the big USE cruiser as she bore down upon them. The eight-inch rifle of Mount One spoke, putting a spout in the water at least eighty yards astern of the galleon's port quarter. The second shot was somewhat better, but not by much. The third rolling report was followed by a white plume erupting thirty yards aft and ten yards wide of the target's rudder.

When the fourth round overshot the ship by fifty yards, Eddie closed his eyes, fearing that he knew what was transpiring on board the *Resolve's* bridge at that very moment. Eager to draw first blood, thrilled but also anxious about taking the up-time ship into combat, the typically unflappable Dirck Simonszoon had given in to the temptation to show everyone in the fleet, and perhaps most particularly Eddie, that he was indeed the right commander for *Resolve*. And so, at the longest range yet attempted, he had started firing at the lumbering Spanish galleon. But since there was no ammunition to waste, he'd had only enough actual gunnery practice to familiarize himself with the inclinometer and the exacting nature of the deck-guns. So in his eagerness to prove himself quickly and decisively, he'd missed.

And then missed three more times. And no doubt felt that if he was proving anything to the rest of the fleet, it was that he did not belong in command of *Resolve*. After all, the young up-timer Cantrell rarely missed more than three times. Unfortunately, the subtleties of wave height, speed, target profile, and the differences between effective and practical range were probably not at the front of Simonszoon's awareness where they belonged, but following behind his increasing frustration and realization that he had engaged the enemy too soon. And even further behind that thought was any latent cognizance that Eddie and Pros Mund had made it look so easy because when they fired, they had always enjoyed the advantages of optimal sea conditions, close range, and significant training.

No doubt Rik Bjelke was trying to provide a patient voice of experience, but Simonszoon, for all his many intellectual virtues, was also a proud man who had never, it was said, encountered the situation that he could not handle. As uncomfortable as the fifth and sixth misses were to watch from the deck of the *Intrepid*, Eddie could only imagine the torture of suppressed counsel and soaring frustration that predominated upon the bridge of *Resolve*.

The *Resolve*'s guns stilled after the sixth miss and, soon after, a prodigious increase of smoke started pouring out her stack. The cruiser jumped forward at what must have been full steam, bearing down upon the Spaniards at almost thirteen knots, her prow slicing through the seas so sharply and powerfully that she was less susceptible to the chop. At eleven hundred yards from the Spaniard, her forward mount fired again, missed long by only fifteen yards, and then the rear mount put a solid shell through the galleon's stern windows.

There was no discernible response from the Spaniard other than a slight loss of speed. Within forty seconds, the *Resolve*'s forward eight-inch rifle spoke again, and this time, an explosive shell blasted a raging furrow three-quarters of the way across the galleon's quarter deck. Fires sprang up in several places, and the ship sheered sharply to starboard, losing way.

Showing the tactical aptitudes that made him such an excellent commander in even these unfamiliar circumstances, Simonszoon immediately ignored that crippled ship, understanding she would not be able to keep up with her fleet and was therefore no longer a threat. Closing to nine hundred yards with his next target, Simonszoon began firing again, but this time, more slowly and steadily. This time, he was probably taking more time to gauge swells, make sure he kept his course and speed rock steady while the gunners adjusted their firing solution, and was listening to the advice of Rik Bjelke. The forward mount's second shot fell just short of the next galleon's prow and the third struck her dead amidships in the gun deck closest to the waterline.

At this range, the impact looked simply like a puff of dust. Seen through Eddie's binoculars, it would have been a split-second tornado of shattered strakes, planking, and gunners. A moment later, secondary explosions started erupting from within the ship. One sent out a brief flicker of orange flame, hastily superseded by a vast plume of gray smoke. While her magazine did not go up, fires built rapidly in her lower decks and she, too, lost speed and heading.

As Simonszoon shifted course to bring his cruiser closer to a third target, Svantner muttered, "Commander, two points off the port bow: *patache* breaking back in toward *Resolve.*"

Eddie shifted his glasses and saw the Spaniard in question. She had been one of the half dozen lighter fore-and-aft rigged ships that had scattered like startled doves at the white-waked approach of the *Resolve.* Since then, she had slowly, casually reversed course, and was now angling in toward the lead USE ship. Behind that *patache,* Eddie saw two more sails slowly tilting over in the same direction, the ships beneath them heeling over into a close-reach to double back in a way that the square-rigged galleons of the Spanish fleet could not.

Eddie felt a painful pulse of premonition flare up in the same, chest-center spot that older men complained of heartburn. He dropped the binoculars from his eyes and scanned the horizon and flanks. Ove Gjedde was doing the same thing, squinting and frowning ferociously.

"You see it?" he asked the old Dane.

Gjedde nodded. "Yes. The smaller ships have not been keeping up with their fleet as swiftly as they did at first. They have been dropping back."

"Into a position from which they can pull just that kind of flanking maneuver." Eddie pushed out his chin. "Well, let's make them think the better of it. Helmsman, bring us two points to starboard so that both our rifles will bear on that *patache.* Intraship, message for Mounts One and Two: Get me a firing solution for that *patache*. And be careful to lead her. She's at speed and leaving a bone-white wake."

"Aye, Commander!"

Gjedde was peering around more aggressively. "Commander, I think you were right."

"Right? About what?"

Intraship interrupted. "Commander, Mount Two reports it has a solution."

"Fire when ready and continue tracking. Same order to Mount One when it reports a solution."

"Aye, sir." And the deck shook as Mount Two, only thirty-five feet behind them, roared.

Gjedde shook his head. "This *patache*, and the others, they are not receiving signals. They are pressing the flank of *Resolve* without orders."

Eddie nodded. "Which is to say, they *already* have orders to do so."

"Yes. This is part of the Spanish plan."

Mount One's discharge sent a shudder back under their feet and a long gray-white plume out over the port bow.

Eddie nodded. "Yes, but the plan is not complete."

"What do you mean?" Gjedde asked.

"I mean there's something missing. They must know we're not stupid enough to charge straight into them"—*well, except van Galen*—"and even at this close an approach to their van, they still can't flank us beyond our steamships' abilities to turn around and both flee and shoot our way out of any attempt to trap us."

As if to prove that point, Mount Two's second shot went through the mainsail of the *patache*, which sheered off to port and away from the two USE ships.

Gjedde nodded. "Yes, that is true. Presuming this is part of a larger trap."

Eddie stopped and felt his misgivings suddenly coalesce into a hard, sharp, painful point directly behind his sternum. "Of course. These light ships, these fleeing galleons: they're not the trap. They're just flypaper."

"What do you mean?" asked Gjedde, but it was the maintop lookout who shouted out the answer that Eddie dreaded hearing.

"Enemy sails off the port beam, coming over the southern horizon! Dozens of 'em and closing quickly!"

Eddie turned to Gjedde. "Now, their trap is complete."

Chapter 49

Slopes of The Quill, St. Eustatia

For the fifth time in as many minutes, Michael McCarthy, Jr., wished he had his father's .45 with him. Two Kalinago warriors appeared out of the trees just ahead of him, making for the antenna's ninth array line. But with the phenomenal senses of jungle-trained hunters, one heard a pebble snap out from under the up-timer's boot and turned.

Mike cursed, both at having to kill again and not having the best tool with which to do it. He raised his Hockenjoss & Klott .44 caliber black powder revolver and brought his left hand in for a two-handed grip. He fired.

The first warrior didn't seem to know he'd been hit square in the sternum. He managed to take two leaping steps, war club raised, before his eyes opened wide. He flinched and fell with a strangled cry.

But Michael missed his first shot at the other, who had either more presence of mind, more experience with firearms or both. The hatchet-armed warrior ducked, sidestepped, then charged.

The sidestep fooled Mike, who missed again. But the Kalinago had probably not encountered a weapon capable of so many shots and charged Mike directly, evidently believing himself safe.

At only four feet range, he learned his error. Mike, gritting his teeth to firm his nerve, fired twice. The Kalinago, hit in the shoulder by the first round, lagged and turned slightly in that direction, just before the next round hit him high in the diaphragm. He fell, bleeding heavily, but still trying to sweep his hatchet at Mike's tibia.

Mike stepped back and moved around the warrior, whose attempts to yell for help and more warriors were no more than hoarse wheezes. Mike, panting in the heat and humidity, crossed to the other side of the ninth and last spokelike array line that descended sharply from the summit of The Quill to its rain-forested skirts. He slipped into the trees and continued to run like hell.

Heading down the slope that would ultimately bring him to the western outskirts of Oranjestad's tent city, Mike finally reached what he'd been striving toward since the attack had begun almost half an hour ago: the groomed *ghut* his workers used as both a run-off sluice for their construction camp, and a wide and direct porter's trail when it was dry. It was hardly an ideal arrangement—almost nothing in the seventeenth century Caribbean seemed to be—but it was a less treacherous path when moving heavy, cumbersome, and yet fragile equipment.

But that wasn't the reason Mike had made for it in the middle of what seemed to be a widespread sneak attack. Instead, he had been told by some of his African workers—well, New World-born *cimarrons*, according to them—that the Kalinago would not suspect a *ghut* to be usable as a trail. The Kalinago were the masters of these islands; they were intimately familiar with how to look at a patch of jungle or the side of an overgrown mountain and predict where the streams and run-offs, or *ghuts*, would be, as well as the game trails, the rocky versus loamy slopes, and the rough gradient of them all.

However, the notion of a *ghut* being widened, groomed, and used as a trail would not be a part of their compendium of natural clues. In fact, quite the contrary, since the courses of most *ghuts* were narrow, rocky, and treacherous. Accordingly, Mike had reasoned it was likely to be the safest path down the western side of the mountain. And from the look of it, he'd been right.

He hadn't been the only person who'd reasoned this out, apparently. Approximately fifty yards farther down the *ghut*, he caught sight of two figures making their way swiftly downward, one a broadly built white man, the other a lithe and muscular black man. Not daring to shout, Michael doubled his already headlong pace, and before long, the other two, hearing the noise, turned toward him, weapons ready.

Mike waved a greeting, got a wave in return and the two waited, crouching cautiously. They rose when he approached, and Mike couldn't help but smile. "Good to see you made it out, Bert, Kwesi."

Bert Kortenaer took his left hand off his musket's forestock and shook Mike's hand. "And good to see you, too, Mike. I confess, I feared you might be one of the first killed."

"Huh. Let's get going while I learn why you were in such a rush to see me hustled to my eternal reward."

"Now, Mike—" started Bert.

"He only means, Michael, that we knew you were restringing wires on the fourth array, today." Kwesi frowned, moving swiftly, steadying his progress with his left hand, his wood axe ready in his right. "How did you get here so quickly? I mean no disrespect, Michael, but you are more of a thinker than a runner."

Michael considered his medium build and less than flat stomach. "I don't know how much of a thinker I am, but you're right that I'm no runner. Never was. But today, it wasn't my head or my feet that saved me."

"No?" asked Bert. "Then what was it."

"Luck. In my case, dumb luck. Literally. I was halfway to array four when I realized I'd forgotten my toolkit back at my tent near array seven. I didn't make it back down yesterday, so decided to stay overnight on the slopes. I was just picking up the tools when I heard the first gunshots."

Kwesi seemed to shiver. "What is happening, Michael? We have seen both Kalinago and white men attacking workers. Together. The white men are French, Mr. Kortenaer says. What are they doing here?"

Mike almost twisted his ankle between a stray root-end and a boulder that had been too large to lift out of the *ghut*. "Trying to destroy our radio, from the looks of it. They've been cutting wires as they go, and if they hadn't stopped to do that, they might have overrun us all before we get to town. Which we need to do as quickly as possible."

"To push them off The Quill?"

Mike stared at Bert. "To keep them from rolling

Oranjestad into the sea. When I came to the clear ridge-line near array eight, I got a chance to look down the eastern slopes." Remembering the sight made Mike shiver slightly. "I didn't know what I was seeing at first. It looked like the ground between the trees was rippling. Then I realized: all those were men, moving up the slopes from wherever they landed on the windward side of the island. Which is why they must be here to knock out the radio. They came ashore where we couldn't see, where Oranjestad would not have any eyes or ears."

"There are some farmers near the eastern shore," Kwesi said grimly. "It's where I must work when I am not working for you, Michael."

"Yeah, I know, but all the farms are farther north, in the cross-island fertile belt. I'm guessing these attackers, who must number over a thousand, came ashore farther south, right at the foot of the mountain."

"That's nothing but rough surf and rocks, there, Mike," Bert observed.

"Yeah, but the Kalinago were born to them and they were willing to take the chance to get the jump on us. Which they've pretty much done." Mike's recent memories seemed to flit across his present vision like the images of an old-style slide projector skipping along a wall. He saw three of his most reliable and agreeable workers hacked down to the ground by half a dozen Kalinago who seemed to appear like ghosts out of the wood, the blood flying up with every backswing of their axes. He saw David, the silent Dutch sailor who had come to love the radio and everything about it, running to alert the camp at array seven, shot in the back by a Frenchman. And when the tow-headed youngster got up, blood smearing the front of his shirt, to try to continue raising the alarm, four Kalinago arrows burrowed into his back with singing whispers. Mike, not thinking clearly, had emptied his revolver at the first attackers who came close, improbably causing a brief lull in the entire attack. But in hindsight, that had been nothing more than the enemy mistaking the revolver's rate of fire for an unexpected number of defenders on site.

"Who else made it out?" Bert asked quietly.

Mike shook his head. "Don't know. All I saw were people running every direction. Some were us, some were them. Most of our technical crew was not on the mountain last night. Just you, David, and Gerben were up there. But our workers—"

Kwesi shook his head. "My people will flee if they can, but will not die without a fight. Particularly not now that they can hope for freedom in a few years."

Mike nodded as they skittered down the last few yards of the *ghut. And if we hadn't made sure of that eventual freedom, your people might be joining forces with the Kalinago right now. And hell, who could blame them if they had done so, anyway? Not like we colonizers have a long, proud history of keeping our promises.* "A lot of the workers were going toe-to-toe with the Kalinago, machetes against hatchets. Gave at least as good as they were getting. I shouted at those guys to run, but a lot just smiled and kept swinging."

"They are warriors, most of them," Kwesi explained quietly. "They were sold to your slave-traders because they were taken prisoner by victorious tribes. Given the promise of freedom, there is honor to be reclaimed in defending the ground they worked with you, Michael."

Mike felt suddenly shamed that he had not stayed on the slopes of The Quill and died with them. Even though he had known, from the moment he saw the invaders, that he had to perform an even more important task: alert Oranjestad. "Let's go," he said as the *ghut* leveled off, leading to Oranjestad's outskirts. "I figure we've got about ten minutes to raise a defense."

Jean du Plessis peered down from the western slope of The Quill, watching the handful of survivors scatter away from its base toward Oranjestad. Behind him, almost all the long, coated wires had been hacked down from there they were secured to high, straight, well-pruned trees. "We are done here then? The radio is disabled?"

D'Esnambuc's nephew, Jacques Dyel du Parque, frowned at the swinging wires. "For now."

"Well, that is as we wanted it, yes?"

Jacques nodded. "Yes, Monsieur du Plessis, but I am concerned that it may not be enough."

"What? Why?"

Jacques pointed at the dozen mite-sized figures sprinting toward the outskirts of Oranjestad. "If they succeed in raising a defense, we may not be able to hold this position. Or remain on St. Eustatia at all."

Du Plessis almost sneered. "And what defense could they raise?"

Jacques raised his finger toward the west as de l'Olive approached, half of his French musketeers just behind him. "Monsieur du Plessis, how many ships do you count in the bay?"

Du Plessis scowled, covered his eyes, although fortunately, the sun was not too far advanced. "About twenty. About a third are jachts. At least three are simply fluyts. None have even weighed anchor, yet."

"Quite true, monsieur. But we did not expect to see so many here, according to the landholders who responded to our bribes. They thought that only a handful would be left."

"What's your point, Jacques?" De l'Olive sounded far less impatient than du Plessis felt.

"Only this, my friend: how many ship's troops would be upon them?"

"A few hundred, at least," de l'Olive murmured with a nod.

"So even though we might prevail in Oranjestad, we might not be able to hold it."

"They shall not shell their own town, even with us in it," du Plessis sniffed.

"No, but you mean to burn it, monsieur. And if you do so, there will be no town left for their guns to spare, and so, no reason for them to remain silent. However, the fort will remain. Which, if my spyglass shows me correctly, is still manned. I would say close to a hundred troops, from what I have counted over the past half hour. They will delay us considerably, no?"

Du Plessis wanted to disagree, but thought the better of it. First, the otherwise ruthless and hard-nosed d'Esnambuc doted on his nephew like a pampered puppy. Second, the young fellow was making sense. Unfortunately. "So what are you suggesting, Monsieur Dyel du Parque?"

The nephew shook his head. "I am loath to say it, for it runs counter to my uncle's fondest hopes, but I do not think we can afford to save the radio. I suspect we will not be able to hold Oranjestad, once we take it. And if my reading is correct, a radio so large as this one will be too cumbersome and fragile to move."

Du Plessis glanced at the wires behind him once again. "Are you saying that we will now have to cut up all these—?"

Jacques shook his head. "No. There is neither the time for that, nor will it serve our purpose. The wire is not irreplaceable. But I suspect the radio itself is. So we must attack Oranjestad, burn it, but make sure we find the radio and demolish it. Then, if we must withdraw, we will still have crippled our adversaries. As we must, if we are to take all of St. Christopher's and expand throughout these islands."

Du Plessis was still getting used to the conceptual changes when de l'Olive nodded and smiled. "You are your uncle's boy, all right. He'll approve. I know it. So, how do we find the radio? What will it look like?"

Jacques gestured toward the cluster of wires that ran down the hill along several converging paths. "We follow the wires. Like the heads of a hydra, they can be replaced. But at the root of them all is the heart of their operation. Which will look like a large machine with wires going into it. And hooked up to some kind of electrical power source."

"Electri—what?" De l'Olive stumbled over the words, gave up.

"More wires," Dyel du Parque supplied, "which carry the energy that the radio uses to receive and send signals. Those wires will be hooked up to a steam plant, or a windmill, or something that takes the work of a turning wheel and turns it into the needed energy."

"And once we find it? Hammers?"

Jacques seemed to flinch in regret. "Yes. Hammers will do."

Du Plessis sheathed his sword, checked his pistols. "Well, then, de l'Olive, you have the information you need. Gather our musketeers and the Kalinagos so armed, also. I suspect we'll need them to break through whatever defense these lazy Dutch manage to throw up in the next few minutes."

Cuthbert Pudsey was gasping for breath when Anne Cathrine bid him enter. "My ladies, make haste! Ye've got to get to the hidey-holes we have built into the—"

"Mr. Pudsey, you may see for yourself that we will not be requiring that protection." Anne Cathrine had already made a trip to the secondary arsenal and returned with an armload of new flintlock muskets, percussion cap pistols, and powder flasks.

"But ladies, your safety was placed in my care, and besides, you are—"

"Mr. Pudsey," Anne Cathrine said, straightening up, "we are able-bodied persons who may help defend this largely unpopulated town. Unless I am wrong, there are but ninety-five men in this fort, true?"

"You are correct, but—"

"And presuming my husband tells me the truth, and my own eyes have not been lying these past weeks, we have few more to spare. Twelve hundred embarked to do battle at Santo Domingo. For which three hundred were furloughed from their defense of the English properties on St. Christopher's, which now has only one company scattered among its many plantations. Furthermore, almost half of the Irish Wild Geese are defending their fort on Trinidad, along with one hundred and fifty Dutchmen. And almost three hundred and fifty more are, necessarily, embarked upon our ships in the bay, should they be required to sail to repulse a Spanish attack. Are my numbers accurate?"

Pudsey swallowed. "I-I think so, Lady Anne Cathrine, but the officers aren't in the habit of informing me—"

"And allow me to conjecture that the landowners have not yet begun to gather in defense of the town," added Sophie.

Pudsey blinked. "How did you know—?"

"Mr. Pudsey," Anne Cathrine snapped, "you may or may not have noticed that the largest landowners are also the largest slave owners, and that none of them are fond of Admiral Tromp or the policies he has championed for their slaves' eventual transition to freepersons. Clearly, they did not respond when the alarm bell on The Quill was rung earlier this morning, nor to the musketry we heard there. Nor have they come here to help defend the town, or secure their own safety. Possibly because many of them have no reason to fear the attackers."

The implication of treason hung unspoken in the air for a second. "And so," Sophie finished calmly, "if we cannot expect help from many of the landowners, how will we defend the town? I know Captain Arciszewski has signaled for Admiral Banckert to send some of his troops ashore, but the attackers will be in our streets before those boats are through the surf." She slipped two decidedly nonmilitary fowling pieces over her arm and walked toward the door in which he was standing. "So, with your permission or without it, Mr. Pudsey, the king's daughters and I will take our places among what few defenders we have."

"I'll get Captain Arciszewski to send fifty men from the fort," Pudsey sputtered hastily. "And I'll come along wid' ye to—"

Anne Cathrine shook her head. "And then who shall defend this fort if half its soldiers leave, simply to protect us? The captain, and you, and all the others must man these walls until Admiral Banckert's relief arrives. Because if we do not succeed turning back the invaders at the outskirts of town, this fort will be our last foothold in Oranjestad, and her guns must not be turned on the fleet."

"But . . . but who shall take charge of the defense of the outskirts when—?"

Leonora shrugged. "Unless I am much mistaken, I believe I have heard Mr. McCarthy all the way from the other end of the town, just before the fire bell began ringing there."

"You did? What was he saying?"

Leonora blushed. "As a lady, I may not repeat it. But we are responding to his summons. All of us."

Hugh O'Donnell glanced at the young man—just a boy, really—who was piloting the *Orthros* at least as much as the man at her whipstaff, a Dutchman simply named Aart. "Are you sure of the depth here, Mr. van der Zaan?"

The lanky, tow-headed adolescent smiled a wide, bright smile. "Oh, Lord O'Donnell, you can call me Willem. Or just Willi. That's what Admiral Tromp calls me."

"Very well, then, Willi," Hugh responded with a

similar smile. "Now tell me, how close can we come to the shore in that bay?" Hugh pointed to an inlet just south of the wide sweep of the anchorage in front of Oranjestad proper.

Willi tapped the helmsman on the shoulder, indicated he should sheer to port half a point. "I'd say about ten yards from shore, Lord O'Donnell. But your men will be in five feet of water, there."

Aart shook his head. "Though you've dumped all the ballast on the way here, you'll still run her aground if you go that far into Gallows Bay."

"I don't think so," Willi mumbled with a faint frown. "Right now, the tides give us a little more leeway. And if we did get caught, it would be by such a small bit that we can kedge ourselves off the sand. There's a patch of rocky bottom just a few yards away, if we keep ourselves due west of that driftwood cask on the beach."

Hugh nodded at Aart. "We're going to follow Willi's advice." He looked back into the faces of both the veteran and newly recruited Wild Geese, as well as the Dutch soldiers crowded upon the deck. "All armor off. Bag your weapons and your powder, and hold them over your head. It's not far to shore, but some of you will be up to your eyebrows for a moment or two."

"Lord O'Donnell," appealed Aart, "once again, please consider landing on the main strand just to the west of the town. It's smooth sands there, easy for your men, and easier for me to sail in and out."

"I know," Hugh answered, "but you heard what our lookout spied before we reefed sail and starting hiding our approach. The attackers are approaching the east edge of Oranjestad. If we port to the west, we'll be doing no better than the boats we've seen Admiral Banckert lowering into the water. We'll get there too late. And we'll be coming from the direction that they expect. And there's one thing I've learned in my years of soldiering, Aart—never, ever do what your enemy expects. Which means that as soon as you drop us in the briny, you come about and head back south around The Quill and worry them from the windward side of the island. But don't shell their boats. Give 'em room and the ability to run. We don't want them bottled here on this island with us." He turned to the men behind him. "Now, boys, ready along the starboard gunwale. We go in smooth and silent, make for land, regroup and then fast march. And remember, you don't shout or shoot until I tell you to."

Chapter 50

Oranjestad, St. Eustatia

Anne Cathrine nodded to Michael McCarthy, Jr., who had seemed fairly calm until he caught a glimpse of the three Danish ladies entering the makeshift defenses. Their arrival had elicited the same degree of desperate solicitousness that had so afflicted Cuthbert Pudsey only five minutes earlier. Strange. Although up-time men were so ready to confer equality upon women in so many matters, they were no different than their down-time brothers when it came to the matter of combat. In some ways it made up-time male attitudes towards women frustratingly inconsistent and yet, familiar.

But the three Danish ladies had stood their ground against Michael McCarthy's objections. They pointed out that a dozen other Dutch women were in the defense lines, mostly to reload the muskets of the men who were sheltering in the trenches or behind the hasty, flimsy barrel barricades that flanked them. Michael had countered that those women were the exception, not the rule, and that most of the women had complied with his order to stay away from the coming battlefield. Anne Cathrine had listened through to the end of his exhortations, and then promptly turned on her heel, but not to depart the defenses. Rather, she began crying an alarm among the tents, calling specifically upon women to come out and take their places along the barricades or in the ditches. Michael had rolled his eyes but had been too busy, or maybe too sensible, to waste any more time trying to end what he could not even forestall.

Looking out toward the dust cloud being raised by the approaching enemy, Anne Cathrine surveyed their defenses. Two ditches guarded the eastern approaches to the town. Each offered waist-deep cover for fifteen men, at most. Most of the soldiers were there, along with a few of the townsmen who had turned out to help. The barricades were manned by the balance of the soldiers and townsmen, the workers who'd made it off The Quill, and those few landowners who had decided to throw their lot in with their neighbors.

She approached the northern trench, where Sophie was calmly surveying the enemy's approach, a fowling piece in her long, slender hands. Leonora waited just behind her, ramrod, powder and balls at the ready. Anne Cathrine wondered if there was some argument, any argument, that she could use to get Leonora off the line. At least one of them should take care to survive this battle and so, be a consolation to their father. "Leonora," Anne Cathrine murmured, "should you not be in the infirmary, ready to help Dr. Brandão with the wounded?"

Leonora's smile was small as she shook her head. "I think not, Sister. If these attackers break our ranks here, they will be upon the infirmary in three minutes and slay all there. So here is the best place where I may work to ensure that the wounded actually have someplace to be treated. Besides," she said, patting the closest powder horn, "I have made a study of the loading and reloading actions undertaken by the soldiers at the fort, when they are at drill. I think I shall make a useful reloader for Sophie."

Sophie nodded. "She seems quite adept."

Anne Cathrine raised an eyebrow. "And you? You are a soldier, too, Sophie?"

"No, Anne Cathrine, but I grew up on wooded estates with a father who, as sheriff, took pleasure in hunting for much of the meat that graced our table." She smiled. "He took great pains to pass some of those skills on to me, at least when it came to shooting waterfowl. So, I suspect I may be of some use, here."

"I'm sure you shall be. I wish *I* was of more use."

Sophie stared at her. "You really do not see how the other women look at you?"

"What?"

"Anne Cathrine, they see you carrying that pistol, walking behind these trenches. They do not think, 'there walks the king's daughter, who knows not how to help.' They think, 'there walks the king's daughter, who gave us the courage to join our men here on these lines, who moves behind us like our better conscience, proof that to be a woman is not to be weak.' If you were not here, and visibly so, there would be far fewer women here now. And our numbers may yet help decide the outcome of this battle."

"I truly hope so, Sophie, I truly—"

With a savage cacophony of war cries, shouts, and

taunts that shared not a single syllable in common, the Kalinago warriors began sprinting across the three hundred yards between them and the meager defenses of Oranjestad. Following them a hundred yards farther back at a modest trot were what looked like musketeers, some European, some native.

Michael McCarthy's voice was loud and surprisingly authoritative. "Hold your fire till they clear the stubble of the closest canebrake. That's about one hundred yards. Reloaders, you need to grab the shooters' spent muskets right away and reload them quickly. If you do that, we'll get off three volleys, which might break them. If you don't, we'll get off two and they're likely to overrun us. Now stay down and under cover until you get the order to fire."

Anne Cathrine rushed into the rear of the trench, next to Leonora, and watched the horde of Kalinago warriors approach. They wore little, bore brutal-looking clubs, stopped here and there to fire their bows. They were good marksmen, but only a few shafts found flesh through the gaps in the cover, and only one of those hits was fatal.

Seeing the Kalinago looming like a wave, and the arrows flying towards them, many of the defenders became restless. One of them in the southern ditch raised up on one elbow, sighted his wheel lock rifle, eased the hammer back—

"You there!" shouted Michael. "You can track a target, but if you fire, I swear to God, I'll shoot you myself." The restlessness in the trenches subsided slightly.

The Kalinago came on, the volcanic cone of The Quill rising up behind them like a green pyramid erected by a cockeyed, atavistic island god. It seemed impossible that the near-naked warriors could run so quickly, so far, and it defied belief when, as they cleared the canebrake, the first of the mob redoubled their already considerable speed into a flat-out charge.

Anne Cathrine watched McCarthy, who, tensely watching the approach, waited two more seconds before he cried. "Fire!"

Almost a hundred muskets spoke in a loose sputter along the barricades and trenches. Perhaps a third that number of the natives staggered, cried out, or fell limp. However, the Kalinago had done battle with Europeans before and expected no less. And today, they still had at least seven hundred warriors in the field.

Anne Cathrine raised her pistol, knew not to fire until the third volley, felt her underarms, back, and brow awash with sweat that owed nothing to the heat of the sun. McCarthy's voice grew increasingly stentorian. "Swap muskets! Reloaders, we're depending on you. Shooters: aim . . . and . . . fire!"

The second volley was even more ragged, but did more damage, in part because the persons using fowling pieces and musketoons were now at range. Only fifty yards away, almost forty of the Kalinago went down. Many of the survivors drew up short—but not because they intended to flee, but rather to return fire.

Arrows keened among the barricades and clipped into the edges of the ditches. Several found their mark, promising the fate that was now overtaking those who had been hit earlier: poison-inflicted convulsions. The leading edge of the warriors was now ragged where it had been chewed at by the Dutch musketry, and none of those natives still had bows in hand. Instead, their war clubs were held far back, primed for skull-crushing blows.

Anne Cathrine raised her pistol and looked for a warrior who was either larger or more adorned than the others. She found one, cocked the weapon's hammer, then gripped the handle of her gun with both hands, just as Eddie had taught her. She wished—very strongly, and throughout her whole body—that she could have seen and held Eddie just one more time. Then she was aware of nothing except for the Kalinago warrior she could see over the brass bead atop the end of her pistol's muzzle. To either side of her, the reloaders were pushing the first muskets back into the shooter's hands, then drawing their own pistols or swords. She wanted to glance at Michael McCarthy, wondered if he hadn't called for the last volley because perhaps he'd been hit with an arrow, feared that maybe someone else—she herself?—had to take charge now, give the final order to—

"Fire!" shouted McCarthy.

Anne Cathrine was both too relieved and too focused to double-guess her aim. She fired the double-charged pistol, saw the male torso upon which the muzzle was superimposed stagger and fall out of the sight picture. Along the line, the blast of musketry was more uniform, and louder, with the loaders' pistols contributing to it. And from behind, she heard the sound of running feet approaching—but only a few. Had some of the natives gotten behind them, sneaked in through town from the north—?

She hadn't the time to think. Although the Kalinagos had taken horrible losses with this volley, many of the charging warriors were too far ahead of the wave of casualties to be stunned or panicked by that destruction. They sprinted closer, racing toward the trenches and the barricades, suddenly so near that Anne Cathrine could make out the individual teeth in their mouths as they shrieked their war cries and thirst for mortal vengeance—

From behind, a fusillade of pistol fire startled her. Had the rest of the soldiers been sent from the fort? Turning, she discovered the gunfire was coming from fewer than a dozen men: the Wild Geese who'd still been in the infirmary, now wielding their revolvers with deadly, much-practiced precision among the Kalinago who most closely approached the defensive lines. Several made it to the northern barricade, but there, Michael McCarthy's own, larger cap-and-ball revolver sent out a steady stream of thunderclaps.

Its leading lines of skirmishers slain, the main body of the Kalinago broke and ran for the rear, suddenly silent in retreat. But they did not go far. Upon encountering the musketeers behind them, they formed up into a mass once again. Voices that both berated and encouraged them in two foreign languages—Kalinago and French—soon had them turned back around, crouching as they sorted themselves into archers and skirmishers. Soon, arrows were sailing across the two hundred yard gap. The whining shafts did not find any victims—it was well beyond the optimum range of what were essentially self-bows—but they were keeping the defenders pinned down. Hearing the dying gasps and shuddering cries of even those who had been modestly wounded by the arrows, the allied defenders were unwilling to expose themselves, making communication and movement difficult.

Sophie turned around, a long bang of sweaty hair hanging down in front of her face. "I do not think we will survive the next attack," she commented with what Anne Cathrine heard as her surreal Norn-calm.

"Why?" asked Leonora.

"They know where we are, they know what weapons we have, and they will bring up their musketeers, this time. When we rise to fire at them, they will no doubt fire at us." Sophie shrugged. "How many times can we afford such an exchange?"

The Kalinago, now aided by the French, were obviously eager to find the answer to that very question. With the rain of arrows still coming in at a shallow arc, the skirmishers began arranging themselves into rude ranks.

As they did, one of the most plainly dressed loaders rose up from her position further down the trench to dig a pistol out of a bag she had left unattended a few yards away. When her plain workman's hat fell aside briefly, it revealed the smoke-smudged face of Edel Mund.

"Lady Mund!" Anne Cathrine exclaimed. "What are you—?"

"I am doing the same thing you are, Lady Anne Cathrine. I am fighting to defend this town."

"Then get down, Lady Mund! One of the native arrows could easily—"

Edel's mouth was a brittle-lipped line as she muttered. "I do not fear that."

"Granted we might die here, but none of us deserves to—"

Edel Mund wheeled on the younger woman. "You are wrong. Some of us do deserve to die. Particularly those of us who caused the deaths of others."

Leonora gaped. "But what—what are you saying—?"

"Do you really not understand? Do you not see that it was I who killed my own husband?"

Anne Cathrine blinked, then realized she'd half forgotten about the regrouping Kalinagos. "You—?"

"A fief on Iceland. A generous gift, I suppose, your father intended it to be. But—Iceland. As grim and life-less a place as God or devil ever conceived or created. And then, Pros was given the chance to come here, to lead a fleet to the New World. To please your father, the king. Perhaps we would have been given land somewhere near Skaelskor, or maybe even here in the New World."

"And how," Leonora asked as the native war cries began rising again, "did that hope kill him?"

Edel Mund glared at her. "The hope didn't kill him, because it wasn't important to him." She closed her eyes. "It was my hope, mine alone. And *I* was what was important to him. Me and my happiness. Pros was determined to do anything to please me, to allow me to escape our fief on Iceland forever. And I"—her eyes became fixed and bright—"and I let him. Did I forbid him to take the risks that I knew—*knew*—he planned to take? To seize Spanish ships for his king to purchase my happiness with those war-prizes? No. I allowed him to destroy himself. All because I wanted a little more sun, and a little less ice, I allowed my husband to go to his death. As fine a man, as good a man, as caring a man as ever lived, despite his stoic silences. And my pettiness killed him, just as certainly as had I driven a dagger into his back myself."

"But Lady Mund—" began Leonora.

Whatever Anne Cathrine's sister had intended to say was lost when, with a single shout that sounded a great deal like "Tegreman!" the Kalinago skirmishers started forward. Now in loosely organized ranks, they came on at a slower trot, closely followed by almost two-hundred native and French musketeers. To Anne Cathrine's eyes, the French were armed with quite modern weapons—snaphaunces and even a few percussion-cap rifles, from the look of them—whereas most of the natives were armed with older Spanish pieces. They would not fire so quickly or so accurately as their French allies, but given their numbers, it would hardly matter.

Even now, as the leading Kalinago skirmishers reapproached the stubble of the last canebrake, the reloaders were just finally passing weapons back into the hands of the shooters. The Wild Geese had taken cover among the crates surrounding the radio shack, and both they and McCarthy were busy reloading. Sophie was right. The defenders would not fire so many times, nor so well, this time, and would be facing a hail of musketry while doing so.

Someone tapped her on the arm. It was Leonora, holding up Anne Cathrine's reloaded pistol. Startled, Anne Cathrine looked down at her younger sister. "But I didn't hand you my—?"

"No, I just slipped the weapon out of your fingers. You were inspecting the battlefield. Confirming Sophie's assessment of our chances, I suspect."

Anne Cathrine nodded, then reached down and gave her sister a fierce hug. She shot a glance at Sophie, meaning to put the same affection into it, but the Danish noblewoman was already facing the Kalinago, fowling piece raised to her shoulder.

"Ready on the line!" shouted a new, authoritative voice: Aodh O'Rourke's.

The lead skirmishers of the Kalinago, now about seventy yards away, were beginning to separate. If the two ends of their lead rank kept splitting farther apart, neither would be funneled by the barricades into the closest approach to the tents of Oranjestad. Rather, they would flank the defenders on either side and bypass the trenches at the center of their line. And if that happened—

O'Rourke and McCarthy perceived that the danger to their flanks would increase with every passing moment. "Fire!" they cried in unison.

The defenders did, and many of the Kalinago sprawled headlong. But the others did not break stride, and now, advancing at a faster trot through the open space vacated by the two halves of the front rank, came the French and native musketeers. As they raised their pieces, McCarthy shouted, "Fresh muskets! Reload the empties! Quick or they'll—"

A well-coordinated volley split the humid air, more coordinated than Anne Cathrine had been expecting, and she fully expected it to be the last sound she ever heard. But instead, she opened her surprise-shut eyes and discovered that the French and native musketeers had not fired, but, in fact, had been mauled by the volley she had heard.

Turning to look south, she saw more than a hundred men emerging from the virgin forest that hemmed in Oranjestad at the south and which extended to a point within eighty yards of attackers. The new defenders—a half company of Wild Geese—was heading for the lead ranks of the enemy musketeers, led by a tall, auburn-haired man whom the others followed with a surety and confidence that was tangible, even at this range.

Anne Cathrine jumped to her feet and shouted for joy, just as O'Rourke's cry rose up, "O'Donnell *abu*! Now one more volley into those musketeers and break 'em!"

But that's not quite the way things worked out. The volley from Oranjestad's defenders, more ragged and ill-timed than before, was less focused than O'Rourke had hoped. At least half of the muskets were fired at the Kalinago who were trying to flank the barrel barricades. The other half did hit the enemy muske-teers while the French leaders were trying to turn that mass to face the new threat coming out of the trees to the south. It did not drop many of them, but it sent ripples of irritation and dismay through their ranks. The natives might have been familiar with their muskets, but not with moving in ranks and certainly not withstanding flanking fire while doing so. A large number of Kalinago angrily turned their pieces back toward the town's defenders, discharged them, and hit close to a dozen of that thin line.

But in the meantime, Dutch musketeers emerged from the wood behind the Wild Geese and discharged a flanking volley into the rearmost ranks of the attack-ers. The front ranks, when finally dressed, turned toward the loose skirmish line of Wild Geese, raised their weapons, and fired. At almost the same moment, the Irish mercenaries dove into the stubble of the canebrake. Nearly a dozen did not dive down in time, but the rest rose up swiftly, and charged until they were only twenty paces from the furiously reloading French and natives. The pepperbox revolvers were in their hands now and, collectively, the sound they made was even faster and more raucous than when the *Intrepid* was test-firing one of her mitrailleuses.

French and Kalinago alike, the musketeers went down in windrows before this point-blank fusillade. Order disintegrated swiftly. Unwilling to keep reloading in the face of such sustained fire, and surrounded by so many casualties, the Kalinago cast aside their cumbersome matchlocks and came at the Wild Geese with their war clubs. That was when they discovered that perhaps one in five of the Irish mercenaries had not been contributing to the general fire, but waiting, kneeling, to break just such counterattacks.

O'Rourke, hoarse and still pale from his slow recovery, vaulted over the ditch in which Anne Cathrine was taking cover, shouting "O'Donnell, *abu*! McCarthy, if you're an Irishman true, now's the time to show it!"

Michael yelled an answering, "O'Donnell *abu*! For Tromp and Oranjestad!" which brought the Dutch soldiers boiling out of the thin defensive line and at the Kalinago.

Strangely, to Anne Cathrine's eyes, that charge by forty or so defenders did more to break the spirit of the natives and the French than anything else. Maybe they reasoned that the defenders would not charge unless they had seen reinforcements approaching from the rear. Maybe it was the audacity of the countercharge. Maybe they thought the defenders of Oranjestad had gone insane with a berserker death-lust. Whatever the reason, the Kalinago and French broke ranks, shooting as they streamed back toward the low humps of The Quill's northern foothills, apparently intending to reach their boats on the windward side of the island by the swiftest possible route.

The Wild Geese took the opportunity to swap new cylinders into their revolvers and renew their charge, the tall, auburn-haired man leading them after the repulsed invaders. Sophie rose slowly, looking at that man, head forward as if her eyes were straining after the sight of him, as if her ears were straining after his voice.

As she and Anne Cathrine watched, several of the French attackers turned, hurled something small and round at their pursuers just as the auburn-haired man stopped to help up a fallen comrade. One of the small black dots thrown by a Frenchman landed next to him. In the next instant, there was a small flash and a vicious puff of smoke, and Anne Cathrine could not tell if the man had leaped, or was blown aside, by the grenade.

Chapter 51

Off Vieques, Caribbean Sea

Maarten Tromp read back across the recent and voluminous wireless exchanges. With his new executive officer peering over his shoulder, he shook his head and muttered, "I can find no flaw in Cantrell's reasoning." Tromp looked up at the skies, looked out over the three-foot seas. "We must split the fleet. And you must stand by the signalman to provide an explanation to our captains."

Whereas Kees Evertsen would have launched into an animated inquiry as to why the fleet must be split in the face of two larger enemy formations, Adriaen Banckert showed that he was indeed his father's son. The taciturn nineteen-year-old executive officer merely frowned. "Why, Admiral? Cannot we stay close to the USE steamships while they defeat the closest group to the west, and then the next one to the south?"

Tromp shook his head. "We cannot put that measure of faith in their guns, not in these seas. Their aim will be less accurate, and so they will not be able to effectively close with and destroy one enemy force without offering the other their stern."

"So the enemy planned this to be able to inflict more damage upon the steamships?"

"Cantrell thinks that is only a secondary concern for the Spanish. And I think he is right."

Adriaen put his hands behind his back. "Admiral, like the captains with whom I must soon communicate, I must wonder: what, then, are the Spanish after?"

Tromp looked up with a bitter smile, looked over his shoulder and the taffrail. Stretching into the far distance, the long line of Dutch warships gave way to an even more extended line of her supply fluyts. "They are after our conventional, sailed ships. But especially our supply ships." Seeing no change on Banckert's face, he sighed and gestured to the last visible sail of their formation. "The Spanish have been more crafty, and have learned more quickly, than we conjectured. They realized after the Battle of Grenada Passage that the steamships cannot be attacked directly. To do so is to commit suicide. So the main fleet before us has only been bait, a lure to get us to keep chasing the galleons of their fleet. But all the while, what they were really after was to pull us out of formation so that they could threaten our slowest ships. The ships that are carrying the thirteen hundred troops with which we mean to raze Santo Domingo and its facilities. The same ships that are carrying all our spare powder and balls, and which are carrying the extra ammunition and coal for the steamships."

Now Adriaen Banckert's beetled brows rose in understanding and alarm. "Of course. But how did they manage to coordinate the appearance of this second

fleet?" He gestured to the rapidly growing mass of
fore-and-aft rigged ships approaching out of the south.

"That is indeed an excellent question, Adriaen.
But given our current position, I think they used the
western mountains of St. Croix as a kind of marker,
a place that their line of ambushers were to form up
against. I suspect that is why they started approaching us along such a broad front. They were signaling,
up and down that line, to maintain position and pass
the word to begin their attack."

Banckert nodded. "Still, it is a difficult feat."

Tromp nodded. "It is indeed, even were those attackers as disciplined as the ships of a legitimate navy."

Adriaen's left eyebrow rose. "What do you mean,
Admiral? How are the approaching ships not a 'legitimate navy'?"

Tromp smiled. "Oh, they are a force to be reckoned with, but those ships are not in the rolls of any
nation's fleet. They are pirates. Well, privateers now,
I suppose."

Banckert was so surprised that he forgot to address
Tromp with an honorific. "What?"

"Adriaen, tell me, do you imagine the Spanish have
ready access to so many fore-and-aft rigged vessels as
are approaching us from the south? Perhaps if they
drew in all the hulls of the *Garda Costa* and all their
advice ships, but that would take more than a year
to coordinate. No, the Spanish *recruited* the fleet we
see coming from the south. And, I begin to suspect
Cantrell is right in guessing that many of the smaller
craft in the fleet to our west have the same origins."

"But the Spanish detest pirates. They almost never
grant them letters of marque—"

"Adriaen, we confronted them with an entirely new threat at the Grenada Passage. And they have formulated an entirely new response. They set aside their old prejudices to find a means to reduce the effectiveness of the steamships' new weapons. Pirate ships are smaller, faster, more maneuverable, all of which makes them harder to hit. It also means they do not require fair breezes from the stern like galleons, but may sail close to the wind, tacking through it at their leisure. No, Cantrell's analysis is correct. And I think he is also correct in speculating that their nature *as* pirates did help us in one way: they lacked sufficient discipline to wait a few more hours."

Banckert looked at the sun, now well past the midday point. "But Admiral, if they had waited a few more hours, they would have been engaging us at dusk."

"Precisely. Enough light to see us, but not enough light for us to maneuver against them, regroup, or unleash broadsides at a distance. Adriaen, the dark is their friend. And they need not sink or disable many of us to win a great victory here. For if we flee these waters, and we must, then any hull that straggles behind will be fodder for these sea-wolves."

Banckert nodded, understanding Tromp's strategic decision at last. "And so, in order to escape, we must sail south by southwest. That will give us a reasonable following wind, give us the wind-gauge over the more nimble ships to the south. And will bring us away from any threat that the main fleet to the west might pose, should it turn about. Although, Admiral, the wind is against them."

"Against the main fleet's galleons, yes. But all her fore-and-aft rigged vessels can tack and make headway

against it, could get in among our square-rigged warships, maybe our supply ships."

"Unless the steamships hold these waters long enough
for the rest of us to sail southward, out of—what did
Cantrell call it, this 'L-ambush'?—and punch our way
through the second fleet."

"The lower and weaker jaw of the Spanish trap,"
Tromp affirmed with a nod. "Now, send the signals,
Adriaen. If our captains wish to have the orders
explained, do so once, and succinctly. And in such a
way that they know that this flagship neither has the
time nor the interest in answering further inquiries.
And once we are tightening up our formation, we'll
need to ready the steam pinnaces for towing both
Amelia and *Gelderland*. We'll be pulling ahead along
with the jachts to serve as a vanguard."

"Yes, sir." He looked over the bow, toward the big
USE cruisers. "At least, with their speed and their
guns, they should be safe."

The admiral merely motioned Adriaen toward the
waiting signalman. Maarten Tromp knew all too well
how easily such confidence could turn out to be wrong.

"Commander Cantrell, Captain Simonszoon has sent
a reply to your fuel inquiry."

Well, about bloody time, Eddie huffed silently while
he maintained an impassive exterior. Simonszoon's delay
wasn't a good sign. If he'd been running his ship right,
he should have known how much coal he had left in
the bunker. He shouldn't have had to send someone
below decks to get a count. "What's his reply?"

"*Resolve* has twenty percent fuel remaining."

It was not terribly surprising that the down-time

commander had burned through so much coal. Conserving fast-consumables other than powder and shot could be tricky to gauge, since the depletion accrued as a constant trickle rather than in a few dramatic gulps. But it was damned inconvenient, given the kind of maneuvers the cruisers might have to perform in order to keep the main Spanish fleet from turning about and closing in.

Which might not prove to be as easy a tactical objective as it sounded. As soon as the *Amelia* turned her prow south by southwest, and the jachts began hurrying to form a flying wedge at the head of the formation, the western progress of the main Spanish fleet had slowed noticeably. And although he wanted to keep the pressure on them, Eddie did not dare call on Simonszoon to keep her steam up, or even to make reasonable headway with the favorable wind. Because when the time came to turn and flee, that new heading would put the cruisers in a close reach. If the two big ships were going to get meaningful distance from the smaller *pataches* and jachts of the western Spanish fleet, they'd need to have steam left to make it happen. Possibly more steam than *Resolve* could raise.

Which meant that only *Intrepid* could afford to edge forward and keep the Spanish galleons somewhat at bay. "Svantner, half reef the sails."

"Sir?" asked the startled Swede.

"You heard me, Svantner. We can't afford to move too far ahead of *Resolve*. And she can't afford to move ahead at all."

Ove Gjedde's voice was quiet, ominous. "They will turn upon us, then."

Eddie shrugged. "Captain, with all due respect, they're starting to turn on us already. Chasing them isn't what will buy us most of the time we need. It's the range of our deck guns. Look at the enemy formation. Their admiral is smart enough to be approaching on a broad front."

"But none too quickly, even so," Svantner offered. "They won't engage us until an hour before dusk."

"Yes," Eddie agreed, "and that's just what they want. They're scared of our eight-inch rifles, but even if they weren't, they won't want to arrive at their useful ranges much before dark. If they do, our main-battery carronades will tear them to pieces at five to six hundred yards."

"But then how will they fire on us, sir? It will be dark for all of us."

"Yeah, but there are lots of them and only two of us. And luck is on the side with the most hulls in the water."

Gjedde nodded. "And see what they are beginning to do. The fore-and-aft rigged ships are tacking in irregularly."

Eddie nodded. "Tactically, we up-timers call that a 'serpentine' approach. Usually used to describe infantry movement, but it holds here, too."

"It does indeed." Gjedde exhaled slowly. "It will be hard for our gunners to predict their turns and adjust in time."

"It will be damned near impossible. Which is why we're going to ignore them for now and go after the galleons as soon as they come within thirteen hundred yards."

"So far?" Svantner murmured.

"Yes. If they don't feel safe edging closer to us now, they'll be too far away to trouble us when the light is failing. We can hit them occasionally at thirteen hundred yards, which is all we need to do to maintain their fear of our firepower. And yes, Svantner, I think Dirck Simonszoon has learned his marksmanship lessons pretty well today."

Gjedde nodded. "So you are not as interested in sinking them as terrifying them."

"That's the idea. Now, let's get some firing solutions and go hunting."

The Spanish lost a galleon and a galleoncete before they realized that the USE cruisers were pointedly ignoring the more rapidly closing light vessels. But the Spanish admiral—*one hell of a competent and ballsy guy,* Eddie had to admit—did not react as expected. After about a quarter hour of signaling, his larger ships continued to advance, but slowly, maintaining a wide arc that could easily turn into a butterfly net. True, the cruisers would logically be able to tear right through that net, but if they weren't careful, even a small snag might allow more yachts and *pataches* to swarm around them.

Gjedde frowned mightily at the distant, but still approaching galleons. "He gives us big targets at range, to keep us from turning our guns upon the closer and faster ones that will be able to close with us swiftly come darkness. Clearly, he believes the small ships may inflict considerable damage upon us."

Yeah, that, or he simply realizes he's got no choice, that the big ships won't last long enough to get in range. And anyhow, as long as he's stopped us in our tracks, and sees the rest of our fleet trying to break out to the south, he knows he's running us out of the battlespace. And that's probably what's most important to him. But in the meantime—"Well, let's not insult our Spanish host by refusing his *hors' d' oeuvres*. Do we have a firing solution on the next galleon yet?"

Svantner called an inquiry down into the intraship, got a prompt answer. "Yes, and they've been tracking for a minute, sir."

"Very well. Standard nonexplosive rounds from both mounts. They may fire at will, and continue tracking."

A moment later, the two deck guns went off in such rapid succession that the overlapping shockwaves buffeted Eddie's clothes in two directions, whipsawing his trouser legs from one side of the compass to the other. Both shots geysered up the gray-green seawater, but less than twenty yards off-target.

"Load with explosive shell, watch the swells. Correct and fire at will."

"Aye, sir!"

Eddie watched the chief gunner lean over the rim of the pulpit attached to the side of Mount One's gun shield, stare down at the near risers and then bring down his hand sharply. Mount One's naval rifle blasted smoke outward in a long plume, leaping back against its recoil cylinders. Mount Two did the same a moment later—and, for the first time since the *Intrepid* had become operational, both rounds hit the target at the same time. The entire galleon shuddered to port. The first shell blew her bow into a ruin of strakes sticking up like the back of a skinned hedgehog. The second disappeared into her high quarterdeck, which, an eyeblink later, blew outward in all directions. Not much was left there, other than a partial skeleton of its framing timbers, silhouetted by an inferno raging where the officers' cabins used to be.

Resolve's guns spoke a few seconds later, and although both shots hit water not wood, Simonszoon's ability to work with his gunners was clearly improving. The two rounds bracketed the galleon he'd targeted and Eddie would have taken odds that if he didn't score a hit with the next pair, he would with the third.

As he watched his own gunners crank their pieces around to access the next proximal target, he crossed his arms, felt his stump tired and cramping in the prosthesis for the first time in weeks. *Okay, Mr. Spanish Admiral, if you're willing to put your galleons in range, we'll keep smacking them down. Until your faster ships get inside of five hundred yards, that is.*

Maarten Tromp watched smoke jet out of the steam-pinnace's funnel, and a second later, felt a tug in the deck beneath his feet. "Are we matching pace with the jachts, now?"

Adriaen Banckert nodded. "Yes, sir. They've reefed sails enough that we can keep formation with them."

Tromp looked starboard. *Gelderland*, also under tow, was abeam at three hundred yards. The jachts *Fortuin*, *Zuidsterre*, and *Pinas* were approximately three hundred yards ahead in a rough arrowhead pattern: a wedge to drive through the pirate ships now two miles ahead. Or so Tromp hoped.

He looked astern. The rest of the Dutch warships were making good speed, the wind having freshened and come into a friendly compass point. But they would not be able to add their weight to any engagement that the advance guard initiated for at least an hour.

Meanwhile, the enemy ships to the south had closed ranks, but probably not as much as they had wished. Having sprung their trap early, they had begun in a wide, dispersed arc. Now, closing ranks came at the expense of forward progress, and vice versa. Tromp could only hope that, despite their greater numbers, they were spread too far and too thin to resist the lance-point that he hoped his fleet would be.

"Admiral Tromp?" Willem van der Zaan's replacement, a fourteen-year-old former native of Recife improbably named Brod, arrived with a strip of paper: a communiqué from the ship's wireless.

"Who from, Brod?" asked Tromp.

"Commander Cantrell, sir. Answering your message."

Tromp nodded, watching Adriaen descend to the main deck to inspect the arms and armor of the ship's troops. It would be a miracle indeed if the slower Dutch ships managed to pass through their antagonists without repulsing at least one boarding attempt. "Read the message, Brod."

The lad complied. "Cantrell commanding *Intrepid* to Tromp commanding *Amelia*. Message begins. Now shifting fire to small vessels. Stop. Unable to estimate time remaining before disengagement. Stop. Cannot predict ETA at rendezvous point one. Stop. Sail for home and do not look back. Stop. Message ends."

Commander Eddie Cantrell was busy scanning and describing the new hulls for *Intrepid*'s growing target list, his runner scribbling furiously.

"Target seven. Currently bearing 284 on the compass rose. Range: 800 yards. Approximate speed: four knots. Type: thirty-foot *piragua* with single lateen sail.

Armament: two swivel guns. Complement of twenty. Unusual feature: prow-mounted pole or boom.

"Target eight. Currently bearing 294 on the compass rose. Range: 950 yards. Approximate speed: five knots, making three knots headway with tacking. Type: Bermuda-style sloop. Armament: eight demi-culverins, four falconets. Complement of thirty-five.

"Target nine. Currently bearing—"

"Commander Cantrell!"

"Yes, Svantner?"

"Targets three and four have sheered off, given us a wide berth."

"Heading back for *Resolve*?"

"That or looking to get behind us, sir."

"Does sub-battery three have them in range?"

"Aye, sir!"

"The gun chief may fire his carronades both with my compliments and expectations of success."

"Yes, sir!"

Gjedde had been giving the sail handlers sharp, fast orders. He now looked up in a lull as the *Intrepid* came back before the wind, steadying so that the main batteries would have a stable platform from which to fire. "They are playing with us, you know."

"Of course they are. But they're paying, too." It was true enough. After sinking four galleons outright and damaging another seven, the two cruisers' guns had turned upon the fore-and-aft rigged vessels and, since doing so, had sunk three and damaged two. Being small—everything from twenty-gun Dutch jachts that had been cut down to follow the sleek lines that pirates preferred, to ten-man *piraguas*—many of the ships were as lightly built as they were nimble. The smaller ones often capsized after a single hit because the shells from the rifles over-penetrated, punching through the strakes on one side, and blasting out a spray of hull chunks as they exited the other.

Gjedde nodded. "Yes. But without our steam, they are more maneuverable, may exploit more points of the wind. We will not be able to keep the water between ourselves and the *Resolve* clear much longer."

"That's why I sent Dirck instructions to come about and start heading after the main van."

"So soon?" Svantner stared nervously at the smaller ships swarming and circling toward their flanks like distant sharks. They stayed just outside the six hundred yard limit, which was where the spread and accuracy of the carronades could begin to reasonably cope with the speed and evasive tacking of the small boats.

"Yeah," Eddie sighed as the portside carronades spoke. "He's got to get going now." Target four—a small *patache*—skipped ahead of four balls that plunged into the sea behind her like a line of foam-spurting exclamation marks. The little ship heeled over and reopened the range to the *Intrepid*. "We've held them here for two hours and by the time Simonszoon gets enough wind in his sails to make a good pace, it'll be the better part of a third. And he doesn't have enough coal to steam away. He may need that later to close with the main van, or help them out if that southern pirate fleet manages to jam them up. Either way, he's got to rely more on the wind than we do, a lot more, which means he's got to get going sooner."

"Which leaves us on our own," Gjedde said quietly.

Eddie didn't respond. He was afraid that instead of calmly acknowledging the threat implicit in that situation, he'd start shouting: *Well, of course we'll be on our own! And why is that? Because some downtimer hot-shot captain got a little too steam happy, that's why!*

But this was no time to publicly vent his feelings. He wasn't really being fair to Simonszoon, anyway. The Dutch captain—born, bred and raised in the seventeenth century—was having to learn lessons under fire that any up-time teenage kid had learned by the time he got a driver's license. *Always keep an eye on the gas gauge, stupe.* You didn't run out of wind the same way you ran out of fuel.

Still, unfair or not, the situation *was* aggravating. Since they had to stay here another hour or so to cover the *Resolve's* withdrawal, could they expect the privateer ships to get bolder? *Unquestionably.* And if they hadn't extricated themselves by dusk, would this fine naval engagement devolve into a confused brawl? *Absolutely.* Would blunders occur right and left? *Assuredly.* Was this all to the advantage of the outgunned and usually outmaneuvered foe? *That's why the enemy is doing it.*

A mechanical flaw or trick of fate only needed to strike them once, only needed to cause them to stagger, to stumble. Because if they did, these little jackals would be on them in a minute with cannons, cutlasses or whatever else might work.

But all Eddie said was, "I share your reservations, Captain Gjedde. But do you see any other reasonable options?"

Gjedde watched the ship's troops—several dozen of which were Wild Geese—mounting the mitrailleuses and immense "Big Shot" scatter guns on the four heavy-weapon mounts, one located at each quarter of the ship. "No," he answered. "But I recommend that we bring the regular ship's troops on deck. And keep the Wild Geese below, as a reserve."

Eddie nodded to Svantner to comply, who had just received a slip of paper from the runner. "I will muster the regular troops at once, Commander. And sir, a reply from Captain Simonszoon."

"Read it."

"From *Resolve* to *Intrepid*. Message starts. D. Simonszoon hereby relinquishes local command to E. Cantrell. Stop. E. Cantrell is, by my command authority, and if acceptable to Captain Gjedde, hereby brevetted to post-captain. Stop. Apologies and bitter regrets that *Resolve* must withdraw before her sister ship. Stop. Shall not rest easy until we see your lights closing on our stern. Stop. Message ends."

Eddie glanced at Gjedde. Whose lips seemed to crack as he smiled faintly. "Well, are you going to reply—Captain?"

Eddie sighed. He'd always thought ascending to that proud rank and title, even as a temporary brevet, would be an event he savored. But right now, he just wanted to get the hell out of the situation that had caused it. "Runner, send this reply. We'll be right behind you. Protect the rest of the fleet. See you in Oranjestad."

Or, added Eddie silently as the runner disappeared down the bridge stairs, *I'll see you in the next life*.

Chapter 52

The steam pinnace that had towed the *Gelderland* into the fray had barely cast off when a barca-longa crewed by pirates-become-privateers heeled over toward her, firing swivel guns. Several of the Dutchman's crew went down as she labored back through what had been, until she turned, following seas.

"Adriaen," Tromp shouted, "do we have grape loaded?"

"In three of the starboard guns."

"Excellent. Fire at that barca-longa. We need to protect our tugs." Tromp started counting down the seconds he had left to make up his mind about *Amelia*'s next course change, which was largely based upon how long it would take for his gun deck to send a load of moaning grapeshot at the privateer. From what he could make of the swirling hulls in front of him, two of his jachts—the *Zuidsterre* and the *Pinas*—had drawn at least six of the enemy ships to them. Too eager to wait to distribute themselves more evenly among the approaching Dutch ships, the raiders had pounced with the blood-eagerness of their kind. In consequence, they had weakened this part of the net they were trying to cast before the Dutch van.

Amelia's three starboard guns spoke, most of the grape falling short, kicking up a fuming lane across the swells. But the end of that lane rode right up over the low-gunwaled side of the barca-longa and mauled men, mast, and canvas alike. The stricken boat swerved away from *Amelia* and the steam pinnace.

But Tromp hardly noticed that. Only three hundred yards ahead, the *Zuidsterre* had managed to slip out between a pair of small *pataches* and was no longer enmeshed with the enemy. But *Pinas* was pinned in the middle of a triangle of their hulls, taking what modest pounding their batteries could deliver.

Tromp saw her crew falling aside among the smoke and splinters and resolved that her sacrifice should prove to be the means of their escape. "Adriaen!"

"Sir?"

"Do you see the gap between the sloop and *patache* hemming in *Pinas*?"

"Yes, sir."

"Crowd sail and make for it, best speed. And double-charge both batteries. We are going to open a wide hole for the rest of our fleet."

"Sir, Captain Gerritsz signals from *Gelderland* that he is making for the western edge of that melee. We might come under his guns, if we follow the course you order."

"Then signal Hans to either hold his fire or be damned careful with it. We've got to break these ships. The wind is failing us, so we can't wait on a careful duel while their fore-and-aft riggers dance around us. This group has been greedy for our blood and has trapped themselves. We must capitalize on that. So, when you're done warning Gerritsz, signal the rest of the warships to converge here. This is where we are going to break through."

Or die trying, Tromp amended.

At eighty yards, the heavily modified ex-Dutch jacht pulled hard over to starboard, bringing her portside battery to bear on *Intrepid.*

"Mount Two has a firing solution," cried Svantner.

"Fire!" yelled Eddie over his shoulder, not bothering with the intraship relays.

The two ships traded shots simultaneously. The eight guns of the privateer made a broad, throaty blast, but the gunners had waited a moment too long as the jacht recovered from her turn, rolling slightly above level. Their balls whizzed overhead, one putting a hole in the foremain sail, the other clipping the mainmast's spencer mast clean off. The spencer's foldable sail tumbled, fluttering, into the dark like a half-spined pterodactyl with one shattered wing.

The eight-inch naval rifle repaid the privateer by driving an explosive shell into her, amidships. The shell didn't go off until it was well inside the light-hulled vessel, blowing out a wide spray of wood, cannons, bodies, and dunnage into the failing light. As the smoke cleared, a strange, guttural growling rose up. It was the water rushing into the savage bite that had been taken out of the jacht's side, and which stretched slightly below the waterline. The ship began to roll in that direction as the risers lapped into her greedily.

"Commander," snapped Gjedde, "*patache* coming up from the port quarter. At sixty yards."

Damn it. The ones who had swept wide around *Intrepid* were now coming out of the near-darkness to her east, easily finding and steering for the big USE ship's silhouette against the increasingly cloudy western horizon. "Anything else closing?"

"Not at the moment." Gjedde's tone put a discernibly dark emphasis on "at the moment."

"Then Captain, if you would be so kind, send the order to fire all, portside battery, when she's abeam."

Gjedde nodded, leaned toward the intraship comms tube.

For the first time in twenty minutes, no one was asking for orders, which allowed Eddie to take in the bigger picture. Up on the starboard bow position, the mitrailleuse was firing athwart the rays of the setting sun, its rounds chasing after a *piragua* that had ventured inside one hundred yards range and was now hurriedly rowing back out. Just behind the mitrailleuse, near the forward companionway, a junior lieutenant of the Wild Geese was hunched down on weather deck, alert-eyed and waiting for orders to bring up the forty or so of his men whom Eddie had put in reserve as an anti-boarding fire-brigade. Their training, experience, and armament—double-barreled musketoons and pepperbox revolvers—were a final insurance against what the pirates-turned-privateers obviously wanted to achieve: a run in under the effective lower arc of *Intrepid*'s guns, and then, to board. Normally unthinkable, the dying light, massed and maneuverable opponents, and isolation had combined to make it a distressingly reasonable possibility.

The majority of the ship's troops—German and Swedish musketeers—were already on the weather deck, stalking along the gunwales, watching. Most of their attention was directed into the darkness behind the *Intrepid*'s stern, where dusk had already pulled all the light away from the eastern horizon. That was the direction from which small privateers, and a few Spaniards, too, had been trying to surprise them, running dark. Several had almost chased in under the arc of the steamship's guns.

The *patache* that had approached from the port quarter was the boldest of this group of ships that increasingly tested and baited *Intrepid*'s gunners as the sun's rays ceased to glint off the swells of the wide seas. However, at sixty yards range, the Spaniard's sails still caught a good amount of the dying light and the cries of her gun crews told Gjedde that they were preparing to fire. He did not give them the chance. "Portside battery, fire all!" the Norwegian cried.

The volley had a few trailing discharges. Probably the forward guns were a second late, being muscled into rearward angles to fire before the enemy ship drew fully abreast of them. Of the fourteen regular eight-inch projectiles, five struck along the hull of the ship, which quite literally came apart. There was no dramatic explosion or burst of flames. The tremendous overlapping force of those hits—along with several more that ripped through masts, sails, and rigging—simply shattered the frame of the ship. The strakes and deck-planks split even where they had not been hit: the shock waves, traveling through the wood from two opposed directions, met and tore them apart. The ship rolled even as its keel started groaning; she was at beam-ends within twenty seconds.

Gjedde's voice was anything but elated. "Our carronades were at minimum elevation, resting on their bases. Because so many of their ships sit so low upon the water, we will be fortunate to put any shot on the smallest of them if they reach twenty yards."

Eddie nodded. "That is undeniably true, Captain." The mitrailleuse at the starboard bow was once again stuttering into the setting sun. A sloop that had approached to one hundred yards listed, taking water as the high-velocity .50 caliber bullets punched a trail of splinter-edged holes in her hull and deck.

Svantner was standing just over Gjedde's shoulder. "Shall I ask if the chief has raised enough steam, yet?"

Eddie shrugged. "Might as well."

"You do not think that this might be a wise time to withdraw?" Gjedde asked with one silver-white eyebrow raised.

Eddie sighed. "Oh, I think it would be a great time—Mount One! Jacht inbound on port bow! Acquire solution and fire!—but we can't withdraw yet." When Gjedde's other cloudlike eyebrow rose to join the first, Eddie handed him the note that the runner had pushed into his palm just before the modified Dutch jacht had made its starboard approach. Eddie recited it from memory. "*Amelia* to *Intrepid*. Message begins. Winds from east weaker and less favorable. Stop. Neither side possesses wind gauge. Stop. Combat continues. Stop. Uncertain if we will break free before night falls. Stop. *Resolve* will not arrive in time to accelerate outcome. Stop. Need an additional hour to secure escape. Stop. The fleet salutes you and your heroic crew. Stop. Tromp, commanding *Amelia*. Message ends."

Svantner swallowed. His eyes were much larger than they had been before Eddie had started reading the message. Gjedde simply looked off into the approaching dark. "How long ago was that sent?"

Eddie shrugged. "About twenty-five minutes ago. In thirty more, we can show these jackals our tail. But until then, we must hold this patch of water. If they are allowed to start southward any sooner, they could catch the rest of our fleet during the early hours, or sometime tomorrow. Between the two Spanish vans, they could keep our conventional ships tangled up long enough to inflict damage to the supply ships and transports, or even our warships. And then we'd no longer be a force they'd fear."

Gjedde nodded. "Within months, we'd see their sails approaching St. Eustatia."

"Exactly. So we have to keep that from happening." Eddie looked to where the sun was finally setting. "Meaning that we have to pin them in place, have to stay here for another thirty minutes."

Gjedde looked down into the lightless depths. "Let us just hope that duty does not mean that we shall stay here permanently."

The next ten minutes were unusually calm, as though the Spanish and their privateer allies had heard the resolute words and tones of the *Intrepid*'s command crew and had slunk away from any further battle with so determined an adversary.

Eddie conceded that that had been a nice fantasy, but he knew that the Spanish weren't daunted by their adversaries' courage. No, they were simply waiting for the arrival of their most decisive ally: nightfall.

And once the sun had fallen beneath the far western waters, the enemy ships made their own mortal
resolve quite clear.

They were not brash about resuming their attack but
began circling in closer slowly. Like nocturnal sharks
cautiously approaching a wounded killer whale, they
could smell the blood, but knew that the immense
predator still had teeth which could rip them open if
they were incautious. And so, just as Eddie gave orders
to douse all lights on *Intrepid*'s decks and in her cabins,
the privateer and Spanish boats began probing at the
rapidly shrinking edge of visibility. Hulls flashed here and
there, but were gone before a gun could be trained upon
them. And as the final hazy, gray-and-salmon smudge
of sun-lit cloud bottoms also shrank down behind the
arc of the wide world, they came closer and closer still.

The sound of sails luffing as the ships tacked to and
fro became the typical first warning of their direct
approaches. Three piraguas swept in from the north,
small lights flickering along their lengths. A moment
later those lights were arcing through the air toward
Intrepid: flaming arrows, most of which sunk into the
side of the big ship, guttering. But the oil-soaked rags
affixed behind their points quickly flared again.

Svantner almost laughed. "Do they mean to burn us?"

"No," Eddie said, restraining himself from snapping
at the lieutenant. "They mean to mark us. As a target
that they can all see. Get the ship's troops to douse those
damn arrows, and prepare to deal with more. Captain
Gjedde, we'd best find the wind and give the Spanish a
more lively target to chase until we break off and run."

Gjedde looked aloft. "Admiral Tromp isn't the only
one whose breezes have weakened." And it was true

enough: *Intrepid*'s canvas was either lank or luffing, no matter how wind-master Gjedde turned her. "The Spanish have lighter ships with more canvas than hull. They'll be slowed, too, but less so than us. And their piraguas move as much by oar as sail."

"Well, get me what speed you can, in any direction but west."

"That risks collision."

Eddie shrugged. "Standing still makes us an easy target. We'll have to take our chances. At least they are small boats."

Svantner leaned over from working with the helmsman as they tried to find a point of wind that would give them some headway. "True, but if we hit a *patache* or *jacht*, we could be severely damaged, start taking water."

"Which is why we have pumps. Get me a little more speed, no matter how you do it." More arrows came out of the night, this time from off the port beam. Several found their way up into the sails, but the heavy, fluttering canvas knocked them aside. This time. A crackling of German muskets reached back along the fiery paths that the arrows had followed. If the ragged volley hit anything, there was no sight or sound to indicate it.

As men leaned over the side to pour water and vinegar mixtures down upon the arrows still burning against *Intrepid*'s dark hull, muskets flared in the darkness about seventy yards off the port bow. One of the fire-control party flopped to the deck with a cry, a dark stain spreading across his shirt from the vicinity of his breastbone.

The runner next to Eddie turned wondering eyes into the dark as more German rifles fired at where the enemy muskets had so momentarily bloomed. "How did they see to shoot at our men?" he asked.

Eddie leaned against the railing of the bridge, taking the weight off his cramping stump. "Probably saw a shadow in front of or at the edge of the light from the arrows. They fired at the movement. Enough muskets, and a little luck—"

"*Patache*, bearing on our port bow," came a cry for the foretop.

Eddie swung in that direction and saw the enemy ship approaching, her sails luffing as she struggled to maintain headway against the shifting wind. Which bought Eddie the time he needed. "Svantner, is the port battery reloaded?"

"Yes, sir."

"Very well. If that *patache* comes alongside, fire the first half of that battery. Mount One," he directed into the speaking tube, "do you have a shot?"

"Barely, sir," replied a tinny, indistinct voice that would have been drowned out had any of *Intrepid*'s guns been active at that moment, "and only the quarterdeck."

"That's good enough. Lay open sights upon her and fire as soon as you can!"

"Yes, sir!"

The mizzen lookout cried about more boats approaching from the port quarter. "How are they coordinating this?" Svantner yelped.

"They're not. But when they see the silhouettes of one of their own approaching us, others try to join in, to swarm us. We can't shoot in all directions at once." *But we're sure as hell going to try.* "Lookout, what manner of boats on the port quarter?"

"Sloops, sir," came the voice from aloft.

"Very well. Mr. Svantner, warn the port quarter mitrailleuse that it looks like they'll finally get some action, too."

"Aye, sir," Svantner said with a nod, just as Mount One roared. Eddie swung around in time to see the eight-inch shell plunge into the low poop deck of the *patache* and planks fly up, the mizzenmast having been sliced through an instant beforehand. Severed only five feet above the weather deck, the mast was blown aside so forcefully that she ripped clean out of her stays.

But the wounded *patache* kept coming. Boarders, Spanish troops judging from their glinting beetlelike morions, were clustered in her bows. "The Big Shot on the forward swivel: is she ready?" Eddie cried at Svantner.

"Aye, sir. They're drawing a bead now. Fire at ten yards?"

"Five!" Eddie corrected as the rear mitrailleuse began chattering, presumably at the sloops drawing close to the port quarter. And from the sound of it, that gun crew might burn through their current cassette of ammunition before dissuading the enemy ships from closing. "Aft port battery!" Eddie howled into the speaking tube.

The battery chief's reply came after a moment. The background furor almost drowned it out. "Yes, sir?"

"Your two fastest crews: have them swap out their current shells for canister shot."

"Canister shot, sir? That hasn't tested too well."

"I'm aware. We'll give it a try at point-blank range, Chief. The two sloops approaching from astern are your targets. Once they're within forty yards, fire at your discretion."

"Aye, aye, sir!" The battery chief sounded strangely delighted. Perhaps, being below decks, he didn't have a complete appreciation of just how close the Spanish sharks were circling.

The report from the forward swivel sounded like a shotgun amplified by a bull-horn. Most of the first three ranks of morion-helmeted boarders on the approaching *patache* went down or over its bows, cries and splashes lost in the dark and ridden under her keel. The Big Shot's crew struggled to get another charge into their weapon, did so, fired just as some of the waiting boarders did, dropping one of that crew.

Damn it. "Gallagher!" Eddie shouted at the junior lieutenant of the Wild Geese who had remained in his motionless crouch throughout the entirety of the battle thus far. "Give me a squad at the port bow, on the double!"

As German musketeers began clustering to contest the boarders as well, the after-half of the port battery roared, the carronades' fiery tongues briefly illuminating the sloop that received the majority of their fury. Although only one of the shells hit, the canister-shot stripped away the vessel's sails as if they had been snatched up in a tornado. A dozen of her boarders and crew sprawled across the narrow deck with ghastly, blood-spraying wounds from the lime-sized balls. Then, the flaring muzzles of the *Intrepid* dark once again, there was only the ruined outline of the sloop and the moan of her wounded.

Well, that decides it. "Svantner, pass the word to all batteries. When next they reload, all odd-numbered guns are to reload with canister-shot. It is to be reserved for use on targets within fifty yards."

"Aye, aye, Commander." As Svantner passed the word, a sustained spatter of muskets up near the bow was joined by the rippling coughs of the Wild Geese's musketoons. Grenades went between the ships, without many casualties being inflicted on either side. The *patache*, with most of its crew dead and whipstaff in splinters, was adrift when she bumped her bow against *Intrepid* with a final desultory kiss. The Spaniard swung away from the light impact. "Looks like we'll pass the *patache*, sir. She's got no grapples on us."

"Very well, but I want deckhands with hatchets out to cut any they might land over our stanchions. And do we have those burning arrows put out?"

"Yes, sir, but we've taken a few more. Working to douse them, now, sir."

"Work quickly. I'm going to call for steam in a few minutes and I'd like to be dark when we do it, not surrounded by another swarm of these damn small boats. They're getting too close for—"

Eddie could not distinguish all the cries that started up, almost simultaneously. There were two more contacts off the starboard bow: a piragua and a barca-longa, both sizable and loaded with boarders who did not appear to be Spanish, let alone part of any civilized army in or out of Christendom. At the same time, the second sloop that had been approaching the port quarter, and which had presumably withdrawn after seeing what happened to her sister ship, had swerved in close to the still-reloading port-side after-battery. And, last, appearing from behind the shadow of the almost derelict *patache*, came a lateen-rigged pinnace, loaded with Spaniards.

Eddie gave the orders he could. *All swivels and mitrailleuses should engage all targets upon which they could bear. Raise steam. Ready the rest of the Wild Geese.* But then events took over and finally, the well-coordinated battle fought by the *Intrepid* devolved into a series of desperate brawls. The sloop fired her sakers and demi-culverins at the after-battery that had savaged her sister ship. Balls bounced off *Intrepid*'s hull timbers, but several smaller ones from the pirate's swivels played across the gun crews. The two carronades that had been reloaded replied, one landing a solid shell amidships. The sloop heeled away from the threat of further fire.

At the port bow, the boarders from the pinnace threw grapples from a distance of five yards, as did a few doggedly courageous survivors aboard the *patache* that was falling behind, still adrift. The ship's troops and Wild Geese aimed their fire down into the ferocious faces lining those decks, who returned the deadly compliment at the defenders some six-feet over their heads.

As that firefight raged and grenades started flying between the bows of the two ships, the starboard bow mitrailleuse yelled a report quickly down the speaking tube. But Eddie, distracted, missed the words which rolled out of the metal horn and which were clotted in a thick Swedish accent. "What?" Eddie asked.

His runner tugged his sleeve. "He said 'petard,' sir. And 'boom.'"

For one sliver of a second, Eddie froze, then ordered his runner forward to call up another squad of Wild Geese, this time to the starboard bow. The boy leaped down to the busy weather deck and began slaloming his way around deckhands and ship's troops to deliver the summons.

"What is the matter?" Gjedde asked.

"Spar torpedo. Like the ones you Danes used against our ironclads last year. We've got to make sure they don't—"

The starboard side mitrailleuse stuttered its way through one of its cassettes, riddling the new torpedo-armed piragua with bullets. Thank God. "Svantner, call for full steam. We're going to get out of here as soon as—"

But as the second ship off the starboard bow, the overpopulated barca-longa, drew closer, the mitrailleuse did not resume speaking. Eddie looked in the direction of the weapon's mount, saw the loader struggling to get the new ammunition cassette into the weapon, then begin struggling to get it out. It was clearly jammed, and the first grapple lines were already coming over the starboard bow.

And a new squad of Wild Geese had not yet risen up to reinforce that weapons mount. Eddie scanned, saw the commander of the Irish mercenaries waiting for just such an order, then sought his runner—and saw the young fellow, writhing in pain, just aft of the bows. Apparently, one of the few Spanish grenades that had cleared the bedroll-lined stanchions had put some fragments into the poor lad, who was leaving a spattering of blood to either side as he rocked to and fro, clutching his left thigh.

Damn it. Eddie spun on his real leg to look for Svantner—who was ringing up the steam and directing the helmsman. He turned quickly toward Gjedde, who was already staring at him. The Dane moved as if to head to the bows himself. "I shall take care—"

"No, Captain. You keep piloting the ship. I'll be back soon."

Gjedde winced, but nodded as Eddie pounded down the bridge stairs and limp-loped toward the starboard bow, shouting as he went. "Gallagher! Lieutenant Gallagher!"

He had closed half the distance before the young, anxious Irishman waiting at the companionway heard. "Sir?"

"Starboard weapons mount! Boarders!"

Gallagher turned, saw the frenzied activity in that direction, ducked his head into the companionway and started yelling orders.

By which time, Eddie was past him. Clumping up the stairs to the low fo'c'sle, he saw the last of the mitrailleuse's crew gunned down by a volley of pirate pistols and blunderbusses. The same fate had befallen most of the German musketeers, who, having fired their last charges, drew swords as Eddie came amongst them.

"Captain, what are you—?"

"Stand aside. Send the Wild Geese up toward me as soon as they arrive." Eddie stepped up into the mount, pushing aside the bodies of the mitrailleuse's slain crew.

Two grapples were already hooked over the gunwale of the reinforced pulpit in which the weapon was situated. Two Jacob's ladders had been hooked alongside them. Boarders were on their way up. But they weren't the immediate worry.

Eddie had read, and had since seen evidence, that the best marksmen in the Caribbean were not the soldiers of any nation, but pirates. Prizing unusually long French rifles, many pirate crews relied mostly on musketry to take ships, being both so accurate and able to mount so withering a hail of fire, that many merchantmen dared not handle sails or man a tiller. So they surrendered their ship, and usually lived or were, at worst, ransomed. Which, by logical deduction, made the most dangerous men in the barca-longa the musketeers who had wrought such death among the mitrailleuse's crew and nearby ship's troops.

Eddie unholstered Ed Piazza's HP-35, leaned over the heavy-timbered pulpit of the weapon position and, both hands on the pistol's grip, began unloading its thirteen-round magazine down among the pirate-crowded thwarts of the barca-longa.

Bodies started falling, men cursing. Not more than half of Eddie's shots were hits, and less than half of those were lethal or even extremely serious. But the sudden and unexpected volume of fire from so strange-sounding a weapon—each report as sharp and spiteful as a cracking whip made of lightning—almost froze the pirates. In the very next second, they were diving for cover as they became aware of the murderous swath the weapon was cutting among their crew.

Eddie fished in his ammo pouch for the next magazine as he pressed the magazine release. The old box slipped out just in time for him to run the next one up and into the handle—and the first pirate face appeared over the gunwale.

Fortunately, it wasn't a face alone that could kill him—*although this one is damned near ugly enough!*— but rather, the weapon-filled hands that were soon to follow it. Eddie thumbed the slide-lock, brought up the pistol as the slide rammed forward and primed it, and fired twice into that ferocious, nearly animalistic face. At a range of two feet.

Eddie did not see the effect of the bullets. The

weapon bucked and the face disappeared. He leaned back out over the pulpit-mount to unload the rest of his second magazine down into the barca-longa—and discovered just how combat-hardened and reactive pirate crews were.

Had he not stumbled a bit on his weakening left leg, the first volley of counter-fire from the pirate musketeers below him would probably have been lethal, or at least debilitating. As it was, one ball came close enough to audibly whisper past his right ear. Tempted to duck down, Eddie forced himself to assess the scene in the boat: no other readied pieces. The rest of the pirates were either reloading or getting on the Jacob's ladders to board.

Eddie steadied the HP-35 with both hands, tracked along the men who were reloading the muskets and two-tapped each one of them. Again, after the first two seconds, pirates were diving in every direction for cover. And just as the HP-35's slide came back and stayed back, two pairs of grimy hands came up over the gunwale, one holding a long, wicked-looking knife.

Eddie gulped, ejected the second magazine, fished around for the third one. He took a quick step back—

—and ran into buff-coated Lieutenant Gallagher. "We'll take it from here, if't please you, Commander."

Eddie nodded as two other Wild Geese pushed past and slashed at the grimy hands with their sabers. Shrieks of agony plummeted toward the water as the Irish mercenaries drew their pepperboxes and, hugging low to the rim of the weapon-mount, sent their deadly waves of fire down into the barca-longa. Cries rose up in three different languages to back oars and get the hell away from the steamship.

Eddie half stumbled down the stairs to the main deck, where Svantner was running toward him, a hand extended in concern. Eddie waved it off. "That runner—that boy—he needs help. He was—"

"Already attended to, sir. And you? Are you unhurt."

"Yes, damn it. Now stand still for a second and report. Are we at full steam?"

"Yes, sir. We should be able to pull away and—"

Looking over Svantner's right shoulder, scanning to see how his ship was doing, Eddie caught sight of the rear end of a piragua disappearing beneath the arc of the starboard quarter gunwale, heard the Big Shot swivel gun covering that section of the ship fire. Bodies splashed in the water, but not all of them seemed to have been hit by the immense gun. It looked like some of the piragua's crew had jumped in. And Eddie realized: the piraguas were too low to the water to have any chance of putting boarders on *Intrepid*'s decks. Which meant, if they closed in this far, and their crews were jumping out—

"Spar torpedo! Sink that *piragua*! Any gun that can bear! Sink—!"

Eddie, running stiffly in that direction as he shouted the warning, heard a dull *th-tunk*, as if a spear or hook had embedded itself in the hull timbers. The piragua, rowed at speed, had probably lodged a prow-spike into *Intrepid*. "Shoot the torped—the petard!" Eddie changed in mid-sentence, realizing that older word would be more immediately understood. "Or shoot the boom it's on! Just shoot—!"

The Big Shot spoke again, but its discharge was drowned out by a roar that shook the deck out from under Eddie's feet and sent part of the quarterdeck's stanchion-and-bedroll sides flying up among the mizzen sheets. The hazard bell began ringing in engineering and as Eddie picked himself up off the deck, he couldn't be sure if he was staggering or *Intrepid* was listing.

An iron hand grasped his arm, steadied him. Eddie looked round: Gjedde. "Captain. Are we—?"

"I know nothing more than you. Go to the bridge. I will see. You, sailor! Help the captain to his post. Svantner, do we still have steam?"

"No, sir."

"Why?" yelled Eddie, trying not to sound like he was watching his child, his creation, die beneath his feet. Which was exactly what he was in terror of.

"I do not know, sir. No comms from Engineering."

Damn it. The piragua had hit back by the engines. "Svantner, get below. I'll see to guiding the pilot, but we've got to get solid information about our engines. If we can't steam out of here—"

Svantner nodded his understanding of the mortal consequences of that scenario and was then sliding down the handrails of the companionway into the darkness of the lower decks.

Gjedde reappeared from back near the transom, scanning the near waters for the outline of any approaching ships. "Captain Cantrell, it is as you surmised. We were struck by a spar torpedo."

"Damage?" Eddie found he couldn't breathe, watching Gjedde as he chewed his lower lip.

"Less than I expected, frankly," the Norwegian answered. "I cannot tell if it was because of the inferiority of their bomb—it was simply a petard, I think—or the stoutness of *Intrepid*'s timbers. But other than some shattered strakes, the hull held up remarkably well."

"And for that, you may thank the ship's design," added Svantner, who came bounding breathlessly back up to the weather deck. Gjedde frowned.

Eddie smiled explained. "He means the citadel design: the armor housing we put around the engine and boiler."

Svantner, panting and doubled over, nodded weakly. "Aye, sir. Because of the inner armoring, the hull could not compress too much at that point, and that second layer, so to speak, made any spalling or shattering of the internal timbers almost impossible."

"So the engines—?"

"Are fine, Captain Cantrell. The chief engineer shut them down because he wanted to ease the pressure, just in case any damage had been done to the rivets, seams, or tubes. He brought the steam down to diagnostic levels and is pleased to report all normal and that it shall be restored within the minute. As far as the hull damage is concerned, the pumps are keeping well ahead of the leaks coming in through the seams that the explosion sprung." A gout of new smoke erupted from the *Intrepid*'s stack as if to punctuate the engines' readiness with an exclamation mark. "Orders, sir?" Svantner asked with a smile.

"As if you need to ask!" Eddie said. "Bring her to south by southwest and let's get the hell out of here—full steam ahead."

Part Nine

January 1636

The unity and married calm of states

Chapter 53

The coast of eastern Texas

Larry Quinn raised his hand and pointed to a darker skein of water on the left side of the narrow inlet they were approaching. "There's the deeper water. Steer to that."

Karl Klemm nodded. "Will there be a countercurrent, Major Quinn?"

Larry shrugged. "I doubt it. The mouth of the Calcasieu shouldn't be putting a lot of water out into the Gulf."

Kleinbaum, a woodland and jungle scout who had come highly recommended from his time working for the Dutch in the jungles of the Pernambuco, stared backward from the bow. "We're going *into* the mouth of the Calcasieu? You said we were beaching east of it."

Larry didn't like his tone, but was willing to let it slide. Once. "That's *not* what I said, Sebastian. I said we'd look at the inlet and make a final call when we got here. Needed to look at the land, see if it has regular visits from the natives. Sure doesn't look like it."

"Yes? Well, I think it is unwise to move inland at

all. We should stay on the coast, where we can move away more quickly if we encounter the cannibals."

Larry sighed but held his ready temper in check. "First, we have no proof that the Atakapas are cannibals or that they are in this area at all. Which I've repeated at least a dozen times in the past three days. And second, you've shared your thoughts on what we should do quite clearly already—three times on the way in. Any more, and I'd be tempted to construe that as disrespect for your commanding officer."

Kleinbaum stared at the approaching sands of the East Texas coast, slightly roseate in the setting sun. "You brought me along to provide you with my best assessment of the lands we are in," he muttered, his voice as stubborn and retracted as the hunched curve of his back.

"Yes," replied Larry. "But we're not on the land or anywhere near its flora, fauna, or inhabitants, yet. Unless you are telling me that your expertise starts from three miles off shore?"

Kleinbaum clearly did not want to respond, but knew he had to: he shook his head. "But going upriver always invites trouble—no matter where you are."

"Does it?" Larry countered quickly. "Kleinbaum, just so you know, I'm going up into the inlet a few dozen meters so that we'll have some depth in which we can anchor and sleep aboard. Yeah, it will be crowded, but we can scoot in a minute. Whereas if we pulled onto the beach on either side of the inlet, we'd have to haul the boat back into the surf before we could get away. Does that sound like a better idea to you?"

From behind, Larry could see Kleinbaum's jaw working angrily. "No, sir," he answered finally.

Quinn leaned back, raising his binoculars again. On either side of the narrow inlet that ultimately led to Calcasieu Lake, low sand-and-scree shores stretched straight and narrow into the vanishing-point distance of either horizon. Beyond them, low scrub brush and occasional stunted trees gave the land the appearance of having a youngster's tousled head of hair. Nothing foreboding. Hell, nothing much at all.

"Major Quinn," Karl said so quietly that he was almost inaudible over the surging growl of the Sportsman's engine, "I think I remember reading that the Atakapas have an extensive coastal range."

Leave it to Karl to read all *the supplemental briefing materials.* "That's correct."

"Then why did we start toward the Mermentau River before the *Courser* left Galveston Bay, sir? If something should go wrong—well, there aren't many of us to handle any unexpected problems."

"Karl, that was very tactfully put, but I'm not a particularly tactful person, so I'm going to answer your real question. Yes, this boat and its small crew will head up the Mermentau as soon as we reach it. Alone. Because even once the *Courser* joins us, her forces will be too far away to make much of a difference. Not unless we wait for them to paddle the ship's boats upriver with us. Which rather defeats the purpose of having a motorboat: to explore and make contact quickly. And to be able to leave quickly as well, if need be."

Karl swallowed; he glanced back at Wright and Vogel's lever-action rifles. "I understand, sir. But wouldn't the natives be more inclined to, er, diplomacy if they understood, from the start, that we had a strong force at our disposal?"

Quinn smiled ruefully. "You know, Karl, that was pretty much the first-contact philosophy throughout the colonization of the New World. And most of the time, it set exactly the wrong tone. Can we awe them? Sure. But there are two problems with that strategy. First, they are the masters of this country, not us. So if they want to stay unfound and unmet, they'd have no trouble doing so, particularly if we bring a company of troops to blunder around in the bush and the swamps that they grew up in.

"Second, if we do meet them, do we really want to awe them? Awe is the first cousin to fear, which has its roots in threat. If you consider the accounts of first contact in this part of the country, the smaller the contacting group, the more personal the interactions. You bring too large a group, and you look like invaders or a warchief with an escort. But if you come in smaller numbers, you look like explorers and are treated more as individuals, which is how friendships start." Quinn rubbed his close-cropped hair. "My ancestors spent two hundred years trying to intimidate and control the natives in the New World. And yeah, they got their way, but killed whole nations in the process. This time, knowing a little bit about the different tribes in advance, we're going to try a different approach."

Karl nodded. "This sounds most prudent—and ethical. Although even if they are our friends, that does not mean they will be willing to let us drill holes in their land."

No, thought Quinn, *it doesn't. Which could put one hell of a giant wrinkle in all our fine plans.* But all he said was, "Give it a little more throttle, Karl. Take us in."

Chapter 54

Santo Domingo, Hispaniola

Fadrique Álvarez de Toledo, Admiral of the Armada de Barlovento, hearing the sudden increase in gaiety in the villa's great-room beneath them, raised a glass of rioja toward his host, who sat opposite him at the table in the well-appointed study. "Happy New Year, Don de Viamonte. A fine party, worthy of the grandees of Madrid."

Juan Bitrian de Viamonte y Navarra, who was still flushed from the exertions of dancing the evening's first extended *rigaudon*, waved away the compliment. "First, the party is not so fine as you say, and you know it well. Second, if I am to be able to deflect your tiresome courtesies with good nature, we must agree to first names. And last, the party is not a half-worthy celebration of what you accomplished, my dear Admiral."

"What I accomplished?" Fadrique scoffed. "Now you mock me—Juan."

"I do not—Fadrique," responded the half-crippled captain-general with a warm and genuine smile. "Santo

Domingo still stands today because of your triumph at the Battle of Vieques."

"The Battle of Vieques, as too many are styling it, was no victory," countered Fadrique. "It was at best, a stalemate. And we paid for it with eight galleons, two galleoncetes, and three *pataches* sunk or irreparable. All this while running away from a fleet we outnumbered, three ships to one, for almost three consecutive days. And you will note I do not include the losses among our 'privateers,' losses which numbered well over twenty hulls, when we include the actions to the south, where the Dutch escaped." He irritably sucked in a full-cheeked swig of the red wine, as he had not done since resolving to regain his fitness and the finer form of his youth. "Another few 'victories' such as the one off Vieques and we shall be done for, in the New World."

Juan shook his head. "You are wrong, Fadrique. Wrong in so many ways, I do not know where to begin enumerating them. Let us return to my first comment. Had your stratagems not repelled these so-called 'Allied forces,' they would have reached this city. And we have all heard what similar up-time naval rifles did to the fortifications at Hamburg last year. They were reduced to rubble in half an afternoon. Had that happened here, how many more ships would we have lost? How many thousands of men? How many slips in which we may build the ships with which we must fight this new menace? And, perhaps more importantly, how would we have fought a war against them in the Lesser Antilles when our next stronghold truly worthy of that label is Havana, far to the west? How could we have hoped to contest their further expansion, and ultimately, contain and suffocate them on the few islands they currently hold? No, my dear Fadrique, you may have lost ships, but you won the battle. Any outcome which did not end in the leveling of Santo Domingo is a strategic victory of the first order. And yours is the mind and will that produced it."

"Well, I—"

"I am not finished, Admiral!" Juan remonstrated histrionically, his color becoming more normal. "Since I have returned to the topic of lost ships, I concede that yes, you did lose many. But you presumed that from the outset, did you not? And many of those lost used to be piratical scourges that are no longer a worry to us, are they not? You need not answer. I know the rightness of my assertions. And what did you accomplish with those losses?" Juan leaned forward and raised his wine-glass toward the man who had become a friend over the past five months. "You drove off those two steamships, and even significantly damaged one. The same ships which sunk and captured so many of our vessels at the Battle of Grenada Passage and routed all the rest. Your strategy—to bait them onward until the weather, sea, or light were unfavorable to their guns—was decisive. They did not discern it quickly enough to counteract it. They were lucky to escape, as it was."

"Not so lucky, Juan," Fadrique insisted, emphasizing his disagreement with a jabbed index finger. "The objective was not merely to deflect their probable strike against this city, but to inflict losses among the slower hulls in the rear of their formation. Every fluyt we sink of theirs reduces their ability to project power, to sail great distances with the troops and supplies and powder and coal that they require. It was unfortunate that we tangled with their steam behemoths at all, and see what it cost us! They were cautious enough not to give chase as ardently or swiftly as they might have,"—*as* I *might have*!—"and so we were not able to strike them at their weak point: support ships. Logistics. And now that we have tipped our hand, strategically, we must expect that they shall not give us such an easy opportunity again." He set down the empty glass. What he really wanted to do was shatter it on the table. "The flaw was in relying upon the pirate bastards in the south. They grew too eager, sprang the trap too early. In another hour, they would have regrouped properly and been abaft the beam of the rearmost Dutch fluyt. Our foes' escape would have been far more difficult and costly, then."

Juan frowned, nodded sympathetically. "Do we know what happened, in the south?"

"What else? Their spleen and bloodlust got the better of them. And I was foolish not to put more of our *patache*s in with them. Equiluz had to hold the mountains of St. Croix in his spyglass toward the far eastern end of our ambush line. Only he was reliable enough to accomplish that. Without him there, the whole sorry lot of them would no doubt have drifted apart in a few hours. And our privateers proved indifferent at sending signals clearly and promptly."

Juan shrugged. "You did the best you could with the resources you had. The Dutch lost a few ships, got a good scare that should give them pause, and ran away. Now, we have coast-watchers who may give us more timely warning of any subsequent approach. And soon, we shall bring the war to these pestiferous 'allies.'"

"Yes, and we've some good officers with which to do it. You know, Juan, I shall confess: I had my reservations about de Covilla when you first introduced us. But beneath that refinement, he's a good soldier. Last one off his galleon before it sank. His men admire his cool demeanor under fire, and they came under fire enough, from those steamships."

Juan traced the rim of his wineglass with his finger. "I have meant to ask: why did you put him up at the head of the van, closest to the steamships? Particularly if you had reservations about his, er, puissance?"

Fadrique shrugged. "By that time, I had revised my initial opinion of him. I also needed a person who knew our entire strategy to manage the pace and range of our retreat before the up-time ships. Most commanders would either have run, or turned and fought. And died. I needed a commander who could resist those two extreme impulses, and who was in our confidence regarding the trap we were setting with the southern privateer force." Fadrique snagged the decanter and poured another two fingers of rioja. "Now, de Covilla has seen combat, has had a ship shot out from under him, and did not flinch. And I know I have an excellent officer, in the bargain."

"Who seems to be making excellent progress with the ladies of my city, this evening."

"Well, it always helps to be a dashing, well-dressed war hero with one's arm in a sling, but with all his pieces still attached. As I said, a fine celebration you have hosted, Juan. And I would rather be here, in good, trustworthy company, than among the viperous grandees that will be clotting the king's ballroom in Madrid."

"Yes, and I wonder how welcome either one of us would be there, given what news we would have to report, and what Olivares might think of our resolve to renew our shipbuilding."

Fadrique frowned as he rolled the glass between his palms meditatively. "Since most of the ships we are building shall not qualify as workhorses for La Flota, and since they are coming from our own pockets, I wonder how much he can object. Although it will be the devil's own work getting him to send over the chandlery and cannon we need for them. But I think he will see the merits of spending a few thousand *reales* once in order to secure the delivery of several millions of them every year. Olivares is often foolish, but still, is no fool. He must know that we cannot brook a serious naval rival in the New World and be able to assure the safety of his treasure fleets. Thanks to your first message, and the one just sent, he should have time to add extra galleons to the fleet he is sending in March. That way, the Dutch and their 'allies' will find it painfully difficult to plunder it when it finally departs Havana with its riches, in late summer."

Juan shrugged. "That presumes he has the ships to spare. So long as Olivares is committed to blockading the English Channel as close as we can to the Dutch coast, too many of our ships are tied down to their duties in Europe."

"Yes, but if Olivares lifts the blockade it will go even worse for us." Fadrique leaned forward. "From what I hear, the Dutch continue to build ships in Amsterdam's ways. As it is, more of their ships will begin appearing in these waters. If Oquendo's fleet is called away or significantly reduced to assist with matters elsewhere, the Dutch will come here in still greater numbers."

Juan nodded. "And then our ability to wear this Allied fleet down will be seriously reduced."

"Exactly. Which are just a few of the reasons why we must push Havana's Captain-General Gamboa to bring de Armendáriz and New Spain in line with our resolutions. He must add the weight of his funds and his shipyards to our own. Similarly, we must get the viceroy of Peru, and de Murga in Cartagena to awaken the slumbering *audiencias* of Tierra Firma and make their own contributions." Fadrique lifted his glass. "Coordination and cooperation, my dear Juan. In the months to come, these must be our cardinal virtues. And if we would hope to see another New Year, we must accept that we will live or die by how well we achieve them—or not."

Oranjestad, St. Eustatia

In Oranjestad's newly completed governor's house, Eddie retreated from the dance floor, assisted by Anne Cathrine. His stump, still recovering from the long hours on deck and the constant tension of both actual and impending battle, was not cramping yet, but he could tell that if he didn't give it a rest, his wife would spend the rest of the evening without a regular dance partner.

The great-hall/ballroom/dining room of the governor's house was airy and clean, but sparsely furnished. The foods and drinks were quite predictable, but the plenitude of rum on this evening either dulled the

sensibilities of the attendees or simply induced them
not to give a damn. It was a party, there was music,
and best of all, it was a new year and they were still
alive. Just a month ago, that last fact had remained
very much in doubt.

The ratio of men to women was actually much
better than usual. No more than five to one, this
night. But that had been achieved through a variety of
careful machinations. First, many of Warner's English
ladies had been invited up to St. Eustatia. Which was
to say, they had been furnished with a *gratis* yacht
ride to-and-fro, and gifts beside. And even some of
the island's French women had made the journey
as well, most of them having been unceremoniously
abandoned when d'Esnambuc was forced to flee on
his one remaining ship without returning to Dieppe
Town. Many of the ladies were widows, many had
been abandoned years ago, many more were mixed
race orphans whose situation in the French colony
had always been delicate.

The English governor Warner had accepted the
invitation as well, and had brought his wife, children,
and several influential members of his now-expanded
colony. For the first time in years, it was relatively safe
for many of the leaders of the English colony to be
absent, in large part due to the repulse of the ships
and soldiers of its French neighbors. The troops that
the captured French bark had already put ashore near
Bloody Point had been tracked down swiftly enough
in the nearby hills. Most of the other French forces in
the colony had been aboard d'Esnambuc's own bark,
the *Bretagne*, which had withdrawn. Once free of
pursuit, she had swept around the southern end of St.

Christopher's to head up along the island's windward side and so get news of the attack upon St. Eustatia. What d'Esnambuc got instead was a view of du Plessis' ship, the *Main Argent*, fleeing southward toward him, flanked by native piraguas. In the distance, several Dutch jachts, along with the *Orthros*, had been in hot pursuit or landing their ship's troops along the French colony's strands. Seeing that, d'Esnambuc and du Plessis had turned their bowsprits southward and vanished into the gathering night.

On the dance floor, almost a third of the men in semi-finery—Tromp's command staff, a few troopers from the Wild Geese, and officers of various ships of the USE flotilla—made regretful bows and were ushered out the door by an honor-guard led by Cuthbert Pudsey. That bandaged worthy then admitted an equal number of men of similar rank, and in similar partial finery. Eddie smiled. This had been the other method of ensuring that the male to female ratio remained beneath the testosterone-alert levels. The men attended in shifts, while the ladies were allowed—indeed, encouraged—to stay for the duration of the evening. Or, now, morning.

Anne Cathrine surveyed the beginning of the next dance with a high-necked and utterly regal expression of immense satisfaction. "It is a fine celebration."

"It sure is." Eddie craned his neck. "But where are your ladies-in-waiting?"

Anne Cathrine swatted his arm lightly. "I am but a king's daughter. I do not have 'ladies-in-waiting,' or are you implying that I am taking on airs?"

"You? Absolutely not, your Royal Exalted Highness of the Universe and Empress of Supreme and Sultry Sexiness."

"Sshhh, Eddie! People will hear!"

"Let 'em. I'm a truth-telling man, by nature," he half-lied. "But seriously, where are Sophie and Sis?"

Anne Cathrine suddenly looked as coy as a debutante and crafty as a cat. "Well, Sophie chose to forego the festivities."

"What? Why?"

"She's in the infirmary."

"Now? Couldn't they get someone else to cover it?"

"Actually, no. And she was quite willing to make the sacrifice."

Eddie was impressed. "Well, that's a hell of a noble gesture."

"Oh, yes. Most certainly." She actually hid the lower half of her face behind her fan and tittered. "Quite noble indeed!"

"What—? Oh, wait a minute."

"Ah, has my war-wizard genius-hero from the future figured it out at last?"

"The earl of Tyrconnell is still recovering in the infirmary, isn't he?"

Anne Cathrine nodded. "Yes, although his wounds seem almost fully healed to me. Except where he lost the last joint on his little finger; that still requires some care. Which Sophie takes every opportunity to provide, you understand. And when I say she takes every opportunity, I mean she seizes it violently, if need be. She almost pushed poor Dr. Brandão aside yesterday, in order to get to Lord O'Donnell first."

Eddie almost chortled at the sudden mental image of tall, fine-featured, almost severe Sophie Rantzau hip-checking wizened little Brandão out of the way to get dibs on her favorite patient. "And is Hugh—er,

Lord O'Donnell—showing appropriate appreciation for her nursing skills and dedication?"

"I cannot tell." Anne Cathrine smiled. "But he has apparently started crafting some verses that he will allow no one else to see."

"Because he's a lousy poet, or because they are about her?"

Anne Cathrine's positively feline leer was back. "His men tell me he is actually a fairly gifted writer of odes."

"Huh. A man of many talents, I guess. And where's Leonora?"

"With Rik Bjelke."

"Really?" He scanned the dance floor but did not see them. "Where are they?"

"Oh, they're gone."

"Gone? Why?"

Anne Cathrine shrugged. "Well, you know Leonora. She got bored with the dancing. So she went outside to show Rik the constellations that we can see here, but not in Denmark."

"You're kidding. She took him out to star-gaze?"

"Yes. And he seemed genuinely interested."

"In the stars or in her?"

Anne Cathrine actually giggled. "Both, I think." She scanned the nearby crowd. Her laughter became a genuine, but very public, smile as two men emerged from the festive throng. "Admiral, Governor. How wonderful to see you this evening. And our thanks for this lovely celebration."

The two Dutchmen had emerged from behind a cluster of officers signing their names on a tired but cheery young lady's dance card. They approached and bowed to Anne Cathrine—a little more deeply now,

Eddie thought. Van Walbeeck straightened up with a smile almost immediately. "I saw you two dancing earlier. I must say, you are a handsome couple! Well, you would be if Eddie wasn't half of it."

Eddie almost gargled his rum punch. Anne Cathrine smiled. "Oh," she said, slipping a shapely arm through her husband's, "on that point, Governor, I must disagree."

"Ah, well and loyally spoken, my lady. You are having a good time, it seems."

"Wonderful," Anne Cathrine replied. "And you and your men seem quite jovial, Admiral."

Eddie didn't think Tromp looked jovial. Hell, Tromp *never* looked "jovial." But the Dutchman certainly looked pleased and relaxed. "We are glad to be on land, together, and alive to greet the New Year. And to be in the presence of such beauty as you bring to this party, Lady Anne Cathrine."

Van Walbeeck poked Maarten Tromp in the arm. "Here, now, you sly sea-dog! *I'm* the shameless flatterer. Do not presume to usurp my role!"

Anne Cathrine smiled beatifically. "You gentlemen are both so gallant. You are also so thoroughly under the influence of rum that your eyes have grown kind and easily pleased. Now forgive me as I ask my husband if he is ready to dance again?"

Eddie listened to the opening chords or the next dance: a *gigue*. And a pretty lively one. He shook his head sadly. "Honey, if I dance to that, I won't be dancing again for a week. How about the governor, here? Mijn heer van Walbeeck looks like he could bust a few moves."

"Bust a few what?"

"Like he'd be an excellent dancer. Now, go have fun!"

Tromp stared at Eddie, at the new dance partners who were making their way out on to the floor, and shook his head with a smile. He raised a small snifter of schnapps toward the up-timer. "*Proost*, Eddie. And a very Happy New Year."

"You, too, Admiral."

"I am Maarten, please. I am not so formal as all that. Particularly not with my colleagues."

Eddie thought he'd choke on his punch again or laugh. Or maybe shout with a mix of triumph and pride. Maarten Tromp, an admiral out of the legends of history, had labeled him a colleague and suggested they proceed on a first-name basis. How cool was *that*?

"Well, Happy New Year to you, too, Maarten. I'm just sorry we can't be celebrating it in Santo Domingo."

Tromp stared down at his schnapps. "Not me. That would have been a very bloody business. Even if your guns had reduced the city as quickly as you projected, I suspect we would still be there, up to our knees in refugees, and bodies, and debris, and the misery of the people whose city we had destroyed. No, I think it is better to have New Year's here."

"Well, I certainly agree with that, Maarten. But I can only hope they have the same tender consideration for us when they come after Oranjestad."

Maarten stirred his rum punch. "And they will come, of course."

"Yep. And by deflecting our drive on Santo Domingo, they debuted a new playbook. And whoever's authoring it is one smart cookie."

"You mean by deferring engagement until night, or by going after our Achilles heel: our support ships?"

"Both, and more besides. The Spanish have never

given lighter, fore-and-aft rigged ships any serious consideration as combat platforms. They got into the galleons-as-sea-forts mentality about a century ago, and haven't budged. But this guy, whoever he is, threw that out after one nasty surprise off Grenada." Eddie shook his head. "The Spanish admirals are usually not out-of-the-box thinkers. But this guy is, and that makes him dangerous. Hell, he was even willing to recruit pirates to get enough of the right kind of ships and crews for his ambush. And he almost pulled it off."

"Well, at least we know what to look for, in the future," Tromp offered. "Although I suspect that this fellow had alternate tactics in the event of bad weather, since poor visibility favors his ships in other ways."

"Yeah, I'm sure he had a Plan B. And probably a Plan C for really high seas. Either way, until we retrofit our ships with a fire-control system that's electronically triggered by our interferometers, and also come up with some night vision gear, they're going to try to engage us in unfavorable fighting conditions. And as long as they keep a lot of their lighter ships around to run interference, it's going to be pretty hard to pin down their heavies and sink them."

Tromp nodded. "Yes. He made quite an accurate study of both your gunnery, and the conditions that will nullify its superiority. And he deduced he needed lighter ships to 'run interference' as you call it. And I am not sure how we can parry his riposte. Unless we find some pirates of our own to recruit."

Eddie smiled. "Or even better, some disaffected Englishmen. They do run quite a number of sloops and yachts between here, the Bahamas, Bermuda, and even Barbados."

Tromp smiled and raised his schnapps snifter in a toast. "An excellent project and New Year's resolution." He took a sip, grew somber. "It would certainly have been helpful to have even four or five more such ships when we tried to push through them to the south. We sank or disabled enough of them, but our warships were too slow to exploit the gaps we punched in their trap before they filled it with more of their swift ships. As it was, we were still fighting when light fell. Thank God that the *Resolve* showed up when she did and made steam. The lights from her, and her funnel, gave us a gathering point, kept us from scattering further. By following her, we got moving in the right direction even though we couldn't see each other's signals. By the way, I am now a convert to your insistence that every ship has a blinker tube. It would have been an immense help at the end of that combat. And perhaps we might not have had to lose the *Pinas* and the *Zeeland*."

"Why?"

"Because they were not sinking so much as they were damaged, unable to make headway. Had we been able to find them in the dark sooner, we might have been able to assess the damage and effect enough repairs to allow them to keep up with the rest of our ships." Maarten flipped one impatient palm upward. "But instead, by the time we found them, we were already worried about not getting far enough away, by becoming embroiled in a second day of combat. There wasn't the time to fix much, and we couldn't afford to leave the crews behind. So we had to scuttle them. Such a waste. We need every hull we have. And more."

"No argument from me on that point, Maarten.

Are your folks finished refitting the Spanish ships we took off Grenada?"

"Not quite, but soon. Frankly, the Spanish ships are so slow that they will not be much use to us when we sail to war. But they will be serviceable enough as part of our defense forces, either here or at Trinidad, I think." He smiled. "They do quite well as floating batteries, at least."

"What about giving them a better fore-and-aft rig on their mizzen? Or spencer masts?"

Tromp shrugged. "One has clean enough lines to warrant such modifications, and we might do so, if time permits. But the others—they are fortress-scows to carry silver back to Seville."

Eddie finished his drink. "I suppose, all things considered, we came out of it well enough. Even if we failed in our main objective."

Tromp seemed to study him closely, for a moment. Then said: "I think you underestimate what we gained, Captain Cantrell. As a result of the battle off Vieques, we have resolved what may have been the single greatest weakness we had."

"Which was?"

"You. Or more precisely, everyone's assessment of you."

Eddie must have looked startled, because Tromp's face was briefly creased with an outright grin—very unusual for such a reserved man. "Come now, Eddie. Surely you understood the predicament we were all in—you more than anyone, perhaps. On the one hand, we were dependent on your knowledge and skills. On the other . . ."

Eddie understood. "I had no . . . the term we uptimers use is 'track record.'" Seeing Tromp's slight frown of puzzlement, Eddie clarified the term. "That means personal—no, more like professional—history. You knew nothing about my . . . well, courage, I suppose."

"Not exactly that." Tromp's grin half-reappeared. "The Danes are quite fond of you. Not only married to one of their king's daughters but, in an odd sort of way, they seem to have transmuted your somewhat suicidal ramming of one of their ships at Wismar into a Danish feat."

Eddie didn't bother trying to explain that the supposedly "somewhat suicidal ramming" at Wismar had been entirely an accident. He'd fought and lost that battle too many times already. Legends could have the thickest hides in creation.

Tromp shook his head. "But frenzied berserk courage is not the same thing as cool control under fire, maintained for hours. That, more than anything, is what a commander has to have—and that is what you displayed at Vieques. Displayed in full measure. So no one has any questions, any longer, about your fitness for command. Which means"—he issued a slight chuckle—"that the next time you try to caution us that we don't understand some subtlety of the way up-time technology affects naval tactics, everyone will listen respectfully. Even Johan van Galen. That may prove critical in the battles still to come."

A little embarrassed, Eddie didn't know quite how to respond. Luckily, an interruption came. A side door into the ballroom opened and a squarish man entered. He was not dressed for the party. Rather, he looked like a workman, perhaps come to fix one of the storm shutters.

Eddie smiled: Mike McCarthy, Jr. "Hey, Mr. Mike!"

Eddie cried out, reverting to the form of address he'd used as a kid, "over here!"

Mike scanned for the source of the voice, spotted Eddie, nodded curtly, and began the laborious job of winding through the dense throngs of men clustered about any woman on or near the dance floor. When he finally extricated himself from the eager, sweating, would-be swains, he looked about in exasperation. "Jeez," he exhaled, "I really am glad I decided not to come."

"And yet, here you are," observed Tromp with a small smile. Then the admiral became quite grave. "Mr. McCarthy, before the moment slips away, I want to say that this colony owes you a singular debt of gratitude, although not all of our citizens are comfortable admitting, and therefore, expressing it. So allow me to say this for every man and woman on St. Eustatia: had our landowners' slaves not been converted into bondsmen with freedom in their future, I am quite certain they would have either joined the Kalinago during the attack, or simply stood aside. And that would have been the end of this colony, given how very many of our troops were in service elsewhere or embarked on the transports heading for Santo Domingo."

Mike did exactly what Eddie expected: he waved it off. "I'm just a guy with a big mouth, Admiral. Sometimes that big mouth is helpful, sometimes it's harmful. No reason to get worked up too much, either way. I'm just here to drop off a few pieces of news: the radio is working again. I've got two messages that came through clearly from Europe. We were trying to trade signals with Vlissingen all afternoon, which was working as a priority relay to the naval radio shack in Luebeck."

"So you were swapping Morse code with headquarters, but not Grantville," Eddie clarified.

"Yep. First item relevant to our mission: on Christmas Eve, the new rotary drill prototype got down to almost seven hundred feet before breaking down. But the crew was able to save the rig, contain the damage, and protect themselves. By this time next year, we'll be digging holes a whole lot faster and deeper in Trinidad."

And, more important, in Louisiana too, if Quinn's expedition is successful, Eddie thought behind the cover of his broad smile and approving nod. "And the other message?"

Mike smiled. "The other message is for you, Eddie. Personally. From Simpson."

"A personal message for me? From the admiral?"

"Yep. Because it summarized a bunch of politicking back home, it kind of rambled, so I only brought the last part on paper. But I can pretty much synopsize the rest. Simpson sends his warm congratulations on all that you and the 'Allies' have achieved. It is his pleasure to promote you to full commander on the basis of meritorious action. Furthermore, due to the death of Admiral Mund, he agrees to extend your brevet rank of post-captain indefinitely." Mike noticed Eddie's broad grin and shook his head. "Y'know, Eddie, you never get a promotion without new headaches."

Eddie found he was no longer smiling.

"Simpson went on to say that 'growing developments' back home in the USE make it 'imprudent' for Simpson's own new fleet to set sail for the New World. First of all, it's not ready yet. He's still overseeing the first production runs of the improved cruiser and destroyer classes that you auditioned here. He also cited 'uncertain international situations' as a reason to keep the strategic power of the new fleet close to home."

"What kind of international situations?"

"He didn't say, and with Simpson, you don't ask. Know what I mean?"

"Do I ever. Go on, Mike."

Mike shook his head, reached into his pocket, pulled out a telegrapher's sheet and handed it to Eddie with a crooked smile. "I figured you might want to read the rest of it yourself."

Eddie, nodding dumbly, took the sheet and read Admiral Simpson's closing remarks:

> *Collectively, these circumstances require that the core of the USE fleet remains in Luebeck. Logically, this compels a strategic revision of the mission profile of Reconnaissance Flotilla X-Ray. Specifically, it is no longer a mere reconnaissance-in-force. It is, de facto, the USE's Caribbean fleet-in-being, and the only tool available to accomplish this nation's critical objectives in that region. Consequently, so that our command-grade contribution to what is being called the composite Allied fleet enjoys equal standing with the senior staffs of the other participating nations, King Christian IV of Denmark is pleased to confer upon post-Captain Edward Cantrell the acting rank of Commodore in Danish service. He has confirmed that this rank shall be recognized by all the nations signatory to*

> *the Union of Kalmar, as well as the armed*
> *forces of the U.S.E.*
> *So I wish you good hunting in the New*
> *Year—and Godspeed, Commodore Cantrell.*

Still staring at the sheet without really seeing it, Eddie murmured. "Hell. I've been promoted. Several times."

"Yeah," commiserated Mike. "Ain't it a bitch?"

Cast of Characters

Álvarez De Toledo y Mendoza, Fadrique	Admiral of the Armada de Barlovento
Anne Cathrine	Oldest daughter of Christian IV by his morganatic marriage to Kirsten Munk; "king's daughter" but not "princess"; married to Eddie Cantrell
Aossey, Lolly	Geologist
Banckert, Adriaen	Dutch naval officer
Banckert, Joost	Vice Admiral of the Dutch Fleet
Barto	Pirate captain and privateer
Bjelke, Henrik	Norwegian nobleman, officer in Reconnaissance Flotilla X-Ray (RF X-Ray)
Brandão, Ambrósio	Sephardic physician
Calabar	Brazilian soldier, freedom-fighter, plantation owner

Cantrell, Eddie	Lieutenant Commander, USE Navy; assigned to RF X-Ray
Christian IV	King of Denmark
Corselles, Pieter	First Governor of Oranjestad, later local director for the Dutch West India Company
De Burgo, John	Soldier, Wild Geese
De Cárdenas y Manrique de Lara, Jorge	Captain-General of the Armada de Barlovento
De Covilla, Eugenio	Captain of Spain
De l'Olive, Charles Liénard	French adventurer, assistant governor of Guadeloupe
D'Esnambuc, Sieur Pierre Bélain	Governor of the French colony on St. Christopher
De Viomante y Navarra, Juan Bitrian	Captain-General of Hispaniola and Santo Domingo
Doyle, Thomas	Lieutenant and field engineer, Wild Geese
Du Parque, Jacques Dyel	Administrator of Martinique; nephew of Pierre d'Esnambuc
Du Plessis d'Ossonville, Jean	French adventurer, governor of Guadeloupe
Fernando	King in the Netherlands, House of Hapsburg, younger brother of King Philip IV of Spain; married to Maria Anna of Austria

Floriszoon, Pieter	Dutch captain
Gerritsz, Hans	Dutch captain
Gjedde, Ove	Captain of *Intrepid*, RF X-Ray
Haakon, Gorm	Officer in RF X-Ray
Isabella	Archduchess of the Spanish Lowlands, House of Habsburg
Jol, Cornelis "Houtebeen/Peg Leg"	Dutch captain
Klemm, Karl	Technical expert and oil prospector, special operations group, RF X-Ray
Kortenaer, Bert	Radio construction foreman
Koudsi, Ann	Oil drilling expert
Leonora	Second "king's daughter" of King Christian IV of Denmark by his morganatic marriage to Kristen Munk; sister of Anne Cathrine
Maria Anna	Wife of Fernando; Queen in the Lowlands; Archduchess of Austria, House of Hapsburg
McCarthy, Jr., Mike	Technical instructor
McCarthy, Mike	Elderly invalid ex-miner and Fenian
Morraine, Paul	Captain, *Fleur Sable*, expatriate French naval officer
Mulryan, Tearlach	Ensign, Wild Geese

Mund, Edel	Wife of Pros Mund
Mund, Pros	Captain of *Resolve*, and Admiral of RF X-Ray
Murrow, James	Soldier, Wild Geese
O'Bannon, Kevin	Captain, Wild Geese
O'Cahan, Daniel	Ensign, Wild Geese
O'Donnell, Hugh Albert	Earl of Tyrconnell, Colonel of the Wild Geese
O'Rourke, Aodh	Aide-de-camp to Hugh O'Donnell and Senior Sergeant of the Wild Geese
Piazza, Ed	President, State of Thuringia-Franconia
Preston, Thomas	Colonel of the Wild Geese
Pudsey, Cuthbert	English mercenary in Dutch service
Quinn, Larry	Major, USE Army, special operations group commander, RF X-Ray
Rantzau, Sophie	Danish noblewoman, companion to Anne Cathrine and Leonora
Riijs	Leader of Barto's landing force
Rohrbach, Ulrich	Oil drilling foreman
Schooneman, Jakob	Captain of the *Koninck David*

Sehested, Hannibal	Danish nobleman travelling with RF X-Ray; agent of King Christian
Serooskereken, Philip	Councilor of Oranjestad
Simonszoon, Dirck	Dutch captain
Simpson, John Chandler	Admiral, USE Navy
St. Georges, George	French expatriate naval officer
Stiernsköld, Tryggve	Captain of the *Tropic Surveyor*, RF X-Ray
Svantner, Arne	Officer in RF X-Ray
Touman	Kalinago cacique from Guadeloupe
Tromp, Maarten	Admiral of the Dutch Fleet
Turenne, Henri de la Tour d'Auvergne	French general
Van der Zaan, Willem	Dutch cabin boy
Van Galen, Johan	Dutch captain
Van Walbeeck, Jan	Governor of St. Eustatia
Von Holst, Hjalmar	Dutch captain

𝕲𝖑𝖔𝖘𝖘𝖆𝖗𝖞 𝖔𝖋 𝕹𝖆𝖛𝖆𝖑 𝕿𝖊𝖗𝖒𝖘

Ship Types

Note: Ship designs and designations were not stan-dardized in the early seventeenth century. The defi-nitions that follow are therefore approximations that are generally accurate but from which any particular ship might deviate to one extent or another.

Barca-longa	A two- (sometimes three-) masted lugger, a vessel using a lugsail, which is a modified version of a square sail. Often used as fishing vessels.
Bark (or Barque)	A small vessel with three or more masts, the foremasts being square-rigged and the aftermast rigged fore-and-aft.
Fluyt	A Dutch cargo vessel, generally two to three hundred tons, at least eighty feet long, and with a distinctive pear shape when viewed fore or aft.

Galleon

A three- or four-masted war-ship developed from the heavy carrack cargo ships, but with a longer and lower design. Not usually more than six hundred tons. Typically, the mizzenmast was lateen-rigged.

Galleoncete

A smaller galleon, generally of one hundred to two hundred tons. Many were designed to be able to use oars.

Jacht

Agile and fast vessel with very shallow draft, originally developed by the Dutch to hunt pirates in the shallow waters of the Low Countries.

Nao

A galleon adapted for cargo-hauling.

Patache

A light two-masted vessel with a shallow draft, often favored by pirates and privateers.

Piragua

One- or two-masted native boat that was also adopted by Spanish and pirates. It was narrow, often made from the trunk of a tree, and could be sailed or rowed. Commonly for a crew of six to thirty.

Yacht

English version of the *jacht*.

Gun Types

Note: As with ship types, naval ordnance was not yet standardized in the early seventeenth century. It varied widely over time and between nations. The definitions reflect this extreme diversity.

Cannon	In general use, any type of artillery piece. Specifically, a very large gun that typically fired a shot of 32 pounds or more.
Carronade	Short-barreled gun firing shot that ranged from 6 to 68 pounds. Much lighter than cannons firing an equivalent weight of shot, but had much shorter range. Predominantly used as a broadside weapon, it was originally designed specifically for naval combat.
Culverin	More lightly constructed than cannons, guns of this type fired shot from 16 to 22 pounds.
Demi-cannon	Gun firing shot weighing from 22 to 32 pounds.
Demi-culverin	Slightly larger than a saker, this weapon fired shot from 9 to 16 pounds.
Saker	A small carriage-mounted gun, firing shot of eight pounds or less.

Rigging Terms

Fore-and-aft-rigged	A sailing rig consisting mainly of sails that are set along the line of the keel rather than perpendicular to it.
Foremast	The mast nearest the bow of a ship.
Lateen-rigged	A type of fore-and-aft rig in which a triangular sail is suspended on a long yard set at an angle to the mast.
Mainmast	The principal mast of a sailing vessel.
Mizzenmast	The mast aft or next aft of the mainmast.
Square-rigged	A sail and rigging design in which the main sails are carried on horizontal spars that are perpendicular, or square, to the keel of the vessel and to the masts.
Stay	A strong rope or wire supporting a mast.
Yards	The spars holding up sails.
Yardarms	The tips of the yards, beyond the last stay.

The following is an excerpt from:

1636
THE CARDINAL
VIRTUES

ERIC FLINT
WALTER H. HUNT

Available from Baen Books
July 2015
hardcover

Chapter 1

Late July, 1635
Outside of Paris, France

The need for secrecy was constant. No one
believed that more strongly than Armand-Jean
du Plessis, Cardinal-Duke de Richelieu, Principal Minister to His Most Christian Majesty
Louis XIII, king of France. Within the palace
of the Louvre as well as at his own residence,
the Palais-Cardinal, secrets were guarded most
jealously. They were a valuable commodity,
esteemed by the cardinal and protected by those
who surrounded him—those particular to the
crown and those plucked from other nations.

However, the secret now contemplated was
too sensitive even for those protected within the
halls of king and cardinal; an even more private
venue was required. Thus it was that when the
king of France rode to the hunt on a sultry,
humid July morning, his entourage included his
minister astride a fine horse, riding at his side.

The courtiers and servants gossiped about it
among themselves—quietly, of course, out of the
sight and hearing of their betters. Whenever the
searching glance of Cardinal Richelieu settled
upon them they fell silent and avoided his eyes.

For his part, King Louis—always at greater ease on the hunt than at court—was pleased to have his minister by his side. Those usually accorded the privilege of taking up the position had to remain at a respectful distance.

The morning was not productive, the hounds and beaters flushing only inferior prey: a few rabbits and foxes, nothing worthy of His Majesty's attention. But it was the hunt itself and not the results that pleased the king. Toward midday Louis called a halt. The royal stewards began the process of laying out a repast for the gently-born in a beautiful clearing, while grooms attended to their mounts.

Minister and king walked away from the crowd, seeming to enjoy the scenery. But far from the court and away from prying ears, their conversation turned to more serious manners.

"I trust all is in—in readiness," the king said.

"I am pleased to say that it is, Majesty. We have secured the Château de Baronville in Beville-le-Comte for the queen's use during her seclusion; and I have engaged the services of an up-timer physician."

"Is he anyone I know?"

"She, Majesty. And no, I do not believe that you are acquainted with her. She is a distant relative of the Masaniello family."

"The Steam Engine people."

"Exactly, Sire. She has put certain up-timer protocols into practice that have caused marked improvement in the health of the technical center employees. The queen will be in good hands."

"Their midwives qualify as physicians also?"

"Up-timers," Richelieu said in response, as if that was sufficient explanation.

"Is my lady wife prepared?"

Richelieu permitted himself the slightest smile. "I daresay that her work does not come until somewhat later. The other participant in the event is ready to do his duty, however. He will be at the Château Fontainebleau, where you and Queen Anne will be making a progress."

"When?"

"Whenever you are ready, Sire, but if I may suggest that the Feast of Saint Louis—the twenty-fifth of August—might be a propitious occasion."

"Our noble ancestor and namesake. We can hear Mass and wave royally. At least it's less unpleasant than Saint Denis. The sight of some peasant dressed as the saint, carrying a plaster head under his arm, always disturbed me."

"As Your Majesty says," Richelieu said. "The people will enjoy being reminded of the divinity of kingship."

Louis shrugged. "As you say. So—the Feast of Saint Louis it is. You will inform Queen Anne that we shall progress to Fontainebleau. But . . . why not, why not simply complete the matter at Baronville?"

"Ah." Richelieu removed a speck of dust from his soutane. "I would think, Sire, that we would prefer the location to remain secret, to be used when Her Majesty is more advanced in her pregnancy. There is no reason to reveal it sooner."

"Yes. Quite—quite correct. You have been most thorough, Monseigneur."

"I thank you, Sire." Richelieu inclined his head. "I seek only to serve; and in this instance I wish to leave nothing to chance."

"Nothing . . . other than the occasion itself. And that is in the hands of God." He crossed himself and looked upward.

Richelieu followed the gesture, but refrained to mention to the king the many methods the up-timers knew about to help assure success.

"God will smile upon France, I am certain," he said after a moment.

Chapter 2

August, 1635
Paris

On the morning of the Feast of St. Louis, the king of France awoke in the darkness. He was unable to sleep any longer. By the time he rose and shrugged into his robe, his ever-attentive valet Beringhien was already in his bedchamber, building up the fire to help his master ward off the unexpected late summer chill.

Beringhien knew better than to ask Louis why he was up and about at this hour. The king had long since ceased to observe the hours an adult man would normally keep. The *lever* and the *coucher* took place at the appointed times, so that the gentlemen who had the honor of assisting with the royal robing and disrobing could be present as needed. But what took place behind the door of the king's cabinet was entirely different.

This was a special morning. Beringhien had laid out some of the king's wardrobe when he retired just before Matins, and as soon as he dealt with the fireplace he retired without a word to complete the task, leaving Louis to attend to his duty with the chamber-pot.

In his dressing chamber, the king yawned, removing his robe and dropping it on the ground so that he could stand in his small-clothes. As he noted the attire that his valet had chosen he favored Beringhien with a slight smile. Even in the chilly pre-dawn dark it warmed the valet's heart to see it. So little brought his royal master to smile these days, with the press of duty and the swirl of intrigues and the weight of the crown upon Louis' brow.

"Send word to Father Caussin that I desire to have him hear my confession," he said when he was done. "And present my respects to my lady, my lady the queen and inform her that I wish to call upon her when she is ready to receive me."

"Majesty—" Beringhien began to reply, and then saw the expression on his master's face: excitement, tinged perhaps with impatience. "Sire. It is two hours before dawn."

"You do not think that my confessor will be, be ready to serve me at this hour?"

"No, Sire...but the queen..."

"When my spiritual duty is done she shall receive me. See to it, see to it," he said, waving the valet off.

"As you wish, Your Majesty," Beringhien answered, and bowed himself out of the king's presence.

The stern voice of Père Nicolas Caussin, the king's Jesuit confessor, pronounced the absolution upon the king as he knelt in the confessional. After a few polite words thanking His Majesty for his piety and his goodness in setting an example, Caussin withdrew from his side of the screen, leaving the king alone.

He offered up a private prayer and rose, stepping back into his private chapel, and then made his way along a corridor, just beginning to brighten with the first rays of sunlight. Three of his gentlemen-in-waiting kept a respectful distance from the king as they followed. In the distance, the first lauds-bells were chiming across the city, calling the faithful to prayer.

Presently he came to the apartments in the Louvre set aside for the queen. The outer door was already open. As he walked through, he received a low bow from François de Crussol, the duke of Uzès, gentleman-in-ordinary to the queen. He was of an age with the king and had been in Anne's service for a dozen years, attending her before and at the *lever*—when she rose from bed and emerged to greet her courtiers. He had received word from Beringhien, and though he appeared to have scarcely performed his morning toilet, was alert and ready to receive the king.

"Sire," Uzès said. "Her Majesty humbly begs her pardon as she is not yet ready to receive you, but asked that I present you in just a few minutes."

"Very well, very well. It is—it is quite early."

"Indeed so, my lord. I trust you rested well, Sire?"

"I could hardly sleep. A great day, a great day, Uzès." The king shifted from foot to foot, then turned suddenly to his entourage. "My good gentilhommes, your service is not required—I shall call for you at once if you are needed."

The three young noblemen offered deep bows and withdrew, scarcely concealing their delight in being released from the royal presence. They knew not to stray far, since the king's mood might suddenly change, but they were clearly eager to be away from his sight.

The king turned again. "And how do you, Monsieur le duc? Are you well this fine day?"

"I thank Your Majesty for asking. I am quite well."

"And the queen?"

"I believe she does well also. I—"

His reply was interrupted by the opening of the inner door of the chamber and the appearance of Marie-Aimée de Rohan, the Duchess of Chevreuse, the principal lady-in-waiting for the queen. The king disliked the duchess. At one time they had been very close, when she was married to Charles d'Albert, duc de Luynes—the king's falconer and favorite, who had died fifteen years before. Since then she had descended into various intrigues, primarily aimed at Cardinal Richelieu. She had even been dismissed and exiled at one point, only to be reinstated earlier this year at the request of his queen.

As in so many things, Louis felt that circumstances had trapped him into such a decision—but it would soon be of no matter.

"Madame," the king said, removing his hat. "Is Her Majesty ready to receive me?"

"Yes, sire," the duchess answered. "She has just risen from her bed and made her morning prayer. She begs to receive you in her cabinet."

"Splendid, splendid," Louis said. "I would speak with her alone."

The duchess de Chevreuse let one eyebrow drift upward, as if it were the strangest thing in the world for husband and wife—king and queen—to be alone together. But she had no inclination to gainsay her sovereign, and merely stood aside as the king entered the chamber. Uzès remained without, and the duchess closed the door behind her and looked at him.

"Do you have any idea—" she began.

"I have found that it is best not to ask, Madame," the duke answered. "I am sure that if it is intended that I know, that I shall learn in due time."

"Aren't you the least bit curious?"

"Do you wish the polite answer or the truth?"

"The truth, of course."

"I am insanely curious. The king here, at dawn? I have no idea why he might come, and then seek private audience with our mistress. But it is his right. Perhaps they want to—"

"On a feast-day? Really, François—"

The duke shrugged, with a slight smile at her shocked look. He thought she was being quite disingenuous. When they were much younger they had both seen the loose morality of the court when Louis' father was king. There had been eight légitimés, the recognized offspring of Henry IV with his various mistresses, and God only knew how many other by-blows that had never been brought to court.

"The calendar is stuffed with feast-days, Marie. I rather think the saints turn a blind eye to it all."

She gave him another shocked look, which he continued to disregard. She reached for the door-handle as if preparing to stalk back into the queen's inner chambers, then, realizing the order for privacy, let her hand drop to her side, and settled with as much dignity as she could manage into a chair.

Louis stood just inside the doorway for several seconds. Anne—who at court was called Anne of Austria though she was a Spanish princess—his wife of more than twenty years, sat at her toilet-table, her back to him; her long tresses lay loosely on her shoulders rather than being bundled up in a chignon or elaborately pinned in a coiffure, as she preferred and as court style demanded. She was dressed in a long plain underdress, and was examining herself in the mirrors at the back of the table.

She had seen him there; but it was some sort of game for her to pretend she had not. At another time, with an audience, this was something she might have prolonged to keep him waiting—to make sure he understood that he moved in her realm, that in these rooms he followed an orbit around her rather than she about him. But the time for such artifice and entertainment was past, if indeed it had ever been the true course she had wished to follow.

"Madame, I—"

"Sire." She turned on her backless chair,

affecting to see him for the first time, and allowed herself to fall to one knee. "I beg your pardon. I did not hear you come in."

"It is nothing. A few moments." In a few steps he was before her and extended his hand, which she took. He assisted her to rise.

"I do not wish Your Majesty to think me discourteous or ill-bred." She smiled.

"I could not imagine such an accusation. You are my queen, my betrothed, and . . ." It was his turn to smile. "A true daughter of Hapsburg. I am pleased that you would receive me so early."

"I am at Your Majesty's service, as he knows."

"Yes. I know." He let go of her hand and walked slowly toward the patio doors, closed against autumn morning chill. Beyond, a beautiful day beckoned, the leaves on the trees in the enclosed garden just beginning to turn.

She followed, stopping at a respectful distance.

"We have not spoken for some time," Louis said. "Not like—like this. The two of us. No courtiers, no cardinal. No confessors or—or—others."

"As you wish."

"Not as I wish: not, not just as *I* wish, Anne. I would have wished otherwise, I think, if things had been different." He turned to face her. "I have reached the conclusion after many years that—that you have been ill-used. Perhaps I have been as well. When we married . . . when we were first together . . . we were not ready. Neither of us."

Anne looked down at her hands, folded in front of her. She wanted to say, I was ready: I was trained to be ready. You were...

You were your mother's son, she thought to herself. Marie de Medici, the domineering, controlling, manipulative queen mother who was Regent of France during Louis' minority had done everything in her power to make sure she maintained that situation, even as she stunted the maturity of the king of France. Indeed, they fought two wars in the space of a year, his partisans on one side and hers on the other. But it took a personal, direct conflict to make him decide between mother and minister.

And to many, she thought, you simply became the cardinal's creature. Weak, indecisive, tongue-tied...and even now without an heir of your body, or mine.

I was ready, she thought. But she did not say it.

"Things have not gone as planned, Sire," she said at last.

"Louis."

"Louis," she repeated, and though she spoke French very well it still sounded like Luis. "My king. I consented to this arrangement so that there might be a future for the royal house, but it would not have been my decision if it had not been decided for me. The...Cardinal, your servant, saw it as a practical solution, and I allow that it is so."

"It was his arrangement, Anne," he said. "But it is—it is my will."

She looked down again at her folded hands. "I know it is your will, Sire. But you asked my consent—or, rather, your . . . servant . . . asked it, and I gave it. It is my choice to participate."

"My servant loves France, and so do I."

"And so do I, Louis. I am its queen. Though you sometimes doubted it, though there have been times that my actions and words have not truly convinced you that it is true, I love France." She was not looking down now: she was looking directly into his eyes. She had not meant to be so emotional, but she felt that it was time for truth. After all of the intrigue, all of the scheming, all of the failed pregnancies and petty jealousies and court rivalries—after all of that—it was time for truth.

"I want—I want to believe you."

"Do you not?" She continued to stare at him. "I cannot imagine what I must do to convince you that I speak the truth. Words fail me. Only deeds will do." She reached forward and took his hand in both of hers. He did not pull away: there was no one to see the gesture, no one to titter at her sentimentality or at his discomfort. Perhaps Madame de Chevreuse or one of the other ladies of her chamber was watching the scene—or perhaps one of the cardinal's spies, for that matter: they said that his eyes and ears were everywhere. She had already decided that she did not care. "We will undertake this and we will do it for France. For you, Sire, and even for . . . for your servant."

"It is not for him."

"Then it is for France, My Lord."

"I can accept that. We do this for France, My Lady. For the France that will be—not what the up-timers speak of in their mysterious future past, but for our, for our France of the near future. I ask for a son, Anne, who will be king after me—another Louis. Louis the Fourteenth, when I am in my tomb."

"I pray that is far from now, Sire. After all of this time you deserve to see that son, and perhaps many more."

He smiled slightly, wistfully. "The nation has not always done well when there are many sons."

She lifted the hand she still held between her own, and softly kissed it. His lip trembled as she did so, but he did not pull it away.

"For France," she repeated, and let go of his hand, offering him a deep curtsey that would have made the sternest instructor in Madrid beam with delight.

—end excerpt—

from *1636: The Cardinal Virtues*
available in hardcover,
July 2015, from Baen Books